Sebastien de Castell had just finished a degree in Archaeology when he started work on his first dig. Four hours later he realised how much he hated archaeology and left to pursue a very focused career as a musician, ombudsman, interaction designer, fight choreographer, teacher, project manager, actor and product strategist. After a year in the Netherlands, he has recently returned to Vancouver, Canada, where he lives with his wife and two belligerent cats.

You can visit him at www.decastell.com or talk to him on Twitter @decastell.

Also by Sebastien de Castell

Traitor's Blade
Knight's Shadow
Saint's Blood

TYRANT'S THRONE

SEBASTIEN DE CASTELL

Jo Fletcher
BOOKS

First published in Great Britain in 2017 by

Jo Fletcher Books
an imprint of Quercus Editions Ltd.
Carmelite House
50 Victoria Embankment
London EC4Y 0DZ

An Hachette UK Company

A CIP catalogue record for this book is available from the British Library.

HB ISBN 978 1 78206 683 5
TPB ISBN 978 1 78648 323 2

10 9 8 7 6 5 4 3 2 1

Typeset by CC Book Production
Printed and bound in Great Britain by Clays Ltd, St Ives plc

For my esteemed editor, Jo Fletcher,
surely the best sort of Tyrant . . .

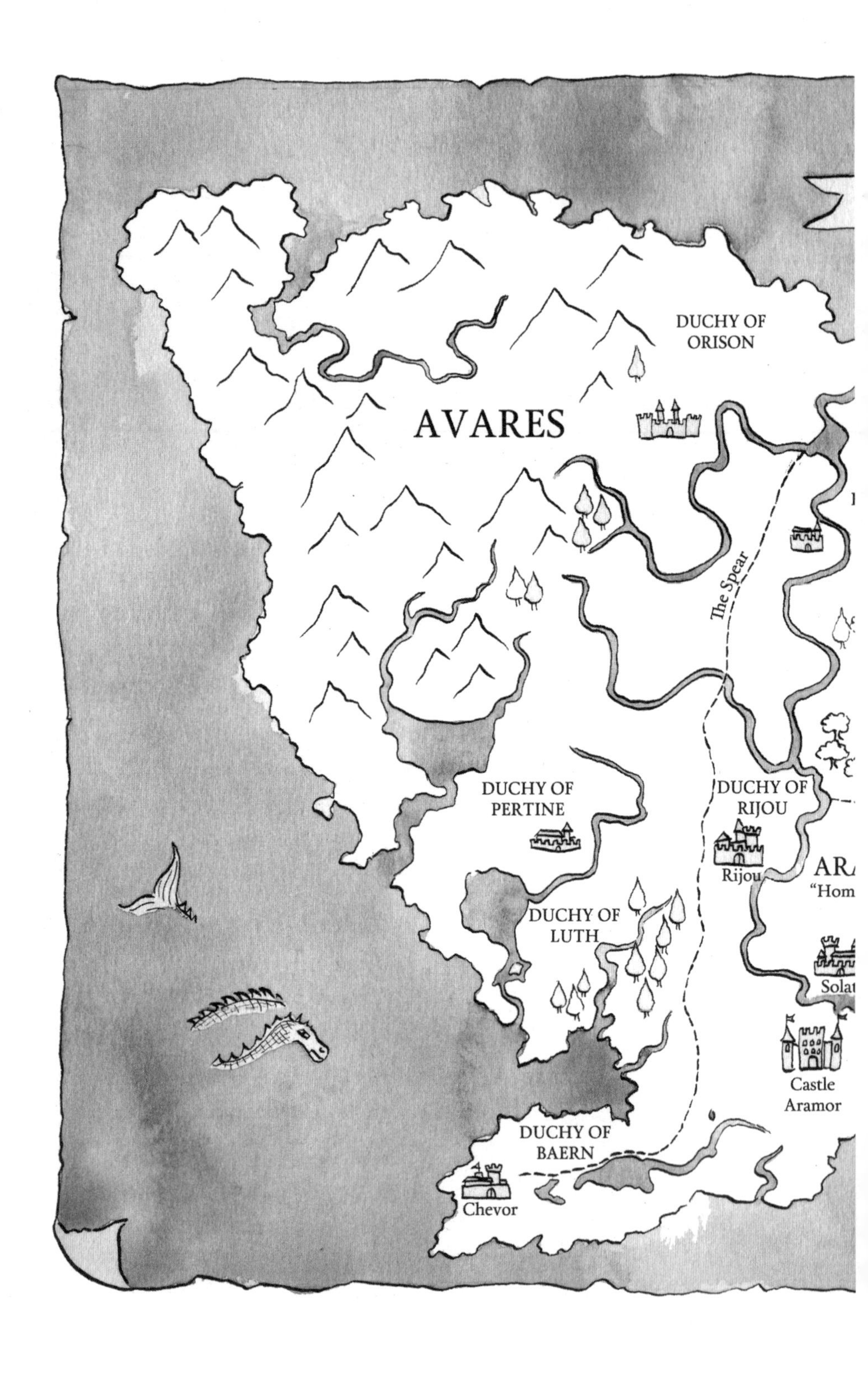
DUCHY OF
ORISON
AVARES
The Spear
DUCHY OF
PERTINE
DUCHY OF
RIJOU
Rijou
DUCHY OF
LUTH
Castle
Aramor
DUCHY OF
BAERN
Chevor

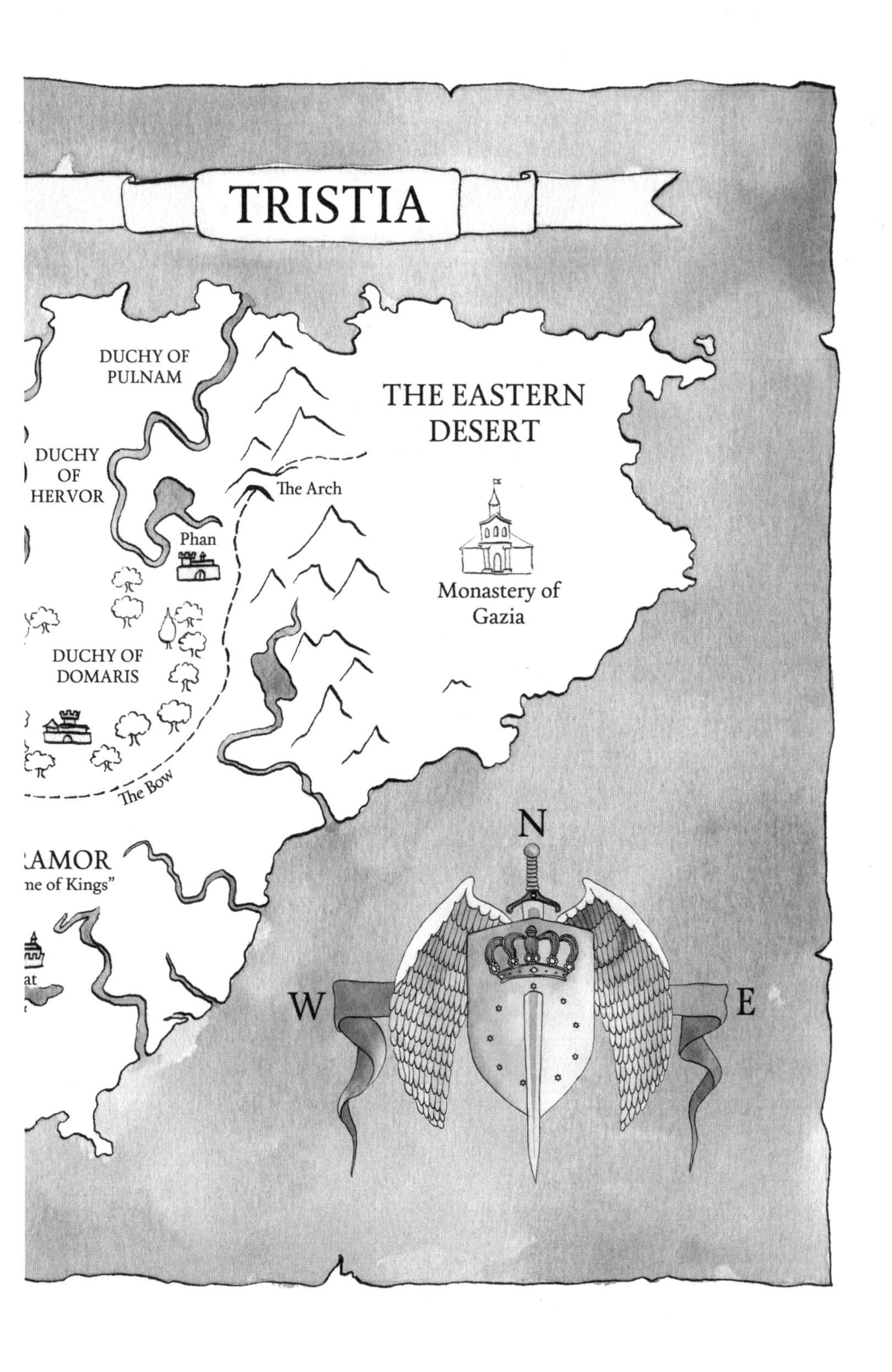
TRISTIA
DUCHY OF PULNAM
THE EASTERN DESERT
DUCHY OF HERVOR
The Arch
Phan
Monastery of Gazia
DUCHY OF DOMARIS
The Bow
AMOR
ne of Kings”
N
W
E

CONTENTS

CHAPTER ONE

THE WEDDING PLAY

A trial is a performance, no different than a stage play or a wedding. The script may be dramatic or dull, the players captivating or hesitant, the spectators enraptured or bored, but by the time the curtain falls, everyone gets up to leave knowing that the conclusion was never really in doubt. The trick, of course, is figuring out the ending before it's too late.

'I don't suppose any of you gutless rat-faced canker-blossoms would like to surrender?' The young woman in the travel-worn leather coat was armed with nothing but a foul tongue and a broken cutlass that she swung in wide, desperate arcs as more than a dozen guardsmen closed in on her. Step by step they drove her back with the points of their castle-forged swords, until she was forced to duck behind the yardarm of the main mast.

'We can't see!' a nobleman called out from his seat at one of the tables set at the rear of the wedding barge's vast deck.

'This isn't a play, you fools!' she shouted back. 'I'm a Greatcoat! A Magister of Tristia, here to enforce a lawful verdict – and just to be quite clear, these swords being waved at me? They're *not* props – these men are going to kill me!'

'She doesn't look like a proper Greatcoat to me,' Lady Rochlan observed to the man in livery refilling her wine goblet. 'Her coat is far too shabby – and that hair! Honestly, it looks as if she cuts it herself.'

'And without the benefit of scissors, it would appear, my Lady,' the servant added.

Lady Rochlan smiled, then asked, 'Are you quite all right, young man? You look a trifle seasick.'

'Quite all right, I assure you, my Lady. I merely . . . Pardon me.'

The servant ran to the back of the barge just in time to vomit over the side and into the calm river waters below, drawing chuckles from nearby guests who wondered aloud how anyone could be seasick without even being at sea.

Still backing away from her pursuers, the Greatcoat growled in frustration. 'Step aside!' she commanded the guardsmen. 'By the laws set forth by King Paelis and reconsecrated by his heir, Aline the First, withdraw, or face me one by one in the duelling circle where I'll gladly teach you the first rule of the sword.' The threatening tone she had adopted was sadly undermined both by her obvious youth and by the way her blade trembled in her hand.

The guardsmen maintained their slow, patient approach, and even the seasick servant shuffling behind them in search of more wine for the guests could sense their excitement. The chance to kill a Greatcoat, to be forever remembered as one of those few who'd brought one of the legendary sword-wielding magistrates to a bloody end? That was enough to make any man reckless. But these were Guardsmen of the March of Barsat, disciplined soldiers one and all, and so they awaited their master's order to strike with the forbearance of Saints.

A soft laugh broke through the tension. Evidalle, Margrave of Barsat, began speaking in tones so light they might have been the opening notes of a love song. 'I believe, my Lady Greatcoat – how does one address a female magistrate, anyway? "Mistress Greatcoat"? Or perhaps "Madam Greatcoat"?'

She shook back a lock of reddish-brown hair that was threatening to fall into her eyes. 'My name is Chalmers, also called the King's Question.'

'Chalmers? Odd name for a girl.' Evidalle furrowed his smooth brow. 'And did Paelis really refer to you as "the King's *Question*"? I wonder, was his query perhaps, "If I were to dress a homely waif in man's clothes and hand her a rusted blade, would she really be any worse than the rest of my tatter-cloaks?"' The Margrave laughed heartily at his own joke. Like a pebble dropped in the middle of a pool, his mirth spread in waves, first to the guardsmen encircling the Greatcoat and then beyond, to the guests in their finery seated at their white and gold tables beneath the long ribbons of silver silk hung from the masts to celebrate the Margrave's nuptials.

As if on cue, a beautiful Bardatti at the very front of the barge struck an opening chord on her guitar and led the three violinists beside her into a jaunty tune fit for the occasion. The guests – Lords, Daminas, Viscounts and other minor nobles, smiled and whispered conspiratorially to their companions as they luxuriated in the shade offered by the stiff white parasols held at careful angles against the afternoon sun by impeccably turned-out servants. Each noble had brought a Knight from their personal guard, both for protection and decoration, their livery proudly displaying their house colours and sigils as they stood at attention, stiff and silent as statues. Now even they began to laugh at the scene playing out before them.

The attending clerics, instantly recognisable by the robes of red or green or pale blue they wore to mark whichever God had, in theory at least, chosen them, smiled knowingly to each other – all save one, standing inconspicuously behind the others, his arms folded within his sleeves, wearing the grey rough-spun robes of an unchosen monk.

Only the servants kept their silence as they scurried between nobles and their Knights to bring plates of roast pig and poultry prepared by a small army of cooks working spits dripping hissing grease onto the flames below. One of the cooks' assistants, apparently oblivious to the anxiety of his fellows, sliced morsels off the chickens turning on one of the spits and popped them into his mouth as he watched the events unfolding.

As the laughter settled down, the guardsmen's eyes returned to the Greatcoat, anticipating the signal to strike – but the Margrave's performance was only just beginning. 'I believe, my dear "King's Question", that your unfortunate appellation may be to blame for your current predicament. You see, when the High Cleric of Baern asks whether the Gods or Saints have any cause to bar a marriage, it's actually considered quite impolite to speak up.'

'The Gods are dead,' Chalmers said, 'and so are the Saints, from what I've heard, and this wedding of yours is nothing more than a sham.' She gestured at Lady Cestina, who stood silently by Evidalle, her eyes downcast, as they had been throughout the ceremony. 'You had her true husband killed so you could marry her, and even now your soldiers hold her mother and father, beaten and bloody, prisoners in their own keep!'

The specificity of the accusations drew uncomfortable titters from the guests, some of whom were no longer entirely certain that what was taking place was the promised wedding play that usually accompanied a nobleman's nuptials.

'You forgot her sister, Mareina,' Evidalle said. 'Clever girl – she's actually quite pretty, too. I'd considered her as an alternative to Lady Cestina but then she came at me with a knife, so . . . well, you know how that goes.'

'She wastes away in a cage beneath the deck of this very barge, you bastard,' the Greatcoat said. 'You're forcing Lady Cestina into marriage by threatening her own sister's life!'

'I *am*?' Evidalle put on a show of shock and confusion as he turned and surveyed his guests. 'You must all think me a truly wretched creature.' He stepped gracefully to where the Lady Cestina was trying, unsuccessfully, to avoid notice and extended a well-manicured hand towards her. 'My Lady? Is there any truth to this *terrible* accusation? Can it be possible that you do not wish to marry me?'

Lady Cestina, who might otherwise have been quite beautiful had her face not been a picture of fear, with smudged blue *maschiera* paints running from her eyes down to her chin, her long blonde hair wet where it stuck to her cheeks, accepted the Margrave's hand.

'No, my Lord,' she whispered, 'the accusations are false. I wish nothing more than to be your wife.'

'You see?' Evidalle said, turning back to the Greatcoat as if expecting her to agree that the matter had been amicably resolved. When she glared at him instead, he nodded sagely. 'Ah, but of course the lovely Cestina might simply be saying this out of fear for her sister's wellbeing, no?' He turned back to his bride. 'My dear, would you kiss me?'

'Of . . . of course, my Lord.' Lady Cestina leaned in towards the Margrave and kissed him. Everyone could see her lips were trembling.

Evidalle shook his head in mock dismay. 'That won't do at all, my darling. I fear our Lady Greatcoat will think you are simply *pretending* to love me – you must do better.'

The Lady Cestina looked around anxiously before kissing Evidalle again, this time pressing her lips hard against his, keeping them there a long time.

'Better,' Evidalle said, pulling away to smile at the audience, who gave a smattering of applause. He held up a hand to quiet them. 'I think we can improve on it, though.' His gaze returned to Cestina. 'This time, use your tongue,' he ordered, then asked sweetly, 'Would you like that?'

The fear was joined by humiliation playing across her face. Her eyes were those of a rabbit caught in a trap. 'Yes, my Lord . . . I would . . .' Tentatively, she opened her mouth and extended her tongue to his lips.

Evidalle grinned and leaned back a bit, making her reach for him, to the ribald laughter of the crowd. After a moment he opened his mouth to receive her tongue.

'Enough!' the Greatcoat shouted. 'Leave her be, damn you!'

Evidalle kept the peculiar kiss going a while longer before pulling away. '*Enough?*' he asked the Greatcoat. 'You do realise she's going to be *my wife*, don't you? We'll soon be doing a great deal more than kissing. But perhaps you're right . . .'

He turned back to the wedding guests. 'My Lords and Ladies, has this demonstration of our love been enough for you, or do you require more evidence?'

For a moment the guests looked at each other in confusion, unsure of what response was expected. Evidalle stared at them and finally someone shouted, 'Er . . . more—?'

At the Margrave's approving nod this soon grew into a rousing chant, 'Give us more! Give us more!'

The clerics stood placid and unmoving, the hems of their robes flapping in the breeze – all but the monk at the back, who had his eyes fixed on the guardsmen; he appeared to be examining each one in turn. The servants were doing their best to feign ignorance of what was going on, save one refilling a flagon of wine, who paused to scowl at the cook's assistant who had stopped turning the spit but was still slicing pieces of chicken for himself.

The chanting grew in volume. 'Give us more! Give us more!'

Evidalle gazed lovingly into his young bride's eyes. 'It seems our guests demand a grander gesture from us, Lady Cestina. We must provide them with a more . . . ah, *complete* demonstration of our love.'

The young woman's eyes went wide as she finally worked out what was to come. Her lips parted and a single word came out, silent as a whisper to all but those nearby. 'Please,' she said. 'Please—'

Margrave Evidalle laughed. 'You see? She's begging for it!' He turned back to her. 'Take off your dress.'

'Please, no, not here,' the Lady said, even as her hands, as though no longer under her control, began to undo the laces fastening the bodice of her wedding gown. 'Please,' she said again, each repetition carrying more trepidation, more desperation.

The curve of Evidalle's lips remained the same, yet his smile grew dark, ugly, his eyes more intense. 'Faster,' he said, a hand already reaching out for her.

'Touch her even once,' Chalmers warned, her voice thick with rage, 'and I swear by Saint Zaghev-who-sings-for-tears, those tits will be the last thing your fingers ever feel.'

'Isn't Saint Zaghev one of the dead ones?' Evidalle asked, his expression turning from desire to mild annoyance. 'I doubt he'll do you much good now.'

The Greatcoat gave out a shout and swung her broken cutlass at the leg of the guardsman closest to her. The tip of the lightly curved blade was missing but the jagged end remained sharp enough that it gashed the man's thigh, sending him tumbling onto his backside. Chalmers had already brought her blade back up in front of her and was swinging it wildly at the faces of the men nearest her, forcing them back. For a brief moment it almost looked like the young woman's ferocity might break their line – until a long-limbed guard reached over her and struck the back of her head with the pommel of his sword. Two other guardsmen grabbed her arms and held on tight, rendering her as helpless as the woman she'd come to save.

The man whose leg Chalmers had cut got back on his feet, ripped the blade from her hand and tossed it to the deck. He drew his own thin-bladed dagger and pressed it against her throat.

The Margrave gave a small cough and the guard froze. He dropped to his knees immediately. 'Forgive me, my Lord. I was—'

'It's perfectly understandable,' Evidalle said, waving him away. 'At times like these one can sympathise with the overwhelming desire for immediate ... *gratification.*' Evidalle signalled to the musicians to resume their tune as he took over the unlacing of Lady Cestina's gown.

Chalmers howled in frustration as she struggled in vain to pull free from her captors. The man she'd injured used this as an excuse to strike her across the face, but to her credit, the Greatcoat didn't beg or plead or moan, but shouted, 'Kill me then, you dogs, but know that a reckoning comes to Tristia. Retribution rides on a fast horse and wields a sharp blade. So go ahead, you foul-breathed bastards, slit my throat if you dare.'

Evidalle sighed. 'Are you just about done, Lady Greatcoat?' He removed his fingers from the laces on the front of Lady Cestina's wedding dress. 'Forgive me, my love, but I fear that the Greatcoat's caterwauling is making me lose my enthusiasm for our little performance.'

Her reply was oddly plaintive. 'You mustn't stop now, my dear.'

All eyes turned to stare in surprise at the young bride. Beneath the tears and smudged *maschiera* paints, Lady Cestina's expression had changed; the mask of fear and sorrow had been replaced by what looked suspiciously like a self-satisfied grin. Eyes bright with mischief, she added, 'We're just getting to the best part.'

Very slowly, like a dancer taking her first few steps onto the stage, Lady Cestina walked over and extended a hand to caress the chin of her deeply confused would-be rescuer.

'My valiant Greatcoat, I must apologise. You see, I'm afraid this really *is* a wedding play ... only you were never meant to perform the part of the daring hero. You're here to play the villain.'

CHAPTER TWO

THE RELUCTANT JURY

'This man had your husband killed!' Chalmers cried out, still straining against the grip of the guardsmen holding her. 'His troops surround your parents' keep even as your sister languishes in a cage below this very deck. Would you betray your own family for—?'

Lady Cestina gripped the Greatcoat's jaw with her hand, pressing her fingernails into the flesh. 'My family betrayed *me* – they refused to even listen to my plans; instead they fawn and cower before that old crone Duchess Ossia! The bitch trades away the future of our Duchy to that foolish child in Aramor – but she will *never* be crowned Queen, not as long as those of us with noble breeding stand up for our freedoms.'

Evidalle took this as his cue to address the assembled nobles. 'Lords and Daminas, Viscounts and Viscountesses, we have brought you here not only to witness our wedding, but to unite with us in a far greater purpose.'

The scraping of chair legs against the polished oak deck drew attention to a man of middle years with streaks of grey in his dark hair rising to his feet. 'You intend to take Duchess Ossia's throne for yourself?'

'I intend something far grander than that, Lord Braimond. I would see us put an end to the reign of the Dukes once and for all!'

The musicians stopped playing as astonishment spread across the wedding barge, the guests erupting in furious whispers.

'Hear me out,' Evidalle said, raising his hands for quiet. 'We have a chance, right now, while those who have held us beneath their thumb for too long struggle to restore order to the country. Castle Aramor is in ruins, the Dukes of Hervor, Orison and Luth are dead, their thrones sitting empty – so let us ensure they remain so. Let us become once and for all masters of our own domains, free from interference by the Crown, free from the petty, intrusive demands of weak and ageing Dukes who understand nothing of our lives and needs.' He strode over to where his guards held Chalmers and wrapped a hand around her neck. 'And above all, free from the tyranny of those who would seek to impose *their* laws on *our* lands.'

Lord Braimond shook his head in disbelief. 'Have you lost your mind? You would set us at war with the Greatcoats: the very men and women who not three months ago fought and killed a God!'

'Theatrics,' Evidalle countered, his eyes still on Chalmers. 'Stories. The Trattari are flesh and blood, just like this one. The Bardatti turn their petty exploits into legends to instil fear in us – well, we too can turn such tales to our benefit. I spread the story of a delicately nurtured girl, stripped of her rights and soon to be ravaged by the big bad nobleman, and sure enough, one of the Trattari comes running right into my little trap.'

Lady Rochlan set down her wine goblet and rose from her chair, signalling with a shake of her head for her Knight to remain where he was. 'What purpose has this ploy of yours served, Evidalle? You cannot expect us to believe that this rather shabby Greatcoat you have captured was your intended prize.'

'My venture was a fishing expedition, I admit,' Evidalle said, keeping his hand around Chalmers' neck. 'I would have preferred to have reeled in a nice big trout, perhaps even their so-called First Cantor, or the one who once claimed to be the Saint of Swords –

but see how easily my lure has taken this little catfish? She will do just fine for a start.'

Chalmers, struggling to speak, wheezed, 'The start of what?'

The Margrave leaned in closer. 'War, my little minnow. When word of what I have begun here spreads, nobles across the country will set their own traps. The would-be Queen and her puppet Dukes won't be able to protect their precious Greatcoats, and they will soon see that the only laws we will abide on *our* lands are the ones *we* choose for ourselves.'

He turned his gaze back to his guests. 'Who will join me in the fight to free our country? Who will be the first to drive their dagger into the Trattari's heart before we send her body floating along the river that it may find its way to Duchess Ossia's doorstep?'

'You—' Chalmers started coughing.

Evidalle lightened his grip. 'What's that?'

'You forgot something,' Chalmers spat, 'you repulsive man-child – you damned, *damnable* dung-eating worm—'

Several of the guardsmen raised their weapons to strike, but the Margrave shook his head and they stayed their hands. The smile he gave Chalmers was almost generous. 'Go on, then. You're bordering on poetry now. What final devastating curse would you utter for me?'

Chalmers tried to draw breath, but Evidalle had begun squeezing again.

'The Greatcoats are coming.'

Evidalle stared at Chalmers – who looked surprised herself, for she was too busy being choked to have spoken. The Margrave spun around and started peering into the crowd of faces.

'Show yourself,' he demanded. 'Who dares to say those words in my presence?'

No one answered. No one moved.

The Greatcoats are coming.

The words hung in the air like an incantation meant to conjure up swordsmen from thin air. The guards and guests had started looking around themselves, as if at any moment the sounds of horses' hooves might echo along the wedding barge's highly polished oak planking. The Knights kept their hands on the hilts of their swords, awaiting an invasion that never came.

Finally Evidalle broke the silence with a dismissive snort. 'By the Saints dead and living, just look at all of you! Does the mere *mention* of their names steal the air from your lungs? *Greatcoats?* You fear a paltry few disgraced magistrates who march to the tune of the bastard child of a dead King?'

'It's not only the Greatcoats,' Lady Rochlan pointed out. 'Many of us have had to deal with their juries even after the magistrates themselves have left our lands. You play a dangerous game, Margrave.'

With his free hand, Evidalle grabbed at the front of Chalmers' coat and tore a button free. 'Is *this* what concerns you? These little symbols of their office?' He tossed it on the deck and watched it roll away. 'Come then, let us see who picks up the coin and swears themselves to the Trattari's cause. Let us see what kind of jury she will find here.'

One by one, Evidalle tore off the remaining buttons, throwing them to the deck as the wedding guests watched in uncomfortable silence. He was about to throw the last button when he paused to look at it, then let go of the girl so that he could peel away the leather shell that covered the gold coin underneath: the payment every juror would take in exchange for their vow to uphold a verdict.

When nothing came away, Evidalle stared at the young woman's coat. 'This isn't even a true coat of office!'

Chalmers looked stricken, but her voice remained defiant. 'I may not have the clothes, you bastard, but I am as much a Greatcoat as any of you have ever known.' She turned her gaze to the wedding guests. 'I have come to enforce a lawful verdict against this man. Those few among you who still remember a time when your heart knew honour and duty are hereby summoned to serve as my jurors.'

Evidalle's fury wiped out any trace of refinement as he screamed, 'You *stupid child*, you've wasted my time! All my efforts, for *nothing*!' He threw away the remaining button and it hit the seasick servant who had been doing his best to keep the guests' goblets filled with wine.

The Margrave caught sight of the cleric in grey robes standing a few yards away. 'You, cleric, what number is most sacred to the Gods?'

The hooded monk tilted his head slightly. 'That's . . . an excellent question. One could argue that six is the number most beloved of the Gods, for that is how many we recognise in Tristia. On the other hand, since by all accounts they're now dead, it's hard to say whether—'

'Just give me a number, damn you! A bigger one.'

The cleric paused. 'Twelve – if for no other reason tha—'

'Fine.' Evidalle turned to his guardsmen. 'Release her.'

Chalmers immediately reached down to grab her weapon from the deck, but one of the guards kicked her in the arse and she fell to her hands and knees.

Evidalle turned to the audience, the smile returning to his face. 'Well, my Lords and Ladies? The Trattari needs twelve jurors. Who among you will take up her cause? Who will—?'

A rustle of cloth nearby caught the attention of both the guards and the Margrave. The monk in grey was kneeling to pick up one of the buttons from the ground.

'What do you think you're doing?' Evidalle asked.

'Taking my payment,' the monk replied, carefully examining the plain round piece of leather-covered wood as he held it up to the sun. 'I'll serve on her jury.'

One of the clerics in green, a servant of the dead God Coin, stepped forward and grabbed the monk by the front of his robes. 'What heresy is this?' he demanded. 'Who are you, that you would dare risk the wrath of the Gods?'

The monk in grey shrugged. 'Alas, I've never had much use for religion, your Holiness.' He pocketed the button and then placed his hand on the cleric's wrist and gently but firmly removed it. 'However, if any deity wishes to register a formal complaint, they may meet me in the duelling circle at their convenience. As it happens, I've already seen at least one God die that way.'

The cleric in green drew away in disgust. 'You're no monk, to speak such blasphemy.'

'I confess, you are correct, Venerati.' The monk raised both arms above his head and his sleeves slid down, revealing that he was missing his right hand. With his left he tore off the robes, uncovering the long leather coat beneath and the shield strapped to his back. As he walked past the shocked guards to stand with Chalmers, he said, 'My name is Kest Murrowson, a magistrate of the Greatcoats.' He paused for effect, before adding unnecessarily, 'And I am the Queen's Shield.'

The guards began to close in on the two Greatcoats.

'Thanks for the support,' Chalmers said. 'Though it would have been more helpful if you'd brought, you know, a sword or something.'

Kest removed the shield from his back and slipped it onto his arm. 'I do all right with this.'

Lady Rochlan strode forward. 'You see now, Margrave Evidalle? Already your arrogant scheme has put all of our lives in danger.' To Kest she added, 'I have no part in this, Trattari. I am loyal to the Duchess Ossia.'

Evidalle's face grew ugly at this first tentative hint of rebellion. 'You *stupid* cow – you think this one man changes anything? You think the Greatcoats will save any of you from *my* wrath?' He reached to grab at her, only to scream with such anguish that the seabirds went fleeing from the topmast.

The Margrave stared down in horror at the arrow sprouting from his hand.

'I believe this Chalmers person did, in fact, warn you about what would happen if those greedy fingers of yours went places they didn't belong,' said the cook's assistant. In his left hand was a short bow made of pale yellow wood. His right reached down to pick up the remainder of a roast chicken.

'You know, they have plenty of poultry at Aramor,' Kest said.

One of the guardsmen strode over to the cook's assistant. 'Who the devil are you?'

'Just a minute,' the assistant replied. 'Kest, chickens in the south just taste better. You know that. Besides, the new royal chef over-spices everything.' He turned his attention back to the guardsman and tossed him the carcase of the chicken before wiping his hand on his shirt and absently pulling another arrow out from behind the spit. 'To answer your question, friend, my name is Brasti Goodbow, and I am the Queen's Jest.'

'Treason!' Evidalle squeaked, his voice breaking. As a squat man carrying a healer's silver case started making his way towards the Margrave, several clerics fell in close behind, all muttering prayers to their various Gods. Evidalle's eyes went to the guardsmen. 'Kill them, you fools,' he commanded. 'There are only two real Greatcoats to deal with—'

'About that,' Kest said. He picked up another of the buttons and tossed it over the heads of the wedding party towards the back of the ship. The eyes of the assembled guests followed its trajectory until a hand reached up and snatched the button from the air.

Shocked gasps erupted from the crowd, who'd all risen from their seats to see who had dared to catch it.

I stuck the button in the pocket of my livery and returned to refilling Lady Rochlan's wine before setting the flagon down on the table beside her, being careful to prevent its contents spilling on her fine white feather-trimmed dress. She'd been polite to me all afternoon, despite thinking me a servant, and besides, the wine looked like a decent claret and there was a reasonable chance I'd soon be thirsty. Also, I was still feeling a bit seasick. 'Pardon me, my Lady,' I said, and reached past her leg to where one of my rapiers was strapped under the table.

She put a hand on my arm. 'There are far too many of them, you silly fool. You'll only die here if you try to fight.'

I patted her hand before removing it, oddly touched by her concern, though I wasn't entirely sure that she'd figured out who I was; maybe she simply didn't want to lose a reasonably competent servant.

I withdrew my blade and leaped onto the table, knocking over a full plate of duck – but not spilling the claret and, most importantly, not falling on my arse.

Evidalle grimaced in pain as the healer poured a dark, viscous fluid around the spot where the arrow still pierced his hand. 'Who in all the hells are you?' he asked.

I smiled. 'My name, your Lordship, is Falcio val Mond.' My throat felt a bit dry, a product of having to maintain a servant's silence all day, so I reached down and took a swig from the wine – and I was right, it was an excellent vintage – before I added, 'I am the First Cantor of the Greatcoats, also called the King's Heart. You might not know it yet, Margrave Evidalle, but you are having a very bad day.'

CHAPTER THREE

RUNNING THE TABLES

There's a trick to fighting on the deck of a ship. I don't know what it is, but I fully intend to find out one day. I imagine it requires not being seasick whilst trying to evade the attacks of a rather large group of enemy guards and nobles – oh, and an enraged bride.

'Take them!' the lead guardsman shouted. A gold stripe around the collar of his black and yellow livery marked him as either their captain or perhaps just the most stylish dresser among them. His voice wasn't especially commanding, but it was insistent, and combined with his bushy red hair and buck front teeth, made me think of a particularly angry squirrel.

All sixteen guards were now staring at me, so I took off at a run, charging straight at them across the tops of the tables beautifully dressed in white and gold, screaming obscenities at the top of my lungs and knocking over translucent porcelain plates and golden goblets as I went, much to the consternation of the noble guests and their attendant Knights. This tactic – and it is an *actual* tactic, which we in the Greatcoats call a 'Wanton Dancer' – distracts the enemy by focusing their attention on the wrong target, in this case, me. One day soon I plan to rename this particular version the 'Suicidal Idiot'.

Brasti took advantage of the momentary diversion to grab his quiver and sling it over his shoulder before running to the raised foredeck where he could rain arrows down on our opponents. Kest slammed the rounded front of his shield across the face of the man closest to him before driving the edge into the stomach of the next. 'Falcio, coming in low!' he shouted.

I leaped up from the table and heard the whoosh of a broadsword stroke that could have cost me my ankles pass harmlessly beneath me. The agility and grace of my manoeuvre became marginally less impressive when I landed and the tablecloth slipped out from under my feet, sending me tumbling backwards, shattering crockery and sending half-eaten chicken legs and chewed ribs flying into the faces of those guests who hadn't yet had the presence of mind to move away.

With the wind knocked out of me, I struggled to draw breath into my lungs, much to the grinning satisfaction of the guardsman who had raised his broadsword high for the killing blow. He was so convinced he was about to end me that I hadn't the heart to tell him that what I lack in luck and skill, I make up for in sheer bloody-mindedness – well, that, and the fact that a rapier thrust moves at twice the speed of a broadsword stroke. Wincing through the pain, I drove the point of my blade through the leather of his jerkin and into his belly. From the expression on his face, it was clear that he'd found the outcome of our exchange exceedingly disappointing.

I tossed the bleeding man a clean linen napkin from the table. 'Keep pressure on the wound. The blade missed your stomach, so you still have a chance to live.' Believe me, I'm no Saint, but I'd dealt with so many monstrous individuals lately that I was developing a fair amount of sympathy for the people forced to work for them.

I rose to my feet in time to face the rest of the guards, who'd been wrestling their way through the crowd to get to me. I'd chosen my terrain carefully: by fighting on the tables in the midst of the guests, I'd made it almost impossible for my opponents to swarm me without accidentally skewering the nobles. Hard to believe, but some of them still appeared to think this was some elaborate wedding performance – Viscount Brugess came within inches of being decapitated as he leaned forward to grab another leg of chicken, clearly sharing Brasti's enthusiasm for southern spit-roasted poultry.

The Knights were taking a more pragmatic view: they'd already begun dragging their noble employers to the relative safety of the back of the barge, clearing the way for the guards to close in on me. As that made the field of battle less favourable – to me, at least – I jumped off the table and began running along the barge's wide railing.

Don't fall. Don't fall. Don't fall. Brasti will never let you forget it if you tumble into the water and drown.

'Protect the Margrave!' Captain Squirrel shouted, cleverly guessing at my destination.

As it happened, I had no false illusions about my chances of reaching Margrave Evidalle in time to deliver the death he so richly deserved, but my *apparent* intentions were enough to convince the guards currently cornering Kest, Brasti and Chalmers that I was the more urgent danger, and with everyone's attention once again on me, Kest moved on to Part Two of the plan.

'Find the sister,' Kest told the young woman who'd been posing as a Greatcoat.

She didn't move. This 'Chalmers' had likely never been in a battle this full of chaos and mayhem before – more evidence that she wasn't a proper Greatcoat, since chaos and mayhem were pretty much our stock and trade. As if to prove my point, one of the guards got the brilliant idea to drop his sword and instead try to swat me off the railing using a long bargepole. I squatted down, grabbed the other end and jumped off the rail, then ran to the other side of the boat. With the bemused guard clinging manfully to his end of the pole, I managed to knock the swords out of the hands of at least two of his fellows before he yanked, *hard*, and I dutifully let go – sending him crashing backwards into yet more of his unfortunate comrades.

'Cestina's sister,' Kest pressed Chalmers. 'You said Margrave Evidalle was holding her captive on the barge – is she truly his prisoner, or might she be part of his scheme too?'

'I . . . no, the Lady Mareina is innocent in all of this! They've got her below in the—'

'Don't *tell* me, just go and get her! We'll keep the guards busy.' Kest shoved her unceremoniously towards the stairs leading belowdecks before coming to my aid.

Brasti joined us. Sighting along the line of his arrow at a group of guardsmen who were preparing to make a run at us, he asked, 'Tell me again why we didn't bring fifty Greatcoats from Aramor on this little pleasure-cruise?'

'Perhaps because we don't *have* fifty Greatcoats?' Kest suggested.

In fact, we had less than a dozen at Castle Aramor, despite all the Bardatti we'd sent out in search of them. But that wasn't the reason why I'd brought only Kest and Brasti with me to Margrave Evidalle's wedding. 'We're here to send these bastards a message,' I reminded them.

'A sternly worded letter wouldn't have sufficed?' Brasti grumbled.

A massive brute of a man grabbed one of the tables by two legs and held it out in front of him like a kite-shield, and more guardsmen rushed to take up position behind him so that they could rush us without fear of Brasti's arrows. Brasti tried sidestepping, looking for a clear view of their flank, but the table was too wide and the big man holding it too wily to give him a target.

'I hate the big ones,' Brasti complained. 'Since we're likely to die here, Falcio, do you mind telling me what message we were supposed to deliver?'

'It's simple,' I replied, reaching up to wrap the end of a rope hanging from the yardarm about ten feet above me around my forearm.

Once it felt moderately secure, I leaped from the raised foredeck, the point of my rapier aimed at the face of the man carrying the table. I'd never tried anything like this before, but if I was stuck having to fight on a boat, I'd damned well try and enjoy it. When the guardsman tilted his makeshift shield over his head to protect himself, I let go of the rope and landed squarely on the middle of the table. Before the big man could shake me off, I'd hopped to the other side of his little squad and by the time the man at the back had turned to face me, I'd already stabbed him in the arse.

'Think twice the next time you decide to ambush a Greatcoat, gentlemen,' I suggested. 'We're better at this than you are.'

Believe it or not, that got a smattering of applause from the wedding guests.

The rich really are different from the rest of us. They're insane.

'Seems a little unfair to punish these poor fellows for ambushing this Chalmers person,' Brasti said, taking advantage of the confusion to fire an arrow into the thigh of the man holding the table. 'She wasn't even wearing a proper greatcoat.'

'Neither are you,' Kest pointed out, joining us at the barge's centre mast.

'You know perfectly well I couldn't wear my coat under my disguise. You're being intentionally abstract.'

'I think you mean obtuse,' Kest said, parrying an opponent's clumsy swing with his shield and sending the blade screeching along its surface. By the time the guard had his weapon back under control, Kest had already bashed him across the face hard enough to send him toppling back into his fellows.

'I need help – *now*!' Chalmers shouted.

'I'm on it,' Kest said calmly as Chalmers came struggling up the stairs, hampered both by the young woman in torn, filthy clothes who was clinging desperately to her and by the two guardsmen intent on blocking their escape. Chalmers was waving around that broken cutlass of hers, but she couldn't even get a decent swing at her enemies for fear of hitting Lady Cestina's terrified sister.

Speaking of whom . . .

'Face me, Trattari!'

I was barely in time to parry what I thought was a pretty impressive lunge by the bride-to-be. Her smallsword was a lovely piece, the glittering gold inlay positively gleaming, which reminded me that my own rapiers were in sorry need of some love and attention. I felt decidedly shabby next to the radiant bride.

For her part, Lady Cestina was full of passionate fury as she came at me. 'Your tyrant Queen's laws will never take root in our lands while I live,' she cried. For someone who'd apparently been deeply involved in the conspiracy, not to mention the murder of her former husband and the kidnapping of her own family, Lady Cestina's outrage sounded positively noble.

I deflected a series of thrusts aimed at sensitive parts of my body as I said, 'Forgive me, my Lady, but there *is* one law we all must obey.'

The tip of her sword whipped out suddenly, leaving a tiny cut on my cheek. 'What law might that be, *Trattari*?'

She pressed her attack, and I felt a strange mixture of admiration and sorrow for her. When you spend a good part of your life studying the sword, you like to think it somehow makes you a better person, but the look of glee on Lady Cestina's face, presumably at the prospect of killing me, was rapidly disproving that theory.

On the other hand, I've always argued that there are differences between an experienced duellist and someone who just happens to be good with a sword – differences such as knowing to pay as much attention to the changing terrain as you do to your opponent. When people get stabbed, they bleed, and that blood has to go somewhere. In this case, I'd noted a nice little pool of it on the deck between us, so I gracefully allowed her to press me back – and just at the moment she started smiling at my apparent retreat, she slipped on the slick surface. I contented myself with a gentlemanly thrust to her shoulder – although it was her sword arm, naturally.

'The law we must all obey, madam, regardless of rank or privilege, is the first rule of the sword: whoever's first to put the pointy end in the other guy wins.'

She dropped her weapon, grimacing in pain. Margrave Evidalle, who'd thus far been too busy nursing his own injured hand to pay attention to anyone else's situation, shouted in despair, 'Monster! What kind of man are you, to wound a lady?'

I assumed he was being ironic, but Brasti said, 'Actually, he used to be offensively squeamish about fighting women as equals.' He clapped me on the shoulder. 'You're really growing as a person, Falcio.'

'A little help here?' Kest called out.

The last of the guardsmen were now focusing their efforts on keeping Kest from helping Chalmers to rescue Lady Mareina.

'Hey,' Brasti called, 'you men attacking those nice ladies—!'

Much to everyone's surprise, several pairs of eyes turned towards him.

'Want to see a magic trick?'

The absurd question was delivered with such ebullient confidence that I swear some of the guards were about to nod yes.

'Watch closely now, because I'm about to make you disappear.'

Despite the fact that I suddenly found myself occupied with a stubborn opponent who was unreasonably good with a mace, I couldn't help but spare a quick glance. Like a weaver spinning silk in the air, Brasti's hand whisked back and forth from his quiver, each time sliding an arrow gracefully into place on the string of his bow, pulling, aiming and releasing, all in one smooth action, then repeating the motion. By the time I'd thrust my rapier into the leg of the man with the mace, Brasti had taken down three of the guards harrying Chalmers. '*Ta-da*,' he said.

I hate Brasti sometimes.

'Regroup! Regroup, damn you all!' Captain Squirrel shouted.

'He does a lot of shouting,' Kest observed.

'He's their commander,' Brasti said. 'Isn't shouting part of the job?'

'Perhaps – but have you noticed? His orders don't have much thought behind them. He just barks out vague commands and expects everyone else to figure out what they mean.'

Chalmers and the young woman stumbled towards us as a number of the Margrave's other functionaries reluctantly obeyed the urging of their Lord, armed themselves with the weapons of the dead and injured and joined the remaining guards, inconveniently making a force larger than the one we'd started fighting in the first place.

'Form up!' Captain Squirrel shouted. 'Run these bastards down!'

'I see what you mean now,' Brasti told Kest while nocking another arrow. '"Form up" – into what? Run us down – *how*? He's really not giving these poor fellows much to go on, is he?'

The guards, however, didn't appear to require much in the way of guidance. Two men with crossbows moved to either side of the main group, while three more settled long halberds into position and took the front of the line where they could use the longer weapons to keep us at bay while their fellows outflanked us. The rest lined up behind them, clearly waiting for the moment to overwhelm us with their superior numbers.

'How would you rate our chances?' I asked Kest.

'Not good. Six of them will die before they manage to down one of us, then three more, but after that we get overrun,' he replied without any discernible concern. 'Brasti will fall first.'

'What? Why is it always me?' Brasti tossed his bow behind him and drew his sword. We were in too close for archery now. 'Why not Chalmers? She's not even a proper Greatcoat!'

'At least she doesn't hold her sword as if it were a snake about to bite her,' Kest pointed out.

'Stop saying I'm not a Greatcoat,' Chalmers growled, bringing her cutlass into a forward guard as she pushed the emaciated Lady Mareina behind her. 'And leave me out of . . . whatever this gabbling thing is that you're doing.'

'It's called "strategy",' Brasti explained kindly. 'Kest tells us how bad our odds are of survival, and then Falcio finds a way to make them worse, usually by—'

'Shut up, Brasti.'

The wedding barge was beginning to look like one of those terribly complicated board games King Paelis used to make me play while expounding on military theory until I threatened to arrest him for violating his own prohibitions on torture. Kest, Brasti, Chalmers, Lady Mareina and I were boxed in near the front of the boat. Opposite us, the eight remaining guards, bolstered by a dozen of the Margrave's other retainers, were wielding a variety of swords, maces, crossbows and knives of varying lengths. Behind them were some twenty wedding guests, many of them armed as well, and each with their very own armoured Knight for protection.

No way to fight them all, and nowhere to flee.

'Surrender,' Evidalle called out, his voice no longer quite so musical as it had been before Brasti shot an arrow through his hand.

I wasn't above trying to take Evidalle or his young bride captive in order to escape, but they were too well protected behind their guards. In fact, had this been one of the King's game boards, you'd have come to the inescapable conclusion that we were well and truly buggered.

'Falcio?' Kest said. 'They're getting ready to—'

I cut him off with a wave of my hand. The problem with games of war is that they're deceptive precisely because they presume that there are rules to be followed. But this is Tristia, after all, and corruption runs deep in the bone.

'Everyone shush now,' I said, taking a step towards the guards. 'I'm about to be impressive.'

CHAPTER FOUR

CHANGING THE GAME

'I come to you with a remarkable offer,' I said, my voice warm enough now to give it the air of command the moment called for. 'A chance to control your destinies – at least for the next five minutes.'

My eyes drifted from the rows of the Margrave's men to the Knights who were now standing in front of their nobles, preparing to shield them from the battle. 'I propose you sail this lovely boat back to shore and allow us to take Lady Cestina's sister away from here; that way everyone gets to walk away alive.' I gestured to where Margrave Evidalle and his charming bride were huddled together. 'If it sweetens the deal, at this point I'm even willing to let those two marry each other.'

'He's stalling,' Captain Squirrel announced. 'Prepare to strike on my command!'

I ignored him, focusing my attention on his soldiers instead. 'Reconsider, gentleman, or I promise by every God and Saint dead and living that you'll end up bleeding all over the Margrave's lovely wedding barge, which will quite ruin the ceremony.'

'Shouldn't the wedding be off anyway?' Kest asked.

'I thought it had already happened,' Brasti said. 'The cleric said a prayer a—'

'You're ruining my speech,' I said testily.

'Sorry.'

Captain Squirrel took a step towards me, brandishing his long curved blade. 'There are more than twenty of us and only three of you, Trattari. A smarter man would—'

'Four,' Chalmers said, irritated. 'Am I being ignored because I'm a woman?'

'There are a great many women in the Greatcoats,' Kest observed. 'Some rank amongst the finest fighters you'll ever meet. Quillata, for example, was devastating with a—'

'Kest?' I said.

'Oh, sorry. You're still giving your speech?'

'Yes, actually.'

'By all the Gods and Saints, will someone damn well kill them?' Evidalle shouted.

The guards took another step towards us, which irritated me no end. No one ever lets me finish a speech any more. 'Gentlemen, you've sorely misjudged the situation. You didn't think we'd come here alone, did you?' Before he could answer I shouted to the Knights standing behind the line of guardsmen, 'Sir Henrow, Sir Evan, Sir Floris, the order is given! By command of Valiana, Realm's Protector, and Aline, heir to the throne of Tristia, *attack!*'

The rear line of guards spun around, fearing an assault from behind, and at the sight of a lot of men in armour with drawn swords facing them, Captain Squirrel screamed, 'The damned Knights have betrayed us!'

In fact, none of the Knights had moved, probably because, to the best of my knowledge, there were no Sir Henrow, Sir Evan or Sir Floris present – and even if there had been, like as not they'd be siding with the guards. However, since the Knights were all from different houses, they didn't know each other, or who might be hiding among them – and as soon as the Margrave's guards started raising their swords and shouting, the Knights instinctively moved into position, apparently confirming that this was all an elaborate trap.

'They're going to attack – protect your Lords!' one of the Knights shouted.

I could have kissed him.

'It's a trick, you fools!' Lady Cestina screamed, but her warning was too late: the Knights, trusting each other more than petty guardsmen, had formed up into a solid line, while the guards had split into two separate groups, half ready to fend off the Knights while the rest came at us. We were still outnumbered, of course, but with the guardsmen all in disarray, their tactics were useless – and the noble guests were helpfully shouting incoherent orders at their Knights and at each other while reaching for their own highly decorative weapons as they tried in vain to make sense of who was actually fighting whom.

'Interesting,' Kest noted absently, taking a short step to the left as one of the guards made a thrust for his chest. As the man overextended, Kest grabbed him by the shoulder and pulled him off-balance, using his own momentum to send him tumbling over the railing and into the water. 'Was the bit with the Knights part of your plan all along?'

'Of course,' I lied.

Chalmers ducked under an opponent's wide slash. 'So it's true what people say about the great Falcio val Mond.'

'What do they say?' Brasti asked.

'That he talks people to death.' She rose up and drove the heel of her boot into the knee of her attacker and the man obligingly screamed, but the slightly awkward move left her unprepared when, despite the crack of his kneecap, the man managed a glancing slash across her right arm. The thin leather parted under the force of the blow, leaving a line of blood in its place.

'You need a better coat,' I said, piercing the man's good leg and kicking him off the point, sending him falling backwards.

'This was the best I could afford.'

'Then you should stop crashing weddings,' Brasti suggested, slashing his sword across the chest of one of the guardsmen. The cut didn't get through the leather cuirass but it did make the man stumble, and Brasti kicked him hard enough in the belly to send him sprawling to the deck. 'I quite like this barge, though. Do you suppose the Margrave would consider letting me borrow it once he's done with it? I was thinking of asking a certain former assassin to marry me.'

'You want to propose? To *Darriana*?'

The idea sent such a chill through me that I nearly got eviscerated by an axe. I countered with a thrust to the man's hand and got lucky; his weapon went crashing to the deck while he fled out of the way, leaving someone else to come forward and try to finish the job he'd started.

Even Kest seemed perturbed by Brasti's sudden revelation. 'You do realise that, other than Trin, Darriana is quite possibly the deadliest woman alive?'

'I can't very well spend the rest of my life letting the two of you try to get me killed, can I?' Brasti replied. 'Time I let someone else have a go.'

I knew their strange relationship – she a former assassin with a jealous streak and he congenitally incapable of fidelity – had somehow continued despite the natural order of the universe, but I had no idea Brasti might ever seriously consider matrimony – to *anyone*.

'Will you both please shut up?' Chalmers asked, slicing open a guardsman's hand with the broken end of her cutlass. 'Some of us would rather *not* die today if we can avoid it.'

The guard howled in pain, but he cleverly grabbed at Chalmer's face, and smeared the blood over her eyes to blind her as he cocked his other fist. Good move. Almost a shame Brasti had to drive his shoulder into the man's side, pushing him over the railing and into the water.

'If living matters to you then I'd suggest you stop running around pretending to be a Greatcoat,' Brasti told her.

'I'm just as much a Greatcoat as you are,' she countered. 'The King named me so himself, on his last day.'

That took me aback. Was this a lie, or yet one more decision King Paelis had made without telling me? I spared Chalmers a glance. There *was* something vaguely familiar about the girl, but I still couldn't quite place her. Also, right now I had other concerns: the Knights and their Lords had formed their own little troop and were looming over the bodies of several dead or wounded guardsmen. By now most of them had figured out my ruse, but it was too late; only four of Evidalle's guardsmen remained standing. Seeing the odds had turned against them, they dropped their weapons and sank to their knees next to their fallen comrades.

'Stand up, damn you!' the Margrave screamed, but no one moved, which was entirely sensible. Nobody ever wants to be the last person to die right before the battle ends.

Shattering the silence, Brasti slapped a hand on his thigh. 'Now I remember you! Chalmers – the annoying little girl who used to hang around the King's cook – what was her name? Zagdana?' He turned to Kest. 'You know what? This is proof the Gods do still exist. I may have finally found someone who knows how to cook a damned chicken.'

'Her name was *Zagdunsky* and she was the Royal *Quartermaster*, you arse,' Chalmers said to Brasti.

The Knights, none of whom appeared to be hurt, looked warily at us from across the pile of dead and injured guardsmen. One or two shuffled, as if they might be inclined to come for us, but I shook my head. 'I wouldn't recommend it, gentlemen. Not your fight.'

'I remember you now as well,' Kest said to Chalmers. 'Though I seem to recall you looked quite different then.'

'That's right!' Brasti said, pointing an accusing finger. 'You were a tubby little thing, weren't you?' He looked her up and down appraisingly. 'My, my, haven't you grown up nicely . . .'

'Didn't you just announce your intention to propose to Darriana?' Kest asked.

'Yes, well, I can't help it: beauty is in the eye of the beholder.'

'That's not what that sentence means.'

'Is there any reason I can't kill him?' Chalmers asked me.

'Wait until we're sure the fight's over.' I called out to the Knights, 'The fight *is* finished, isn't it, gentlemen?'

A few of them glanced over their shoulders at the nobles they served, none of whom looked eager to take the chance that their man would fall to our blades and leave them vulnerable.

'This is treason!' Evidalle bellowed without the slightest trace of irony as he pounded his non-bleeding fist against the railing. 'I will have justice for this!'

'Well, well,' Brasti said to me. 'For once your plan hasn't got us into worse trouble than we started with.'

'Don't speak so soon,' Kest said, and pointed past the barge's railing to the open waters beyond. In all the chaos of the battle none of us had noticed the ship rounding the bend in the river: a galleon was coming up fast behind us, flying a banner bearing the image of an eagle with talons extended over a field of blue and white.

'Which one's that?' I asked.

'I believe that the eagle is the symbol of the Margrave of Val Iramont,' Kest replied.

As the galleon gradually drew closer, a slender man with a slight stoop and thinning grey hair approached the side. He was in his late fifties, I estimated. He ignored us and looked to the other end of the barge, where Evidalle was kneeling with his bride. 'Margrave Evidalle,' the man called out courteously, 'my profound apologies for arriving late to your blessed day. We had some rather inclement conditions navigating the Red Bay and then ... well, never mind now.' He glanced at the rest of us: three – *four* – Greatcoats, the frantic guests, and finally the dead guardsmen. 'I appear to have missed the festivities ...'

Evidalle rose to his feet and minding his bandaged hand, adjusted his coat before making his way to the side of the barge and greeting the newcomers with as much grace as his dishevelled condition would allow. 'Margrave Rhetan, how wonderful to see you, regardless of the hour.' Then, in a rather impertinent stretching of the truth, he added, 'As it happens, we delayed the ceremony until your arrival.'

Margrave Rhetan gave his own perfunctory bow and motioned for his men to extend a narrow boarding bridge from the deck of his galleon down to the wedding barge. Without showing a trace of concern over the blood, fallen guardsmen, and rather large numbers of drawn weapons, he stepped across and said, 'I hope there's food left. My men haven't eaten.'

I looked past him to see the rows of soldiers, weapons at their sides, preparing to come across. I guessed there were around a hundred.

'What now?' Chalmers asked.

'I'm not sure. I didn't plan on another Margrave showing up with his own private army.'

'You know all your plans are terrible, don't you?' Brasti asked.

'That's not true,' Kest countered. 'A number of Falcio's schemes have proven to be ingenious.'

'Thank you.'

'Mind you, this isn't one of them.'

'Well,' Brasti said, retrieving his bow from the deck and nocking an arrow to the string, 'maybe we'll be lucky for once; maybe Margraves Evidalle and Rhetan don't like each other very much.'

Evidalle caught my eye and it became clear to me that whatever numbing salves the healers had given him to ease the pain of his wounded hand had kicked in because he could barely contain his laughter.

As Margrave Rhetan stepped onto the deck of the wedding barge, Evidalle embraced him and said, 'It really is wonderful to see you, Uncle.'

CHAPTER FIVE

THE MARGRAVE OF VAL IRAMONT

When someone holds your life in their hands, they become remarkably impressive to behold.

At first glance, Rhetan might easily have been mistaken for a peasant farmer or a village shoemaker. He had the lined, leathery skin that comes from age and too much sun; his posture was that of a man whose fight with time was being lost by degrees. His hair was thin and mostly white, only a few stubborn strands of black remaining, and cropped close to his head. Stripped of his galleon and his hundred-odd soldiers, Rhetan would have been an altogether unimposing figure.

Of course, he *did* have a galleon, and he *did* have an army.

A dozen of his men accompanied him down to the wedding barge while the rest remained behind, leaning up against the railings of their ship and making sure we all got a good look at their assortment of crossbows and more than a few pistols.

Rhetan's men wore leather armour studded with steel rings sewn onto the surface, making it durable without adding weight or bulk: an efficient choice – perhaps less grand than the plate worn by the Knights, but better suited to the dangers of fighting aboard ship. More importantly, each man's cuirass was properly sized to his chest and torso. Rhetan clearly took care of his people, and they, in turn, looked upon him without the disdain that soldiers so often held for their Lords.

It was the soldiers' obvious respect for Rhetan that transformed his appearance in my eyes.

The wrinkles that might otherwise have suggested a doddering old man now looked to me as the mark of keen intellect and long study. His slightly stooped posture wasn't the sign of failing muscles exhausted by a long voyage; it was evidence of a man fully at ease in the world. The lack of notice he gave to potential threats all around him didn't signify a deficit of observation but rather served to illustrate a single, incontestable fact: Rhetan was in control.

'Breathe, everyone,' he said. 'You'll live longer.'

The entire company – wedding guests, Knights, guards, and even Margrave Evidalle – watched as Rhetan wandered over to the cooking spits. He picked up a dinner knife from a nearby table and cut a piece of pork off the carcase. 'The meat's overdone, I'm afraid.'

'Try the chicken,' Brasti suggested. I elbowed him in the ribs.

From behind the spits I could hear the quavering sound of the cook's voice. 'Forgive me, your Lordship . . . I . . . there was so much—'

'Relax,' Rhetan said, still chewing on his piece of pork, 'if I killed every chef who overcooked my dinner there wouldn't be a man left in Tristia who knew how to light a fire.' A smattering of nervous laughter rose up, but Rhetan cut it off simply by ignoring it. He turned to survey the crowd. 'You're scared. That's fine. Use it to make yourselves smart. Keep your mouths shut until you have something useful to say and you might just survive the afternoon.'

Such a bold statement would normally have elicited a blistering response from the noble guests, several of whom were Viscounts and Viscountesses of large condates and thus of equal rank to the Margrave. These men and women, who normally took poorly to being told to shut up, kept remarkably silent.

In fact, no one moved so much as a muscle – except for one of Rhetan's own soldiers, a black-haired, broad-shouldered man in his late twenties, who came forward to kneel before Rhetan. 'Margrave? The men await your orders.'

'The men can relax, too, Pheras.' He wagged a finger in mock reprimand. 'Patience. You can't have too much patience.'

'Patience ruined the meat,' Brasti said.

I whispered in his ear, 'It's rather important that you stop talking now.'

'Better overdone and a little chewy than so raw it makes you sick,' Rhetan said as he grabbed a silk napkin from the nearby table and began cleaning his dinner knife. 'Patience is always the wiser course. I had four older brothers. The eldest two were twins, though there was some dispute as to which of them emerged first from our mother's womb – they killed each other when they were twelve, before either was even of age to take the title. The third, determined to prove he was too strong to be challenged by the fourth, died from heat and exhaustion practising with his sword one particularly hot summer's day. Weak heart.' The corners of his lips turned down. 'I always liked Pieten best. I miss him still.'

I generally dislike listening to noblemen wax nostalgic about themselves, but since he had an army and I had yet to figure some way out of this mess, I kept quiet.

'What about the fourth brother?' Kest asked. I didn't bother to elbow him; it wouldn't have done any good: Kest's obsessive need to know the answer to completely pointless things vastly outweighs his survival instincts.

Rhetan didn't seem to mind. 'Astaniel? Ah, he did in fact become Margrave after my father died. He took the seat of Val Iramont at the age of fourteen and held it for nearly five years, every day of which he spent fearing that I was secretly planning to have him killed. He used to wake me up in the night, after our mother had retired for the evening. "I can see how you hunger for what is rightfully mine, little Rhetan", he would say, and hold a knife to my throat.' He frowned. 'He could have killed me at any time, but he was so convinced that I had some devious plot against him that he feared my death would trigger his own.'

'And you killed him?' Kest asked.

'Good Gods, *no*. After a few years his constant paranoia made him so stressed that he too suffered a heart attack, in the middle of the night. They found him dead, his body lying across a table strewn with sheets of paper upon which he had listed his enemies, real and imagined. That's when I became the Margrave. I was never a particularly bold warrior, nor even very clever, but I've always been patient. Patience is what gets you ahead in life.' He turned to Pheras, who was still waiting for his orders. 'Take two dozen of ours below to man the oars and steer us back to shore. Have the galleon follow. Once we're all back on dry land, have our doctor look to the injured. Afterwards you and the others find something to eat at the palace – I'm sure my nephew won't mind if you raid his stores.'

Evidalle looked as if he did mind, very much, but he was wise enough to let it pass. 'The hospitality of Barsat awaits you, Uncle,' he managed sulkily.

Pheras nodded and ran back up to relay the orders, and during the hustle and bustle, Kest whispered, 'Falcio, if we're going to make a move, it has to be now, while Rhetan's men are busy dealing with the boats.'

'What can we do?'

'If we get into position, we can jump over the side just before the barge reaches the dock. Evidalle's wedding carriage is waiting there – you, Chalmers and I can unhitch the horses while Brasti provides covering fire. The odds aren't great, but the four of us might—'

'What about her?' I asked, looking down at Lady Cestina's barely conscious sister, leaning against Chalmers for support. The Lady Mareina shared her sister's colouring and features, but her beauty was marred by extensive cuts and bruising and the effects of being half-starved. She was in no shape to be leaping over the side and running through the shallows, and even if she could, she'd never be fast enough to escape enemy fire.

Kest shook his head. 'This comes down to moving between the ticks of a clock, Falcio. You know that. If we let anything slow us down, we'll be dead before we reach the carriage.'

'You'd leave an innocent victim behind?' Chalmers whispered furiously.

'We won't do her much good if we're dead.'

'Keep silent a moment,' I said, surveying the scene aboard both the galleon and the wedding barge, searching for some opportunity that Kest might have missed. But he was right: Rhetan's soldiers were disciplined and efficient, and far too numerous for any of our usual tricks. Even with some form of distraction, it would be all we could do to escape *without* hauling the half-conscious Lady Mareina with us. The young woman's eyes caught mine; her fear was justified – and contagious. For a moment I worried she might try to make her own desperate run for it, even though she must have known she'd be dead before she hit the water. Perhaps that was preferable to being held captive by her sister and Margrave Evidalle.

'Just wait a little longer,' I whispered, as much to myself as to her.

Evidalle made a token effort to regain control of his own wedding. 'Uncle, we have much to discuss. I suggest we put the Greatcoats to the sword, allow the clerics to complete the ceremony, and then you and I can sit down with a nice glass of brandy and discuss business. With this marriage, my standing in the Duchy will be vastly improved.'

As if he'd only just then noticed the existence of Lady Cestina,

Rhetan said, 'So you managed to seduce the girl after all. You proved me wrong, Evidalle. I never thought it would work.'

Evidalle grinned. 'Did you ever doubt my powers of persuasion, Uncle?'

'I certainly doubted her husband would approve the match.' Margrave Rhetan walked over to Lady Cestina and bowed. 'My dearest girl, forgive the unseemly manners of an old man tired from the travails of too many sailings in too short a time.'

Despite the bandaged wound on her shoulder, she responded with an impressive curtsy. 'Margrave. We are delighted to have you here. As my fiancé says, there is much to—'

'I understand your first husband met with an unfortunate accident,' Rhetan interrupted, raising his voice loud enough to be heard all across the wedding barge. 'And here your poor sister appears to have missed the luncheon.' He went to stand before Lady Mareina, the dinner knife still dangling loosely from his hand, as if beckoning the girl to take it. She could have, too; she was near enough, and Rhetan showed no sign of being aware he still held it. 'You appear to have been ill of late, my Lady. How unselfish of you to rise to the occasion of your sister's wedding.'

Lady Mareina, visibly shaking, took slow, deep breaths as her gaze went from the knife before her to Evidalle, and then to her sister, just a few feet away. The depth of anger she must be feeling, to have been so utterly betrayed by her own blood, had to be overwhelming. I could see the fingers of her right hand twitching, desperate to grab the knife from Rhetan, but when her eyes found the guardsmen all around us, tears of frustration began to slide down her cheeks. 'My sister is well matched to Margrave Evidalle, my Lord,' Mareina said, her curtsy made possible only by Chalmers holding her tightly enough to keep her from falling down.

Margrave Rhetan could have let it go – whatever defiance Lady Mareina might have managed had already slipped away – but he kept at her anyway. 'And your parents? I worry for them, my dear. Yours is a prosperous family, is it not? And yet they too have suffered some recent . . . losses.'

'Bandits, my Lord,' Mareina said, her voice low, but without hesitation. 'These are uncertain times . . .'

The old Margrave smiled. 'No doubt the presence of the bulk of my nephew's forces stationed outside your parents' keep will ward off any more such . . . *bandits*.' He reached out and gently patted the girl's cheek. 'You're a smart one. You know how to read the lie of the land. I imagine that with a little patience you'll find contentment with your circumstances.' He turned to face the rest of us. 'You see? A little discretion, a little wisdom, and all is well.'

Evidalle's pleasure was evident in the tone of his voice and the confident manner in which he spread his arms wide as if he were acknowledging a cheering crowd. 'As you can see, Uncle, I've brought peace to once warring families.'

'And doubled your holdings in the process,' Rhetan noted.

'Now, let us deal with these Trattari and begin the next step in my great plan to—'

Rhetan cut him off. 'No, let's not create trouble where none is needed.'

'What? Are you mad? The Trattari came here to arrest me!'

'Oh, I'm sure it was nothing of the sort.' The old man glanced over to me. 'You merely came to bless the happy occasion, isn't that correct?' Before I could answer, he turned to Captain Squirrel. 'Too bad the temporary miscommunication caused a bit of a fuss, but these things happen during such turbulent times. Best to leave any little transgressions forgotten, I suggest.'

Captain Squirrel bowed. 'I . . . Yes, Margrave, it is as you say.'

Rhetan walked over to me, deliberately stepping over a dead guard in the process. 'Of course, I might have the situation confused. Perhaps you were here to arrest my nephew for . . . what would the charges be, I wonder? The unlawful confinement of Lady Mareina? Or the accusation could be something more severe – treason, perhaps?'

There was something very dangerous at play here. Rhetan wasn't simply speculating; he was laying out options for me, pushing me to see which one I would choose. *What exactly is your game here, old man?*

'The situation is complex, your Lordship,' I said. 'We're still . . . investigating.'

'Really? The question is a simple one, surely? Have the Greatcoats come to arrest the Margrave of Barsat, and if so, on what charge?'

Chalmers started to speak, but I held up a hand to keep her silent. Rhetan was prodding us for a reaction, but I hadn't yet figured out why. He pointed with his dinner knife at the bodies on the ground. 'Frankly, if this is what comes of your "investigations", one has to wonder what *outcome* might result from an actual trial.'

It was the way he said the word 'outcome' that gave me the first clue as to what was really going on. 'Outcomes vary, my Lord, depending on the circumstances and, of course, the presiding magistrate.'

'No doubt, no doubt. I suppose any number of—'

'Enough!' Evidalle shouted, and strode towards us. His four remaining guards stomped behind him, crossbows in hand. 'I suggest you move out of the way, Uncle.'

Rhetan's men looked poised to attack, but the old Margrave waved them off. He let out a long sigh and stepped aside. 'Your impatience is making you sloppy, Evidalle. I suggest you take a moment to fully appreciate the situation.'

'Patience is the shackle that binds the timid, Uncle.' Evidalle grabbed a crossbow from one of his men. 'Only the daring know glory.'

'I suppose you have a point,' Rhetan said without enthusiasm.

Brasti chuckled. 'Hah – that's a good one.' No one else laughed. 'You know, because of the point on the crossbow bolt – wasn't that meant to be funny?'

With Evidalle's weapon trained on me, it was difficult to sound flippant, but I made the effort anyway. 'There's something you should know before you fire, Margrave Evidalle.'

The Margrave of Barsat was nothing if not gracious. 'Speak then, Trattari. Beg. Threaten. Make your accusations. No one will listen.'

I forced myself to focus on what I was about to say, rather than the steel tip of the bolt aimed squarely at my face. 'Well, to begin with, I am the First Cantor of the Greatcoats: I don't *make accusations.* I *issue verdicts.*'

'Do so, then, if it gives you any solace. Let the Gods hear your blasphemy before I end you.' He wrapped his finger around the trigger of the crossbow and began to squeeze, very slowly.

I had to speak quickly now. 'My verdict is this, Margrave Evidalle: I judge you guilty of commissioning the murder of the young man Udrin, rightful husband of Lady Cestina. I further find you guilty of assault upon her parents and of the unlawful confinement of her sister, Lady Mareina, all in furtherance of your attempt to stage a coup against the throne of Baern and to incite insurrection against the Crown.

'The punishment for those crimes is death, and every man present is bound by law to assist in your capture.'

'Goodbye, Trattari, your death will launch a revolution.'

'Sounds grand. One piece of advice then, my Lord?'

This took him aback. 'What?'

Saint Birgid, I know you're dead, but if you'd be inclined to lend any assistance from beyond the veil, I'd very much appreciate it right now.

I looked at Margrave Rhetan, who was now standing next to his nephew. 'Never trust a man who brings a hundred soldiers to a wedding.'

It's odd how quickly the mighty become less remarkable to behold once they realise that all their power has been taken away. Margrave Evidalle's luxuriant hair had gleamed like a golden crown upon his head, but now sweat dripped from his brow and it began to look limp, in fact, positively foppish. His eyes, so full of fire and certainty before, became those of a boy who has just lost his favourite toy. When he opened his mouth – which only moments ago had been full of confident smiles and easy laughter – all that emerged now was a soft gurgle and the tip of Rhetan's dinner knife as it completed its journey through the back of the Margrave's throat.

CHAPTER SIX

THE VIRTUE OF PATIENCE

For all of Margrave Rhetan's sermonising on the virtue of patience, events moved remarkably quickly after that. The wedding guests, gasping, huddled behind the Knights who once again readied themselves to protect their patrons, while Rhetan's men busied themselves ensuring that none of Evidalle's remaining guardsmen attempted anything untoward.

The erstwhile Margrave of Barsat hadn't even finished falling to the ground before his uncle had moved on to other business. 'The Greatcoats will make no efforts to bar my annexation of Barsat into the March of Val Iramont,' he said to me, as though we were halfway through an afternoon of negotiations. I suppose in some sense we were.

It was my turn. 'The troops occupying Lady Mareina's parents' keep will leave immediately.'

'Already done.'

'And they will be compensated for their suffering, as will Udrin's family.'

Margrave Rhetan waved a hand. 'Of course, of course. Besides, the cost will be more than made up for by the temporary reduction in taxes you will be persuading the Realm's Protector to grant me.'

Great. Another reason for Valiana to yell at me. 'Lady Mareina,' I said, pointing to the girl who was gazing at the scene before her in utter disbelief, 'needs support. You'll be apportioning a third of your new lands into a separate condate and naming her Damina of . . . Well, let's call this little spot Revancia, shall we?' *Revancia* was an old Tristian word that meant *righteous vengeance*.

Rhetan's eyes narrowed. 'You do realise that poor Evidalle was my nephew? He had no heirs, so as his closest living relative, his property is legally mine.'

'Ah, but you appear to have overlooked something yourself, Margrave.'

He looked quizzical.

'While the ceremony was not yet completed, the marriage contract was already signed, and so there *is* in fact an heir to your nephew's lands.'

'Which would be Lady Cestina, not . . .' But by then Rhetan had caught my meaning. He turned his gaze on the new bride and would-be-rebel. 'Of course, we've all heard of brides dying of grief over the loss of their beloved: a tragic outcome – although I think in this case it would bring with it a certain poetic symmetry.'

The Lady Cestina had a far quicker mind for political calculation than Evidalle; she took two steps towards the nearest cleric and dropped to her knees. Gripping the hem of his pale blue robes, she started, 'I wish to dedicate my life to . . .' She paused, staring at the handful of cloth, no doubt trying to remember which God was associated with the colour. '*Phenia!* Yes, Phenia, Goddess of Love.'

The cleric looked dumbfounded. 'My Lady . . . you wish to—? Such a life does not come—'

'Oh, shut up,' she said, rising to her feet and turning back to address the entire audience. 'With my spiritual life now dedicated to Phenia, I hereby name my beloved sister, Lady Mareina, as beneficiary of my—'

'As *immediate and irrevocable* beneficiary,' I suggested helpfully.

Lady Cestina's eyes sent daggers my way. It was a good thing the

God of Love was already dead, for I do believe her new priestess would otherwise have been invoking any number of curses. 'As *immediate and irrevocable* beneficiary of all my lands and holdings from now unto the end of time.'

'Marked,' Rhetan said. He went to stand before Lady Mareina. 'You, girl. Will you, in front of all these fine people, and in your capacity as the new Damina of—'

He turned to me. 'What did you want to call it again?'

'Revancia.'

'Right. In your capacity as the new Damina of Revancia, do you swear fealty to me as your Margrave, giving unto me all such duties required by law and by tradition?'

Lady Mareina, whose world had been destroyed and rebuilt and destroyed again all during the span of an hour, somewhere found the strength to support herself and with remarkable poise, announce, 'As Damina of Revancia, it is my most heartfelt honour to be the first to swear fealty before your Grace, the Margrave of Val Iramont, Lord of the proudest territory in all of Baern.'

The wedding guests finally had a situation for which they knew the appropriate response; they didn't even need the tiny prompt from Rhetan's soldiers to burst into wild applause.

Rhetan acknowledged their cheers with a bow that lasted less than a second before turning back to me. 'I'll expect to receive word of the tax exemption within the week.'

Captain Pheras stepped forward and motioned to Evidalle's body. 'What should we do with him?'

'Take him ashore with the rest of the dead. You can bury him after everything else is dealt with.' Rhetan looked down at his nephew's corpse. 'Impatient fool. He could easily have been Duke one day, but he had to play the rebel hero.' He shook his head. 'You can't just go around killing people in a blatant bid for power.'

Most days I know when to keep my mouth shut, but in this instance

I couldn't stop myself. 'You do recall that you stuck a dinner knife through the back of your nephew's neck just a few moments ago?'

'True – but you were the one who declared my nephew guilty of treason, invoking my legal responsibility in front of all present. I really had no choice but to assist you.'

'And gain all of Margrave Evidalle's lands in the process,' Kest noted. 'And anyone aggrieved by the outcome will blame the Greatcoats, not you.'

Rhetan, Margrave of what was now the largest and most powerful territory in the Duchy – and by extension, the presumptive future Duke, once Ossia either abdicated or died, set his gaze on me. He finally gave a wide smile that looked as if it had been waiting patiently for years to show itself. 'As I told you: patience reaps rewards – especially when folly paves the way.'

This is why I despise the nobility.

Evidently my distaste showed on my face because Rhetan was staring at me with one eyebrow raised. 'Don't get all pious with me, Trattari. You don't seriously expect anyone to believe that Duchess Ossia – a *very* patient woman, I can assure you – sent you here just to rescue the poor, pitiful Lady Mareina?' He gestured at the wedding guests who were even now hastening to disembark from the barge. 'I'm not a gambling man, but if I were, I'd wager my new lands that your orders were to spy on the assembled nobles and quietly report back who was showing any enthusiasm for Evidalle's conspiracy and who might remain loyal to the heir.'

He clapped me on the shoulder and added cheerily, 'I expect you'll have some explaining to do once you get back to Aramor.'

CHAPTER SEVEN

THE WEDDING CAKE

The execution of a Margrave creates a surprising amount of paperwork. Military forces, for example, can't simply be dumped together like vegetables in a stew: each side's officers must now begin vying for command of the newly combined force, while the common soldiers, always convinced that the other guy's troops get better pay (and even if they don't, *they* should), will immediately start demanding higher salaries. Not that more money even begins to deal with the possibility that you're suddenly part of the same squad that just killed your comrade or even one of your brothers.

Then there's the matter of taking over the palace, eliminating anyone related to (or having sex with) the deceased Margrave, and most important of all, securing the treasury before its contents mysteriously disappear. A great many people need to be bribed, especially the clerics – even in a country where the Gods have been murdered, you still don't want to be on the wrong side of the Church.

And, of course, when wedding celebrations come to such an unexpected and bloody end, you have to decide what to do with the cake.

'It's not bad, actually,' Brasti said, licking his fingers as he sat back down on the edge of the dock.

The narrow beach was littered with wounded men awaiting

treatment, lying groaning amidst the decorative silk streamers meant to guide the happy couple along the gilded path that led up a gentle slope to the Margrave's summer palace.

Kest looked up from cleaning the edge of his shield. 'You should probably leave the cake alone,' he warned Brasti.

'Why, is it bad luck?'

Kest pointed at the remains of the cake, sitting unceremoniously next to a pile of dirty dishes. 'I suspect that's *not* raspberry sauce.'

Brasti looked at the red splatters on the icing, momentarily horrified, then he shrugged and used the head of one of his arrows to slice himself a second piece, this time taking care to cut around the red parts. 'I'm going to miss this, you know.'

'Desecrating dead men's wedding cakes?' I asked, following Kest's example and carefully running a cloth along the blade of my rapier. The problem with killing people is that if you forget to polish the blood off your weapon, you're liable to find it stuck in its sheath the next time you need to take someone down.

Brasti kicked an unconscious guardsman. '*This*. Travelling around the country together, beating the hells out of corrupt nobles and their thuggish lackeys.' He let out a sigh. 'Mark my words, Falcio, life will become terribly dull once Aline becomes Queen.'

'You foresee a shortage of corrupt nobles and thuggish lackeys in our future?' I asked. 'Or is this because you're going to abandon Kest and me so that you can run off and marry Darriana?'

He turned abruptly serious. 'Come on, Falcio, it had to end sometime. You've done your duty: you've fulfilled the King's last request; you've found his "Charoite" and pretty soon she's going to be taking the throne. Our time is over. Let someone else take a turn at judging whose sheep ate whose grass.'

There was a certain logic to his words, of course, but it still struck me as highly optimistic – or pessimistic, perhaps, depending on your point of view. I didn't really have the energy to contradict him, though, so I looked at Kest, who shook his head at me. 'You forget, Falcio, when the King was in power we weren't constantly racing about the country trying to save it. Most of the time we just rode our circuits, heard our cases and delivered our verdicts.'

Brasti blew a strand of damp hair out of his face. 'Gods, those circuits: twice a year, the same bloody route, the same wretched towns and villages, and the same pressing need to work out how to saw a cow in half in order to settle some bloody-minded farmers' dispute. I swear they glued the damned things back together after we left just so they'd still have something to fight over.'

Some part of me knew that Brasti was right – although hopefully, not about the cow. I felt an odd pang in my chest just then; I'd only recently discovered that I had a habit of remembering the past somewhat more . . . well, *romantically* than perhaps it deserved. Whenever I thought back to the early days in the Greatcoats, I remembered the deviously complex cases, the perilous duels and daring escapes. There'd certainly been a fair few, but they'd taken place over *years*, not weeks. Believe it or not, most trials *don't* end in swordfights. Once Aline became Queen, the fate of the country would no longer be in our hands at every turn – we'd go back to being judicial functionaries. *Bureaucrats.* I'm sure I used to enjoy that life . . . so why did the mere thought of it feel so foreign now?

I felt Kest's hand on my shoulder. 'It's not just you, Falcio. The mind can become accustomed to almost anything, even the chaos of an interregnum and the daily struggle to avoid death.'

Brasti jumped to his feet. 'I have an idea.'

No good has ever come from those four words coming out of that particular mouth.

He waited patiently to be asked – almost a full second – then pointed at the deceased Margrave's wedding barge. 'We should become pirates!' He caught my expression and hastily amended his suggestion. 'I mean, *good* pirates, of course. *Noble* pirates.'

'"Noble pirates"?' Kest asked.

'How would that work, exactly?' I asked, having already forgotten my rule about Brasti and ideas.

He looked thoughtful, as if he'd given the matter extensive consideration. 'Well, we only attack the ships of excessively rich and venal men, and then we . . .' He made a series of gestures with his hands that made no sense to anyone, then explained, 'We sort of . . . well, *redistribute* what we took, give it to those in the greatest need. Minus a reasonable commission, of course.'

Kest tilted his head. 'You're suggesting we switch from *enforcing* the laws to *actively breaking them* by stealing from those with wealth to give it to those without?'

'Minus a reasonable commission,' he repeated. He saw me staring at him and added quickly, 'Not a *big* commission, of course! I'm sure Kest could come up with a suitable formula.'

'"The Greatcoats",' I announced, '"stealing ships from the wealthy to give unto the poor . . . minus a suitable commission".' I slid my squeaky-clean rapiers back into their sheaths. 'Not exactly the most memorable catchphrase.'

Brasti sulked. 'Not the way you say it.' He looked past me and grinned. 'On the other hand, perhaps you can ask Rhyleis to come up with something more poetic.'

I turned to see the beautiful – and dangerous – Bardatti guitarist from the wedding walking towards us.

Brasti was suddenly close behind me. 'You really should bed that woman, Falcio. I warn you, I won't wait much longer before I make her a better offer.'

'You already did,' Kest said. 'Five times, by my count.'

'How dare you, sir!' Brasti said, doing his best impression of a gentleman whose good name has just been slandered. He has to do it as an impression, of course, because he's never actually *had* a good name. 'I will have evidence from you, Kest Murrowson, or have no choice but to challenge you to—'

'When we first saw her in that tavern on the road back to Aramor,' Kest said, putting down his shield so that he could keep a tally using the fingers of his left hand. 'You hadn't even asked her name before you made some rather elaborate suggestions as to how the two of you might pass the time together.'

'Aha! You see? I didn't know her name, so it didn't count.'

'Then there was the moment when Falcio left the common room and you asked her again – we all knew her name by then.'

'An innocent misunderstanding.'

'Also at the Busted Scales, shortly before the battle against the Blacksmith and his God, then again *during* the fight.'

'You propositioned Rhyleis during a battle against an actual God?' I asked.

He shrugged. 'The rest of you were busy.' He turned to Kest. 'That was only *four* times. I'll have my apology, oh Saint-of-remembering-things-no-one-wants-remembered.'

'Wait for it,' Kest said to me.

Rhyleis approached us, hands on her hips. 'Well, if it isn't the King's Heart, the Queen's Shield, and . . . the other one.' She looked up at Brasti. 'I forget, what is it you're known for, again?'

He grinned salaciously at her. 'Why, I'm an explorer, Rhyleis, and if you'd like to come for a little walk inside the palace with me, I promise to explore you most thoroughly.'

'And there's number five,' Kest said.

'You're a terrible friend, you know that?' Brasti asked. 'I expect recompense in the form of strong drink.'

The two of them headed up the path towards the former Margrave of Barsat's summer palace. I briefly considered running after them, but Brasti would never have let me live it down, so instead I turned and faced Rhyleis: musician, actress, spy, and some day soon, quite likely the death of me. The smile on her face and the curve of her hips filled me with more trepidation than all of Evidalle's men combined.

CHAPTER EIGHT

DUELLING FLIRTATIONS

'Why Falcio,' she began, turning my name into the opening of some kind of tune, 'you look like a frightened cat backed into a corner by a bloodthirsty hound.'

Even I wasn't going to fall into the trap of admitting that her words perfectly summed up the situation. 'Rhyleis, you are, as always, a delight to the eyes, music to the ears and an unspeakable terror to the hearts of innocent men everywhere.'

All right, so poetry isn't a weapon with which I'm particularly skilled – but I still thought it a passable opening salvo.

'The same could be said of all women, don't you think?' she asked.

Another trap. Never let yourself be tricked into comparing one woman with all others; it rarely turns out well. 'Rhyleis, is there any chance I could convince you to punch me in the face now rather than spinning out whatever torment you've got planned for me?'

The Bardatti looked utterly crestfallen. She took a shallow breath. 'Oh, Falcio, is *this* to be our relationship? I come to you with adoration and you spurn me until my heart grows so fragile it awaits only one final snub before breaking entirely?'

And here it was: the ambush.

Any time I *think* I have Rhyleis figured out, she turns this petty flirtation of hers around on me and the next thing I know, I'm apologising for having hurt her feelings. She's just too damned good an actress – but for all her teasing, there's always a subtle question beneath her words, played out in brief flickers in her expression that makes me wonder if – *just perhaps* – this game of hers might mask a genuine affection that she's otherwise unable to express. If I push her too far, I risk hurting her feelings.

That's assuming that she *has* feelings.

I held up my hands in surrender. 'Can we not simply agree that you've got the better of me once again? That I look like a fool while you are charming, witty and devastatingly brilliant?'

She tumbled into my arms as if we'd come to the romantic climax of the play. 'Falcio, oh my Falcio! You always know just what to say to make a girl melt . . .'

I stood there awkwardly, trying to find some configuration of embrace that was neither inviting nor callous. She nestled closer to me. Apparently in my efforts not to offend, I'd overshot the mark considerably.

'You should be nicer to me, you know,' she said, reaching up a finger to tap my nose. 'Wasn't I the one who brought you word of Margrave Evidalle's little revolution in the first place? Just think how much fun you'd have missed without me.'

'I came here to *enforce the laws*, Rhyleis. Despite what you might think, I don't actually go around *looking* for trouble.'

She tilted her head, just a little, and whispered, 'Are you sure? Trouble can be rather fun, in the right company.'

Her breath was a mixture of sweet and spice that sent my heart racing. The moments after you've just survived a battle are a poor time to resist temptation. 'Rhyleis, please . . .'

She placed her hands on my chest and arched her back to look up at me, briefly dropping the role of seductress. 'Oh, Falcio. Am I really so menacing? Must you always act like the innocent boy, pining away on his lonely farm, dreaming of the day when the Saint of Mercy will finally come back to him?'

'Could we leave Ethalia out of this?'

She raised an eyebrow. 'I would dearly love to, Falcio, but you appear to be incapable of letting her go.'

Though I wished it weren't so, there was some truth to what she said. I *did* miss Ethalia. Our romance might have ended, but the ache of being apart from her hadn't gone away.

'Has Ethalia-who-shares-all-sorrows returned from her Saintly pilgrimage?' Rhyleis asked innocently.

'You know she hasn't,' I replied.

Rhyleis ignored the bite in my remark. 'I wonder, in her quest to find the other remaining Saints, if she might fall in love with one – what a remarkable song that would make, don't you think?'

'Rhyleis, is this some bizarre effort to make me get off my arse and go chasing after Ethalia, or are you just trying to get me into bed again?'

She laughed enigmatically, in the way of actors, poets and other liars. 'Can't it be both?'

I felt her hands reaching up behind my neck, pulling me down into what would soon be a kiss. Our lips moved closer and my body politely requested that my mind stop getting in the way.

'Perhaps it's time you stopped confusing sex with love, Falcio val Mond,' she whispered.

I felt my body, quite of its own accord, start to give in. Rhyleis was wild, unpredictable, clever, beautiful, and any number of other things that would make anyone feel lucky to be in her company. On the other hand, it really pisses me off when people try to manipulate me. The instant before our lips would have met, I turned my head and whispered in her ear, 'Maybe it's time you stopped confusing being beautiful with being desirable.'

She stiffened. For a moment I feared I'd gone too far, that my cruelty would be repaid with a devastatingly biting remark paired with a slap in the face. Instead, Rhyleis laughed, her voice neither cruel or mischievous, but light and winsome, like a bird taking flight. '"Stop confusing being beautiful with being desirable",' she repeated. 'I love it! I *must* use that in a song some day.'

I let out a breath I hadn't realised I'd been holding in.

'Oh,' she said, patting me on the chest, 'I almost forgot why I came to find you in the first place.'

'That seems unlikely.'

'Don't be like that. This is important. Duchess Ossia requests that you rendezvous with her at Werta's Point, three days north of here.' Rhyleis shook her head mournfully. 'I believe you've got rather a severe scolding coming to you.'

'But . . . but how could she possibly know already that we didn't exactly follow her orders?'

Rhyleis tilted her head at me as if it were an odd question. 'When do you *ever* follow orders, Falcio?'

I suppose she's got a point.

'Now, I must go and write down that wonderful line of yours. As always, you are an inspiration to me, Falcio.' She gave me a peck on the cheek and momentarily pulled away, fooling me into thinking the moment had passed and the danger averted, but then her hand snaked behind my neck, she pulled me closer and kissed me full on the lips. I doubt a dozen such kisses have ever existed in the history of the world.

'Why did you that?' I asked, when the kiss was over. For all her games and flirtations, Rhyleis had never pushed things this far before.

She looked up at me and something in her gaze had changed – it wasn't love or ardour or even mischief, but a kind of sorrowful compassion. She reached out a finger and traced the line of my eyebrow. 'You are too serious, Falcio. When the bad days come, I want you to remember that there can still be bright and playful moments, even in the darkest of times.'

She kissed me once more, on the cheek this time, and started up the path towards the palace.

'Wait,' I called out to her, 'what do you mean, "the darkest of times"? What do you know that I don't, Rhyleis?'

The Bardatti turned her head and flashed me that roguish smile of hers, as though nothing had happened between us. 'A great many things, Falcio val Mond. A great many things.'

I stood there like an idiot watching her saunter away until Chalmers came up alongside me. 'Is she really a Bardatti?'

'As far as I know. They don't exactly wear insignia.'

Chalmers gave that some thought. 'It's just odd, because she was talking to me earlier.'

'And?'

'Well, I've never met a Bardatti before. I always assumed the experience would be . . . I don't know. *Different.* Mystical somehow?'

'Was that not the feeling you came away with?'

Chalmers shook her head. 'By the end of the conversation I found myself with a profound desire to punch her in the face.'

'Ah,' I said.

She looked up at me. '"Ah"? What's that supposed to mean?'

'As far as I can tell, that's one of the only two sentiments one is meant to experience after an encounter with the Bardatti.'

'What's the other one?'

'None of your business.'

I heard Brasti and Kest's footsteps coming up behind us and Brasti announced bitterly, 'Well, they've managed to lock up all the liquor – I mean, you can steal the deeds to half of Evidalle's estates right now if you've a mind to, but don't bother trying to get a drink in this damned place.'

'That's probably for the best,' I said, and repeated Ossia's enigmatic command to present ourselves at Werta's Point three days hence.

'Why would you be taking orders from a Duchess?' Chalmers asked. 'You're supposed to be Greatcoats. Since when do the Dukes get t—?'

'Please don't get him started,' Brasti warned. 'Some bears you do not poke.'

'We need Ossia to persuade the rest of the Ducal Council to accept Aline's coronation,' Kest explained. 'But we have a different problem now, Falcio.'

Excellent. Because I didn't have enough of those already. 'What is it?'

He pointed towards the water. 'The ship that was supposed to take us to Aramor hasn't arrived, which means it was scared off by Margrave Rhetan's galleon. It's three days to Werta's Point by sail, but if we have to go on horseback it'll take us more than a week to get through the mountain passes and we'll never get to the meeting on time.'

'Perfect,' Brasti said. 'Let's *really* piss off the Duchess of Baern, right when we need her most. Unless . . .' He paused for a long moment, apparently deep in thought – which, I'll point out again, is *always* dangerous – then suddenly grinned at me.

'What?' I asked, but I'd already guessed. 'No. *Absolutely not!*'

Brasti gestured proudly to Margrave Evidalle's gaudy – and now empty – wedding barge. 'Pirates!' he declared proudly.

CHAPTER NINE

SANVERIO GORGE

The problem with ships is that they spend entirely too much time on the water. Having spent my life making my way through the world on foot and on horseback, with my only forays off dry land being the occasional – and completely involuntary – dunkings into various ponds, canals, lakes and rivers, I find the sensation of being perpetually surrounded by something that will drown you if you fall into it to be uniquely disconcerting.

'Look,' Brasti said, pointing at me as he hopped up and down like a giddy child, 'he's going to be sick again!'

Kest lifted his nose from an old book of maritime navigational theory – because *of course* he could read for hours on this nightmare vessel without ever getting even remotely seasick – and peered over at me. Narrowing his eyes, he said, 'That's not the look he gets when he's about to throw up. I think he's just having some sort of philosophical crisis.'

Chalmers looked down on us from her perch in the rigging. 'Does he have many of those?'

Brasti rolled his eyes. 'You wouldn't believe how many.'

'You know what I find relieves the symptoms of both seasickness and philosophical discomfort for me?' I asked, lending an edge to my voice that any reasonably aware person might have recognised as a sign to stop talking.

Brasti looked thoughtful, then raised a finger. 'Getting into fights and killing people?'

'Exactly.'

He looked around at the sailors quietly going about their duties. 'Well, I don't think any of the crew are particularly expendable, so we'd need to find you someone t—'

'He means you,' Kest said.

Brasti guffawed. 'Hah! Don't be ridiculous – just look at him. He's got the worst sea legs of any man alive. If the barge had actually been *moving* during the fight with Evidalle's men, he wouldn't have been able to draw even one of his rapiers without falling flat on his arse.'

I would have been keen to test out his theory but just at that moment there were other things concerning me. Two days of sailing had brought us to the Southern Sea and I now found myself looking out onto the endless expanse of water. 'Are we . . . going the right way?'

Chalmers looked down and asked Kest, 'Is he truly this stupid?'

Since my twentieth birthday, I've fought seventy-six judicial duels (not that I'm counting. Kest does that). I've been on the 'vastly outnumbered' side of more than a dozen different battles, thwarted numerous assassinations and faced an uncountable number of other attempts on my life. The fact that I'm still here and the majority of my opponents aren't should say something about my capacity for both survival and violence. And yet I swear there isn't a single person in this damnable country who's afraid of me.

Chalmers climbed down to stand alongside me. 'Look over to port.'

'Which one's port again?'

'The left.'

'Then why don't they just call it left?'

Kest put down his book. 'Because it's only on the left if you're facing the prow.'

I sighed. 'The prow is the front, correct?'

He extended his hand in each direction while reciting them aloud: 'Prow, port, stern, starboard.'

In a fit of pique I repeated his gestures, saying, 'Front, left, back, right.'

'Oi,' one of the sailors said, an offended expression on his face, 'show some respect for the lady.'

'The lady' refers to the ship itself. That's right: sailors are sufficiently stupid and superstitious to confuse a large, loosely held together heap of planks and canvas sheeting with a 'lady'. I let the comment pass and turned my attention back to Chalmers. 'You were saying, about my stupidity—?'

She pointed to the left – the *port* – side of the barge. 'See that big puddle of water out there?' When I nodded, she said, 'That would be the Great Bay of Pertine.' She turned to the right. 'And that large patch of—' She motioned to the sailor, who was still standing there, a wooden barrel on his shoulder, apparently awaiting an apology on behalf of ships everywhere. 'What do you call that non-watery thing over there again?'

The man looked confused. 'What? You mean the *land*?'

'*The land*,' Chalmers repeated to me. '*That* would be the Western Cliffs of Luth. So given that we have water on one side and land on the other, how exactly could we be going the *wrong* way?'

'You know,' Brasti said to Kest, 'I'm starting to believe she *is* a Greatcoat. She might be too young for the job, and absolute rubbish with a weapon, but she instinctively shows just the right amount of deference due to the First Cantor.'

I stared up at the cliffs a few hundred feet away – I couldn't even begin to think in terms of knots or nautical miles or whatever the hells they used instead of normal distances – and felt profoundly uncomfortable. I'd been to Luth dozens of times – it borders my own Duchy of Pertine – but this didn't look anything like it to me.

'It's a different view of the world, isn't it?' Kest asked as I clung onto the side.

'I feel like a foreigner. I thought I'd walked or ridden across every inch of the country, and yet . . .'

'Thirteen per cent,' Kest said. 'I worked it out once, in the map room at Aramor. In my life I've seen thirteen per cent of the villages, towns, cities and hamlets of Tristia.'

I stared at him. 'You're joking.'

'That was a few years ago, of course, but since the King died we've spent most of our time in places we'd already been before, so I doubt it's much higher than fourteen per cent now. Maybe fifteen, at a pinch.'

Tristia is a small country, or so I've always been told. I've seen maps of the known world, of course, and I can even name half a dozen other countries, but I've never been to those places – I've never left the land of my birth. To find out I knew barely a sixth of my homeland was troubling.

'We'll be entering Sanverio Gorge soon,' Chalmers said, pointing at the high cliff. It looked like a giant had riven the coastline with an axe, leaving an impossibly narrow passage into the land itself.

'How will we fit?' I asked.

The sailor behind us put down his cask and joined us. 'We're still a ways off. It looks narrow here, but it's actually a good half a cable across.'

'Half a what?' I muttered.

'About three hundred feet,' Kest translated.

'Won't it be too shallow?'

'Nah,' the sailor said, 'most of the river's twelve fathoms.'

'Seventy-two feet,' Kest said before I had to ask what in all the hells a fathom was.

As the barge sailed slowly towards the gorge it did eventually become clear we *weren't* going to be crushed, which allowed me to relax just enough to feel seasick again. But the sense of being lost remained. I looked up at the Luth side of the gorge, trying to re-establish some sense of location. 'The nearest town's Elean, isn't it?' I'd actually been there once.

'That's *miles* away,' the sailor replied cuttingly. 'You've got a dozen villages between here and there.'

'Vois Calan is the closest, I think,' Chalmers said, peering at the cliffs looming over us.

The sailor nodded appreciatively. 'Exactly right. Well spotted, little girl.'

'I'm eighteen, and I'm a Greatcoat.'

He laughed. 'Well then, well spotted, *Trattari*.'

'Use that name again and I'll—'

Chalmers and I both stopped, realising we'd both spoken at once.

The sailor threw up his hands and walked away as she and I shared a brief nod of acknowledgment.

Maybe Brasti was right. Maybe Chalmers *was* a Greatcoat.

'Anything interesting about this Vois Calan?' Brasti asked. He'd hopped up on the rail and was hanging on to a piece of rope tied to something called a 'mizen'. 'I mean, other than the fact that they have a chair at the top of a cliff?'

The rest of us shielded our eyes from the sun overhead and followed his gaze. I couldn't see any chair, but I did make out what looked like a small crowd assembling near the edge.

'Look at the path,' Chalmers said.

It took me a moment to make out the steep path carved into the rock; it was almost hidden in the shadows and scrub. There were two people slowly making their way from the shore, dragging what looked suspiciously like an unconscious or dead body behind them.

'Well, that isn't polite,' Brasti said.

'What are they doing with him?' I asked, wishing my eyesight was even half as good as his.

'Looks like he's being taken for trial.'

'How can you be sure?'

'Well, first of all, I think the chair is a magistrate's throne, and second . . .' He pointed a little further along, away from the crowd. At first it looked like a row of little trees along the edge, but they were far too straight – and trees don't usually have ropes dangling from their tops.

'One usually doesn't hang quite so many people at once without a trial,' Brasti finished.

I grabbed a passing deckhand. 'Tell the captain he needs to stop—'

'—weigh anchor,' Brasti said helpfully.

'—*now*.'

The sailor stared back at me.

'You mean "drop" anchor,' Kest said. '"Weigh" anchor is the other one.'

'I don't give a shit.' I motioned for the deckhand to move. 'Just tell the captain to make the damned ship stop and give me something that floats so I can get to the shore.'

Kest glanced up at the late afternoon sun. 'We'll have to move fast. Village trials in Luth take place at sunset.'

'Why's that?' Chalmers asked. 'There's nothing in the legal codes about—'

'So they don't lose time working the fields.' Brasti was already packing up his quiver. 'And so it's over before supper. Nobody likes to watch an execution on a full stomach.'

My mind had already turned to the problem of the time it would take to get up the cliff path. I've always had a dislike for hanging – apart from anything else, it tends to make appealing the verdict difficult. But more than that, I was sick and tired of seeing the law twisted into a means of bringing more death and destruction into the world. I needed to have words with this so-called 'magistrate'.

On a more positive note, I wasn't feeling seasick any more.

*

'You see, *this* is why we ought to take up piracy full time,' Brasti said, pulling himself up the slippery path. 'We could spend our days relaxing on our lovely barge, enjoying the fresh salty air, drinking, carousing with other pirates, and hardly ever have to slog our way up a cliff only to face a mob who will doubtless be trying to send us right back down, only much faster.'

'We're *not* being pirates,' I panted, wiping my sleeve across my forehead. The sun was dropping fast.

Brasti paused to glance back at me. 'Why not?'

'Because pirates are outlaws and we're fucking magistrates, you twit.'

As he turned back to the climb, he added, 'Sorry, my mistake. I must have forgotten about us being lawmen on account of all those years we spent, you know, running from the law.'

'He has a point,' Kest said from behind me.

'I should have left you on the ship instead of Chalmers.' I looked up the steep slope at the backs of the people dragging their intended victim to the top. 'How far ahead of us would you say they are?'

'About a quarter-cable,' Kest replied.

I turned back to him. 'Are you trying to be funny?'

'Sorry.' He didn't sound in the least bit sorry. 'Roughly a hundred and fifty feet.' He peered past me. 'They'll get to the top before we do.'

I gave Brasti a push. 'Hurry up.'

He groaned in reply, even as he started jogging. 'What damned good will it do, getting there faster, if we're too shattered to fight when we reach the top? And anyway, who the hells goes to the trouble of dragging a man all the way up there just to hang him?'

As Kest had predicted, our quarry finished the ascent a few minutes ahead of us, which gave them more than enough time to alert those waiting up top to our presence, and we arrived to find ourselves facing a crowd brandishing boar-spears and pitchforks.

'What in hells is going on?' I asked no one in particular.

Having an angry mob ready to send us to our deaths wasn't all that unusual for us, but your typical mob isn't usually made up of some fifteen women and children.

'You know what's odd?' Brasti said.

'What's that?' I asked, unsheathing my rapiers.

'This isn't actually the largest group of women I've ever had try to stab me at once.'

CHAPTER TEN

THE MAGISTRATE OF VOIS CALAN

A stand-off is a particularly important moment during a fight, though to an onlooker it might appear to just be two groups of angry people glaring at each other, shifting their feet, gripping their weapons and, of course, hurling insults. I'm usually quite partial to that last part, but this wasn't my usual sort of angry mob.

I counted eleven women, none wearing armour or carrying themselves like trained fighters, two girls no older than ten holding rocks and two boys, even younger, hanging onto their mothers' skirts. All of this presented a bit of a problem for me, not least because my usual repertoire of threats and insults included things like, 'Drop that sword before I use it to cut off your balls and make you wear them like earrings!' or 'You've got until the count of three before I tell Brasti to fire an arrow right up your arse and out your cock!' which struck me as particularly inappropriate things at this moment.

Don't get me wrong: I've fought – and been nearly killed by – any number of women, just not those who looked so utterly unprepared for violence. Somewhere nearby, a guitar played sombre chords, which was unusual, but not really my top concern right then.

'Now, let's be reasonable,' I suggested, and that did the trick: the massed faces in front of me now looked completely comfortable with the idea of doing serious violence to me.

Brasti snorted. 'Did you just ask a crowd of angry mothers facing off against three pirates to be reasonable?'

'We're not fucking pirates!'

'Perhaps we should tell them that,' Kest said as he lifted his shield up just a hair. One of the women had pointed her boar-spear at our faces.

She looked young to me, perhaps in her mid-twenties, although the years were already wearing hard on her body, if not her spirit. 'You'll not touch one scrap of what's ours,' she said defiantly, gripping her spear tightly in her hands. 'Not our food, not our girls – so just you walk back down that cliff-path with your lives and count yourselves the richer for it.'

'We aren't pirates,' I said.

One of the little girls peered at our coats. 'Then why are you dressed as pirates?'

It hadn't occurred to me before, but actually, our greatcoats didn't look all that different from the one worn by an actual pirate I'd duelled years ago – though his had been a good deal more colourful, with a lot fewer pockets full of useful things, and luckily for me, a lot less effective in stopping a blade.

'You see?' Brasti said. 'We've already got the ship and the clothes for it. The Gods themselves are practically *begging* us to take up piracy!'

'The Gods are dead,' I reminded him.

'On this we can agree,' said a new voice, and the crowd drew back a step and parted to make way for a white-haired older woman, likely well into her sixties, though still strong of body and with a posture that suggested she wasn't anywhere near done with life yet.

'Who are you?' I asked.

'I am Olise, magistrate of Vois Calan, and you are interfering with a lawful trial.' Rather than wait for any reply of mine, she turned and gestured to the two women who'd dragged the unconscious man up the cliff-path. 'Prepare him for the noose.'

'Brasti . . .' I began.

'Let me guess: shoot the first person who tries to put a rope around his neck?'

'Exactly.'

'I wouldn't bother,' Kest said.

'Why?'

'Because if you look a little closer you'll see he's already dead.'

I looked past Kest's shield to the body being dragged across the rocky ground towards the roughly made gibbets. Kest was right: the man in question wasn't unconscious at all. His limbs trailed awkwardly across the ground, most likely because every bone in his body was broken.

'What happened to him?' I asked.

Olise looked at me as if I'd just asked why water is wet. She motioned to the gibbets and now I was studying them, I could see the rest of the occupants looked the same, as if their bodies had been crushed before being hanged.

'He jumped off a cliff,' she said.

A couple of the women gave dark laughs at that, and the guitar played a sad counterpoint to their grim mirth. But most of them looked stricken, and one of the children began wailing.

'It is a bleak humour you have here,' Kest said.

'These are bleak times, and an even bleaker place,' Olise replied. 'I suggest you make for happier shores and leave us to our trials.'

I gazed at the bodies hanging from the gibbets. Every one of them was male. 'And in all of these "trials" of yours, how many of the defendants were found innocent?' I asked.

'None.'

'What madness has overtaken this place?' I demanded. 'You drag dead men up from the shore and hold pretend trials, only to find them guilty and hang them? This isn't justice, it's a sham!'

Olise glared up at me. 'You're damned right it's a sham – and it is also justice. The only kind we can afford.'

Her calm determination and the way the other women were looking to her for leadership despite the senselessness of what was going on here was maddening – although not half so maddening as the damned music. 'Would someone please shut that minstrel up?'

The guitar stopped and a figure rose up from behind one of the gibbets. 'No one may tell a Bardatti to stop playing, Falcio val Mond. Be thankful I don't play a snake melody to slither its way into your dreams and drive you insane.' No sooner had I registered the deep, feminine voice than Nehra stepped into view, guitar still in hand. 'On reflection, a snake melody probably wouldn't have any effect on you, given how insane you already appear to be.'

'What in the name of—?' Once again I struggled for a Saint's name. Since the Saints I'd grown up with had all been killed and I didn't know any of the new ones, cursing had become a real trial.

'Go with "Saint Drusian-who-falls-amongst-the-dead",' Kest suggested. 'Apparently he's the new Saint of Sorrow.'

Unlike Rhyleis, who looked exactly like the seductive portrayals of Bardatti troubadours immortalised in the tapestries of wealthy nobles and the imaginations of young men and women everywhere, Nehra could easily have been mistaken for a farm labourer: she was stocky, with plain features and short hair kept tidy without any attempt at style. She neither dressed nor acted the part of a Bardatti – but when she played, the beauty and power of her music was almost frightening. If there was anyone more highly respected amongst the Bardatti, I had yet to encounter them.

'What are you doing here, Nehra?' I asked.

She raised an arm and motioned at the scene before us. 'Witnessing the end of a people,' she said. 'Writing their last song.'

'If I want poetry I'll ask a—' I stopped. 'Actually, I almost never want poetry. Just tell me what's happening here.'

Nehra turned to Olise. 'Tell your folk to stand down. These three truly are Trattari, not pirates or brigands. They aren't trying to take anything of yours.'

The other women looked at her, then at their magistrate, but only on Olise's signal did they set down their weapons. The strain on their faces gave way to sorrow as they walked back to the magistrate's throne.

'Just watch, and listen,' said Nehra. 'There is no battle to be fought here, no victory to be won.'

I stared at the scene playing out before me, at the grey wood of the gallows and the grey faces of the dead hanging from them. The magistrate's throne was little more than a few rough planks hammered together; it would give no comfort to whoever sat there. The air felt heavy, like a fog weighted down by the numbness and desolation all around us.

'Come with me,' the Bardatti said, pulling at my arm. 'Keep silent, and bear witness to what justice is left to those without hope.'

Kest, Brasti and I stood at the back and watched as the self-proclaimed magistrate of Vois Calan took her seat and read aloud the charges. The dead man's body lay on the ground by her feet, a broken doll being summoned to justice.

'That you did, with full will, understanding and intent, flee from your debts, from your oaths and from your duties,' Olise proclaimed. 'That you did, without just cause, abandon your wife and child to starve, leaving them without even the meagre solace your small labours could provide.'

'What is she on about?' Brasti asked, his voice low.

'The man committed suicide,' Kest whispered back.

Olise looked down at the dead man. 'Hearing no plea, I deem the defendant's response to the charges to be a claim of innocence.'

'That's generous of her,' Brasti whispered. 'But since when is suicide illegal in Luth?'

'It's not—'

Nehra gave us an angry look and mouthed, *Shut up.*

The magistrate leaned back in her throne. 'Who will prosecute these charges, and bring forth what evidence can lend them weight?'

The crowd shuffled about a bit as a young woman emerged from their midst, holding one of the little girls by the hand. 'I will prosecute, and I will give evidence.'

Olise said, 'And would any come forward in defence, to plead this man's innocence?'

No one spoke, nor made any move to stand opposite the young woman.

'Falcio,' Kest whispered, 'we could still—'

'I know,' I said.

As Greatcoats, representatives of the Crown in matters of law, we had the right to serve as advocates in any trial in Tristia. This wasn't simply privilege; one of the most pernicious judicial problems in the Duchies was that no one would dare serve as a prosecutor or advocate if it would set them against the wishes of the local nobility. So if we wanted to, Kest, Brasti or I could act as the advocate here, and it was highly unlikely the young woman standing as prosecutor could win.

It was likely Olise knew this – after all, she'd made a sufficiently convincing show of being a magistrate thus far – and the question was answered when she caught my gaze. 'Well, Trattari, will you invoke your right to advocate for the defendant?'

The women in the crowd turned, their faces full of confusion and no small amount of trepidation.

'Don't,' Nehra said quietly. 'Please, just trust me and for once don't try to fix the world all by yourself.'

I'd managed to get through most of my life without being caught up in the tangled ways of the Bardatti. Apparently that time was at an end. 'We defer to your wisdom, Magistrate of Vois Calan,' I said after a tense moment.

The old woman gave no acknowledgment, but said to the younger one before her, 'Let us hear the evidence.'

'I am Janelle Turisse. This man was my husband. He swore before the Gods and Saints alike his faithfulness and devotion. He gave his life to me, as I gave mine to him.' She looked down at her daughter, who clutched at her leg as if she was afraid the wind might blow her away. 'When Dia was born, we gave our lives to her . . .' The young mother's voice trailed off, sadness and futility overcoming whatever need had brought her here.

The magistrate gave her sorrow no ground: she banged her fist against the rough wood of her chair and cried, 'The witness will continue her testimony or else as prosecutor she must withdraw her case.'

Janelle sobbed for a moment longer, then swallowed and whispered, 'When our crops failed again this year, for want of better seed, he fled in the night, taking with him our last few coins.'

Olise banged her fist. 'To claim that this man fled is to accuse him of leaving the jurisdiction of your contract. Do you stand by this testimony?'

'Forgive me,' she said, 'I misspoke. He left our cottage that night, but he did not flee the village.'

'Tell us, then, what he did upon departing your home.'

The woman's back was to me so I couldn't see her face, but the pain and anger in her voice were palpable. 'He took our coin with him to the tavern and ate a meal of good, rich beef: three thick slices, the tavern master said.'

Here a murmur passed through the crowd. Beef wasn't cheap in these parts.

'I'll have silence during these proceedings,' Olise commanded.

To Janelle she added, 'Tell the court what he did with the rest of the coin.'

'He drank himself merry, and bought drinks for his friends, that they might toast his generosity. Then, when the coin was all gone, he . . .' Her voice faltered.

'Tell the court what he did then,' the magistrate prodded.

'He said the Gorge Prayer.'

More grumbling came from the crowd, and when several women spat on the ground, the children copied them, although I doubt they understood why. I didn't yet, not exactly, but I thought I was beginning to work it out.

Nehra whispered into my ear, 'When the men of these villages believe they can no longer provide for their families, they leap from the cliff at dawn. They believe if they can catch the very first light of the sun on their bodies as they fall to their deaths, they will attract the Gods' attention and bring good fortune to those they leave behind.'

'Someone should probably tell them the Gods are dead,' Brasti said.

I'd been about to make that very point, but I doubted these people would truly believe it. And to be honest, I wasn't convinced the Gods would stay dead. Despite the Blacksmith's machinations, faith in Tristia was inexorably drawn to take physical form, and if that was true, wouldn't Death himself be one of the first Gods to return?

Something else was troubling Kest. 'I can understand the emergence of this sort of ritual suicide cloaked as sacrifice – but why the expensive meal and drink?'

A shadow passed over Nehra's features. 'Because the Gorge Prayer is all shite, that's why. The men tell themselves they must eat and drink well so that the Gods will know this is what they wish for their families.'

I glanced around the crowd. No men had attended this trial. 'What about the rest of them?' I asked, keeping my voice low. 'Or are there any left? I can't believe every man in the village got drunk and jumped off a cliff—'

'Many are already dead,' Nehra replied. 'Others fled the hard times, some with their families, some without – they take work as soldiers or guards, but these days they're lucky to be paid at all, and there's rarely enough to send any back to their families. From time to time a man will return, but most stay away unable to face the destitution that awaits them here. Some even start new families, new lives, leaving their cast-off wives and children to their misery.'

I found myself breathing heavily, full of futile sorrow and rage, with nowhere to direct it, as Nehra went on, 'It's an easy enough lie for a man to tell himself that by taking the Gorge Prayer he relieves his family of the burden of one more mouth to feed. He tells himself that perhaps Death will accept his sacrifice with good grace, and in turn provide prosperity for those he has left behind.'

'Then they are fools,' I said uselessly. 'Death is always glad for a sacrifice, but I've never known him to pay for it.'

Nehra shook her head. 'Again you miss the point, First Cantor: the practice of the Gorge Prayer isn't a delusion, but rather, a convenient fiction. It provides an excuse to flee from the burdens of life, cloaked in noble intent.' She gestured at Olise and Janelle. 'These women hold trials for the dead to show there is *nothing* virtuous or honourable about the Gorge Prayer, to stop their children growing up thinking that this is how you deal with hard years.' She gripped my arm, so tightly I could feel her fingers pressing through the thick leather. 'Falcio, these women are fighting for the very survival of their villages.'

My attention was pulled back to the trial as Olise rose from her chair. 'Having heard the crime of abandonment well proven, its foul nature compounded and aggravated by the harm done to the victims, I am prepared to render my verdict.' She stared down at the broken body at her feet and addressed the man as if he could hear her from whatever hell he now made his home. 'Cyrin Turisse of Vois Calan, through cowardice and greed you have stolen that which you swore to give: support, strength and life. Thus will your own life be taken from you. Hear now my verdict' – for an instant her eyes went to me – 'as true and sanctified as any in the land. You are guilty, and the sentence is to be hanged by the neck and remain that way until Death himself is sick of you and sends you back to face true justice.'

She rapped on the seat again and this time four women stepped forward, lifted up the body and carried it to the gibbet. Janelle watched as they went, but now her daughter, crying, broke free of her mother's grip and ran towards her father's corpse.

But Brasti was already on the move; he raced to her and picked her up in his arms. 'There now, my love,' he crooned, 'let's you and I look out on this fine ocean together and sing a merry song and leave this bothersome business to others.'

The child sobbed, but she melted into his arms, and that reminded me how quickly Aline had come to love Brasti when she had been equally frightened and full of grief. For all his brashness and ego, no one could match the unquenchable warmth of Brasti's heart.

'Stop!' Olise commanded. 'Set the child down.'

Brasti turned his gaze towards her. There was no warmth in his eyes for the magistrate. 'You would force a child to watch her father die a second time?'

The girl's mother came and pulled at her arm. 'Give her to me.'

Brasti looked at me, waiting for a sign, an excuse to take the child and run, but when I shook my head, gently, he carefully passed the girl to her mother.

Janelle held her tight in her arms, just for a moment, before setting her down and facing her towards the gibbets.

'Why?' Brasti asked.

The young woman blinked away her own tears. 'So that she will see cowardice for what it is. So that as she grows, her eyes will never fall with favour upon those whose hearts are not as strong as her own.'

Brasti turned and stood to face the clear waters and the open sky. He never could stand to see the horrors our world forced upon our children. Kest and I left Nehra to stand beside him, and the three of us pretended not to hear the grunts of effort, the squeal of the rope against the pole, and the quiet sobbing of the children.

When it was done, Brasti said, 'Falcio, what's happening to our country?'

We left the women of Vois Calan with what supplies there were in the hold of the Margrave's wedding barge. Kest, Brasti and I offered up what little coin we could spare as well, in case someone from the village might be able to travel far enough to buy seed with it.

None of these things were in as short supply as hope.

'How did it come to this?' I asked Nehra as we stood on the shore together. The others had remained on the ship after the last delivery, leaving me to row back by myself.

'It was the war against the Saints,' she replied. 'Men abandoned their homes to kneel and moan outside palaces, heeding the call of clerics who insisted that if we all just prayed a little harder, then surely the Gods would favour us again. Each pilgrim was a strong back taken from the fields, a pair of sharp eyes to watch out for thieves and bandits, gentle arms to hold a sick child until the fever passed.'

'But we beat the Blacksmith and his God,' I insisted.

'And many pilgrims returned – but not all, and those who did came too late to help with planting and harvesting.'

'One bad harvest won't break a village,' I argued. 'I was a farmer – we *prepared* against the hard times . . .'

But Nehra was shaking her head. '*Think*, Falcio: it was barely six months before the war against the Saints that we had Dashini masquerading as Greatcoats while they were killing off the Ducal families – and each noble death caused a hundred different failures of government, which in turn triggered a thousand different problems for the common folk. And before that? Have you forgotten Patriana trying to put Trin on the throne? I fear the country has been going to the hells for a very long time, First Cantor.'

'But we—'

'Yes, Falcio, you cleverly unwound the conspiracy, and you put a blade through Shuran's guts: good for you! I'd call for a parade, but there isn't anyone left to carry you down the streets in celebration.' She gestured at the waves splashing against the rocky wall of the cliff. 'It's only water, Falcio, barely a breath against the hard stone of this land, and yet give it enough time, it will wear this place down to nothing.'

'You make it sound hopeless.'

She gave me a rueful smile and held up her guitar. 'I am a Bardatti, Falcio: a troubadour. I play hope every night, and joy twice on weekends. But when the hour grows late and the work day approaches, even I must play the ugly truth for all to hear.'

I wanted to dispute Nehra's gloomy assessment, to tell her that my wife Aline and I had lived through times just as hard as these and had still made a happy life together – but the Bardatti *wasn't* wrong. Those years had felt hard, but they weren't nearly as chaotic as now: we hadn't had to deal with civil wars and intrigues, with black-tabarded Knights and monstrous Gods.

'Tell me what I have to do, Nehra,' I begged. 'Tell me how to put an end to all this madness.'

She waved a hand at the gentle waves that were slowly destroying the cliff wall. 'There is the enemy, First Cantor. Will you challenge it to a duel?'

'Maybe I'll take up the guitar,' I said, frustration seeping into my words, 'and pretend that sweet music and poetry will stop the sea.'

Her eyes narrowed as she stared back at me. 'You know *nothing* of the Bardatti, most especially how dangerous we can be. Learn the ways of your own Order before you mock . . .' She stopped then, and sighed. 'Clear the roads, Falcio, if you want to make the country better. Bring seed from one place to another, deliver crops and cattle to where they are most needed. Move iron and copper from Orison down to Domaris and beef from Aramor up to Phan. Find labour where it is plentiful and move it to where there is land and money but not enough strong backs.' She looked up at me. 'Give us peace and time and prosperity.'

'I'm a magistrate, Nehra – you know I can't do any of those things.'

'No,' she said, 'you can't, and neither can I.' She turned and began walking back to the path that led up the cliffs. 'But you can bring the laws back to us, Falcio. Convince the Dukes to put that damned Queen of yours on the throne. Let us hope she can provide the rest.'

CHAPTER ELEVEN

THE INCOMPETENT SPIES

Another day and a half of seasickness aboard our stolen barge brought us to the middle of nowhere, as planned. Werta's Point was named after the former Saint of the Seas – though I'm told it's also sometimes referred to as Zaghev's Point, after Saint Zaghev-who-sings-for-tears, on account of the torturous rocks hiding in the shallows. Neither name made much sense any more, since both Saints were dead. More pertinently, while Werta's Point had once been a fishing village, decades of war, disease or perhaps just a lack of fish had reduced it to half a dozen cottages worn down by wind and water and salt.

Duchess Ossia's tent was a beacon amidst these desolate ruins.

Well, perhaps 'tent' is the wrong word. The twenty-foot-high pavilion was made of what looked like extremely costly red velvet, with gleaming cloth-of-gold trim.

Chalmers, Kest, Brasti and I stared up at the centre poles that seemed determined to prod the clouds above.

'It's like a gargantuan toy castle meant for some obscenely wealthy child.' Chalmers sounded genuinely offended.

'Try not to open with that when you meet the Duchess,' I said.

'How about "Your Grace, what an honour it is to visit your moveable monstrosity of wasted textiles"?' Brasti suggested.

'That isn't better.'

'Actually,' Kest said, 'the correct architectural designation would be a "twin-peaked pavilion with central marquee".'

'I think mine is more accurate,' Brasti said.

The front flaps opened to reveal a red-haired man about my age, an inch or two taller, dressed in a long brocade coat of red and gold that matched the tent.

'I am Fentan Tuvelle,' he informed us portentously, 'Chamberlain to the Duchess Ossia of Baern.'

'Falcio val Mond, First Cantor of the—'

He cut me off. 'Did you think me unaware of your identity?'

'I just assumed we were being polite.'

A thin but strident voice called out from inside the tent, 'Fentan, just get those damned fools in here!'

'At once, your Grace.' He turned back to me, his features settling into a weary expression. 'I suspect you'll find little concern for politeness inside.' He looked the four of us up and down as if trying to estimate how much dirt we were going to be tracking into his lovely tent. 'You'll have to leave your weapons outside,' he said finally.

'We're magistrates,' Chalmers protested. 'By right and tradition we—'

'Leave it,' I said. This wasn't my first scolding by an angry, self-important old crone and experience had taught me it was better to get it over with quickly and as painlessly as possible.

I unbelted my rapiers and handed them to Fentan, then signalled for the others to do the same. When Kest started to unstrap his shield, the chamberlain motioned for him to keep it. 'Best hang onto that,' he said. 'Maybe if you're quick enough you can keep some of the tea from staining the carpets.'

To no one's surprise, Kest proved remarkably adept at using his shield to deflect all manner of projectiles, ranging from several varieties of almost (but not quite) lighter-than-air scones to gold-edged porcelain plates to any number of cups of scalding hot liquids.

'You know,' he commented, holding the shield out in front of us as the Duchess disposed of what was no doubt intended to be a lavish luncheon, 'this is actually more difficult than trying to block normal weapons.'

A shard of broken pottery glanced off my cheek, drawing blood. 'Why do you suppose that is?'

'It's the angles,' he explained. 'An arrow or a knife travels along a discernible arc and all you have to do is to consider distance and velocity. The Duchess' weapons' – he barely deflected a saucer that had been thrown with remarkable force and accuracy – 'are rather more difficult to predict.'

'Be thankful I didn't think to bring my hunting bow,' Ossia, Duchess of Baern bellowed – although somehow she still managed to sound elegant. 'I'd have given that simpleton archer of yours a run for his money in my youth – and even now, in my autumn years, I'm confident I have the skill to dispatch Tristia of three of its most pernicious burdens!'

From her refuge behind one of the thick, elaborately carved mahogany poles that provided the tent's main supports, Chalmers asked, 'Is this the kind of reception you usually get from the Dukes?'

'Only the ones who actually *like* us,' Brasti replied grimly, his red hair sopping from some kind of soup that smelled deliciously of cardamom and chicken. I contented myself with a scone that had rolled along the carpet close enough to reach, figuring it was probably the only food Ossia was going to offer us today.

'Your Grace?' I called out from behind Kest's shield.

'Please don't make it worse, Falcio,' he whispered. 'She hasn't started on the cutlery yet.'

For all his intellect, Kest has never really understood the nobility. In his mind, the benefits of breeding, expensive education and advanced age should amount to some degree of adult behaviour. He forgets that being waited on hand and foot one's entire life can turn anyone into a petulant child.

Something hard and heavy clanged against the shield. The Duchess had apparently reached the fruit bowl.

'Duchess Ossia,' I said, more firmly, 'in five seconds I'm going to come out from behind this shield and when I do, if so much as a grape touches my person, then Kest, Brasti and I will take our leave of this hideous velvet monstrosity of yours, and we'll confiscate its main support poles as compensation. Then you can see how much you enjoy parading around the countryside in a tent that won't stay up.'

The barrage paused, and after a moment to make sure she wasn't just looking for new projectiles, I stepped out from behind the shield.

Ossia was staring up at the decorative fringes that surrounded the tapestries. 'It is rather grotesque, isn't it?'

I gestured to the extravagant mess she'd made of the inside of the tent, which was now covered in bits of food and shards of broken porcelain. 'Your peculiar choice of redecoration hasn't much improved it, I'm afraid.'

She turned her gaze to me and favoured me with a brief, light laugh. 'I do enjoy your wit now and again, Falcio.' The smile disappeared. 'However, I was illustrating a point.'

'Which was?'

Duchess Ossia knelt down to pick up a wine glass that had escaped destruction. 'That every time the three of you enter my Duchy you wreak havoc and leave behind a bloody awful mess.'

'If this is about Margrave Evidalle—'

She reached for a teacup and I flinched involuntarily. '*Of course I'm referring to the Margrave, you blithering idiot!* I sent you there to do *one* thing: all you had to do was to *discreetly* learn his plans – *not* to contrive to have his own uncle *murder him!*'

Brasti stepped out from behind Kest's shield to pick up a cloth-of-gold napkin from one of the serving trays. As he set about wiping broth from his hair and beard, he pointed out, 'Well, once you knew his plans you'd've wanted him dead anyway, so we just skipped a step. It's like you just said: we're pernicious.'

'He means "precocious",' Kest explained.

'Saints save us from would-be heroes and travelling magistrates!' She rose, walked back to the centre of the pavilion and sat on a smallish but intricately carved mahogany throne that matched the tent's supporting poles. 'The three of you disobeyed a *direct order* from the Ducal Council, and in the process, you've made a shambles of our strategy for dealing with the lesser nobles.' She paused a moment before adding, 'You are, without question, the worst spies I have *ever* seen.'

'Actually, I suspect we're only the second worst, your Grace,' Kest said, his infatuation with accuracy overwhelming any sense of diplomacy, 'since you apparently couldn't trust your own spies to do the job.'

Duchess Ossia clacked her fingernails against the arms of her throne in barely contained frustration. 'I will confess that of late I have found that men and women who spy for money can often be purchased by more than one buyer. Thus am I forced to choose between disloyalty and incompetence.'

She motioned imperiously towards a small table nearby upon which sat a teapot and the last intact cup. Whilst I disliked her propensity for treating everyone like a servant, she was, in fact, Aline's closest ally among the Dukes and the nearest thing to a decent human being Tristia's nobility had ever produced. So I served the old bag her tea.

She took a long sip, then set the cup down on the arm of her throne. 'The country's minor nobles – and *damn* the Gods for saddling us with all these wretched Margraves and Margravinas, Viscounts and Viscountesses, Lords and Daminas! – have been waiting for an opportunity to betray both me and the Crown for years.'

'Then what's the problem?' Brasti asked. 'We ended Evidalle's little revolt for you.' He spread his arms wide. 'Let there be wine and scones and celebrations for all!'

Ossia turned her gaze on me, revealing a mountain's-worth of weariness, and too late I understood why she and the Ducal Council had wanted us to *investigate* the conspiracy, rather than try to put a stop to it. 'Revolutions don't end with one man's death,' I said. 'Those nobles who were prepared to support Evidalle will just take cover for now and wait for a better opportunity to come along.'

The Duchess of Baern sighed. 'Why must you always be clever *after* the fact, Falcio? With a list of the names of the noble houses who were discomfited by Evidalle's plans, I might have quietly set up alliances with them; that would have ended the reigns of those who supported treason. Then we could have distributed their holdings to those nobles most loyal to Aline and begun—'

'How easily you all discuss these filthy schemes and machinations,' Chalmers interrupted, the look in her eyes making it clear she included me in her disdain. 'We're supposed to be *magistrates.* What happened to *administering the law* in Tristia?'

Chalmer's indignation awoke some of my own, though I quickly tamped it down. *Put Aline on the throne. Worry about the rest of it later.*

Duchess Ossia took notice of Chalmers for the first time. 'Who is this child you've brought before me, Falcio?'

'I am Chalmers, called the King's Question, and I can bloody well answer for myself.' She turned a scathing glance at me. 'Seriously, do you people have *any* idea how often you talk as if no one else is in the room?'

Ossia opened her mouth to reply, but then she paused and leaned forward to peer at Chalmers. 'I know you, girl.'

'I very much doubt that, your Grace. I rarely travel in company such as yours.'

The Duchess' eyes narrowed. 'The stores at Castle Aramor – you were always scampering about the skirts of that old woman, the quartermaster. What was her name again?'

Chalmers looked surprised. 'Zagdunsky, your Grace.'

'I remember now. I consulted with her extensively some years ago, when I was considering the administration of my own palace.'

'You tried to hire the King's own quartermaster away from him?' Brasti asked.

'Indeed – and I made a generous offer too, but as I recall, we caught a certain red-faced little hellion spying on our conversation who was apparently unhappy at the possibility of being removed from the home of the Greatcoats. She made a great fuss about it, until Zagdunsky assured me she couldn't leave her current post.'

Chalmers looked pale. 'That was more than ten years ago – I was just a child! How could you possibly recognise me?'

Ossia smiled. 'A woman of noble birth rarely survives to old age in this country unless she soon learns to see more deeply and remember far longer than her enemies do.' She rose from her throne and stood in front of Chalmers, examining her as if she were a painting. 'I remember that look, too,' – she raised a finger – 'there, in the eyes. You have gained in years, but not in wisdom, I see.' Ossia turned to me. 'You will leave the girl in my care, Falcio. Perhaps there is still time for me to train her to—'

'I'm afraid that won't be possible,' Chalmers said.

'Oh? And why not?'

'Well, for one thing, I don't like you.' Chalmers set her sights on me. 'For another, *he* doesn't get to tell me what to do.'

The Duchess apparently found that amusing. 'How trying it must be, First Cantor, to have those beneath you so stubbornly refuse to follow your orders.' She pinched the lapel of Chalmer's coat between thumb and finger. 'Though it appears you've forgotten to give her a proper coat.'

'It's complicated,' I started.

The Duchess turned her glare on me. 'You're a bloody fool, First Cantor. So desperate to reunite your lost magistrates that even once you knew – you *knew* – that this child wasn't a proper Greatcoat, still you broke cover to rescue her, with no regard for the—'

'Tell me I'm not a Greatcoat again, your Grace,' Chalmers said, pulling away from the Duchess, 'tell me twice more for luck – and then go back to your palace and retrieve that hunting bow of yours. I'll meet you in the circle at your convenience, you sour old—'

'Ha!' Brasti chortled. 'She sounds just like you, Falcio.'

'Shut up,' Chalmers and I said at once.

Duchess Ossia took her teacup and lifted it up in a mock toast. 'And so ends Tristia, once the very pinnacle of culture and civilisation, dissipating in misery while the great Falcio val Mond rushes across the land in search of anyone in a long coat who happens to share his fanatical devotion to a dead King's dream.'

I'd long ago come to the conclusion that one of the duties of the First Cantor of the Greatcoats is to subject oneself to the mockery and insults of the nobility in the interests of keeping the peace, but the memory of Vois Calan and the women struggling to keep their families and their villages alive clashed violently with the obscenely opulent setting in which I was now being told off.

'Perhaps, your Grace, the country would be doing better if the Dukes were to devote more of their wealth to taking care of their people and less to—'

Ossia laughed. 'Is *that* what you think? That the country falters because of my tent? No, First Cantor, if you want to see the treasury of Baern at work, go back to Aramor and ask that pitiful handful of soldiers Valiana has managed to assemble to show you the swords and crossbows we've sent. Examine the tools and forges the crafters are using in their desperate attempts to rebuild the castle. Go to the infirmaries and look closely at all the medicines in the crates marked with my seal.'

'I didn't—'

'Didn't what? You didn't know that Baern was the *only* Duchy paying its taxes to the Crown these past months? Why should you? You've been far too busy chasing rumours of lost Greatcoats to worry about the *cost* of holding a country together. But tell me, First Cantor, how long do you think I'll be able to continue after I lose control of my own Duchy?' She looked at all of us. 'Don't you understand, you fools? I'm hanging on by a thread here – and what good will it do to put Aline on the throne if her closest allies lose all power to support her?'

Chalmers looked aghast, the fierceness draining out of her. 'Oh, Gods . . . it's *my* fault – I was the one who fell for Evidalle's trap. If I hadn't gone to that wedding, the rest of you wouldn't have had to save me. None of this would have happened if only I'd—'

'Don't torment yourself, child,' Ossia said, reaching out a hand and holding her chin, just like Cestina had. 'Had you not taken the Margrave's bait, some other fool in a long coat would have done so, and Falcio val Mond, being what he is, would have leaped to their aid just as he did yours.'

'And what would you have me do instead?' I asked quietly.

I hadn't meant the question as a signal of my surrender, but Duchess Ossia took it so. 'The Ducal Council meets in ten days' time, Falcio, to vote once and for all on whether or not to put Aline on the throne.'

'What choice do they have?' Brasti asked, looking at me. 'Aline's the heir, so it's her or—'

'Secession,' Kest replied. He was watching Duchess Ossia closely. 'That's what you've been avoiding saying outright all this time, isn't it, your Grace? That's why you're so concerned with the minor nobles rebelling, why your fellow Dukes have been slow to pay their taxes.'

She nodded. 'Tristia wasn't always one nation; it began as separate city states, each with its own sovereignty, its own laws.' She took a long sip from her tea. 'Dukes were called Princes in those days. That has an appealing ring, don't you think?'

The weight of her words came crashing down on me. *Saint Zaghev-who-sings-for-tears, if you're dead, how is it you manage to keep torturing me?* 'What's the price?' I asked. 'What will it take to make the other Dukes vote our way?'

'That is precisely what my fellow Dukes are negotiating amongst themselves even now, Falcio. But whatever their list of demands, I can assure you of two things: first, they will be offensive to you, and second, you'll have no choice but to agree.' She rang a small silver bell and a moment later her chamberlain appeared at the entrance to the tent and held the flaps open for us to leave.

The Duchess sighed. 'We enter an age of politics now, Falcio, not of outraged idealism, nor daring deeds in search of perfect justice. The time for preposterous heroics has passed.'

'Well, if that's true, then we're in for a spot of trouble,' Brasti muttered once we were outside.

'Why is that?' Kest asked.

'Preposterous heroics are the only things we've ever been good at.'

CHAPTER TWELVE

THE FALLEN CASTLE

Politics and sailing have a great deal in common. They both require complex navigation skills, they both feel slow yet actually move quickly, and they both make me nauseous.

'We could have accepted Duchess Ossia's invitation and travelled with her,' Kest reminded me.

Moonlight shimmered on the surface of the river, reflecting the stars as they began to appear overhead, the beauty of the image marred only by the food currently departing my stomach at speed. He stood next to me as my latest meal become part of the waters below. It had become a familiar sight. It was probably a metaphor for something.

'M'fine,' I mumbled.

Taking the river route saved us a day or two, but that would hardly justify arriving back at the castle to present myself to the heir to the throne in substantially worse condition than when I'd left. Ossia's caravan would have been the wiser choice – or at least the more comfortable choice – but I couldn't bring myself to suffer ten days of the Duchess pointing out every weed-filled field or broken-down barn as further proof that nothing the Greatcoats had done since the King's death had made the slightest difference to the country's wellbeing. Puking up my guts every two hours was a pleasant occupation by comparison.

I was more concerned with how little I was sleeping. The ever-present queasiness left me in a constant state of hazy confusion. Days and nights flowed into each other without my notice: light bled into darkness, clear skies dissolved in rain and then faded into fog, and over it all came the incessant bellowing of sailors unfurling this or belaying that . . . it all blended together into a thick soup, punctuated by my periodic vomiting.

'You don't have to babysit me all day and night, you know,' I told Kest as I wiped spittle from my lips. Whenever I looked up from the railing, he was there, standing next to me with a book in hand. He'd lift his eyes from the page and raise an eyebrow to see if I needed anything, then go back to his reading. By now I was fairly sure he'd memorised the barge's entire collection of navigational manuals.

'Really?' He did me the service of pretending this was some new idea and not something I'd repeated daily. 'I suppose it's just a habit I've picked up over the last fifteen years.'

It was a plain statement of fact; it would have stung, had it come from anyone else. But Kest said it like a kind of promise: he'd kept me alive this long – despite my many poor choices – and would continue to do so for as long as he could. I found the thought both poignant and somehow heart-breaking.

'Go fuck yourself,' I said, by way of reply, and went back to staring at the river passing beneath us.

More troublesome than seasickness was the echo of Ossia's words in my head. '*We enter an age of politics now. The time for preposterous heroics has passed.*'

Preposterous heroics. Was that all we'd managed, all these years since the King's assassination? Had I really been doing nothing more than racing from one crisis to another, facing off against each new threat and pretending that somehow *this* fight, *this* duel, *this* battle would be the last, the one that solved all the complex problems of my troubled country with a brilliant *coup de grâce*?

Most days I could convince myself that it *did* matter, that if Trin had succeeded in taking the throne, she would have held all of Tristia in her iron grip, just like her mother Patriana had ruled the Duchy of Hervor. She would have been a tyrant unlike any the country had ever seen.

Only . . .

When I thought back now to my travels to Hervor, that harsh northern Duchy rich in mining but poor in everything else . . . the people there had appeared to be no worse off than in many other parts of the country. Patriana might have treated them more as indentured serfs than free men, but for all that, they never went hungry.

Nehra's exhortation came back to me: *Get labour to where it's needed, bring seed and move crops, keep the roads clear and trade flowing.*

Might as well ask me to duel the ocean.

Aline could do it, though. She was quick and clever, and with Valiana's help, she could navigate the dark arts of economics and politics to put in place policies that would set the country on a path of recovery. Someone just needed to put her on the throne first.

I could do that – I *would* do that. Even if it meant giving the Dukes whatever it was they wanted from me first.

'Not long now,' Kest said, pulling me from my reverie.

'Really?' I looked up from the railing to a dark sky full of stars. How many hours had I been standing there? Along the river-banks, cottages began to appear in the pale light cast by the moon overhead.

'Look over to starboard,' Kest said, gesturing to the right, and in the distance, past the next winding turn in the river up ahead, I could just begin to make out lights from the city itself. My eyes followed the path up the hillside to where Castle Aramor had once stood.

Until a few months ago, nine great towers, one for each of the Duchies of Tristia, had topped that hill, connected to each other by a massive curtain wall built to withstand a siege . . . then the Blacksmith's God had raised his fist and just like that, the castle had come tumbling down, leaving only a single tower and part of the original keep standing. Even in darkness and from this distance I'd swear I could make out the grey haze that permanently smothered the ruins.

'It's a trick of the wind,' Kest said, following my gaze. 'All the dust and debris from the shattered stones and mortar swirls around the hilltop, then it falls to the ground, only to be picked up by the next breeze – one of the stonemasons working on the repairs told me it might be years before the cloud dissipates for good.'

I guess that too was a metaphor for something.

'Well, well,' Brasti said, the heels of his boots clacking against the deck as he approached. 'Home again, boys.'

'You look rested,' I said, hating him for it.

He took in a deep breath and grinned. 'Must be all this fresh sea air. Well, that and the gentle rolling of the ship. It's like being rocked in a cradle – I swear I've slept like a baby this entire journey.'

I thought about taking a swing at him but I was too close to the edge and there was a decent chance that I would miss and end up falling over the side.

'Saint Anlas-who-remembers-the-world,' a voice swore from above us in the rigging, and the three of us looked up to see Chalmers nestled among the ropes on the crossbeam of the mizenmast.

'Anlas is definitely one of the dead ones,' Brasti pointed out. 'We saw the body.'

'How long have you been up there?' I asked her.

She didn't reply, or even acknowledge that she'd heard me; she looked at once spellbound and horrified, and only then did I remember that Aramor had been her childhood home.

'I . . . I haven't been back since the King died.' Her voice sounded very small. 'How could . . . how could it all just come down like that?'

'A God,' Kest answered simply.

Her eyes found mine. 'And *you* killed him?'

'It's not like he didn't have help, you know,' Brasti said, irritated.

The sailors started bustling in that carefully orchestrated chaos which involves them doing whatever it is sailors do in preparation for landing a ship – rolling up sails and dropping anchors, or something along those lines. I watched the crew for a while until I noticed Brasti in the periphery of my vision alternating between stretching his arms up high and then folding over at the waist to reach for the tops of his boots.

'What in all the hells are you doing?' I asked.

He stood back up and began lifting one knee at a time, hugging first one to his chest, then setting his foot back down on the deck and repeating with the other. 'Limbering up, of course.'

'I can see that. The question is *why*?'

'We're going to be docking in a few minutes. Assuming the stablemaster hasn't sold our horses, we'll be riding up to Castle Aramor within the hour.'

'A fifteen-minute ride on horseback requires limbering up?' Kest asked.

Brasti rolled his shoulders. 'No, stupid, but then we'll be back at the castle.'

'And?'

'When have we ever come home without ending up in a huge bloody fight?' He stretched one arm, then the other, across his chest. 'No point pulling a muscle in the process.'

Oddly, he turned out to be right.

If there's anything more depressing than returning to a once-magnificent castle that's now reduced to ruins, it is surely to find the guards refusing you entry.

'Explain it to me again,' I said.

'Told you: *nobody* enters the castle after dark.' The guardsman gestured with his spear to rows of tents set up on the field behind us. 'Go and sleep it off and come back in the morning to see if the Captain will clear your credentials.'

'*Sleep it off?*' I asked. 'What in all the hells is that supposed to mean?'

'He thinks you're drunk,' Kest explained.

The guard smirked. 'Yeah, on account of the way you keep stumbling around – you know, like a drunk.'

Sadly, he had a point. Turns out, spending time on boats plays havoc with your sense of balance once you get back on dry land, and it really was all I could do to stay on my feet. Brasti and Chalmers looked equally unstable. Kest, of course, stood as straight as the iron gateposts. I would have asked how that was possible, but the prospect of a lecture on the various techniques for countering the effects of recent sea travel was almost as unpleasant as the thought of being forced to wait outside in a tent, like someone come to beg for food.

Bloody castle guardsmen. Even when King Paelis was alive and the Greatcoats were going in and out of this damned fortress on a daily basis, they *still* acted as if we were unwelcome guests come to steal the silverware. And if that wasn't enough, only two of the soldiers barring our way wore the faded purple livery of Aramor. The other two wore yellow.

'What in the name of—?' I paused and turned to Kest.

'Eloria-whose-screams-draw-blood?' he offered.

'Which one's she?'

'According to the Bardatti, she's the new Saint of Torture.'

'That works.'

I spoke to the one in purple with a Sargent's insignia on his collar. 'Why in the name of Saint Eloria-whose . . . whatever he said . . . are soldiers of Luth standing guard outside Castle Aramor?'

'Pastien, Ducal Protector of Luth, is within on a diplomatic visit,' the younger of the two said proudly, as if this revelation should send me genuflecting at the mere mention of that glorious name. 'By order of the Ducal Council, we have permission to establish a perimeter to ensure his safety.'

Through tight lips the Aramor Sargent said, 'I'm afraid my . . . *colleague* . . . is correct.'

'We have a right to defend our Lord,' the second soldier in yellow insisted, brandishing his crossbow to emphasise his point. Then he smirked. 'Besides, wouldn't want to risk the heir to the throne being assassinated by intruders now, would we?'

I took a deep breath and counted very slowly as I let it out, giving peaceful, reasoned debate the chance to prevail. 'Listen, you blithering idiot: *we're the Greatcoats* – *we're* the ones who protect the heir!'

The Sargent coughed. 'Well, actually, sir, the last time someone came dressed as a Greatcoat, they did try to kill her.'

'That was completely different,' I said.

It wasn't, of course. It was only a few months back that a man wearing Harden Vitale's greatcoat had insinuated himself into the castle and nearly managed to slit Aline's throat before Mateo Tiller had stopped him.

The second Luth guard, sensing their imminent victory, then made the mistake of pointing at Chalmers. 'Look, that one's not even wearing a proper greatcoat.'

'Oh, that's it,' she said, trying to push past me.

'Don't,' I warned. 'It won't get us anywhere.'

I glanced back at the rows of tents behind us. No doubt someone would come along shortly, offering to charge us an exorbitant fee for using one, but at this hour, everyone we needed to see would already be asleep anyway. 'Fine,' I said at last. 'We'll sleep outside tonight, but I damned well better see someone ready to let us in at first light.'

The guards looked relieved, and Chalmers looked as if I'd just sacrificed one more great and important principle on the altar of expediency. Kest went off to deal with the horses, leaving Brasti to stand next to me looking oddly confused.

'What is it?' I asked.

'I can't believe I wasted all that time stretching.'

'Not everything ends in a fight, Brasti.'

He shook his head. 'The whole world's stopped making sense, Falcio.'

I clapped him on the shoulder. 'You'll get over it.'

We turned and started towards the tents when the sounds of muffled shouts reached us and without a word I ran back to the castle gate to find the Sargent opening the door to the castle. 'What in hells is going on in there?' he demanded of the guard inside.

Over the frantic sounds of boots on marble and weapons being drawn the guard replied, 'We're not sure yet, sir – we think there's been some kind of attack inside the keep.'

As the others joined me, I drew my rapier. 'Gentlemen, time we all stopped playing "Who's King of the Castle?".'

The two Aramor guards looked ready to give way, but the soldiers from Luth raised their crossbows.

'Look, friends,' Brasti said amiably, 'here's what's going to happen. Falcio's going to talk a lot of nonsense about having to save every endangered soul in the world, then one of you is going to say the wrong thing, and then the four of us are going to knock the lot of you on your arses. Since none of you look like you've limbered up, you might as well just let us pass and save yourselves a lot of pain and trouble.'

'Let them pass,' the Aramor Sargent said.

'We don't know who these people are,' the older of the Luthian soldiers declared, adding smugly, 'They don't get in until their credentials have been established to *our* Captain's satisfaction.'

'We're four of the most dangerous people you've ever met,' I told him, 'so get the hells out of my way or we'll establish our credentials to your eternal *dis*satisfaction.'

'See?' Brasti said, elbowing Chalmers. 'That's the kind of threat you need to have at the ready if you want to be a proper Greatcoat.'

The Sargent, clearly as keen as we were to get on and deal with whatever was going on inside, shouted at the men in yellow, 'I'm the senior officer here and I'm ordering the two of you to step aside. *Now.*'

The younger guard turned his crossbow towards the Sargent. 'You don't command us—'

An instant later he was stumbling backwards. His weapon dropped to the ground as he slumped down against the stone wall, blood spurting from his nose. 'Been waiting to do that for weeks now,' the Sargent said, rubbing the knuckles of his right hand and looking deeply satisfied. He turned to the second soldier from Luth. 'Care to register a complaint?'

The guard set down his crossbow and the Sargent motioned for us to enter.

'Thanks,' I said as I passed him.

'Just protect the heir – and try not to steal anything, Trattari.'

CHAPTER THIRTEEN

THE ASSIGNATION

We ran through a maze of dark halls hazy with dust, past ungainly supports propping up the damaged walls and roof.

'Saint Laina's cold dead tits!' Brasti swore, coughing as the dust got up his nose. 'Did something *explode* in here?'

'No, it's all the people,' Kest said, gesturing to the motley collection of nobles, retainers and guards clogging the halls, trying to find out what was happening. 'They're stirring up the debris from the repair work.'

I ignored everyone; I'd trained myself months ago to navigate the path to Aline's rooms blindfolded, in case of yet another assassination attempt.

Why must they always come after you, sweetheart?

'First Cantor!' a young voice shouted, and a boy wearing a page's uniform started waving furiously at me.

'Bendain, isn't it?' I asked.

The boy nodded. 'Thank the Saints you're here, sir – but you're going the wrong way!'

I glanced at the intersection of hallways, momentarily confused by the chaos around me. 'What do you mean? Aline's rooms are—'

'The attack isn't on Aline, sir.'

'Then who—?'

'I'm not sure.' The page pulled at my coat, leading me down a side passage. 'I think something's happened to the Realm's Protector.'

I suddenly recognised where I was, and grabbing Bendain by the shoulders, said, 'You've brought us to the diplomatic wing – why would Valiana be here in the middle of the night?'

'Weren't these rooms set aside for Pastien and his entourage?' Kest asked, noting the soldiers' yellow livery.

I was starting to really hate that colour.

The boy didn't meet my eyes. 'I don't want to be indiscreet, sir, but—'

'You think I give a damn about discretion right now? The whole damned castle's awake. Where's Valiana?'

'She's . . .' Bendain hesitated, then muttered, 'She was . . . er . . . *visiting* the Ducal Protector, sir.'

Saints, but I'm thick sometimes.

One of Pastien's personal guard caught sight of Bendain and grabbed him by the collar. 'I told you before, runt, keep clear of this area. No one gets in or out until we—'

'Remove your hand from that boy,' Chalmers said, coming up beside me, her hand on her cutlass, 'or I can cut it off for you. Your choice.'

Her threat drew a half dozen other soldiers to us, all with weapons at the ready. The man holding onto Bendain tightened his grip.

Saint Eloria-who-is-clearly-going-to-be-my-patron-saint, I really don't need this now.

If Chalmers drew her blade, not only would we stumble headlong into a pointless fight, but the boy would likely be the first one killed. With my free hand I grabbed Chalmers by the shoulder and hauled her back, then dropped her and slapped the guard across the face, hard enough to make him let go of the page.

The boy had the good sense to immediately get out of the way.

'Trattari bastard,' he growled, raising his weapon high. 'Just wait—'

'Look down,' I said, and when he did, the first thing he saw was the point of my rapier at his crotch. 'Laying hands on a royal page inside Castle Aramor is considered an attack on the Crown, you know.'

Bendain was dusting himself off. 'Sir, that's not technically—'

'Shut up.'

'Men of Luth, stand down now!' commanded a deep, rumbling voice, and the soldiers immediately made way for a man bearing a Captain's insignia on the collar of his yellow livery. 'You're Falcio val Mond, right?'

'I am.'

'Good. Figured I'd save you the time of one of your legendary introductions. I'm Gueran Lendale, Captain of the Ducal Protector's Guard.' He gestured at Pastien himself, looking rather pale and ungainly in his nightshirt, standing ringed by an assortment of servants and soldiers. 'There's been some sort of incident. No one's dead, but I need to secure the area so that I can determine what is to be done.'

'Who attacked him?' I asked. 'And more importantly, where is Valiana?'

'That will be determined once I've—'

Bendain spoke up. 'He's lying, sir. I heard his soldiers saying that Valiana tried to kill the Ducal Protector. They've got her locked in a room. They said they're going to—'

'Be quiet, boy,' Captain Lendale said. 'No one's going to do anything until I've properly secured the prisoner and investigated the assault.'

'Actually,' Kest said, 'if the alleged assault has taken place within the castle, jurisdiction would fall under the purview of the highest magisterial authority in Aramor.'

'That's us, by the way,' Brasti said, no doubt pleased with himself for knowing that much about the law.

The Captain shook his head. 'I'm afraid not, no; without a monarch on the throne we're within our rights to—'

I cut him off with a gesture, then considered my next words.

Despite my history, I really *don't* go around trying to get into fights with Ducal guardsmen on a regular basis. 'I understand your desire to protect your Lord, but there are three things you need to consider.'

'What would those be?' he asked, visibly determined not to give ground.

'First, Valiana is Ducal Protector of *Tristia*. She's not subject to arrest by anyone without an edict from the Ducal Council.'

'That's debatable,' the Captain said.

I sighed. I sometimes think it's like they *want* to be beaten senseless. 'Second, as First Cantor of the Greatcoats, I have no intention of leaving this in the hands of a bunch of thick-witted grunts from a backwater Duchy whose sole distinction in the judicial arts has thus far been its occasional efforts to exceed Rijou in the practice of torturing suspects.'

'Falcio . . .' Kest began.

'Does he do this all the time?' Chalmers asked. 'He just hauled me off for threatening a guard and now he's ready to start a war?'

I kept my eyes on the Captain. 'Third, and of vastly more consequence to your current predicament, Valiana val Mond is my daughter.'

'Guess that explains it,' Chalmers muttered.

'You have no idea,' Brasti said.

Captain Lendale seemed a reasonable enough man, and from the expression on his face, I suspected he might have a daughter of his own. 'Look, Trattari, I mean no disrespect to you, or to the Realm's Protector, but my orders are—'

A woman's voice boomed from behind me, 'Who the *fuck* do I kill first?' and Darriana came striding down the hall towards us, that long, thin blade of hers in hand and a fire in her eyes more black than red.

'Oh, hello, dear,' Brasti said. 'I promise I was coming to visit you first, but circumstances—'

'Shut up.' Darri turned to me. 'Valiana's in there?'

'I believe so.'

She looked at Captain Lendale and his soldiers, who probably outnumbered us three to one. 'Why haven't you killed them yet?'

'I was getting around to it.'

Kest came to stand next to me, examining the assembled guardsmen and doubtless assessing the best lines of attack.

When I looked at the Captain, I saw that he too had a keen eye for the logistics of violence. 'Soldiers of Luth, form up,' he said grimly.

'You'll lose,' Kest warned.

'Not before I take you lot down with me.'

Kest raised his shield and Brasti took up position behind it, resting an arrow just above the circular rim.

'Captain,' I said, 'in about five seconds I'm going to give the order and Brasti will begin to fire. Several of your men will be injured trying to get to him, but I promise they won't get past Kest. In the meantime, I'm going to do my best not to kill you while Darriana takes out two of your—'

'Three,' she said.

'Sorry, *three* of your soldiers.'

'You forgot about me,' Chalmers said, her cutlass in hand. 'Again.'

'None of us want to spill blood tonight, Captain, but this hall is crowded and with these narrow angles, several of you will be sleeping six feet below ground when we're done.'

To his credit, Captain Lendale looked fully prepared to test my calculations – but fortunately for all of us, Pastien, Ducal Protector of Luth, finally managed to rouse himself.

'Let them through, Lendale,' he murmured, and the Captain instantly stood down, his soldiers following suit a beat after.

'What happened here, Pastien?' I asked, stepping past them, 'and more importantly, where is Valiana?'

The handsome young Lord managed to look both ashamed and

defiant as he pointed to the barred door a few feet away. 'She's in there, but I can't allow you to—'

I pushed past him and confronted the two men determinedly guarding the door. 'I'm told good soldiers are hard to find, Pastien. It would be a shame for you to lose two of yours.'

'You don't understand, Falcio. Something's happened to her. She . . .' He paused, giving his best impression of a man torn in two. 'Very well. I would have preferred to keep this matter quiet, but—'

'You've done a fine job of that so far,' Brasti said, waving airily at the assembled mob of nobles, servants and guardsmen who formed Pastien's entourage. From their faces I could see that they had already formed their own opinions: some looked horrified, some offended – and the rest were smirking.

'*Talk*, my Lord,' I said.

'Valiana and I were . . . That is to say, we have grown close of late and . . . although I respected her modesty without question, we were . . .'

'The word you're looking for is "fucking",' Brasti offered helpfully.

'*Not* helping,' I told him.

Pastien swallowed and located the balls he'd apparently not had any trouble finding earlier. 'We were sharing an intimate moment when she . . .' He looked at me and swallowed again, then turned his back to me. I could see thin tracks of blood beginning to stick to the inside of his shirt. 'I'm sorry, First Cantor, but she went insane. I believe the adoracia has taken hold of her again.'

I felt something tearing at my guts. *No, she overcame the Adoracia fidelis. She proved she could withstand it.*

'Valiana *attacked* you?' Kest asked.

Pastien nodded. 'I barely managed to get out – I had my men bar the door from the outside so she could do no further harm to anyone.'

Several of the nobles snickered and someone remarked, 'A bitch in heat is often hard to contain.' I thought about killing him, but that would have to wait; I had bigger problems to deal with right then.

'Tell your men to move aside and unbar the door, my Lord. I will see to Valiana.'

He stepped in front of me and put a hand on my shoulder, which would have been brave, had I not been able to feel him shaking. 'You cannot, First Cantor. The madness has taken her. She is like a mad dog now. We must wait until morning and hope it passes.'

That was the second time someone had referred to her as a dog.

I can't have been doing a very good job of hiding my reaction, because a moment later Pastien stepped aside and motioned for his men to do the same.

As I reached up to lift off the bar they'd wedged between two brackets that normally held lanterns, I felt a hand on my arm.

'Falcio . . .'

'Don't start with me, Kest.'

'I know, but just tell me you've got a plan in case things go badly in there.'

I lifted the bar and leaned it against the wall. 'When do I ever have a plan in these situations?'

CHAPTER FOURTEEN

THE MADWOMAN

I entered into near darkness, the only light coming from a candle that had been knocked to the floor and was now threatening to set the rug aflame.

'Stay away,' Valiana said. Her voice was growly, rough, as if she'd been screaming. 'I don't want you to see me like this.'

'Aline's already inheriting a rather shabby castle, sweetheart,' I said, kneeling by the candle on the rug. 'I really can't have you going around setting what's left of it on fire.'

'Leave it,' she said. 'Let me burn. Let the flames drive away the madness inside me. If you come closer, you may have to kill me yourself.'

Wax dripped on my hand as I picked up the candle, but I ignored it. 'If Kest were here, he'd tell you that burning is considered to be the most painful way of dying.'

'I told you, stay away.'

The tiny wick didn't do much to light the room, but I could see Valiana sitting up in the bed, her back against the headboard, cloaked in shadow.

'Now, I know what you're thinking. You're thinking, "Well, if fire is the *most* painful way to die, then what's the *least* painful?" Luckily for you, I've given this a great deal of thought and I believe the answer is: in your sleep, at a ripe old age, surrounded by those who love you best.' I walked to the bed. 'And that, Valiana val Mond, is the only death I will grant you.'

Strands of sweat-dampened hair were sticking to her face and tears tracked misery down her cheeks. She was naked, which made me uncomfortable, and filled with sorrow and self-hatred, which was infinitely worse. She pulled the sheet up as I approached. 'I went mad, Falcio – I thought I could control it, but the adoracia was too strong for me.'

'Nothing is too strong for you,' I said, too quickly.

Sometimes I say these things, and I swear that in my own head they make perfect sense and should, if the world functioned in any sort of logical way, make the people I care about feel better. Only they don't; somehow, I just make things worse. In Valiana's case, that manifested as her covering her eyes, her fingers curling into her dark hair, and sobbing.

I set the candle down on the flat corner-post of the bed and sat down, not too close, for fear of . . . well, making things worse again. Despite my general ineptitude in all matters pertaining to women, I was about to try consoling her again when the sound of a commotion outside reached us. My hand went to my rapier: at least if we were being attacked I'd be of some use.

The noise went away, and a moment later we heard a quiet knock at the door.

It's odd to say that you can recognise a knock when most people do it pretty much the same way, but I knew this one instantly.

'Make them go away, whoever it is,' Valiana sobbed.

'It's Ethalia.'

Valiana looked at me. I knew she didn't want anyone to see her this way, but she needed help. 'She's the Saint of Mercy,' I reminded her. 'She was able to reduce the effects of the adoracia before – perhaps she can do so again.'

It took a while, but eventually Valiana nodded and I opened the door to reveal Ethalia, surrounded by a pale white glow. Behind her, the hall was filled with people on their knees, including Kest and Brasti.

'Could you please tell her to stop doing that?' Brasti asked.

Ethalia entered the room and I closed the door behind her. 'It's the adoracia,' I warned. 'Valiana attacked Pastien.'

'So he tells everyone who will listen,' she said.

Ethalia is, most days, the most peaceful and gentle person you will ever meet. I suppose that goes with being a Sister of Merciful Light – and now she's the *actual* Saint of Mercy, so it goes double. Right now, though, she wasn't striking me as all that merciful.

'I didn't know you were in the castle,' I said.

'I returned a few days ago.' She briefly put a hand on my arm and squeezed it, recognition that there was no time for us now but we would talk later. 'Wait outside, Falcio.'

'But what if—?'

She left me standing there as she went to Valiana's bedside, the glow around her lighting up the room.

'Well?' Brasti asked as I left the room. 'Is Valiana a complete lunatic now, or just a mostly crazy person?'

I glanced around the hall. Pastien and his retainers were gone, though several of his guards remained, along with some of the nobles housed in this wing. They were all staring at me, awaiting an answer.

'I don't know,' I replied. That was the truth.

Whatever goes to make up raw courage, Valiana had more of it than any person I'd ever met. Two months ago she'd done the impossible: she'd overcome the effects of *Adoracia fidelis*, a poison that would drive anyone – well, anyone except a Saint – to utter madness. Except, of course, she hadn't actually *overcome* it; the adoracia still raged in her veins, which meant that she had to continually push the madness aside, every second of every minute of every hour of every day, a feat I could barely imagine. When my wife Aline died,

I'd embraced insanity with both arms rather than face the world. I doubt I'd have lasted five minutes with *Adoracia fidelis* in my blood.

Kest came and stood next to me. 'Her strength has surprised us before.'

'Ethalia is with her; with any luck she'll help her regain full control of herself again.' I noticed Darriana was nowhere to be seen. 'Where's—?'

'Who knows?' Brasti said, sounding annoyed. 'Once she heard Valiana wasn't in danger she just took off.'

A noblewoman in her nightclothes whose name I'd forgotten approached me, her husband, similarly attired, close behind. 'That creature should be locked up in a cell, not running around attacking the Ducal Protector of Luth!'

'I take it you're fond of Pastien, then?'

The husband gave one of those noises nobles make that's supposed to make you realise you've overstepped the bounds of propriety. It sounds a lot like *harrumph*, only with more phlegm. 'We are loyal and patriotic citizens of Luth,' he announced portentously.

'That's odd,' I said. 'I seem to recall the Ducal Protector being in rather dire need of loyal citizens a couple of months ago – I can't say I remember any of you stepping up to defend him when the Prelate and his Church Knights came to call.'

I felt a sharp sting on my left cheek: the man had *slapped* me. I mean, he'd *really* slapped me! This crook-backed, pot-bellied nobleman had brought his arm back, opened his hand and cuffed me as if I were an errant child.

'You dare to laugh at the Viscount of Destre?' his wife demanded.

Truth be told, I hadn't even noticed I was laughing. 'Your pardon, my Lady.' I looked at the Viscount. 'My Lord. I regret my hasty and thoughtless words.'

There followed a bit more *harrumphing* and a few choice insults about the Greatcoats' lack of manners and courage, but at last they retired back to their chambers.

I leaned back against the door of Pastien's room and noticed Chalmers was staring at me with one eyebrow raised. 'Since when do the Greatcoats take shit from petty noblemen in their nightshirts?'

I took in a breath and let it whistle out through my teeth. 'Do you suppose you could resist the urge to remind me what a disappointment I am just long enough for me to find out what's happened to my daughter?'

'Don't take it personally,' Brasti told her. 'Ever since Falcio figured out the country's going down the toilet he's convinced it's all his fault.'

'We have to make peace with the nobles,' I said, 'at least until Aline is crowned and gets the economy working again.'

That didn't appear to satisfy Chalmers, so Kest added, 'Luth is a major agricultural provider and one of the few Duchies whose support we may be able to secure for Aline.'

Brasti snorted. 'So is that why these arseholes get to sleep in the nice rooms with proper beds and I'm supposed to sleep outside in tents?'

'Yes, Brasti,' I replied, 'that's exactly why you'll be sleeping on the cold, hard ground tonight and why I'm letting venal old men slap me in the face and call me names.' It was also the reason why I hadn't already gone to find Pastien to beat him senseless for having abandoned Valiana in the midst of an adoracia attack.

I suddenly stumbled forward as the door behind me opened and Ethalia stepped out.

The glow was gone, but her eyes burned white.

'Ethalia?'

She ignored me and turned to the few remaining stragglers in the hall. 'Go back to bed. *Now.*' To the soldiers she said, 'You can fulfil your duties just as easily at the end of the hallway.'

A couple of them didn't look pleased to be addressed in such a fashion, but she said, '*Now!*' and whatever they saw in her eyes was enough to make them reconsider any potential obstinacy.

'What is it?' I asked her urgently. 'Is Valiana—?'

'Bide,' she said.

To anyone else, Ethalia would have looked calm, fully in control of herself. To me, she might as well have been on fire.

Once the guards had made their way to the end of the hall, she said, 'Valiana is fine.'

'*Fine?*' Brasti asked. 'She attacked the bloody Ducal Protector of Luth. Not that I mind, given what a twat he is, but still, it can't be good for business to go about—'

'You should be silent now.'

He shut his mouth. For about a second. Then the essential nature of Brasti Goodbow reasserted itself. 'Listen, Ethalia, since I haven't had the pleasure of your company in bed, I'd as soon you not play the shrewish wife with me—'

It's true, he's rude and offensive, but you really have to admire someone who can stand in the presence of a Saint and still be an arrogant twit.

'Let's focus on Valiana,' I said. 'How can she be fine if—?'

'It's *not* the adoracia poisoning,' Ethalia said.

'Then what?'

'I prefer not to say.'

That threw me for a moment. 'Ethalia, if there's some danger to Valiana or to those—?'

'There is no danger. I told you, it's not the adoracia.'

'Then—'

'Aha!' Brasti said, his mouth breaking into a wide grin. 'I figured it out.' He looked from me to Kest as if to ascertain that we didn't know what was going on. 'It appears our little Valiana has something of the vixen in her. Who would've thought she—?'

He stumbled backwards and fell to his knees. At first I thought it was Ethalia's power, but then I saw blood spout from Brasti's nose. Kest had just punched him in the face.

'You shouldn't speak of Valiana that way,' Kest said, his voice perfectly calm.

'Thanks,' I said.

'Oh, that's just great,' Brasti said, checking his nose to make sure it wasn't broken. 'Falcio gets slapped in the face and won't retaliate, but I make one innocent comment and get a bloody nose for it!'

'I guess you don't have any important agricultural holdings,' Chalmers said.

'Also, you're behaving like an idiot,' Kest added.

I turned to Ethalia. 'So this . . . *thing* with Pastien – the scratches on his back? This was all just . . .'

'It was her first time,' Ethalia said. 'Not all women are delicate flowers during lovemaking. Some have an . . . especially strong ardour. *That* is what overtook her, not adoracia poisoning.'

'So Pastien just—'

'He was scared,' she said. Her eyes narrowed. 'Which is no crime. He too is young. However, he has chosen to deal with the embarrassment caused by his overreaction by claiming that Valiana has lost her mind, and I suspect word is spreading quickly.'

Brasti got to his feet and looked at me, still holding his nose. 'Right, so, simple then: Valiana was a little rowdy, Pastien got scared and now he's trying to cover up having run naked into the hallway by telling everyone she's nuts. So which one of us is going to pay him a visit first?'

'Weren't you mocking Valiana just a few seconds ago?' Kest asked.

'First of all, you celibate barbarian, I wasn't *mocking* her. I consider sexual passion to be an outstanding quality in an individual. Second, Valiana's family: *we're* allowed to mock her. It's practically a law.'

'It really isn't,' Kest said.

'Well, it should be, along with an attendant penalty that says anyone who does what Pastien did gets his arse kicked up and down the stairs a few times until he fully appreciates the consequences of his actions.'

The door swung open again, this time revealing Valiana herself. She was dressed now, thank whatever Gods or Saints remain, and had cleaned herself up. 'No,' she said.

Brasti nodded. 'Quite right. You should get to beat him up first.' He looked thoughtfully at the rest of us. 'Then Falcio.' He tapped his nose and turned to Kest. 'Then Chalmers. You go last because you already got your aggression out tonight.'

'That's fair,' Kest replied.

'No!' Valiana's voice was a mixture of frustration and heartache. 'No one goes near Pastien. Regardless of my personal relationship with him, Aline needs him on her side. We can't risk the chance that—'

'I'm sorry,' I said.

She turned to me. 'It's not your fault, Falcio. I'm a grown woman and—'

'No, I mean, I'm sorry, but if you think I'm going to allow that primping fop of a man to wander around masking his own inadequacies by telling lies about you, then you really are suffering from adoracia poisoning.'

She shook her head, closing her eyes to stop the tears. 'I don't want this – don't you understand? I don't want you running off fighting my battles for me. I'm trying to do what's right for the country and you're just making it worse.' When she opened her eyes she looked straight into mine. 'You're not my real father. Don't pretend to be.'

'I'm not trying to—'

She cut me off, and in that voice she had perfected for just these occasions said, 'Until a new monarch sits the throne, I am Realm's Protector of Tristia, First Cantor. You may not give that title the respect it warrants, but rest assured, the soldiers who guard this castle do. Touch one hair on Lord Pastien's head and I will have you arrested.'

She turned and left me feeling like twice the fool I usually am.

'Give her time,' Ethalia said, watching as Valiana strode down the hall away from us. 'For a brief moment she saw a future that might be hers, one that might not be governed by the toxin in her veins or the circumstances of her birth.'

'I'm not the one denying her that,' I said, 'but her situation won't get better with Pastien running around saying—'

'When she is in pain, Falcio, she hides from her fear by retreating into the one thing she knows: duty.' Ethalia let her fingers graze against mine. 'You of all people should understand.'

I tried to take her hand in mine but she pulled away. 'I have duties of my own to which I must attend,' she said, and left.

I cursed myself for misreading the moment.

After the fall of the Blacksmith and his God, Ethalia and I had spent what little free time we'd had together, walking among the broken remains of the castle, exploring the town or wandering the nearby hills. I found myself fascinated by all those things we'd foregone in our rush to become lovers: we talked about books we'd read, foods we loved or hated, places we hoped one day to visit. As a Sister of Merciful Light, Ethalia had received a wide-ranging education in the arts and sciences, but she'd never travelled outside of Rijou and Aramor. The little island off the coast of Baern she spoke of so often was just a place in a story to her. So I told her about the nine Duchies, and in return she instructed me in botany, chemistry and any number of other subjects I was woefully ignorant of. It wasn't a promise of anything beyond friendship, I understood that, but nothing I did felt complete until I'd shared it with Ethalia. I found it a strange and confusing compulsion, but I hoped perhaps it was simply how people who don't spend every waking minute of their lives fighting go about the business of falling in love.

Except maybe it wasn't that at all.

'Well?' Brasti asked, bringing me back to the present. 'What's your plan now, First Cantor? Do we go and beat the shit out of Pastien anyway, or find some other nobleman's arse to kiss?'

Lack of sleep and seasickness must have caught up with me,

because I'd actually forgotten that he, Kest and Chalmers were standing there, waiting for me to say something. Saints! Why do people keep looking to me for answers when every decision I make just creates more problems?

'Part of caring for Valiana is respecting her decisions,' Kest said to me. 'She's asked you to stay out of this.'

'It's the logical thing to do,' I agreed.

Brasti was unconvinced. 'Except that now we're saying it's okay for a nobleman to besmirch Valiana's reputation just because we might need his vote . . .'

'That's politics,' Kest said. 'We may not like it, but since none of us are very good at it, we're going to have to trust in Valiana's judgement.'

A refined, deeply self-satisfied voice replied silkily, 'Any man who uses the words "politics" and "trust" in the same sentence has disqualified himself from talking about either.'

Jillard, Duke of Rijou, was leaning against the wall a few feet away. For a nobleman, he had a remarkable ability to move silently.

'Who's he?' Chalmers asked.

Brasti snorted. 'Oh, just a lying, vicious, self-important lunatic who's tried to murder Falcio on more than one occasion.'

'Let me guess: that makes him one of our closest allies?' she asked.

'Now you're catching on.'

'You look well, your Grace,' I lied. While Jillard retained his immaculately styled hair and fashionably cut red and silver brocade coat, his eyes looked just as they had the last time I'd seen him, standing over his son's dead body: emptied of all joy and filled instead with a hollowed-out darkness.

'As do you, Falcio,' he said.

That was okay; I knew I looked like shit.

I felt an odd kinship with the Duke of Rijou, and occasionally had to remind myself that Brasti was right: he was as much a monster as anyone else in this benighted country. I had hoped that grief might improve him somehow, but as he approached us, I saw Bendain had been hiding behind him.

'You've added bribing royal pages to your list of crimes now?'

'Don't think poorly of the boy, Falcio. He wasn't spying on Valiana.'

'Then who—?'

Jillard spread out his hands and gestured: the rooms around us were occupied by the various nobles who made up Pastien's entourage. 'What you imagine to be a private matter between young lovers is, of course, nothing of the kind.'

'You're saying this situation was . . . *arranged* somehow?' Kest asked.

'Don't be silly,' Jillard replied. 'Those skilled in the arts of manipulation don't stoop to anything as simplistic as *plans*. Rather, they set up the conditions necessary to ensure they can take advantage of otherwise unpredictable events. For example—'

'A young, naïve nobleman panicking at his lover's ardour?' I asked.

Jillard smiled in that way of his that signals neither pleasure nor friendship but simply the satisfaction of knowing something you don't. 'That, or a dozen other outcomes, all of which Valiana's enemies would be happy to use to damage her standing among my fellow Dukes, lessening her influence with those whose support she needs most if Aline is to be crowned.'

I tried to ignore his smugness as I made sense of his words. 'Let me guess: if we don't do something about Pastien, the nobles around him will encourage him to keep spreading this story of Valiana's madness. And if we do—'

'They'll say she's using the Greatcoats to threaten nobles.'

'So, either way I'm damned, is that it?'

Jillard turned and headed back down the hall. 'I would think you'd be used to it by now, Falcio.'

CHAPTER FIFTEEN

SUBTLE FORMS OF PERSUASION

The one good thing about having two equally terrible options is that you needn't waste time considering your choices. I followed the others outside and arranged for space in one of the tents, then used my well-deserved reputation for brooding and pacing to go for a walk through the castle grounds.

The next two hours involved a great deal of crouching and silently padding past guards too busy gossiping about the recent excitement and sharing their own rather unsavoury predictions for Valiana's future to pay attention to their duties. Finally, I reached the spot where I could climb up the back of the keep to the window that led to the antechamber next to Pastien's bedroom. With no other suitably grand apartments available within the castle, I reasoned that the young Ducal Protector would have to end up back there eventually, ready to snuggle down in his bed and dream of new ways to be a pain in my arse.

It was only a paltry fifteen feet, but the climb was a slow, painstaking process and by the time I had worked the window open and squirmed through it into the little side room I was so exhausted I had to sit down to catch my breath. Breaking into a castle is a lot harder work than the ballads suggest – it's no wonder spies and assassins are so expensive.

Once I'd settled myself, I approached the adjoining door between the antechamber and the bedroom. For a heartbeat I considered knocking, before deciding that quietly turning the handle just enough would enable me to kick it open; that would be, I thought, a suitably grand and menacing entrance.

Except that Pastien wasn't alone.

I found the Ducal Protector of Luth standing naked on his bed, pressed against the wall behind him, his arms stretched out wide. His eyes were shining with terror as he tried very hard not to look at the small woman standing on her tip-toes in front of him and whispering in his ear, the very sharp blade of a poignard held to his genitals.

'You're late, Falcio,' Darriana said. 'You can have him when I'm done.'

'Please,' Pastien pleaded with me, quickly deciding I was the lesser of two evils, 'make her stop!'

'I sympathise, my Lord, I really do.' I thought about that for a moment, then corrected myself. 'Actually, no, I don't at all, you feckless piece of dung.'

Darriana whispered something else into his ear and I saw her blade move just a hair.

His eyes widened. 'Saint Laina-who—'

'Wrong choice of Saint in this particular situation,' Darri warned. 'Also, Laina-who-whores-for-Gods is one of the dead ones.'

'*Please*,' Pastien whispered, 'I'll do anything.'

'Oh, don't trouble yourself,' she said. 'I'll take care of the hard parts.'

'Darriana?' I said casually.

'Yes, Falcio?'

'What if – and I'm not trying to interfere in your personal affairs here – but what if the Ducal Protector were to swear to us that he would go round and personally tell the truth to every single person he's impugned Valiana's name to and promise to never do it again?'

'He can still do that with just the one testicle, can't he?' she asked.

'In theory,' I conceded, 'but I suspect that would require a certain period of convalescence and I'm sure we'd all rather this was wrapped up quickly.'

Darri looked up into Pastien's eyes. 'Is that true, my Lord? Would it really be that much more difficult to make up for your little . . . *mistake* . . . if you had only one testicle?'

'I'm sorry,' he said, looking miserable enough that I almost believed him, 'I was scared, all right? I hadn't expected . . . I just thought, she always seemed so demure and then when she—'

'Go ahead,' Darriana said, 'don't be shy: tell us what horrible crime the *slut* committed upon your person.'

'I didn't know what to do! Like a fool, I ran, and then all of a sudden I was in the hallway, standing there with guardsmen who don't respect me and my nobles coming out of their rooms, already laughing at me – I knew they'd use it against me.' He looked at me. 'Falcio, you *know* how hard it is, trying to keep my nobles from conspiring against me—'

'Indeed – and imagine how hard it would be if you were a young woman,' I said, 'one whom everyone knew to be of common blood and who was, according to someone – oh yes, that would be *the Ducal Protector of Luth* – a madwoman.'

He hung his head. 'I know. I'm sorry – I'll do whatever must be done to make up for this, I swear.'

I let his oath hang in the air for a while before I said, 'Darriana?'

She glanced back at me with that look in her eyes that most days just means she thinks I'm a gullible fool but one of these days will mean she's about to try and kill me. 'Are you going to give me the "I'm the First Cantor of the Greatcoats" speech?'

'Only if you don't let him go now.'

She sighed theatrically, then said to Pastien, 'It's very important you don't move now.'

'What? Why?'

Suddenly her blade whipped up and out and an instant later it was back in the sheath at her side. Pastien had gone completely white. He didn't dare to look down, but gingerly let his right hand feel around his private parts to make sure everything was still attached.

'I'm thirsty,' Darriana said, punching me in the shoulder far harder than was necessary. 'You owe me a drink.'

Finding alcohol proved to be more difficult than either of us had anticipated: apparently neither wine nor ale flow from magical spigots embedded into castle walls. Imagine this: someone has to actually grow stuff – things like grapes and wheat – and then spend weeks working some sort of alchemical miracle to make them drinkable.

As we searched high and low, Darri told me about the Dashini's own favoured drink. It sounded like more of a poison to me, but what else would one expect from the Dashini? Its effects included hallucinations and a powerful urge to commit suicide. I'd spent much of the last fifteen years experiencing both those phenomena and had never needed alcohol to achieve them. Darriana didn't appear to find that funny. I'd noticed she only normally laughed when someone had embarrassed themselves horribly – or if a great deal of blood was involved.

It was strangely awkward, wandering the ruined halls of Aramor with Darri. We had never spent much private time together before, and I doubt either of us had any particular desire to do so now, but our need to find alcohol had become a kind of holy quest. We would not rest until we had our drink.

Eventually I remembered that the King had had a small collection of bottles he'd received from foreign dignitaries, kept in a cabinet in the fifth tower – and it just so happened that part of the fifth tower was still standing. Anxiously, I counted the remaining boarded-up windows. The good news was that I reckoned that particular room was still there. The bad news was the tower stairs had fallen when the Blacksmith's God had wreaked his wrath upon the castle, which meant there was no safe way to get there.

I took this as a sign we should look elsewhere. Darriana took it as a challenge.

'Come on, old man,' she called from her perch several feet above me on the outside of the tower. She claimed it would be easier and safer to climb from the outside; I suspect she just thought it would be funny if I fell. 'Weren't the Greatcoats supposed to be good at sneaking in and out of places? Castles, palaces, pig-pens, that sort of thing?'

'You're thinking of the Dashini,' I replied, clinging to a narrow ledge. It says something about my vanity that I'd allowed her to convince me to climb a second time in one night. I had a nasty moment when I groped for my climbing spikes and came up empty, only then remembering I'd changed pockets after sharpening the metal spikes and replacing the leather straps used to tie them to our palms in these situations, figuring it would be easier to grab them in a hurry from the back. Without them, I'm quite sure I'd have fallen when the stone crumbled beneath my boot.

'I could come down and carry you if you want,' Darriana offered.

I didn't dignify that with an answer but hauled myself up a few inches more, found a gap to jam in a toe and resumed the climb. There was a limit to how much abuse I was willing to take from her – also, at this point it was probably safer to finish the climb than it was to try to get back down.

Eventually we reached the highest surviving floor and forced the window open. I pulled out a piece of amberlight and by the light of the torch Darriana produced I recognised our surroundings: one of the many storage rooms the King had used for unwanted gifts. Sure enough, the little cabinet with all the bottles from Saints-knew-where was still there – and it wasn't even locked.

'Why would the King keep these here?' she asked. 'Didn't he have a wine cellar?'

'A vast one,' I replied. 'But these were all gifts, so he could never be sure they weren't poisoned.'

'Makes sense,' she said, picking out a bottle. She twisted the cork out and handed it to me. 'You first.'

'*Me?* Aren't you supposed to be a Dashini? Don't you go through some kind of mystical training to make yourself resistant to poison?'

'Yes – but I reckon you've been poisoned so many times your body probably doesn't care any more.'

'Good point.' I took a swig, and the taste of summer peaches woke up my tongue, closely followed by a burning sensation – but it could have been worse. 'Not bad,' I said, passing her the bottle.

She took a drink. 'Sweet,' she said, then a moment later, '*Oh* . . . I quite like that.'

I extended my hand for the bottle but she pulled it away from me and threw it against the far wall. It smashed into a thousand pieces, the delicious peachy liquor pooling on the floor.

'Why *in hells* would you do that?' I growled, glaring.

Darriana picked out another bottle. 'We already tried that one. Let's push our luck a bit, shall we?'

Reluctantly, I accepted the bottle. And the next. And the one after that.

An hour or so later, sitting on the floor with our backs to the wall, somewhat drunk and still alive, she said, 'I wanted to ask you something.'

'Go ahead.'

She turned to me, her eyes a little blurry from the booze. 'You came back to find Pastien – why?'

'The same reason you did. I was going to beat some sense into him.'

'But weren't you risking the nobles getting pissed off with the Greatcoats?'

'I suppose so.'

'And isn't Aline likely to need Pastien's support in the coming days?'

I was a little confused about where this was going.

'And didn't Valiana *specifically* tell you to leave him alone?'

I nodded again.

She leaned her head back against the wall. 'So you risked creating all kinds of inconveniences for yourself and the Crown, in full knowledge that Valiana would be furious with you, just to slap that git around a bit.'

'Except you got there first.'

She grinned. 'Yes, but I'm crazy. Everyone knows that.'

'True.'

'So why did you do it? Why go there, knowing you'd likely only make things worse?'

I rubbed my shoulder while I thought about that. The climb had been harder than I expected and the soothing effects of the alcohol were wearing off. 'I don't know,' I said finally. 'No, wait, that's not true. I do know. Valiana said something to me. She said, "You're not my real father. Don't pretend to be".'

'So?'

I shrugged. 'I don't give a shit if I'm her father or not. She's my daughter, and no one gets to treat her like dirt while I'm alive.'

Darriana gave a little snort, then looked up at the ceiling. After a few seconds, she turned and kissed me on the cheek.

'What's that for?' I asked.

She leaned her head against my shoulder. 'For knowing that sometimes the right thing to do happens to be the wrong thing.'

CHAPTER SIXTEEN

THE PRICE OF A CROWN

The next morning I was summoned before the Ducal Council. I could think of two reasons, and I prepared a response for each one. If they'd heard about my shenanigans with Pastien and wanted to take the opportunity to dress me down or threaten me with one punishment or another, well, fine: I could live with that. I'd prostrate myself, apologise and beg forgiveness, and as long as that over-manicured piece of shit never tried humiliating Valiana again, I was happy to let him kick me around a bit.

The second possibility was that the Dukes had a list of demands in order to put Aline on the throne, as Duchess Ossia had predicted. They would seek to curb the Greatcoats' influence in their territories, or maybe demand we stamp out a problem or two. I had little doubt that whatever they wanted from me would involve a combination of humiliation and life-threatening danger. I could live with that too. The country's need was far too great, and the salvation of seeing Aline crowned was too close for me to screw things up out of pride or indignity.

Whatever they demanded, *this* time I was going to keep my temper. I would honour my commitment to maintain my calm and give offence to no one, remembering the times when Paelis had been King and I'd been able to sit quietly and speak diplomatically, regardless of whatever asinine proposals the Dukes had in mind for me.

A magistrate is, first and foremost, a man of words.

Peaceful words.

'Are you absolutely fucking mad?' I shouted, slamming a hand down on the new large round oak table inside the council chambers. I suspected the table's shape was to prevent anyone – especially Valiana or Aline – from ever being at the head of the table and therefore being seen to have greater status than the Dukes.

'It's a perfectly sound request,' Hadiermo, Duke of Domaris, said for the third time. He was, notably, the man who'd lost most of his men to Trin's army in less than a week of fighting.

'*None* of you,' I said, pointing to each one of them in turn, 'not *one fucking one of you* is ever going to marry Aline.'

'It needn't be one of us,' Duke Jillard said, with the calm that comes from already knowing that even if you haven't quite won yet, your opponent has lost.

So much for my new best friend, I thought.

'She. Is. Too. Young,' I said, emphasising each word to see if I could, through sheer effort, make them understand.

Erris, Duke of Pulnam, the brave leader who, having largely lost his own battles with Trin's forces, waited until we had saved his bony arse before making a pact with the bitch to betray us, creaked his way to a standing position. This was, apparently, a time for the sage wisdom of elder statesmen. 'She is of marriageable age,' he said, and promptly sat back down again.

'Well argued, Duke—'

'I'm not finished,' he said. 'Like it or not, First Cantor, the girl is old enough – by the Saints, man: you want to make her Queen of Tristia and give her the whole country, but you say she's too young to manage a *husband*?'

'There's a side to this you aren't seeing, Falcio,' said Duke Jillard, looking for all the world as if he were magnanimously trying to reason with me. 'For the sake of the Kingdom, Aline must take a husband so that she can produce an heir.'

'And when she does you'll have no more use for her, will you, your Graces?'

'You tread close to a dangerous accusation,' Hadiermo said. 'Do the Greatcoats suspect this council of wrongdoing?'

'I suspect you of little else.'

'There!' Erris said to Valiana. 'You see? You ask us to permanently reinstate the Greatcoats but you see how they seethe with desire for petty revenge? How can we ever trust them to fairly adjudicate the laws in our Duchies when this barking dog is their leader?'

'Have you forgotten that you killed our King, you fucking senile bastard? Why should *we* ever trust *you*?'

Normally at a time like this, Valiana would have stopped me – she knew exactly what to say to get me to back down – and yet she was silent. If I had been in a saner frame of mind I might have taken this as a warning that something wasn't right here, but, of course, I was nowhere near in my right mind.

Jillard stood, with considerably more calm and grace than the others, and asked, 'So what is your solution, First Cantor? We deposed the King, that is fact, and it will not change. To you, he was a visionary – a Saint. To us, he was a tyrant, shaping the world to his own liking. We fought over the matter and our side won. Now the country is weak and we must either stand together or fall apart – you've said it yourself. There are many who would see Aline dead. So again I ask, what is your solution?'

'Simple,' I said, belligerence rapidly overtaking my earlier commitment to calm, reasoned debate. 'I'll just find every man who wants to harm her and I'll teach them the first rule of the sword.'

'And so barks the dog who does not see the hammer coming down upon his own head,' Erris said.

Valiana placed her hands on the table and the gesture somehow brought the room back to order. 'Gentlemen, let us set this particular matter aside for now. There are other issues which concern us.'

'Like Orison,' Jillard said.

I looked at the Duke of Rijou with what I hoped was a sufficiently threatening expression. 'What exactly about Orison would you like to discuss, your Grace?' *And if you think I'm going to support whatever little plans you have now, you're crazier than old Erris is.*

Valiana surprised me when she motioned to a small stack of papers on the table. 'There have been a number of reports of Western villages claiming the right to secede.'

'Secede? Why bother? And why now?' I asked. 'There hasn't even been anyone to annoy them since Duke Perault died.'

'We don't know,' she replied. 'We haven't had many dealings with the Duchy of Orison for precisely that reason. But if there really are villages threatening to break away . . .'

'Break away *where*? They don't grow enough of their own food – who will they join with? Avares?'

'We don't know,' Hadiermo admitted. 'That's why we thought it might be prudent for the Greatcoats to—'

'Forget it,' I said. 'I'm not sending men to be spies or tax collectors for you. Besides, don't you have your own men you could send?'

Valiana spoke up before the Duke of Domaris could reply. 'I believe it's unwise to send soldiers, especially Ducal soldiers, into a situation that may require investigation before action.'

Again, she surprised me: she knew how much I hated the Greatcoats being used to suppress rebellion amongst honest people who had genuine grievances with their Dukes. 'Send someone else,' I said. 'I'm staying here until I see Aline seated on the throne.'

'Falcio,' Valiana said warningly, 'it would be a mistake to imply that the Greatcoats might defy the Ducal Council's direct order.'

I let it go. I'd come here to make peace, and while I was doing a lousy job of it so far, I knew it was time to step back. 'You're right. My apologies, your Graces. I'll . . . I'll find someone to send north to investigate these villages you've talked about.'

'Good,' Jillard said. 'Then I suggest we adjourn.'

'What of the matter of finding a husband for the heir?' Hadiermo said.

'I'm sure we can leave this for another time and allow the First Cantor to adjust to the idea.'

'No!' Hadiermo said, his voice suddenly raised to a shout, 'I'll not see council business ignored simply because it offends the Trattari's sensibilities.'

This was another of those times where Valiana would usually step in and calm everyone down, and then we'd work something out – and yet again, she stayed silent.

Great, so I have to actually be reasonable of my own accord.

I took in a breath and held it as long as I could before letting it out. When I was confident I could speak rationally again, I said, 'I mean no offence, your Grace, but I still fail to understand why it's so important for Aline to marry, never mind immediately give birth to a child.'

'Falcio,' Jillard said, 'if we put her on the throne . . . if something happened to her and there wasn't another heir . . .'

Saints, I thought, *he's right – it would be* chaos. *It would mean civil war for generations.* How had I not seen this before? Was my own determination to protect Aline blinding me to the country's plight?

'See?' Hadiermo said triumphantly. 'The dog has finally learned to add two and two together. That's right, First Cantor. It's time to decide if you're fighting for the safety of your King's bastard child or for the survival of your country.'

'That "bastard child" is your rightful Queen, and Aline will marry *when* she wishes, and to a man she loves,' I said.

Hadiermo rose to his feet. 'She'll marry whomever you damn well tell her to and you bloody well know it! Let us not pretend you aren't the one who can pull her strings whenever you wish, First Cantor. So now, tell us: do the Greatcoats work for the people of Tristia, or do they exist solely to act on your petty vows and passions?'

'Enough, Hadiermo,' Jillard said. 'The First Cantor understands now. It's enough.'

'*Pah!*' he said, sitting back down heavily on his chair. 'Look at you, coddling the fucking Trattari. Shall we sing sweet songs to the heir to soothe this fool's nerves?' He turned to look at the other members of the council. With a ribald laugh, he added, 'I tell you this: I'll wed her and I'll see her pregnant within a fortnight, whether she wants it or not.'

'Say that again,' I said. 'Get back on your feet, Duke Hadiermo, and tell me again how you'll bed Aline whether she wishes it or not—'

'Do you threaten a member of the council in open session, Trattari?'

'Hadn't I made that clear?' My right hand reached down to my side and drew one of my rapiers. The hell with the people who say I threaten too much. 'Does this clarify my intentions, *your Grace*?'

Erris slammed a fist on the table and shouted, 'How *dare* you come into this council chamber and—'

'I'll come and threaten you in a different one, if you prefer, your Grace. For example, I'd be happy to turn up in your Ducal bedchambers the next time you—'

'Falcio, be silent,' Valiana said, her voice even.

I turned to her, my earlier regret over my harsh words vanishing. 'Oh, now you've found something to say?'

'Keep silent, I said.' She turned and walked to the door. At first I thought she was leaving the meeting, but instead, she signalled for the guards to enter, four men in armour, war swords at their sides. It took me a moment to realise what she'd said – and the guards themselves were so surprised that she had to repeat herself.

'I said, arrest him.'

The guard in charge hesitated. 'Realm's Protector, you set an order that prisoners were to be taken to the Greatcoats for trial – so how am I to—?'

'Just take him to the damned dungeon,' she said. 'Let him sit there a while and recover his temper, if not his senses.'

The guards took a step towards me and I raised my weapon. 'Think carefully, gentlemen,' I said. 'People are prone to get hurt in these situations.'

Valiana stepped in front of the guard so that the point of my sword touched her chest. 'Then start with me, Falcio. If you really want to kill someone, start with me.' When she saw me hesitate she batted my blade out of the way with her hand. 'Or else follow these men down to the dungeon and wait until I see fit to have you released.'

I considered my options, which amounted to harming the young woman to whom I'd given my own name and made my daughter, or allowing myself to be arrested. I sheathed my rapier and let the guards lead me away, pausing only to say loudly, 'No wonder those fucking northern villages want to secede. I'm starting to think it would be a good idea myself.'

CHAPTER SEVENTEEN

THE KING'S GLAIVE

With as much gentleness as men of violence could manage, they led me down the three flights of stairs to the dungeons of Castle Aramor. I suffered the indignity of it all with as much good grace as I could, given that it was entirely my own fault that I was in this situation. I knew it would take all of an hour for Kest and Brasti to find out what had happened and either convince Valiana to have me released or simply break me out themselves.

Castle Aramor's dungeon is about as pleasant a place to pass the time while incarcerated as you could hope for. Unlike most dungeons, the King had installed long diagonal vents in the stone walls so that there was some natural light in the cells. There were actual beds, with thick woollen blankets, and the food was tolerable, so it wasn't until we reached the end of the long row of cells that I seriously considered resisting my arrest.

'Well, well, if it isn't the world's dumbest man come to pay me a visit.'

The walls of the last cell were lined with books, and ensconced in what looked like an excessively comfortable chair, sewing pieces of leather, sat the Tailor. Several bottles of wine were grouped on a small table in the corner. Apparently Aline and Valiana had decided to make what remained of the Tailor's sentence for having nearly destroyed the country only slightly less comfortable than if they'd simply given her the crown and seated her on the throne of Tristia.

The guards ushered me into the cell opposite hers before I had a chance to protest.

'So it took almost a whole day, did it?' Her voice was always full of grit and sand. 'I bet Gerrald here a silver stag that it would take you no more than an hour to force Valiana to have you arrested.'

'Who's Gerrald?'

'I am,' said one of the guards, reaching a hand, palm-up, through the bars of the Tailor's cell.

She snorted and said, 'I'm imprisoned, ye great twit. Where would I get silver?'

Gerrald said nothing, but kept his hand where it was.

Finally the Tailor reached into a pocket of her coat. 'Greedy bastard. I should have you killed.'

The guard smiled. 'My missus thanks you, ma'am.'

He and the other guards left us there.

'I thought you were pardoned,' I said.

The Tailor shrugged. 'I was, but these accommodations suit me fine and sometimes it's useful for people not to know one's true status.'

'Does Valiana know where they've put me?' I asked.

The Tailor gave me a wink.

'I'm sorry,' I said, 'but I don't speak crazy old bat. Is that a yes?'

'It's a yes,' Valiana said, coming down the hall. She had a man with her, tall and slender, with long, shaggy blond hair and a bushy beard that made him look older than I suspected he actually was. He wore a greatcoat like mine but his collar and cuffs were lined with thick grey-white fur. He carried a tall staff shod with bands of iron at one end and an eighteen-inch curved blade at the other. 'Falcio, this is—'

'Son of a bitch,' I said. '*Morn?*'

He nodded.

'The beard is new. Makes you look uglier than I remember.'

Morn, once called the King's Glaive after the weapon he habitually carried, raised a hand to his chin and grinned. 'Gets cold where I've been these past few years.'

'And where is that?'

A loud clang followed by a crash drew everyone's attention towards the entrance to the dungeon. I stuck my face up against the bars, but I couldn't see what had happened . . . then I heard the voices and the 'what' didn't matter.

'I told you it would work,' Kest said. 'It's just a matter of calculating the force required against the weakest point on the door.'

I heard a loud snort that could only have come from Brasti. 'Wonderful. Perfect. It just happens to make enough noise to bring the castle down on us.'

They came into view, the pair of them carrying a log which Brasti promptly dropped when he saw who else was in the dungeon. 'Saint-fucking-Zaghev, if it isn't Morn the King's Arse-Licker come for a visit.' He pointed at Morn's glaive. 'Still carrying that ugly thing instead of a proper weapon?'

Morn looked to me. 'So he's still insulting other people's weapons and thinking it's clever?'

'Yes,' Brasti said before I could respond, 'but this time it's true: a glaive really is the ugliest weapon ever devised.'

Morn grinned. 'I'd beat you senseless for that remark, Brasti, but it looks as if you've got enough problems.'

He reached out and pulled Brasti into a rough bear hug and then turned and did the same to Kest, who was still hanging onto his end of the log with his one hand. It was a nice moment, when seen from inside a cell.

'Oh, by the way,' Brasti said to Valiana, 'the Saint of Mercy asked me to convey to you that if Falcio isn't released within the hour she's going to bring what's left of the castle down on everyone's heads.' To me he added, 'Sainthood is *really* making her moody.'

I let that rather terrifying thought slide because something else was bothering me. 'Why wasn't I told Morn had returned?' I asked Valiana. 'And why did you bring him down here?'

It was the Tailor who replied, 'Because he has something to tell us.'

I sat back on the bed in the cell, finally putting the events of the last hour together. 'Shit. It's not by accident that I find myself in this cell, is it?'

'We needed a meeting,' the Tailor said, 'one that wouldn't arouse suspicion or bring too many ears.'

I looked at Valiana. 'So you goaded me into threatening the Dukes as a pretext for having me arrested just so you could bring me down here.'

'I didn't have to push very hard,' she pointed out, and I could see she was still hurt by my behaviour. Hells, how was it she had me sitting in a cell and I got to feel guilty for it?

I looked at Morn. 'What was the King's last command to you? Was it something to do with Orison?'

'A little further west,' he replied.

'There is nothing west of Orison,' Brasti said, 'just mountains and . . . *Oh* . . . fuck me.'

'Avares,' Morn confirmed. 'Land of piss-drinking barbarians and not a single decent beer for three hundred miles.'

I stood up from the bed. 'King Paelis sent you to Avares? To do what?'

Morn leaned on his glaive. 'Oh, you know how the King was. Brought me into the library on his last day, took a drink from his glass and said, "Need you do to a little ranging for me, Morn." Then he pointed on a map and said, "Keep an eye on this for me, will you?"'

'"Ranging"?' Kest asked.

It was an odd word to use, since normally it meant sighting distance in preparation for launching an attack. It also sounded a lot like ... *Ah.* 'The King told you to join the Rangieri?' The word sounded odd on my tongue.

Morn pulled at the fur collar of his coat. '*Join* them? When's the last time you saw any Rangieri running around? I doubt there are ten left in the whole Western Mountains. I spent the first year just trying to find one to get him to teach me how to survive in all that damned freezing wilderness. I swear the King picked me for this mission because I used to complain about having to go on those damned long journeys up the trade routes.'

'And you're sure he was pointing to Avares on that map?' Brasti asked.

Morn stopped for a moment, then his eyes went wide and he stood up. 'Hells! You know, I think he might have been pointing at Hervor – Saint Gan-who-laughs-with-dice, have I just spent six years in the wrong damned country?'

'All right,' the Tailor said, 'if you're done having your fun, we need to get down to business.'

'Wait a minute,' I said, 'I still don't understand. Why would the King send you to spy on Avares?'

'Because no one else would,' Valiana said. 'The Dukes recalled all of their diplomats and spies after the King was deposed.'

'Why in hells—?'

'They needed them here, close to home, so they could keep track of their enemies within Tristia.'

Here we were in a castle infested with spies, but we had none in the country that might actually decide to invade us one day soon. As if I needed another reason to be annoyed with the Dukes ...

'The King had some of his own spies in Avares, of course,' Morn said, 'but the Dukes ratted them out so they all died.'

'And yet you survived?'

He smiled and made a show of inspecting his fingernails. 'They don't call me the King's Magic for nothing, Falcio.'

'Nobody ever called you that,' Brasti said. 'He named you for that stupid stick with the knife on the end of it – and anyway, with all that fur on you we ought to change that to the King's Rug.'

I shook my head in disbelief. 'Are you telling me that for all these years we've had *one man* keeping an eye on the country that's gone to war with us seven times in the last hundred years?' I looked at Morn. 'Okay, so what's going on in Avares?'

For a moment he didn't speak, then he sighed. 'I'm not exactly sure.'

'You're not sure?'

'It's a big country, Falcio, and not an easy place to blend in.' He rubbed his jaw through the beard. 'But I'll tell you this: it isn't the country it was.'

'Meaning?'

'Over the last five years their warbands have become better organised, and more dangerous. They're actually forging their own steel now.'

The Tailor stood up and leaned close to the bars. 'There's no way in any hell they should be working in steel, Falcio, not for at least another ten years. They lack the organisation to mine properly, to work forges, to . . . well, I won't waste my time explaining it all, but it's enough to say that moving this quickly isn't natural.'

'Falcio,' Morn said quietly, 'I'm fairly certain I saw cannons.'

That hit me like a blow. We had cannons, of course, but not good ones, not the kind you hear about from across the sea in Darome.

'And that's not the worst of it.'

'Fantastic,' Brasti said, throwing his arms up in the air. 'Let me guess, whatever Gods are still living have taken a vote and decided to side with the barbarians?'

'Not quite,' Morn replied, 'but there is a new Warlord in Avares, a man they call the Magdan – which means "King of Battle", by the way – and he's started uniting the tribes.'

'Have you seen him?' the Tailor asked.

'No, he's too clever. His men know how to run a camp. You'd never get within a mile of him without being caught.'

I stood up and pushed at the door, only then realising the guards hadn't locked it. 'So you came back to warn us. Have you told the Ducal Council? They should send troops to the borders.'

Morn looked at the Tailor.

'Go ahead,' she said.

'That's not why I came back. I've been crossing the border back and forth every few months for years to keep up with what's happening here in Tristia as well. The last time I snuck into Avares, I got captured by another of these Avarean Warlords: a big brute of a man with the sense of a donkey but with an army of two thousand warriors. I managed to convince him that I was just a travelling merchant, someone willing to risk the dangers of trading across the border for the profits that such trips can bring. When I was in his camp, a woman visited him: an impossibly beautiful woman with a smile that made my blood go cold. She offered him a great deal of money, payment to bring his army on as mercenaries. Falcio, her name was—'

'Trin,' I said with a shudder. 'Trin is hiring mercenaries from Avares.' I looked at Valiana and the Tailor. 'You want me to go to Orison. You want me to pretend to go and settle the villages down for the Ducal Council when in reality I'll be tracking down Trin.'

'You'll also be looking into this new Warlord Morn's been telling us about,' Valiana said.

Hells. If Trin really was hiring Avareans as mercenaries, they could wreak untold damage on the country. We couldn't stand another civil war, not this soon after the last one. As much as I hated the thought of leaving Aline alone, this was a threat we couldn't ignore. There was another reason I would go, though: for the chance to kill Trin, to rid the world of her and Patriana's vile line once and for all.

'Falcio, there's something else,' Valiana said, catching the look on my face. 'I need you to bring her back alive.'

'*Alive*? Are you *insane*? Even the Dukes wouldn't want her brought back alive – Saints, Duke Jillard is her father and he'd be the first to congratulate me for putting a blade in her belly.'

'He might,' she said, 'but that would send the message that we're scared: that we had to resort to assassination because we feared one woman so much. Worse, it will confirm the fears of those who believe the Greatcoats are nothing more than Aline's private army. Falcio, if we bring Trin back to Aramor and make her stand trial for what she's done, the country will know that justice is still alive in Tristia.'

I turned to the Tailor in disbelief. 'You *agree* with this? You'd let Trin come back here and—?'

The old woman spat. 'I'd rather rip out that little bitch's cunt with my bare hands just to make sure we never see another like her.' She let out a long breath. 'But Valiana's right, and wiser than either of us, thank Saint Felsan-who-weighs-the-world – oh, wait, he's dead, too, isn't he?' She stood up and rested her hands against the bars of her cell. 'This country is on the brink of failing, Falcio. You've seen this. There are plenty of reasons, but the most insidious is that the people of Tristia have no faith in their leaders and even less faith in our so-called laws. Given nowhere else to turn, they'll simply follow whichever fool talks the loudest.'

Brasti groaned. 'So this was just a way to get Falcio down here to appeal to his love of suicide missions? Now we're supposed to invade a foreign country and, while avoiding capture, simultaneously track down and kidnap Trin and then somehow bring her back alive to stand trial?'

'He's right,' Kest said. 'The Greatcoats weren't meant for operating inside a foreign country. We don't know the people or the land – our chances of being captured and killed once we cross their borders are . . . significant.'

The Tailor ignored them both and favoured me with a sour grin. 'Think of this as an act of daring and valour, Falcio. You've always been fond of those.'

CHAPTER EIGHTEEN

THE STONEMASON

Freed from my very temporary captivity, I spent some time in the Greatcoats' wardroom preparing for the journey: packing my clothes, re-sharpening my climbing spikes, oiling throwing knives and hunting around for supplies to refill the dozens of now-empty pockets in my coat.

King Paelis, back when he was still alive, appointed Magisterial Valets: specialists whose job was to prepare our coats before each journey. They'd oil the leather using compounds formulated by the Tailor for whichever climate we were heading for. The bone plates would be inspected and replaced where necessary, and each pocket would be checked, all our tricks and traps and weapons carefully maintained and replaced as needed. One of our pockets is designed especially to carry writs for our forthcoming cases, and sometimes the King would sneak in a little note – and he was fond of the odd practical joke too (one circuit, I spent days trying to work out why I smelled so powerfully of lavender). Those childish pranks of his reminded you that he cared – he knew he was sending you off into danger, and he would be so proud when you returned. It was for that reason, as much as the bone plates and the weapons, we felt almost invincible when that greatcoat was on our shoulders.

Rummaging through one of the old cabinets near the weapons racks, I scrounged up a few small fragments of amberlight. I had less luck finding any jars of the black salve we use to treat wounds incurred on the road. Worse still, I was completely out of the hard candy that I'd relied upon so many times these past few years. By the time I was done, I felt oddly naked in my coat; far too many of the pockets were empty. Not for the first time, I worried about how the other Greatcoats – those who'd yet to return to Aramor – were faring without the means to replenish their supplies.

Deal with the problem in front of you, I reminded myself. *Get Aline on the throne, then you'll have all the time in the world to find the rest of the Greatcoats and get the things we need to make us functional again.*

With my preparations complete, I spent a few restless hours wandering the halls of Castle Aramor, which had been my habit in the old days on the night before a long journey. Kest used to spend that time reading – travelling through rain, cold and muck with books is seldom a good idea. Brasti would get drunk or seek out . . . *other* diversions. But me? I liked to remind myself that we weren't entirely alone out there and to take with me some small sense of this strange castle where I'd first snuck in, a madman, covered in filth and bent on revenge, and had left months later as a King's magistrate, with a sword at my side and a greatcoat on my back.

I could almost imagine Paelis himself following me down the halls, making fun of my penchant for nostalgia, but sometimes just feeling the stone flags beneath my feet gave me the sense of solidity that was absent in every other part of my life.

'Take another step and you're dead,' a woman's voice called out.

My rapier was in hand even before I turned to face whoever had come for me. I was in one of the passageways that ran behind the throne room, the few lanterns casting more shadow than light. 'I only just cleaned this blade,' I said, 'so I'm going to be even more pissed off than usual if I have to kill someone with it tonight.'

A figure stepped into view – a woman in a stonemason's heavy leather apron, carrying a mallet in one hand and a chisel in the other. 'Reckon you're going to duel in a hole in the floor, do you?' She gestured with the chisel to the patch of shadow where I'd been about to step.

The stonemason was far enough away that I allowed myself a glance back. Sure enough, I'd nearly walked right into a three-foot wide hole in the damned floor.

'Goes down nearly twenty feet,' she said, coming to join me. 'The rubble below is so damnably sharp your skin would be cut to ribbons even before your bones broke from the impact, you blind idiot.'

'Thanks,' I said, resheathing my rapier. 'For the warning, I mean, not for calling me an idiot.'

She stuck her tools into the leather loops attached to her apron. 'Midreida,' she said, offering her hand. 'Chief Stonemason. I'm the one who's keeping your castle from falling down.'

'Falcio val Mond,' I said in turn, 'First Cant—'

'Everybody knows who you are, you blithering—'

'For someone whose job is to keep this place standing, perhaps you should fix the fucking gaps in the floors rather than casting aspersions at others.'

'You might have a point there,' she conceded, staring down at the hole in front of us. 'But almost nobody uses this particular passageway anymore, so we've just been using it to store our tools at night. We'll get to it eventually, but there's only so many hours in the day and this whole place is a wreck.'

'You and the others have been working on this for two months already – shouldn't things be—'

'"Two months",' Midreida repeated in a tone laden with sarcasm. 'Two *whole* months? Has it really been that long? Hard to imagine how we couldn't have finished rebuilding the single largest structure in the entire fucking country in that time, isn't it?'

'Yes, fine,' I said, irritated by the woman's apparently endless derision, not to mention the way she kept snorting as though I had no comprehension of how castles were constructed – I didn't, of course, but she didn't have to remind me of it with every twitch of her lips. 'What if we hired more people to speed things up?'

'*What* people?' she asked. 'With *what money*? This isn't digging trenches we're talking about, First Cantor. This is skilled work.' The stonemason spread her arms wide, gesturing at the passageway as if she herself had carved it from solid rock. 'A castle like this takes a generation to build! It takes specialists in a dozen different crafts; can you not understand that?'

Before I could answer, she grabbed me by the arm and hauled me through the servants' entrance into the throne room. 'There,' she said, pointing at one of the heavy marble tiles on the floor. 'You see that? And there? And again there?'

I peered down at the marble. 'Er . . . the ones in the middle of the room are a little lower than the others. So what?'

'*So what?* That marble rests on a stone floor above the lower levels of the keep: *it's not supposed to sag*. Tell me, have you ever seen rock bend?'

'Well, no, but—'

'That bloody God of yours somehow weakened the foundations holding up the entire bloody castle.' She looked away as if addressing someone else – someone considerably less ignorant than me. '"How soon can the castle be finished?" he asks me.' She turned back to me. 'First Cantor, right now it's all I can do to make sure what's left of the fucking thing doesn't fall into the dungeons the next time more than twenty people come begging favours from the crown!'

Saint Eloria-who . . . whatever she does. It never occurred to me that the keep could actually be in even worse state than it looked from outside. What had once been the proudest castle in the country was now little more than a husk; it shared so much in common with the broken, rotting nation itself that I wondered if the damned Blacksmith hadn't done it this way on purpose.

'Oh, now he gets it,' the stonemason said. 'Now the true state of things is seeping into that mighty magistrate's brain of his. Now he understands why asking me how soon I can be done is the most idiotic question of the age.'

I didn't feel like I was going to develop a good working relationship with Midreida, so I waited until she stopped railing at me, then a little longer before she finally let her arms drop by her sides. Then I asked, 'So, next week is no good then?'

With only a few hours left before daylight, I should have made my way straight to my bed, but instead found myself continuing my lonely meanderings in the castle's halls (although this time I was paying more attention to where I stepped). I kept hoping I might run into Ethalia; I still hadn't exchanged more than a few words with her since my return. The stupid thing was, I knew where she would be: inside what was left of the broken-down old chapel she'd taken as her bedroom in the same way I'd moved into the Greatcoats' wardroom. We'd both made homes out of our respective professions, and somehow that had created another barrier between us. Although I must have walked past the chapel a dozen times that night, my uncertainty over the state of our relationship kept me from just knocking at her door. Instead, like an unwanted puppy, I returned to the wardroom, tail between my legs, and hoped that she might come to seek me out. So there I sat, on my dusty cot, waiting like a lovelorn fool for a knock at the door.

Unfortunately, when the knock finally came, it wasn't Ethalia.

'Rhyleis,' I said wearily, 'I don't know how you got to Aramor so quickly, but I swear if this is another—'

She reached up and briefly placed a finger against my lips. 'Shush, my darling, no time for your usual flirtations tonight. I'm here on important business.'

'Which is?' I asked suspiciously.

'I bring orders from Nehra.'

I sighed. 'You know what I wonder sometimes?'

Her mouth lifted in a salacious smile. 'I know *exactly* what you wonder about.'

I let that pass. 'Why is it that the Greatcoats are literally the only people in the country who are never required to bend a knee to anyone and yet everyone and their cat think they can order me around?'

Rhyleis pinched my cheek. 'You have a very *orderable* face, Falcio.' Before I could protest, she blithely relayed Nehra's command. 'When you get to Avares, it's very important that you bring back any warsongs that you can. The Avareans don't write them down, but their warriors often sing them during training. Have Kest take note, since he's got the best ear for music of the three of you, and make sure you—'

'Hold on,' I said, barely keeping up, 'how does Nehra even know we're going to Avares?'

Rhyleis arched an eyebrow at me. Not many people can do that, and few so superciliously. 'Falcio, please, we're the *Bardatti*.'

'You say that like I should give a damn, which I don't. Anyway, if you know where I'm going you probably have some idea of *why* I'm going, and you'll then understand why I don't have time to bring back any tunes, poems, ditties or other nonsense.'

Something changed in Rhyleis' expression and it took me a moment to recognise it for what it was. I guess I'd never seen her angry before. 'Be very careful how you speak of songcraft, Falcio val Mond. The spread of a single carefully worded scorn poem has taken the crown from a Prince's head. Generals have watched their infantry run screaming from the field as the effects of a true warsong broke their spirit. *We are the Bardatti*, and we are not to be trifled with.'

There was a fire in her eyes and it was an impressive speech, but I have a low tolerance for excessively flowery threats when I'm tired.

'No, of course not. The Bardatti are too busy trifling with everyone else.'

For some strange reason, Rhyleis took this as submission. 'Now remember, it's not important to get the words, but we need the melody and rhythm – as many Avarean warsongs as you can, every single one you hear while you're away on your little holiday.'

Holiday. 'Right. I'll get on that straightaway. Warsongs. Rhythm. Melody. Tell Nehra it's as good as done.'

Rhyleis smiled. 'Excellent. Now that we've got business out of the way . . .' She brought her fingers to the collar of her shirt and undid the top button, then nodded for me to do the same.

'Rhyleis . . .' I said.

'Yes, Falcio?'

The thing about being a duellist is that you learn to sense when someone is testing you with a feint rather than preparing an actual lunge. 'Get the hells out of my room.'

CHAPTER NINETEEN

THE UNANSWERED WHISTLE

It was cold outside, the morning of our departure – colder than it had any right to be for the time of year. I'd risen later than I'd intended, the result of yet another frustratingly sleepless night, and by the time I walked out of the front gates I expected to see Kest, Brasti and Morn waiting impatiently for me. Instead, I found Aline standing alone in a pale grey robe far too thin to protect her from the wind.

She whistled into the empty air, then fell silent as the sound floated off into the distance. She stared down the main road and after a moment she whistled again and once more stood quietly, as if waiting for a reply.

'You'd make a terrible bird,' I said, and when she didn't reply, I tried a sterner tone. 'You shouldn't be outside alone.'

She motioned absently off to her right and now I spotted the three guards standing a discreet distance away, doing their best to blend into the gardens while still keeping an eye on her.

Aline started whistling again and at last I realised this wasn't an idle tune; it was more like an urgent call. A summoning.

I bridged the distance between us to take a position next to her. 'What are you—?'

'I come out here every morning and call her,' Aline said, 'but she never comes.'

'Call who?'

She didn't answer at first, until I leaned over and saw the deep sadness in her eyes and the set of her mouth. 'Monster,' she whispered.

I hadn't thought about the Fey horse in almost a year. She went on, 'We aren't that far away from . . . from where I made her go away.' Aline turned to me at last. 'I said *horrible* things to her, Falcio. I threw rocks at her and called her . . . but I *had* to make her go. She wouldn't . . . she was causing problems with the other horses – she just wouldn't fit in. All she wanted to do was fight, to charge into battle . . .'

I was about to say that I knew that feeling, but somehow, I managed to keep my mouth shut. Was that what I was now: a mad beast who just wanted to kill his enemies, who had no place in this new world? I wanted to say something reassuring, to myself as much as Aline, but what came out was, 'Maybe she doesn't come because she can't. Maybe she's . . .' I paused in my headlong rush to a bad ending.

'Dead?' Aline shook her head. 'No, I don't think anything can kill her. The Tailor says that Monster is all gristle and iron on the inside. I just wish I could see her one more time – to apologise. All she ever did was try to protect me, and I . . .'

'And she did, sweetheart. No doubt Monster's off somewhere raising seven hells against the world.' I took a chance and reached an arm around Aline's shoulders.

She surprised me by turning and grabbing onto me, her face sinking into my chest. 'I'm sorry I wasn't there when you arrived, Falcio. I'm sorry Pastien was so foul to Valiana – I should have—'

'Wait now, sweetheart,' I said, holding her close. 'The weight of the world will be on your shoulders soon enough.'

She pulled away and took my hand. 'I have something for us,' she said, and pointed to a small table set a little ways inside the gate with two chairs, set for tea, with a flagon of wine besides.

As we sat there, she poured tea for herself and wine for me, and I had a momentary stab of panic. There had been times in the past when Aline had reverted to a child's innocence – but then she set the wine in front of me and I remembered something.

'You know, your father did this sometimes,' I said.

'Did what?'

'Tried to get the other guy drunk while he stayed sober.'

Aline blew on her tea before bringing the cup to her lips. 'Did he? From the stories I've been told by those eager to tell them, my father was usually the one who was drunk.'

That made me smile. 'He certainly liked to give off that impression.' The wine in the glass decanter looked to be a pleasant claret and I started to reach for the goblet, then thought better of my choice and picked up the teapot to fill the second cup instead. 'In truth, he was rather fond of drinking himself into a stupor, but those who claim to have seen him do so are usually lying.'

'Why do you say that?'

'Because your father knew he had to stay sharp, keep his mind clear. He never knew who his enemies were, other than the fact that almost *everyone* was his enemy in one way or another. Even the most innocuous of conversations could end up being used against him. He could rarely afford to let down his guard in the company of others.'

Aline seemed to consider that. 'But he did so with you.'

I nodded. 'With me, and Kest, sometimes with Brasti and a few of the others.'

'So he only felt safe with the Greatcoats?'

I was about to agree, but something about that struck me as wrong – or at least, incomplete. 'It's more that . . .'

'He saw you as friends?'

The sentiment still wasn't quite right. 'King Paelis was trying to do something *big*, trying to . . . change the way the country saw itself. The Greatcoats were part of that, but I think the real reason he felt comfortable in our presence was because we were the only people who shared some small part of that vision – we saw the world in the same way.'

'What about Grandmother?'

'The Tailor? She . . .' I searched for the right words. Even when the Tailor isn't in the room, if you say the wrong thing, you're likely to get a sudden slap across the back of the head. 'She supported the King's dream, to be sure – I think in many ways she understood how to make it come to life better than he did . . . but she never took any pleasure from it.' I shook my head. 'I'm not making sense.'

'No, that makes perfect sense,' Aline said. 'My father could talk about his plans, his vision for the country, and feel as if you and the others shared in the excitement it brought him.'

'Exactly. I suppose you could say that King Paelis liked to drink around us because somehow our presence made him feel a bit like celebrating.'

She gave me a small smile. 'Then there's at least something I have in common with my father.'

I smiled back. 'You have at least one other thing in common with him.'

'What's that?'

'You both think that a little wine and pleasant conversation will somehow make me less prone to wanting to tear the walls down once I hear what you actually sat me down to say.'

She hardened a little. 'The walls have already been torn down, Falcio. You'll have to find some other way to express your displeasure.' The words were spoken lightly, almost as a jest, but there was an edge there I recognised as a warning not to overstep: a third tendency she shared with her father.

From my chair, I bent at the waist and gave a small bow. 'I await your command, your Majesty.'

'Don't do that, Falcio.'

'I wasn't mocking you.'

'Yes, you were. You might not think it, but when you play the loyal servant with me, what you're really doing is saying that if you don't like what I have to tell you than you'll just find some way to subvert me without explicitly disobeying me.'

I tried a smile. 'See, when you say it like that, I don't sound very clever at all.'

'You aren't,' she said. 'You just rely on the fact that most of the world is even stupider and more stubborn than you are.'

'Perhaps, *your Majesty*, my reticence to follow a monarch's commands is because the last time I did so, I found myself standing outside these very walls while Ducal Knights came and dragged him to a cell.'

She sighed. 'I'm not about to commit suicide, Falcio, I promise you.'

'Excellent.' I reached for the goblet and the wine. 'In that case, what would you like to discuss?'

She shook her head, but there was a smile in there somewhere. 'You obstinate arse! I need your advice.' She held up a hand. 'Not to mock me or complain or make threats against the rest of the world. To *advise*.'

I considered where this might be heading. Despite my better judgement I took a sip of the wine. I was right: it was an outstanding vintage. Just as well; I was fairly sure I was going to need to be very drunk to get through this conversation. 'You're going to do as the Dukes demand and marry.'

She put her teacup down on the table. 'I'm fourteen – it's not unheard of, especially in a royal line.'

'To whom should I send my congratulations?'

'That is precisely what I need your advice for, you great oaf!'

I nearly spat out my mouthful of wine. 'You want *me* to help you choose a husband?'

'Yes,' she said, so quietly I barely heard her. 'When you return from this mission, I mean.'

'*Me*? Why me?'

She shrugged, the gesture of a nervous child, and for the first time since we sat down, I found myself facing not the determined and clever future Queen of Tristia, but a fourteen-year-old girl forced to make a choice that clearly terrified her. 'Because when I think of asking anyone else to help me choose, I feel sick to my stomach. Even Ethalia . . .'

I felt a stab of guilt at the way I'd spoken to her. I'd been wrong about the nice chairs and the wine and the pleasant conversation. She hadn't been trying to ease me into this horrible subject. She'd been trying to build up her own courage to face it.

I tried to imagine what it must be like, to be young, beginning to see your own talents emerging, to see the world full of possibility – and yet have to set that aside, to prepare yourself for a marriage whose only purpose would be to ensure you never fully met your own potential. To consign yourself to be less than you could be in order to satisfy the machinations of old men.

'I'm sorry,' I said.

'It's not your fault—'

I reached out and took her hand. 'Well, then, I suppose I'll have to make a list of suitable candidates.'

Aline lifted my hand and kissed it. 'Thank you, Falcio.'

I gave her my best smile and tried to mentally prepare for what would one day soon be a horribly awkward and uncomfortable conversation for both of us. I consoled myself with the fact that I was about to travel into enemy territory and face what would quite possibly be my death. If that didn't work, I'd have plenty of time on the return journey to come up with the required list of prospective husbands, each of whom I would soon be visiting in order to explain the finer details of stab wounds.

'Oh, I met with Chalmers, by the way,' Aline said.

I was taken aback by that – we'd only arrived yesterday – but then,

Aline always took such pleasure in meeting with every Greatcoat she could. What did you think of her?' I asked, genuinely curious.

Aline took another sip from her tea. 'She's rude and obstinate and she clearly suspects everyone who *isn't* a Greatcoat of being morally compromised.' She put down the cup and grinned. 'I adore her already.'

Before I could provide my own assessment, Aline rose from the table. 'I should go. I have to meet with some of the Dukes before the council adjourns.' As she walked back through the gates, the guards quickly following behind, I thought she might have whispered, 'I'm sorry.'

I wasn't sure who she was talking to.

I walked out of the gate and found myself staring at the same point off in the distance that had transfixed Aline. Maybe if I delayed my journey north I could . . . I don't know, go out there and find the damned horse? Maybe that would make things better. Bloody creature.

Who told you that you could run off and leave Aline alone like that? I thought we had a deal.

'She'll be all right, Falcio,' said a voice somewhere off to my right, and when I turned, I saw Valiana sitting a few yards away on the stone foundation that supported the long iron gate into the castle. How is *everyone* able to sneak up on me lately?

'How long have you been sitting there?' I asked.

'An hour or so. Aline comes out here around the same time every morning, so I try to keep an eye on her when I can.'

'"When you can"?'

She winced. 'There are seven guards watching her at all times now, Falcio. Two of them are Greatcoats.'

'Which ones?' I asked, looking out to see if I could spot them. I couldn't.

'Lately, Mateo and Quentis Maren. They work well together.'

I found it odd that Mateo, about as heretical a man as I'd ever met, and Quentis Maren, a former Inquisitor, had become such close friends, but really, it was none of my business. Besides, knowing they were watching Aline made me feel much more comfortable about leaving; that was a much more practical solution to ensuring her safety than trying to lock the heir safely away in an impregnable iron box until I could get her seated on the throne.

'I'm sorry about the ruse,' Valiana said.

I waved a hand. 'It's all right. You did what needed to be done.' That sounded like a credible response, but . . . no.

'You could have told me, Valiana. I could have given just as good a performance for the Dukes – or hells, we could have found a different way to meet . . .'

'I was wrong,' she said. 'I should have trusted you.'

'Damned right . . .'

Only she wasn't wrong; that was the thing. I would have railed against meeting with the Tailor. I would have refused and stomped around and . . .

What the hells is wrong *with me lately?*

'You're trying to keep us all from danger,' Valiana said, as if she could hear my thoughts. I suppose it wasn't that hard; I felt like anyone could read my face these days. 'This . . . it's just a different sort of danger.'

When I didn't reply, she rose from the stone foundation. 'Anyway, I'm sorry if I've disappointed you,' she said, and walked past me into the castle courtyard.

'You haven't—'

But she was already gone.

Negotiations. Intrigue. The dark arts of politicians. The tactical deceptions and secret deal-making that were needed to make a country run. I don't think I'd ever really appreciated the way the King used to deal so masterfully with such problems, all the while letting the rest of us run off on our righteous quests to bring justice to the people of Tristia. Did he ever resent the way we left him behind to deal with the mess? Did Valiana? She had to work every day to keep the Kingdom running, and every day she had to use a hundred different tactics to fight off a hundred different enemies and always come out the winner.

While my only job involved going around stabbing people with swords and giving long-winded speeches that no one wanted to hear any more.

The sound of hooves shook me out of my introspection. Kest, Brasti and Morn rode up to the gates with my own horse, Arsehole, alongside. 'Why in all the hells can't Trin launch her conspiracies in the spring?' Brasti said. 'It's colder than the Tailor's heart out here.'

Morn chuckled. 'You think this is cold? This? You should see the frozen shithole we're headed to.'

Brasti gave me a dirty look.

'Leave him be,' Kest said, attaching his shield to one of his saddlebags.

'You know you've got a lot slower since losing your hand, Kest. You're not a Saint any more—'

'I'm still fast enough to knock you off your horse three times before you draw your weapon.' Kest leaned over on his horse to peer at Brasti's waist. 'No, you're still hanging your sword belt too far to the back. Four times.'

Brasti threw up his hands. 'Will I ever get any respect from you damned bastards with your stupid pointy sticks? Has everyone forgotten that *I'm* the one who killed an actual God? In fact, I'd like someone to explain why *I* haven't become a Saint yet. Is there really no justice in—?'

I turned to see why he'd stopped talking and saw Ethalia walking towards us. She was wearing a blue woollen sweater over her usual simple cotton dress, and she looked ... well, I've probably said enough about how she looks. If it helps, Brasti and Morn shared my reaction as they suddenly became very quiet. Kest is always quiet, so it's hard to tell whether anyone's presence makes a difference.

'I won't keep you,' Ethalia said. 'I know you have a long journey ahead, but a note came for you, Falcio.'

She handed me a folded slip of paper. It wasn't sealed. I unfolded it to find a single line written in her own hand: *Be wise, rather than brave, prudent, rather than bold, and don't let the complications between us keep you away too long*, the note read. I looked into her eyes and tried to make sense of the word 'complications'. What precisely was that supposed to mean?

'My darling Ethalia,' Brasti said, 'when will you finally rid yourself of this drab and inconsolable fellow and make your way to a warmer and more welcoming bed?'

Ethalia turned and looked at Kest, sitting astride his horse. 'Kest?' she asked innocently.

'Yes?'

'Might you, as a fellow – if former – Saint, consider knocking some sense into Brasti for me? It's just that, as Saint of Mercy, I'm not supposed to do it myself.'

'Give me a moment to consider it,' he replied. Suddenly his arm flew back and sent Brasti tumbling off his horse. 'Ah. It appears the answer is "yes".'

Ethalia took advantage of the ensuing swearing and chaos to place both her hands on my cheeks. Her skin was warm against mine as she kissed me, and my troubles lifted away from my shoulders like ravens frightened off by her presence. Surprised as I was, I held that kiss for as long as I could, because I knew those ravens would return soon enough.

CHAPTER TWENTY

THE ROAD NORTH

The road north felt strange to me . . . or no, not strange, *wrong*.

I tried to blame it on lack of sleep – in the mere two days we'd spent in Castle Aramor since our return I don't think I'd slept a full night; that and the after-effects of a week of raging seasickness made riding a real chore. Of course, it didn't help that Arsehole, my copper-coloured Tivanieze, insisted on prancing about unpredictably, as if every flower, bird or butterfly was calling him over to play.

'You really should have taken up the stablemaster's offer to trade him in,' Kest said, noting my discomfort.

I'd tried, seriously. Tivaniezes are rare enough that I could have exchanged him for a more reliable and less exuberant horse – one who, for example, didn't object to galloping in a straight line. But for all his faults, I just couldn't bear to give him up. Arsehole is an unfathomably strange horse, but he and I had come to a more or less cordial understanding over the past few months: I would do my best to ignore his preposterous behaviour and he, in turn, would do *his* best not to throw me from the saddle more than once a day.

'I'm fine,' I said, which was something of a lie. Despite my efforts to pin my discomfort on exhaustion and ill-bred horses, the problem was not so much that we were riding towards an undesirable destination, but rather that we were riding away from the poor, battered castle that still felt like home. The sensation was especially troubling because I could remember with aching clarity why I used to love setting out on my judicial circuits.

For all the complaints about the danger, drudgery and distinct lack of proper beds that came with our tours of duty, there was a kind of magic in the roads we travelled. Tristia is a relatively small country, and yet every Duchy, March and Demesne – along with its people – is strange and unique, with its own customs and traditions. It's as if Tristia is made up of dozens of tiny foreign nations all packed in together. You could visit every part of the country a hundred times over and never fail to be surprised at how different they all are from one another.

Everywhere we went in those days trials awaited us: complex legal disputes and thorny criminal cases that required our expertise and sometimes our blades. Men and women ensnared by the legal machinations of neighbours, relatives or even their Lords told me they'd felt frozen in time, trapped in ice, and it was only the King's Travelling Magistrates who'd been able to shatter their bonds and let time tick forward once again, freeing them to get on with their lives.

Riding north now brought those memories back in a rush of desperate longing that nearly overwhelmed me. It wasn't simply nostalgia: I needed that sense of *rightness* again. I didn't care if a mission was hard and dangerous; I just needed it to be *right*. Instead, here I was travelling to Orison, a Duchy without a Duke, now that Perault was dead (and thank the Gods dead and living for that small mercy), to persuade some unruly villagers that they did not, in fact, have the right to secede from Tristia. It was a pretty safe bet no one would be cheering our arrival there.

And afterwards? Afterwards I'd be sneaking into Avares, a country with which we could not risk war, so that I could capture *and not kill* the woman who had decided it was her Gods-given destiny to destroy everything King Paelis had built.

'You look twitchy,' Morn said, bringing his horse alongside mine.

Arsehole reacted with unexpected glee to this new companion and proceeded to bop the muzzle of Morn's horse, confusing that poor beast no end.

'I was just thinking,' I said.

Morn smiled as if I'd actually said something meaningful. 'You're thinking about the circuits, aren't you?'

'How the hells did you know that—?'

He chuckled. 'It's what we all think about whenever we set out on a journey, Falcio: how much has changed, how much we wish it were more like the old days . . . the anticipation of adventure, the sense of . . .'

'Rightness?' I suggested.

'*Rightness*. Damn me, you always know just the perfect word.'

'We'll have that again,' I said. 'Things won't all go back to being the way they were, but once we have a Queen on the throne, we can get back to the work of making Tristia a just society again. Aline is—'

Morn held up a hand. 'Please, Falcio, don't start singing this girl's praises to me. I've heard the stories already. "Aline who defied a God to reconsecrate the laws in Tristia; Aline who commanded her people to rise and never kneel again; Aline who sprouted wings and flew up to the heavens to push away the clouds and let through golden sunlight"—'

'You know what, Morn?' Brasti asked, riding up behind us. 'I forgot what a jackass you are.'

Morn chuckled. 'Well, the rest of us never forgot what utter zealots the three of you were, that's for sure.'

'You've seen the others?' I asked. 'Quillata? Old Tobb? Senneth?'

His expression darkened a little. 'Some. I saw Bellow a couple of years ago, in a village in Domaris – he'd lost both his legs. You probably know Cunien started his own little band of vaguely noble brigands a few years back and set about redistributing the contents of caravans run by particularly venal nobles amongst the poorest. He's something of a legend along the northern trade routes.'

'Damn it, Falcio,' Brasti said crossly, 'I *told* you we needed to get a move on with this piracy plan of ours.'

'What about the other Greatcoats?' Kest asked. 'Falcio sent Bardatti out months ago with the call to reassemble at Aramor, but few have come. Where are the rest?'

Morn shrugged. 'How should I know? I've been living like a half-wild animal, sleeping in caves and walking hundreds of miles through mountains and forest ever since the King died, which hasn't exactly made for easy socialising with my fellow magistrates.'

A moment later he reached over from his horse and clapped a hand on my shoulder. 'Don't look like that, First Cantor. The rest of the Greatcoats will turn up eventually.'

'Sure,' I said, forcing a smile I didn't feel. 'In the meantime all we have to do is invade a foreign country, sneak into the camp of some devastatingly brilliant new Warlord and kidnap the world's most dangerous woman – oh, and bring her safely back to stand trial.'

'You're forgetting that first we have to go negotiate with a bunch of petulant citizens of Orison and get them to stop threatening to break up the country,' Brasti added.

Secession wasn't actually an uncommon problem in Tristia; far too often people got the idea into their heads that separating from their home country would make them rich – or at least, less poor. I knew how to deal with people like that; it always involved a lot of listening, a lot of negotiating and the occasional threat.

It wasn't until we arrived at the gates of Den Chapier that I discovered a slight setback to my tried and trusted method for securing a deal: there was no one left to negotiate with.

CHAPTER TWENTY-ONE

THE SEDITIOUS VILLAGE

Like many towns and villages in the northern Duchies, twin statues of the God of Making guard the entrance to Den Chapier. In much of the south he's known as Mestiri, which means 'one who masters', whereas in my home Duchy of Pertine, Craft has always been depicted as a young woman named Feturia. No wonder the people of Tristia have never been able to get along: we can't even agree on what any particular God looks like. Of course, no one will ever know who was right in Craft's case, because by the time I met the God, there was nothing left of him (or her) but a skeletal wreck hanging from the Blacksmith's gibbet.

'They call him Duestre in these parts,' Morn said, standing between the two statues. The one on the left depicted the God as a muscular young man drawing iron from a vein of ore inside the stone on which he stood. That rock had probably come from the hundred-mile-long mountain range that divided the Duchy of Orison from Avares. On the right, Craft appeared as a stoop-backed elder, hammering the iron into a sword.

'Falcio?' Morn asked. 'Why are you just standing there?'

'I . . . nothing. I just—'

'Give him a moment,' Kest said. He and Brasti walked over and stood next to me at the entrance to the village. We were all a little hesitant about taking that next step. Brasti held an arrow and his longest bow, Intemperance, but he hadn't drawn it yet, perhaps because his hands were shaking almost as much as mine. Memories of Carefal – the charred corpses, the stench – played out in my mind. They had worshipped Craft too, but he hadn't cared; his only concern was the *making* of things. The *unmaking* he left to humans.

'Come,' said Kest gently, 'we need to see what's happened.'

I forced myself to take a breath, to dispel the stench of burning flesh from my memory, and arranged us in a diamond formation with each man facing a different direction. We moved at a snail's pace through the narrow, unpaved streets, but the emptiness was absolute: no people, no livestock, no sounds, no smells . . . nothing. We walked like ghosts haunting a place that no longer existed.

'Saint Shiulla-who-bathes-with-beasts,' Brasti muttered, 'how many people lived in this town?'

'Three hundred and twenty, last time I was here,' Morn replied. 'Miners and their families, mostly.'

'*Three hundred*,' Brasti repeated. The muscles in his jaw worked awkwardly, as if he were trying to speak but something was lodged in his mouth.

'Split up,' I said, once I was confident no ambush was awaiting us. 'Check the cottages.'

I headed for the town square: there were no signs of violence, no bodies or blood, no broken weapons, nor even signs of scuffles preserved in the cold, hard dirt.

'No corpses so far,' Kest said, coming out of a cottage. 'There's nothing in the streets on the other side, nor in any of the homes. Might they have been captured?'

Brasti, walking towards us, heard. He shook his head. Kneeling on the ground, he said, 'There are no signs of struggle, or tracks to indicate anything unusual.' He looked up at me. 'It looks as if they simply walked away.'

'Look here,' Morn called out. He stuck his head out of a cottage door and gestured for us to join him.

Inside, it was just as you'd expect: three small rooms, one with beds along each of the four walls. The main room had a wood-burning stove. The clothing chests were empty.

'There's nothing here,' Brasti said, coming up behind me.

'That's the point,' I said. 'They haven't just left, they've *moved*.'

'Perhaps the mines ran out?' Kest asked.

'Most of these people would have been born here,' Morn explained, 'like their parents and their parents' parents – whole generations never travel more than five miles from their homes. They don't just pick up and leave . . .'

'Let's search for any signs that might indicate a struggle – or even some idea of which direction they went,' I suggested, and chose a narrow alley that ran between two rows of cottages. I was running a hundred scenarios in my mind, but none of them made any sense. In the village of Phan, in Pulnam, the villagers hid out in broken-down old cabins in the hills when raiders came from the Eastern Desert – could something like that have happened here? But this was no rushed departure, and there were no signs of panic.

I heard the whisper of a sword leaving its sheath behind me and didn't hesitate. I knew if it had been one of the others, they'd have announced themselves first. My rapier flew from its scabbard as I spun around, bringing up the true edge to strike where I guessed my opponent's weapon-hand would be – barely managing to stop the momentum of my blade before it hit the boy standing behind me holding a child's wooden sword. My entire arm shook from the effort of holding my rapier still as it lightly kissed the boy's neck.

He was small, perhaps seven years old, with skin a little darker than the curls of his light blond hair. He looked at me, his own pretend weapon held out front, eyes wide, and stayed very still. A tiny trickle of blood slid down the side of his neck where my rapier had made the tiniest of cuts.

'Don't move,' I said, and slowly took my blade away. *Fool*, I cursed myself. *Another half-inch and you'd have killed a child.*

I sheathed my rapier and knelt down so I wasn't looming over the boy. 'You're not in any danger,' I said. 'My name's Falcio. Can you tell me your name?'

'Tam,' he said, and threw his wooden sword at my face before turning tail and pounding down the alley.

I followed as fast as I could, but slipped on the dirt as I swerved onto the wider street. By the time I recovered my balance, the boy was gone. Kest came running towards me from the left and shouted, 'He went down to the other end of the village—'

We checked at every junction to see if he'd turned, but saw no sign of him. Brasti and Morn, drawn by the sounds of our chase, soon joined us.

'A boy,' I panted, 'maybe six or seven—'

'A boy? What's a boy doing here on his own?' Brasti examined the tracks in the dirt. 'I can find him.'

Tam's footprints wound their way around the village until they finally led into one of the last cottages on the lane; we'd not yet got as far as checking that end.

The door was open and I called into the shadows, 'We're not here to hurt you.'

'Then walk away,' said a voice behind us, and I turned and saw a woman in hunter's greens standing on the opposite side of the street. She had a longbow in hand and an arrow trained on me. The boy had led us here on purpose, I realised belatedly – stupidly – giving her the opportunity to come up behind us. The routine struck me as practised, and I wondered how many times they'd done it before.

Of the three of us, only Morn had his weapon out, but even his six-foot-long glaive wasn't long enough to reach the woman before she fired. Brasti had his own bow in his left hand; his right was halfway to the quiver on his back.

'If your bowman moves another inch, I fire,' the woman said. 'Better for you if you turn and leave.'

'What happened here?' I asked. 'Where did everyone go?'

'Away – same as you'll do if you don't want an arrow sprouting out of your chest.'

'Just put the bow down and we can talk. I swear to you we won't move from this spot.'

'Who are you, that you parade about like bandits coming to steal what isn't yours and then act as though I should believe for a second that you won't have your way with me and the boy the first chance you get?' she asked.

'My name is Falcio val Mond,' I replied. 'I'm—'

'You're him,' she breathed, almost as if I were some Saint come to her village. 'The one they talk about – the First Cantor of the Greatcoats.'

I started to nod in agreement as her left eye closed and her mouth tightened, only slightly. She let loose the arrow and I watched as it slammed into my chest.

CHAPTER TWENTY-TWO

THE HUNTERS

It's at times like these that I find myself conflicted about my relationship with the Tailor. On the one hand, she's a conniving monster who manipulates everyone around her to achieve her own ends, which are always just slightly more vile than I can actually live with. On the other hand, that woman really knows how to make a good coat.

A loud crack filled the air as the arrow struck the front of my greatcoat, shattering one of the bone plates protecting my chest – but it stopped the steel head from driving straight into my heart. It still hurt like seven hells.

Before the scream had even left my mouth my attacker had another arrow ready – but so did Brasti.

'Unlike Falcio, I can spot your muscles tightening just before you fire,' he said. 'You won't get another shot out.'

The woman bit her lip, uncertainty and fear playing across her face.

'Don't,' Brasti said wearily. 'Just don't.'

Whatever sign he was looking for, he must have seen, because I caught the slight motion too – just as he fired. 'No!' I shouted, far too late to do any good. The woman fell backwards, hit her head against a stone wall and slipped down to the ground. 'Brasti, damn you—'

From behind us I heard the boy scream as he ran out from his hiding place to where the woman was lying.

'She was going to fire again,' Brasti said. 'I heard the plate break in your coat, and she did too – and she's good enough to hit the same spot twice. Besides, I didn't kill her.'

The boy was standing in front of the woman, his fists in the air as if he would fight us all.

'I'm . . . all right, Tam,' the woman said. 'Just hit my head.' She stood up and I could see now that Brasti's arrow had carefully grazed her right arm, just enough to leave a nasty cut. 'Damn you,' she said, glaring at Brasti. 'It'll be days before I can hunt again.'

'Well, maybe you should have thought of that before—'

'Who are you?' I asked. 'Why are you and the boy here when everyone else has left?'

She moved protectively in front of the boy. 'My name is Rhissa. The boy is Tam. As to your other question, go fuck yourself.' Her bravado lasted a few more seconds before she broke. 'Do what you must with me, but I beg you, let the boy go free – I don't have much, but I won't resist if you—'

'We're Greatcoats, woman,' Morn said angrily. 'We don't harm innocents.'

Despite the fear and pain on her face, she spat on the ground. 'Greatcoats! How many good and decent men and women of Orison have you killed in the name of your child Queen?'

'None,' Kest said. 'We didn't—'

'Where do you think all those soldiers come from? When you and your Trattari thugs attacked our Duke last year, who do you think bled and died for him? Did you think he summoned demons from the pits of the thirteenth hell to fight you? When there is war, it's always the common people who pay the price.'

'Duke Perault was trying to help Duchess Trin take the country,' Kest explained.

'Politics and power – what the hells do we know of these things?' she snarled. 'And why should we care?'

I felt a powerful desire to argue with her, to tell her how wrong she was, but hadn't I just been thinking the same things?

'My mother needs a salve for her arm,' the boy said.

I reached into my coat. 'I have something that will help.'

'We have our own medicines. Why would we want yours?' He didn't wait for an answer but instead took his mother's left hand and led her past us and into the cottage where he'd been hiding.

'What now?' Morn asked.

I rubbed at the spot on my chest where the arrow had struck. It was going to be bruised and painful for a long time. 'We still need answers,' I said, and turned to follow the boy and his mother into their home.

'What happened to the rest of the villagers?' I asked as Rhissa spread a clear, sticky salve on her wound. With visible reluctance, she accepted a length of bandage from Brasti.

'They left,' she said.

Morn's voice was impatient. 'Yes, damn you, we got that part. But *why*?'

'This is a mining village,' she said. 'The mines produce good iron ore, but it's not a place for raising crops or beasts. Duke Perault took all of the ore we dug out of the mountainside, and in return he made sure we had food and supplies and the equipment we needed. Then he died, and everything vanished: no one sent us beef and barley, and there were no traders, neither. We nearly starved last winter.'

'But evidently, you *did* survive,' I said. 'How?'

She eyed me suspiciously. 'We had help.'

'Yes, but from whom? Was it—?'

'Avares,' Morn said. 'The help came from Avares, didn't it?'

Brasti snorted. 'What would they provide? Goat turds to eat and jars of their own piss to drink?'

'Tomatoes,' Rhissa replied, 'and bush beans. They brought us meat, too, when they could.' She stretched out her right arm to test it and winced. 'Some of us hunted – there are mountain goats up there, if you're lucky. It was a hard winter, but our cleric kept telling us the Gods would protect us. He said everything we needed to survive was waiting for us in those mountains.'

'And was he right?' I asked.

'Not at first. We were having to go further and further to find anything, until one trip we realised we'd gone too far and we didn't have the food or the strength to get back home. When the men from Avares found us, we were starving, huddling like children in the snow, waiting to die. They could have killed us, but they didn't. Do you know what the phrase "tennu ti sinne" means in Avares?'

'"Brothers and sisters",' Morn replied.

'Yes. "Brothers and sisters" is what they called us. I suppose many people here are just that: there're plenty of folk in Orison with more Avarean blood than Tristian.'

'We've been at war with them for more than three hundred years,' Kest said.

'*Your* war, not ours. They could have killed us and taken what little we had, but instead they called us "tennu ti sinne" and gave us food and drink. They made dozens of trips across the mountains over the next months, and thanks to them, we survived the winter.'

A chill breeze seeped through the gaps between the wooden slates of the window set into the stone wall of the cottage. 'And with winter coming again?'

'The men from Avares said we could move, live in their villages – maybe just for the winter, maybe longer.'

'That would . . .' Kest looked at me. 'Wouldn't that technically be a crime? We're still at war with Avares, theoretically, at least . . .'

Rhissa snorted. 'Go and arrest them if you want.'

I turned my attention back to the question of Avares. What did they have to gain by giving away their own resources? Were they nobler than we'd ever been led to believe? Somehow, I doubted it.

'The mines,' I said. 'Are they empty now?'

Rhissa shook her head. 'There's plenty of iron ore left, but the equipment needs replacing and men need full bellies to work.'

'Who makes your equipment?'

'We do, given time and supplies, but much of our gear is broken and we've been waiting for someone to send us what we need, but no one has.'

'So they all went?' Morn asked. 'Every one of them?'

'Not everyone; some went east, to family in Orison or Hervor or Pulnam. Most, though . . . they took the trip over the mountains.'

I looked at her, sitting here in this dark cottage with her boy. 'But you stayed.'

She gave a strangled laugh. 'I'm not even from here, you know? I came from Domaris, years back, with my father – he was a trader. I met a man from the village who fancied me, and I him, and soon we had Tam.' She looked away, but I'd already caught sight of the expression on her face.

'My husband was a strong man,' she said. 'When they came looking for soldiers he had to go.'

'But that was well over a year ago,' I said. 'He must be—' I shut up abruptly.

She glanced briefly towards her child and muttered, 'I'm not stupid. I know the odds. But there've been other men who've come back, as recently as six months ago. He might have been injured and still be making his way home. If . . .' She started to cry, then managed, 'He'll be tired, hungry, hurt . . . I'll not have him be alone.'

It was a foolish dream; the man was almost certainly dead – and yet weren't there widows all over the country still waiting for their loved ones to come back? And if you let go of the dream, what was left?

'I'm sorry,' I said, but even as I spoke, I sensed Rhissa was holding something back, using her tears to keep me from pressing further. There was a practicality to this woman that reminded me too much of my wife to believe she would stay here this long merely on a false hope.

'What else holds you here?' I asked bluntly.

She looked at me as if waiting for some sign of deceit on my part to reveal itself. After a few seconds she rose from the narrow bed and gestured for us to follow her.

'One of us had to stay behind,' she murmured.

She led us to the door of the next cottage, but held out an arm to stop us entering. Instead, we crowded around the doorway and gazed inside.

The room was identical in layout to hers, but here, the smell of sweat and sickness hung in the air. Heavy fabrics had been hung at the door and windows to keep the heat inside. I could just make out a man lying on the bed, cocooned in blankets. Only the ragged cough and the sheen of sweat on his skin revealed he was still alive, though I doubted he'd be for long.

'Who is he?' I asked.

'We don't know,' Rhissa replied. 'He was grievously wounded when he arrived here. Our healer did his best, but he said the wounds were too deep, and cruelly placed to ensure a slow, painful death.'

'So when the others left . . . ?' Brasti asked.

She sighed. 'I couldn't leave him to die alone like that.'

'Why did he come here?' Kest asked.

'I don't know. He just keeps repeating the same two words over and over. It sounds like "Sheen Shitaley".'

The language was archaic Tristian, but the meaning escaped me. I turned to Kest who was looking equally confused. '"*Sien Sitale*". I believe it means "Noisy Footsteps".'

At his words, Morn gave out a sudden cry and pushed past us, shaking Rhissa off as she tried to stop him, but he stopped at the bedside and stared down at the man – or boy, for with the curtain pushed aside, I could now see he couldn't have been more than seventeen or eighteen. He had long russet hair and the sharp, broad features of an Avarean.

Morn's fists were clenched and there was a terrible rage in his eyes.

'Morn, what in hells is going on?' I asked. 'Who is this man?'

'Sien Sitale,' he replied. '"Noisy Footsteps".' It's what the Rangieri call their apprentices. It's what my teacher called me – before this Avarean bastard killed him.'

Morn appeared to be wrestling with the question of whether he should just strangle the boy, or let him die of his wounds. I hauled him out of the cottage before things got out of hand. It took some time to get the story out of him.

'How did he come to be here?' Morn demanded of Rhissa.

'He stumbled into town, terribly wounded, as I said.' She was standing her ground despite the uncertainty now clouding her features. 'He was near death – we thought we should try to help him. We had no idea that he had . . .'

'It's not your fault,' Morn said, though his jaw was so tight you could tell it hurt to say so.

'Will you . . . ?' Rhissa hesitated, then she lowered her voice. 'Will you kill this man now?'

Morn stared out at the empty street. 'I don't know. Let me think.'

'Since when do we execute people without a trial?' Brasti asked. 'Not that I'm against it, mind you; it's just that Falcio usually has a problem with that sort of thing.'

Morn didn't look as if my approval was a necessary precondition for his vengeance.

'You didn't tell us your teacher was dead,' I said.

'There are any number of things I didn't tell you, Falcio.' He took in a deep breath and let it out slowly. 'I'm sorry – I'm just surprised, that's all. My teacher, Yimris, was an old man – he may well have been the last Rangieri master in the entire country.'

'The boy—?'

'Don't call him a boy!' Again, Morn had to calm himself. 'Any Avarean who can wield a knife is a warrior, and any man who would kill his teacher is a damned murderer.'

'So he was also a student of this Yimris?' Kest asked.

'His name is Gwyn,' Morn said, 'and he was Yimris' student long before I met the old man. He took in the bastard when he was just eight years old, after his parents had been executed for treason against their own warband. By his people's laws, the child should have died too, but Yimris took him and trained him in the ways of the Rangieri.'

'If Yimris saved the boy, then why would he kill the old man?'

Morn gave a smile that had no joy in it. 'Because Gwyn wanted to prove himself worthy of rejoining his people, and killing a Tristian Rangieri was his ticket back into Avares.' Morn's hands clenched at empty air. 'By the time I found Yimris, he was near death, but he still made me promise not to go after that damned traitor.'

'Why?' Brasti asked, looking puzzled. 'Why would your teacher—?'

'Because the Rangieri are stupid that way.'

Oddly, it was the boy, Tam, who spoke first. 'I will kill him if you ask, sir. Murderers should be punished.'

Morn looked at the child for a long time, then he reached into his coat and took out a small jar of black salve, the ointment we carry to treat our wounds. 'Do you know what this is?' he asked Tam, and when he shook his head, Morn put the jar in his hand. 'It's medicine. You put it on wounds, even the ones that have gone green and stinky, and sometimes it can make them better. Mostly, though, it will ease the pain.'

'I don't understand, sir – you want us to put this on his wounds?'

Rhissa took the jar from her son. 'Why would you have us treat this man if he's a killer?'

'He won't attack you or your boy,' Morn said. 'It's not his way. He's unlikely to survive, but if he does, he'll go back to his people, or perhaps just disappear into the mountains and live alone.'

'I don't understand,' Tam said again. 'Don't you hate him for killing your teacher?'

Morn ruffled the boy's hair. 'Hate is a heavy load to carry around with you. Rangieri are travellers by trade and by nature, and a traveller cannot afford to carry wasted burdens.'

He rose to his feet and I could see the anger was still there, burning underneath his skin.

'You'd like the Rangieri, Falcio,' he said to me as he set off down the empty street. 'They're full of stupid sayings like that.'

CHAPTER TWENTY-THREE

THE DESERTERS

Men and women of all ages trudged along the craggy trail that wound its unrelenting, monotonous way through the sparse grass and over the rocks. They moved so slowly that further up the line they looked more like distance markers than people.

'You soldiers?' an old man asked, ambling up behind us, his walking stick providing a clacking counterpoint to the slap of his thin-soled shoes on the rough ground.

'Just labourers, looking for work or food,' I replied. 'Or both.'

'Sure. Sure you are.'

I gave the old man my best attempt at a menacing glare. Judging by the easy smile he offered in return, it hadn't been particularly persuasive. Morn could pass well enough, but Kest, Brasti and I didn't make convincing villagers. We'd had to leave our horses back in Den Chapier with Rhissa and Tam, although Arsehole had promptly run off to who knows where, no doubt in hot pursuit of a particularly intriguing butterfly. I hoped he'd find his way back at some point. We'd hidden our greatcoats in our packs before we'd joined the long line of those who'd left their villages and were heading for Avares, like pilgrims in search of a newer, better God to worship. The heavy woollen cloaks we now wore felt flimsy and awkward in comparison, hardly more than blankets tied at the neck with cord to keep them from falling off. I felt horribly exposed, both to the increasing cold as we plodded our way to higher altitudes, and to the stares of those around us.

'Look like soldiers to me,' the old man went on. His own cloak was practically threadbare, and I wondered how he planned to make it through the mountains. Those born and bred in the north must be better able to tolerate the cold than I could.

'Labourers,' Brasti said. 'You know how I know? Because I'm listening to you flap your mouth and it's quickly becoming labourous.'

'He means laborious,' Kest corrected.

The old man's laugh followed us as we walked around a boulder that must have fallen from the mountain eons before. Brasti had a way of setting people at ease that I really envied at times like these. He would have made a half-decent spy, if not for the fact that he'd likely have walked around bragging about being a spy all the time.

'A little help here?' the old man called out, and I looked back to see the end of his walking staff was caught between two rocks. 'Thought I saw something shiny in there. Damn fool that I am, I poked my stick inside. Now it's stuck.'

Kest gave the old man a shoulder to lean on while Morn pulled the staff free. 'Best not to poke at things,' he said, handing it back before coming over to where I was waiting.

'Fair enough,' the old man said, rushing to catch up to us, 'but since you helped me out of a little jam, let me help you avoid one: when we get to the border, just tell them the truth – that you're *former* soldiers.'

'We're lab—' Brasti began.

'Won't they kill us if they think we were soldiers?' I asked. Telling people we were just farm workers clearly wasn't going to work. We could try to act a bit, maybe attempt talking like labourers, but the chances were we wouldn't be able to keep it up. Better to go with a lie that fit people's expectations.

'Not if you're truthful with the bordermen,' the old man said. 'A soldier's back is just as strong as a farmer's, and there's plenty of hungry veterans struggling after their discharge who've headed into Avares. That what happened to you four?'

My first instinct was to just agree with his assessment and leave it there, but that might have made us look too eager to follow the explanation he'd given us, so I embellished a bit. 'We weren't discharged, well, not exactly . . . damned captain decided he could make us tend his fields if he said our unit needed to stay together. That's why we said we're labourers.'

'Son of a bitch. How can he get away with that?'

'There were no generals left,' Kest said, picking up the story. 'And no Duke. Who's going to tell him otherwise?'

'So . . . I don't mean any offence, but doesn't that make you . . . ?'

'Deserters?'

He nodded a little cautiously.

'No. It's like I told you, we're just labourers.'

The old man gave a laugh. 'Fair enough, fair enough. Still, though, best to just tell the warriors in Avares that you're former soldiers. There's a phrase they use in that rough tongue of theirs: "Tota valha, maksa verta".'

'What does it mean?'

'"The truth will set you free, the lie will cost you blood".' The old man paused a moment to lift a flask to his lips. 'The Avareans don't take kindly to deceivers and spies.'

Brasti shrugged it off. 'Well, I've never been a soldier and I don't plan to be. I'm a poacher, born and bred.'

That statement had the virtue of being the truth and looking at Brasti, the old man believed it readily. 'You should probably lie, then.'

'Lie? I thought you said—'

'The bordermen hate poachers worse than liars.'

That set off one of Brasti's favourite rants, the one Kest and I like to call 'Requiem for the Sainted Poacher'. It has no particular tune, the words are largely incomprehensible and it can go on for several hours. On the positive side, Brasti's determination to convert the old man banished any questions he might still have had about Brasti's background and, by extension, our own. We were soldiers, right enough, and although we might not be particularly honourable, we were clearly nothing to be concerned about.

'Hells of a war that was,' the old man said, probably more to change the subject from Brasti harping on about ancestral hunting rights than out of any genuine interest.

'I imagine all wars are hellish,' I said.

'Maybe. I'm no soldier, never have been, but seems to me, we've never come so close to ruin as when that bitch decided she wanted to make the world her own. Saints' praise to the man who one day puts the tip of a sword through her heart. Doubt I'll live to see it, mind you.'

'You never know,' I said, giving myself a moment to savour the idea. *Give me one chance, and with it, one moment of perfect clarity. Give me that, you Gods and Saints, and I'll rid the world of half its evil in one strike.* 'Perhaps that day will come sooner than you expect.'

The old man clapped me on the shoulder. 'Ha! Look at you now. Maybe we've got a hero here with us, eh?'

'Not me,' I said, cursing myself for showing my true desires . . .

'Ah, I can see it now: you'll ride south on a fine horse, ride right through the gates of Castle Aramor and past the bastard Trattari.' He spread his arms in a ludicrous impression of a fencer. 'Then you'll bound into the throne room where you'll cut the little bitch's head off in one clean strike.'

I felt Kest's hand on my arm before I could even make sense of the old man's words. *Aline. He's talking about Aline . . .*

'Ah, don't be sore, lad,' the old man said, catching my expression. 'I'm not mocking you. Hells, I'd be the first to call you Saint if you did do the deed.'

Whether to distract attention from me or simply because he never pays any attention to the dangers in such talk, Brasti said, 'You know, that's the King's true heir you're talking about.'

The old man spat. 'That's for the King's heir.'

A worn-down family passing us looked up momentarily at his words. 'Come on now, she's just a little girl,' said the father, reaching out to touch the girl trudging along beside him. 'There's none of this her fault.'

'You really think the girl's to blame for all this?' Brasti added. 'She had no say in her parentage. It was Duchess Patriana who set about killing off King Paelis' children – it was she who gave us Trin.'

'Watch yourself now,' the old man said, but I could tell he was still full of good humour. This was the kind of political discussion the common folk delighted in, taking opposite sides of grand arguments about who deserved the throne and who deserved the noose. 'Duchess Patriana kept all of Hervor running like a well-timed clock. She was sent by the Gods to rule, that one. Harsh, sometimes, but ain't that the way of those with power? No, I lived half my life in Hervor. Damned Greatcoats came and now the place is a mess. Thought if I went west to Orison, things would be better but, well' – here he motioned to the mountains ahead – 'you see where that got me. No, I'd take Duchess Patriana back anytime – and as to killing off the tyrant King's bastards? Well, you know what we say in Hervor?'

'What?'

'Too bad Patriana missed the last one.'

The trail carried on its dull and mildly treacherous way for another three days before turning steeper. It was much colder now, and the pilgrims dragged themselves along like dead men not quite ready to fall down. At night we huddled together for warmth in ragged tents. Unlike travellers in the south, who'd have passed the time getting to know each other and trading stories about their home villages, these people appeared to be content to just listen silently to the wind whistling through the holes in their thin shelters while they waited for the sun to rise.

'It's hard to imagine anyone's ever come this way before,' I said as we renewed the march on the fourth day. I was used to long periods of travel but my mood was starting to take on the same grey hue as the landscape.

'What do you mean?' Brasti asked.

I hadn't really meant anything; I was speaking more to remind myself I could than for any particular purpose. 'Just that it's a long way on foot and I doubt anyone's come this way for years.'

'This path is fairly well-worn, Falcio. I'd say people have been going back and forth between Orison and Avares for generations.' He gestured at the people walking ahead of us. 'They probably share more blood with the people of Avares than those of southern Tristia.'

'That's a troubling thought.' It was, too. There were enough complications plaguing the country already without having to worry that a large number of country folk identified more with the barbarians over the mountains than with their own people.

A problem for another day, I thought. For now, all that mattered was keeping our heads down, getting through the mountain pass and finding Trin. We could investigate the latest beard-braiding fashions in Avares later.

'Falcio . . .' Kest warned, but I could already hear the commotion up ahead.

We ran a few dozen yards and found a young woman who'd taken a fall. A girl of six or seven, likely her daughter, was trying to help her up. The other travellers walked past them without a word. *So much for the warm hearts of the north.*

As I knelt down to look at the woman's ankle, which was clearly sprained, the little girl started beating me away, crying, 'Leave us alone!'

'I'm trying to help,' I said, holding her off with one hand while I reached into my pack.

'Tillia, stop!' the woman said. Her plain brown hair matched her plain brown clothes; everything about her spoke of poverty. To me she said, 'We're fine, sir. I'll be fine.'

'You won't get very far on a sprained ankle.' I pulled out a length of bandage, careful not to let the coat itself be seen, and started fumbling about to find my black salve. 'This will help keep it from swelling,' I said, showing her the salve on my fingers before working it into her ankle. I bound it up, winding the cloth around the ankle several times to give her a little support.

'Thank you,' she said suspiciously once I was done, ignoring the hand I'd reached down to help her up. She winced as she stood.

'Thank you,' the little girl repeated, as though hoping they were magic words that would make me disappear. When they didn't, mother and child began plodding along the path.

'Helped a nice lady in trouble, did you?' Morn asked, after the others had passed us by.

I turned to look at him. He was smiling, but not with his eyes. 'That was stupid,' he said quietly.

'How is helping someone in need stupid?'

His gaze went to the other travellers, who were staring at us as they passed us. '*Being noticed* is stupid. How much black salve do you think these people have ever seen in their lives? That bandage you took from your coat? It's made of hemp from Baern, treated with wormroot from Luth: a ten-foot length of it costs more than these people would earn in a month and it might as well come stamped with the King's crest right on it.'

He was right, of course. If the wrong people got a good look at the bandage, it would raise questions for which we wouldn't have very good answers. But what was I supposed to do? Leave the woman to stumble around in pain until she couldn't go on any more? Leave her and the child to rot amongst the rocks and dirt?

As if he sensed my uncertainty, Morn said, 'You're a decent man, Falcio.' He clapped me on the shoulder and set out ahead. 'You'd make a terrible spy.'

'Well, I'll leave that to you, then, shall I?'

He looked back at me uncertainly. 'You know that the odds are that we're going to get captured, don't you?'

'I do,' I said. Now it was my turn to smile. 'And you know what that means, don't you?'

He caught my expression. 'Oh, hells. Why me?'

I shrugged. 'You're the only Rangieri here, Morn. That makes you the natural choice.'

'Great,' he said. 'I knew you'd find a way to kill me before long.'

I spent the next few hours largely alone with my thoughts. The old man – called Clock, although I hadn't worked out if it was because of the *tick-tock* sound his cane made, or because he was constantly asking how long it was until the next break, matched pace with me. 'Won't be long now,' he said. 'A day or so before we reach the true mountains and then it's just a hop over and we'll be in Avares.'

'A hop over?' I said, surprised at his optimism. 'Surely once we start getting into those mountains proper, people will start dying. It's going to get colder and more treacherous – hells, how much have these people climbed before now?'

'People don't die where you're from?'

'We try as a rule to avoid it.'

'Not all of us,' Brasti said bitterly, a little way ahead of us.

Clock laughed. 'You've got too much of the south in you, boy. Afraid of a little cold and hardship.' He pointed to the long train of travellers ahead. 'We're hardy people – practically mountain-bred ourselves. We drink the cold and shit out warm sunshine. We're as sure-footed as mountain goats. The hills are no threat to us.'

He was wrong. Not two hours later, as the sun was starting to set, the woman I'd helped earlier stumbled as she passed the edge of a fifteen-foot drop. She recovered her balance, but her daughter, who'd immediately grabbed her mother to keep her from falling off the path, slipped on the loose shale and slid down into the gap below.

CHAPTER TWENTY-FOUR

BROKEN BONES

'Tillia!' the woman screamed over and over again as I ran to the edge and looked down. It wasn't a long way down, only about fifteen feet to a shallow ledge, but below that was another fifty-foot drop that would most certainly be lethal. The child was lying unmoving at the edge. 'Someone give us some rope,' I called out to the villagers – surely someone must have rope amongst their supplies? But everyone passed us by, shaking their heads and trying hard not to meet our eyes. A couple of people pressed a piece of fruit or hard cheese into my hand as they shuffled onwards, but that was it.

'What in all the hells are they doing?' I asked Clock, who was patting the young mother's shoulder.

'Walking on,' he replied, the sanguine humour gone from his voice. 'They've got families too, and they can't risk getting hurt. They're leaving the food so Yelena here can stay with her girl a while longer.'

'They'd abandon her to die here?'

'It's cold on the mountains, boy. You said it yourself.'

'So much for your northern sunshine,' Brasti said.

I stood up and shouted to the villagers ahead of us, 'Walk on if you want, but one of you must have a length of strong rope. Just leave us that.'

None of them acknowledged my words, or looked back.

'You're wasting your time,' Clock said. 'A piece of rope might be the one thing that keeps them alive on this journey. Anyroad, there's nowhere to tie it. They won't want to see it slide down the mountain for no purpose.'

Kest, Morn and Brasti joined me at the edge. 'It's only fifteen feet,' I said.

'Might as well be fifteen miles,' Morn replied. 'You'd have a devil of a time getting back up, even if we did have rope – which we don't.'

I looked at Kest, but he was shaking his head. 'Falcio, don't.'

He was right, of course. If we did what he knew I was thinking, any pretence of being deserter-soldiers would be well and truly gone. I wasn't worried about the mother and child, but the old man could rat us out as soon as we reached the border. 'Go ahead with the others,' I said to him, my tone grim. 'I'll wait it out with Yelena here. I don't think it'll be long now.'

I looked back down at the overhang. The child's leg was bent at an impossible angle and blood was dripping from her forehead. She was making her way slowly, painfully, towards the edge.

'Tillia, *no*!' her mother screamed.

'Girl, stop!' I shouted. 'Just *stop*.'

'It's our way,' the old man said softly. 'The girl knows she's just holding her momma here. It's better this way. *Our* way.'

I growled, 'Shut your fucking mouth—' but Kest laid a hand on my shoulder.

'Falcio, stop. This isn't helping,' he said, but I shrugged him off.

I looked into Clock's eyes. 'I'm going to save that little girl now. If you utter one word of what happens here I'll beat you blind, so no one will believe what you claim you saw. The Gods themselves won't be able to save you if I find out you had a rope in your pack.'

I let him go and turned to Yelena. 'Call to your daughter – keep her from going over the edge.' I opened my pack and pulled my coat out. 'Get your coats out,' I told the others.

The old man's eyes widened. 'Greatcoats . . .' he whispered.

'Damned fool,' Morn muttered. 'Worst bloody spy I ever met.'

We tied three of the coats together, connecting the sleeve buckles from one to the other for added protection. Kest was about to start adding my coat when I stopped him.

'It won't be long enough with just three,' he said.

I took the coat and put it on. 'You won't be able to pull me up – the leather will get caught on the rocks – so I'll need to climb, which will take both hands, leaving me with no way to carry the girl.'

'You're going to use the coat to carry her?' He looked over the edge. 'It's hard going, and slippery. The odds of falling are—'

'Not helpful,' I said, and motioned for Brasti and Morn to hold one end of our makeshift rope while I began to ease myself down.

The descent was awkward. The coats are a tremendous advantage in battle, but turns out, the stiff leather and bone plates that keep us safe from edged weapons also make the coats pretty useless as a rope. I was gripping, white-knuckled, as they lowered me a few inches at a time, and by the time I reached the bottom the muscles in my hands were already exhausted, shaking from the effort.

Thankfully, Tillia had passed out from the pain. It was already getting dark and there was nothing there I could use to splint the leg, but if I didn't get her back up to the path it wouldn't matter anyway. I pulled out my black salve – it wouldn't knit bone, but it would help the pain and ward off infection for now – but as I carefully spread it on her skin, Tillia's eyes opened and when she saw me kneeling over her in my coat she started screaming and tried to push herself over the ledge.

'It's all right!' I cried, and grabbed her. 'It's okay, I'm going to get you back to your mother.'

The girl didn't stop trying to get away from me until she passed out again. I took off my coat and carefully eased her onto it, then buttoned it around her and tied the sleeves together to create a makeshift sling: an awkward thing, but better than nothing. I stuck my head through the loop formed by the sleeves and lifted her up. She weighed almost nothing, and as I reached for the coat-rope and began the slow, dangerous process of working my way back up the side of the cliff, I felt like I were carrying a delicate glass figurine, one that would shatter at the slightest impact.

Fifteen feet isn't a great distance, but everything was conspiring against me. This would have been a hard enough slog unencumbered, but carrying the girl made it murderously difficult. The cold air made it hard to feel my hands, which were constantly slipping on the smooth leather. It was almost impossible to find anything resembling a secure foothold on the mountain, an unhelpful mix of sharp, jagged rocks and fragile shale that meant I couldn't use my climbing spikes either. The others couldn't just pull me up in case the coat-rope got caught on the overhang.

Four feet from the top, my hands stopped responding completely.

Through sheer force of will I managed to keep them clenched enough to stop me slipping back down, but I couldn't seem to make my fingers work any more.

'Nearly there,' Brasti called down. 'What are you waiting for?'

I didn't reply; that small effort might draw away the last shred of strength from my arms. And of course, that's when the girl came to again, and began to cry.

'It's all right,' I whispered. 'Go back to sleep.'

'It *hurts*,' she said. 'I'm *scared*.'

'I know, sweetheart . . .'

I started to pray to Saint Birgid-who-weeps-rivers, but of course she was dead and somehow praying to her successor felt odd since I was quite sure Ethalia wasn't going to suddenly appear and save us. I hadn't had much luck with Gods lately – although to be fair, they hadn't had much luck themselves. *Where are you, Valour? Too busy saving fucking alley cats to lend a hand?*

The hells for Saints and Gods; I'll do this myself. My hands were *so* cold, though – colder than they had any right to be. I tried to think about things that might inspire my body to be stronger. I thought about Aline, and Valiana. I thought about the mission ahead of me. I thought about Ethalia and what she would think if she knew I'd failed this child, and all these things went through my mind in the few seconds, the ticks of the clock, between near success and abject failure.

I was about to tell Kest that I couldn't do it, that I'd try and slide back down and make the attempt again later, when my hands had warmed up and stopped shaking . . . But when I looked up to tell him, I saw the girl's mother, barely more than a child herself, lying on her belly watching me, her face full of a thousand sorrows, already resigned to her daughter's fate. What happened to *hope* in this damned country? When did we let go of all faith in ourselves?

I *hated* this woman lying there like a dead tree, so quick to give up on her daughter's life. What was *wrong* with these people?

Maybe it was the momentary respite, or perhaps the muscles in my hands unlocked, but an angry fire seared my flesh, burning through the cold: a *different* kind of pain, and almost without my volition, the fingers of my right hand unclenched, reached up and wrapped themselves around the next length of coat and a hand's-grip at a time, I made my agonising way up until, two feet from the top, I felt Kest grab one of my wrists and Brasti the other and the two of them hauled us the rest of the way.

I knelt there, unable to move, so Kest carefully undid my coat and took the girl. Her mother's face was a mixture of desperate relief and terrible guilt as she looked at me and asked, 'How will I carry her?'

'Falcio, come on, we have to get going,' Brasti said.

I was still on my knees at the edge of the cliff, so I think only a few minutes had passed, but it felt like a lifetime. There's a strength when you're exhausted that comes from beyond sore muscles and aching bones: it's all in the heart's need to keep beating. I kept reaching for that need.

'You did a good thing there,' the old man said.

It was a nice thing to say, but he wanted to see Aline dead. 'You've seen our coats. You know what we are. If you tell the bordermen, I'll kill you.'

Before the old man could reply, Kest said, 'He won't.' He reached out and rested his hand on Clock's shoulder. 'Look at me. Falcio won't kill you. He doesn't have it in him to murder an old man. But I do.'

'I believe you,' Clock said, and walked on ahead.

I felt Brasti hauling me up. 'Where's Morn?' I asked.

'He splinted the girl's leg and now he's taking his shift carrying her and muttering about what an idiot you are.'

'That's fair.'

We stuffed the coats back into our packs – might as well try to keep anyone else from seeing them – then followed the path for another hour into darkness, until a shout from Morn brought Kest, Brasti and me running.

We found him lying on the ground, his leg twisted, holding Tillia – somehow he'd managed to fall without hurting her.

'Is it broken?' Brasti asked.

'It wasn't my fault,' the girl said defensively. 'He just slipped on a rock and fell.'

I reached out a hand to comfort her and she flinched. 'It's all right,' I said, 'wc know it's not your fault.'

Kest was examining Morn's leg. 'It's not broken, but he's sprained both his left knee and his right ankle. There's no way he can walk.' He glanced around us. 'And there's nothing to make a litter from either . . .'

Clock came back and joined us. 'You'll never get there if you try to carry him,' he said pragmatically, 'and there's nobody will take turns humping him along.'

'No one?' I asked.

He shook his head. 'Look around. Everyone's exhausted – they're all of them near the end of their strength and their supplies. There's no room for charity now.'

'Leave me,' Morn said, his jaw tight. 'I'll camp here, join you when I can walk again.'

Clock leaned over him. 'You'll die out here, son. If the cold doesn't get you, wolves or something worse will. Best your friends stay with you.'

'No,' Morn said, 'I can take care of myself. I know how to stay alive in the mountains. Just go,' he said firmly.

'Is there anything you want from our supplies?' I asked.

'I've got my own – just get out of here.'

I exchanged glances with the others. 'All right. We'd better do as he says.'

Clock looked surprised. 'I thought you Trat— I thought you types . . . were all loyal to each other?'

'It's too cold for loyalty,' I said, walking past him to rejoin the line.

We plodded along with the rest of the travellers for the next two hours, our way lit only by the moon above us.

'Why aren't we stopping?' I called out to Clock at last.

'No protection from the wind,' he replied. 'We'll rest when we get to the base of the mountain.' Despite our earlier threats, he smiled at me. 'Tomorrow we go up the mountain, easy as can be.'

'Are you mad? It's hardly been steep until now and people are still barely making it – how in all the hells will they get up a mountain?'

He laughed. 'Look,' he said, and pointed.

It was too far for me to make out what I was supposed to be seeing but Brasti's eyes are better than most.

'Saint Brughan-who-chews-stone—' he swore.

Kest looked at him. 'Which one's that?'

'Saint of Mountain. Or rocks. I don't know, I just made him up. It's too much work trying to keep track of which Saints are still alive and which ones aren't.'

'What am I looking at?' I asked him.

'Ladders,' Brasti replied. 'There are ladders bolted onto the mountainside, and what looks like long sections of steps cut into the rock. And look there—' He pointed to something else I couldn't make out.

'I'm not seeing it. Still.'

'I do,' Kest said. 'Pulleys and winches – is that a *platform*?'

'It is,' Brasti said. 'Looks to be at least fifteen feet square. How did they ever engineer all that?'

Clock smiled at us, oblivious to what was troubling me. 'See? Most of us can climb those easy enough: a few hours to the top, then it's a straight road to the next mountain and just a day's march to the first town in Avares. Those pulley systems can help get the injured up there.'

But that's not what they'd been built for. Kest and Brasti had understood immediately, too: Avares had put in a highly effective system to move men and equipment back and forth across the mountains – across the only barrier that had impeded their attempts at invasion in the past – *and Tristia knew nothing about it.*

'Ah, look, see?' Clock said. 'There's a greeting party now.'

I saw big men with torches up ahead, handing out flasks and food to the weary travellers.

'Remember what I said,' Kest warned the old man.

'Don't you worry about me, son. I'll keep my mouth shut. I don't know why you're here, Trattari, and I don't imagine I'd like it if I did, but it's my own life I'm concerned with, not whatever plans you have.'

I wasn't sure if I believed him but in the end, it didn't matter. By the time we reached the camp, twelve Avarean warriors were waiting for us. We'd already been betrayed.

CHAPTER TWENTY-FIVE

THE ART OF TAKING A BEATING

There's an art to taking a beating.

Lying there on the ground as brutes of men punch and kick you into oblivion might not seem as complex a skill as wielding a sword, but trust me, it is. I'm a master at it.

'All right, gentlemen,' I said, as the Avarean guards began circling us, 'we surrender.' The rough-looking men in thick woollen kilts and furs had axes of varying sizes strapped across their backs or hanging at their sides; their odd shape and slightly serrated edges made me think they were for breaking through ice as much as cutting off heads.

One of the guards stepped to within a foot of me. He had lustrous blond hair falling in waves over his massive shoulders to his equally massive chest. I wondered briefly how he could keep his hair so healthy and shiny in this environment, but decided it probably wasn't the right time to ask. I decided to call him Princess.

'Se–renn–dur?' he said.

'Surrender. Yes.'

Maybe he didn't appreciate my correcting his pronunciation or (more likely) he had no idea what the word meant, but Princess delivered an impressive punch to my jaw. It was a solid hit – but it didn't do much damage, as I'd seen it coming. It's the ones you don't see coming that do the most harm. I let the impact swing me around a bit and tumbled impressively to the ground.

'Se-renn-dur,' Princess repeated.

You might be wondering why I didn't duck his first blow and follow up with some impressive feat of martial prowess – well, first, because there were twelve of them and three of us; second, because there were dozens more armed men all around, and third, we hadn't completed the mission yet, and being captured was far more likely to get us to where we needed to be than climbing the mountains and then trying to navigate the freezing wastes of Avares by ourselves.

'*Whoof!*' I said dramatically as the man I dubbed Goatface, with curly black hair and a magnificent forked beard, delivered the first good kick to my belly, sending me rolling over onto my side, icy snow sneaking its way down my collar and cuffs. While I was down, I noted that Kest and Brasti were also on the ground, pursuing similar strategies to mine. Goatface laughed and repeated, 'Se-renn-dur.'

The ground is a good place to be during a beating. It's like having a massive shield protecting one side of your body. Granted, it's not great for manoeuvrability, but if you try to move about too much, someone will invariably hold you so the others can continue the beating, and that can get painful.

My third man, Rosie, on account of his flaming red cheeks, tried a face-stomp. There's always someone who goes for the face-stomp, and that's the one thing you really must avoid. Rosie's heavy-booted foot would have landed squarely on my right cheek, breaking my jaw and sending half my teeth flying across the frozen ground, had I not twisted out of the way. Of course, this earned me a nasty kick to the back from Princess, who I guess was starting to feel he was missing out on the fun.

In a situation like this, it's helpful to determine the purpose of the beating. Committing an act of violence against another human being without intending to kill them requires either moral or pragmatic restraint – Avareans have never shown any discomfort when it comes to killing Tristians (or even each other, really) so morality was unlikely to keep them from hacking us to bits. And since our captors' axes hadn't yet made an appearance, there had to be some other reason for the beating.

If, say, your attackers wanted to rob you but would rather avoid a messy family vendetta, or maybe greater punishment from the law if they were caught, they'd go for a good old pummelling, rather than a stabbing or hacking. But Avareans love blood-feuds, because they add to their personal prestige, and given that the men duffing me up at that precise moment probably *were* the law, I doubted they were much worried about being charged with any crime.

Goatface lined up his foot with my stomach and brought it back in preparation for another good kicking. I curled up, getting my forearms low, ready to take most of the hit and avoid any more damage to my gut, then rolled onto my back and let out a big moan, so as to not offend him. I caught a glimpse of Kest, who was in middle of a 'cow-hop' – that's when you're on your hands and knees and your opponent tries to kick up into your stomach. The trick there is to push off on all fours so you come up in the air a few inches, thus allowing your aggressor to feel extremely powerful while ensuring they make barely any contact at all.

Kest caught my eye and let out a yelp that was louder than necessary, which I correctly interpreted as a warning, and sure enough, Rosie had come around and was gleefully intent on driving his foot down upon my face again – I don't know why, but some people are just obsessed from birth with the desire to stomp another man's skull in. Once again I rolled out of the way just in time and heard his boot thud into the ground just behind my head. If that had connected with my face, I wouldn't have been much use for interrogation.

Eliciting information is another common reason for a beating. We were Greatcoats, so the three of us had plenty of information the Avareans might want – but since all they were doing was laughing and saying 'se-renn-dur' over and over again, that wasn't the likely reason.

On the other hand, the laughter suggested our current situation might just be down to the fourth purpose of a beating: to have some Gods-damned good fun. This made the most sense, but as all the other men were doing actual work – lifting cargo, helping the migrants with their things – I didn't think it likely that they'd let a few of their fellows have all the fun.

That left only one reason for the violence, and having worked it out, I allowed myself a private little smile on the inside. They were softening us up, a time-honoured and entirely practical application of violence. The last thing you want when transporting prisoners is any chance that one might escape their bonds and get in a lucky shot that leaves you or your fellow guards wounded or dead, so a few judicious boots to various parts of the anatomy serves to lessen both their capacity and their enthusiasm for escape.

What's good about figuring out what the beating's for? It gives you control of the situation.

'Aarrghhh,' Brasti screamed, a couple of feet away from me. He began letting out little puffs of breath, then his head lolled to the side. I was a little disappointed that he'd figured it out at the same time I had. The scream was to let his captors know that he was now severely injured, and the panting and lolling was to make them believe he couldn't take much more.

Princess grunted something at Brasti's opponents and one of them replied with a string of Avarean I assumed to be a commentary on the weakness of Tristians in general and his in particular.

First Kest and then I followed Brasti's lead, and before long the Avareans were standing over us, laughing to each other as they doubtless commented quite unfairly on our lack of fortitude. Then

Rosie – *of course it had to be Rosie* – lifted his woollen kilt and pissed on me. I'd had just enough warning to roll over, sobbing in agony, so I got it on my back rather than in my face.

We got to lie there for some time getting our breath back while they fetched chains for us, and in the meantime, the villagers just walked right on by. Some looked sympathetic, some looked smug. But it was the girl, Tillia, whom I had carried up the cliff-face in the makeshift sling of my greatcoat, now cradled in the arms of an Avarean warrior, who looked down at me and said, 'My daddy was killed by Trattari.'

It's the blows you don't see coming that do the most damage.

CHAPTER TWENTY-SIX

SHAN STEEL

'I have a question,' Brasti said, his words a trifle slurred. He'd had less practise in the whole 'taking a beating' thing than I had and was looking a little the worse for wear.

'Ask it.'

'We're magistrates, right? I mean, we're the ones whose job it is to consider complex legal issues and render verdicts.'

'True.'

'And sometimes that verdict involves sending people to gaol, yes? Sometimes even to dungeons?'

'Also correct. Where are you going with this?'

He pushed himself upright until he was standing on the rough platform, trying to avoid leaning against the freezing iron bars. 'So why the fuck are we always the ones who end up in a cage?'

The Avarean warriors had tossed us like sacks of grain into one of the eight-by-four-foot metal and wood cages I'd assumed they used to haul supplies up and down the sheer mountainside. Thick ropes ran from heavy iron rings welded on top of the box to the pulleys that creaked and whined as we clattered our way up into the air.

'Nice view, though,' Kest said.

Watching the ground get further and further away from us left me considerably less enthused. I tried very hard to stay in the middle of the cage – it made no sense, but somehow it made me feel better.

After a moment I realised Kest was right: looking through the bars at the slopes below as the first hints of sunrise began to illuminate the icy landscape was an experience both inspiring and humbling – at least until Brasti moved to the front of the cage to get a better view, setting the whole thing swinging wildly.

'Stop it!' I moved backwards, trying to balance the box as it inched up the mountainside. 'Saint Zaghev-who-sings-for-tears, you're going to make me lose my dinner!'

'Still dead, and we didn't have any dinner,' Brasti reminded me. 'Besides, I think I'm having fun now. Those hairy barbarians should turn this into some kind of amusement for children. They'd make a fortune.'

'I think they intend to use it for other things,' Kest said, 'such as moving troops and equipment quickly and efficiently when they invade Tristia.'

Brasti grinned at us. 'That's the genius of my idea, don't you see? They could make so much gold from paying customers that they wouldn't need the war.'

In addition to the joys of our mode of transportation, we had been assigned a guard, a great burly man with braided dark brown hair and a long, reddish beard, also braided, who sat on top of the cage, apparently much less concerned with the prospect of falling than I was. Reyek or Rayicht (I wasn't clear on either pronunciation or spelling) was taking great pleasure in talking to us – or rather, *at* us, since he'd clearly overestimated his ability to speak Tristian.

'I speak you language,' he shouted down to me, as he did every time he began a sentence. 'I speak you language. We near top, see?'

As the cage clattered to a stop some hundred and fifty feet up, it occurred to me that dealing with spies by opening the cage and pushing us out would be highly efficient – but I suppose they could just as easily have made us climb the damned mountain and *then* pushed us off the side rather than have some poor bastard pull us all the way up. That made me feel better.

'Well?' Brasti asked, once six men had heaved the cage onto the flat area beside the winch. 'Shouldn't you let us out now? Or are we going back down?'

'I speak you language. We take you now to the Magdan.'

'Who's the Magdan?' I asked.

Reyek lifted his arms and shook them as if declaring victory. 'Big fighter: fighter of all fighters.'

'You mean one of your Warlords?' Kest asked.

Reyek looked confused for a moment, then he grinned. 'Magdan *is* Warlord. Only need one now.'

I found that hard to believe, but thought better of challenging Reyek's obvious admiration of this new Warlord and instead asked, 'Where will we find the Magdan?'

Our guard signalled to the men and only then did I see the large cart being pulled by two huge horses. I had to admire the ease with which the six men lifted our cage onto the back of the cart. Within moments we were rolling smoothly over the packed snow along a wide, well-made road.

'Not far,' Reyek said, pointing to a fort nearly hidden behind walls made from logs and ropes. 'There you will see the Magdan. There he will see you. Then we will see.'

It was almost poetic in its odd foreign fashion.

'I feel it's necessary to point out that once again we're headed for trouble because Falcio couldn't keep his heroism under control,' Brasti said as the cage bounced unnervingly on the back of the cart. The horses here had longer hair than our Tristian beasts, doubtless bred to deal with the colder weather. They were bigger, too, and made me think of Monster. I wasn't yet sure how Kest, Brasti and I were going to make our escape, but I would have dearly loved Monster's brutish strength and vicious temper on our side right about now.

As we approached the fort, Reyek pointed unnecessarily towards the open gates set in the great wall surrounding it. 'We go inside now, Trattari?' From his mouth the word sounded more like Traii-taraii. I didn't bother to correct him.

'We're not Traii-taraii,' Brasti said. 'We stole those coats from men on the road. Killed them.' He patted his own chest. 'We good men – kill bad Traii-taraii. I personally have slain nearly fifty nasty Traii-taraii.' He gestured to Kest then added, 'He only kill twelve.'

'You're wasting your time,' Kest said, the fingers of his left hand twitching as he limbered them up for when the time came to fight.

Brasti gave Kest a dirty look. 'Hey, Saint Kest-who-fucked-the-plan, why did you give it away? You think these barbarians are too clever to be fooled? Or is it that you can't follow any idea unless it's Falcio's?'

'Neither,' Kest replied. He looked at Reyek. 'He has no clue what you're saying.'

'I speak you language,' Reyek said, his face belying the statement.

'Four words of it, anyway,' I muttered to myself.

The cart pulled inside the walls, we got our first look at the fort and for the longest time, none of us spoke. Kest stopped moving his fingers, Brasti stopped complaining. I stopped thinking about escape.

The fort itself was plain enough – a hastily constructed affair made from felled timber lashed with ropes and seamed with some kind of thick glue maybe made from sap. It was typical of what we knew of Avares construction: sturdy, simple, and by and large looking like it had been designed by a child. Outside the fort proper was a vast courtyard of hard-packed snow marked by hundreds of wheel tracks. Perhaps two hundred men milled about – big men like Reyek, all with long hair and thick beards, sporting a motley collection of furs. Some were moving small carts laden with supplies in and out of the fort; others were practising with canfreks, the Avareans' favoured blade: straight wide swords that came to an abrupt, almost flat end where the point of a normal sword would be. These were cutting weapons, meant for chopping off a man's head or limbs. I watched as one of the men swung his canfrek and took a foot-long piece off a log. The sun glinted against the steel of the weapon.

That was my first sense that something was badly wrong.

'Where are they getting proper steel from?' I asked out loud. Avarean weapons are usually made of bronze, or a weak iron they mine that's too full of impurities to smelt into proper steel.

'That's not just steel,' Kest pointed out, 'it's *Shan* steel.'

'How in hells would *barbarians* get hold of Shan steel?' Brasti asked, staring through the bars. 'Don't those little bastards kill anyone who turns up on their shores?'

The Tristians might consider the Avareans uncivilised, but the Shan believe *everyone* who isn't Shan to be barbarians. Though their small island lacked some resources, still they rarely traded with other nations.

'You're looking at the wrong thing,' Kest said, taking my attention away from the blade.

'What do you mean?'

He pointed to the other side of the courtyard where a group of about three dozen men were drilling with spears inside a hundred-foot training square. 'So what?' I asked. 'They have Shan steel spearheads, too. I hardly think . . .'

My words trailed off as I realised that the problem wasn't the weapons. The men were practising *in formation*, their every movement matched to the rhythm of a jaunty tune they were all singing as they stepped forward, thrust their spears then returned to guard, moving in perfect time. I remembered then that Nehra had wanted us to memorise any of their warsongs that we heard – despite my knowing barely enough about music to sing a verdict.

But watching the Avarean warriors on the training ground, I realised I now had much bigger problems to deal with.

'What's the problem?' Brasti asked. 'They're big men, but they're not doing anything different; that's just how any fool group of Ducal foot soldiers would do it.'

'That's the point,' I said. 'Since when do Avarean warriors fight in formation?'

Brasti looked like he was about to make a joke, then he stopped. '*Shit*.'

King Paelis' best estimate had been that the population of Avares was only about a third of Tristia's, but they had two warriors for every one of our trained soldiers. The only thing that kept them from overrunning our borders was a mix of tradition, religion and their unsophisticated military practices, which meant they had no inclination or idea how to fight in formation. There's some saying in Avarean which I'd never learned, because – well, why would anyone want to learn their language? But the gist of the saying is, 'No glory comes from more than one arm.' They'd always fought individually, believing their singular God favoured only the boldest warriors.

Our cart stopped not far from the entrance as a small group of women came out lugging baskets that proved to have food for the training warriors. Then three more women came out, these wearing furs banded by leather and carrying their own canfreks.

'Well, there's something else I never expected to see,' Brasti said. Avarean women are almost as big as their menfolk, but I'd never heard of any being allowed to take up arms.

'It appears there have been a number of changes here in recent years,' Kest remarked. I could see him thinking the same questions I was: how many of their women were now warriors? Ten per cent? Twenty per cent? How many battles would be won by that difference? How well could Tristia, with its broken Knights and ill-prepared soldiers, now fight off an invasion from Avares? How well would our idiot generals – mostly wealthy men with no real skill in strategy or experience in battle – fare against a real army for the first time in two hundred years?

As the women passed our cage I studied the little carts sitting inside the walls of the fort, until a clang startled me and the cage door opened. Reyek gestured at the four men with spears at his side, then motioned for us to come. 'I speak you language,' he said.

He surely did.

CHAPTER TWENTY-SEVEN

THE MAGDAN

I expected them to put us in a cell in the fort, but instead we were prodded to the edge of the training square as the warriors ended their formation exercises and began to assemble along the heavy wooden fencing.

'If this is summary execution, then I'm going to be very disappointed,' Brasti warned Reyek.

The red-bearded man just pushed him forward. The warriors had left their formations and were now taking up positions around the square. A low humming sound, almost a rumbling, began to arise from the onlookers and soon took on the shape of another song, or perhaps just the beginning of a song. The slow, thick notes evoked in my mind the tense moments just before a battle.

'Odd buggers,' Brasti commented.

Kest concurred. 'They do appear to be almost as fond of singing as they are of killing.'

'Oh, hells,' I swore. 'I almost forgot. On the off-chance we don't die up here, Nehra wanted us to try and learn the tunes to their warsongs. I don't suppose you could . . .' A glance at Kest's face told me he already *had* been memorising the songs. 'She had Rhyleis ask you, too?'

'No.'

'Then why—?'

He shrugged. 'Force of habit.'

Reyek gave me an extra-hard prod in the back. 'I speak you language good,' he reminded me.

'I don't suppose they plan to have us duel?' Kest wondered aloud. His tone was wistful, and not just because it had been days since the last time we'd nearly been killed, but because the warriors of Avares, with their obsessive need to prove their pre-eminence, might just be stupid enough to give us back our weapons, let us kill off a few of their best warriors and then release us after we'd embarrassed their people enough.

We all get a little unrealistically optimistic sometimes.

'There's a chance we can fight our way out,' Kest added.

'Really? How in the world would that work?'

He looked briefly at the men with the spears. 'I take one of the spears and kill two men. The others will converge on me, which will give you time to get over there.' I followed his gaze to where a number of swords were sitting on a small bench. 'The other men will chase you, but if you can take down the first few quickly enough, then I might be able to evade the ones trying to kill me in time to grab that fire bucket and throw the embers up through that window. I can see cloth there. If it catches fire then—'

'What are the odds of any of this happening before we're killed?'

He did that counting in his head thing. When he was done he admitted, 'Not good.'

Reyek put a big hand on my shoulder and pointed past me at a warrior walking into the training square. He wore brown and black furs and stood well over six and a half feet tall. He was bigger than Reyek, bigger than the spearmen behind us – hells, he was pretty much bigger even than bloody Shuran had been. The double-sided axe he bore would have sheared through a tree trunk with ease.

'You stand here,' Reyek said. 'Watch. Not move. Watch the Magdan kill.'

'Who's the Magdan going to fight?' Brasti asked.

Reyek shook his head. 'Not say fight. I speak you language. Kill is kill, is not fight.'

So, an execution then, not a duel at all. So much for Avarean honour.

A second man entered the training square from the opposite side, his appearance obscured by one of the braziers billowing flame and smoke onto the field. He was tall, but slim for an Avarean, and shirtless. Four warriors with spears followed behind him, no doubt ready to stop him trying to escape his inevitable death.

'Why is the Magdan doing this? What crime has this man committed?'

Reyek looked thoughtful for a moment then said, '*Kriukath*.' He repeated it several times as if waiting for the word to translate itself.

'*Kriukath*,' Kest repeated. 'I think it might mean . . . craven? Cowardice?'

Reyek nodded, but then tilted his head and frowned as if the word wasn't quite right. His tongue worked its way awkwardly inside his mouth and finally he said, 'En-sab-ard-ena-shun.'

'Ensue *what*?' Brasti said.

'I think he means "insubordination",' Kest replied.

Reyek grinned. 'En-sab-ard-ena-shun, yes. I speak you language good.'

I looked up at Reyek. 'Seriously? You speak all of ten words in our tongue and one of them is insubordination?'

The big man nodded. 'I speak you language good.'

'Not that good,' Brasti said, peering towards the square, 'because I don't think insubordination is what he meant.'

The two fighters approached each other and only then could I make out the blond hair and beard on the unarmed shirtless man walking to his death.

It was Morn.

*

The big brute calling himself the Magdan gave a roar and Morn skipped back a step and crouched low to keep out of the way of that heavy doubled-bladed axe. His opponent laughed and gazed out at the crowds of warriors lining the square as if waiting for them to cheer him on. A few did, but the rest stood in solemn silence. Perhaps they were wondering how mighty a Warlord could truly be if he had to find his amusement in the slaughter of an unarmed man. Morn stayed on the balls of his feet, knees bent, ready to move quickly once his enemy started his attack.

The Magdan shouted something at the crowd, the guttural words sounding as much like growls as words to my ignorant ears. 'Something about keeping their traditions alive,' Kest said. 'And I think . . .'

'Let me guess,' Brasti said, 'a lot of stuff about breaking backs and crushing spleens and various stomping-on of limbs?'

'That's not . . . actually, some of that's pretty close.'

'Focus,' I told them. 'We need to find a way to get Morn out of this mess before it's too late.'

Damn you, Morn. The reason I'd ordered you to fake an injury was so you could help us escape when we inevitably got captured, not the other way around. But after months of searching for my fellow Greatcoats, I was damned if I'd let the first one to turn up at Aramor end up dead in this frozen hellhole.

I followed Kest's eyes as he scanned the crowd, the square, the buildings in the compound. He kept returning to the dozens of Avarean warriors all around us. 'There's nothing we can do for him, Falcio.'

'You always—'

'It's not just a matter of being outnumbered,' he said, cutting me off. 'The terrain doesn't favour us. There's nowhere to run and nothing to use as a distraction that won't get us killed quicker than Morn.'

'You could give a speech,' Brasti said. 'Oh, but you don't speak Avarean.'

'*Really* not helpful,' I said, and turned my thoughts to what we carried in our coats. I had amberlight, which could spark a decent fire, but wouldn't do much good in this cold. The bracers in my breast pocket were half-full of the lightweight throwing knives I preferred, but I doubted they'd penetrate the fur of our enemies' cloaks, never mind the thicker leather armour underneath. There were climbing spikes, sharpened caltrops, yellow-fen oil to darken skin for night work, green periden powder to blind an enemy – all good things to get *out* of a jam, but nothing that was going to get through so many enemies in time to help Morn.

'You watch,' Reyek said to me, grabbing my head and turning it back towards the square. The Magdan had finished his little speech about devouring his opponent's entrails and now the real fight was about to begin.

Brasti scowled at Reyek. 'So much for Avarean courage.'

Reyek smiled as if he'd just given him a compliment. 'The Magdan mighty.'

In a last moment of silence, the warriors assembled around the square halted their soft, rumbling song, the big brute in the square stopped talking and Morn shouted something in reply, his voice sounding perilously small by comparison. 'What did he say?' I asked Kest, but by then the answer no longer mattered, for the Magdan shouted and ran for Morn, swinging his heavy twin-headed axe up high over his head, then bringing it back down in a perfect diagonal arc – harder by far to dodge than a straight vertical blow. But somehow Morn had managed to leap up and to his left, passing over the axe blade and coming down the other side, then somersaulting and coming back up on his feet before spinning around to face his enemy once again.

The instant the fight had begun, the song had changed as well, becoming a fast, almost rousing chorus. 'It's "Seven for a Thousand",' Kest said, tilting his head just slightly as he listened.

'What's that supposed to mean?' Brasti asked.

'It's—' Kest paused to listen again. 'I think it's the story about seven Avarean warriors facing off against a thousand enemies. It's about courage in the face of impossible odds.'

Sure, like a massive axe-wielding brute bravely fighting an injured and unarmed man.

The Magdan gave a loud, barking laugh and cried out, just a single word this time, before once again lifting his axe up high and launching into a series of whirling manoeuvres both terrifying in their ferocity and strangely beautiful in their efficiency. The big man made it look elegant, as though his weapon were a puppet he'd set to dancing for the audience. Morn was fast, and far better at this than I would have been, ducking and dodging, staying in close when he could, leaping away when there was no other choice. Step by step, though, the Magdan was driving him across the square, forcing him back towards the spearmen. Again and again Morn narrowly avoided death, but even from this distance, I could almost count the moves left to him. In three, maybe four strikes at most, he was going to be dead.

I stood uselessly. I was the First Cantor of the Greatcoats: it was my job to protect my people, to think past the obstacles and find a solution even when one didn't appear possible.

Brasti tried to turn away, not wanting to witness the butchery the moment Morn stumbled, but Reyek grabbed his jaw and forced it back around. 'You *watch*.'

'Why?' Brasti demanded. 'Is this "Magdan" of yours so vain that he thinks killing an unarmed man will impress us somehow?'

'You stupid,' Reyek grunted.

The Magdan continued to press his attack, now wielding his axe in a figure-of-eight pattern to force Morn closer to the edge of the training square, giving him no chance to escape to right or left. I reached into my coat for the yellow-fen oil. If nothing else, I could try to distract them long enough to run onto the square – that might give Morn a moment to catch his breath. *If they like stories about seven fearless warriors facing a thousand enemies, maybe they'll appreciate one suicidal idiot running at them while screaming like a maniac.*

Kest caught my arm. 'Falcio, something's not right.'

'What is it?'

'Morn's moving too slowly.'

'He's tiring, you idiot,' Brasti said.

Kest shook his head. 'Look at him. He's not breathing hard – if he were desperate, his movements would be rushed. He's not panting, his eyes are clear. Falcio, I think he's waiting for his moment.'

A hoarse laugh escaped my lips. 'Then he's spent too long in these damned mountains,' I said, pointing to the massive black-haired monster pursuing him. 'The Magdan's about to decapitate him with that bloody axe!'

Reyek looked over at me, a confused expression on his face as he tried to make sense of my words. 'You say stupid things. Magdan—'

I missed whatever it was he was saying next because the low-level roar of the crowd grew into a cacophony of shouting and cheering as the black-haired brute raised his weapon up high. His opponent had nowhere left to run. The sunlight overhead glinted on the axe blade in that brief instant before it came crashing down on Morn, who was now far too close to dodge. But instead, Morn stepped forward, placed his hands around the Magdan's arms and lifted a foot to hip-height – I thought he was going to kick his opponent, though I couldn't work out what that would achieve – but instead Morn fell backwards, still gripping the Magdan's thick arms, and they went over like a wheel, propelled by the bigger man's momentum. The spearmen guarding the square were suddenly forced to back up a step, and in the blink of an eye, the Magdan was on his back with Morn on top of him – and with a great heave, Morn tore the axe from the stunned man's hands and brought it over his head so their positions were reversed. Without a moment's hesitation or mercy, Morn brought the axe blade down on the black-haired man, cleaving his face in two.

Even from this distance my eyes closed reflexively to avoid the spray of blood. When I opened them again I saw Morn, his chest now dripping red, pushing his foot against the remains of his enemy's chin to tear the axe free. He turned to the crowd and held it up high.

Silence enveloped the square, just for a second, then the warriors began cheering, the shouts so loud I thought the snow would cascade off the mountains, sweeping us all away in an avalanche.

Morn pumped his fist in the air as he walked towards us, his eyes seeking me out – and it was only then I realised what it was the Avareans were chanting.

'Magdan! Magdan! *Magdan!*'

Reyek pounded me on the back. 'See? I say to you, the Magdan *mighty*.'

Morn discarded the axe and stood before Kest, Brasti and me. 'Smile, Falcio,' he said. 'I'm about to give you everything you've ever wanted.'

CHAPTER TWENTY-EIGHT

THE WARLORD

The cheering and celebration continued all around us, and as they left the square some Avareans even smiled at me, as if Morn's victory had settled some long-running argument between us, fought over beer and boasts in the local tavern.

He isn't an outsider to them.

That realisation shook me to my core. I'd always believed the Avareans to be barbarians: tribes of inbred mountain men steeped in brutality and bloodshed in the name of their clans. I doubt you could find five people in all of Tristia who had a different impression of them.

Morn wiped the sweat and blood from his bare chest with a towel, then reached for the shirt and coat being handed to him by a grinning man.

Kest was watching as a quartet of warriors carried the corpse of the black-haired brute from the field. 'Insubordination.'

Reyek nodded, clapping him on the back. 'En-sab-ard-ena-shun!'

So that really *was* one of the ten Tristian words he knew.

'You'll have questions, I imagine,' Morn said, picking up the discarded towel and wiping his face. 'You wouldn't believe how much of a sweat you can build up, even in this cold.'

He said something to Reyek, who ran off and returned with our weapons. Kest strapped his shield across his back, though he was still watching Morn and I could see him re-evaluating our fellow Greatcoat in that strange mathematical way of his. 'I would have thought the thinner air at this altitude would be the greater challenge.'

Morn chuckled. 'Of course you would be the one to notice that, Kest.' He tossed the towel to Reyek. 'The body gets used to it after a while, but I'll admit I was worried that perhaps I'd spent too long away bringing you here.' He tilted his head back and took in a series of staggered breaths through his nostrils. 'Fortunately, there are ways to adapt more quickly.'

'That old man you talked about,' I said. 'He really was Rangieri?'

He nodded. 'Yimris could do things that would amaze you. Walk for days without rest, sleep in ice-cold snow without getting frostbite – one time I came upon him and his heartbeat was so slow that I thought for sure he'd died in the night. I actually started crying. All of a sudden one of his eyes opened and he said, "Rangieri don't waste water," and then went back to sleep.'

I knew almost nothing about the Rangieri – even less than I did about the Bardatti or the Dashini. All these ancient Orders with their secret ways . . . what was it all for?

'That's a nice story, Morn,' Brasti said. 'Is it supposed to make us ignore the fact that you apparently fucked off and became an Avarean Warlord while no one was looking?'

Reyek, who'd been watching us through the squinting eyes of someone trying to keep up with a conversation he couldn't hope to follow, nonetheless caught the edge in Brasti's words. He cuffed him across the back of the head and said, 'I speak you language good. You speak to the Magdan good.'

'*Jas beyat*, Reyek,' Morn said, motioning for him to be calm. '*Jas beyat*.'

'"Rest easy",' Kest translated.

'Yeah, I figured,' I said.

It's not as if I'm uneducated. I'm fluent in modern and archaic

Tristian, I can manage a fair bit of Shan and can even puzzle out ancient Tristian if need be, which I promise is a lot more than most people. But this language of grunts and growls and words that all sounded like they meant, 'Come over here so I can beat your brains in'? I felt woefully unprepared for this mission. *Then again, I'm supposed to be a bloody* Tristian *magistrate. What business do I have in this Gods-forsaken country?*

'Brasti's right,' I said. 'What in all the hells are you doing here, Morn?'

His eyes narrowed – only momentarily, but long enough for me to see he didn't appreciate being questioned. I supposed that came with the territory: he was a Warlord and he'd just killed the last man who'd challenged his authority. But Morn's jovial smile quickly returned. 'Now *that* is a much longer story than we have time for right now.'

All right, so you don't want to talk about it – is that because you're waiting until we're alone? Or because you just don't want us to know?

'Wait, let me have a try.' Brasti turned to Morn. 'You went north as the King ordered and almost died in the mountains, only to be saved by the old Rangieri, who taught you his ways. Somehow you wound up in a duel with an Avarean Warlord who underestimated how dangerous you were because he'd never fought a Greatcoat before – even one who mostly fights with a big stick with a knife stuck on the end.'

'Brasti . . .' I warned, but he ignored me.

Gesturing at Reyek, he went on, 'Then you convinced a bunch of these great big bastards to follow you, and using a combination of the tactics we learned in the Greatcoats and somehow finding a way to bring Shan steel weapons to Avares, you gradually took over several other warbands.' He poked a finger at Morn's chest. 'How am I doing so far?'

Morn had to wave off Reyek a second time, then admitted, 'Pretty damned close, actually.'

Brasti turned to Kest. 'See, I can be clever, too, sometimes.'

'You should try to do it more often,' he replied.

Morn gave a big, deep-throated laugh. 'Ah, see? This is what I missed. The three of you! Your little travelling comedy routine, the masterful heroics, the speeches.' He looked down at me. 'Those things don't work quite so well in the north.' Without another word he took off for one of the large wooden buildings inside of the compound, not even bothering to make sure we followed. Mind you, he didn't need to, because several of his warriors immediately started prodding us with their spears until we set out after him.

'The Avareans aren't like us, Falcio,' Morn said as he walked. 'War isn't a means to an end for them; it's not an act of anger or hatred. It's *religion*. It's the way they show their worth to their Gods, and the way they measure one another. There are no games, no politics.'

'You sound as if you admire them,' Kest said, keeping an eye on the men behind us.

Morn stopped, forcing us to do the same. 'I do, in a way. There's a kind of . . . *purity* to their ways that's different to anything we have back home. Justice is absolute for them, unyielding. It's a far cry from all the corruption and manipulation we deal with in Tristia.' He glanced back at me. 'I'll bet you think that's terribly militaristic, don't you, Falcio?'

I hate it when people know exactly what I'm thinking.

The inside of the building was larger than I'd expected. The walls, beams and supports that held it all together were made of massive logs. The men, women and children we'd come over the mountains with were being attended by Avarean warriors, men and women, who were feeding them and dealing with the wounds of the injured.

'The Avareans are remarkably skilled healers,' Morn commented.

'That's charitable of them,' Brasti said. 'Do they have to bandage one wound for every five people they eat?'

'You still don't get it,' Morn said. 'Those people who came over the mountains with you? They risked *everything* to get here. The Avareans call that *rokhan*.'

'"Spirit"?' Kest asked.

'Almost: mix courage and daring and faith all into one and you have *rokhan*. To an Avarean, it isn't a favour or even a duty to feed and care for someone with *rokhan*. It's an honour.'

I looked at the men and women of this place, struggling to reconcile Morn's words with the impressions I'd grown up with. Apparently Brasti found it impossible. 'All sounds very admirable,' he said, 'except I don't recall Avarean warbands ever taking prisoners when they've attacked Tristian villages. They kill them all.'

'Kill cowards,' Reyek rumbled from behind me.

I turned. '*Cowards?* They're *farmers* and *craftspeople*, not soldiers.'

The big man showed me his teeth. 'They not fight. *Cowards*.'

'I told you, the Avareans respect courage and daring,' Morn explained. 'They treat their prisoners commensurate with the degree to which they are willing to face fear. Put up a brave fight? Show them *rokhan*? They'll still wipe out your army, but they'll treat your people almost as equals. Retreat, or surrender? Then you die, and all your kin become slaves and sometimes worse.'

Reyek poked me with a finger. 'Cowards. *Spies*.'

'And here I thought we were all going to be such good friends,' Brasti whispered to Kest, not very quietly.

'Oh, we are, Brasti, I promise you.' Morn led us out of the infirmary and along the wall of the compound to another building, its construction almost identical but its contents very different. Racks of weapons awaited us: swords, spears, shields, and a variety of pole-arms, including an entire rack just like Morn's.

'You really do love those fucking glaives, don't you, Morn?' Brasti asked.

Morn ignored the jibe, saying to me, 'This is just one camp. One armoury.'

'How many do you have in all?' Kest asked.

'Six.'

Hells. Six might not sound impressive, unless you considered just how poorly armed Tristia was right now. When the Knights had abandoned their Dukes and Lords, they'd taken their weapons with them. What few soldiers we did have left were neither well trained nor well armed.

'What are those?' Kest asked, pointing to a row of canvas-covered carts in the centre of the building.

Morn signalled to one of his men, who wheeled one of the carts over to us. Morn removed the tarp to reveal that what was underneath was not, in fact, a cart at all.

'*Oh*,' Kest said.

The machine before us was a long wide iron tube set on top of a set of small wheels. A little wooden box shaped like a small trench was attached to the side. Inside was a set of six black iron balls around six inches in diameter. 'A cannon,' I mumbled, my eyes going back to the others all in a row, trying to count how many they had here, and how many in their other five encampments. 'Morn . . . what are you doing with all these cannon?'

My reaction was clearly exactly what Morn had been waiting for – what he'd been building up to all along.

'I'm going to save Tristia once and for all.'

Things went downhill after that.

CHAPTER TWENTY-NINE

THE NEW COUNTRY

I had to run to keep up with Morn as he walked out the building and towards the front gates of the encampment, my boots crunching over the densely packed snow, making me feel like a child chasing after his father. 'Tell me how this works,' I demanded. 'Tell me how this can end in something other than violence and bloodshed!'

'Stop being so melodramatic, Falcio. It's not nearly so terrifying as you make it out to be.'

Then why are you doing your best to terrify me, you arsehole?

Morn didn't speak again until we were past the gates and on our way up a small hill nearby. My lungs were pumping hard in the cold, thin air of the mountains. *Should've joined the damned Rangieri instead of the Greatcoats*, I thought.

Morn finally came to a stop and pointed east. 'Those mountains? Those are the ones we crossed together. On the other side are Orison and Hervor: two Duchies whose rulers have never brought the rest of the country anything but oppression and villainy. Both Duchies are without Dukes right now, and their people are suffering. *Those people*' – he accentuated the last words – 'have as much Avarean blood in them as Tristian.'

'So you plan to annex Orison and Hervor as part of Avares?' I asked.

'Of course.' Morn spread his arms wide. 'Strike me down here and now, Falcio, for I am a traitor to our country, to our King, to our cause.' He dropped his arms and shook his head, his eyes never leaving mine. 'You think I'd go through all this just to take from one country to give to another?'

'Then what—?'

'To create something *new*!' He gripped me by the shoulders. 'Don't you see, Falcio? This is our chance – our *one* chance. We're going to create a new country, one founded on unshakeable principles of justice. Every man and every woman will be judged on the way they live their lives, not on how much wealth or power they've accumulated. It will be a nation without Dukes or Kings.'

'Or Warlords?' Kest asked.

'The Avareans don't seek territory, only glory. I will give them the glory they seek, the chance to prove their *rokhan* and do something their parents and their grandparents never did: to help liberate a people and change the shape of a continent.'

The excitement in his voice, the ardour with which he spoke, was seductive almost beyond imagining. Orison and Hervor: two Duchies I've hated as much or more than Rijou; two ruling families who had brought Tristia nothing but strife and warfare.

'Imagine, Falcio,' Morn said, sensing my weakness, 'the Law as the very *foundation* of a country, not some gilding painted on too thinly to stretch across its surface, but the very rock upon which it's built.'

The depth of passion gleaming in his eyes was hypnotic, blinding. I could barely hold his gaze.

'Oh, do fuck off.'

Brasti was staring at us, his arms folded across his chest. 'There's no such thing as a country without rulers. Eventually some arsehole comes along and—'

'Morn doesn't intend this new nation of his to lack for rulers,' Kest said. 'Do you, Morn?' He turned to me. 'He means the Greatcoats to have dominion over an entire country.'

Far from being insulted or trying to deny Kest and Brasti's

accusations, Morn was so sure of the incontestable rightness of his plans that I don't think he even recognised the scepticism on their faces. I doubt it would have mattered anyway, because it was *me* he was seeking to convince.

'It's what we always talked about, Falcio,' he said seductively.

His final words hit me like a mallet to the stomach. Those days leading up to the Dukes' war against the King, to the imminent destruction of everything we'd fought for . . . we *had* said it then: why not a country with magistrates in charge? Who better to rule for the good of the people than those very judges who administered the laws?

Was *this* what the King had wanted? Was this why he'd sent all of us on these strange missions, to set the stage so that Morn, always one of the King's favourites, could do the one thing that Paelis himself could never hope to accomplish in his own lifetime?

A petty thought occurred to me then: *why not me?*

If this was your great plan, your Majesty, why not entrust it to me?

'It can't be done,' Kest said, the dispassion in his voice drawing me out of my own small-minded thoughts.

'It can,' Morn countered, making his way up the hill along a path pounded into the snow. 'I promise you, all of you, every detail has been considered.'

Kest shook his head. 'Even a single Duchy isn't ruled by one Duke; the territory is simply too big, the administration too complex – we have Margraves and Viscounts, Lords and Daminas . . . even a country made up solely of Orison and Hervor would need more Greatcoats than we have at Aramor.'

Morn stopped at the top of the hill and turned back to face us. 'I know.' Then he smiled and gestured for me to join him. 'Come.'

I walked up the few remaining yards to stand with him at the summit of the small hill and looked past him to the other side. The sun was high up overhead and the glare off the snow was blinding me. All I could make out at first was a sea of brown and black.

Coats, I realised. Not fur, not armour. *Coats.*

I'd been fooled before, in Rijou, by the so-called 'new Greatcoats', and later by the Tailor with her Unblooded Dashini – but this was no trick, no deception. As my vision cleared I began to make out faces of people I *knew*: Quillata, her long dark hair wild as always, the scar across her cheek new, but unable to hide her smirk. I remembered the day I'd met her: the King's Sail. Next to her stood Ran, the King's Silence – one of the original twelve like Quillata, and next to him, Judian, the King's Hammer. Face after face, almost all of them familiar to me, every one of them a spark in my heart. How long had I been searching, hoping, even praying that I would see them again – and here they were.

'I told you I was going to give you everything you ever wanted, Falcio,' Morn said, his voice filled with more pride than the Gods should ever allow one man. 'The Greatcoats are here.'

CHAPTER THIRTY

THE FIRST CANTOR

I couldn't move, couldn't speak. All I could do was stand there and watch them, the sight of their faces washing over me like the tide.

I should be happy, I thought. *I should be running down to them, shouting their names, making stupid comments about how beaten up and downtrodden they all look. I should be punching them in the arms, demanding to know why they hadn't heeded my call to come to Aramor, instead joining up with a loud-mouthed fop like Morn and coming up with this preposterous plan to save the world without me.*

Quillata, Ran, Old Tobb, Shana: the men and women who'd joined us in those early days when it had been just me and the King. And others, too: Jakin, whom Kest had recruited. Murielle de Vierre – I couldn't remember who'd brought her in, but I could still picture the look on her face when Paelis had asked her to take the oath and become the King's Thorn.

Saints, but I loved them all.

So why was I just standing there, silent, frozen in the snow?

Was it the thick fur cloaks I only now noticed hanging off the shoulders of their coats like an admission that the things we believed kept us safe in our own land were insufficient in this harsh northern country? Was it the way they were looking back at me, not smirking or smiling, not overjoyed to see us, but rather, cautious . . . reserved . . . *waiting*, I realised suddenly. *They're waiting to see what I do.*

'I count forty-two,' Kest said. There was something unusual in his voice. Fear? No. *Dismay.*

Why dismay?

It was only when I looked in his eyes and saw something of myself reflected there that I began to come to my senses. I remembered the one question every magistrate asks of themselves every time a case comes before them, whenever there's a possibility of using the verdict to shape the world not by the law, but by their own vision of justice. The King used to ask this question sometimes when the two of us got particularly drunk and I'd start going on yet again about venal noblemen and how much better someone like me might do in the top job.

What do you call a judge sitting on a throne? he always demanded, and he always answered his own question: *A fucking tyrant, that's what.*

'Don't, Falcio,' Morn said, staring at me, although I hadn't yet said a word. 'It doesn't have to be this way. That little girl you admire so much can still hold onto the south if you want – but Hervor and Orison will be *ours*: the beginning of something new, something *untainted*.'

The beginning. I wondered if Morn even understood the implication of what he'd just said.

The Magdan, I reminded myself then. *Stop thinking of him as Morn and instead call him the Magdan.*

'Falcio, look around you. This isn't a trick. These are our fellow Greatcoats. *Our friends*.'

Our friends.

How long had I been searching for them? How many times had I laid my head on my pillow, unable to fall asleep as I worked out which backwater town or village I'd missed, which damned corner of the country I had failed to search? All these months I wondered why even the Bardatti couldn't find them.

The answer was simple: they hadn't wanted to be found.

The Greatcoats weren't lost. They were *here*.

'You look sad, Falcio,' said the man who had once been Morn, not sounding the least bit sympathetic.

'I am sad,' I admitted, my eyes still on the Greatcoats waiting for us below. Had the Magdan told them when to wait there, and for how long, just so he could build up to this moment?

Let them see it, I thought. *Let them see the disgust on my face and hear the heartache in my voice.*

'Damn you, Falcio,' the Magdan said, already walking over to join the others. 'This isn't logic or idealism whispering in your ear, it's just your damned stubbornness.'

I ignored him and turned to look at Kest and Brasti, suddenly terrified by the possibility that they might be wavering as I had been. My heartache eased, if only by a fraction, to see the pain that they felt too – the absolute certainty that what the Magdan proposed wasn't some grand plan to solve the world's problems or create a wondrous nation founded on justice rather than power.

This was the death of my King's dream, plain and simple.

I looked down at our fellow Greatcoats. I think they must have known all along that we wouldn't go along with this – *that's* why he brought us here, far away from Mateo and Antrim and the few who'd come to Aramor, the few who still honoured the King's memory.

'You're making a mistake, Falcio,' the Magdan said, standing with the others now. He spread his arms wide, a generous King offering to embrace his lowly subject. 'We should be celebrating. The Greatcoats are reunited.'

'Did they teach you magic when you came here?' Brasti asked.

'Magic is considered a sometimes necessary but largely cowardly pursuit in Avares,' he replied. 'Normally only those born with deformities study it. So no, Brasti, I'm not a wizard. Why would you ask?'

Brasti looked out at the other Greatcoats. 'Too bad. I was hoping maybe all you fucking cowards were under some kind of spell.'

Several hands went to hilts of swords; a few raised bows or crossbows. Old Tobb still had that ridiculous pistol of his; nobody else could shoot straight with them, but he'd always managed to hit his target. Quillata still had her sling.

They're the same people they've always been. That thought nearly sent me to my knees.

Brasti nocked an arrow to the string of his bow. 'The problem with the bone plates in our coats is that they don't cover your face.'

'Falcio . . .' Kest said. 'Our chances aren't good here.'

'When are the odds ever in our favour?' Brasti asked.

'Compared to right now? Every single time.'

'Then why haven't you got your damned shield up?'

'Because he knows,' the Magdan said, his voice deep and resonant, as if he'd been born to make words echo across the mountaintops. 'Kest knows what Falcio's going to do next, just as I do.'

He walked to a spot halfway between his Greatcoats and us. 'You know what I always used to wonder about the King?' he asked me.

I didn't bother to reply; I knew his question because I'd asked myself the same thing the last time I'd been in this situation.

'How is it,' the Magdan began, looking up at the sky as if King Paelis were sitting upon a cloud holding court, 'that for all our study of the King's Law, of the workings of the country, of the ways of its people, that the First Cantor was selected by something as crass and unsophisticated as a contest to see who was the best fighter?'

'That's simple,' Brasti replied. 'The King was drunk the day he had to pick a leader for the Greatcoats and he wanted some amusement.'

The Magdan laughed. 'You know, I used to think that, too, sometimes.' His eyes went to me. 'But that's not why, is it, Falcio?'

'You know,' I said, shaking off the stupor that had been paralysing me until now, 'as someone known to enjoy a good speech, I hate to interrupt your carefully crafted script. But it's cold out here, so why don't you just get on with it.'

The Magdan stripped his fur cloak from his shoulders and tossed it aside. 'I think the reason the King made us fight was because for all his fine words and lofty ideals, he understood the most basic principle of justice: the only laws that matter are the ones you've got the strength to enforce.' He unstrapped the glaive from his back, its blade glinting in the sunlight. 'Do you still think you have what it takes to be the First Cantor of the Greatcoats, Falcio?'

I drew my own rapier. Kest put a hand on my shoulder. 'Falcio, don't, it's a—'

'A trick?' I looked back at him and smiled just before setting out to meet the Magdan in the snow. 'Of course it's a trick, Kest. It's always been a trick.'

I took my time drawing a duelling circle in the snow with the end of one of my scabbards. The Magdan watched, amused by my efforts. 'So formal, Falcio?'

'Wouldn't want you claiming the court was rigged once I've kicked your arse,' I replied. The truth was, I was hoping some of the other Greatcoats would protest, but they didn't. I glanced at them as I trudged around the space. I'd known almost all of them, but I'd been genuinely close to a few and they didn't look particularly happy. Quillata looked the most uncomfortable; I remember telling her that I'd told the King that if I ever got killed, she should be his next choice for First Cantor. Yet even she kept silent, which meant they had all known this was coming. The Magdan had told them ahead of time and made them agree not to interfere. *Because you are a predictable idiot sometimes, Falcio val Mond.*

'I'm starting to wonder if perhaps you're just playing for time,' the Magdan said.

He was right, but I wasn't just vainly hoping for a last-minute protest from my fellow Greatcoats; I needed to get used to moving in snow. I've always relied a great deal on my footwork when fencing, and falling flat on my back in the middle of the fight wouldn't do. 'Almost done,' I said. 'Have you chosen your second?'

'I hardly think we need to—'

'Just do it,' I said.

He glanced around the other Greatcoats, almost as if he was going to pick someone at random. He wasn't, though; this sort of thing mattered, which is why I'd forced the issue.

'Quillata,' he said.

She was a natural choice: strong, fast, and utterly incapable of giving up a fight when it came to it. Most importantly for the Magdan, it would prove to me whose side she was on.

'Pick someone else,' she said.

I smiled. So while they might be committed to his cause, they weren't necessarily happy with everything he was doing.

Quil must have caught my expression. 'You're an idiot, Falcio. He'll turn the snow red with your blood before this is done.'

'See? I knew you still cared.'

'Fine,' the Magdan said. 'Ran, you're my second.'

Ran was also one of the original twelve, but unlike Quillata, he'd sort of hated me from the start. So the Magdan had gone from the bold choice to the safest one. *He's not completely certain of their loyalties and he can't risk embarrassing himself twice.*

I felt a small surge of hope, if only because I was finally thinking clearly again.

'Choose your own second, Falcio,' the Magdan asked. He sounded considerably less amused.

I was tempted to ask Quil, if only because it would be funny, but I knew she'd refuse. So would anyone else with a lick of sense in them – if any of them were still on my side, agreeing to be my second would just reveal them to the Magdan. So I did what I always do in these situations. I went to Kest.

'Hey,' I said.

'Hey?'

'Are you busy right now?'

'Not especially, why?'

'Well, I was thinking of kicking the Magdan's arse all over this mountain, then challenging the rest of those turncoat bastards one by one until they surrender so, you know, I'm going to need a second.'

'What will you do if you win?'

I glanced over at them. 'Probably take all their coats from them and start a really big bonfire.' I turned back to Kest. 'Unless you think that's a bad idea?'

'It's a terrible idea. So is challenging Morn. Falcio, look at his face. He's absolutely convinced he can win.'

I wiped the snow off my rapier and drew the second one. I don't always fight with both since that's got its disadvantages, but the Magdan had a great big fucking glaive. I'd need all the steel I could get between me and my opponent. I looked back at him. 'He does look rather confident. Why do you suppose that is?'

'I don't know. That's what worries me.'

I smiled as I turned to go. 'How bad can it be? I once beat you, remember?'

Kest didn't have a reply for that one, but as I entered the circle, the Magdan said, 'You know the one question every Greatcoat used to ask themselves, Falcio?'

'"How did I ever get tricked into accepting this horrible job?"'

A few of them laughed at that.

'No,' he said, bringing his glaive up into a high guard, 'we all used to wonder how in the world you could possibly have beaten Kest.'

I brought my own blades up into a staggered guard, one blade high, the other low. I started to say, 'You know, it's kind of a funny st—' just as someone else shouted, 'Begin!'

CHAPTER THIRTY-ONE

THE DUELLIST'S DECEPTION

'Begin!' the King shouted.

He always yelled far more loudly than was appropriate in these situations. Sure, he was a brilliant and visionary monarch who'd read more books than anyone alive and could speak any number of languages, but as a referee in a fencing match, he was a rank amateur.

Kest winced as he brought his sword into a high side guard, the blade held horizontal at the height of his right shoulder. 'I really wish he wouldn't do that.'

'He just gets excited,' I said. Just before the last word came out of my mouth I lunged, my right rapier aiming at his chest. Just as he went to parry it, I thrust my left one at his thigh.

Damn, he's fast, I thought as I watched my left-hand rapier go spinning through the air and out of the duelling circle. 'Did you want to go and get it?' he asked politely.

'No, I'll stick with the one,' I said, delivering a whip-cut towards his right cheek that was a feint so that I could actually flip the point over his head to go for the left. That didn't work either, of course.

'You don't seem to be taking this very seriously,' Kest observed, delivering a rapid series of fluid cuts that flowed in and out of each other, forcing me to back up almost to the edge of the circle.

I could already hear coins changing hands as close on a hundred other Greatcoats watching began paying off their bets. I didn't take this early prediction of my demise personally – frankly, I was surprised anyone had bet on me in the first place.

Kest was wrong, though: I *was* taking this fight seriously. The moment the King had announced he was going to hold a competition to decide who would be the First Cantor, I knew it had to be me. Don't ask me why – I'm not normally particularly competitive, let alone all that confident in my abilities, especially compared to the other Greatcoats. More importantly, I knew better than anyone that there wasn't a person alive who could beat Kest in a fight.

The rest of the Greatcoats knew it, too. So did the King.

So he'd called this competition, and I had to win.

You see, Tristia's never been short of powerful men armed with deadly weapons. We've never had a problem determining who's got the biggest army or who's most willing to unleash it on their neighbour. But how can you expect laws to be followed in a country where the strongest man always wins? If a legal dispute can come down to a single fight – and it almost *always* comes down to a fight – then what kind of justice could we ever hope to achieve?

That was why King Paelis had decreed this idiotic contest to determine the First Cantor. The question wasn't who was the best fighter; it was who could win *regardless* of whether they were the best or not. Some day, in one lousy Duchy or another, we were going to find ourselves outmatched. On that day, would we be forced to concede and let the laws fall by the wayside? Or would we find a way to win? It was a fundamental test of whether the very idea of the Greatcoats made any sense. How do you bring the rule of law back to a country where the most fundamental equation of justice amounts to the fact that even those who are right will always be overwhelmed by those of greater might?

You have to change the equation.

I knew before I walked into the duelling circle that there was no way in all hells I could hope to beat Kest today.

That's why I'd beaten him yesterday.

'Again,' I grunted, sweat pouring down my face and burning my eyes as I stumbled back to my side of the duelling circle. We had nine of them in the old training hall, each one an exact replica of the different duelling courts in the nine Duchies, so we'd be prepared for the varying sizes and shapes.

Kest had a disapproving look on his face. 'Falcio, I hardly see the point in—'

'Again. Unless you're too scared I'll score a lucky cut on that pretty face of yours. You'll look awfully silly walking into the duelling court tomorrow covered in bandages.'

He stared at me and I knew – I just *knew* – he was trying to figure out if perhaps I was losing my mind. 'Falcio, by my count I've beaten you twelve matches in a row. In the last five you haven't scored a single hit. You've got two cuts on your left arm and one on your right, you're limping on your left leg and you've nearly run into my blade three times now.'

I wiped some of the sweat away from my brow with my shirt-sleeve. It came away bloody. Evidently Kest had been too polite to mention that one. 'Well, you haven't impaled me yet, so I must be doing something right.'

'You haven't done *anything* right! Every time – *every* time! – I've had to hold myself back to keep from stabbing you through your stomach. You need to pay more attention to—'

'Again,' I said.

'Falcio, how is any of this going to help you in the competition tomorrow? You'll be so tired you—'

'Again.'

He hesitated, but Kest's known me for a long time and he could tell I wasn't going to back down. We began our thirteenth match and I changed up my style, using a set of swirling forms of more use to a cutting weapon than a rapier, which is most suited to thrusting.

'That's a Shan style of fencing, isn't it?' Kest asked.

I didn't respond; he already knew the answer and I was short of breath.

I'd never visited the Shan people, mostly because there was a small ocean between us and them and I'd never left my country before, but I'd often wondered if their culture matched their fencing style. There are as many ways of Shan fencing as there are Tristian, but what's interesting is that they don't parry; they don't try to stop an attack. Instead, the Shan use either a complex, dance-like series of postures and steps to avoid the blade, or they push into the attack. In theory, it's simple enough, in effect boiling down to *always thrust on an angle that forces your opponent's attack out of line*. It's a logical enough approach, since there's no virtue in wasting time with a parry-riposte when the counter-attack both deflects and strikes at the same time.

In theory.

As Kest came in for a cut to my left shoulder, I brought my left-hand rapier up high and caught his blade in the rapier's wide quillons as I rotated my hand clockwise – yes, it forced me to partially turn my back to him, but it did let me thrust before he could withdraw his own weapon. For most opponents, that would have been enough – unfortunately, Kest isn't most opponents, and of course he's an absolute master at hand-parries. Even without gloves on, he slapped my blade with his right hand, sending it out of line as he swiftly pulled his own back. I spun around quickly, but not fast enough to stop him from very nearly driving his war sword straight into my guts.

'Saint Birgid-who-weeps-rivers, Falcio, you nearly ran into my blade again,' he said.

'Guess we'll call it your point then.' I brought my rapiers back into guard. 'Again.'

'Thirteen matches, and each time you've tried a different style of fencing. What are you up to, Falcio?'

I smiled, which was a mistake because I was huffing and puffing so hard that spit came out the sides of my mouth. 'Can't you guess?'

His eyes narrowed. 'If you were any other opponent I'd assume you were trying to find a style that I'd have difficulty countering.'

'Sounds like a smart enough strategy.'

'Except you know perfectly well that there *are* none that would achieve that objective.'

'Must be something else then. Ready to begin again?'

'A moment,' he said, stepping back as if he needed a wider view of me.

Watching Kest try to figure something out is oddly mesmerising. You don't normally see someone look at the world with such perfect focus that he doesn't bother to hide his own thoughts – you can practically see them drift across his forehead like clouds. I especially enjoy watching Kest when I'm absolutely certain he won't figure it out, because Kest is congenitally incapable of believing he can't come up with the right answer.

'I believe I have it,' he said.

'Do you mind if we talk and fight at the same time?' I asked.

'As you wish.' He came into guard. 'Since you know there's no one style with which you can beat me, it's possible that the reason for all these bouts is you're trying to identify a set of moves and attacks I'm less skilled at defending against, and thus construct a sort of mélange with which to defeat me tomorrow.'

I delivered what I thought was a lovely triple-lunge, shifting targets with each one, my steps short, both to keep me from extending myself too far and to trick him into backing up more than he should. It's a style they use in the desert whilst fighting on sand, which has too much give to allow you to do long lunges.

Kest had no trouble dealing with my magnificent triple-lunge, of course.

'This won't work either, Falcio.'

'No?'

He batted my blade aside and pulled the same manoeuvre on me. Even though I absolutely knew it was coming, I still didn't manage to evade him, and he struck me three times, his touches so light he wouldn't have dented the skin of an overripe strawberry.

'No,' Kest said, 'Falcio, this isn't arrogance on my part; I'm just telling you there's no—'

I whipped my blade in a wide arc, going for a circular cut at his temple, and just as he brought up his blade to parry, I dived forward, rolling to his right and coming up on his unguarded flank. I began a thrust that should have hit him, but he batted it away with the back of his hand even as his own sword came right at my belly, too fast for me to parry and almost too fast for him to stop in time.

'Damn it, Falcio! You're going to get yourself killed tomorrow—'

I waved him off. 'I'll be fine. I can't very well be the First Cantor if I'm dead, can I? So I'll just have to win.'

He stepped back and stared at me again. 'You aren't trying to find one style and you're not trying to create a new one.'

'Really? Then what am I going to all this trouble for?'

He smiled. There was some admiration there. 'You're using all these different forms to see if you can triangulate a vulnerability that wouldn't show up if you used just one style. That's very clever.'

'Well, I don't know what triangulation is, but I'll accept the compliment.'

This time, I didn't ask if he was ready; I just went at him, using all the styles we'd used, but putting pressure on his defences on the same side and at the exact height where he tended to be weakest with his parries. For a brief instant, I nearly had him – but he got out of the way. I wasn't letting him – or me – off that easily, though, so

I did a grand jeté (basically a big leap that looks rather poncy) and came over the top of his blade. He countered, and yet again beat my blade aside as he brought his own into line. Unfortunately for both of us, I'd been coming at him too fast for him to pull back in time.

'Saints, Falcio!'

I looked down at the blood starting to trail from my belly down the line of his blade. 'Just a scratch,' I said – well, *moaned.*

'You bloody fool!' he said, carefully withdrawing the half-inch of steel from my side. 'If I'd been a fraction of a second slower or you faster, you'd have impaled yourself!'

'Sorry to inconvenience you,' I said, grabbing for a clean cloth and pressing it to my side. 'I'm afraid that will have to be all for today.'

'Falcio, you can't compete tomorrow, not like this. You're exhausted and wounded.'

'A few stitches and I'll be fine by morning.' I tried to sound insouciant, and before he could argue, I turned and headed out of the hall.

He shouted at me, 'If it comes down to you and me, Falcio, and you know it will, presuming you don't die of infection overnight, I'm going to beat you. I didn't set the rules, but if the King believes the finest swordsman should be the First Cantor then that's exactly what I'm going to be!'

It wasn't like Kest to yell and I felt bad for upsetting him. Still . . .

I paused at the door and turned back for a moment. 'You're going to lose tomorrow, Kest. You may well be the greatest swordsman in the entire country, but you're going to lose and you'll never even know how I did it.'

CHAPTER THIRTY-TWO

VICTORY & DEFEAT

You would think from the number of people who have asked me over the years how I could possibly have beaten Kest in a duel that I must be blind in both eyes and perpetually drunk. It's not that they think I'm incompetent – after all, you don't survive as many swordfights as I have without developing something of a reputation as a fencer. It's just that everyone is convinced that Kest is better than I am.

That part is undoubtedly true.

The thing is, I don't rely on skill alone in a fight – I never have. A duellist who spends his life trying to be better than all his opponents either turns out to be a once-in-a-generation swordsman like Kest or, more likely, ends up dead by the age of twenty-five. I'm somewhat older than that, and I've survived because I never try to be better than my opponent. I find a way to make them defeat themselves.

When you're fighting a Knight, for example, you use their armour against them. Some people think this means you should make them move around a lot to tire them out, but that's a mistake – your average Knight spends hours *every single day* training in full armour. If they can fight for an entire day on a battlefield, they can easily outlast you in a duel. No, with Knights what you want to do is get them turning around as much as possible, constantly shifting direction: every time they have to readjust their stance, they get a little more off-balance and their muscles get a little more tense. If you can do this without them being aware, they'll get so stiff it's as if they'd tied themselves up in knots. Then it's just a matter of going for one of the gaps close to the knees. Every armoured Knight's biggest nightmare is falling onto their backs and not being able to get up in time.

With a city guardsman, you use their (perfectly reasonable) fear of someone coming up from behind – a not uncommon occurrence in the streets and alleyways they patrol. With a Dashini, you have to turn their own mind-games against them.

With Kest? Well, with Kest you run into a problem, because he doesn't have a single weakness as a fighter. His mind is always focused, his movements always swift and sure. He doesn't make mistakes. In the middle of a duel he thinks twice as fast as you do, he can swing a heavy war sword almost as fast as I can thrust with a rapier, and he's trained himself to learn new techniques so quickly that he need practise a new move only a few times to get it down perfectly, and then to use it without thinking about it.

And *that's* how you beat Kest.

'You really don't seem to be taking this very seriously,' he said, sliding the blade of his war sword along my rapier's and suddenly circling his point underneath, only to flip it up an instant later. My own point was driven up high and out of line, opening me up for a thrust to my belly that was so fast and light I didn't even feel it before I heard the King shout, 'Fourth touch to Kest!'

'Nicely done,' I grunted. He hadn't actually cut into me, but the pain from yesterday's wound was intense. A few seconds later, spots of red started to seep through the bandage.

'Yield, Falcio,' Kest advised.

'Here's a thought: how about you yield instead?'

He shook his head. 'If you're hoping I'll concede just to avoid hurting you, then you've miscalculated. The next Lord's champion we face in trial by combat isn't going take pity on you, and neither can I.'

I went to grab my other fallen rapier, took up a double high guard and smiled through the pain. 'I haven't miscalculated at all.'

'One more touch and the match is over,' the King said, winking at me.

For a moment I wondered if he had discerned my plan, then I dismissed that idea. King Paelis was clever, but even he couldn't possibly have worked it out.

'I'll try to make it quick,' Kest said, noting that more blood was seeping through my bandages.

We were at four to one in the match (I'd tripped, which was how I'd ended up with my single point). All Kest needed to win was one touch, anywhere on the body – hells, if he tapped my arm with the blade of his sword, I'd lose. For me to win, I'd either need four points in a row – an impossible task, given how tired I was – or to score what's called a 'master's stroke'. I don't know why it's called a 'stroke' when it's actually a thrust. To be First Cantor, I'd have to place my point perfectly at his throat, forcing him to concede. The odds of anyone doing that to Kest? Only one Greatcoat had wagered their coin today on *that* bet.

'*Vata!*' the King shouted enthusiastically.

'Vata' is archaic Tristian for 'I'm a pompous arse of a monarch and don't want to just say "go" like a normal referee'.

I had both my rapiers whirling in a swift figure-of-eight pattern before the King had even finished uttering the second syllable. I knew Kest would want to end this quickly and I couldn't take the risk of trying to parry an attack that I probably wouldn't even see coming. In case you're ever in this situation, you should know that *real* fencers will mock you unmercifully for spinning your blades 'like a child with a skipping rope' – but ignore the insults; sometimes this is the only way to delay your opponent's attack. No matter how fast they are, they still need to get into the right position to get past your defence.

There's a problem, though, because you can't really attack like that, and the moment you try, your opponent will see it coming. That's why I didn't thrust or cut but instead threw my left rapier at him. Technically, if it hit, I could count it as a point, but that wouldn't do me much good since he'd counter-strike me within the measure and his point would count too. So as he beat aside my tossed sword, I dropped down low and swung my right rapier in a wide arc at his ankles. Kest leaped neatly over it, bringing his own sword up high in preparation for a downward cut, but instead of parrying, I came in close and punched him in the stomach with my left fist. His blade overshot, though I got a pommel in the back for my troubles. As he stepped back to regain the distance, I repeated a move from yesterday, diving into a shoulder roll on the ground to come up on his right flank, rising up so fast my head was swimming as I readied my rapier to cut at his unprotected side. I'd done it faster this time than ever before.

Not fast enough, of course.

Kest, annoyed that I'd punched him in the middle of a match, already had his war sword in line. His reflexes took over and he began his thrust even before he noticed that the buttons of my greatcoat had come undone and he was about to stab me through the belly from far too close. I think even he surprised himself when he managed to stop the thrust in time to not kill me. '*Saints, Falcio!* That stupid move of yours doesn't work!'

I smiled at him. Kest rarely gets angry, and a man has to be pretty pissed off to not notice the tip of a rapier sitting a hair's breadth from the ball of his throat.

'Touché dei Maestre!' the King shouted. That's the pretentious way of saying I'd landed the master's stroke.

Kest was now looking down at the blade of my rapier, eyes wide with disbelief. 'How did you—?'

'The problem with you, Kest,' I said, carefully pulling my weapon back and dropping it on the floor so that I could devote both my hands into pressing against the now sopping wet bandage around my belly, 'is that you're almost as damned fast as you think you are.'

That part was a lie. Kest was every bit as fast as he believed. What he hadn't yet figured out was that yesterday I hadn't been trying different styles on him, nor figuring out which moves he was slower at defending, nor even trying to discern some broader weakness in his own style. I had been *training him*! I had spent the whole day schooling his reflexes – those same reflexes that let him master new moves so quickly – to stop short when he was about to thrust at my belly.

There was no way in any hell I would be able to defeat Kest on the day of the competition. So I'd defeated him the day before.

The King came into the circle, separating us. There was a good deal of cheering and yelling as my fellow Greatcoats tried to settle up bets or, more likely, dispute them (we may be judges, but that doesn't mean we don't try to get out of paying our wagers just like everyone else).

'You know,' Paelis said, quietly enough that no one else would hear us over the racket, 'if Kest weren't, in fact, the best damned swordsman in the *entire* country, he would have ended up stabbing you right through the stomach, and you'd have wound up dead and bleeding all over my nice new duelling court.'

I smiled. 'Then I suppose it's a very good thing that he *is* the best swordsman in the country, your Majesty.'

The King chuckled. 'He's going to be pretty pissed off when he figures out how you won.'

'He'll never figure it out,' I said. 'His mind doesn't work that way. He'll assume I got my point at his throat first – that it was some weakness in his style or some superior timing on my part. He'll spend the rest of his life imagining different ways I could have won before he ever figures out that he actually had me first but his own reflexes stopped him.'

The King locked eyes with me. 'You beat him using a strategy that will only ever work on him. What happens when you're in the ring with the next swordsman who's better than you?'

I shrugged. 'I'll figure out a different way to beat that guy.'

'So damned cocky, aren't you? I have half a mind to void the bout. What do you think about that?'

I grinned. 'To be honest, your Majesty, I've always suspected you had only half a mind. It speaks highly of you that you can admit to it.'

He didn't laugh at the joke, but he did grab my hand and raise it high overhead. 'Ladies and gentlemen, duellists and magistrates one and all, I give you Falcio val Mond, an arrogant bastard and the First Cantor of the Greatcoats!'

While the other Greatcoats shouted my name – and Kest loudest of all – the King whispered to me, 'Be careful, Falcio. The higher you rise, the greater the fall.'

I wasn't thinking about King Paelis' words as I circled the Magdan in the snow. I was thinking about the cold; it was a danger, but once we got moving I'd warm up quickly enough. I was also keeping track of the snow, which wasn't especially deep, but would still be enough to throw me off-balance if I wasn't careful. Finally, I was paying close attention to the Magdan himself.

In the old days, Morn had been a skilled fighter, if a little reckless and rough around the edges, but he was better now. Much better. He'd long since mastered the southern styles of pole-arm fighting, and he'd clearly been training in the Avarean way, which was vastly more elegant. Within a few exchanges I knew him to be twice the duellist he'd been before.

So was he better than me? He was probably a little faster, and quite a bit stronger – but my technique was still better, and more important than technique, my *style* was more effective. Whatever I might have lost by the years of rough living and being knocked around, beaten up, tortured and poisoned with alarming regularity, I'd made up for in experience and tactics.

The two of us were almost perfectly evenly matched, even factoring in the cold and the snow, which he was used to and I wasn't.

Through blow after blow, attack, counter-attack, thrust, cut and parry, our eyes kept meeting, over and over, and that's how I knew that the Magdan was fully aware of our relative strengths. I also began to realise that none of that mattered; there was no way he could beat me that day. That's why he'd beaten me the day before.

'Be careful, Falcio,' the King had said that day, unaware how prophetic his words were. 'The higher you rise, the greater the fall.'

The only reason I'd remembered the King's warning was because I was starting to pass out, and I tend to get nostalgic when I'm about to fall unconscious. You see, the problem wasn't the Magdan's skill or strength, nor the cold or the snow.

It was the fucking altitude.

CHAPTER THIRTY-THREE

THE UNFAIR DUEL

'It's nasty, isn't it?' Morn – the Magdan – asked, bringing his glaive back into a high guard, ready to attack with a diagonal slash that would be challenging to avoid while I was struggling just to stay on my feet. 'The dizziness, the sudden fatigue . . .'

As I'd expected, his blade came crashing down towards my right shoulder and I tried to get my sword up deflect it, but I was moving too slowly and had to settle for falling back out of the way, losing my balance in the process. Trying to get as much distance between us as possible made me stumble, and I landed painfully on my back. 'You forgot . . . the nausea,' I panted, which was probably a bad idea. My pulse was far too fast and I was breathing too quickly.

'Oh, Saint Zaghev-who-sings-for-tears,' he swore, laughing, 'the *nausea*. I did, I almost forgot about that. First time I came to this place I couldn't keep my food down for a week.' He began walking towards me, the blade of his glaive resting lightly on his shoulder. 'The good news is that it does pass, eventually. You become acclimatised to the mountains.' He took in a deep breath, then puffed it out all at once. 'Actually, I've come to enjoy it up here.'

He was almost within striking distance of me. *Get up*, I told myself. The problem wasn't just that I was having trouble thinking straight, but that I knew he wasn't planning to kill me. No Greatcoat had ever killed another. However confident the Magdan was in his support from the others, he wouldn't risk going too far – so my body apparently considered this an excellent reason to lie down for a nap.

With a huge effort, I forced myself back to my feet and held my rapier at full extension. The Magdan took a swipe at it with his glaive, but I'd been expecting that and brought my tip under in a semi-circular disengage, allowing the bladed end of his weapon to pass mine by while I kept my point on him. Foolish hopefulness led me to put everything into my lunge, hoping I might get lucky.

I'm not sure why, after all these years, I still kid myself that luck will suddenly come to me.

My lunge was not just slow, but clumsy. The Magdan barely bothered to sidestep out of the way. Then he laughed as I lost my balance and fell flat on my face.

'You could stay down, you know,' he said, standing over me. Struggling to lift my head, I snorted snow out of my nose. 'Just lie there. It's cold at first, but soon you'll feel a wonderful warmth spread across your limbs.' His voice sounded far away, muffled. 'There are those who say that drowning is the most peaceful way to pass out of this world but they have never tried falling asleep in the snow.'

'I think once you're dead it's hard to compare it to something else,' I said. Only I hadn't said it; I'd *thought about* saying it – but I'd forgotten to make my mouth move. I'd fallen unconscious for a brief second.

Get up, you idiot.

I kept expecting King Paelis to appear before me with some acerbic remark about getting my lazy arse off the ground, or my dead wife Aline to remind me that it was time to beat up the bad man, but neither of them showed up.

That was somehow fitting: *all* my illusions were being shattered now.

Suddenly I rose up, almost effortlessly – but no, it was *entirely* effortlessly, because the Magdan had grabbed me by the collar and hauled me to my feet. 'Wake up now, Falcio. Let's do this properly, shall we?'

He gave me a push and I stumbled around, trying to find my balance like a drunk whose eyes weren't focusing in the harsh light of morning. I got myself into a half-decent forward guard, both rapiers extended, although for some reason, I couldn't see the blades. That was because my hands were empty. I'd dropped my weapons somewhere in the snow.

'You're really not doing well, are you, First Cantor?' the Magdan said.

'Enough,' Kest said. 'There's no fair match to be had here.'

'*Fair?*' the Magdan asked. 'Since when is the law fair?'

I knelt down to pick up my rapiers; for once I'd leave the philosophical debate to the others. My hands tried to grasp the hilts, but for some reason I kept missing them. *Your vision is failing you*, some more astute part of my mind informed me.

'For Saints' sake,' Brasti cried out, 'he can barely stand!'

'Really?' the Magdan asked. He came into view as he walked around me, apparently inspecting me. 'He's standing just fine, as far as I can see.'

I gave up on the rapiers and took a swing at him. I swear I saw my fist go right through his face as if he were nothing more than an apparition.

'See?' he asked. 'He's just getting his second wind.'

Suddenly he swung the bladed end of his glaive right at my stomach, turning it at the last minute so he hit me with the flat. My stomach muscles were too slow to clench, so he knocked all the air out of me, leaving me gasping for breath. I sounded like an old man wheezing in his last moments of life.

'Whoops – I suppose I should have said his third wind.'

'Enough, damn you!' Kest shouted.

The Magdan leaned forward to peer at me. 'What do you say, Falcio? Is it enough?'

I started to say something very clever, but he struck out with his free hand, catching me in the throat – reflexively, I tried to catch my breath, but I failed: my throat wouldn't open.

The Magdan stood back and shrugged. 'I can't seem to get a straight answer out of him.'

For several harrowing seconds I stood there choking, until finally something unclenched and I sucked in a desperate gasp of air.

I heard the sound of a bow being bent. 'Touch him again and it'll be the last thing you do,' Brasti said.

Even dazed as I was, I saw two clear rows of white teeth as the Magdan smiled. 'Interfering in a lawful duel, Brasti? Is there truly nothing sacred to the three of you any more?'

All of a sudden, the other Greatcoats had surrounded the Magdan and me. The duelling circle looked as if it were made up entirely of leather-clad columns. I'm pretty sure they had their weapons out, so it was clear that if Brasti or Kest tried to interfere with what was happening, the pair of them would go down as well.

'How about this?' the Magdan began. 'As long as Falcio remains standing, the match continues. If he falls, we'll call it a day.'

Excellent suggestion, I thought, letting myself start to collapse – but without warning, the blade of his glaive was inches from my neck and I was about to fall right onto it. I forced myself back upright.

'See? There's still some fight left in him,' the Magdan said. Then he smacked me across the face with the back of his fist.

I spun around, too fast to keep my balance, but as I started to go backwards, he flipped his weapon around and smashed the shaft into the small of my back. The force stopped my descent, pitching me back forward, and I felt the cold blade at the back of my neck, catching the inside of my collar and pulling me back again, choking me, but keeping me upright.

'What a remarkable dancer you are, Falcio,' the Magdan said. 'How long can you keep this up, I wonder?'

He kept striking me, first on one side, then as I started falling, on the other, moving me as easily as if I were a puppet.

'Stop it, damn you!' Kest screamed.

I realised I was dribbling vomit from my mouth – I think that was the result of the butt-end of his glaive driving into my stomach. Then my back seized up as he slammed the shaft across my spine, so hard that for a moment I couldn't feel my legs at all. That was a bit of a relief, but he kept hitting me, over and over, and the pain quickly came sweeping back in as he kept me upright like a child's spinning top.

'*Please*,' Kest begged.

'"Please"?' The beating paused for a moment, and I felt the Magdan's hand on my chest, holding me upright. 'Is that what you say to the Dukes when they take more and more power for themselves? "*Please, sir, may we have just a little bit for us?*" Or do you suppose that's what the common folk say as they slowly watch their children starve to death? "*Please, all you Gods and Saints, give us a little food today.*" Or maybe what they really plead for is a quick death?

'Honestly, what good has all this pleading ever done for Tristia? Day after day, year after year, the country loses more and more of itself. It's drying up like fruit left too long in the sun.' He brought his hand up to my throat. 'Is *this* how you bring justice back to Tristia, Falcio? By *begging* for it?'

For the first time I saw his confident, urbane mask slip, revealing nothing but the deep-down anger I recognised all too well: a red-burning rage that could melt even the ice of this frozen hell. After all, I'd found it many times in my own heart.

'*This* is what you have done for your country, First Cantor.' He spat in my face.

To Kest he said, 'What is it you would plead for, Kest Murrowson?'

'For mercy,' he replied.

The Magdan held me up, his stare somehow commanding my own

eyes to focus upon him and his superiority. I could feel the heat coming off him, warming me as if he were a God come to grant clemency upon the icy damned.

'Very well. I think we're all sick and truly tired of holding you up anyway.'

He let go and walked away from me, the snow crunching beneath the soles of his boots. After a few steps, he stopped; he must have realised he hadn't heard me fall.

Very slowly, very carefully, so as not to lose my balance, I turned to face him again. My rapiers were on the ground at my feet but they might as well have been a thousand miles away. I raised my fists in front of me, trying to remember not to squeeze too hard, for fear of hurting my hands on what they held in each palm.

It took almost everything I had to remain on my feet, and even more to cough out my next words. 'We're not done yet.'

'Falcio, no!' Brasti shouted, and Kest caught my gaze and shook his head – he understood what I was doing and wanted me to know it wasn't worth it. He was probably right.

The Magdan smiled and let his glaive fall to the ground. He started back towards me, his own fists closing so tight I could almost imagine I was watching the blood fleeing his fingers. 'I could not adore you more right now were you the Goddess of Love, Falcio.'

The first blow struck my ear and a ringing filled my head. It didn't dissipate. The second caught me just below my right eye, the blood and swelling blinding me. By then I was desperately grabbing onto his coat to keep me upright. The third blow caught my lower lip, leaving me gagging on the blood that was pouring down my throat. The cold was completely overtaking me now, destroying my sense of touch. The world retreated further and further away, but somehow I stayed on my feet as the Magdan beat me senseless.

Brasti was crying, I knew – I couldn't see it or hear it, and yet I felt it just as truly as I did Kest's heart breaking when I finally held up my now empty hands and dropped to my knees in the snow.

'Enough,' Kest said, pleading, to the others. 'He's given up. It's enough.'

'One last thing,' the Magdan said, coming up behind me. He tore the coat off my back and dumped it in the snow, then stood over it – I think he was about to piss on it, until he realised what poor taste that would be.

'Burn it,' he ordered. *Okay, so being tasteful wasn't the issue.*

I smiled up at him – or at least, I think I did. 'You can have it. I'm done with it.'

I let myself fall back in the snow for a moment, but someone came and lifted me back up. I didn't care. I was tired, and I'd done what I'd come to do. Neither Kest nor Brasti looked as if they understood why it had taken me so long to fall, but if I'd been able to speak, I would have told them that I lost this fight yesterday, when I'd allowed myself to be tricked into coming up into these mountains, to a place my body was not adapted for, where I had no hope of winning.

What I had to do now was win *tomorrow's* fight.

CHAPTER THIRTY-FOUR

THE UNEXPECTED CELLMATE

I drifted in and out of consciousness for a while after that. I was still trying to keep my one good eye open for more than a few seconds when two Avarean warriors grabbed me by the shoulders and dragged me through the compound. Looked like none of my fellow Greatcoats had wanted the job.

'Your people have an unusual way of escorting prisoners,' Kest said, looking back at the guard behind them; he was resting the end of his sword against Kest's right shoulder as they walked; Brasti's guard had positioned his blade the same way.

'An Avarean technique; it's extremely effective,' the Magdan said chattily. 'No matter how much you might try to hide your intentions, the muscles in your shoulders will tense before you make a run for it – the guards will see that, and it's child's play to pull the sword back a few inches and stab you before you move.'

Kest stared straight ahead, but I knew how his mind worked. They'd taken his weapons, and Brasti's too, and their coats, so there weren't exactly a lot of options for resistance. 'And yet, if the prisoner were to take a more unorthodox action—?' Kest quickly lifted his hand to grab the sword while taking a small step backwards; it should have prevented the guard from withdrawing the blade, but the warrior was too quick for him.

For an instant I feared Kest was about to be stabbed through the back, but the guard just struck him lightly on the top of his head with the flat of the blade before resting it once again on Kest's shoulder.

The other guards laughed.

'Forgive their manners,' the Magdan said, 'but this is a game Avareans play as children.'

Kest gave a nod. 'So, an unconventional means of control to everyone but their own people. Surprisingly effective.'

'No doubt if you had more practise, you'd be able to evade the sword,' the Magdan said, giving Kest a friendly slap on the back.

Brasti snorted. 'Isn't that sweet? We're all becoming fast friends again.'

We passed twenty or thirty cannons lined up down the centre of the main hall of the fort, each one with its accompanying small cart on heavy wheels. They were all filled with leaded balls and small barrels, which I assumed must contain pistol powder.

'What do you plan to do with us?' I asked. My throat was barely able to conjure more than a hoarse whisper. I wasn't expecting an honest answer, of course, but sometimes the choice of lie can be instructive.

The Magdan stopped and turned to face us. For a moment I saw the old Morn there, though I didn't like it any more than the new one. 'You'll be our guests for a long time, I'm afraid: you'll watch as we do the things the Greatcoats should have done years ago, and when it's all over and you've seen what we've accomplished, I'll set you free.'

'That's decent of you,' I said.

It would be, if it were true, only I was fairly sure it was nonsense intended only to reassure the other Greatcoats.

'I apologise in advance for the accommodations,' he said as we reached a long hallway barred with a heavy iron gate. I didn't need to examine it to know it would be easier to cut through the wooden frame than to attempt to break through the gate itself. Inside were ten cells, each sealed with more bars.

All right. Time to get on with it, I thought, and prayed to no one in particular that I could summon the strength for what had to happen next.

I slumped, not even bothering to attempt to hold myself up – the two warriors holding onto me were doing a good enough job of that – and the instant I felt their guard dropping just a fraction, I used their shoulders to help me propel myself at the Magdan. I got one half-decent blow, tearing at his coat and screaming, 'You don't deserve to wear this, you bastard!' before he grabbed me by the neck. Despite my injured throat, I'd shrieked so loudly I'd actually made him wince.

I kept pawing at him even as he slammed me back against the wall. 'Enough,' he said. 'You're testing my patience, Falcio.'

I spat in his face – it seemed only fair, after all he'd done to me – but more importantly, it made him throw me to the floor by the bars. I lay there for a bit, showing them all that I was finally spent – and because I was, in fact, completely spent. I had no idea how I'd managed that last effort. Now I just wanted to sleep for a year.

'Saints, his head is bleeding,' Brasti cried. '*You've killed him—!*'

'Stop being so damned melodramatic, Brasti,' the Magdan said. He kicked me with the toe of his boot. 'I'm disappointed in you, Falcio. All those stories people tell about you back home? The only thing you appear to be any good at is getting hurt.'

Despite how horrible I was feeling, I couldn't help but chuckle at that. *You can say that again.*

One of the guards took out a heavy key with four different lengths of teeth on it and used it to open the iron gate.

I kept silent as two men dragged me into the hall of cells.

'Just like being back in Tristia,' Brasti muttered as he entered behind me. 'Who says our two peoples are so different?'

The hall grew darker as we moved away from the gate. There was only a single torch lighting the space at the end.

'I wish it didn't have to be this way,' the Magdan said.

Sure, I thought, *only you pretty much engineered it to all happen just like this.*

I heard the Magdan's sigh carry along the corridor. 'Despite everything you've done, I still have one gift to give you, Falcio.'

'Is it a set of lockpicks?' Brasti asked.

'No,' he replied. 'Something Falcio wants even more.'

Now I could see the two cells at the end weren't empty; each held one prisoner. Both had their wrists bound with thick rope attached to chains above their shoulders, and a noose around each neck was connected to a pulley attached to the ceiling and then out into the hallway, where the ropes were wound around hooks – a handy contraption allowing you to pull on the ropes and choke them without exerting too much effort yourself. One of the prisoners, a young man, was so covered in filth and bruises I doubted his own mother would have recognised him.

The other had also been beaten, although not nearly as badly – but it was by her voice that I recognised her the instant she spoke.

'Hello, my lovely tatter-cloak,' Trin said. 'Did you really come all this way to rescue me?'

The guards didn't even bother to lock us in our cells. They just closed the iron gate behind us with a great *clang* that echoed down the hallway.

'You see, Falcio?' the Magdan said. 'I told you I'd give you everything you ever wanted.'

Trin looked at me, and despite her playful words I saw that she was, for maybe the very first time, truly terrified.

So I suppose it wasn't all bad news.

CHAPTER THIRTY-FIVE

THE FAMILIAR SMILE

You would think that the sight of my worst enemy would have sent my heart pounding and my muscles clenching in anticipation as my mind started wrestling with my orders to bring Trin back to Aramor for trial and my deep-seated desire to kill her the moment I laid eyes on her.

Maybe I did feel all those sensations – but I can't be quite sure, because it was around then that I finally passed out completely.

When I awoke the next day, someone had bandaged me extensively, and from the tingling sensation all over my body, I guessed the Magdan must have graciously allowed Kest a jar of black salve to patch me up. By the time I'd risen unsteadily to my feet, I'd half-convinced myself that I'd only *imagined* seeing Trin inside that little cell.

Nope, I thought, staring into the endless cold of those eyes. *That's definitely her.*

Kest and Brasti joined me and the three of us stood in silence, looking at her. None of us wanted to speak our thoughts aloud – we could see the guards just beyond the gate and it was a safe bet that at least one of them spoke Tristian. After a few moments, Kest helped me into one of the cells midway down the hall. It was almost completely dark inside, but I hoped it was far enough away that the guards couldn't hear us.

'Morn wants us to kill her,' Kest said.

'Well, that works perfectly for us, doesn't it?' Brasti asked. 'Because I'd rather like to get on with killing her myself.'

I peered out into the dimly lit hall. I could see the two ropes, each attached to a hook outside the cell door. I could almost feel the rough texture of the rope in my hands, the way the muscles in my fingers and palms and wrists would tense as I secured my grip. I'd taken a bit of a beating, true, but I was not so shattered that I wouldn't be able to string her up and watch her twist and dance in the air. How much pain had her family brought into my life – into the lives of so many others, so many *innocents*?

I found myself trying to work out what I would say to her just before she died.

'Falcio,' Kest said softly, 'Morn *wants* us to kill her.'

Brasti threw his hands in the air. 'And again I ask: why is that a problem?'

'Why doesn't he do it himself?' Kest asked. 'Why is it so important that *we* do it?'

I thought about the village back in Orison, and the long march. I thought about old Clock and his running commentary about everything political. Those people didn't hate *Trin*; they hated *us*. They'd been well served by Duchess Patriana, and it sounded like they'd supported her daughter's efforts to win the North. 'The Magdan wants the people of Orison and Hervor to support his plans,' I said finally. 'Killing her might create bad blood between him and the people he wants to rule.'

'But if we do it—' Brasti began.

'—then he can lay the blame squarely at our feet.' I thought about it for a moment longer. 'In fact, he can drag us back to Orison and summarily execute us in front of the locals, which will make him a hero in their eyes. I imagine he'd like to be seen as a hero instead of a traitor.'

'I was wondering how long it would take you to figure that out, my love.' Trin was doing an excellent job of burying her fear beneath that sweet, melodic voice of hers, every syllable as clear as if it had come trickling from a silver flute. I staggered out of our cell, grabbed the rope hanging outside hers and gave it as hard a yank as my screaming body could manage. I watched her body stretch up towards the roof and it took every ounce of self-control I had in me to stop from lifting her off the ground by her neck.

'Stop!' a thin voice shouted from the cell next to hers. 'Touch her and I'll kill you, I swear I will!'

The raw innocence and determination in that voice lit a flicker of guilt in my chest, but it was Kest's hand on my arm that brought me back to my senses. 'You can strangle her any time you want,' he said gently. 'Just make sure you do it for your reasons and not Morn's.'

Slowly, reluctantly, I eased my grip on the rope. Kest took it from me and tied it back round the hook.

'Ah, I've missed you Falcio,' Trin said, her voice scraping a little. 'I'm so glad you finally arrived.'

'You sound as if you have been expecting us,' Kest said.

'Well, of course. When that fool Kragven – that's the first Warlord I tried to hire; I assume he's dead now – failed to keep control of his own warband, I knew Morn would want me dead. But how to do it? The Avareans dislike executions; they prefer bloody combat to the death – but little old me? Why, there isn't a man or woman in this whole damned camp who would find *rokhan* in fighting me – and more importantly, there are a great many people from Orison and Hervor here, and they *like* me. If Morn were to have me killed, he'd lose more than half of them. No, he went about killing all the birds clouding his sky with a single stone the *right* way, by revealing my presence here to Valiana. Now that you've given her that preposterous title, *obviously* the puffed-up little girl would send someone to bring me back to Tristia so she could put me on trial before the entire country and show her absolute commitment to justice. And who else would she send but you, my noble, beautiful Falcio. My oft-fated companion: *my hero*.'

I had a hard time resisting the overwhelming urge to grab the rope again and shut her dulcet tones up once and for all.

Trin shook her head at me. 'Don't give me those nasty looks, Falcio. You need to concentrate and find us a way out of here – although that might have been easier had the three of you not been so foolish as to lose your little coats somewhere along the way.'

'We fully plan on escaping,' Kest said. 'I wonder, though, why you would think we would bring you with us.'

'Not just me, silly.' She pointed towards the cell opposite. 'You'll bring my charge and me safely back to Aramor.'

'Why would we do that?' I asked.

'Why do you do anything? Because I have information about Morn that your precious Realm's Protector will want to hear. Because you'll believe it's the right thing to do. But most of all, because of the question you've yet to ask me.'

'Who is this boy you've got with you?' I asked.

'Why don't you go and see? The cell door isn't locked, is it? He doesn't bite.'

I took the torch from the wall and shuffled slowly into the other cell. Her companion was shaking, but he didn't say a word. I checked him first, in case he might have a weapon of some kind – his hands were bound, but there might have been a knife-edge on his boot soles, or some other means of doing me grievous harm . . . but all I saw was a scrawny figure trying hard to pretend he wasn't shivering in fear.

'Who is he?' Kest asked.

'His name is Filian,' Trin replied.

'Your new lover?' Brasti asked from behind me. 'Looks a little rough. You've come down in the world; Duke Perault was a good deal more handsome.'

Brasti was right: beneath the blood and the bruises, the face staring out at me wasn't anything particularly special. Filian was young, perhaps sixteen or seventeen. Though his eyes struck me as full of intelligence, he was a little plain-faced – his nose was sharp, as were his features. He blinked a good deal, and his mouth twitched a little, as if he were embarrassed and maybe trying to say something funny or clever. After a heartbeat his lips settled into an awkward smile, as if he hoped we might be friends.

It was the smile that did it.

Trin gave a tinkling little laugh, as if she'd heard the sudden breaking of my heart. I'm usually the last to figure these things out, but this time I knew I was the first.

To anyone else, Filian would have looked like an ordinary young man – Trin's lover or servant, maybe no one important, just her next victim.

But he must have seen my flicker of recognition, because his gaze settled on me and his expression became a little sad as he said, 'Oh, Falcio, I am so very sorry.'

All the boy said was, 'Oh, Falcio, I am so very sorry.'

The sound of the torch clattering to the floor was followed by the sensation of falling and then a sudden pain in my knees as they struck the hard stone floor. My arms hung useless at my sides.

'They're dead,' I whispered. I hadn't breath enough to speak any louder. 'Patriana told me she'd killed all the others—'

Brasti was shouting behind me, 'What's *wrong* with him?'

I saw the noose pull tight around the boy's neck as Kest took hold of the rope outside the cell. 'If this is magic,' he said, 'I would suggest you stop it now.'

The boy said nothing. He didn't need to.

'Maybe it's not magic,' Brasti said. 'It's probably poison. Falcio's always getting poisoned.'

It was neither of those things. It was the smile.

It's always the smile.

Trin's voice was odd, almost soothing as she said, 'Don't be sad, my dearest Falcio. It was long past time that you met your King.'

CHAPTER THIRTY-SIX

THE CHAROITE

Seven years ago I ruled on a legal dispute involving a portrait of the late King Gregor. The painting's value came principally from the rumour that his wife, Queen Yesa, had been the artist. Despite her terrible taste in husbands, Yesa had been, by all accounts, a lovely woman: bright, kind, and according to those who'd heard her play, an excellent musician.

Saints, she was a terrible painter, though.

True, on his best day Gregor's face displayed all the beauty of a barrel mastiff cross-bred with a tree stump, but this portrait looked like a one-eyed child had dumped his fingerpaints on a canvas and promptly vomited on it.

You would think such an eyesore would be soon forgotten, but in fact a rather brisk trade in forgeries of portraits of Gregor had been building in Domaris of late – no doubt fuelled by nostalgia for the old King now that his son Paelis (and his annoying travelling magistrates) were getting in everyone's way. So it was with some amusement that I had found myself asked to rule on which of two versions of the painting was authentic.

I stopped being quite so amused when I heard the price paid for them.

Any good forger knows to never sell the same work in the same – or even adjoining – territories, so it was by sheer accident that Viscount Pluvier happened to stop by for a visit with his second cousin, the Margrave Boujean, at his newly constructed palace hundreds of miles away from Pluvier's own lands. Civil war threatened to break out when Pluvier found, there on the wall of the map room, a near-perfect copy of his own prized portrait of King Gregor. With neither party trusting the dubious allegiances of their fellow nobles, Pluvier and Boujean transported their paintings to neutral ground and then, for quite possibly the only time in our country's history, two aristocrats actually *asked* for a Greatcoat to rule on which work was authentic.

It may surprise you to learn that I know slightly less about art than I do about surgery or romantic relationships, so staring at the nearly identical portraits did me little good. Solving the case – and here's where I'll get to the point of all this – required ignoring the paintings entirely and instead watching the eyes of *the owners* of the works of art. You see, people rarely buy forgeries unknowingly; the price of such an original is high enough that tracing the provenance is worth any extra expense. So I stood the two men next to their paintings, instructed them to keep their mouths shut and watched and waited, and waited some more.

All men know how to lie, and nobles better than most, but the human face is a canvas upon which our true thoughts are painted, and after enough time, an expert in such matters can always spot the fakes.

In case you're wondering, Pluvier had bought the forgery; he'd hoped that by challenging his cousin he could, as part of the settlement, somehow swap the paintings beforehand, then demand the forgery – which would now turn out to be the Margrave's – be destroyed. I never said it was a good plan.

So what did any of this have to do with a battered and bruised young man chained to a wall in a cell over the border in Avares? Simple: it's how I figured out why my life was about to become vastly more complicated than I'd ever imagined possible.

Like a brilliant forgery, Filian displayed all the characteristics of the original. He had King Paelis' slouch – even with his arms being bound high over his head – and you could see some of the King in his eyes, too, if you knew what to look for. Of course, these could easily be dismissed as common enough traits, just as one could ignore the sharp nose and ever-so-slightly jutting jaw. The subtle twitch of his mouth when he spoke, though? That was so much a part of the man I'd known and loved it was impossible for me to ignore.

It's a trick, I told myself, and I silently repeated the words once, twice, a hundred times until I was almost convinced my eyes were deceiving me. I had to, because if this boy was whom Trin claimed, then *everything* I had fought for was about to come to ruin.

When I was almost positive it was all a deception, I turned to stare at Trin, chained and roped in her cell, and held her gaze for as long as I could stand to. She's a masterful liar, perhaps the finest ever to emerge from a class whose very essence is deceit. But discerning truth from falsehood had once been the most important task of my life, and while I've been fooled any number of times since I put on the greatcoat, I'm very hard to trick when I know *exactly* what I'm looking for. I searched Trin's face for the little things – the subtle tightening around the corners of the mouth, the minuscule tremors in the skin that pass so quickly you'll miss them if you blink. People make sounds when they're deceiving you, even when they aren't speaking: the little grunts and squeaks, the uneven breathing. Kest once read a book that claimed the trained nose could *smell* a person lying. Whilst I didn't have that particular ability, I felt sure the author of that book would have taken a long, deep inhale of Trin's skin and sworn she was telling the truth.

By the time I forced myself to my feet and went to the open door of her cell, I knew I had to stop myself from entering. If I got too close I was afraid I might pull on the rope the Magdan had so kindly left for me and hanged Trin until I felt the last gasp of air leave her body.

'How did you do it?' I asked.

She smiled. 'You should be gratified, Falcio. Wasn't the grand quest King Paelis set for you to find his . . . what did he call them again? His "Charoites"? Well, now you've found one. In fact, you've found the brightest gem of the lot.'

'You're lying,' Brasti said, then to me, 'She's lying, Falcio. This is just another one of her tricks.'

I ignored him. Whether or not I believed Filian was the son of King Paelis or not was no longer relevant. There were only two questions that mattered now: would the Ducal Council support the boy's claim over Aline's, and was I willing to murder him to prevent it?

'Tell me the rest,' I said to Trin.

'The rest?'

'How did it work? How did you—?'

'Ah.' She leaned back against the wall of her cell as far as the rope would allow her. 'My mother divined the King's plan, of course. He was, after all, a very clever man, and he knew that any woman he chose to marry would meet with an accident sooner or later, as would any child she bore. So he . . . how shall we say? He *spread his lineage* across a number of noble households, thanks to a number of especially *patriotic* ladies.'

'And their husbands?' Kest asked.

'Most of the noblewomen involved were recently widowed, so the child could conceivably be the late husband's get, as long as no one looked too closely. As to the rest? Well, I never understood it, but Paelis did always inspire rather excessive loyalty in some of his subjects.'

There was a question burning in the back of my mind – it had been there since the day I'd finally figured out who Aline was. To ask it would be to reveal a weakness to my enemy, but I couldn't hold it back. 'Why didn't he tell the Greatcoats?'

Trin laughed. 'Why didn't he tell *you*, you mean? I asked Mother the same question. At first she thought he *must* have told you – that the lot of you were simply keeping his secret. But after she interrogated you in Rijou, she realised you really *didn't* know, and she quickly worked out why Paelis had kept the Greatcoats in ignorance.'

I reached out for the rope that hung around her slender neck. 'Tell me.'

She didn't sound at all scared; if anything, her expression was pitying. 'It was because of *you*, Falcio. The King couldn't tell you because he was ashamed of what you would think of him. You always wanted him to be so noble, so perfect – and yet here he was, using his position of power to have his way with women for no better purpose than to preserve his own line. Oh, they were willing, I've no doubt, but really, how consensual can it be when it is a King doing the asking?'

This I refused to believe; this part of her story was a lie meant to make me question Paelis, question myself. 'He – and they – did what was necessary to protect the country from your mother.'

'Tell yourself that if it helps,' she said sweetly. 'All of this must be *terribly* hard on you – I promise you, it was difficult for my mother as well. She went to no end of trouble trying to figure out who the eldest child must be.'

'To kill him?' Kest asked.

She shook her head, making the rope sway. 'No, to save his life. My mother wasn't the only noble trying to discover the King's plan. A number of the Dukes were also working on ferreting out these secret heirs.'

'Which Dukes?' I asked.

'Issault of Aramor certainly suspected,' Trin replied, 'although he was too fat and lazy to do anything about it. Duchess Ossia of Baern. My father, of course.'

Trin must have seen something in my expression. 'Jillard would have killed them all, Falcio: every single one.'

'Duchess Patriana beat him to it,' Kest said.

'Oh no, Mother was far cleverer than that. She wanted to find them and force Paelis to acknowledge them publicly, to reveal his fickle, feckless nature, and in so doing, she intended to extract certain promises from him over Ducal rights.'

'Such as rolling back the King's Laws?' I asked. 'Eliminating the Greatcoats entirely?'

'Oh, we're not against *all* laws; I'm sure we'll keep a few around. In fact, magistrates can be useful, as long as their conduct is suited to the practical needs of a nation. You aren't a *bad* man, Falcio – even my mother knew that. It's just that your more extreme ideas about justice represent a luxury that none of us can afford.'

I let that slide, knowing she was only trying to anger me – that had always been the first step in her manipulations. Damn, but it was hard not to kill her then and there.

'There's a flaw in this story of yours,' Kest said. 'Your mother tried to put *you* on the throne, not this boy.'

Filian spoke up for the first time. 'I'm no boy, sir. I'll thank you to—'

'Shut up, *boy*,' Brasti said.

Trin's next words carried an edge to them. 'You really shouldn't speak to your King in such an insolent fashion.'

'Why not?' Brasti said, undaunted. 'I spoke to the last one that way. Besides, this *boy* is never going to be my King.' Brasti turned to me. 'Please tell me he's not going to be my King.'

'Tell me the rest,' I said to Trin. 'So Patriana kidnaps the boy from his mother—'

'I wasn't *kidnapped*,' Filian said. 'I would have died, had the Duchess

Patriana not saved me. She protected me, ensured I learned the ways of a monarch.'

'Really?' I asked. 'And what exactly did she teach you?'

'I know the laws,' he replied, 'all of them. I've read the histories and studied economics and warfare. I know what brought the country to its current state. I know what my father was trying to do to fix it.' He paused for a moment, then added, 'I know how much he loved you, Falcio.'

Brasti snorted. 'If you know so much about Paelis then you must know how much he fucking *hated* Patriana.'

'I . . . I'm not so foolish as to think they were friends, but I believe it was political circumstance that kept them enemies. Both loved their country, both wanted to protect its people.' Filian leaned forward against his ropes, trying to catch my eyes. 'I will be a good King, Falcio, this I swear to you. I've never met Aline, but she is my sister and I will protect her every day of my life. Put me on the throne and you will see I can—'

'Aline will sit that throne,' Brasti said. 'You know how I know? Because we've all bled a dozen times to put her there.'

'She can't be Queen,' Trin interrupted. 'Filian is a full year older than her, and thus has precedence.'

'That's horseshit,' Brasti said.

'No, it's the *law*. You remember the law, don't you, Falcio? It's that thing you've been telling everyone you've been fighting for all this time. It's what you and every other Greatcoat *swore* to uphold.'

She locked eyes with me as if she could hold me there against my will, as if she could force the truth of her words into me like the needles the Unblooded had used to pierce my flesh.

That was her first mistake.

I knew what to watch for, and for once, I was looking for it. Filian *was* the son of King Paelis, of that Trin was absolutely certain. But she *wasn't* sure if he was older than Aline – oh, he might look a little older, but that could simply be the difference between boys and girls in any family. Trin had been trying to provoke me in order to distract me from the one possible flaw in her plan. She didn't know Filian's true age.

'Falcio?' Kest said. He had his hand on my arm. I hadn't even noticed. 'None of this matters right now.'

'You don't think who sits the fucking throne of Aramor *matters*?' Brasti asked. 'What have I been risking my life for all this time?'

Kest shook his head. 'Right now Avares is planning on annexing Orison and Hervor. There's precious little Valiana can do about it if she doesn't know it's about to happen. We need to get back to Aramor and warn her.'

'Which we can do faster with Trin and her little boyfriend dead,' Brasti said, warming to Kest's way of thinking.

They were right, of course: three could travel faster than five, especially since Filian didn't look especially hardy. Did I really owe this boy anything? Was the law nothing more than a noose to be placed around my neck so anyone who wanted could tug me towards whatever doom they chose for me and the country?

Again Kest tried to bring me back. 'Falcio, Morn doesn't know who Filian is, but he put us in here with Trin because he wants us to kill her. He needs her dead and us blamed for it so that he can strengthen his support in the northern Duchies of Tristia.'

'Fine,' Brasti said. 'We kill the boy, then knock her unconscious and drag her back to—'

'Enough,' I said, careful not to shout and risk attracting the attention of the guards outside. 'I don't know what to do about Avares or the Magdan or even the damned Greatcoats any more. All I know is that I woke up this morning as a magistrate. Valiana sent us here to arrest Trin and bring her back to Aramor for trial and so that's what I'm going to do.'

I went back to her and looked deeply into her eyes, making sure she had all the time she needed to assure herself that what I said next was the absolute truth.

'After that I'm going to find a way to prove that this boy is just one more of your many ploys to take the throne for yourself, and then I'll add another count of treason against you.'

CHAPTER THIRTY-SEVEN

THE ART OF THE PRISON BREAK

'How do you intend to effect our escape?' Filian asked.

'Shut up,' I replied. In addition to all the other reasons I had for disliking Trin's would-be heir to the throne, I found his manner of speech deeply annoying.

'I merely wish to ascertain whether there are ways in which I might serve in the endeavour.'

See what I mean?

'I'm sorry, I'll be quiet now,' I said.

'What?'

'"I'm sorry, I'll be quiet now".' I held up a hand before he could speak. 'Those are the only words I want to hear coming out of your mouth whenever I tell you to shut up.'

His eyes and cheeks went bright red then white as he went from confused to hurt to angry and finally to quiet acceptance.

'Kind of reminds me of Paelis when he makes those little faces,' Brasti remarked.

'Shut up.'

The thing about ingenious plans is that they often turn out not to be quite so ingenious if you fail to notice small but important details. I looked at Trin again: her clothes were dirty and ragged, her hair matted against her face. I could see the strain of days, maybe even weeks of captivity in the bruises on her arms and in the grey pallor of her face.

'Enjoying the view?' she asked, as placid as if we were sitting on the grass under the warm sun by a lake about to share a picnic lunch.

'How did they catch you?'

'It's sweet that you hold me in such high regard, Falcio, but as I already told you—'

'You bet on the wrong Warlord, yes, I heard you. But what happened to all your tricks? Your magic? Couldn't you' – I waved my fingers in the air – 'cast a spell or something?'

She laughed. 'Please, Falcio, never talk about magic again. It makes you sound like a child. I'm not a mage. I can't "cast spells" as you put it. Those tools I've used in the past were secured the old-fashioned ways: I either bought them or stole them.'

'Great,' Brasti said, 'so she's no good to any of us. Can we kill her and move on?'

'Actually,' Kest said, 'we may need her.'

When he saw the two of us staring at him he said, 'What? There are only three of us and the boy and we're surrounded by hundreds of warriors in enemy country. In all likelihood, we're going to need her help to escape. For better or worse, we're allies now.'

Brasti went to stand by the iron gate. 'That's a thought that's going to freeze my balls at night.'

'Your balls will have to sort themselves out on their own,' Kest said. 'The guards left a moment ago to go on their rounds. Based on the last time, I estimate that they walk the perimeter of the lower floor of this fort twice every hour, and each circuit takes them roughly ten minutes.'

I joined the two of them at the gate. 'So we have about nine minutes to work out the details of our escape and then wait for the next cycle.'

'There's no guarantee that they won't leave at least one guard watching us, Falcio. This is the first time they've all left at once – this may be our best chance.'

'How?' Filian demanded from inside his cell. 'The gate is locked and far too strong to break. How can you hope to open it without tools?'

'We're the Greatcoats,' Brasti replied. 'You think this is the first time we've ever been beaten to within an inch of our lives, stripped of our weapons, deprived of our coats and locked up in a cell? The Tailor practically included a pet rat with every coat just to keep us company in situations like this.'

Sadly, he was only mildly exaggerating.

There are, for those who make a study of this sort of thing, three basic ways to break out of a prison. The first – and generally the best – is to bribe the guards. If you happen to be a powerful noble, or have one or two nearby who owe you a favour, this has an excellent chance of success. Alas, that solution was unavailable to us since we were in a foreign country with no allies, not to mention the fact that Trin's efforts to bribe one of the local Warlords had resulted in that poor bastard's death as well as her current incarceration inside this fort.

The second method for escaping a cell is to somehow get the guards to open the door and then overwhelm them. Unfortunately, despite the many and varied ways in which prisoners have, throughout the ages, sought to lure their captors into opening the cage, few of them tend to work – I mean, your average guard might not be a genius, but nobody's actually dumb enough to fall for the old 'help-he's-choking-on-his-food' trick. No, the only way this approach works is if you're being transported from one place to another, or when the guards happen to be drunk when they're coming to feed you, beat you up for the hells of it or kill you because it turns out you don't have a rich uncle who likes you enough to part with sacks of gold just to return you to the bosom of the family.

The third method of escape – and the subject of many a delightful literary romp – is to slowly, over the course of weeks, months or even years, find the single flaw in the prison's design and work away at it until you can effect your escape. Unfortunately, while Avarean hospitality was turning out to be no worse than anyone else's these days, I was fairly sure that our relationship with the Magdan was only going to go downhill once he realised we weren't going to kill Trin for him, which meant we were unlikely to have time enough for Plan C.

'We're going to die, aren't we?' Filian asked from inside his cell, sounding as if he was trying to summon the courage to face his end. The idea that there's some virtue to bravely facing death is another literary device best left to Bardatti romances. Besides, I had no intention of letting a damned traitor like Morn – I mean the Magdan – take my life. Not until I'd killed him first.

Did I say there were only three ways to break out of prison? Actually, there is a fourth: arrange your escape *before* they lock you up. That's why I'd dropped my rapiers in the snow and goaded the Magdan into beating me up with his fists: I'd needed to get close to his pockets.

Morn was a Greatcoat, so of course he knew all the tricks and tools we kept in our coats, and there was no way he was going to leave Kest, Brasti and me with ours. So while he'd been busy pummelling me a bit more, I'd taken a couple of small tools from my own pockets and dropped them into his. Then in the hallway outside, when I'd thrown myself at him one last time, I'd retrieved what I could.

See? I'm not *always* a reckless idiot.

'What did you bring?' Kest asked.

I reached down to the corner of the floor just on our side of the gate and lifted up a set of three small, flat pieces of shaped steel attached to a narrow ring. 'It's only the small set of lockpicks,' I said, 'but there's a rake, a hook and a double-ball.'

'I thought I saw you placing something else in Morn's pockets,' Kest said.

I nodded. 'A caltrop. Couldn't get it back out when I jumped him, though.'

'I'm surprised he didn't figure it out,' Trin said from her cell. 'It all sounded rather theatrical from in here, Falcio.'

I smiled. Many of our former fellow magistrates used to chide Kest, Brasti and me for what they called our 'childish antics'. People like Morn thought we were trapped in the past, trying to emulate the Greatcoats of legend rather than dealing with the dark realities of the present. But there are times when a fast blade simply isn't enough.

'So what did you bring to the party?' I asked Brasti.

He knelt down and picked something up from a pile of dust and dirt. 'Amberlight,' he said. 'Managed to toss it there when I threw my hands up in what I feel was a highly underrated performance of "just look at the mess Falcio's got us into this time".'

'Not bad,' I said. 'A shame we don't have some kind of knife, though.'

'I have one,' Kest said. 'The rope blade from inside the left cuff of my coat.'

'Where in the world did you hide that?' Brasti asked.

Kest opened his mouth and extended his tongue. Sitting there was a narrow black blade just under two inches long. It might be small, but those serrated edges were razor-sharp.

'How in hells did you manage to keep that there without cutting yourself?' Brasti asked.

Kest carefully removed the blade from his tongue. 'You just have to concentrate, that's all. Actually, I'd almost forgotten it was there.'

'You really are a freak of nature, you know that?'

'All right,' I said, 'so while Kest uses the blade to cut Filian and Trin free, Brasti, you get to work on the gate.'

He knelt down and inspected the lock. 'It's not complicated, but the mechanism looks heavy. I should be able to do it in about ten minutes.'

'We need it done faster.'

He shrugged. 'Complain to the Magdan.'

'Okay, just get started,' I said, turning over options in my head. 'We'll need to take out the guards. There's four of them, so we'll want a moment when they're distracted, then we boot the gate open as quickly and forcefully as possible.'

Brasti was already at work on the lock. 'It won't work. When the lock is open, the bolt is retracted. If I open it before they get here they'll see that the gate is unlocked.'

Hells. Hells. Hells. Why must everything be so damned *complicated*?

'Then it's hopeless,' Filian said. The boy appeared to have a finely tuned sense of the poetically tragic.

'We could always go back to my plan,' Brasti suggested.

I glanced over to check on Kest's progress. He was nearly done cutting through the boy's ropes.

'What was *your* plan?' the boy asked.

'We kill you and Trin and then let the Magdan throw a feast in our honour,' Brasti replied.

'You will not—'

'This works faster if you aren't pulling at the ropes,' Kest said. Once he'd freed Filian, he moved into Trin's cell to work on her bonds.

I knelt down next to Brasti, who was humming a tune as he worked. It took me a moment to recognise it. 'Are you seriously going to sing that fucking "Seven for a Thousand" song while we're trying to escape Avares?'

'I don't know. Are you seriously going to berate me for my choice of music while I'm trying to pick a lock that can't be picked in the time I have?'

He had a point. A thought occurred to me. 'Do you think you

can get the first three pins on the lock and then ready the pick on the fourth?'

He pulled on the tiny rake and I heard part of the mechanism shift. 'I suppose so – but what good will that do? Won't the guards wonder why you're holding a little piece of metal against the lock of the gate?'

Trin emerged from her cell rubbing at her wrists. 'More importantly, how do you plan to get us out even after we escape from this cell? There are four hundred men and women in this compound and it won't take long to rouse them. There are guards outside too – and even then, we're miles from the border.'

'That's my job. You just be ready to do yours.'

She curtsied. 'And what would my job be, First Cantor?'

I walked back over to the iron gate and stared out through the bars at the Magdan's display of weaponry, and those damned cannons.

Hells. Hells. Hells.

I went back and took the small blade from Kest and handed it to Trin. 'Once Brasti has the gate ready, you're going to help me with the distraction.'

There's really no feeling quite like knowing you're about to put your life in the hands of the woman you hate most in the world.

CHAPTER THIRTY-EIGHT

THE DARING ESCAPE

As terrible plans go, it began not too badly.

Through the bars to our cell I could just about see the guards coming down the hall with food and drink for us, laughing to each other as they took turns spitting in our bowls. There's precious little difference between a grown-up prison guard and a particularly mean-spirited six-year-old.

Brasti was holding the last pick in place in the lock; I carefully closed my fingers around it as he removed his hand and stood up.

As he let Trin pass by he whispered, 'It's been nice knowing you.' He slipped into the shadows of the nearest cell.

Trin smiled and held up the little blade, ever so lightly tapping the serrated edge with the tip of her finger. 'It really is wonderfully sharp, isn't it?'

As the guards approached the gate, Trin placed the edge of the blade against my throat.

The guards caught sight of us and started shouting in Avarean – I don't know what they were saying but I'm guessing it was something along the lines of, 'Goodness, that Tristian must be truly, truly stupid to have allowed this woman to get out of her bonds and put a knife to his neck.'

'Damn you!' I shouted to the guards. 'You left her in here with *a knife*?'

Trin gave me her best lunatic smile. 'I'll kill him here and now if you don't get the Magdan here. Tell him my terms are—'

'Terms?' the guard laughed. 'No terms. You kill Greatcoat, we kill you, then we say Greatcoat did it. Everybody happy.'

'That's pretty much what I thought,' I said, then with my left hand I twisted hard on the pick and felt the lock click open. 'Now!' I shouted.

Brasti leaped out from the shadows behind me and kicked hard at the iron gate, smashing the bars into the face of the nearest guard. As he fell back, the others tried to get around him to push it back closed, but Trin had already removed the blade from my neck and she, Brasti and I shoved hard together, pushing the gate all the way open, leaving a path for Kest.

He was halfway down the hall and had started his run forward just as I'd unlocked the gate. Now he used that momentum, building up so much force that when he jumped up and kicked out at the nearest guard, the man stumbled back several feet.

It wasn't a bad start to an escape, but of course, we still didn't have any weapons.

'Now!' I said, this time to Trin.

She tossed the two-inch knife to Kest, who caught it neatly out of the air with the thumb and forefinger of his left hand and as the third guard began to draw his sword, swept the little blade across the man's wrist, sending blood spurting in the air and the man scrambling to stop the flow. Kest reached down and drew the man's weapon. Although he was grimacing at the pain touching a sword brought him ever since he'd stopped being the Saint of Swords, there was no hesitation as he slashed it across the shoulder of the next man.

It was largely chaos after that.

We'd counted on other guards being near enough to hear the commotion, and prepared for it. The moment Kest had a weapon in his hand he used it to take out another two of our guards, while Brasti and I overwhelmed the fourth. Now we all had swords, although they were the heavy kind I've always disliked; they don't have the elegance of the rapier, or the manoeuvrability. Trin took a dagger from one of the fallen guards and motioned for Filian to do the same.

'I estimate two minutes, Falcio,' Kest said.

Two minutes? Saints, that was worse than we'd anticipated. Our next problem was going to be one of increasing numbers: the rate at which people heard the racket and came running would speed up quickly and soon we'd be overwhelmed – which meant we needed a bloody big distraction.

Fortunately, the Magdan had provided us with the means.

With my free hand I took the amberlight out of my pocket and raced over to the cannons. 'Quick now,' I said to Filian. Somewhat against my better judgement, I'd given him a job to do and now he grabbed one of the great stone balls whilst Trin was pouring pistol powder into the tube. I was pretty sure the Avareans would keep the wicks separate and we didn't have time to search for them, so instead, I carefully jammed a sliver of amberlight down the wick hole.

On my signal, Filian rolled the ball down the tube, leaving Trin and me to push it into position so it was aimed at the front gates of the fort. She handed me the blade and I was just about to strike it against the exposed amberlight when Kest kicked aside one of the two Avarean warriors who had arrived and were going for him and shouted, 'The angle's too high!'

He dropped his stolen war sword, grabbed a shield from the wall and took the first attack on its rounded front, then after driving the edge into the throat of the other man, he began weaving through his opponents, dodging attacks where he could, deflecting them when he had to. 'Three inches lower,' he added a moment later.

I didn't bother wondering how Kest could possibly have had the time to calculate the exact angle at which to position a cannon in order to hit a door some thirty feet away, let alone *how*; it's just how his mind works. We dropped the barrel by three inches and at Kest's approving nod as he drove his right elbow into a guard's stomach, I sliced across the amberlight with the little blade.

It started burning with a bright, sparking flame. *Okay, either I'm about to fire my very first cannon, or this escape is going to rapidly come to a sputtering, humiliating end.* Either way, I had a few seconds on my hands, so I grabbed my own stolen sword and ran to help Brasti.

A broad-shouldered Avarean woman was in the process of wearing him down, her powerful blows making his parries ever more desperate. I brought my war sword down hard on her back, feeling a little guilty at my unfair attack – but what the hells, it's not as if anyone was offering us a fair chance to duel our way out.

A crack of thunder, louder than I'd have thought possible, reverberated through the hall and just about made my heart stop. Fortunately, it had the same effect on everyone else. When I turned, I saw smoke and chaos, and through the gloom, not only the main doors but most of the supporting wall of the fort lying shattered in front of me.

'Time to go!' I shouted.

'Hate to think what that'll do to our armies if we do end up at war,' Brasti remarked as he ran past me.

Kest and I followed, Trin close behind me. We were almost at the gap where the doors had been when I heard her scream, 'Filian—? *Where's Filian?*'

For a happy moment I thought we'd lost him, but then I caught sight of him through the swirling fog, running towards us with something bundled in his arms.

'What in all the hells—?'

'I thought you'd want these, First Cantor,' he panted, proffering our coats and smiling with such . . . I don't even know what the word would be, but it broke my heart a little because it reminded me so much of someone else.

CHAPTER THIRTY-NINE

THE TRUSTED FRIEND

A successful escape requires four things: the right plan, the right tools, a willingness to die, and a little bit of luck.

It's that fourth part that's always been the problem for me.

'Saint Bog-who-shoves-hot-needles-up-his-own-arse,' Brasti swore as he padded lightly back to where the rest of us were hiding behind a row of outdoor privies.

'Saint "Bog"?' Kest asked. 'You're not even trying any more.'

'What's the point in making up a proper Saint when you're going to die before you can trick anyone into believing in him?'

'The stables are guarded?' I asked.

The one part of our getaway we couldn't plan for was horses. The chaos we'd set off in the armoury had been an effective enough distraction to get us this far, but it was only a matter of time before someone got up a coordinated search for us. What we needed now was transport. Normally in a camp this size someone leaves a few horses tethered somewhere accessible, but apparently not in this damnably organised compound: warriors and workers littered the place but there wasn't single horse outside the stables.

'*Guarded?*' Brasti spat in the snow. 'No, the stables are practically *surrounded*. Morn's got a dozen soldiers at every damned door.'

'What now, then?' Trin asked. Despite our imminent risk of discovery, she showed not the slightest concern. Doubtless part of that was because she's absolutely insane, but I couldn't help but wonder if she had her own plan, just in case I failed her. 'One presumes we can't *walk* all the way through the southern passes into Tristia?'

'We could try a Blushing Bride,' Kest suggested. 'It's worked for us before.'

I considered it, but quickly shook my head. 'We've already blown up part of the armoury. Even if we could set one of the other buildings on fire, there are just too many soldiers here – they wouldn't need to leave the stables unguarded to deal with it.'

'The Sewer Rat?' Brasti offered.

'You want to dig a tunnel under the stables?' I asked incredulously.

'I thought that was a Burrowing Weasel.'

'No,' Kest said, 'the Burrowing Weasel is when you bury yourself in a pit and wait for the pursuers to pass you by.'

'Then why isn't *that* one called a—?'

'Shut up,' I said absently, trying to run through possible options in my head. Even without the distraction of Kest and Brasti bickering, that didn't take long.

Time was the problem: we couldn't afford to hang about. If this were a city or even a castle, we'd likely be able to find somewhere to hide, perhaps even disguise ourselves, but anyone who saw us here would instantly know we weren't Avarean. And since the only Tristians here were Greatcoats . . .

'All Hail the King,' I said suddenly.

Brasti's eyes narrowed as he looked at Kest. 'Is he talking about the one where—?'

Kest nodded.

'Forget it,' Brasti said. 'There's no way we can pull off an All Hail the King.'

'It's our only choice,' I said. 'Look, Morn must have had the other Greatcoats here for ages, and they're not prisoners, which means they must have the run of the place. I'll bet they take out horses all the time.'

All Hail the King isn't one of the most devious tactics we'd ever come up with, but every once in a while it does actually work. And the rest of the time there's usually enough confusion amongst the people you're trying to deceive that at least you get a head-start running away.

'The problem is,' Brasti argued, 'that we're *not* Morn's Greatcoats.'

'The Avareans might not know that,' Kest pointed out.

'You think one Tristian looks like another to them?' Trin asked with a light chuckle.

'Well, *they* all look the same to me,' Brasti said.

'Perhaps, but from what I gleaned during my negotiations with the poor dear Warlord who died this morning, your former colleagues started arriving two years ago, so a great many of them are well-known to the Avareans by now.'

'Which means some aren't,' I said, stepping carefully towards the end of the row of privies and staring at the nearest stables. If I just walked right up to them, not a care in the world, and pushed past them into the stables, would they buy it?

'As much as I do love watching your little feats of daring,' Trin said, 'I'm afraid this one will end in tears.'

I hesitated, but as I couldn't come up with another approach, I worked on convincing myself this one would work. *Time*, I reminded myself, *is working against us.* Then again, what *wasn't* working against us?

A voice called out softly from behind us, 'I'm afraid the bitch is right, Falcio.'

I spun around, but at first I couldn't see anyone – until a woman stepped out from behind the privies, her long black leather coat etched with a ship on the right breast. Quillata, the King's Sail. The Seventh Cantor of the Greatcoats and once one of my closest friends.

'Hello, Quil,' Brasti said, taking a step towards her and bringing his stolen sword into guard. 'Goodbye, Quil.'

'Please,' she snorted, looking at his blade, 'don't embarrass yourself, Goodbow.'

'You know, I might have to kill you with this stupid metal stick just to get people to stop mocking my fencing skills,' he said.

Quillata ignored him. 'The All Hail the King won't work, Falcio. These people aren't stupid. They don't panic just because of a little noise and fire.'

I kept my own weapon light in my hand, measuring the distance between us. Quil was a ferocious fighter and I didn't particularly want to test myself against her if I had any other choice. 'Don't suppose you have any suggestions?'

She looked at me for a long while, as if weighing her own options. 'How about a Trusted Friend?'

There's no tactic in the Greatcoats' repertoire called a 'Trusted Friend'.

'Haven't had one of those in a long time, Quil,' I said.

'Do you wonder why?' The look she gave Trin suggested she was seriously considering murdering her on the spot. 'Allying yourself with Patriana's daughter? The King would be ashamed.'

'He surely would be,' I said evenly.

That set her off. '*Don't!* Don't you dare for even one second to play the martyr with me, val Mond! You're not the one who had to watch Bellow get his legs sawed off by Viscount Croisard's soldiers. You weren't there when six of my own Greatcoats were hung by the neck, the knots left just loose enough to make them dangle for a good long time before they finally died. You weren't—' She held up a hand, as if stopping herself. 'No. I won't do this with you.'

I let my hand grip the hilt of my sword a little tighter. 'Then what *are* you planning to do, Quil?'

She sighed. 'I'm going to go and create a second distraction by telling the guards I've just spotted you going over the western wall.' She pointed to a small building across the compound. 'Get yourself over to that maintenance shed. There's a ladder hanging on the outside; it's long enough to get you over the wall. On the other side I've left three horses for you. You'll have to double up on two of them, so you'll need to swap riders regularly. That's the best I could do.'

I felt something like relief seep into me, just for a moment. Sometimes you need to fool yourself that your world hasn't *actually* been turned upside down just for the sake of getting air into your lungs. 'Come with us,' I said.

She shook her head. 'No, Falcio. You and I are done. The others are done with you as well. And you can stop calling yourself "First Cantor" from here on out.'

'Why?' I asked, straining to keep the pleading out of my voice, trying instead to focus on the sounds of men running through the compound, of the imminent threat, of the need to escape. 'Just tell me why, Quil.'

'Because Morn's right, Falcio. If you'd just listen to his plan, take the time to hear about the numbers of lives that could be saved, you might finally let go of this insane obsession with the King's last wishes and realise that this is the only way to save our country.'

'Then why give us the horses?' Kest asked. 'Why not try to make us stay?'

She stood there a moment longer, the cold breeze lifting her dark hair. She looked sad, and tired. 'Because even after all the stupid things the three of you have done these past years, I can't stand to watch any more Greatcoats die.'

CHAPTER FORTY

THE LOVELORN SACRIFICE

The horses Quillata had left for us were heavy beasts, well-chosen for riding long distances in cold weather. They wouldn't be very fast, but endurance would soon become more important than speed. I was pleased to see the saddlebags were well supplied too.

'And here I forgot to bring her anything,' Brasti said, examining the bow hung from a strap on his horse's saddle before putting a foot into the stirrup.

'Oh, I don't think that's true,' Trin said, reaching down a hand to help Filian mount up behind her. 'Apparently you've brought her and the other Trattari quite a bit of misery.'

I took the reins of one of the shaggy creatures. 'We'd better go. There'll be plenty of time for you to mock us *after* we've saved your worthless life.'

We raced for the thick forest running between Avares and Tristia. Going east might have got us out of the country faster, but that would have meant taking the mountain passes again and I doubted anyone was going to let us use their platforms and pulleys to get down the sheer cliffs. Instead, we'd have to go the long way round, easing our way down to the border with Pertine, where we could finally leave this damned country where everything turned to ice in one way or another.

We rode hard and fast, the horses falling into a steady pace –

though not one they particularly enjoyed. Despite the effort, mine was particularly responsive and well-behaved, which, oddly enough, made me miss Arsehole. I guess I'm just used to horses that don't obey me. *I hope you found that butterfly, you great big idiot.*

Two hours into our journey, I began to believe we might have managed the impossible and escaped – until my horse reared up suddenly, tipping me unceremoniously into the snow as a figure appeared from the trees in front of us.

'I've got the son of a bitch,' Brasti said from behind me, his words accompanied by the creak of a bow.

Kest had already dismounted far more gracefully than I had and I could see him approaching from the corner of my eye.

The figure before us shook off his covering of snow, revealing a long coat made from heavy wool, trimmed in fur as white as the landscape all around us. A hunting knife, the blade a good ten inches long, gleamed in his hand. 'It is a trap,' he said in a thick Avarean accent.

'Yes, we know it's a trap,' Brasti observed. 'That's why I'm about to shoot you.'

'It is a trap,' our apparent ambusher repeated, as if he weren't sure we'd understood him the first time. He pointed in the direction we were headed. 'Ten miles ahead, they have a camp. They wait for you.'

'Who waits for us?' I asked.

Anger stirred on the young man's features. 'The traitor's soldiers – twenty, perhaps a few more. They have nets and *danfangsten* – you would call them . . . man-catchers.'

I *hate* man-catchers. Actually, I'm fairly sure *everyone* hates man-catchers: eight-foot-long poles with spiked two-pronged heads that close around your neck; they're painful, and make it incredibly easy for your opponent to keep control of you. Slavers are very fond of man-catchers, though they're much less common in Tristia; say what you want about my country – for it is corrupt, venal and generally despicable – but at least we don't have slavery. I stared into the endless barren terrain ahead of us. If what the boy said was true, then the Magdan had fully prepared for our possible escape. *Which means he really is better at this than I am.*

'Hang on a minute,' Brasti said. 'Why in the name of Saint Dreck-who-pissed-in-the-snow should we believe some bloody Avarean?'

Kest took another step closer, peering at the young man. 'Falcio, I know who he is. This is—'

'Gwyn, isn't it?' I asked, recognising him myself now. 'You were lying feverish in a cot, covered in sweat-soaked blankets and near death back in Den Chapier. You appear to have recovered rather swiftly.'

He shrugged as though it were nothing of note, although now that I was really looking at the young man, I could see how pale his skin was, and how gaunt his features. 'Fever broke five days ago.'

'How did you get here so quickly?' Kest asked, echoing my own concern. 'Five days isn't long enough to make the trip on foot and the mountain passes are too rough for horses.'

'Not for a *braijaeger*.' Gwyn gave a short, sharp whistle and a moment later a copper-coloured blur burst out from the forest. Before I could get out of the way, the blur had leaped towards me then abruptly stopped, nose-to-nose with me.

It licked my face.

'Arsehole?'

Gwyn frowned, apparently thinking I was referring to him. 'I did not mean to steal him, but I needed to get here quickly, before—'

'He's not calling *you* arsehole,' Brasti explained. 'It's the horse's name.'

The young Rangieri stared at me, wide-eyed and a little offended. 'You named a *braijaeger* "Arsehole"?'

'We call them *Tivanieze*,' I replied, a little defensively. 'But yes.' I patted Arsehole's neck and told him, 'And you and I are going to have a conversation about how you never listen to me but seem perfectly content to follow the commands of a possible Avarean assassin.'

The horse nuzzled me in reply.

'If we could get off the subject of horses,' Brasti said, still eyeing Gwyn warily, 'are we really supposed to believe you jumped off of your deathbed to come all the way here to warn us about Morn's trap just to piss him off? Weren't you content with killing his old Rangieri mentor?'

A leather sling suddenly appeared in Gwyn's other hand and I found myself reflexively raising my arms to protect my face. Slings are funny things: you wouldn't *think* a child's toy would be especially dangerous in actual combat, but you'll change your mind the first time you see a one-inch rock bury itself in a man's skull.

'Yimris was my teacher, my . . .' Gwyn struggled to find the right word. 'My *zedagnir*.'

'"*Dagnir*" is the Avarean word for father,' Kest explained, 'so I would guess that "*zedagnir*" must mean foster-father.'

'The one you call Morn,' the boy growled, 'the *traitor* – he *betrayed* Yimris, stabbed him, left him for dead.'

Trin came up close to me, which always feels like someone dropping a dozen spiders down the back of your neck. 'This boy speaks rather good Tristian for a mountain man, Falcio. This could easily be a trick.'

'Yimris teached me . . .' Gwyn paused then corrected himself. 'Yimris *taught* me.'

All right, so, either this young Avarean was sincere and we had to change course, or this was all some elaborate deception that would result with me right back in that damned cell in the Magdan's compound, only this time with even more bruises. I watched Gwyn carefully, searching for some sign of deceit or ill-will. He cut an odd figure, standing there before me in the snow: a slight young man, not as tall as most of the Avareans I'd met, and much leaner of build. I doubted he was more than eighteen years old, though he carried himself with a kind of ease and confidence you rarely find in anyone other than Kest. The coat he wore . . . it was very much like the one depicted in the only book I'd ever read that mentioned the Rangieri. Moreover, it was clearly fitted to him, so either he *was* a proper Rangieri – the first I'd ever met – or he'd cleverly found one who had the *exact* same build and killed him for it.

Hells. For all my staring, the only thing I could say for sure about Gwyn was that he genuinely despised Morn – which was as good a reason as any for trusting someone. 'All right,' I said finally. 'We can't go forward along this track and we can't turn back. Any suggestions?'

Brasti shaded his eyes and peered ahead of us. 'I think that set of hills off in the distance might be the start of the Degueren Steppes.'

'Yes. Here they are called the *Svaerdan*,' Gwyn said, 'but it is the same thing. You must make for them quickly and quietly, then head east back through the passes to your own country.'

'Good,' I said, 'then let's get—'

'It won't work,' Kest said. I turned to see what he meant and found him staring back the way we'd come. He was making that face of his – the one that means he's working out things in his head that would take me a week to figure out. 'We're never going make it.'

I followed his gaze, half-expecting to see Morn with a hundred soldiers at his back coming over the ridge. 'They can't be that close already, can they?'

Brasti dismounted. Motioning for us to be silent, he ran a few feet back and listened. 'Nothing yet,' he announced after a minute. 'This area is pretty barren. If they were within half a mile of us I'd hear it.'

'It doesn't matter,' Kest said, and gestured to one of the horses. 'We've been pushing our mounts faster than they're bred to travel. They're already tired. If Morn is smart – and it's fair to say that he's proven that he is – he'll have doubled up on horses: they'll be able to move twice as fast as us, and we're only going to get slower.'

'How long till we reach the Degueren Steppes?' I asked Gwyn.

He didn't answer at first, but instead walked up and examined my horse, placing his hand on the beast's side. 'Their coats are wet from riding too fast. You must walk them a while, then ride, then walk again. Three hours, I think.'

'Too long,' Kest said, locking eyes with me. 'I'm telling you, Falcio, I've worked this through: there are simply too many of them coming for us.'

'Then we split up, take different routes and—'

'There are no other paths,' Gwyn interrupted. 'Not until you reach the *Svaerdan*.'

I was really starting to dislike this damnable country. I reached for the sword strapped to my saddlebag. 'Well, if we can't run, then I guess we'll have to fight.'

Kest grabbed my wrist. 'I'm telling you, *this won't work*. They won't be coming after us with just a few soldiers, Falcio: they want Trin far too badly. We're on cold, rocky terrain here, which gives the Avareans the advantage. None of our usual tactics are going to do us any good. This is going to come down to a pure numbers game, and we're going to fail.'

'I will stay behind,' Gwyn said, coming closer, his voice full of righteous anger. 'I will kill the Magdan for what he did to my teacher. That will give you the time you need to—'

The boy fell face-first in the snow, and it took me a moment to realise what had happened: Kest had thrown him.

'You're still weak from the fever you suffered,' he said dispassionately. 'Your reflexes are slow, and even if you were in perfect health, you wouldn't be one-tenth the fighter Morn is. He'd kill you without bothering to dismount.'

Gwyn rose to his feet, his sling already spinning in his hand. I caught a sudden motion out of the corner of my eye and watched the sling fall unceremoniously to the ground. Kest had knocked it from the young man's hand with a snowball.

'Enough,' I told Kest. 'Stop humiliating the boy. You've made your point.'

'Good, then you and the others go on ahead. When Morn and his soldiers come, I'll keep them busy and buy you a little more time.'

'Forget it. I'm not leaving you here.'

'Falcio, it's the only way—'

The tinkling sound of Trin's deeply annoying laughter caught me off-guard. 'My, my, this is just like watching one of those lovely military plays about honour and duty.'

'If we're all going to die anyway,' Brasti began, 'does anyone mind if I kill Trin first?'

She put a hand on Filian's chest to stop him from once again declaring his willingness to protect her no matter the cost, then went to Kest and standing up on her tiptoes, kissed him on the cheek. 'It's kind of you to offer, dear Kest, but it won't work either, and you know it.'

'What?' Brasti said. 'Why not?'

'Because they don't want Kest – they'll either overrun him with sheer weight of numbers, or more likely, they'll ignore him and keep right on after us. We need to give them a more tempting target to pursue.'

'Which is?'

She took in a deep breath and let it out slowly. I think it was the first time I'd ever seen real sorrow in her eyes. 'Me.'

'No!' Filian said, rushing to her. 'No, you cannot—!'

Trin was right: Morn wasn't worried about us – our escape would annoy him, that's all – and he didn't know who Filian was. But Trin? She commanded immense loyalty in Hervor and Orison ... he couldn't afford to lose her.

'I'll stay behind,' she continued. 'As soon as they're within sight of me, I'll ride as fast as I can – I'll head for the hard ground to the north of here.'

'They'll catch you,' I said.

'Of course they will. But all I need to do is draw their pursuit long enough for the rest of you to escape.'

I found myself peering into her eyes, searching for the trick, the deceit. 'This is suicide,' I said at last.

'Why, Falcio, I didn't realise you cared.'

'We're wasting time,' Kest said. 'Whatever we're going to do, we need to do it now.'

'I'm not leaving her!' Filian shouted.

'Here, my darling,' Trin said, and reached out to hug him. She caught my eyes and nodded faintly and I knew exactly what she wanted me to do. I took the sword I'd stolen and struck the back of Filian's head with the pommel.

The boy fell like a sack of wheat into my arms. I handed him to Kest who lifted him back onto his horse. He took out a length of rope to start strapping him in place.

'Take care of Filian,' Trin said. 'He really is a sweet boy.'

As soon as he was fast in the saddle, Kest made Gwyn mount up behind him, and he and Brasti started riding down the road. I climbed up onto Arsehole's saddle, but found I couldn't leave; I needed to try and understand what was driving Trin. 'You're going to die,' I said. 'The Magdan won't risk losing you a second time.'

'Perhaps,' she said, 'but I'm a survivor.'

Again I found myself looking into her eyes, convinced that I would see signs of trickery there, but I found nothing but fear mixed with determination. 'Why?' I asked at last.

'I'll never sit the throne of Tristia, Falcio: you know that. So what is left for a woman born and raised to rule yet denied all power, except to make that one last decision of consequence left to her?' One corner of her mouth lifted. 'I may still surprise you, Falcio.

I'm not without my own tricks, and these barbarians are fools.' She came over and reached up a hand to caress my cheek. 'Go, my lovely tatter-cloak. Tell Filian . . . Well, I'm sure you'll think of something suitably poetic.'

I pulled away from her and nudged Arsehole into motion. We pounded down the road that would lead us to Tristia and to Aramor. I was confused beyond all measure.

My world had stopped making sense.

CHAPTER FORTY-ONE

THE BOY AND HIS DOG

We stopped sooner than we should have, Filian being too tired and too heartbroken to continue. A better man than I would have been sympathetic to his plight. A more practical one would have killed him.

'You don't like me, do you.' He didn't bother making it a question.

I stared at him, willing his mouth to tighten into a sneer or his chin to inch up into a haughty scowl, giving me the excuse to slap him across the face, but he was too smart – or too innocent – to provide me with the necessary provocation.

'I don't know you,' I said at last.

'And you don't want to.'

I kicked at a mound, stubbing my toe on the broken branch concealed by the snow, then knelt to pick it up. 'Find more of these,' I said. 'We need wood if we're to have a fire.'

He did as he was told, staying close and often looking back to make sure I hadn't left him alone in this wilderness. His entirely natural and sensible fear bothered me; no one raised by Patriana, Duchess of Hervor, had any business exhibiting normal human emotions.

More troubling was that I found myself making dark calculations: at fifteen paces away from me, with his attention focused on the ground in front of him, it would take me four seconds to bridge the distance between us. Even with my hands firmly at my sides, the urge to draw my rapier, to let that swift, fluid motion extend into a killing lunge, gnawed at me. The tip of the sword would slide so easily through the boy's back, just to the left of his spine, and come out the other side with his heart's blood dripping along the length of the blade.

I tried to shake the image away, but that made the bracer of throwing knives inside my coat rub against my chest, reminding me that I needn't even get close to the boy to do the job; he'd stuck to the little path and there was a clear line between us, no trees or branches to shield him. My first throw would embed a knife between his shoulder blades – enough to incapacitate, not kill – but the second and third would finish the job. Aline would be crowned. The country would be safe. And Filian wasn't facing me, so I wouldn't even have to see his eyes when the light left them.

The vividness of my visions unsettled me and I didn't know if it was the traditional Tristian aversion to shedding royal blood, or because despite all the violence in my life, I had never before contemplated the murder of an innocent.

Saint Birgid, where are you when I actually need someone to scold me for thinking a blade could solve all the world's problems?

A polite cough pulled me back: Kest, alerting me to his presence, which I'd managed to miss entirely – a sure sign that I was unlikely to make a good assassin. The urge to yell at him for sneaking up on me quickly faded when his expression made it clear he'd not put any particular effort into moving silently; if I did bring it up, he'd just ask if I'd prefer that he clomp through the snow more loudly from now on.

One day I would find something that Kest Murrowson was bad at, and on that day all of Tristia would breathe a sigh of relief.

'Any signs of pursuit?' I asked.

He shook his head. 'Brasti and Gwyn went nearly a mile in each direction. No one is following us.'

'So Trin was right: the Magdan doesn't yet know who Filian is.'

'So it would appear.' Kest tilted his head as he watched me. 'You're troubled that Morn hasn't sent any of his men after us.'

I sighed. I suppose the logic was simple enough: he had more than forty Greatcoats on his side, so Kest, Brasti and me escaping would make little difference to his master plan. 'Is it possible that the world doesn't actually revolve around us?'

Kest reached into his pack, pulled out a strip of dried beef and handed it to me. 'I don't know, but if it doesn't, at least you could stop trying to carry it on your shoulders.'

I accepted the food although I wasn't hungry and tried to do the same with the implied criticism. I was less successful at that. '*Forty Greatcoats*, Kest. How did I lose that many?'

It's not Kest's way to offer words of comfort, especially not platitudes – it doesn't occur to him to consider someone's feelings because, really, what difference would it make? The situation is what it is. 'Forty-two, actually,' he said.

Forty-two. Take the few who had come back to Aramor and those we knew were dead and forty-two amounted to just about everyone left. 'Is that supposed to make me feel better?'

Kest shrugged. 'They made a choice, Falcio, the same as you and Brasti and I do every day of our lives. Do we keep following the strange, winding path the King set us on, or do we allow ourselves the luxury of expediency and just kill our way to a better world?'

He made everything sound so simple: a straightforward choice. Go left or go right. Examine the evidence, analyse the testimony, weigh the truth as if it were little wooden blocks you could sit on either side of a scale and then either set a man free or sentence him to death.

'I could do it, you know,' I said, my eyes returning to Filian, who was walking towards us. 'I could kill him right here and now and no one could stop me.'

'Perhaps,' Kest said, 'but then you'd have a different problem.'

'Just one? What would that be?'

He unslung his shield and before I even understood what he was doing he'd set it on his right arm and slammed me so hard in the chest I went flying back three feet and landed on my arse in the snow.

'I'd have to arrest you,' he said, slinging the shield back on his shoulder. 'My First Cantor takes a dim view of murder.'

I stared up at him, dumfounded. For the life of me I couldn't remember Kest *ever* striking me outside of a bout. So why now? Was it to make the point that even without his right hand, even without a sword, he could still take me down if he had to?

I decided to try and lighten the mood. 'Hey, *I'm* not the one who wanted to kill Valiana back when we thought she was Patriana's daughter.'

'That's true. You didn't *want* to kill her.' He paused a moment, then said, 'All these years, Falcio, for all the danger, for all the horrors you've endured, you've never once had to choose between the King's laws and your own sense of what was right.' He glanced back at Filian, trotting towards us with a pathetically small bundle of kindling in his arms. 'You can't have it both ways this time. You're going to have to decide whether to follow the law or save the people you love.'

I imagined that scale with Aline, Valiana, Ethalia and everyone I cared about on one side. The other side was empty. *The Law*. The King's Dream: words with no more weight than the breath it took to utter them.

'How do I choose?'

Kest chuckled, which was unusual for him. 'If I knew the answer to that, *I'd* be the First Cantor.'

'Do you require my assistance, First Cantor?' Filian asked, clutching his bundle of sticks.

'Why would I need *your* help?'

'You appear to be lying in the snow. I thought you might be injured.'

As I rose to my feet, snow slid down the back of my neck, making me shudder. 'Give me those,' I said. I took the branches from him and set about making a fire – well, I set about doing all the things that eventually lead to a fire. I've never been any good at fires, so usually I cheat and use a fragment of amberlight, but I'd used it all up for our escape. I'd end up having to let Brasti do it, which inevitably meant enduring a lecture on the importance of basic woodcraft.

Filian was standing mute, his lips moving silently ever few seconds, as if he were rehearsing lines for a stage play. He was really getting on my nerves. 'What is it you want to say?' I asked curtly.

'Do you . . . ?'

He hesitated – was he worried I might hit him? *Oh, please,* I thought. *Give me an excuse.*

But then he blurted out, 'Do you think she's still alive?'

I might well have struck him, or at least mocked his concern; I might possibly have listed all the people Trin had killed or had horribly murdered in the short time since I'd been unlucky enough to make her acquaintance, starting with a hapless Lord Caravaner who'd been in her way. But staring at that face which shared so many of the features of my dead King, I said instead, 'I don't know. The odds aren't good, but she said it herself: she's a survivor.'

He looked for a moment as if he might start bawling her name and praying to the Gods, then he visibly pulled himself together. 'You really hate her, don't you?'

He doesn't know, I realised for the first time. *He's never met the woman I know, the one who's come so close, so many times, to killing the people I care about.*

'Do you love her?' I asked back. I needed to know his true feelings for her if I was to be able to gauge what kind of man he might become.

Filian's cheeks turned an awkward sort of pink. 'I know she's done terrible things, if that's what you're asking. Neither she nor Patriana ever hid from me the ugly truths of politics and warfare.'

'So how is it even possible that you love her? She's not just *conspired* against her own people – hells, she's killed a fair number of them!'

'Can I ask you a question?' He didn't wait for permission. 'How many men have you killed, First Cantor?' Before I could reply, he said quickly, 'Let me ask it differently. Do you think you—?'

'There's a difference between killing a man in battle and murdering him in cold blood.' My voice was firm – and no, the irony of my reply wasn't lost on me.

The little smile on his face made me want to punch him. 'You think this is funny?'

'I'm sorry,' he said hastily, backing away, 'it's just that Duchess Patriana used to say that when a man kills, it is always "in battle" but when a woman kills, it's always murder.'

His attempts at cleverness were intensely irritating – then an odd thought occurred to me: *I wonder if this is how people feel around me?* I ignored it.

'Patriana killed your father, you know. Did she tell you that when she was filling your head with clever platitudes?'

'I was nine years old when she and the Dukes overthrew my father.'

Nine years old. It had been six years since the King's death, which would make Filian fifteen now, a year older than Aline. So was this true, or simply a carefully practised lie to establish his age for me, as he surely would do for the Dukes when he presented himself before them? If I ever gave him the chance.

I think the boy must have interpreted my scowl as a response to his casual mention of overthrowing his father. 'It was a *coup*,' he said quickly. 'A change in government.'

'Well, that does sound much nicer than conspiracy, insurrection and beheading, doesn't it.'

Filian set down his sticks. 'Have you read the histories of the Kings of Tristia?'

'Several different versions – I used to read a chapter when I needed something boring enough to put me to sleep.'

'You must never have got past the first few pages, then.' He sounded surprised. 'Every chapter ends in blood and violence – few monarchs ever died of natural causes.'

'That doesn't speak well of your future, then, does it?'

He took in a breath and stood a little straighter. 'I am prepared to pay the price a King must pay when the time comes.'

I found his veneer of nobility both pretentious and cloying. 'Did Patriana teach you that? One of her lectures on how to pretend to be a well-behaved little monarch?'

'You mock her and me but she raised me in the ways of kingship.'

It was hard not to shudder at the thought of Patriana's notion of raising a King. 'Care to share some of her lessons with me? Or am I too lowborn to understand?'

He looked thoughtfully at the snowy ground for a moment. 'When I was seven years old she brought me a puppy. He was a Sharpney. Have you ever seen one?'

I had, though at first I couldn't remember where – then it came to me: Rijou, at the end of Ganath Kalila, the Blood Week. Mixer was his name; he'd belonged to that little tyrant Venger and his group of miscreants. Mixer had raced to grab one of my gold buttons from the ground at the Rock of Rijou. I chuckled: technically speaking, that dog was one of my jurors.

Filian mistook the cause of my laughter. 'I know,' he said ruefully, 'it sounds utterly banal – a boy given a puppy to look after. But Duchess Patriana told me it was part of my training.' He looked wistfully up at the sky. 'Gazer.'

'Excuse me?'

'The pup. I called him Gazer – Stargazer – because I'd always find him outside the cottage at night staring up at the stars as though they were something he could chase.' He sighed. 'I loved that dog.'

I could guess where this story was going. In Avares they were reputed to give puppies or kittens to children to raise and love until the child was old enough to begin training as a warrior. 'Is this the part where you tell me she made you slit the dog's throat to prove how strong you were?'

Filian looked horrified. 'No, of course not! She made me care for him – she said love and loyalty are one and the same, and to prove myself a man, I must prove that loyalty every day.'

'Then what—?'

'Sharpneys are good dogs, loyal to a fault. But they can be aggressive, go a bit mad sometimes. Gazer . . . well, he attacked a boy in the village . . .' Filian's voice dropped. 'Nearly tore his arm off.'

'What did Patriana do?'

Filian looked ashamed. 'Nothing, at least at first. I lived with a servant, Mully, who pretended to be my father. Duchess Patriana always made sure I had plenty of money, so I had Mully pay the boy's family. They kept it quiet.' His look of shame deepened. 'But Gazer got worse – not with me, but he hurt another child, and then another. I paid their families too, but then Duchess Patriana found out.'

'What did she do?'

'She asked me if I thought people's lives could be bought for a few coins; how many more boys and girls should suffer before I did what needed to be done.' He clenched his fists. 'I yelled at her. I threw her own words back at her: "You said love and loyalty were the same thing, and that a man had to always be loyal!" but she told me, "And a King must ask himself if he is to judge himself by the standards of a man or by something more." She said a King always had to ask what price others would pay for his love.'

'You killed the dog.'

'Trin offered to do it for me, but Gazer was my responsibility.' Filian looked over at me. 'Do you think that if my father had been in my place he would have done differently?'

'I don't know,' I replied, but I was lying. Paelis would have looked for another way around the problem, even if it was doomed to fail. He had never been very good at sacrificing those he loved.

I wasn't sure what to make of this little tale of sick dogs and hard decisions. If I closed my eyes and imagined Patriana, I saw a monster in woman's form, capable – no, *desirous* – of succumbing to every conceivable act of cruelty.

And yet . . .

The men and women who'd left their villages in Hervor and Orison had told us she'd been good to them, she'd kept them safe and fed while the south never spared a second thought to their wellbeing . . .

'She liked you, you know,' Filian said, pulling me from my reverie.

'She *tortured* me.'

'She said you were the best man she'd ever known.'

'*Patriana?* I think she must have been referring to a different Falcio val Mond.'

'You can't reconcile her different aspects, can you?'

'Not really, no – if she admired me so much, maybe she shouldn't have put quite so much effort into killing me.'

He bit his lip for a moment. 'She liked you, but she didn't *admire* you. She said you wanted to be a good man but you didn't care what your goodness cost the country. Like all the Greatcoats. Sometimes rulers must be harsh, even . . . well, evil, I suppose, because sometimes that's what the country needs.'

'Spoken like a true noble,' Brasti said, coming up behind us. He put the back of his hand on his forehead. 'Oh woe is me, for the good of the country I must torture and kill a few more villagers today.'

Filian stared at me, trying to make me understand his point. 'When Patriana was alive, her people were safe and prosperous. Now she is dead and those same families starve while you race around the country righting whichever wrongs please you.'

'You should really shut your mouth now, boy,' Brasti said.

Filian ignored him. 'You wanted to know what kind of a King I would be? I would be a King who put the welfare of his people above my own loves, my own ideals – and if that meant doing things that tied my stomach up in knots, then I would remember Duchess Patriana and Gazer and do what was necessary.'

The sound of yew creaking as it bent filled the air. 'See? Now *there's* something we agree on,' Brasti said, a big smile on his face. 'Which is an excellent reason to get rid of you now, *before* you become an even bigger pain in our backsides.'

'That depends,' Filian said. His voice was steady, but I could see he was terrified. 'If you believe my sister would be a better monarch, then loose your arrow. But if you believe that the law is a necessary prerequisite to a country's survival, then perhaps you should be magistrates and stop trying to set the course of the country's future as though it were yours to choose.'

'Says the boy whose favourite Auntie Patriana arranged to have the King executed – murder's *illegal*, by the way, in case no one's mentioned it to you before.'

The boy chewed on his lip. 'Actually, that's not entirely true. Some of my father's actions technically overstepped the traditional rights of the monarch. Some interpretations of the *Regia Maniferecto De'egro* would suggest that—'

Brasti grimaced. 'Saint Hugo-whose-words-bore-men-senseless, he sounds just like Kest now.' He turned to me. 'Falcio?'

'Enough,' I said. 'Just start the damned fire before we all freeze to death and these questions become moot.'

Reluctantly, Brasti relaxed the tension on his bowstring and put the arrow back in its quiver. Then, with far greater enthusiasm, he set about instructing Filian – who then made up for all of his offences in Brasti's eyes by being an attentive listener – just how easy it is to light a fire, and how only the truly thick could possibly have any difficulty doing it.

In the meantime I turned my attention to our route home. It would be a long, slow trip and some part of me was glad of it, for once we reached Aramor, I would need to make a decision once and for all. Would I be a magistrate, or a kingmaker?

Kest had been wrong. Apparently it was entirely possible for the world *not* to revolve around me while still settling its entire weight on my shoulders.

CHAPTER FORTY-TWO

THE REUNION

The southern passes between the eastern border of Avares and my own home Duchy of Pertine felt longer and more treacherous than I'd expected, and yet it couldn't have been more than fifty miles. I'd spent my childhood on one side of those mountains, listening to stories mangled through repetition about the barbarians on the other side, never really understanding just how close they were to us.

We stayed well away from any populated areas, heeding Gwyn's warning that the Avareans had a system for alerting their settlements about invaders: smoke fires that could be lit to signal across the mountains in case of attempted enemy incursion. I didn't think our little party really qualified, but I also didn't want anyone sending word of our passing up or down the chain to where it might reach the Magdan.

When our food ran out, Brasti and Gwyn set about hunting, trapping just enough to keep us from starving. The Rangieri considered the quantity of game more than sufficient, but it wasn't long before the rest of us took to discussing the foods we missed the most and what our first proper meal would be the moment we set foot back in a civilised country. But by the time we'd entered Pertine and bought extra horses to speed our trip back to Aramor, we were seeing the hunger and deprivation all around us. We stopped talking altogether after that.

It was almost a relief to find ourselves periodically set upon by brigands. As it happened, the roads were filthy with them, and Kest, Brasti and I quickly slipped into our more normal roles, scaring our enemies off when we could, killing them only when they gave us no other choice. Gwyn turned out to be an effective fighter. He could make all sorts of wooden weapons with that great big knife of his, and he used them to good effect in close combat. Now he was fit again, his sling proved to be a remarkably capable weapon for distance work.

At first I wondered why anyone would take the risk of attacking us. It was clear enough we weren't carrying trade goods and certainly didn't look wealthy enough to have much coin. The answer, it turned out, was that the brigands weren't interested in us at all: it was the horses they wanted – and not for riding.

Tristians don't eat horseflesh, not as a rule, but clearly times had changed. The conspiracies, endless battles and betrayals and finally, the loss of their deities had proved to be one too many blows for anyone to endure. I doubted the people in these parts cared anything for Greatcoats or laws or who should sit the Tristian throne, they just wanted food and an end to year after year of things getting worse. If they'd had a choice between Patriana or King Paelis, I don't think they'd have hesitated for one second; it was beginning to look like Patriana would have been a hugely popular Queen.

What if people didn't need outdated heroics and idealism? What if they didn't need Greatcoats at all? What if the one thing my country needed most to survive was a tyrant? That question festered inside me all the way to Castle Aramor, where I found a different kind of mathematics at play.

'Saint Felsan's rotting balls,' Brasti said, staring at the tents littering the castle grounds, 'please tell me this isn't another pilgrimage. I'm too bloody tired to kill a God today.'

The clusters of rake-thin men and women warming themselves

around fires, rusted swords lying unscabbarded on the cold ground, were eating greedily from bowls being handed out by guardsmen from the castle. Gwyn looked around at them with a mixture of disgust and pity in his expression. 'Who are these people?'

'Soldiers,' Kest explained. 'They're conscripts.'

I heard Filian's sharp intake of breath.

'Not quite the royal army you hoped for, your Majesty?' Brasti asked.

'I . . .'

'Shut up,' I said, 'and try not to be noticed until we can get you safely inside.'

As we rode up, I guessed at the numbers around us. 'Two thousand, do you think?' I asked Kest, but he shook his head.

'Less than twelve hundred,' he replied.

Brasti pointed down one of the rows of tents. 'Well, I hope you're not counting him in that number.'

I followed the line of Brasti's arm and saw a one-legged man some distance away, holding himself up with a crutch. He watched us with one eye, the other being covered by a patch. 'How exactly is he supposed to face off against an Avarean warrior?' Brasti asked.

I wondered the same thing myself, but something about the man was bothering me, and not just his infirmity. Despite missing an eye and a limb, he held himself like a soldier and his arms were still showing wiry muscles that defied obvious age and years of rough living. When he caught me staring, he turned away and ducked into his tent.

'We should go,' Kest said. 'Best get inside and report to Valiana as quickly as possible.'

I nodded, but something was keeping me rooted there. I thought at first it was the paupers' army arrayed before us – Saints, how long had it taken Valiana's envoys to collect even these few shabby volunteers? With his four hundred Shan steel-armed and Greatcoat-

and Avarean-trained warriors, Morn would cut through this lot in an afternoon. And there were dozens of other warbands in Avares, each with their own horde of skilled fighters.

'Come on,' Brasti said, 'let's go and see the Realm's Protector so I can ask her personally how she expects a one-legged, one-eyed man to help her "protect" the realm.'

'She wouldn't,' I said, and suddenly found myself dismounting and walking towards the tents.

'Falcio?'

'Wait here and keep an eye on the boy,' I said, and headed straight for the tent I'd seen the man enter. No recruitment envoy, no matter how desperate, would conscript an ageing, one-legged man to be a soldier.

The tent looked empty at first glance, but only because the old man was hiding himself just to the right of the entrance. The flash of a curved dagger flitted into my peripheral vision as he brought it up to my neck. Without hesitation I dropped my own weapon and reached up to grab his wrist. He was a strong devil, but he needed one arm to hold onto his crutch so it took me only a moment to twist the blade from his hand.

'Sorry,' he said, letting the knife fall to the ground. 'Couldn't take a chance it might be one of them bastards from Luth come to make trouble again.'

'Which bastards would those be?' I asked.

He grimaced and reached up a hand to scratch at his scraggly beard. 'Fucking Ducal guardsmen. A couple of 'em come through once in a while looking to see if there's any contraband they can "confiscate".'

As if I didn't already have enough reasons to want to pummel Pastien's guards to a pulp. One more thing to deal with later. Keeping an eye on the old man, I knelt down and picked up his knife. 'You were staring at me,' I said.

He gave a half-grin that didn't do anything to make up for the scars on his face that weren't nearly well enough covered by his beard. 'Couldn't help myself, Trattari. You're pretty damned ugly.'

Despite the crutch, he stood straight-backed, confident, almost commanding. It was his presence, rather than his appearance, that made me recognise him. 'Well, you don't look half-bad for a dead man, General Feltock.'

His smile widened. '*Captain*, as you well know. Wondered when you'd figure out it was me, Falcio.'

'But how—? Duke Perault's soldiers had you outnumbered four to one.'

Feltock nodded. 'Aye, and killed every one of my boys,' he said, an angry edge to his voice. 'Thought they'd killed me, too.' He tapped a finger against the patch. 'Did you know you can survive a crossbow bolt right in the eye?'

'And the leg?' I asked.

He looked down and shook his head as if he couldn't believe the limb was gone. 'A cut – barely a scratch, really. Got infected.' He looked back at me. 'Funny, ain't it? A wound that should've killed me – the shot that convinced Duke Perault's soldiers that I was already dead – saved my life, and a little nick on my thigh cost me my leg.'

'I'm sorry,' I said.

'Not half as sorry as you'll be if you keep looking at me with that pitying expression on your face.'

I was working on a clever reply when suddenly Feltock reached out and grabbed my shoulders with both hands, letting his crutch fall to the ground. 'Thank you, boy,' he said, hugging me roughly.

'For what?'

He looked at me as if I were mad. 'For *her*, of course. For Valiana. You saved her! Despite all that bitch Patriana tried to do, you saved my girl!' Tears welled in his eyes. 'The things she's done . . . becoming Realm's Protector, facing down a God . . . you even made her a Greatcoat!'

It was quite possibly the first time I'd ever heard him refer to us as anything other than 'Trattari'. Then it suddenly dawned on me that I *wasn't* the person who should be having this reunion. 'Damn, Feltock, we have to take you to her! She'll be *so* happy to—'

He pulled away from me, hopping over to reach down and pick up his crutch. 'No.'

'No?'

He used the crutch to help himself back up, refusing my hand. 'Look at me, Falcio. I'm a broken old man, useless for anything but begging my way from village to village. I won't have Valiana see me like this.'

'She wouldn't care,' I said. 'She'd want to . . .'

The deep, unrelenting sorrow in his gaze told me there was no point in pushing him further, and yet I couldn't help but ask, 'Why did you come here, Feltock? If you didn't want her to see you then why—?'

'So I could see her,' he replied, and held the tent flap open for me to leave. 'Just one more time, Falcio. So I could catch a glimpse of our girl from afar and see how bright she shines in all this darkness.'

Though it pained me to do so, I did as Feltock asked and kept his presence secret even from the others. I knew Kest would understand, if I'd explained Feltock's reasoning. Brasti would have listened carefully, nodded his head, and then run off straightaway to tell Valiana. He never did think much of the old tragedies, those stories and plays about honour and dignity. So I kept my silence and made vague excuses as I rejoined the others and we walked our mounts up to the castle where other annoyances awaited our attention.

'You'll have to wait,' a man in the brown livery of Domaris warned, gesturing to his fellows to be ready in case we tried to pass. 'No entrance until our captain—'

Filian started to speak but Brasti blessedly cut him off before the boy could unwittingly draw attention to himself. 'Oh, for the love of Saint Liza-who-shaves-men's-backs,' Brasti swore, 'not *this* again.'

One of the Domaris guardsmen looked at us quizzically. 'Saint who?'

'Don't ask,' I said. 'And we're not here to make trouble.'

'We aren't?' Brasti asked.

'No.' I turned my gaze back to the guardsman. 'I just need you to take a message to Aline for me. Tell her—'

My words were cut off as a blur in a blue gown ran past the guardsmen, shouts following close behind. Something soft struck me square in the chest, nearly bowling me over, and it took me a moment to realise that my assailant was a young woman apparently intent on hugging me to death.

'Tell her yourself, you unshaven, smelly excuse for a magistrate!'

I tried to say something clever in reply, but her hair was covering my mouth, the scent of it filling my nostrils with reminders that not everything in the world reeked of sweat and grime. Aline might be small for her age but her arms gripped me tightly, and I hugged her back just as hard, falling to my knees from the sheer joy of holding her.

'Aline!' someone called, followed by hurried footsteps, and I shook away enough of Aline's hair to look up at the woman standing before me. Gods, but I wanted to grow more arms so I could hold her, too – mind you, I wasn't quite sure if she'd knock me down for trying. She probably hadn't yet forgiven me for my interference with Pastien.

'It's a fine thing that you're back, Falcio,' Valiana said, shaking her head at Aline. 'The heir to the throne has been so focused on your return that she's been quite useless at running what's left of her country.'

'You would speak to your future Queen in such a fashion?' Aline asked, letting go of me. 'You think I can't keep affairs of state in mind even while keeping an eye out for . . . for . . .'

I leaned back to see what was wrong and found her staring past me at the others. I understood then what had caught her attention: that she had seen what no one else had.

I rose to my feet and quickly said, 'This is Filian, a carpenter's boy we saved from brigands on the road. He doesn't speak much—'

Aline silenced me with a shake of her head and walked past me to stare up at Filian.

I'd kept the boy from shaving, reckoning whatever straggly hair he could grow might undermine the similarities to his father, and I'd made sure he had a good coat of grime on him too. Somehow, Aline saw past all that. I suppose it was down to the hours she'd spent staring at portraits of her father and at her own sharp features in the mirror, trying to find traces of him in her own face.

There wasn't even a shred of doubt in her voice when she said, her voice quiet enough to elude the guards but loud enough for us to hear, 'Hello, Brother. Welcome to Aramor.'

CHAPTER FORTY-THREE

THE UNITED FRONT

I had lied to Filian, back in forest when he'd asked if I'd read the histories of the Kings and Queens of Tristia. In fact, Paelis had an entire section of his private library dedicated to books on the rise and fall of monarchs. He'd bring me there sometimes, on nights when I'd just returned from one of my judicial circuits, and do his best to drown me in free wine and extended lectures on the fragile nature of royal lines and the events that led to their creation and destruction. The wine helped a lot. At the end of the evening, he'd offer me one or two of the books – gracious of him, given their rarity and value – and I, for my part, would thank him profusely and then walk over to his fencing and duelling collection and take one of those instead.

In retrospect, I probably should have chosen to wade through those ponderous tomes on monarchical disputes. If nothing else, one of the books might have warned me about the many unpleasant meetings I was in for.

'By the Gods themselves,' Meillard, Duke of Pertine, swore, pacing around the council room table at such speed that I wondered whether the carpeting or his heart would give out first, 'have you lost your mind?'

Since Pertine was the land of my birth, I owed this particular Duke some small measure of deference, and since it was the only honest answer anyway, I replied, 'I'm not entirely sure, your Grace.'

I thought this was a polite response, but apparently I was wrong. 'Disrespectful dog!' shouted Hadiermo, the Iron Duke of Domaris, rising from his seat and nearly colliding with Meillard, who was on his fifteenth circuit of the table. Hadiermo, as was his practice at such times, reached behind him so that the two retainers who carried his massive two-handed greatsword could make a show of preparing it for him.

'Sit down, Hadiermo,' Ossia, Duchess of Baern, said, quietly sipping her tea as if nothing of any consequence was going on around her. That made me feel genuinely uncomfortable. The more Ossia acts as if everything is fine, the worse things usually are.

Pastien, Ducal Protector of Luth, and Erris, Duke of Pulnam, stared at me as if they were waiting for me to confess this was all a terrible joke. Worse was Duke Jillard, who simply shook his head, as if I'd somehow disappointed him.

None of that mattered to me, though. What did I care whether the Dukes disapproved of the choice I'd made, or how they chose to express their condemnation? It was Valiana who broke my heart. She looked stricken, almost lost. The others appeared to be waiting for her to either endorse or refute my actions, but she did neither, instead turning to the current heir as she said, 'Falcio had no choice.'

Hadiermo was still on his feet, one hand on the hilt of the greatsword his retainers were struggling to hold upright. 'He should have killed the damned whelp – hells, he could have simply left him in Avares and let the barbarians do it for us.'

Until that moment Aline had been silent, letting the others posture as they made their displeasure known. Now she rose and locked eyes with the Iron Duke of Domaris. 'Falcio val Mond is the First Cantor of Tristia's magistrates: his responsibility is to the *laws* of this country, your Grace, not to this council's whims or my convenience. What would you have had him do?'

It was Jillard who answered, saying quietly, 'What he's always done. Kill those he deems a threat to your father's dream and find some suitable legal justification for it later.' The Duke of Rijou turned his gaze on me. 'You do realise, don't you, Falcio, that if you'd fallen asleep in the snows of Avares and died there, you would have done your dead King the greatest possible service?'

Actually, that thought *had* occurred to me.

'Enough!' Aline said, a dangerous edge to her tone. 'We are a nation of laws, your Graces. If we have learned nothing from facing the Blacksmith's God it is surely that we cannot set that aspect of ourselves aside. Circumstances have brought us to difficult times, true, but now we must all rise to meet the challenge. We must—'

'*We?*' Erris repeated in that creaky, wheezing voice of his that always suggested he was not long for this world, even though the old bastard showed no sign of obliging. He pushed himself up. 'It seems to me that there is no *we* any more, little girl. Your time as heir to the throne has come to an end and I see no reason to tolerate your prattling wishfulness any further.' He motioned to two of his personal guards. 'Remove the child.'

From the moment the emergency session of the Ducal Council had been called, I'd ignored my usual instincts and instead opted to be polite and take my beating as graciously as possible. Now I found myself staring at the sheaf of paper and the pen used for recording major decisions. I reached over and slid it along the gleaming oak surface towards the guards approaching Aline. 'You'll want to fill out the names of any next of kin before you take that next step, gentlemen.'

Aline rolled her eyes at me. 'You're not helping, Falcio.'

'You expect me to let them drag you out of the room?'

'They wouldn't dare to try.'

'Really?' I said, my eyes on the guardsmen, who were doing an excellent job of ignoring me. 'You think your winning smile will keep them from following their Duke's orders?'

Aline didn't reply, but looked at Valiana, who'd kept silent during this most recent threat to Aline's safety. Her eyes were locked with the guardsmen's and now I understood why they weren't paying attention to me at all. The raw ferocity in Valiana's eyes burned so hot that it could only be the *Adoracia fidelis* running through her veins. Normally she kept it under control, but right now she was letting just enough of it rule her to make everyone nervous. The men Erris had ordered to remove Aline had been here in this same room when the poison had overcome Valiana some months ago during the war of the Saints. Clearly they remembered that little incident.

'That mad dog has no business being here,' Erris declared. 'She should be locked up during these episodes of hers.'

Valiana's voice was surprisingly calm, and dreadfully cold. 'You ought not to trouble yourself with my *episodes*, your Grace. Worry instead over what I will do whilst in full control of my faculties should you ever again command men to set hands on Aline.'

How any person alive could not adore Valiana was beyond me.

The light clack of a teacup being set down on its plate broke the silence. 'Are we all done with the theatrics and posturing?' Ossia asked. 'I imagine this "Magdan" and his army would be rather amused to find us at each others' throats.'

Amused, I thought bitterly, *but not surprised.*

'That presumes this tale we've been spun about a Trattari amassing war bands and arming them with Shan steel weapons and cannons is even true,' Hadiermo said.

Ossia looked over at him with all the disdain he deserved. 'You think Falcio val Mond of all people would manufacture a tale of the Greatcoats joining with Avares, abandoning their King's missions and turning traitor against their own country?' She didn't wait for a reply. 'No, gentlemen, the threat of invasion in Hervor and Orison is real *and* imminent. We need to be redoubling our efforts to rebuild our own military so we can face this Magdan with a united front.'

'And behind *whom*, precisely, shall we unite?' Jillard's tone was perfectly balanced between genuine respect and subtle mockery. 'I take it you have some wisdom to offer on that score?'

'I do.' She let her gaze travel around the room. 'All of you have been operating under the assumption that this boy, this "Filian", is the true son of King Paelis.'

'You haven't seen him yet,' Hadiermo said. 'Take one look at the scrawny runt and you'll have no doubts.'

'Really?' She turned to look the Iron Duke up and down. 'Are you saying that if I travelled the length and breadth of this country I couldn't find some overweight, flat-faced braggart who could pass for your brother in a pinch?'

Even Erris laughed at that one. 'She's got you there, Hadi!'

Ossia went on, 'Patriana loved nothing better than to plot and scheme, to engineer deceit against those she believed had slighted her.' The Duchess gestured towards Valiana. 'Did she not take this orphan child and train her to believe that *she* was a princess?'

Jillard's eyes narrowed as if he was trying to determine if Ossia knew something she shouldn't. 'You're saying Filian is another fake?'

'I'm saying we have no reason to believe he is the true son of King Paelis until we have proof – the kind of proof Tristia has always demanded of its noble houses.'

'You want to summon the City Sages?' Aline asked.

When the two of us had been trapped in Rijou, it was the City Sage, drawing on some esoteric mix of magic and genealogical lore, who'd discerned the true identities of the noble lines assembled before him.

'I do,' Ossia replied.

'I can have the Sage of Rijou here within the week,' Jillard said.

'Precisely why I suggest we don't rely on *one* Sage.' Ossia turned to look at each of the Dukes in turn. 'Gentlemen, this country has seen far too much chaos and uncertainty of late. For the good of the nation, for the assurance that our people will surely demand, I recommend that we summon a Sage from each Duchy.'

'Including Hervor and Orison?' Hadiermo asked.

'*Especially* Hervor and Orison.'

'Clever,' Jillard said, stroking his short beard. 'If our Sages should decide the boy is not the heir, then the fact that those from Trin's territories do swear to his authenticity will be seen as political manipulation on their part.'

'I leave such ploys to you, my lord Duke of Rijou,' Ossia said. 'I only know that this will give us the time we need to explore our options.'

It didn't take long for them all to agree to Ossia's proposal. The one thing everyone wanted was more time to make sense of this development and work out its ramifications. For me, it meant a chance to find some law that might justify putting Aline on the throne even if she did turn out to be the younger.

My sense of relief disappeared when I caught the glance that passed between Hadiermo and Erris. I didn't need to be told they'd be using this time to seek out Filian and see what kind of deal he might offer them for their support.

Ossia was still sipping her tea; Jillard was staring off into space, contemplating, no doubt, the various ways he might arrange for this new heir to suffer a tragic accident before the Sages could be assembled.

And if he did, would I stop him?

Kest's words came back to me unbidden: 'My First Cantor takes a dim view of murder.'

He used to, anyway.

I felt Aline take my hand and squeeze it. 'You had no choice but to bring Filian here, Falcio,' she said. 'Nor do the Greatcoats have any choice but to uphold the law if he truly is the rightful heir.'

I squeezed her hand back and tried to think of something clever and biting to say. I hated it when she knew what I was thinking, and I hated it more when she had to remind me of my duty. In a scarily short time, Aline had gone from a frightened and confused little girl to a young woman who exemplified everything you could hope for in a monarch: she was clever, compassionate, strong when she needed to be, merciful when she could afford to be. In her I saw my King's dream made flesh, and all the things Kest, Brasti – so many of us – had fought to bring about for the country. She was our future.

I pulled my hand away after a few seconds, saying nothing – it wasn't that my sense of humour had abandoned me, just that, for the first time in my life, I was quite sure I had no intention of following the law.

Filian, the man I was absolutely sure was the true-born son of King Paelis, would never take the throne from Aline.

I wouldn't allow it.

CHAPTER FORTY-FOUR

THE DIVIDED ORDER

'I take it *that* went well?' Brasti asked, taking note of my expression as I left the council room. He and Kest followed me as I made my way out of the royal wing and back towards the centre of the keep.

'Well?' Brasti repeated, jogging to catch up to me.

'It took roughly thirty seconds after I gave my report for half of them to begin plotting against us.'

'And the other half?' Kest asked.

'Plotting against each other.' I stopped, waiting as a group of craft-masters followed the labourers carting building materials past us, off to start repairing some other bit of the castle that was never going to be fixed in my lifetime. I was starting to wonder why they bothered.

Brasti opened his mouth to speak, then stopped.

'What?' I asked.

'Well, it's just that . . . if it's down to who can come up with the most vicious, conniving plot, should we . . . ? You know . . .' He seemed to be struggling to meet my eye.

'Spit it out.'

'Well, shouldn't we go and see the Tailor? I mean, aren't vicious conniving plots kind of her stock in trade?'

Even Kest looked uncomfortable. 'That . . . hasn't entirely worked out for us in the past.'

I almost laughed at that. *Almost.* 'You mean, besides the time she sold me out to the Dashini Unblooded so they could torture me to death?'

'Now be fair,' Brasti countered, 'all that torture and poison may well have helped burn the neatha out of your blood – it's pretty much been dead fatal in every other case.'

'There's a different issue we should consider,' Kest said. 'If Filian *is* the King's son, and we all think he is, then the Tailor is his *grand-mother*. How can we be sure who she'll side with?'

And that's the real problem: the reason I really can't trust her. Not with this.

'Fine,' Brasti asked. 'Then what are you going to do now?'

Kest shot me a sympathetic look. He already knew *exactly* what I had to do next, which meant my day wasn't likely to get any better. As much as I'd rued having to tell the Dukes about the twin problems of Filian and Avares, it was the next meeting that I would have done *anything* to avoid.

'Carefully and quietly, I need the two of you to gather all the other Greatcoats still in Aramor. Talia, Mateo, Antrim . . . all of them.'

'What about Chalmers?' Brasti asked. 'She's only really half a Greatcoat, isn't she?'

'Her too – and find out where Gwyn's stashed himself away. We'll need him too.'

'And when we find them?' Brasti asked.

'Bring them to the old Greatcoats wardroom.' I took in a long, slow breath, and yet still felt as if there wasn't enough air in my lungs. 'It's time to tell them what's become of our brothers and sisters.'

'You're either lying or you're stupid,' Talia repeated, slamming the butt of her spear against the already-damaged stone floor of the wardroom for the third time.

Antrim Thomas, who'd always been something of a diplomat, tried to soften the blow. 'I think what Talia's asking is . . . is there any way this might all be some kind of . . . mistake?'

Brasti snorted. 'Morn nearly beat Falcio to death and then locked us all up. No mistake there.'

'Well, in his defence,' Mateo chimed in, trying to make a joke of it, 'who hasn't wanted to beat the shit out of the three of you once in a while?'

Talia rose to her feet, her spear still in hand as if she might have some cause to use it. 'This isn't a fucking *joke*, Mateo.' She pointed her weapon at me. 'He's accusing more than forty Greatcoats of turning traitor. *Forty!*'

'Forty-two,' Kest corrected.

'Shut the hells up, Murrowson! No one thinks you're clever just because correcting people gives you a tingle in your balls.' She turned back to me. '*Quillata.* You're *really* telling me *Quillata* betrayed the King? Do you have any idea how many times she saved my life? How many times Quil saved my *brother's* life when she was his Cantor?'

'I'm guessing you're about to tell me.'

I hadn't meant to sound glib; however much Talia's ferocity sometimes grated on me, I knew it was her way of showing her devotion to the cause. Deep down, I'd always admired her. Shame the feeling wasn't mutual.

'You *arrogant fucking prig*! *Quil* should have been the First Cantor, not you!' Talia started tapping my chest with the head of her spear. 'If Morn and the others really have turned traitor, then it's because *you* damn well pushed them to it.'

Kest got between us. Talia let the tip of her spear drift up to his chin. 'Something you want to say to me, Murrowson?'

He gave no ground. 'Only this: if you think Falcio isn't already eating himself up inside with that thought, you don't know him very well.' With his left hand he batted the head of her spear away. 'And if you think I'm going to let you keep pushing him, then you don't know *me* at all.'

Antrim got to his feet. 'Let's all take a breath. We need—'

'Kest-fucking-Murrowson,' Talia said, bringing her spear back into line, 'are you sure you were the Saint of Swords? Because most of us always figured you for the Saint of Lapdogs, following Falcio around and growling at anyone who got in his way.'

'Keep pointing that weapon at me, Talia, and you'll find out *exactly* who I am.'

Tempers began to flare in the room, everyone shouting – even those calling for calm – except for Gwyn, who sat silently, looking out the window as if he desperately wanted to climb out of it. Chalmers kept staring at me, waiting for me to say something – to *do* something – to stop the situation from getting even more out of hand. But I couldn't. For all Talia's bluster, the reason her words were cutting so deeply was because she was right: if the others had so lost faith in what we stood for that they'd willingly turn their backs on the King's dream, then they had done so because I'd failed to give them a reason to keep believing.

I wasn't the First Cantor any more, not in any way that mattered.

'Enough!' Chalmers shouted, her voice too young to sound anything other than shrill. 'Is this what the Greatcoats have become? Bickering children so eager to assign blame that we can't even focus on the danger to the country?'

'What would you know?' Talia asked. 'Nobody in this room is even sure if you *are* a Greatcoat, little girl, and certainly nobody wants you here. How old would you have been when the King named you? Thirteen?'

'*I* was only thirteen when the King named me his "Patience" and sent me to the Dashini,' Darriana said, although she didn't sound particularly interested in the conversation. 'Would you care to challenge *my* right to be here?'

'I can fight my own battles,' Chalmers said. She pushed Kest aside and took up position just inches away from Talia.

'You should step back, little girl,' Talia warned.

To her credit, Chalmers didn't cede any ground, though perhaps that might have been because she was shaking too much. 'You don't believe I'm a Greatcoat?'

'No, I don't.'

'Tell me this, then: when this "Magdan" comes with his Avarean soldiers and all those other Greatcoats and I go with Falcio to face them, what do you think's going to happen then?'

Talia snorted. 'You'll end up lying face-down in a pool of your own blood.'

Chalmers nodded. 'From what I've heard, we're horribly outnumbered: the enemy has more warriors and more weapons. So you're right, I'll end up dead. Now tell me how that makes you and me any different. Is it that you think you'll defeat them by yourself? Or that you don't plan to fight when the time comes?'

Talia's sneer turned into something darker for a moment, but then something changed in her expression. 'All right,' she said at last, smiling ruefully as she punched Chalmers in the shoulder. 'I guess you really *are* a Greatcoat. Little girl.'

Some of the tension left the air and I could hear the sounds of breaths being exhaled. It occurred to me watching that exchange that there are any number of qualities required to become a Greatcoat: knowledge of the King's Law, skill-at-arms and willingness to risk life and limb to get justice. Sanity, however, always was entirely optional.

'Can we now get on to figuring out what we do next?' Antrim asked. 'Morn is out there with more than forty of our brethren. If they really do try to take over Hervor and Orison, people will never trust the Greatcoats again.'

'They do not trust you now.'

Everyone turned to see who had spoken. It was Gwyn, still looking as if he were halfway to jumping out the window. He'd seemed perfectly at ease in the wilderness, but the moment we'd reached civilisation – and especially once we'd come inside the castle – he'd become strangely uncomfortable. His accent was thick when he said, 'This is a very warm place even in the winter, I think.'

'Is that supposed to mean something, Avarean?' Talia asked.

'It must be hard to leave a place like this, to go where it is cold, where it is dangerous, where a sore foot becomes a sprained ankle, then a broken leg and finally a sleep in the ice that never ends.'

He turned to face us, his young face showing a kind of . . . *disdain*, as though *we* were the callow youths. 'I am Rangieri, and we do not stay where it is warm, where it is safe. We travel the borders of this country. We go to the northern climes, where it is too cold, to the eastern deserts, where it is too hot. We sail the southern coasts, waiting and watching for signs of raiders from across the water. We are the ones who go scouting to other lands – not for days or weeks, but for months, sometimes for years – to witness armies forming and bring warning before they can invade the soft warm belly of this country.'

'Well maybe one of you *Rangieri* ought to have warned us a little sooner this time,' Talia complained.

'We might have,' Gwyn said. He pulled open his strange coat, so like ours and yet so different, and lifted up his shirt to reveal the still barely healing wounds. 'But there were only two of us left in the north, and one of your Trattari killed my teacher before setting his blade on me.'

Even Talia looked chastened by that.

Mateo glanced around at everyone in the room. 'What I want to know is, how come Morn picked all the other Greatcoats, and yet none of us knew? I can understand why he never asked Falcio or Kest or Brasti, but why did he never try to bring any of us over to his side?'

'Maybe it's because he thought you were all too loyal to your First Cantor,' Brasti said casually. 'I guess it just goes to show he's not all *that* clever.'

Talia looked like she might go for him then and there, but another voice spoke up. 'He asked me,' Allister said.

Every eye in the room turned on him.

Allister looked up at me, his face a mask of confusion and self-loathing. 'I swear, I didn't know what he was up to, Falcio. He just . . . he found me in Luth, three years back. I was trying to track down a book Saint Anlas asked me to find. The old man used to do that a lot; I used to think he just wanted to be rid of me for a whi—'

'You *knew* Saint Anlas-who-remembers-the-world?' Mateo interrupted.

Allister smiled sadly. 'That was my mission: the King sent me to watch over him. Anyway, I ran into Morn . . . or maybe he'd been looking for me. He said he had a plan to reunite the Greatcoats and fix the country. I thought it was just Morn, you know, being the arrogant prick he always was. But his ideas did make sense.' Allister's eyes caught mine again. 'A nation ruled by magistrates, where the laws were the foundation of the country, not just an afterthought. It *did* make sense to me, Falcio. After all the horrors I'd seen, after having to stand there when the Dukes and their armies came to kill King Paelis? Morn's ideas didn't sound crazy.'

'So why didn't you go with him?' I asked.

'I just . . . I couldn't bring myself to abandon Saint Anlas. I didn't understand the King's plan for me, not at all, but somehow I didn't want to give it up, not then.' A look of sorrow passed across his features. 'Then he died and I figured I had to find out who could have killed a Saint – and when I got word that you were nearby, I went to find you.'

In other words, it was geography and not faith that made Allister come to me and not Morn. Gods and Saints alike! How had I lost the Greatcoats so completely? What terrible failing of mine had sent Quillata and Jakin and all the others into Morn's camp? Was it truly only down to a quirk of fate that not everyone had gone with him?

'How much did he tell you about his plans?' Kest asked.

'Hardly anything at all,' Allister replied. 'I mean, he mostly talked about his vision for what we could achieve, but he never mentioned how he intended to accomplish it.' Again he looked over at me. 'I swear, Falcio, I had no idea he'd go to Avares and become some kind of all-powerful Warlord—'

'It's not your fault,' I said.

A sombre mood descended over the room. Now the shouting and threats were over and done with, all that was left was confusion, fear and shame.

'What do we do then, Falcio?' Talia asked at last. 'How do we fight our own people?'

Oh, so now you want me to lead you again? It was a petty thought, but one I couldn't quite get out of my head. 'That's simple,' I said, trying to put a light-hearted tone into my words. 'I'm going to hatch an ingenious plan and then, you know, save the day. In the meantime . . .' I walked over to where Mateo and Quentis were sitting on my cot and motioned for them to get up. 'Everyone get the hells out of my bedroom.'

There were a few chuckles and some groans, and soon the others began to leave, all except for Gwyn. With everything else going on, it hadn't even occurred to me that he'd never been to the castle before, and had no place to go. 'Get Brasti to help you find someplace to bunk tonight,' I said, then added, 'Don't let him trick you into going out drinking with him unless you want to end up learning a lot more about . . . southern mating rituals than you might be ready for.'

He did up his coat, then said, 'Thank you, but no. My wounds are healed now and I must return to the north.'

'Wait . . . back to Avares? Why?'

He paused. 'You said the Magdan has Shan steel weapons and cannon in his arsenal.'

'I saw them myself. Apparently he's got enough to outfit an army.'

He glanced around the wardroom. 'And how many Shan steel weapons do you have here?'

That drew a chuckle from me. 'Me? None, of course. Even if you could convince a Shan trader to sell you some, they'd have been too expensive for my salary . . . even when I *had* a salary.'

'And Avares is not one tenth as wealthy as Tristia. We have livestock and farming, yes, and strong backs, but little trade with other nations.'

The implication of his initial question suddenly hit me. 'So how in the name of Saint Zaghev-who-sings-for-tears was Morn able to buy enough weapons to drain a rich country's treasury?'

Gwyn headed for the door. 'That, First Cantor, is what I must go discover.'

He left me alone with my thoughts and far too many questions, which made for rather poor company, so I stripped off my shirt, grabbed a rapier and started practising the eight fundamental forms. Usually half an hour of repetitions will exhaust me *and* bore me into oblivion, but the twin dilemmas of Morn and Filian kept turning over and over in my mind. Every plan I envisioned began and ended with murder.

In the end, I went for two hours before a rapping at my door shook me from my dark thoughts. Recognising Ethalia's distinctive knock, I put away the rapier and was halfway to the door when I stopped to go back and put on a shirt. I wouldn't have bothered for anyone else.

Somehow she noticed it. 'Have I come at a bad time?' she asked. 'Should I go?'

The sight of her standing in the doorway, the white silk of her robes shimmering against her skin, the long dark hair falling in waves past her shoulders, her expression full of compassion, of wit and laughter and all the things a body longs for to make the pains of life fade away . . . how was it possible that every single person who saw her didn't feel about her as I did? How could anyone who spent even an hour in her company, hearing her talk, seeing the way she listened . . . how had I come so close to marrying her and yet managed to screw it all up so monumentally?

And here she was, at my door, coming to see if I was all right. If there was no promise of anything more in her eyes, at least there was the offer of her company and the solace it always provided. I had a joke already prepared, and a smile to go with it. I'd been about to motion for her to enter when something terrible happened – some poisonous combination of exhaustion and confusion and shame over the anger that was burning a hole inside me as I contemplated just how far I was willing to go to put Aline on the throne.

The words that came out of my mouth had no business being spoken by any sane man.

'I'm sorry,' I said. 'I think I need to be alone.'

I saw the skin tighten around her eyes, just for a moment, and her cheeks went red with the humiliation of being turned away – then that thing that sets Ethalia apart from anyone else I've ever known came back and she reached out a hand to my chest, laid her palm on my heart and kissed me on the cheek. 'I understand,' she said. 'We can talk tomorrow, or the next day if that's better.'

My hands tried their best to reach out and hold her; I wanted nothing more than to be close to her. And yet something held me back: the recognition that the man I had to be right now had no business being in love with – or being loved by – someone like her. All of which might have been forgivable had I not said, as she was walking away, 'It might be a few days. Things are complicated right now.'

Saints, but I am *rubbish* at relationships.

CHAPTER FORTY-FIVE

THE UNWELCOME PROPOSAL

I'm not sure why it is that after screwing something up spectacularly, I generally find myself seeking out the company of Jillard, Duke of Rijou. In this case, my excuse was that I needed something from him very badly, and I was willing to pay the price to get it.

'I wondered how long it would take you,' he said. Despite the late hour, the Duke of Rijou looked immaculate. His carefully oiled black hair was perfectly styled in a nod to the current contemporary fashion whilst still retaining its classical foundation, clearly showing a man who moved with the times, although those times did not control him. He wore his usual red and silver brocade coat over silk, and I imagined I could examine every inch with a magnifying glass and never find a single thread out of place.

His smile was perfect too: amused, but not unserious, pleased with the state of the world but not content to leave it be. A man with a smile like that could walk into a palace dressed in rags and covered in filth and still the wealthy and powerful would part before him like water under a cart's wheel.

Standing there in the antechamber, the dust from Aramor's destruction still rising in the air, he looked as if he were about to be immortalised in marble or oils . . . *and yet* . . .

Deceit is Jillard's stock-in-trade. It is his means of protection, *his* greatcoat. Hidden beneath the perfect smile and the perfect clothes and the perfect hair, the pain of loss lingered there for those with the wit to see. His son Tommer had been the one true star in Jillard's firmament; the man who stood before me now was a pale shadow of the Duke of Rijou.

'Are you well, Falcio?' Jillard asked, the corner of his mouth rising just a hair in amusement. 'You look rather senile.'

'Quite well, your Grace.'

He turned, an elegant pivot on one heel, reached down for the two glasses of wine sitting on a silver salver and offered one to me.

Such simple gestures are never simple with men like Jillard. 'Poison?' I asked.

He took a sip from one of them and curled his lip. 'Decidedly. It's a poor vintage. I'm afraid we lost much of King Paelis' legendary wine cellar.' He looked up from his glass. 'Do you know, the cellar was actually underground, the least likely room to be damaged, even during the destruction of the outer walls.' He wrapped his knuckles on the solid stone wall next to him. 'And yet, despite all the rooms surrounding it remaining intact, the cellar itself caved in. Do you suppose the Blacksmith's God had a sense of humour?'

I considered telling him about the King's private stash, but that would have required explaining why Darriana and I had smashed most of the bottles.

I raised my glass to him. After all, Jillard had any number of infinitely more unpleasant ways of killing me, if that were his aim. A sip revealed that the Duke was right: the wine did have the faintly bitter aftertaste I've come to associate with cheap wines and poison; I'd become something of an expert at both. 'To your health,' I said.

He nodded graciously. 'Well, Falcio, we have played our little game and decided not to kill each other yet again. To what do I owe the pleasure of your company?'

'Aline.'

Jillard frowned. 'Please tell me you're not about to start on your usual litany of threats?' He made a show of glancing around the empty room. 'I fear I am too poor an audience for what I have no doubt will be a grand speech on Ducal overreach, the nature of venality and innocence lost.'

'No speeches,' I said, then hesitated. 'I need a favour.'

'Falcio, if you've come here believing I can somehow elevate the girl to the throne of my own accord, then I fear you'll be sorely disappointed. What influence I once had with the other Dukes has largely faded away.'

'Really? Why?'

'The boy, of course. Hadiermo and Erris have already met with him privately, and have taken the liberty of assigning him "councillors" and "advisors" to enable him to navigate the more esoteric aspects of the laws and protocols governing questions of royal lineage.'

Saints. Why couldn't Trin have had the decency to at least rid the world of those two arseholes during her last attempt to overthrow the country?

'Oh, and in case you're wondering,' Jillard went on, 'that Margrave, Rhetan? The one you made the most powerful noble in Baern apart from Ossia herself – and the man now almost certain to replace her when she can no longer hold her Duchy? He's already made overtures to . . . how did he put it? "Our rightful and glorious King".'

Well, fuck me. You can't even trust men who murder their own relatives any more.

'Oh, don't look so surprised, Falcio. If it makes you feel better, I'm sure Rhetan can be persuaded to change sides for the right price. Probably a little more land and a lot fewer taxes.'

'What will it take for Hadiermo and Erris?' I asked.

He looked at me quizzically. 'What will it "take"? You mean, to buy their votes to put Aline on the throne?' He shook his head. 'You will never have their support; they are far too delighted at the prospect of a male ruler. Their inexhaustible determination not to have a woman on the throne is the closest thing either have to a principle.'

'Fine. I don't need them if I have you, Ossia, Meillard and Pastien. Ossia will certainly support Aline, and I'm fairly sure Pastien *can* be bought. That leaves you and—'

'She will never be Queen, Falcio,' Jillard said quietly. Before I could protest he raised a hand. 'It is through no machinations of mine, I assure you. Given the choice between her and Patriana's puppet, I have no doubt that Aline is the best hope the country has for stability.'

'Then—'

He interrupted, asking, 'How many Queens have we ever had ruling Tristia?'

'Three,' I replied. I'd checked.

'Describe them for me.'

'Well, Illenia the First was—'

'No, no, not their names: tell me of their rule. What great and grand things did these Queens do?'

The question took me aback – I'd sought only to make sure that a Queen *could* hold the throne, not study their economic or military achievements. 'I'm not sure I understand—'

'You understand the question perfectly, Falcio. The few Queens we've had sit the throne, some prettily, some less so, have done *nothing* to change the country. They allowed the Dukes to rule as they saw fit; they made no major changes to the laws or the government – in fact, they largely stayed out of politics altogether. Now, does that sound like Aline to you? Does that sound like the girl who – before she was even on the throne – repudiated more than a thousand years of royal prerogative by telling the common folk that they need never again kneel to the monarch?'

I didn't smile; I didn't want Jillard to mock me for my pride in her, but she'd been so brave, so brilliant. In a moment when the whole world expected her to take vengeance on those who'd set themselves against her, she had instead given them not only forgiveness but hope in a single command: *Rise.*

'You are a damned fool!' Jillard said, smashing his wine glass on the floor. Apparently I'm not as good at hiding my emotions as I think I am. 'You see the world in such sweet dreams, Falcio – that alone should tell you that you're asleep!'

'You're saying Hadiermo and the others won't tolerate a strong Queen.'

He waved a hand. 'The hells for the Dukes; I would kill them all myself if I thought it would do any good. It's not just them, Falcio. It's *all* the nobility: the Margraves and Margravinas, the Viscounts and Viscountesses, the Lords and Daminas: none of them will let her do the things she will want to do. Go amongst the Lords Caravaner and the wealthiest of the merchants and ask about your little Queen – in fact, speak to the peasantry. You will find the same thing, Falcio. No one wants a fourteen-year-old girl telling them how to live their lives.'

He stared at me as if he expected me to deny his logic, to shout at him or threaten bloody murder, but I did none of those things.

'Ah,' he said. 'I have underestimated you. You already know this.'

I nodded.

'And you think you have a solution.'

Again I nodded. 'Before I left for Avares, we had been discussing marriage for Aline.'

'Falcio, that ship long ago left its port. You cannot hope to—'

'A Duke,' I said, cutting him off. 'What if she were to marry into one of the Ducal lines?'

Jillard looked taken aback, and I didn't blame him. A month ago I would have cut off my own foot with a rusty blade rather than even *think* about what I was about to suggest.

'Pastien?' he asked. 'He's young and . . . malleable, but I'm not convinced he can be trusted.'

'I wouldn't trust that little shit with passing the salt,' I said. 'Not Pastien.'

'Then I'm afraid you have a poor set of choices, Falcio. Hadiermo and Erris would be monsters to her, Meillard is already married and Ossia is . . . not of the appropriate persuasion, even if Aline *was*. Which only leaves . . .'

This was the part that really made me want to cut my own tongue out. 'You,' I said. 'What if she married you?'

I'd never seen the Duke of Rijou taken by surprise before and I felt I should press the advantage. 'You're unmarried, your Grace – Tommer's mother died in childbirth, didn't she?'

'She did.' His tone was flat, cold.

'Yours is the wealthiest Duchy in the country. Your nobles are among the few who are – well, if not precisely loyal, at least sufficiently cowed not to risk crossing you. The other Dukes would be confident that you'd keep Aline from any excesses of common decency in her governing of the country. Most of all, you have the one characteristic I most desire in a spouse for her.'

'Which is?'

I didn't lock eyes with him, or put a hand on my rapier. I didn't even take a step towards him. I knew I didn't need to. 'You know without a shadow of a doubt what I would do to any man who would lay an unwelcome hand on her.'

He stood there, staring at me – and then he burst out laughing. 'That is quite the proposal you offer me, Falcio: the seething resentment of my allies, the outrage of my enemies and the promise of what I presume will be a most uncomfortable dismemberment should I ever displease my new bride.'

'That's about the size of it,' I said. 'Also, you'll get to help save the country.'

He walked back to the glasses, picked up a clean one and filled it with wine. 'I take it you haven't discussed this with Aline?'

'Not yet,' I confessed.

'So out of your endless love and respect for this girl, you'd push her into marriage with a man three times her age with a history of . . . shall we say, flexible ethical positions? I must confess, the sheer perversity of your willingness to abandon your values holds a certain appeal to me.'

Just so long as she becomes Queen, your Grace. I'll figure out the rest later.

Jillard made short work of his wine, filled the glass a second time, then, moments later, a third. Something was wrong.

'Your Grace, are you—?'

'No,' he said finally, the word coming out almost as a grunt.

'No? You'd have more power than—'

'Get out.'

Before I could even ask why, he threw the glass at me. I ducked in time and it shattered on the wall behind me. 'Get the hells from my sight before I have you killed, Falcio!'

I started to leave, but I couldn't stop myself from asking, 'Why?'

'Because there are some lines even I won't cross, damn you!'

I could hear his guards massing outside, preparing to take me down, but still I couldn't leave. 'That's rubbish! You've never shied away from *anything* that would increase your power and influence. You expect me to believe that somehow *her youth* stops you from this? Try something better, your Grace, because in a thousand years I can't believe you'd—'

'Tommer,' he said, cutting me off. He reached for the bottle of wine, then stopped himself. '*He* would never forgive me.'

'Tommer is dead,' I said cruelly, my need outweighing any common decency left in me.

'He is,' Jillard said. 'So why is it I see his face everywhere, Falcio? I can see him now, if I just close my eyes for a moment. Why does he look at me with such . . . *hope*, as if he expects me to live up to his example somehow?' He shook his head, shame painted across his features. 'I do not know what my dead son expects of me, Falcio, but it is surely not what you ask.'

CHAPTER FORTY-SIX

THE SUMMONS

For the next two weeks I conceived a hundred new and ingenious schemes that would enable me to put Aline on the throne without requiring me to commit murder in the process. I failed, of course; for every political or legal machination I attempted, someone else – Hadiermo or Erris or some other damned noble or Gods-forsaken merchant managed to stop me.

Filian was kept well away from me, and I avoided anyone I cared about. I couldn't stand the thought of them seeing who I was becoming.

The hells for it. Put the girl on the throne and fix the rest later. Those words had become a prayer I found myself repeating with more dedication and fervour than even the most zealous monk.

In the meantime, everything that could go wrong, did. We'd intended to bring the City Sages to Aramor *quietly*, but word of a second heir to the throne had spread – I was pretty sure Hadiermo and Erris had been responsible for that. They'd been busying themselves eliciting support with the usual mix of bribery, blackmail, subtle threats and promises; the two of them were apparently going to become *very* important people one day soon.

Too many people had taken sides for there to be a peaceful resolution to this. The City Sages would soon be assembled, and we would either have a united decision, which might settle matters in the wrong direction, or a disputed lineage, which would mean civil war.

Eventually someone tired of my attempts to subvert the machinery of royal succession and late one night six guardsmen showed up at my door. I'd heard them coming, of course, and had put on my coat and prepared my weapons, although I stopped in time when it occurred to me that there might be consequences for killing Aline's personal guards.

'She wants to see you,' Antrim Thomas said, leaning in my doorway with his arms crossed over his chest, looking nothing like the soldiers standing rigidly to attention behind him.

'You know you're supposed to work for me, right?'

'Really?' he asked. 'I heard you weren't the First Cantor any more.'

I followed him out into the hallway. 'Was there ever a time when my fellow Greatcoats actually respected me?'

Antrim chewed on that as the lot of us walked down the hall and towards the stairs leading up to Aline's private chambers. 'Probably not,' he said after a while, then gave me a wry grin. 'Mostly we just followed your orders because we were afraid Kest would kick the shit out of us if we didn't.'

'I should have you arrested,' Aline said as she motioned for me to sit on a delicate gilded chair next to a small card table.

I looked over at Antrim and his guardsmen, standing just outside the door. 'I'm fairly sure you already did, your Majesty, although no one's yet mentioned any particular crime.' I reached over and picked up a biscuit from the intricate arrangement on a silver tray. 'What exactly am I charged with?'

'Prostitution, I should think. Possibly slavery.' She leaned back in her chair. The way she sipped from her teacup reminded me uncomfortably of Ossia. 'Tell me, First Cantor, what would be the appropriate punishment for attempting to sell a fourteen-year-old girl to the Duke of Rijou?'

'I wouldn't have—'

'Oh, don't bother, Falcio. I knew you'd come up with something at least this stupid the moment you came back to the castle with my brother in tow. I suppose it's my own fault for having asked you to help me choose a suitable husband in the first place. Why did Jillard refuse you, anyway?'

'Tommer.'

That surprised her, and I saw her hand shake as she put the teacup down on the table. 'I . . .'

'I'm sorry,' I said. 'I shouldn't have told you.'

The sorrow left her eyes, pushed out, no doubt, by the enraged irritation that now filled them. 'Falcio val Mond, since when has it been your business to keep secrets from me?'

I didn't have an answer for that, so I busied myself with eating the biscuits at a pace that would have embarrassed even Brasti. *Saints, how long has it been since I last ate?*

'I was proud of you, you know,' Aline said.

'Proud?' Crumbs escaped my lips in an embarrassing spray down the front of my shirt.

She smiled, my awkwardness somehow buying me a measure of forgiveness. 'Yes, you oaf, *proud*. When I saw Filian standing there with you, when I realised what you must have done . . . the choice you'd faced . . . I can't imagine how hard that must have been.'

I poured myself a goblet of water from the flagon on the table. 'It turned out to be rather a stupid choice in the end. All I did was buy us a thousand more problems.'

Aline grabbed my hand. 'No, Falcio, that's *not* what you did. You saved my father's son – and more than that, you proved everyone wrong, once and for all. You showed the nobles and the Dukes and everyone else that the Greatcoats uphold the laws, *no matter the cost to themselves*.'

'Sure, except for the guy who's planning on invading Orison and Hervor and who just happens to have . . . what was it again? Oh yes, *the vast majority of the Greatcoats* on his side.'

'And yet with all that, still the First Cantor found the strength to do what was right rather than what was easy.'

I found the admiration in her gaze profoundly uncomfortable. 'See, when you say it like that, I don't sound nearly as stupid as I feel.'

She grinned. 'Oh, don't worry; you've more than made up for it with all your nonsense these past two weeks. Honestly, Falcio, you really should stick to deciding which farmer gets which part of the cow from now on and stay out of the business of deciding who should rule the country.'

She put on a good show, but I'd known her far too long to believe this act. Aline was as afraid as anyone would be in her position. Unlike me, she was refusing to let it rule her.

'You've spoken to him?' I asked, trying to change the subject. 'Filian, I mean?'

She nodded.

'What do you think of him?'

'I . . . I'm not sure. We've met several times now. He's clever, and certainly knowledgeable. He might make a good King.'

'Or he might be a monster.'

'I don't know. It's true he's difficult to read; what is certain is that he loves my – *our* – father, even though he never met him.' Aline took my hand again. 'That's the one hope we have, if things turn against us: Filian's desire to be connected to King Paelis. *You* could guide him in that, Falcio. Yours could be the voice that keeps him to the path of my father's ideals, rather than Duchess Patriana's cold logic.'

I shook my head. 'Sweetheart, if he becomes King I don't plan on being within a thousand miles of this place ever again.'

'You must,' she insisted. 'Falcio, I'm telling you, the one hope we have is his admiration for you. He looks up to you, just as my father must have done. *That's* how we protect the country, Falcio, that's how—'

A knock at the door stopped her mid-sentence, and I wondered if her raised voice had made Antrim worry about her, but when he opened the door he was holding a note in his hand. 'We have a problem,' he announced. 'A large contingent of soldiers has just arrived at our gates. They're carrying Tristian banners.'

'Isn't that a good thing?' I asked. 'New conscripts arriving – so maybe we finally have some decent troops to work with.'

'Oh, they're well-trained soldiers, that much is certain,' Antrim agreed. 'The problem is more their commander.'

'Who is it?' Aline asked.

'Trin, my lady.' He turned to me and abandoning any pretence at decorum, added, 'Apparently that prick Morn couldn't even kill *her* properly.'

CHAPTER FORTY-SEVEN

THE TRIUMPHANT RETURN

The gleam of early morning sunlight on the shields and armour of the arriving troops was almost blinding. They held their banners high, sable for Orison and silver for Hervor, catching the breeze and contributing to a tableau so magnificent that I couldn't help but wonder if she hadn't timed her arrival just for that effect. Had anyone but her been at the head of this army, I would have felt a surge of relief so overwhelming I'd have been tempted to drop to my knees and thank the Gods dead and alive for their generosity. As it happened, I was spared the need for any display of piety.

'My, my,' Trin said, gazing at the ruins of the castle. 'You've really let the old place go, haven't you, Falcio?'

I ignored the jibe; my mind was occupied with figuring out how she'd got here – we'd not been aware of her presence in the country, which meant Trin had brought her troops down through Domaris, which meant Hadiermo had arranged for safe passage. The second and more pressing issue was the young man who burst from the castle doors and ran past me to embrace her, shouting, 'Tarindelle!' He hugged her desperately.

It was the first time I'd heard her called that, but of course I understood why: 'Trin' was the name Patriana had given her for her role as Valiana's maidservant, but it was hardly the name of a Duchess . . . or a future Queen. *Tarindelle*. Hells, it even *sounded* royal.

For her part, Trin was looking at me over Filian's shoulder as the boy clung to her like a sailor hanging onto a mast in the midst of a storm. She mouthed 'thank you' to me, then she whispered something to Filian, who reluctantly let go of her and went back inside the castle.

'You look remarkably alive for someone who sacrificed herself to the barbarians in the snow,' I said. 'And you made remarkably good time getting back.'

'I did tell you I was a survivor, Falcio.' She looked back at her soldiers, standing smartly at attention, waiting for orders. I guessed there must be two thousand of them, almost twice as many as the rest of the country had sent us. 'The soldiers of Hervor and Orison have always been more loyal than those in the south,' she said, noting the pathetic conscripts gazing out from their poorly constructed tents. 'Perhaps because we treat them better.'

'Let's get back to how you evaded Morn and his warriors,' I said.

'Ah, that. Well, I'd like to say it was some vastly clever ruse on my part, but in fact I got lucky: a passing blizzard took pity on me. It hid my tracks and I took the opportunity to bury myself in the snow until my pursuers had passed by.'

'You *buried* yourself?'

'Well, you can actually keep quite warm if you do it right. Of course, there are risks. You have to make sure you wake up, for one.' She pulled the glove from her right hand and I saw three of her fingers were gone from the second knuckle. 'Alas, I'll never play the harp, I'm afraid. The frostbite was severe, so I had to cut them off before it spread.'

She said all this as if it were nothing at all, merely the cost of doing business. I found that as terrifying as everything else about her. 'You appear to be almost impossible to kill, your Grace,' I said, and I let my hand stray to the hilt of my rapier. 'But you should know I'm willing to try a few more times.'

It was an idle threat. Even if I could have killed her at that moment – an unlikely prospect, given she had an army at her back – that would just prove the Greatcoats couldn't be trusted, I'd end up dead and the others would be expelled by the Ducal council, leaving Aline unprotected.

Trin laughed, as she always did at my threats. I suppose it made sense, seeing that I'd yet to successfully harm her in the slightest. 'Ah, my tatter-cloak. Would that we could be friends.'

'Quite impossible, I fear, given that you're a lunatic monster who wants to take over the country.'

'Why must you always accuse me of madness, Falcio? It's really quite rude.' She looked down at the ruin of the fingers on her right hand. 'I suppose you're right, though.' Her eyes went to me and there was something akin to genuine sorrow there. 'Do you know, I think my mother might have driven me insane as a child *intentionally*? She did all manner of terrible things to me, all part of my training.'

'Hang on,' I said, 'I'm beginning to feel sympathy for you – oh no, it's passed now. Please do go on.'

Trin put the glove back on. 'Whatever her faults, my mother made me strong, and for that, I suppose I must always be grateful.' Again she looked back at her troops. 'It is a bit of a mad world, though, don't you think? I wonder if she understood this at some level deeper than you or I could ever grasp, and perhaps that's why she made sure I'd be willing to do *whatever* must be done to save this poor benighted country of ours.'

Something in her confession bothered me; how many times had someone suggested that to preserve Tristia, one must be willing to abandon decency and reason in favour of black bloody murder? How many times in the past weeks had I let that same thought infect me? I shuddered.

'What do you intend to do now, *Tarindelle*?' I asked.

Her mouth twisted into a smile and her lips parted as if she were going to speak, but then she stopped and stood there silently, as if wrestling with an unseen opponent. Finally she said, 'Go, Falcio, leave this place. Take Kest and Brasti. Take the whor— Take Ethalia.' She hesitated a moment longer. 'Hells . . . you can even take Valiana with you. Take them all, now, today. Run from this place, from this country, and I swear I will never pursue you, nor allow anyone else to do so.'

The sincerity in her voice troubled me, so I countered it with defiance. 'You appear to be forgetting, your Grace, that I've beaten you before. Every time, in fact.'

She reached out a hand and I flinched at first, but then I found myself frozen by the odd tenderness in the gesture. Her fingers brushed my cheek. 'That was a different time, Falcio. You know that now, I think. This is about politics, and the ruthless arithmetic of power. Even after all the terrible things you've seen, the horrors you've endured, your heart isn't near black enough for what comes next.'

Some small part of my mind – the part that managed to invent plans and tactics and could figure out the answer ahead of my enemies – forced words out of my mouth that I hadn't ever wanted to utter. 'Let me take Aline,' I pleaded, 'and I'll do what you ask: I will leave this all to you.'

Trin shook her head. 'I'm sorry, Falcio. I truly am. If I could let you have her, I would, but you know I can't; that's not how this works. There would be confusion among the people, and some would seek to take advantage, to sow discord in hopes of achieving victory at some later date. I have to secure the country's future now, Falcio, and that means there must be one monarch, and it *will* be Filian.'

CHAPTER FORTY-EIGHT

THE PACT

One of the mistakes fencers sometimes make before a duel is to focus too much on their adversary. You can pour over court records, fixate on every detail of your enemy's trials by combat (devoting entirely too much time to their victories and not their defeats – but that's a separate issue). You can even seek out their former opponents and ply them with wine and coin to learn their weaknesses. All of these are fine things to do, but all of them fail to appreciate the true origins of every fencer's style: their teacher.

Anyone who studies the sword becomes both an imperfect reflection and an improvement on their first master – *that's* where you'll find the key to understanding the danger that you face. The problem for me was that Trin's teacher had been Duchess Patriana, the most cunning, brilliant and vile manipulator to come out of Tristia (which is saying a lot). Which meant my best chance was to go see the *second* most cunning, brilliant and vile creature I knew: the Tailor.

That she hadn't already come to me, recounting in agonising detail every mistake I'd made, demanding to take charge and begin setting the world to rights – the way she saw it, anyway – could only be because she wanted the additional satisfaction of seeing me crawling on my hands and knees to her cell to beg for her guidance.

Fine. I could do that. To defeat Trin I would seek the Tailor out, my head hung low and my tone respectful, and take my medicine like an errant child. I'd already been called a fool and worse by my enemies and my allies alike, not to mention almost every member of my own Order. How much worse could this be?

As it turned out, I was never to find out, because by the time I got down to the dungeon, the Tailor was gone, her cell all but bare.

'Where is she?' I shouted back down the hallway to Gerrald, the guard.

'She left,' he shouted back, his footsteps thumping as he came to join me. 'Last night – didn't even say goodbye.'

I raised an eyebrow at that. '"Didn't even say goodbye"?'

He shuffled about awkwardly. 'It's not as if she was locked in, sir. I wasn't even guarding her, really. Mostly I was just bringing her things or delivering messages for her.'

Some of the furniture – the bookshelves and cot and her big leather chair – were still in the cell, but everything else – every book, every bottle, every last spool of thread – was gone.

'She left *nothing* behind?' I asked.

Gerrald held out his fist and opened it, palm up, to reveal a silver coin. 'She finally paid up for our bet.' He put the coin in his pocket and then withdrew an envelope. 'Oh, and she left this for you.'

I tore open the envelope and found a note inside, a few paltry words scrawled in her own handwriting:

> Falcio,
>
> She has won.
>
> Forgive me.
>
> Magrit Denezia

'Who in the name of Saint Ebron-who-steals-breath is "Magrit Denezia"?' I asked.

The guard was silent for a moment, his expression unreadable, then he let out a despairing sob, quite at odds with his deep voice.

'I think that was her name ... before she ... became whatever it is she became.'

I had known this strange woman more than half my life and yet I'd only recently learned that she was the King's mother – and even then, it had never occurred to me to wonder who she'd been *before* she became the Tailor. Now I stared at that name on the paper, *Magrit Denezia*, and wondered why she'd never told me before.

The answer was obvious, of course; it just took me a little while to work it out. *The Tailor* was an *Inlaudati* – an unknowable genius with the ability to cunningly shape events that could change the course of history. *Magrit Denezia* was a *grandmother*, to Aline, and to Filian too. Duchess Patriana had created the perfect trap for her deadliest adversary: she'd given her a choice no woman could ever bring herself to make.

That was why the cell was empty. *That* was why the Tailor was gone, and had written down her old name for me. She needed me to know that she was no longer the Tailor.

I left the cell feeling unmoored, confused and filled with an unexpected sorrow. For all the Tailor and I had fought, and sometimes come perilously close to one of us dying, she had been a constant in my life for longer than I'd been a Greatcoat. Her schemes had more than once come close to killing me, but the coat she'd crafted for me had saved me from death more times than I could count. Now she was gone, and I felt alone.

'The hour grows late for this little country of ours,' Duchess Ossia said.

The surprise of hearing her voice sent me stumbling into the open cell.

'It's time for you and me to save it, Falcio.'

It took me a moment to make out her form, sitting on a chair in the shadows of the hallway leading out of the dungeon. Even in such surroundings, she was a strikingly elegant sight. 'You surprised me, your Grace.'

'A great number of things surprise you of late, First Cantor. You should have anticipated that the Tailor would be removed from the board.'

Excellent. Just what I needed: another talking-down-to by our illustrious nobility. I was still feeling raw, so I retreated into my old defences. 'I am a magistrate, your Grace. My role is to adjudicate the law and see it enforced, not to play games with the future of nations.'

She rose, the heavy fabric of her skirts falling into place as she stepped towards me. 'I think not, Falcio. You gave up the right to such facile answers the day you and the other Greatcoats took up King Paelis' final commands. Or would you pretend that the missions he gave you were simple legal disputes?'

She was right, of course, but still I resisted. 'Each of the King's commands was a step towards restoring the rule of law to Tristia, nothing more.'

'Is that so? We are in an interregnum, Falcio. Since when has the judiciary taken it upon itself to choose the next monarch?'

Why is she pushing me?

'As I have explained to others of late, your Grace, we are *not* in an interregnum. We have a lawful heir to the throne.'

'In fact, we appear to have two: a matter I believe you could have resolved in a cell in Avares. I wonder, did you spare the boy's life because you do not believe he is Paelis' son, or because you do not care and will see Aline crowned regardless?'

'I spared him because I am not a murderer.'

She looked as if she was about to object, so I cut her off. 'I have killed men who were trying to kill me or those in my care, or who were guilty of crimes worthy of death. You know the difference, Duchess Ossia, so please don't waste my time with whatever philosophical speculations on the nature of justice happen to appeal to you today.'

'The deaths which concern me, First Cantor, are those which will flood this place with blood once Filian's lineage is proven.'

'The City Sages have only just begun to arrive, your Grace. Perhaps they will declare that he is not of Paelis' issue. I doubt Trin has spoken an honest word in her life; why should we believe her now?'

'She speaks true,' Ossia said bitterly. 'Damn Paelis and his "charoites": a fool's scheme to keep his line alive. And now, thanks to other fools, we will all pay the price for it.'

'You know, your Grace, I've been on the receiving end of these little chats ever since the day the King died. It occurs to me, however, that both Duchess Patriana and Duke Jillard – among others – knew that King Paelis had sired children and kept them hidden from the world. So while I accept my part in never realising there might be an older child with a stronger claim, I wonder why someone like you – someone who has always been obsessed with bloodlines – managed to miss this possibility.'

She blinked, and *now* I saw that she *had* known; *this* was the true reason for her anger, not that I'd been a fool.

'Patriana,' the Duchess spat. 'She boasted – she *crowed* – that she had killed them all, every one of them. Her own allies believed she spoke truly – after all, why keep one alive when we all knew she was planning to put Trin on the throne? What kind of mother steals another's child only to keep it safe as a spare, just in case her own daughter should die?'

I didn't reply because the answer was as simple as it was horrifying: Patriana understood the ways of power better than any of us. There'd always been a chance that she might be found out and killed, that Trin would be prevented from being crowned. So she'd raised another heir in secret, inculcating him with her values, growing him like a weed hidden amongst the flowers of a garden, so that once it had taken root – once he took power – he would bring Trin with him. They would marry, and Trin would be Queen at last.

Jillard had told me Aline's betrothal would be the first step towards her elimination; that choosing her husband would be her single act as monarch. Would that happen if *Filian* became King? Would he die of mysterious causes shortly after his joyous marriage, his death blamed on . . . well, me, probably, somehow, leaving Trin – *Tarindelle* – to rule alone, as Patriana had always intended?

Ossia caught the look in my eyes, the expression on my face. 'Forgive me, Falcio. We have all of us been played for fools, I more than most.' She took my arm. 'But now we must take action before it is too late.'

I shook my head. 'The matter isn't settled yet. The City Sages might still—'

'I told you, they will not! Filian will be revealed as the true heir and all will be lost!'

'No, listen, Kest has been looking into the matter and it might not be as simple as that. The Ducal Coun—'

The slap surprised me; usually my reactions are better.

'Fool!' she declared. 'You spend your life trying to *protect* this country but you don't *understand* it at all! If Aline were the elder, the other Dukes might well find a way to declare the younger sibling the true heir: *anything* to avoid a woman on the throne! They *will not* go the other way.'

'Jillard knows Trin better than anyone – he'll do whatever it takes to keep her off the throne—'

'The Duke of Rijou is *lying* to you, Falcio. He plays you like a Bardatti drummer, making you dance to his rhythm. He uses Tommer's death as the instrument to control you, through your guilt and your maddening need to pretend that men such as he can be redeemed. Don't you understand, Falcio? He is *playing* you, he has been all along!'

'Duchess . . .' I found myself suddenly weary from the weight of her accusations. What must it must be like to be a noble, to have so much power and yet never feel safe because your fellows are always plotting, always waiting for the chance to work against you?

Not that my life is turning out any better.

I'd always believed the Greatcoats were different, that we were united by an ethos that went beyond our oaths, but Kest had been warning me for years that I was romanticising the past. Maybe this truly was the way of the world: power was a drink that invariably made you thirstier for more.

'What would you have me do, your Grace?' I said quietly. 'Even if what you suspect is true, I cannot . . . I *will not* murder a fifteen-year-old boy who has committed no crime.'

I half expected her to slap me again, but instead, she squeezed my arm. 'I know you can't, and I can't fault you for the decency in your heart.' She sighed. 'In truth, I expected as much. That is why I come to you with an alternative: a negotiation. Shared power.'

'You want Aline *and* Filian to rule? How would that even work?'

The skin around her lips looked tight, as if the words she was trying to get out were distasteful. 'It isn't as unusual as you might think. They are only half-siblings. The old royal lines often had—'

'You want Aline to *marry* Filian? Have you lost your mind?'

'No, Falcio, I have simply run out of options.' She held up a hand. '*Listen to me*. Aline is clever, and wise. She has a strong spirit and she could hold her own in any power-sharing arrangement. She would have the right to her own bodyguards, and you and your fellow Greatcoats would keep her safe from Trin's machinations. After a while, Filian might even become a good King.'

'Trin will never allow it.'

Duchess Ossia smiled. 'That is why we will not give her a choice.'

'Killing her will make Filian into an intractable enemy.'

'We needn't *kill* her. All we need to do is take control of the castle for a little while – a week at most, time for negotiations to take place. I will bring the Dukes to our side by showing them the wisdom of having both heirs share power.'

'So that they have time to decide which one to have assassinated?'

'Perhaps – but more likely my fellow Dukes will see that power-sharing will keep the crown weak, which is, let's face it, our preferred state of affairs.'

I found the idea sickening for a hundred different reasons, but she was right: we were out of options. Although we were ostensibly waiting for Filian's lineage to be proven, the Dukes were already rushing to his side; we had no other leverage. 'All right,' I said, 'how does this work?'

'We need to take control of Aramor.'

I shook my head. 'I have fewer than a dozen Greatcoats and I don't—'

'I have a thousand troops within a day's march,' Ossia said.

'*A thousand?* How—'

'They wear no armour. I've had them travel in small groups, craftsmen and labourers seeking work. Your man Antrim controls the Aramor guardsmen, so all we need is his assistance to get my men into the castle. Once we have control, we can bring the parties together to negotiate a quick and painless peace.'

'Trin's army is larger,' I said. 'Two thousand at least.'

'It won't matter. Once my soldiers are inside the castle they can hold it against five times that number.'

The conversation had moved so quickly: from cajoling and insults to a palace takeover. It required only a word, a nod of my head.

'The other Dukes won't like it – they all have their own troops garrisoned outside the castle. What happens—?'

'The Dukes hold their soldiers by them like precious gems. They won't even notice until it's too late, and they won't want a battle that might strip them of what few troops they have. This is how it must be, Falcio.'

Her words made sense, but my discomfort wasn't going away. 'We're talking about a coup.'

She gave a laugh. '*A coup?* There isn't a monarch yet, so how can there be a coup? In fact, all we're doing is securing the situation so that a lawful solution can be found. Isn't that what you told me King Paelis wanted you to do? Isn't that what his little missions were all about? So that you could secure the country and reinstate the rule of law?'

'You know, it's not polite to use someone's words against them.'

Except that's what this has been about all along. That's why she'd goaded me about the King's missions: she already knew what my answer had to be. By that same logic, I had to admit that what she proposed was no less lawful than any of the commands King Paelis had given us the day before he died.

'I'll speak to Antrim in private,' I said. Even that simple acknowledgment tasted bitter on my tongue. I wouldn't be able to tell Aline or Valiana. They'd never go for it.

And *that* told me that all this talk of interregnum and securing Aramor so that negotiations could take place was nothing more than pathetic self-deception. I was going to turn my back on the law to get what I wanted, which was Aline safe and on the throne. If it had no other virtues, at least Ossia's plan meant I wouldn't have to murder a boy, nor watch my enemy take power. With that realisation came a decision.

I was about to launch my first coup d'état.

CHAPTER FORTY-NINE

THE TRAP

When I went to meet Duchess Ossia in the cells at the lowest level of Aramor, the late afternoon sun was snaking in through the windows mounted high on one side of the sloped ceiling. The King had never wanted anyone, even his prisoners, trapped in darkness. Oddly, the light made me uncomfortable. Treason should happen in the dark.

'What exactly are we doing down here?' Brasti asked as we walked past the heavy iron door and into the long hallway with its rows of cells on either side. How long would I be willing to keep Filian imprisoned here if we couldn't come to some kind of power-sharing agreement between him and Aline?

I hadn't told him or Kest what the Duchess and I had discussed; the fewer people who knew, the less chance we'd make Trin suspicious. Anyway, surprise is the single most important asset in a coup d'état: it's more powerful than any troops, more effective than any bribe. It's the difference between a quick, painless shift in power that would enable us to negotiate the agreement we needed and a bloodbath that would set the country against itself for years. If we wanted to clean up the mess the King had left us, we had to shift the balance of power with the suddenness of a lightning strike coming out of a clear sky.

'Falcio?' Kest said. He knew something was wrong.

'We're taking control of Aramor,' I said. 'Duchess Ossia is going to help us take custody of Filian. Once we have him, we'll establish a new council and arrange formal power-sharing between him and Aline.'

Kest's eyes narrowed. 'You're staging a coup.'

'I'm saving the country.'

'Well, I'm no legal expert,' Brasti said glibly, '—oh, wait . . . I *am* a legal expert. Isn't this illegal?'

'It is,' Kest confirmed. 'Utterly and absolutely illegal.'

'That's debatable,' I said. 'There is a case to be made that we are in an interregnum.'

'Now where have I heard that before?' Brasti asked, cutting me off. He pointed a finger in the air. 'That's right: Morn made the exact same argument to justify his plan to take over the northern Duchies.'

'This is *different*. We're not taking power for ourselves, we're just introducing a temporary security measure so that we can ensure—'

Brasti snorted. 'Hey, I don't need the explanation. I'm fine with us taking over the country and killing Trin.' He folded his arms across his chest and leaned back against the bars of one of the cells. 'I suppose we'll need to kill a few others as well, just in case. Which of our enemies should we start with, do you think?'

'We're not killing anyone. We're just—'

'And should we still call you "First Cantor"?' he asked, prodding me with his finger. 'Or do you prefer "Emperor Falcio" now?'

I'd expected his asinine jibes and yet I still found myself enraged. I grabbed him by the collar and slammed him back against the iron bars. 'I'm trying to save Aline, you fool!'

'Then give Filian the throne and get her out of the country.'

'No! Trin won't allow it – and besides, she's King Paelis' daughter—'

'—and Filian is his son.'

I found his hypocrisy stunning. 'You don't even believe he *is* the King's child!'

'But you do,' Brasti said, 'otherwise why would you throw away the one thing you've been telling us we were fighting for all these years?'

'I told you, it's not that simple!'

Kest grabbed my shoulder and hauled me back, forcing me to let go of Brasti. I stumbled, trying to regain my balance, but he didn't say anything, just stood between us.

'What happened to the man who wanted to murder Valiana when he thought she was a princess?' I asked him bitterly, but Kest didn't even blink.

'He was commanded by the First Cantor of the Greatcoats to follow the law. Was that a mistake? Should I have killed her when I had the chance?'

'She was different. She was—'

'Valiana was raised by Duchess Patriana, just as Filian was, and yet you risked all our lives and the future of the country on her. What great sin has Filian committed that you won't give him the same chance? By what right do you decide that Aline must rule no matter what the law says?'

The sounds of footsteps removed the need for any reply on my part. Duchess Ossia, followed by half a dozen of her men, came down the hall and stopped outside the entrance to the dungeon, waiting for us. 'By the right of a parent,' Ossia said.

I pushed past Kest and walked down the hall towards her. Two of her guards held up their spears before I got too close. Treason always makes people nervous. 'Aline isn't my daughter,' I said.

Ossia smiled, leaning against the iron door to the hallway. 'It is nothing to be ashamed of, Falcio. I know the pain that these actions bring you. Only the obligation of a father is powerful enough to make you set aside your duty as a magistrate.'

I let the comment slide. 'We should get moving. The afternoon court session will end soon and once the throne room empties out we'll have our best chance to take control.'

She took in a breath to speak and I saw the tiniest crack in her composure. She tried to regain her normal calm demeanour, but as our eyes met, she knew I'd seen. 'I'm sorry,' she said, stepped back and swung the iron door shut. The latch clanged into position and the lock engaged.

'What in hells are you doing?' I shouted, banging on the door. 'This was *your* idea! Why would you—?'

'I'm sorry, Falcio. It is the only way.'

I stared at her through the four-inch-square peep-hole in the door. 'The coup . . . You convinced me we could—'

'I needed you to make it possible for my troops to enter Aramor unfettered and to keep as many of the Greatcoats out of the way as possible. I promise you, this will go quickly, and I'll have you freed as soon as it's done.'

'You're *betraying* us?' I shouted. 'Why would you do this?'

Duchess Ossia looked genuinely sad as she said, 'Because I must.'

I didn't understand: Ossia had always been the King's closest ally amongst the Dukes, so what possible reason did she have for betraying him now? Then it came to me – too slowly, of course. There was *one* reason why she would betray Paelis' daughter.

Like an idiot I'd never asked her why she'd been so sure that Filian's parentage would be validated by the Sages when they arrived. 'Filian is your son.'

She began backing away, her guardsmen surrounding her with shields in case Brasti tried to fire an arrow or I tried to throw a knife. 'Forgive me, Falcio. A mother's duty compels me, and a mother's burden always comes to a terrible end in this sad and broken country.'

CHAPTER FIFTY

THE COUP D'ÉTAT

The seconds ticked by as I watched Brasti trying to pick the lock. He'd always been the fastest of us, but it still felt as if he were moving far too slowly.

'Can you—?'

'Yes, Falcio, I *can* pick the lock faster. I'm just doing it slowly to punish you for getting Kest and me involved in a fucking coup d'état which has now turned out to be *against* Aline!'

'I'm sorry,' I said, 'I didn't—'

'Better that you not speak,' Kest said. He didn't sound angry at all, and from anyone else I might have been able to fool myself that he was merely being efficient. But I'd known Kest most of my life. He was *enraged*, and he was right to be. I had allowed Duchess Ossia to use me to set up the coup which would see her son on the throne. When she had control of the throne room as well as the castle, would she murder Aline immediately? Or just lock her up?

Even as I watched Brasti work, my mind started turning, trying to come up with some kind of leverage I could use to negotiate for Aline's safety. A new King would have enemies, and even the Dukes who supported him might be troubled at the manner in which Ossia had secured his rule. She might be open to a deal with the Greatcoats as a means to give some legitimacy to Filian's takeover.

Instinctively I looked at Kest, wondering what our chances might be – of course he'd know what I would be thinking now. But I could tell he was truly disgusted with me: I was already looking for some new way to use the Greatcoats as a tool for my own ends.

Saint Birgid-who-weeps-rivers . . . what has happened to me? How did I turn into this . . . this thing *I've become?*

I heard the click in the lock as Brasti worked it open and a moment later we were racing through the halls and up the stairs. Whatever hopes I'd held for a bloodless transition of power had been dashed. I'd be killing as many of Ossia's men as it needed to win this damnable game we'd begun.

I'd expected to encounter more resistance, but by the time we reached the throne room, chaos had already taken over. Antrim, bless his untrustworthy heart, had obviously failed to follow my orders because he and some thirty Aramor guardsmen were waging a bloody fight against Ossia's troops. When he saw us coming, he barked an order to his men and they made a sudden surge against the opposing force, only to suddenly pull back, leaving a gap for us to race past and into the throne room. The look on Antrim's face told me that he would be holding me accountable, whatever came of this.

The scene inside was even more confusing: several guardsmen were trying to protect Filian and Trin, who was screaming threats at anyone who came near. On the other side of the dais, Aline was rising from her throne; only Duke Jillard was nearby. At first I didn't understand who Trin's men were fighting, since the only Aramor troops I'd seen were still outside in the hall – then I noticed the opposing soldiers' plain clothes. '*They wear no armour*,' Ossia had said.

And at last everything fell into place: Ossia hadn't come to take power for Filian. She'd brought her troops to *kill* him.

'*A mother's burden always comes to a terrible end in this sad and broken country*,' she had said.

This was why she'd wanted the Greatcoats out of the way: not because she was going to betray our pact, but because she was going to take it one step further by killing her own son to ensure Aline took the throne. *She thinks Patriana's influence will have made Filian into a monster*, I realised, *just like Trin*. So Ossia had locked me in the dungeon to prevent me from interfering as she murdered her own child in the name of saving the country.

Ossia's men cut down the guards protecting Filian, and I watched in horrible fascination as the Duchess herself, a poignard in her hand, approached the boy. She was going to kill him herself.

A mother's duty.

I started towards her, but I wasn't running now; I was walking. Some part of me had made a decision. I hadn't wanted Filian to die, but if this was the way of things, then the hells for him and Trin and all their machinations. Aline would take the throne: she would be Queen and I could finally rest, knowing my King's daughter and his country and his dream were safe once and for all.

Trin screamed a curse, but even if there was magic in it, it wasn't enough to stop Ossia's cold determination. Something black and oily glistened on the tip of her blade in the dying afternoon light that poured through the windows. *Poison.* She wasn't taking any chances.

'Falcio!' Kest called out, and when I turned, I saw he and Brasti were caught in the press and fighting to keep from being taken down. I turned back to the dais and the events unfolding there.

'Falcio, this is *murder*!' Kest shouted, and he was right: it *was* murder – but I wasn't the one doing it. Ossia had freed me from that burden. Filian tried to catch my eye and I wondered what he saw in my face: was he expecting me to run to save him, the boy who would destroy my country and the girl the King had named after my wife so I would know I had to protect her? The young fool so in love with Trin that he couldn't see the evil that drove her? Whatever fine intentions he might have, as soon as he took the throne he would marry her and *she* would be the one in control. She would turn this country into a bigger hell than it had ever been.

He was still looking at me but I didn't even bother to mouth the words 'I'm sorry' because in that moment, I wasn't.

A shout from the other side of the dais drew my attention. Aline, her own small belt knife in hand, was running towards Ossia, with Jillard chasing after her, but he was moving too slowly. I was running too, now, realising that in my willingness to forsake the law to save Aline, I'd forgotten the most important thing about her: Aline would *never* allow someone else to be murdered for her, and she would never forgive me for allowing it to happen.

Her courage snapped me out of the fog I'd allowed to envelop me – but it was too late, because Aline failed to reach Ossia in time to stop the attack.

Instead, she got there just in time to get between Filian and the blade.

CHAPTER FIFTY-ONE

THE SOUNDS OF BREATHING

Screams, shouts, whispers, laughter . . . the human voice is capable of a remarkable assortment of sounds when words fail us, when reasoned, ordered thoughts cease to mean anything in the face of a world turned upside down. And yet it was the sounds I noticed most through the chaos and wreckage that was Aramor's throne room.

My other senses had slowed down, coming too late, like thunder preceding the lightning. I knew I was running towards Aline, but only because I could hear the clap of my boots against the hard marble floor. Men had tried to get in my way, but I knew that only because of their groans, the scraping of my rapiers as they slid through leather armour, the wet sigh of steel withdrawing from flesh. I knew Aline had fallen to the floor from the dull crack of her head striking the marble and the soft sigh from her lips. I knew she was still alive, but only because I heard her speaking to me.

'Time,' she said, so softly that I shouldn't have been able to hear the word over the din, and yet I could.

I looked down at her stomach, forcing my eyes to focus, to take stock of the cut that had slashed through her gown just above her waist. The wound was deep, but a cut is not the same as a puncture;

none of her vital organs had been struck. 'It's going to be all right,' I said.

I felt a squeezing of my right hand and only then noticed she'd taken it in hers. 'It will be all right, Falcio.' The tears filling her eyes belied her words.

Someone was shouting over and over for a doctor, swearing all the while. I think it was Duke Jillard.

'Hey,' I said to Aline, trying to keep my voice light even as the clashing of steel came perilously close. A clang, almost like a bell, told me that Kest was nearby, protecting us with that big shield of his. I took a bandage from inside my coat and started to wrap it around Aline's belly. 'It's just a little scrape, barely worth making such a fuss over.'

She gave me a little smile. 'I love how stupid you are sometimes.'

My own tears were tracing lines down my face, but I only discovered that because of the strangled sob that came out of me unbidden. 'I thought I'd lost you.'

She took my hand and placed it over her heart. I'd expected it to be racing, as mine was, but Aline's was slow and steady. That's when the fear tightened around my gut.

Aline spoke to me calmly, almost reassuringly. 'Duchess Ossia is old now, Falcio. Her hands shake sometimes just from holding her teacup. She couldn't trust her blade alone.'

'No,' I said. '*No*. You don't know anything about—'

Aline closed her eyes for a moment. 'It doesn't hurt, not even a little bit. I don't think she wanted him to suffer.'

'Stop,' I said, shaking her until she was looking at me again. 'You don't know what you're talking about. Death and dying are *my* expertise. I'm a proper duellist and you're just a little girl who dresses up like a Queen and pretends she knows things when really she's no wiser than her fool of a father.'

'I wish I'd met him. The priests say we can only meet those in the next life who we've met in this one. That's not fair, is it?'

'Priests don't know what they're talking about either, remember? They're the ones who thought the Gods made us.'

A giggle, like the little silver bell they use in Pulnam to declare the end of a fencing match.

'And besides,' I said, 'even if you were poisoned, which you're not, the only poison I know of which is truly painless is neatha, and if I survived it, so can you.'

She gave me a wan smile, the corners of her mouth only moving a little. 'You *inhaled* Duchess Patriana's poison, Falcio. Do you suppose it's stronger or weaker when it goes into your blood on the edge of a blade?'

'Get me a doctor, damn you all!' I shouted, willing my voice to carry over the sounds of the fighting.

In between clanging sounds I heard Kest say, 'Doctor Pasquine is on her way.'

The touch of Aline's fingers on my cheek made me turn back to her. 'I need to tell you something, Falcio.'

'Tell me later, when you're better.'

She locked eyes with me, her gaze hardening even as her words struggled to find voice. 'Falcio val Mond, First Cantor of the Greatcoats, called the King's Heart, I am Aline, daughter of Paelis the First, heir to the throne of Tristia. You will heed me now.'

Some part of me, the part that was fighting to break through the thick layers of self-deception I was trying to wrap around my breaking heart, forced me to say, 'I'm here. I'm listening.'

'Before my father died he gave you a mission, Falcio. Will you accept mine?'

I felt a hand on my shoulder and nearly reached back to break it when I realised it was Brasti. I glanced around and saw that the fighting had ended. Duchess Ossia's troops had surrendered.

The woman herself was kneeling on the floor like some penitent beggar.

'Let me pass,' a fiery voice called out and the Aramor guardsmen parted to allow Doctor Pasquine to make her way to us.

'Falcio, listen to me,' Aline said.

'The doctor is here, she'll—'

'Please.' And when I reluctantly nodded, she whispered, 'Once I asked you to bury me near my father's grave on that little hill in Pulnam. Will you do that for me?'

Doctor Pasquine knelt down on the other side of Aline, eyes on the slash wound and two fingers already on the side of her throat, feeling her pulse.

'Save her,' I said.

The doctor ignored me, pulling out a thin metal instrument from her pack and pressing it down on the wound. The blood that oozed out was so dark it was almost black. 'My lady,' she said, 'the flesh is already necrotising. You are dying.'

My hand reached up of its own accord and wrapped around Pasquine's neck, squeezing hard enough to draw a broken gasp from her. 'Damn you! Would you take away hope from a child?'

Something painful struck a nerve in my wrist and my hand came loose. The doctor had jabbed me with her instrument. 'She isn't a child and you're not my patient. I owe her the truth.'

'Stop,' Aline said to me. She tried to reach out to me but her arm drifted back to the floor. 'Falcio, please, don't take this away from me.'

Stupid girl – after all this time she still didn't have any clue about life and death. 'What is left to take away?'

Her eyes went to Pasquine. 'I can't feel anything in my limbs. Does that mean . . . ?'

'Only moments now, my lady.' The doctor leaned over and kissed her on the forehead. 'I would have been proud to call you my Queen.'

Pasquine rose and motioned for the others to step away, leaving Aline and me as alone as two people could be in the midst of a crowd.

'It's strange,' Aline said, 'to not feel anything.'

I was so angry, so broken and empty, and yet at the same time I was filling up inside with a rage that was demanding payment for this: to smash everything around me, to destroy every person who dared stand upon this earth as she left it. The only thing holding me back was the fear I now saw dawning in Aline's eyes.

I reached down and wrapped my arms around her, lifting her to hold her close to me. With my cheek against hers, I asked, 'Can you feel this?'

She whispered in my ear, 'I can feel your tears on my face.'

'It's sweat, silly girl. Haven't you noticed how hot it is in here?'

A light chuckle, more a tiny gasping of breath than anything else, but she found the strength to speak. 'I wish you could know how much I love you for what you gave me, Falcio.'

That was too much for me. 'I failed you.'

A breath, cool against my ear. 'I was supposed to die in Rijou. You . . . you gave me the chance to fight for my country, for my people. I saved my brother's life, Falcio. What more could I . . . ?'

The words were getting softer and softer. It was getting hard to hear anything, even the sounds of breathing all around me were overpowering her, like ocean waves drowning out the sound of the breeze. Yet still Aline went on, 'I want you to be the . . .' she began.

'Be the what?' I asked.

In the stories, there's always just enough time for those dying to give some last commandment, some last words of wisdom to the living. But neatha attacks the nerves, smothering them, taking away movement and sensation, leaving behind endless black.

I held Aline in my arms even as I felt her body cooling, my mind so desperately wanting to hear her voice that I imagined all the things she might have wanted to say to me.

Be the man who saved me and not the one who killed those who tried to murder me.

Be the Greatcoat, and not the Duellist.

Bury me next to my father.

I would have kept holding her all night, resisting any attempts to take her from me. I could have held her like that until my last ounce of strength failed me, ignoring the murmurs and cries around me, ignoring Brasti's words of condolence and Kest's of reassurance. I could have ignored them all.

It was the laughter that I couldn't take.

CHAPTER FIFTY-TWO

REGICIDE

Trin stood next to Filian, surrounded by those guardsmen loyal to her, their swords and shields facing out to protect her, and she *laughed*. There wasn't a trace of regret in her eyes, in the curl of her mouth, the rosy flush of her cheeks. Aline's sacrifice had meant *nothing*. Filian would take the throne; he would marry Trin and she would be Queen of Tristia.

Her laughter sounded strange to my ears. In my mind her voice was replaced with that of her mother. Patriana, Duchess of Hervor, had finally won. After all this time, and from beyond the grave, she had destroyed my King's dream once and for all.

The echoes of her merriment and of Patriana's boasts and taunts filled my hearing, making my vision blur, my fingers itch. My tongue was as dry as the Eastern Desert under the burning sun. I have known loss many times in my life, but this was the first time I truly understood the taste of defeat.

Trin didn't even notice me. She was looking down at Ossia, Duchess of Baern, who was still on her knees and would likely remain there until the order came to take her head.

'Forgive me,' Trin said, the lightness of her voice giving the lie to her words, 'it's just that . . . it's like one of the old comedies, isn't it? The ones where identities get confused and everything begins to fall apart until finally one of the Gods descends and tells the audience what happened and then everyone gets married?' She reached out a hand and stroked Ossia's silver-grey hair. 'You're finally reunited with your son, only to trick the Greatcoats into helping you kill him so that Aline can take the throne – and she ends up giving up her own life to save him. It's all so very poetic.'

I blinked the useless tears from my eyes. I would need to be able to see clearly for the next few minutes.

Some two dozen men protected her. They wouldn't be nearly enough. I knelt to set Aline's body gently down on the floor, working through my next moves as I did.

Many of Ossia's soldiers remained, along with the Aramor guardsmen. I would draw my rapiers as I rose, shouting at Ossia's soldiers to attack. Their captain would try to countermand me, but not fast enough, so I could sow confusion on both sides as I'd done at the Margrave's wedding. Trin's men would have to split their focus. She was standing a few feet from the dais, perhaps twenty feet away from me. If I ran up the stairs and onto the throne, I could launch myself from there. The closest men would instinctively raise their shields, which would be a mistake for them. I'd need to land with my feet under me, driving Trin's defenders down, then I'd have to thrust a rapier each at the two men closest to me, one on either side, using the advantage of height to get over their shields. The rest would try to attack me, but they'd be aiming high and I'd duck low under their blades and come up right behind Trin, and only then would everyone realise I'd left my rapiers buried in my first opponents and that I had a knife to Trin's throat. They'd all expect me to make some sort of threat, ordering them to back off or else I'd kill her – I wouldn't disappoint them, of course not, but even as I uttered the words, letting them believe we were in a standoff, I'd be burying the knife in her neck.

It was a good plan.

The sane part of me, the part that had heard the wisdom in Aline's words and followed her train of thought, imagining what she hadn't been able to say, knew there was a problem with my strategy: Trin would die, yes, but Filian would be King and his heart would be hardened against the Greatcoats, against the King's Law, against everything we'd stood for and fought for and bled for: against the very principles Aline had given her life to preserve.

That's why, in those precious seconds when all eyes turned to Trin as she gurgled and bled out, I'd need to kill Filian too.

Let the Magdan have this country. The poor would be no worse off – in fact, their lives would probably get better. The Avareans would take the territory they wanted. The Magdan would likely purge Tristia of its foul nobility and set his own preferred lieutenants in charge; I expected many of them would be men and women I knew, former Greatcoats. The country would live under a kind of judicial dictatorship. It could do much worse. It already had.

It was a good plan. Trin would be dead, the country would be no worse off and I would finally have put an end to Duchess Patriana, her daughter and all their foul conspiracies.

And all it would cost was the last shred of my King's dream and my own life: a bargain at twice the price.

I let Aline's body settle on the ground and rose, my fingers already reaching for my rapiers, the muscles in my calves tensing as I prepared my perfectly planned run up the stairs and over to the throne, then into the chaos that would follow. When I turned, something flat and hard slammed into the side of my head, sending me tumbling backwards. My legs went weak, but I recovered my balance, my rapiers drawn, blinking furiously to clear my vision as I saw the man standing between me and the woman whose death I had so meticulously formulated in my mind.

It had been a good plan. I'd only forgotten one thing.

'I'm sorry, Falcio,' Kest said, standing a few feet away from me, holding his shield in front of him. 'I can't let you do this.'

CHAPTER FIFTY-THREE

FRATRICIDE

My plan adjusted itself without any prompting from me, shifting each detail to accommodate this new inconvenience. It could still work. 'Step aside, Kest.'

His face was ashen, as if with that brilliant mind of his he'd already worked out my every move, as if he'd even calculated what would happen to our friendship if he tried to stop me. 'Please, Falcio, don't make me do this.'

'No one's making you do anything. I'm the First Cantor of the Greatcoats and I'm giving you an order. Step aside now.'

'It's not too late,' Kest said, and I could hear the tiniest fragment of hope in his voice, even as he shifted his shield on his arm to prepare for the attack that he must have known was coming. 'Not so long as we hold to the law, you and I. Don't do this, Falcio. Don't throw away everything you've stood for in exchange for one moment of revenge.'

I closed my eyes for a moment, letting his words wash over me. 'You're right,' I said. 'It's not worth it.'

But when I opened my eyes, Kest hadn't put down his shield – he was too savvy a fighter and had known me too long to be so easily deceived. He knew I couldn't let Aline's death go unanswered. Trin was going to die. Filian was going to die. I was going to die.

What did one more body on the pile matter?

'I won't ask you again, Falcio,' he warned.

'Goodbye, Kest,' I said, and launched myself at him.

A moment before he'd been the finest fighter in all of Tristia and my best friend in the whole world.

Now he was neither of those thing; he was simply an obstacle.

I let him have the first blow. I came in high, my right hand up above my head, the tip of my rapier angled down over his shield while my left was already beginning the thrust that would sneak past his shield once he parried the first attack. Even if he got both of them, I could simply continue the right-hand thrust once the shield was out of the way. There's a reason why people don't go into battle with only a shield.

Kest was too fast for me, of course. He didn't just parry the high attack but knocked my right rapier out of line, and without pausing for an instant he dealt with my left-hand thrust, not by deflecting it, but by allowing the first foot of the blade past, only to drive the edge of his shield down so hard and so fast that he shattered the blade, leaving me with just one rapier and one rather badly balanced dagger.

That would have been enough to knock sense into a smarter man, but Kest was taking no chances. Before I could get myself back into guard, he slammed his shield against the side of my face for the second time and I fell backwards again. Getting hit in the head twice within minutes is not especially good for concentration. When I regained my balance, I spat out blood on the floor.

'You can't beat me,' Kest said. 'Not today.'

I smiled. It was odd how life, once divorced from purpose, could become so much like a game. 'Let's find out, shall we?'

His eyes narrowed, trying to figure me out. 'Even if you got by me, Trin's guards would kill you before you got near her.'

'Maybe, if she'd had a chance to get control of the room.' I tilted my head towards Ossia's guards. 'But now all the other soldiers have had time to consider the future. They've heard all about Trin; they know there's no pardon coming for them. She'll have them executed – but not before she's tortured them into giving up their loved ones so that she can have them killed too.'

'Stop,' Kest said. Of course he knew what I was doing. 'You're making things worse.'

That pulled an unexpected chuckle from somewhere deep in my belly. '*Worse?* You fucking fool, *Aline is dead!*' I risked raising my broken rapier to point it in Trin's direction. 'The daughter of Duchess Patriana is going to take power. How much worse can it possibly get?'

I didn't wait for an answer, but instead ran for him, switching up my guard so that my broken left rapier was high and my right was low. He knew I'd have to try for a long lunge with the right as the left was now too short to get past his shield. I feinted low, then high, then lunged for his left hip, but with the precision of a surgeon, he angled his shield so that my blade slid along its surface. I was too close to recover, and I could practically see the word 'sorry' forming on his lips as his arm came back to smash the flat of his shield into me a third time. The first two blows had been hard, but measured. This time he'd knock me unconscious to avoid having to kill me outright.

That was his mistake.

An opponent who won't kill you limits his options: his strikes have to be precise, measured. Kest wouldn't risk striking me with the edge of his shield, not when I was in so close – he'd end up caving in my skull. So it had to be the flat, which meant he needed more distance, but not so much that I could stab him with my rapier as he prepared his own blow. There wasn't one in a thousand duellists who could do what Kest was planning – he could, of course, because he's Kest. But all that careful timing meant that he'd missed seeing me flip my broken rapier so that I was holding it by the blade, and he didn't see until it was too late that I'd brought it up under his shield and hooked the rim with the quillons, yanking it up high so that all of a sudden we were facing each other like two travellers huddling together under an umbrella against the rain. His eye caught mine, then looked down at the tip of my right rapier touching his throat.

'Yield,' I said.

I could see him working through the possibilities for escape faster than I could envision any counter-manoeuvres, but it didn't matter. He knew I had the one advantage that he had given up from the start. I was willing to kill my best friend.

'What's happened to you?' he asked, the words so quiet I didn't know whether he'd spoken them aloud or I had simply read his lips. I've never seen such agony in a man's face as I did then: Kest, who ignored pain and exhaustion like other men did a light breeze. Kest, who'd barely grunted when I'd severed his right hand from his arm to stop Shuran. Kest, who even now, even after what I'd done and was going to do, still loved me more than any brother could.

Had I a heart left to break, that would have done it, but my voice didn't even quaver as I said, 'They showed me how the world works.'

He nodded, as if somehow that answer made sense. I let my gaze move to Duchess Ossia. The horror of what she'd done was already wearing off and she was rising to her feet. She'd call her men to fight with me – some might refuse, of course; now that Filian was the sole heir, to kill him would be regicide, and everyone fears the curse that comes from spilling a King's blood. It didn't matter, though, because I didn't need them to win, just to create enough chaos for me to finish what I'd started.

Without a word, Kest knelt down, signalling he wouldn't try to stop me again. I glanced at Brasti, who had an arrow nocked. I knew he wouldn't fire. His eyes were filled with tears and so much sorrow that he looked like an old man to me. He removed his arrow from the string and he too knelt down on the floor, and as he did that, others did as well, even some of Trin's men. Perhaps it was because they genuinely didn't know who was in charge any more. Perhaps it was simply that kneeling is so often second nature to us.

'Duchess Tarindelle of Hervor,' I said, stepping past Kest and making my way to her, 'for your crimes against this nation, for murder and conspiracy, it is my verdict that you will be executed.'

Filian tried to stand in front of her. 'Who are you to issue such a verdict without trial?' he demanded.

'I am the First Cantor of the Magistrates of Tristia,' I replied. 'I'm the man with the sword.'

He reached for his belt-knife, but Trin stopped him. She whispered something in his ear and after a few seconds he reluctantly stepped aside. She looked up at me, for once neither smiling, nor making any sly comment or bold threat. Our eyes met, and for the first time I recognised how similar we were: both tacticians at heart, finding the path through obstacles others believed impenetrable. That's why she knew that there was no move, no ploy that would save her now.

Trin went to her knees and spread her arms wide, tilting her head back, giving me a range of options on how best to end her. It was also a clear signal to her supporters not to interfere. I felt a strange surge of gratitude. She could have commanded her men to protect her and made this a bloody affair, but she didn't.

Filian was staring daggers at me and I wondered why *he* didn't command the guards to stop me – I supposed that too was Trin's doing. Perhaps she thought I might not kill him if he didn't interfere.

As I came closer to Trin, my rapier in my hand, I felt an eerie calm take over me. At first I thought it was simply the feeling of peace that comes when you've made your decision and no longer question it, then I realised it was something else. I tilted my blade up a few inches and saw her in its reflection.

'Ethalia.'

'Ethalia-who-shares-all-sorrows,' she corrected me. 'The Saint of Mercy.'

CHAPTER FIFTY-FOUR

THE SAINT OF MERCY

My plan had been so simple, so perfectly clever. I'd considered everything: the room, the furniture, the soldiers and their weapons, Trin, Filian – everything and everyone, except for the woman I loved.

White light reflected off my blade, blinding me for a moment, and the calm I'd felt a moment before began to weigh me down, pulling me to the floor. 'You're making a mistake, Ethalia,' I said. 'I've resisted the Awe of Saints before. I'll do it again.'

I heard her footsteps coming up behind me and I found myself breathing more deeply, wanting to inhale the scent of her. All my talk of 'friendship', of leaving the future uncertain between us, had been rubbish. I loved Ethalia; it was as simple as that. The skin on the back of my neck awaited her touch.

It never came.

She walked right past me to stand in front of Trin. 'Put away your sword, Falcio. Help me take Aline away from all this anger and destruction. Let us grieve for her together, and wait with her until she can be made ready for burial in the green grass behind this castle that she protected from madmen and Gods alike.'

'Pulnam,' I said.

'What does—?'

'She wants to be buried in Pulnam, on a little hill outside the village of Phan. That's where her father was buried. The Tailor knows where it is. She can show you.'

'Then we will take her there together.'

I shook my head. 'You'll have to do it without me. Kest will accompany you, keep you safe on the journey.'

The white light flared. 'I can take care of myself, Falcio val Mond. Who will take care of you?'

'Step aside now, Ethalia,' I said. 'This isn't a place for Saints.'

'Is it a place for murder?'

'Without doubt. Aline died here, like her father before. This place has been consecrated with the blood of her family.'

'And now you'll kill Trin?'

'I will. She caused this.'

'And Filian?'

'I haven't decided yet.'

'And me? Look at me, Falcio.'

I struggled to raise my eyes to see her. Her loose dress was covered with the dust in the air all around us. She looked tired. I caught my own reflection in the blade of my rapier, which I was still holding out in front of me even though every part of me screamed that it was an abomination to brandish a weapon in front of the Saint of Mercy. 'I could *never* hurt you.'

'Of course you could, Falcio. You just need to be angry enough to give yourself an excuse.'

Those were the cruellest words anyone has ever said to me. The thought that she believed me capable of doing her harm, after all the things I'd gone through in my life . . . ?

Then her light pulled back somehow, as if the air was being drawn out of me – but it wasn't air. Something else – compassion. Mercy. I supposed it made sense that the Saint of Mercy might be able to withdraw her nature from a person if she so chose.

So this was how she planned to do it: to make me waver in my certainty by taking away her influence entirely, to make me long for that sense of compassion I always felt around her. How typical. She'd never truly understood the nature of a duellist: that we don't care how we *feel*; we just do what must be done. This was Ethalia in her purest form. Manipulative. Deceitful. Using my love of her – the love she'd *rejected* – to bend me to her will when her Awe couldn't do the job.

I took a step forward, and she flinched as if I'd struck her. I didn't care.

'Falcio, don't,' Kest said behind me.

He'd get up and try to stop me in a moment, once he realised what was about to happen. I was going to kill Trin, as I'd promised to do, as I should have done ages ago. Ethalia thought she could stand there and stop me, but she was wrong.

I'd never realised before just how sick I was of people who were supposed to care about me trying to force my hand, to handcuff me to their own weakness. I could have saved this country years ago, if only the King hadn't commanded me to step aside while the Dukes brought their armies into Aramor. I could have ended this mess and saved Aline if only I'd killed Trin back in Avares. Did Ethalia really think I was going to stop now? *I wasn't.* I wanted to kill her almost as much as I wanted to kill Trin – in fact, I could just drive my rapier through Ethalia's heart and straight into Trin's neck, and then I would be free. At long last, the torment inside me would go away and I would drift back into that blessed madness that had sustained me for so long, before Ethalia had taken it from me.

I took another step towards her, towards Trin, towards freedom.

One lunge. One perfectly executed lunge, just like in the old fencing manuals. Don't think of Ethalia or the future or anything else. Let the explosion begin in the calf of the rear leg, the muscles carrying the force up into the body, the arm forming the perfect line, the tip of the blade piercing skin then flesh, scraping past bone and through the other side and into Trin's neck.

Freedom. Freedom from all of them is one lunge away.

Part of me kept expecting my wife Aline to appear, or perhaps King Paelis: hallucinations, memories from my past, come to haunt me into good behaviour. Nothing.

As I began the strike, I looked into Ethalia's eyes, so sure was I that nothing there could stop me. Her own gaze was peaceful, serene ... no ... it was something else: *confident*. She was *convinced* I wouldn't do this. How *stupid*. Aline, my King's daughter, used to look at me that way, so absolutely positive that I would stop whichever assassin had come for her – and I'd done it, too; time after time I'd found a way to save her ... Until now. Was this all I'd ever been? A reflection in the eyes of others? A man with no dreams of his own, who only tried to live up to the expectations of those he cared for? And if that was true, then this, right now, the one act of my own choosing, the only thing I'd ever done for myself, was going to be an act of murder.

No.

I raised my hand high, letting the tip of my sword point straight down. With all the strength in my body, with every last ounce of rage in my being, I drove it down into the marble floor.

By rights the blade should have shattered, yet somehow I'd found the perfect angle and the tip struck a weak point in the marble. My rapier sank nearly a foot into the floor of Castle Aramor's throne room. I let go of the grip and watched as it quivered from the force of the impact. The stonemason's warning about the castle's weaknesses came back to me and I found myself wondering if we were all about to go tumbling down to our deaths. There would have been a kind of poetic symmetry in that, but death, like life, cares nothing for poetry.

Very slowly, I walked back to Aline's body. I removed my greatcoat and laid it on top of her.

Then I turned and faced the room. 'I'd like to go to my cell now,' I said.

CHAPTER FIFTY-FIVE

THE THREE VISITORS

The first week in a cell is the hardest. Fear is a constant companion, an unwelcome cellmate who talks and talks until you clamp your hands against your ears even though you know it will do no good. Then, when exhaustion finally overtakes you, he whispers such horrors to you that your own imagination seems an insufficient canvas to hold so many dark thoughts.

I suppose it's even worse for those who still care about living.

For someone like me, who, let's face it, has never had the most adamantine grip on reality, the real problem is having my sanity fall out from beneath me like a trapdoor opening onto a particularly deep pit. The sensation felt so familiar that the thought of going mad was almost welcome – it does help to pass the time, after all. However, it's not without its annoyances, specifically, never being sure if the parade of people coming to see you are real or not.

'Food,' my night-time guard said, and I looked up from the darkness of my cot to see him holding a tray beneath the dim light of the lantern hanging in the hallway outside my cell. I checked to see if his appearance had changed; in my experience, imaginary people rarely look exactly the same from visit to visit. In this case, Dezerick was much the same as every other time I'd seen him: a big, burly man with oddly beautiful blue eyes offset by a nose that had clearly been broken more than once. He had thick, curly black hair and a beard that looked like it had been recently been adorning a bear's—

'You're not real,' I said, wagging a finger at him.

He looked surprised. 'I'm not?'

I got up from my cot so I could see him better. 'You've had a haircut – and not one you did yourself – and your beard has been trimmed. Elegantly.'

'A man's not allowed to take some pride in his appearance?'

I kept silent. It's important to remember not to talk back to hallucinations.

'Look, do you want this food or not? Otherwise I'm going to eat it.'

Despite myself, my eyes went to the tray: a bowl of soup that smelled of tomato and basil, a thick slice of bread and a plate that *appeared* to have a slab of actual meat on it (and not rat meat, either). 'Now I *know* I'm imagining you,' I said, breaking my own rule about not conversing with my delusions. 'Who in the hells would bother putting herbs in prison soup?'

'Brings out the flavour,' he said, sounding a little offended. 'Besides, why would the cooks go to the trouble of making especially unappetising meals just for you when they've already got pots of proper soup made for the castle's guests and staff?'

He was right; you really do have to wonder why most dungeons go to all the trouble of serving such unpalatable food to prisoners.

'That doesn't explain the beef,' I pointed out. 'And I couldn't help but notice you're wearing a clean shirt too . . .'

'Look, I'm going to put this tray through the slot and you can either eat it or not as pleases you. Now, do you want to hand me your shit-bucket or is that imaginary too?'

Reluctantly, I picked up the bucket and slid it through the gap in the bars intended for that purpose – and immediately ran to the far corner of the cell. Guards often find it terribly funny when, instead of taking away the bucket, they hurl the contents through the bars and drench you in your own filth.

Dezerick gave me a sour look. 'You really do expect the worst of people, don't you?'

As he started his slow shamble back down the hall I scrutinised the contents of the tray. My inspection lasted less than a second before I grabbed the beef and took a bite, barely bothering to chew before swallowing it. Yes, fine, it *might* have been poisoned, but really, I'd attempted to kill the new heir to the throne so I was going to die anyway soon enough. And in truth, the meals hadn't been bad to start with, and oddly, appeared to be getting better and better. 'A proper haircut,' I called out between the bars. 'Your beard styled and oiled and a nice new shirt. Who's been bribing you to bring me better food?'

The guard came back and folded his arms across his chest. 'Did you just accuse me o—?'

'I'm not complaining. I'm just saying, I hope you made out all right on the deal.'

A wide grin slowly spread across Dezerick's face. 'I've never had so many give me money! I can't walk from my cottage to the castle without someone slipping a coin into my hand. "Show him some kindness," they say, "and there'll be more on the morrow." I swear, Falcio, the missus and I are *this* close to being able to buy a nice little plot of farmland we've had our eye on.' He glanced down at the tray, now mostly empty, as I'd been eating while he'd been talking. 'Want some more? It isn't any trouble.'

I shook my head. 'Thanks, but I'm all right – I don't want to look fat at my hanging, do I?'

'Well, I hope that's not too soon.' His look made it clear he'd hold me personally responsible for any loss of income should I be executed before he'd become the proud possessor of a snug little farm. 'Anyway, if there's anything I can do for you – well, other than letting you escape! – you let me know.'

I considered that for a moment. Books might have been nice, and perhaps an oil lamp to read them by, but that wasn't how I wanted to spend this favour. 'There is one thing you could do for me.'

'Name it,' he said warily.

'No visitors.'

Despite my request, I received a visitor that same night. I suppose given who it was, I couldn't really blame the guard.

'Hello, First Cantor.'

At first I thought it might be Filian, but where his voice had always annoyed me with its supercilious formality, this one was younger, richer, filled with a kind of warm enthusiasm, like that of a child about to set out on their first fishing expedition.

I rubbed the sleep from my eyes and waited for my vision to clear as I stared at a young man of twelve with unruly dark hair and an overly optimistic grin. Tommer, who'd taken a fatal blow protecting Aline from a God, whose hand I'd held as he'd given up his last breath, was standing a few feet away from me, *inside* my cell.

'You'd better be a fucking hallucination, because if you're the God of Valour I'm going to kick the shit out of you.'

He laughed and brought his small fists up into guard. 'Shall we have a bout, First Cantor?'

I was seriously considering punching my God in the face when a loud hiss was accompanied by a sudden painful scratch on the back of my hand. I looked down to see the source of the punishment for my blasphemy.

'You brought the fucking cat?'

'When I told her I was coming to visit you, she wanted to come along.'

As if to prove his point, the little wretch hopped up on my lap and promptly went to sleep. She was warm, though her fur was a little wet and stank of – well, *cat*, which made it somewhat harder for me to convince myself that this was all a hallucination. 'I thought you were dead. I thought the Blacksmith's God killed you.'

Tommer – no, *Valour* – tilted his head as he stared back at me. 'Faith has to go somewhere, Falcio. It can't just disappear. It's not magic, you know.'

'Are you trying to be funny?'

'I died, as did the others, but we come back, over time. Death returned first – of course – and Love was quick to follow. I was perhaps a little late.'

That confirmed something I'd suspected for some time, but still I said, 'You're a liar. You might be a God, but you aren't Valour.'

'Why do you say that?'

'Because Gods appear to us wearing the faces of those who most represent their aspect to us.'

'And who best personifies Valour for you, First Cantor?'

'You know the answer.'

He sighed. 'I would show you her face, Falcio, but you won't let me.'

That drew a hoarse chuckle from me. '*Let* you? Since when do mortals command the Gods?'

'Since always – I thought you understood that.' He reached out a hand towards me. 'Give me leave, Falcio; let me show you her face. She was so valiant, so determined to live up to your example, to—'

'No!' I screamed, and the cat scratched me a second time before leaping from my lap.

'Can you not set aside your anger for one instant? Just for one moment, to marvel at who she was? At what she did? This country you have fought so hard for sits on the precipice, Falcio. It needs valour now more than ever.'

'Then maybe you should stop letting those who show it die all the time.'

'It's not the Gods who commit such acts. No God made Ossia plot to kill her own son, or make you try t—'

'Get out,' I shouted, and then less coherently, '*Get out!* Leave me alone, damn you! Or give me a damn sword so I can kill you myself!'

His expression showed no sadness nor anger as he stared back at me – I suppose neither emotion meant much to him. Instead, he walked to the cell door, opened it as though it were unlocked and walked out. He left it ajar.

I ran to it and slammed it shut, tripping as I did and hitting my head against the bars. I fell to my knees. 'Stay away from me,' I said, more to myself than anyone else, for both Valour and the cat were gone. 'And don't do me any damned favours. I wouldn't need your help if I wanted to escape!'

'Well, I suppose that's good, because I'm not here to break you out.'

I looked up and saw Kest, standing outside the cell in the shadows. We stared at each other for a while, then I asked, 'I don't suppose you saw a God on your way here?' I held out a hand, palm facing down just below the height of my chest. 'Little fellow? Goes around with an alley cat?'

He shook his head.

Damn. I'd done exactly what I promised myself I *wouldn't* do. I'd let myself be berated by my own insanity. I went back to sit on my cot. 'Well, then, what is it *you* want?'

'I meant what I said, Falcio. I'm not here to help you escape.'

'Did I ask you to?'

'You shouldn't need to!' He made the words sound like an indictment.

'I imagine it took some convincing to get Brasti not to do something rash.'

'Brasti saw reason.' Kest paused, then added, 'Once he regained consciousness.'

Despite everything that had happened, the thought of what had doubtless been a number of colourful exchanges between the two of them brought a smile to my face.

'You should know that Valiana wanted to free you,' Kest said.

'You stopped her?'

'I did.'

'Thank you for that.'

'It wasn't easy,' he said. 'When I wouldn't let her, she very nearly allowed the adoracia to take her over so that she could fight me. Still, that was nothing compared to Ethalia.'

I had wondered that she hadn't come to see me, though I had no idea what we'd say to each other, not after what I'd almost done. 'Did she threaten to use her Saint's Awe on you?'

'She threatened a great many things – I have to say, for a Saint of Mercy she's developed a rather loose interpretation of the job.'

I leaned back on my cot, the rough-spun linen sheet cool through the thin fabric of my shirt. 'You have to keep them from trying to free me, Kest – all of them. If they do something foolish—'

He slammed a fist against the bars, sending a clanging sound through the cell. 'I don't need *you* to explain the state of the world to me, Falcio! Do you think I'm unaware how precarious you've made things? They would have rounded up and hanged every Greatcoat in Aramor already, were it not for the dubious goodwill of a boy not yet sixteen who is utterly in love with *Trin*!'

'Well,' I said, allowing my own anger to slip through, 'it probably helps that *you fucking saved her*.'

He gave no reply to that, and for a long while, all I could hear was the soft in-and-out of his breathing, so perfectly even, so controlled. There was something reassuring about that. It was only because I was listening so closely that I realised he'd begun to cry.

'He made me *promise*, Falcio.'

Despite the tears, the words had been spoken without ire, with barely any emotion.

'Who made you promise – promise *what*?'

'The King.'

I got up from the cot and faced him. 'King Paelis made you promise to stop me killing Trin?'

'That night, before the Dukes came for him . . . He called me in before he saw you. He gave me my mission then.'

'You said your mission was to help me,' I said, acutely aware of the accusation in my voice. 'To help me find his Charoites—'

'No, you just *assumed* that my purpose was to protect you, and I allowed you to believe that because I . . .' He hesitated. 'Because that's how it's always been between us. But that's not the command the King gave me.'

'Then what—?'

'"Stop him",' he said to me. '"If the time comes . . . If Falcio abandons the law, *you* have to be the one to stop him. That is the final command I give you, Kest Murrowson though it breaks both your heart and mine".'

I felt something cold and thick in my throat that was making it hard to speak, to breathe. 'The King thought I would—?'

'He had more faith in you than in the all the rest of us combined, Falcio, but he knew there was a side to you . . . a part of you that loved him so much you would do *anything* to bring about the vision of the world you both shared. But a dream unchecked by conscience, unrestrained by the law? That's the first step towards tyranny, Falcio.'

'Then it's too bad he didn't have you follow Morn around, because he's the one who—'

'The King didn't *fear* Morn, Falcio. He didn't fear Patriana or the Dukes or anyone else. He believed in you so much that he trusted you to find a way to stop them. But if *you* went wrong? If *you* turned your back on what the Greatcoats stood for?' Kest looked heartbroken. 'I pleaded with him to pick someone else, Falcio. I *begged* him.'

The guilt and sorrow in Kest's words became a poison in the back of my throat, mixing with my own shame and betrayal. Not only had Paelis so feared what I might one day become that he'd set my best friend against me, but in the end, I'd also proven him right. It took a long time before I could bring myself to ask, 'What happens now? Does Paelis' final mission compel you to . . . ? Have you come down here to kill me, Kest?'

For a moment the old Kest shone through: that laconic demeanour, the dry sense of humour, so subtle that most people mistook it for disinterest. 'I'm fairly sure Trin has that covered.'

The jibe took me unawares and despite myself I laughed and added, 'I almost feel sorry for her; she's already used up the Greatcoat's Lament on me. She must be poring through every book on punishment and torture ever written searching for something new to inflict me with.'

'Ah, that's your one piece of good fortune: Trin intends Filian's first act as King to be your execution: "A show of strength," she said. Her voice had a distinct note of glee in it at the time; I believe she was hoping to goad me into some reckless attempt to rescue you.'

'I guess she's in for a surprise.' It was hard to imagine Filian executing anyone – although he had killed that poor mad dog of his. 'How's our new King supposed to do the deed?'

'With a greatsword. A single stroke, apparently.'

That made sense. Watching your new monarch chopping away at a dying man's neck for half an hour would make for a tiresome end to a coronation. I had a thought then. 'Maybe he could borrow that great big bugger of a sword Hadiermo lugs around with him.'

That drew an unexpected chortle from Kest, who looked both surprised and a little mortified by the slightly high-pitched sound. 'Don't make me laugh like that,' he said, returning to his usual reserved expression. 'It's humiliating.'

'Perhaps you should take a break from mastering fighting techniques one day and spend a little time practising a slightly less embarrassing laugh.'

He hesitated, then, looking a little sheepish, confessed, 'I've tried, believe me. Turns out laughter isn't an entirely voluntary reaction.'

Maybe it was all the days and nights I'd spent sitting alone in my cell recently, but I found Kest's admission unimaginably funny. I started laughing so hard I had to work at getting enough of a breath to mock him further.

'Oh, Saints, just give me enough time before my beheading to tell Brasti that after all these years of being able to master everything from the most esoteric schools of fencing to the most complicated foreign dances, the great Kest Murrowson, the finest fighter in the country, the man who somehow once defeated Caveil-whose-blade-cuts-water himself, who—'

'Falcio?' Kest asked.

Something that had started as a passing thought, a question, really, began to tickle the inside of my mind until finally I stared at him through the bars and swore, 'Son of a bitch. Tell me it isn't true.'

'Tell you *what* isn't true?' he asked, but a moment later his normally serious expression broke into a wide grin and I knew I was right.

Brasti and I had always wondered why Kest refused to tell us how he'd managed to beat Caveil-whose-blade-cuts-water. Considering you usually can't get Kest to shut up about the particular virtues of the various martial strategies he's mastered, he was abnormally silent on the subject of his duel with the Saint of Swords. Privately, we'd begun to suspect that there had to have been some form of divine intervention – which Brasti insisted was preposterously unfair – but this . . .

'How was it even possible?' I asked.

Kest shrugged. 'Right before I was to fight Caveil, when I asked you how you'd beaten me in the fencing match to become First Cantor, you told me you'd fooled me into using my own reflexes against myself. Of course, I didn't exactly have time to trick Caveil into making his muscles memorise the necessary reactions.' He shook his head. 'He was so *fast*, Falcio. I could barely even see his blade moving. Every time I tried to thrust at him, he just batted away my sword before the tip had moved even an inch. There was no way I could win in a fair fight.'

'So you . . . ?'

'Even as he was cutting me to ribbons, Caveil was boasting about the price you and Brasti and the others would pay for my arrogance in challenging him. He was describing the things he'd do to you all – he started saying, "I'll use their stiffened corpses as decorations in my home" – and then . . . just when he was going to deliver the final blow . . .' Kest looked down and leaned his head against the bars. 'Please don't *ever* tell Brasti about this. You have to *promise* . . .'

'Why not?'

'Because at that exact moment I found myself remembering the punchline to that joke Brasti always tells – about three lonely nuns and a dead cleric? You know the one: "Be careful where you sit, sister, or you'll be committing a mortal sin"—'

The snort that came out my nose nearly set the bars of my cell shaking. 'And Caveil?'

Kest looked up and I could see tears in his eyes from trying to hold back the laughter. 'He was so shocked – he tried not to laugh, and he just stood there frozen. It was only an instant – less than half a second – but in that time I got the point of my sword into line and—'

'You killed the Saint of Swords, the greatest fencer alive, with *a dirty joke*.'

Kest was giggling so hard now he had to grip the bars just to stay on his feet. 'You can't tell Brasti. I beg you. If he knew—'

'He'd go around claiming *he* was the one who *really* defeated Caveil?'

Gradually Kest got hold of himself and said, very seriously, 'I can endure almost anything, Falcio, but not having to refer to the worst swordsman I know as Brasti-whose-naughty-jokes-slay-all-monsters.'

That sent the two of us into another fit of uncontrollable laughter that must have made the guard at the other end of the hall wonder if we'd both gone completely mad.

When exhaustion finally settled upon us, I reached a hand through the bars and touched Kest's arm. 'Thank you,' I said.

'For what?'

It was such a simple question, but the answer was far too small to encompass the magnitude of what he'd done for me. Kest had been there for me since we were children. He'd given up everything to stay by my side – and now, having traded every other happiness for what little my friendship had provided in return, he was about to lose that too.

Before I could answer, we were interrupted by the sounds of two sets of footsteps coming towards us, and a moment later, Dezerick appeared, escorting Valiana.

It occurred to me that I'd had entirely too many visitors in one night for a prisoner, so I asked, just to be sure, 'Kest, is there an annoyingly well-groomed guard standing there with my daughter?'

He glanced at them. 'It appears so.'

'All right then.' I let go of his arm. 'I guess you'd better go.'

Valiana waited until after he'd left before gesturing to Dezerick.

He looked uncomfortable. 'Realm's Protector—'

'Do it.'

He brought out his key and unlocked the door.

'Valiana, whatever it is you think you're doing—'

She cut me off. 'Filian knows I'm here, and what I'm doing. Duke Jillard has asked to see you and the heir to the throne has given his consent.'

It made sense that he might not want to alienate the most powerful Duke in the country before he'd even been crowned, but I was sick and tired of political games and machinations. I went back to my cot. 'Tell his Grace that I'm rather busy at the moment. Perhaps we could arrange a later meeting, sometime after the coronation ceremony.'

'It has to be now.'

I sighed. 'Fine. He can come down here then.'

She hesitated for a moment, then said softly, 'Jillard is dying.'

CHAPTER FIFTY-SIX

THE DUKE OF RIJOU

The body is a strange thing. After all, what is the human vessel but an inelegant accumulation of blood and bone, skin and sinew? As a child, long before I learned that it was we who had shaped the Gods and not the other way around, I thought they must have marvelled at their strange creations: these ungainly amalgamations that somehow walked and talked and thought and loved. From nothing we become men and women who write poems and wage wars and conceive of futures both wondrous and terrifying.

When I'd taken up fencing, I came to see the human body differently: as a machine, with levers and gears: a clockwork contraption that could be carefully tuned and oiled to peak efficiency, its purpose to point and swing a blade smoothly and swiftly, to disassemble other machines within the circular confines of a duelling court. Eventually the day comes when the gears turn a fraction too slowly, when the lever sticks at the wrong moment and the contraption itself is dismantled.

'He's in here,' Valiana said, motioning to the half-open door through which I could hear the strains of a guitar. Vibrations became sounds that turned into notes as a melody formed, then into a song I recognised: a lullaby, of all things, a favourite of mine as a child.

I laughed. After all this time, Jillard and I had found something in common.

Valiana's fingers touched my arm and she looked into my eyes, as if measuring how far into madness I had already descended, how much further I might go.

I pushed the door aside and entered the infirmary. Nehra was perched on a wooden chair; it had lost one of its legs and she was keeping herself balanced with her feet while she played that much-travelled guitar of hers. Jillard, Duke of Rijou, lay in a bed, all the regal bearing of his person, the splendid clothes, the carefully coiffed and oiled hair, the fine features of his face, rendered absurd by the ashen colour of his skin. All that he was, all he had done, all he had aspired to, was grinding to a halt.

His eyes found mine as I approached him.

'Did you kill them?' he asked.

'Them' is rather non-specific when one is speaking of death, but I knew exactly who he meant. In this case, 'them' meant all of them: Trin, Filian, Ossia, her soldiers – not to mention the retainers who might have assisted in the plan, minor nobles who might have been consulted, contingencies in case of later complications, innocents who had nonetheless failed to prevent what had taken place.

'Them' meant everyone who had contributed to Aline's death.

'Not yet,' I replied.

A long, slow breath slipped from between his lips and his eyes closed. I thought perhaps he had died, but he had only sighed. 'That's a shame.'

Nehra's playing changed, the notes becoming harder, more precise. I no longer recognised the melody, but I understood the song's purpose. She had been giving him what ease her music could provide to gentle his body and keep him alive as long as possible. Now she was telling us time was growing short.

'I'm sorry I can't shake your hand, Falcio,' he said. He pulled his arm from under the blanket. The hand and forearm had been removed.

'What happened?'

His lips pursed slightly – it wasn't an expression I'd seen on him before. Then I understood he'd tried to shrug, but his shoulders hadn't responded. 'The Duchess planned her attack to perfection. There was a disturbance outside the castle, half the guards left to investigate and by the time we recognised the remaining men were all hers, it was too late.' He sighed. 'Ossia would have made a fine General, I think.'

'I don't remember you being hit, your Grace. You'd think I'd have noticed a Duke's arm falling to the floor.'

He didn't laugh, but one corner of his mouth rose a little. 'My own fault, I'm afraid. I assumed Ossia was planning to move against Aline, so I thought I could win myself favour with our new King by killing her myself – after all, why be a bystander to history when you can get your name in the books?' He gave a little chuckle this time. 'Never made such a bad bet in my entire life.'

'You're lying.' The truth, for once, was written plainly in his eyes. 'You tried to save Aline.'

'He reached for the blade as it was coming for her,' Valiana said softly. 'The doctor hoped that by removing the limb, the poison could be stopped in time.'

The sallow skin and pallor made it clear the doctor had been wrong.

Jillard opened his mouth to speak again and I waited for one of his usual acerbic remarks to emerge. I think he expected one too, but instead, tears formed in his eyes and he whispered, 'I thought Tommer was there.'

'In the throne room?'

His head twitched left, then right. 'No.' He paused, maybe trying to conserve some last vestiges of strength within himself before he continued, 'Aline understood before the rest of us did that Filian was the target, not her. She ran to save him – she was trying to get past one of Ossia's guards – a huge man, so much stronger than her. He looked more like a tree she was trying to climb than an opponent she could ever hope to defeat. She was screaming for someone to help – and when she turned and looked at me—' He stopped abruptly, and I was shocked to hear a sob escape his lips.

'It makes no sense,' he whispered. His eyes caught mine. 'It was as if she was looking at someone else inside me. Someone . . . *different*.'

'Tommer.'

The slight quiver of his head was acknowledgment enough. 'I thought . . . if I do what Tommer would do . . . if I run to her, if I save her life, I'll feel him with me again. If I can be reckless and brave, just as he would be, then when the blade strikes me instead of her, I'll close my eyes and Tommer will be there, watching me – not smiling; he'll be too shocked for that – but his eyes will widen and I will see reflected there the pride of a son for his father.'

The music changed again, the notes becoming heavier, each one filled with regret.

Jillard's bitter laugh came out as a cough. 'I failed, of course. The blade sliced the palm of my hand before it made its way to Aline. All I accomplished was to give the country a death it needn't grieve to balance out the one that will bring sorrow for a hundred years.' He looked up at me. 'I should have known I wasn't meant for heroics.'

There was a longing in his eyes, so I said, 'Oh, I don't know, your Grace. Maybe you just need more practise.'

He laughed then; though brittle, it was genuine. The effort drained the last of the colour from his face. 'I have a joke to tell you,' he said.

'You have at best a dozen good breaths left to you in this life. Do you really want to waste them on telling me a joke?'

'The joke isn't for you,' he said, and his eyes went to Valiana.

'Your Grace?' she asked.

'Come here.'

She hesitated, and although I had no reason to believe he meant her harm, I felt an urge to stand between them. After all, it's not as if he'd ever needed a reason before.

Nonetheless, Valiana went to his bedside and she even took his remaining hand in hers, for all that she loathed him.

'When Patriana first brought you to me, I fancied that you looked more like me than her. Of course, then I learned that Trin was my blood and you were, well, no one.'

Valiana let the insult go by. 'I've come to believe that blood is a poor indicator of virtue, your Grace.'

'I . . . came to a similar conclusion,' he conceded, 'the day I watched you fight in my dungeon to save Tommer's life. I could owe no greater debt than that.'

'He was my brother,' she said, the determination in her voice brooking no dissent. 'And he saved me in return.'

Jillard appeared not to have heard, and I wondered if he was even aware that we were still there. 'I hate debts,' he went on, 'so I thought I could repay this one. I spent a little time and a great deal of money to find your parents. I thought . . . I thought you might like to know who they were.'

Valiana's eyes widened. 'You found my parents?'

'Your mother.'

'Who was she—? Is she still alive—?'

'She is not; she died shortly after you were born. As to her name: she referred to herself as the Viscountess Puchelia, although it was well-known amongst the court that her title was somewhat exaggerated. Her presence was tolerated because of her extreme beauty and her . . . charms.'

'Her "charms"?' Valiana's tone grew harsh. 'Is this the joke you summoned me here to inflict on me, your Grace? Did you expect me to be ashamed to discover my mother was a prostitute?'

'Not a prostitute,' Jillard corrected her, 'a courtesan. But I can see from your face that you're not getting the joke.'

'I don't understand.'

Jillard looked up at me. 'For Saints' sake, Falcio, don't tell me you don't get it either?'

I shook my head. 'I'm afraid your serpentine wit eludes me as always, your Grace.'

By way of answer, Jillard very slowly took his hand, which was trembling badly, from hers, reached up and stroked her cheek. 'She looks a bit like Trin, does she not? Though somewhat prettier, I think.'

It took me a moment more to work out what he was trying to tell us.

Oh . . . hells.

'And there it is,' Jillard said, clearly cheered by my sudden discomfort. 'Patriana's plan had always been to hide Trin in plain sight while she secured the support of the Dukes to put her daughter on the throne. So she needed someone who wouldn't display any of Trin's *darker* qualities, but it also had to be someone who looked as much like her as possible.'

Valiana's eyes narrowed. 'I don't understand. What does all this have to do with—?'

'I believe the reason his Grace knows of your mother's apparent charms was because he was one of her . . . *admirers*.'

Jillard nodded feebly. 'Evidently Patriana made a habit of stealing useful babies.'

Valiana looked at me. 'But . . . but that would mean . . .'

'Tommer was indeed your brother,' Jillard said. 'Well, your half-brother, I suppose.' He let out a breath and sagged deeper into the bed as he took her hand again and held it to his lips. He kissed it. 'I'm afraid you'll have to drop the "val Mond" surname. You will be known from now on as Valiana, Duchess of Rijou.'

He tried to laugh at his own joke, but by then there was no breath left in him. Leaving chaos in his wake, Jillard, Duke of Rijou, my enemy, my friend, died.

CHAPTER FIFTY-SEVEN

THE CORONATION

A guard escorted me back to my cell with Jillard's little joke still ringing in my ears. Part of me hoped Valiana would follow, that she would grab hold of me and whisper in my ear that, despite this news, I was still her father in some way that mattered. It was a petty, selfish thought. Valiana's birth – her whole life – had been a toy played with by others. She'd spent her first eighteen years as the daughter of a Duke and a Duchess, the heir to the throne, a convenient fiction to serve Patriana's purposes, until the day she was no longer needed, and discovered she was nothing more than the daughter of some unknown peasant.

Being Valiana, of course she'd come to see her common birth as a badge of pride: evidence the country badly needed to show that the value of a life was in its living, that nobility was found in courage and dignity, rather than lineage.

Now that too had become a jest. I was certain Jillard hadn't intended his revelation to be cruel, but it was perhaps the cruellest joke of all. Valiana wasn't just the first new Greatcoat since the King's death, but the finest there had ever been. Now the new Duchess of Rijou would instead spend her life dealing with intrigues and conspiracies, struggling to bring some semblance of peace and decency to a violent, hopelessly corrupt Duchy. It was the work of a lifetime – if she was even given enough of a lifetime in which to accomplish it.

That thought alone was enough to make me depsise this country all over again.

I had never been to a coronation before. I'd been a babe in my mother's arms the day King Gregor had ascended to the throne, and I'd missed the next one while I was stumbling through the country in a haze of madness seeking revenge on every nobleman and axeman I could find – I hadn't even known that Gregor had died and his unwanted son Paelis had ascended the throne until the night I'd dragged myself up a long sewer tunnel with a sword in hand, determined to sever a King's head from his neck.

It's funny how these things can come back to haunt you.

From the way people talk about them, I'd always imagined coronations to be grand affairs, weeks-long festivals of pomp and circumstance, grandiose demonstrations of power, conspicuous consumption and compassion, with foreign dignitaries arriving by the boatload, all hoping to curry favour even as they're assessing the new monarch's strengths and weaknesses and working out how best to exploit them.

In one of the guest wings of the castle there was a great tapestry nearly fifteen feet high and more than twice as wide depicting some King from long ago walking barefoot through the city (a peculiar image when paired with the gleaming cloak of purple and gold and a crown that must have felt like an anvil on his head). The streets of Aramor, woven in brown thread, were crowded with craftsmen and merchants, labourers and noblemen, all with hands clasped together in almost religious fervour at the sight of their new monarch. King Paelis had made me stare at that damned rug for more than an hour once, until I'd found the one little boy in the tapestry who was sticking his tongue out at his new ruler. I'd wondered aloud that the embroiderer would dare take such a risk at offending the monarch who'd commissioned the tapestry, but *of course*, Paelis had said, *no one ever saw the little boy*. All they saw was a great King, crowned in gold and revered by the masses. *We crave that which is glorious*, Paelis told me, *and in its presence we will forget everything else.*

The coronation of Filian I, King of Tristia, would no doubt be remembered as many things, but glorious will not be one of them.

The whole affair took place in a single afternoon. Aramor didn't have the money for days-long feasts and parades, and as we were rather short of Gods, even the most basic religious rituals were truncated. Foreign dignitaries were in short supply too: instead of their presence, they sent modest gifts and sumptuous apologies, blaming short notice and urgent matters at home. Most likely their absence had more to do with the knowledge that the Kingdom of Tristia might not even exist by the time they arrived.

Filian the First was crowned King of Tristia in the dusty, damaged throne room of Castle Aramor on a chill autumn afternoon.

By early evening, Tristia was no more.

I had a good spot from which to watch the ceremony. Two guards had lugged in a large piece of carved oak which I mistook at first for some kind of uncomfortable-looking chairt; it was only when they pushed me down until my chest was pressed against it and chained my hands to iron rings on either side did I recognise it as a headman's block, and its purpose to position me for the touching climax of the ceremony. A prodigious number of guards were assembled nearby, apparently to ensure nothing ruined the grand finale.

It didn't take me long to spot Brasti, dressed in Kest's preposterous monk's outfit. It might have hid his quiver, but it made him look like a hunchback. No doubt he'd convinced some of the others to prepare for some preposterous last-minute attempt at saving my life. I really hoped none of them would die in the attempt.

A priest in golden robes stood behind Filian, hands shaking as he held the crown over the boy's head – I doubt he'd expected to have to perform this ritual with nine guardsmen extending longswords over his own head to form a very sharp steel canopy. He'd started Filian's various new titles, increasingly pompous synonyms of King such as 'Defender of the Nation, Overseer of its Affairs, Heart of its People . . .'

That went on for a while.

Kest stood on the other side of the dais next to Nehra, who was representing the Bardatti. Dezerick had told me Trin had forced Quentis into his old Inquisitor's coat, to stand for the Cogneri. Gwyn's plans to ride north had been cancelled – although clearly not of his own volition – because he was standing there, a colourful display of bruises across his forehead and hands tied behind his back, representing what was left of the Rangieri. They'd even managed to get Darriana to stand for the Dashini, which meant some deal must have been struck to allow Valiana to live.

None of them looked very happy.

They'd managed to get a representative from every one of the secular and religious Orders of Tristia too: a Knight for the Honori, the Viscount of Brugess, of all people, for the Nobli, people representing all of the religious Orders, from the lowest Quaesti to a Venerati Magni – and there was even an Admorteo, one of the Gods-forsaken torturers.

And they'd thoughtfully included a confused-looking craftswoman wearing an apron and carpenter's tools to represent the labouring classes. Nice.

The whole thing was a pretty little piece of pomp designed to give the impression that the country was united behind Filian.

The pronouncements reached their end, the priest fell silent, and so did the assembled guests. His gaze passed over the crowd as if he was looking for someone to give him some last-minute reprieve – not everyone was happy about Filian's coronation, and Tristia's always had quite a tradition of assassinating those crowning an unloved monarch. It might be nothing more than a petty act of revenge, but even so . . .

The priest's eyes landed on me.

Sorry, Venerati, I thought, shaking my hands in their chains to remind him of my situation. *Looks like you and I are both on the same fish-hook dangling in the river now.*

The priest sighed and set the crown gently upon Filian's head, announcing, 'Filian Primé, Dei Beadicté.' You could hardly hear the tremble in his voice.

And thus was a child stolen from his mother and raised by her greatest enemy handed the throne of my homeland.

Trin wasted no time. She signalled two black-garbed men who brought forward a lovely shining silver case, just the right size to hold an executioner's sword. Filian's eyes flickered to me and his lips twitched, just the way his father's had whenever he was wrestling with a decision. I was just close enough to hear Trin whisper, 'Look at the nobles, my love. See how their eyes search for the first sign of weakness. It will be his head or ours if you do not act boldly while you have the chance.'

Filian rose from the throne. 'My people,' he began, 'dangerous times are upon us, and so I call upon my Dukes to witness my first act as your King . . .' His words trailed off.

I didn't understand what had happened until I strained my neck to look around the room and realised that Hadiermo, Erris, Meillard and Pastien were all missing. Valiana's claim to Rijou had not yet been validated – no doubt because Trin was in no hurry to let Filian do so – and that meant that there was not a single Duke or Duchess in the room.

'Where are the Dukes of Domaris, Pulnam and Pertine?' Trin demanded. 'Where is the Ducal Protector of Luth?'

A woman's voice called out from the crowd, 'I think they might be busy right now.'

Trin had asked the question, but it's actually considered highly impolite – if not downright suicidal – to speak at a coronation without the express leave of his newly anointed Majesty. The eyes of everyone present turned to a single woman standing previously unnoticed amidst the crowd near the front of the dais. She was wearing a brown leather greatcoat with a ship inlaid on the left breast.

'Quil?' I said incredulously.

She nodded to me. 'Falcio.'

'How did this Trattari get in here?' Trin shouted at the guards.

'I'm a Greatcoat, *bitch*. Getting in and out of places without being caught is our specialty.' She looked back at me, kneeling, chained to the block of highly polished oak. 'Well, most of us, anyway.'

There were a number of calls for her immediate arrest and execution, but Quil didn't even flinch. 'You don't want to do that,' she warned before anyone had even made a move towards her. 'The Avareans take a dim view of those who harm their messengers.' She took two steps forward and extended a rolled-up piece of parchment towards the dais.

She waited for someone to come and take it, and after a hesitation, Filian gestured at one of the pages, who ran down to take it from her and bring it to the throne.

Trin reached for the parchment, but Filian gently pushed her hand aside and took it himself. I was rather surprised that she didn't slit his throat on the spot. *There's love for you.*

When Filian was done reading the document, he handed it to a clerk and said, 'Read it aloud.'

'From the Magdan,' he started, 'Warlord of Avares and First Magistrate of . . . *Boreadis?*'

Boreadis. Land of the Northern Winds. This must be the country Morn plans to carve out of Orison and Hervor. Nice name.

The clerk continued, 'To the tyrant and false-born usurper called Filian—' He stopped again, evidently feeling rather exposed, having just insulted the King, but Filian bade him to read on and he continued, his voice wobbling a little, 'Know that your presence is a blight on a great people with a great history, and that the crown on your head will be justly removed the very hour we come to liberate the Duchy of Aramor from you.'

The clerk was not alone in looking stunned. There were no threats, no demands, no terms set forth; the Magdan had skipped over all the usual diplomatic feints and instead, simply declared war and signalled his intention to invade.

To his credit, Filian tried to make the best of the situation. 'We thank you, madam,' he said politely to Quillata, 'and assure your safe passage back to . . . wherever it is you now return to.'

She gave him a wink. 'Why, that's kind of you, your Majesty. I'd bend a knee but' – and again she looked at me – 'present company excluded, Greatcoats don't kneel.'

Trin looked like she might grab the massive executioner's sword and take a swing at Quil herself, but other events overtook her: as if on cue, five messengers resplendent in Ducal colours made their way through the crowds. The one dressed in the pale blue of my home Duchy stepped forward first, bearing a little stack of vellum scrolls. 'Your Majesty, forgive me, but their Graces have been called away on urgent business.'

Filian kept his calm far better than the crowd of panicked nobles surrounding him. 'What business requires the immediate absence of my Dukes?' he enquired calmly.

'The need to protect their people, your Majesty. Troops must be deployed and borders fortified.'

'The defence of Tristia is in the purview of the King,' Trin started. 'He will decide—'

'Forgive me, your Grace,' the messenger said. His voice was remarkably even, considering he was almost certainly dead. I wondered how much the Dukes had promised to reward the families of these men in exchange for their certain sacrifice. 'The borders we speak of are those of our respective nations.'

'*Nations?*' Filian asked.

The messenger said, 'For the defence of their people, Pertine, Domaris, Pulnam, Baern and Luth can no longer remain Duchies within the country of Tristia, your Majesty, nor are their rulers *your* Dukes. The Princes of our respective nations send their regrets and wish you a pleasant reign.'

Chaos erupted then, although it wouldn't *change* anything. It was more the petulant rantings of children: Trin shouted, of course, commanding the messengers be arrested *immediately*. If Filian had any sense, he'd free them in a few hours; it wouldn't be a great start to his reign, announcing to all and sundry that the Dukes' – or rather, *the Princes'* – representatives weren't safe in his court.

Less than ten minutes after the crown had been placed upon his head, Filian, King of Tristia, had lost more than half his country, without anyone even unsheathing a weapon.

Some clerk I'd never seen before ran onto the dais and began drafting a declaration voiding the secession of the Duchies – but that was a waste of time too. All of this fury and uproar was accomplishing nothing.

Well, maybe not entirely nothing. All the rushing-around of the clerks, the guards and the confused nobles was apparently too much for the already weakened foundations. With a great crack, the throne room began to shift and the crowd fled, pushing and shoving, from the room as the floor slowly collapsed beneath them.

Kest and Brasti hauled me – and the beheading block I was still chained to – out of the room.

As I watched what was left of the dais groan and fall into the gaping pit to the floor below, I wondered if perhaps I'd been a little too quick to decide that life wasn't poetry.

CHAPTER FIFTY-EIGHT

THE UNCOMFORTABLE RESCUE

A rescue – a *proper* rescue, that is – usually takes place in four stages. First, there is the devastatingly clever plan, which requires juggling dozens – if not hundreds – of tiny details involving everything from the position of each guard in the room to the relative slickness of the floors. That's if the circumstances are favourable. In a well-guarded castle, in plain view of hundreds of onlookers, escape is highly unlikely without the aid of a brilliant tactician.

I got Brasti.

As far as I could see, his 'plan' consisted of turning up to the coronation with a couple of only slightly bigger idiots who'd somehow become Greatcoats – namely Matteo and Talia – with the apparent intention of – hopefully – 'working something out' in between me being dragged out onto the dais and the executioner's sword coming down on my neck.

I was almost annoyed that his utter lack of preparation was somehow validated by the sudden political destruction of the nation and the *actual* destruction of the throne room.

He always was a lucky bastard.

The second stage of a rescue is the daring implementation: the carefully timed and perfectly executed actions that will result in the evasion of enemy forces, the outwitting of traps or devices used to secure the individual being rescued and, of course, his or her removal from the scene, preferably unharmed.

'Gods damn you,' I shouted at Brasti after my head struck the edge of yet another doorway, 'that's the *third* time!'

'Oops,' he said, without any trace of embarrassment or apology.

Kest and Brasti had elected not to remove that hells-damned oak headman's block – which was starting to feel like a permanent attachment to my body – and instead were hauling both me and it past confused nobles and servants. There were guards aplenty, but most of them were too busy trying to find the new King so they could make sure no one slid a blade in his back during the chaos. Regicide on the first day always looks questionable on a royal guardsman's work history.

'Not much further now,' Kest said.

The third stage of a rescue is to escape from the gaol, prison, dungeon or tastelessly decorated private torture chamber as quickly as possible.

'Since we appear to be headed *deeper* into the castle,' I noted, groaning in pain every time my jaw struck the oak of the block, 'would this be an appropriate time to make two points?'

'Not really,' Kest said, his attention clearly focused on the path in front of him. Then he added kindly, 'But go ahead anyway.'

'First, I distinctly recall ordering you *not* to rescue me.'

'True,' Brasti acknowledged, huffing and puffing as he struggled with the weight of both me and the heavy oak beheading block. 'But then we remembered that no one really likes following your orders, Falcio.' He and Kest took a sudden right turn and my forehead banged against the oak beheading block yet again. 'What was your second observation?'

'Well, I don't like to sound ungrateful, but you seem to be making a terrible hash of it.'

Brasti managed a snort. 'You have no idea.'

Hanging slightly upside down and being mercilessly jostled is unhelpful to one's sense of direction. Kest and Brasti turned me down yet another narrow passageway (Brasti somehow contriving to hit my head on yet another doorjamb) and a few moments later we entered a dark room lit only by a pair of small lanterns hanging from the ceiling.

'Where the hells are we?' I demanded.

Kest gently set down his side of me and Brasti half-dropped the other to the marble floor. I managed to get myself stood as upright as possible while still attached by the wrists to a heavy piece of wood. 'And would someone be so kind as to remove these damned chains? I'd really like to avoid spending what's left of my soon-to-be-truncated life as a hunchback.'

'Abide a while,' Kest warned.

The fourth stage of any decent rescue – once you've got the prisoner out of immediate danger – is to *immediately* free them from their restraints. It's a nice addition if you also hand them a full wineskin – I'm fond of claret, especially a full-bodied Southern Luthian, but you're welcome to pick your own favourite. Unfortunately, it was clear no one was removing the chains from *my* wrists.

That's when it finally occurred to me that this might not actually *be* a rescue.

'What in *hells* is this if it's not a rescue?' I asked. 'And where have you brought me?'

The expanse of shadows before me combined with the number of times my head had struck doors, walls and doorframes on the way here was making it difficult for my eyes to adjust. Since no one was answering, I passed the next few seconds waiting for my vision to clear and setting my mind to the task of deducing where we were.

When I clanked the chain on my right wrist against the oak, the sound echoed several times, indicating a very large room. We hadn't gone down any stairs, which narrowed the possibilities. There were two ceremonial chambers for civic functions, but their floors are covered in massive rugs representing each of the nine Duchies of Tristia (a common theme in Castle Aramor; visiting Dukes always like to know the monarch isn't in danger of forgetting them). As the throne room was no longer an actual *room*, but more of an over-decorated pit, that meant I could only have been brought to—

'What in the name of dead Saint Felsan-who-weighs-the-world are we doing in the castle's courtroom?' I asked Kest.

He said nothing, but by then it didn't matter because my vision had cleared enough to make out the silhouettes of several figures standing quietly in the shadows.

Here's an easy way to tell you *haven't* been rescued: when your 'escape' ends with you being put on trial.

CHAPTER FIFTY-NINE

THE TRIAL OF THE FIRST CANTOR

'I choose trial by combat,' I declared loudly. It would have sounded more impressive had I not been chained to a lump of tree.

'You don't even know what the trial's about,' Kest said.

My Queen had died, my country had fallen into the hands of the daughter of my worst enemy and now a substantial headache had been brought on by too many blows to the head, all of which meant I really wasn't at my best. 'There's a big white circle over there,' I said, 'so if someone will kindly hand me a fucking rapier I can get on with beating the shit out of you all, one by one.'

'That's quite a temper you've developed of late, First Cantor,' Nehra said, stepping out from the shadows to stand beneath one of the lanterns suspended from the ceiling. 'I wonder, how well has it served you?' Before I could answer, she added, 'How well has it served the country?'

'Oh, go sing a fucking song,' I replied unimaginatively. I really wasn't anywhere near my best; instead, heartbreak and anger were driving me towards petulance. I should have been working to calm myself, to puzzle through what was happening and what I'd need to do next, but even on a good day I tend towards belligerence when chained to a log. 'Why don't you have the rest of your little company step out of the shadow, Nehra?'

'You would already have guessed who they were and why they're here if only your mind were clear, First Cantor. *That* is why no one has yet removed your chains, and *that* is why we need you to master yourself now.'

Seven figures stepped forward, led by Darriana. She looked as uninterested in my welfare as always, but our encounters usually begin with her making rude comments about me, so I found her current silence unnerving. Gwyn followed, his eyes darting here and there, looking almost as confused as I felt. I would have been sympathetic, but *his* bonds had been removed.

One by one the others came into view: Quentis Maren, still in his old Inquisitor's coat, standing next to a young Knight with dark, curly hair and an unfamiliar sigil on his surcoat. Kest took up position on the other side of Nehra, then motioned for a shy-looking woman to join him. I wondered where I'd seen her before, then recognised her. she'd been standing on the dais during the coronation, representing the support of the common folk for their beloved new King.

Valiana stood silently beside Ethalia; the Saint's hard gaze was moving back and forth between Nehra and me and she didn't look especially predisposed towards mercy for either of us. 'Don't goad him,' she told Nehra. 'He has the right to know why you've brought him here.'

'I should think that would be obvious: the First Cantor of the Greatcoats tried to kill the lawful King of Tristia.'

'In my defence, I was mostly keen on killing his lover – he just happened to be in the way,' I started. 'Also, at that time he was still technically just the *heir* to the throne.' I should have stopped then and there but the wounds were too fresh. 'Apparently *no one* minds if you kill a few of those.'

A sob escaped Valiana's lips and I felt vile for having drawn it from her, but I couldn't keep myself from adding, 'Besides, as I understand it, the Ducal Council already held a trial in my absence. I'm told they served cake.'

Nehra nodded to Brasti. 'He's telling stupid jokes again. I think it's safe to remove his bonds now.'

He knelt beside me and started fiddling with the cuffs binding me to the beheading block. A grinding click was followed by one of the manacles coming loose from my wrist. Brasti turned his attention to the other, and a few moments later I had the enormous satisfaction of watching the wooden block crash to the marble floor.

'You know, Nehra,' I began, rubbing my wrists to get the blood flowing to my hands again, 'I'm absolutely positive there was a time when I *liked* you. Mind you, I suspect we were a good two hundred miles apart at the time.'

'Have you figured out why you're here, First Cantor?' she asked.

'Not exactly, but I see a pattern in this little jury you've put together.' I pointed at her. 'Bardatti.' My finger drifted to the Knight. 'Honori.' One by one I called them out. 'Gwyn, for the Rangieri, Darriana, for the Dashini, I assume. Quentis to represent the Cogneri, Ethalia for the Sancti, and finally' – my finger stopped at Valiana – 'a Greatcoat.'

'Trattari,' Nehra corrected. 'Is it really so difficult for you to say the word?'

It is, actually. Usually when people hurl it at me it's a prelude to them trying to kill me.

I gestured to the woman in carpenter's garb. 'Which Order do you represent?'

She stiffened. 'None,' she said, 'but I have as much right to speak at these proceedings as any of these others.'

'Then I suppose we should get started,' I said to Nehra. 'Now, since you're not a magistrate and have no fucking business holding a trial, allow me to help by letting you know that it's customary to begin with a recitation of the charges against the accused.'

Nehra answered my challenge with a question. 'Do you know how the Trattari began, Falcio?'

'The *Greatcoats* began when Damelas Chademantaigne, the King's Hope, swore his oath some two hundred years ago.'

She sighed so I would know that yet again I'd disappointed her. 'The Order of Trattari are *far* older than that, Falcio – as are the Honori, the Rangieri and all the rest.' She turned to the others. 'You have all forgotten your history; time and ignorance have fragmented those who once stood together as part of a vital and more complex design.'

'But *you* remember?'

'Yes, because we Bardatti are the memory of this country! We keep the past alive through song and story, poem and performance. We still remember the rhymes of the Dal Verteri.'

'*Dal Verteri?*' The words were archaic Tristian; they meant something like *the road of the virtuous*, or maybe *the path of the daring*; something about a road or a bridge or a pothole, anyway, and something else that sounded pretentious.

'Twelve ancient Orders: men and women who chose a path of service in defence of this country and its people.'

'We appear to be short a few,' I noted.

She nodded. 'Some of the Orders have lost their way, like the Honori. The rest have faded away completely.' She gestured to the others. 'We in this room, and those we represent, are the last remaining strands of a tapestry that for centuries protected Tristia and inspired its people.'

The words sounded very grand, which, unexpectedly, made me laugh. I pointed to the young man in armour. 'And you're including the *Honori* in this little myth of yours? The fucking *Knights*? When have they been anything more than thugs and bully-boys?'

'My name is Elizar,' the young man said, taking a step forward as if he were giving evidence. 'My fellow Honori weren't always this way. In my youth, my grandmother shared the stories with me of *her* grandmother: a Village Knight who protected the common folk and organised them in times of danger that they might fight together to defend their homes and families.'

'It makes sense,' Kest said, sounding far too earnest given how ridiculous this all sounded. 'Falcio, how many times have we asked ourselves how the notion of "honour" could be so important to Knights when all they ever do is the bidding of their Lords, no matter how unfair or cruel? What if their practices – their very *notion* of honour – has simply become corrupted over time?'

I'd have had an easier time believing the religious torturers known as the *Admorteo* were really just physicians who healed their patients with vigorous massage. I looked over at Darriana. 'How about you?' I asked. 'Since we're spinning fairy-tales, why don't you tell me how the Dashini were really very nice people whose history of assassination is just a terrible misunderstanding?'

The look of shame in her eyes told me she was uncomfortable at being forced to count herself among their number, but still she said, 'The old man . . . the one you met when you found the Dashini monastery? He spoke of a time when the Dashini served as spies, uncovering plots and schemes within the nine Duchies that could threaten the security of the country—'

Gwyn's eyes went wide as he turned to her and finished, '—while we Rangieri scouted those dangers that arose from *outside* of the country . . . Yes! My teacher Yimris always used to wonder why our missions took us always along the borders and outside, never *within* Tristia itself.'

'The Dashini did kill,' Nehra admitted, 'but it wasn't *murder*, not originally.'

'So, mercy killings then? A quick poignard to the heart for those tired of life?'

Nehra was apparently tiring of my belligerence. 'Were you a murderer, Falcio, on those occasions when the verdict you rendered was death to those who had committed the most heinous of crimes?'

I bristled at the comparison. 'When a magistrate sentences a man to death it's because there's no other choice, and because the *law* demands it. That's why only Greatcoats have the authority to issue verdicts of . . .'

All of a sudden the point of Nehra's question became clear. 'You've *got* to be kidding!'

Apparently, she wasn't. 'When the Order of the Dashini was first formed, it executed only those warrants passed to them by the Trattari – by the First Cantor, in fact.'

'That's a *damned lie*! If I have to sentence a man to death I bloody well hold the blade myself! I don't send some assassin out to—'

She cut me off, raising her voice for the first time. 'And what about those occasions when the wealth and influence put a guilty person beyond the reach of even your vaunted Greatcoats? What do you do then, First Cantor?'

Nothing. That was the honest answer. Some people are simply too rich and powerful to kill, so we did nothing – but I wasn't about to admit that to Nehra.

'We would go to the King,' I said at last.

Brasti snorted. 'Yeah, and then Paelis would ask us if we thought executing a Viscount was worth starting a civil war.'

'It was not the King's decision to make,' Nehra countered. 'For the law to be just, it must be independent, and some questions of law have such far-ranging consequences that only the chief magistrate of the country may render the verdict.'

Brasti elbowed me. 'She means you, in case you're wondering.'

'And just what question of law have you brought to me, Nehra?' A terrible thought took shape in my mind, one that I would have believed impossible only hours before. 'Have you brought me here to rule on whether we should assassinate the King in cold blood?' I stared at each of them in turn. 'Have you all lost your minds?'

'Forgive me,' Sir Elizar said, 'but isn't that exactly what you set out to do?'

'You think I *want* some legal justification for what I . . . ?' My voice broke, and I took in long, slow breaths, hoping to steady myself, failing miserably. For all my petulance and outrage, I was like a child trying desperately not to cry, only to realise it was inevitable. 'I tried to commit murder . . . I abandoned *everything* the King ever taught me! I was willing to do *anything* to get to Trin, even if that meant murdering a fifteen-year-old boy.' I looked over at Kest. 'Even if it meant killing my best friend.'

'Aline had just died. You weren't in control of yourself,' Kest said, then, almost glibly, he added, 'Besides, you only beat me with a lucky shot. Next time you do something that stupid I'm going to bash you senseless with my shield.'

The light-hearted words were an invitation to share a moment's laughter together, the opening of a door – but one I wasn't ready to walk through. 'If Ethalia hadn't been there . . .' My gaze went to her, but I couldn't bring myself to meet her eyes. 'If you hadn't stopped me . . .'

She came to me then. 'I did nothing, Falcio, save to make you choose.' She reached out a hand and placed it gently on my cheek. 'You stopped yourself. Even there, in that awful place where she . . .' She stopped, then said, 'Aline would have been so proud of you.'

The forgiveness and compassion in her words were meant as a kindness, but they struck me like an arrow in the centre of the chest, shattering what fragile armour still held me together. 'I miss her, Ethalia – I miss her so much . . .' A pain that had been building inside me minute by minute since the moment of Aline's death radiated out to every part of my being. 'Gods take me, Ethalia, the

King meant for me to protect her and I failed – how am I supposed to go on with this inside me?'

She held onto me, the strength of her arms the only thing keeping me from falling to the floor, and I felt her breath on my neck, heard the warm notes of her voice as she began to speak, but whatever comfort she was about to offer was cut off by Nehra.

'By doing your job, First Cantor,' the Bardatti said.

'Give him time to mourn,' Ethalia implored her.

'No. Forgive me, Sancti.' Nehra's eyes met mine. 'And forgive me, Falcio. I know this grief is more than you deserve to endure, but endure it you must.'

'He's not ready for this, damn it,' Kest said, moving to stand between us.

'You can protect him from me all you want,' Nehra said to him, 'but not from his duty. The Dukes have seceded and Tristia is on the brink of a war that will assure its total destruction. You have all seen the state of Tristia's "army", huddling in threadbare tents outside this broken castle. When news spreads, even those few will refuse to fight.'

'Then let the new King deal with it,' Darriana suggested, for once taking my side. 'Or Trin. She broke the damned country – let her fix it.'

'She can't, and we all know that.' Nehra cautiously pushed past Kest to stand before me. 'Filian knows it too, Falcio. He's going to come to you soon because he needs us – the Greatcoats, the Bardatti, and all the rest of the Orders. Even as few as we are, we're the only ones left the people of this country still respect. Filian will need you to help rally them to his cause.'

'And we're supposed to decide the fate of the country?' Brasti asked.

'No, you fool,' she replied, impatiently. '*We* cannot – it is not *our* verdict to render!' She reached out and grabbed me roughly by the shoulders. 'The country has failed, Falcio – it's failed in every way imaginable. No one is even sure if Tristia is a nation anymore. *That's* why we brought you here. Before the Dal Verteri can fight a war, we need a verdict.'

I stared back at her for a long time, partly because it took me time to make sense of her words and partly because I wasn't at all sure I wanted the responsibility she was putting on me.

'You *are* the First Cantor, after all,' Darriana said with a smirk.

The words practically sticking in my throat, I whispered, 'You want me to put Tristia itself on trial. You want me to decide if my country deserves to fall.'

CHAPTER SIXTY

THE TRIAL OF TRISTIA

King Paelis once goaded me into a night-long legal debate about the limits of royal prerogative. For each supposed 'privilege' – from no taxes to outright murder – he would find some ancient law that could, in theory, justify the action. He kept pushing me, for hours on end, until finally our quarrel ended with me shouting at him, '*Because I'd fucking bring down your country if you tried it* – that's *why!*'

At the time I'd assumed the King had been arguing simply for the enjoyment of it – he always did take perverse pleasure in making me lose my temper – but now, standing there in Aramor's courtroom with everyone awaiting my answer, I realised it was because even he had never been entirely sure of the answer to this simple question: what right does any country have to exist?

By what rights are men and women subjugated, controlled by a government hundreds of miles away? If some form of social order is required, then why can't any village or town simply declare itself a sovereign nation? A thousand years ago there had been no 'Tristia': it had been nothing more than a collection of disparate city-states, each ruling themselves as they pleased until they evolved into the nine Duchies, then ruled by Princes.

Was 'Tristia' such a great idea that it deserved the sacrifice of what few Greatcoats, Bardatti and others we had left, in a futile attempt to save it one last time?

More importantly, which magistrate would ever be so arrogant as to believe him- or herself qualified to make such a decision?

Me, apparently.

'I'll hear evidence,' I said.

The young Knight, Sir Elizar, stepped forward. 'The Honori have failed,' he admitted. 'The great Orders of Knighthood have faded from memory, leaving behind only men in armour who wield their weapons in service of whichever Lord pays for their fealty.' He hung his head, dark hair falling over his eyes. 'And even in this we failed. More than half of my brethren sided with Shuran in his bid to take the country. And then many sought redemption by siding with the Church and the Blacksmith's God *against the Crown*. The rest – well, most of them – have abandoned their Lords and gone to seek whatever fortune a good set of armour and a strong blade can win for them.'

'What would you have me do then, Sir Elizar?' I asked.

The young man pushed his shoulders back and stood up straight. 'This nation is broken, First Cantor. There is nothing left for us to defend but its citizens. Let us turn our efforts to helping those who can flee across the water or the desert—'

'And leave the rest to die at the hands of the Avareans?'

Gwyn stepped forward. 'My people are . . . hard,' the young Rangieri said, 'but they are not the barbarians you believe them to be.' He turned to the others. 'Listen to me, all of you: the Avarean way of war is not like your own. It is our religion, and *rokhan* the only measure; it is sacred to us. When the horde comes, they will offer you the chance to kneel, and in so doing, you will be branded as slaves. My people are not unkind to those they conquer, though it will be a difficult life.'

'Slavery has no place in Tristia,' Valiana said forcefully, 'and nor will it so long as I am Realm's Protector!'

'I suspect they fired you from that job, sweetheart,' Brasti pointed out. 'Probably about two seconds after the crown was plonked onto Filian's head.'

'Then let them keep the title – it won't stop me from fighting.'

'Forgive me, Lady,' Gwyn said, 'but you know nothing of war.' He shook his head as though struggling to find the words to explain. 'Do none of you understand? You talk about "battle" as if it were a simple matter of placing pieces on a board, some sort of game to be won or lost. To an Avarean, the *way* a person fights is the measure of their worth. Courage in war, skill in battle, these are the only meaningful Gods we follow.' He turned back to me. 'If an enemy army fights bravely, cleverly, if they impress the horde with their *rokhan*, then the horde will look upon the conquered as *brothers and sisters. This* is how Avares grew from a small nation to one which encompasses the entire north and west of this continent.'

'What happens if they aren't so impressed?' Brasti asked.

'Then you will wish you had become slaves.' Gwyn's eyes looked haunted. 'We have a word, *kujandis* . . .' He was clearly struggling to translate it. Eventually, he said, 'It means a cowardly opponent, one who is less than an animal. The only use for *kujandis* is for sport: it is no crime to kill one, or to slaughter them all.'

His words hung in the air a while before he asked me, 'Do you believe your people will fight bravely, First Cantor? Do you believe they will win *rokhan* in the face of a hundred warbands?'

A strange question – a foolish question, really, when I was surrounded by the bravest people I'd ever known. But I knew full well they were the exception that proved the rule. 'Not especially,' I replied.

'Then tell your King to submit, quickly, without hesitation or attempt at negotiation. The Avarean horde will reward subservience with mercy. Perhaps then, one day, Tristian blood and Avarean will be so intermixed that we shall truly be one people.'

I saw a shadow cross Nehra's face. Although she remained silent, I knew what she was thinking: *One people. What of our art, our language, our stories?* They would be gone; we would all be singing 'Seven for a Thousand' from now on.

I looked at Quentis Maren, Inquisitor-turned-Greatcoat. 'Well, what about you? I would think the Cogneri would be loath to let the worshippers of foreign Gods take over.'

His expression was thoughtful, serious. 'You know I am no longer one of the Cogneri, Falcio.' He fingered the trim of his coat. 'The Duchess of Hervor bade me wear this again to stand as representative of my old Order, but I am uncomfortable speaking on their behalf.'

'Well, you're the only Inquisitor we have,' I said, 'not to mention the only Cogneri whose judgement I would trust. Speak.'

'I can't advise you on this, First Cantor. I can't imagine how one is supposed to decide the fate of a country – especially when the Venerati – who are supposed to be the religious leaders of this country – are every bit as corrupt as its nobility. Or worse. I see no path to redeem them.'

'I take it you think the same?' I asked Darriana, who was leaning back against the wall, arms folded across her chest.

'I don't give a shit – and I'll tell you something else: the farmers and craftspeople and labourers? They don't give a shit, either. They want food and roads and a chance to survive the next winter. Their local Lords practically treat them like slaves now, so what difference will it make if the guy shouting orders at them does it in Avarean or Tristian?'

The women in carpenter's clothes stepped forward, her fists clenched in anger. '*You* do not—' She stopped abruptly and began to step back, until Ethalia walked to her and put an arm around her shoulders.

'This is your country as much as theirs, Lyssande,' she said. Her eyes went to me. 'Do not let this nonsense convince you otherwise.'

With Ethalia beside her, Lyssande found the confidence to speak. 'First Cantor, do you . . . ?' Again she hesitated.

'Go on,' I said, in as kindly a fashion as I could manage.

'Do you . . . do you have children, First Cantor?'

I thought about Valiana, to whom I'd given my name until Jillard had taken it away, but oddly, it was to Ethalia my eyes went. 'I have no children of my own, no.'

'I have a boy,' Lyssande said, 'six years old, and a girl, a year younger. Life's been hard for my village since before my children were born, and yet they face each day so bravely, smiling when they find a bush in berry, playing at Greatcoats with nothing more than a bit of stick.' She turned to the others. 'I don't know why we lose ourselves so easily in this country, but we are *not* born to be slaves. That is not our way.'

'And who's going to fight for your "way", you silly cow?' Darriana sneered. She gestured towards the door. 'Have you been outside? Those pathetic conscripts? They are the *dregs* – actually, they're the *dregs of dregs*. They're not going to make a good impression on *anyone*.'

Then she turned to face me. 'How many times have these fine upstanding Tristians let you down, Falcio? Remind me: when the Dukes came for the one King who'd actively tried to better their lot, did they rise up? When the Blacksmith orchestrated his takeover and set his little churchmen against this country and this country's Gods, did all these farmers and craftspeople and ditch-diggers fight? No, they *bowed down*.'

She looked back at Lyssande and said, 'I'm surprised you aren't already on your knees. And when the Avareans come and those brave children of yours see every adult in their village bow to the invaders, you can bet they'll learn to be cowards just like everyone else.'

'And how much courage does it take to denigrate those who *haven't* spent a lifetime learning to fight?' Ethalia asked.

Darriana looked chastened, but only for a moment before her

angry, bitter self took over again. 'So look who's found her claws.' She gestured to the duelling circle. 'Is today the day we finally see your full measure?'

'It certainly isn't the day we see yours,' Ethalia said. 'Terrifying this woman who has no sword, no armour? She comes before you asking for hope – an act far more courageous than anything I've seen from you today.' She hesitated for a moment, and I saw her rising fury give way to a gentler impulse. 'I expected better of you, Darriana.'

Darri's face went redder than I'd ever seen it. 'One day,' she muttered. Oddly, it was not so much a threat as a promise.

'One day,' Ethalia agreed. 'But not today.'

Finally Darri nodded, 'Not today.' She turned to Lyssande and said, 'I'm sorry, Sister. I had no business . . . I'm sorry, that's all.'

A thought occurred to me. 'Ethalia, if it comes to war, will the Saints of Tristia fight with us?'

She shook her head. 'The Saints' Awe cannot be wielded as a sword, and should we try, I fear for what might happen.' She stood up straighter. 'But *I* will fight, whether the rest of the Orders unite or not.'

'And you?' I asked Nehra. 'What do you have to say?'

'I have no counsel to offer.'

'No counsel? You arranged this trial!'

'I did.'

'Why? If you don't have—'

'The country is about to change, First Cantor, either because we made a decision and fought for it, or because we sat back and let the winds of Fate decide.' She gave a slight smile. 'I'm a Bardatti. We hate stories where Chance decides the ending.'

Almost as if they'd received a signal, everyone else withdrew a step, leaving only Kest and Brasti standing there.

'Anything you two want to add?' I asked.

Kest looked uncertain. 'It comes down to a choice between Law and Justice – and they are two very different things, Falcio, despite how hard you've tried to unite them. The simple fact is that Filian *is* King now, and so it's every citizen's lawful obligation to defend him, and thus the country.'

'Even if they'll die in the attempt? Even for a country not worth defending any more? How is that—?'

'Justice? It's not. That's my point: if you want *justice*, then go and murder Trin right now. Kill Filian too, and put someone else on the throne – someone you believe will serve the people and not the foul plans of a dead Duchess whose visceral loathing of her own country has brought us here, to the brink of destruction.'

'Except . . .' Brasti began.

'Neither of you are here as witnesses,' Nehra said.

'Oh well, forgive me. In that case . . .' Brasti turned back to me. 'Anyway, what I was going to say – and I can't believe I'm saying it, by the way – is that . . . wasn't Trin ill-treated herself? Wasn't she tormented, tortured and manipulated, forced into this pattern, this life by that bitch Patriana? And had Jillard even a hint of her existence, he'd have killed her as a child, wouldn't he? So she has as much right to demand justice as anyone else, and, Saint Agnita-who-vomits-men's-bones, what might *that* look like?'

'Vendetta,' Valiana said quietly. 'An endless cycle of revenge in which each death is merely fair payment for a previous one.'

Vendetta. How close had I come to triggering one of my own? Had I succeeded in murdering Trin, how many citizens of Hervor might rightfully have sought vengeance for the Duchess they so admired? *This* was why Valiana had been so insistent that we bring Trin back for trial rather than simply killing her on sight.

How did you ever become so wise? I wondered, staring at the young woman who had taken my name. Soon she would have to shed that name and instead become Valiana, Duchess of Rijou. She would never be known by the title I had secretly hoped she would one day take: she would never be First Cantor of the Greatcoats.

Of course, neither title would have much meaning if the country ceased to exist. How, by all the Gods and Saints, was I supposed to choose between ending a country or bringing even greater sorrow to its people?

King Paelis, I don't know if the dead can hear the thoughts of the living, but I really wish you'd picked someone other than me for this job.

I looked at Nehra, then at the others. 'I'm leaving now,' I said.

'Where are you going?' Kest asked.

'Back to my cell.'

'You have to render your verdict,' Nehra said. 'You must decide what course w—'

'Tomorrow,' I said. 'Right now I have one more witness to question.'

Nehra's eyes narrowed as if she didn't quite believe me. 'What witness? Tell us who and we will bring them to you.'

'You won't have to,' I replied. 'The witness will be coming to me.'

CHAPTER SIXTY-ONE

THE ROYAL CONSORT

There's always been a fundamental flaw with the whole idea of the Greatcoats. It all sounds great in theory, of course: travelling magistrates who can navigate not only the esoteric laws of the Kingdom and its nine Duchies, but who also possess the skill with a blade to enforce their verdicts through trial by combat when necessary. In a country like Tristia, where the duel is an almost sacred tradition, wouldn't you want your judges to be able to fight?

The only problem is that the mind of a duellist works very differently from that of a magistrate. When conducting a trial, the judge must be open-minded, able to weigh every aspect of the case, to carefully consider each argument and to withhold judgement until the most balanced verdict can be identified and declared. Any duellist who thinks that way will be killed in the first exchange of blows. To survive as a swordsman, you have to find an opening and exploit it without hesitation, finishing the fight before the opponent even realises it's begun.

For someone like me, this can be problematic.

'A pleasant evening to you, Duchess Tarindelle,' I said, proud of myself not only for remembering to use her full name, but also for keeping my hands from reaching through the bars and throttling her. Although self-restraint in this particular case was profoundly unsatisfying, the country was balanced on a knife's edge, my King's dream was in tatters and my instincts as a duellist had led to no end of stupid mistakes. Time for the magistrate to be in charge for a while.

She curtsied, letting pale blue silk rustle against the stone flags of the dungeon. It was an almost perfect copy in colour and style of Ethalia's favourite gown. 'And a pleasant evening to you, First Cantor. You don't seem surprised to see me.'

'I'm not.' Nor was I surprised that she would use even the clothes she wore as a tool to manipulate me.

Trin tilted her head like a cat, as though she needed both her eyes to see me through the gap in the bars. 'How did you know I was listening to that little sham of a "trial" your so-called *Dal Verteri* friends held? I thought I'd been remarkably silent.'

'You were,' I replied. 'I neither saw nor heard you, nor did anyone else.'

She looked surprised. 'Then how did you—?'

'Because you're *you,* Duchess. Spying and intrigue and murder are what you *do*. You ask how I knew you were there? Because a hundred guards didn't come in to arrest everyone in the room. *That's* how I knew.'

That earned me a smile. 'So clever, Falcio. It's just one of the things I love about—'

'Enough,' I said.

She stared through the bars at me and for once I tried to keep the anger from my features, to remove all the disdain and outrage, the disgust and despair. I wanted her to see me for who I really was – and perhaps she in turn might drop her mask and reveal her true self to me.

The coquettish smile disappeared. 'Enough,' she agreed.

We stood there silently for a long time. There is something strange, almost otherworldly, about being so close to your bitterest enemy. We shared a terrible intimacy in that moment, a brief pause in our endless sparring, and I found myself wondering if in some other life we might have been friends, or more.

'I am pleased to see you,' she said. The words had no inflection, no forced charm or smirking contempt.

The one common bond between magistrate and duellist is that both must be skilled in discerning intent, no matter how well hidden it might be. Trin *was* genuinely pleased to see me; on some peculiar level she really did like me. 'Ask me your question,' she said.

'What question is that, your Grace?'

'Are you testing me, Falcio? You want to know what happens next, if by some miracle you do find a way to save this poor little country of ours. You want some sense of what your sacrifice – and that of all the others – would yield.'

I sat down on the cot. 'And will you answer me truthfully, your Grace?'

'I'm offended, my tatter-cloak.' Trin looked around until she spotted the guard's stool and brought it over. She sat, altogether too elegant for her rough surroundings. 'Ask yourself a question, Falcio: have I *ever* lied to you?'

'Everything about you is deception.'

She spread her hands. 'Then you should have no difficulty naming a single instance in which I lied to you.'

I couldn't, of course: for all her schemes and games, for all the conspiracies she'd hatched, the falsehoods she'd told others – even when she'd been masquerading as Valiana's handmaiden – I realised she'd never actually lied to me.

'Remarkable,' I said at last.

Again that smile. 'I am besotted with you, Falcio val Mond. I honestly can't explain why, but there is something about you that draws me in. I sometimes wish . . .'

She let that word – '*wish*' – dangle before me.

Sitting there on opposite sides of the bars of a cell, I felt like I finally *truly* understood Trin: she was a monster who revelled in destroying her enemies and she was *also* a tormented young woman genuinely able to admire people, perhaps even to love them. And scarily, the two Trins weren't separate sides of a coin but inextricably intertwined with each other.

I really would have preferred it if she'd just picked one side.

'Don't look so apprehensive, Falcio,' she said. 'I'm not *in love* with you – entranced, certainly, but not in love.'

'Well, to be fair, your Grace, you don't know me that well – other than having tortured me and tried to have me killed several times, of course.'

I'd expected a laugh or some clever reply, but instead she shook her head. 'I do know the difference between love and infatuation. I love Filian. I quite expected to hate him, growing up – the idea that my mother was raising the King's son to rule in my stead if her plans for me failed?' She shuddered, very elegantly. 'Believe me, I considered killing him any number of times, just to remove the temptation that she might switch horses in midstream.'

'Why didn't you?'

She sighed theatrically – but for her, *every* move, *every* sentence was a performance. 'You spoke to him, didn't you? On the journey back from Avares?'

'I did.'

'And what did you find?'

'He is intelligent, like his father, and curious about people. He's given a great deal of thought to what it means to rule a nation wisely. He has studied many different philosophies on how to govern, and he balances those against the plight of this country.'

'Does he remind you of King Paelis?'

'Very much.'

'And do you think he would make a good King?'

'He would,' I admitted.

'Then you must—'

'If it weren't for you.'

She smiled then, as if I'd complimented her, before rising from her stool.

'Have you decided not to answer my questions, your Grace?' I asked.

She stopped. 'I've answered the only question that matters, Falcio. You are trying to judge whether it is best for you and the other Orders to fight for Tristia, or whether to let the Magdan and his warriors take it over in favour of a new system of government. Before you can render your verdict, you wish to know what Filian's rule would mean for our people.'

'And how have you helped me make that decision?'

She turned back to me, not smiling this time; there was neither delight nor deceit in her gaze. 'You know that it is in Filian's nature to be a good King, and that the law demands his coronation, yet you fear that my influence will – to *your* way of thinking – *corrupt* him.'

'Succinct, but it hardly leads to a decision.'

'It is simple, Falcio. The daring idealist you once were can't help but believe Filian's intrinsic decency would win out. The bitter cynic swayed by Ossia's cold logic no longer trusts in such things.'

I considered that for a moment, then said, 'If you're counting on my idealism to sway me to your side, your Grace—'

'Trin,' she said.

'Excuse me?'

She looked up and our eyes met across the bars separating us. 'You never call me by my name, Falcio, did you know that? In all our encounters, only once have you called me Trin.'

Oddly, I remembered the occasion: it had been at the Ducal palace of Rijou when I still believed her to be Valiana's shy and innocent handmaiden who I'd offended by refusing her invitation to wander the halls with her.

'Would you call me by my name now?' she asked.

'Why does it matter?'

Her shoulders rose and fell in a barely perceptible shrug. 'Because I liked the way you said it that night in Rijou, because, for reasons I will never understand, such things as words and names mean a great deal to you.'

'Trin,' I said, as much to prove she was wrong as out of any courtesy.

She smiled, just a little. It seemed genuine. 'Thank you, Falcio.' She drew a key from a thin silver chain around her neck and unlocked my cell door.

'I haven't agreed to rule in the country's favour, your Grace.'

'I know.'

'Then why are you unlocking my door?'

'Because whatever your decision, I am done with this game of ours.' She turned and started to walk away, but then she stopped. 'I'm sorry I laughed when Aline died. I know that must have hurt you.'

The words were genuine, sincere, but Trin was in the shadows, facing away from me, so I couldn't make out the expression on her face.

'Then why did you?' Despite all my efforts not to show weakness, a racking sob escaped my lips. 'Aline was bright and brilliant and decent – she ran to save Filian's life at the cost of her own. *How could you laugh?*'

She remained silent for a moment longer, then said, 'Because it was funny.'

CHAPTER SIXTY-TWO

THE VERDICT

You would think, given my propensity for delirium and hallucination, that I would have been visited that night by a host of Gods or Saints, dead Kings or dead wives, all assaulting me with acerbic remarks before gifting me with their enigmatic guidance. No one came – possibly because the dead rarely appear when you actually *want* them too, or maybe because they likely knew that this was a question beyond the legal reckoning of *any* magistrate.

I wondered if Morn, having so effectively predicted and manipulated events thus far, had known I'd wind up in this position. *He must be laughing himself silly right about now.*

You almost have to pity him, I could imagine him telling the other Greatcoats. *Falcio's become so accustomed to following a dead man's dream that now he's awake, he finds himself utterly lost.*

Somehow it wasn't surprising that even in my imagination Morn was an arrogant bastard. I just wished he wasn't right.

Every day since the King had died, I'd fought and bled in a desperate bid to bring about his vision for the country – at least, what I understood of it. I'd searched far and wide for his so-called Charoites, and when I found Aline, I'd become convinced he'd meant me to put her on the throne – only to discover there was a *second* living heir. I'd risked my life – and those of so many others – to save the Dukes from assassination and the country from falling into civil war, only to now have those same Dukes carve up the country for themselves. And if that wasn't enough, Kest, Brasti, Valiana, Aline – we'd *all* had to face the wrath of a God to defend the rule of law. Now it turned out the greatest threat to King Paelis' plan – the one thing I *couldn't* defeat – was his own *loyal* Order of travelling magistrates. It was the Greatcoats who would finally kill the King's mad, hopeful dream.

And what did he expect me to do about it?

I could really use a sign right about now, you skinny bastard.

I rose from the cot, pushed open the door to my cell and walked unhurriedly down the hall.

Dezerick saw me coming. 'Taking your leave of us, are you?'

I couldn't tell if he was being sarcastic. 'Are you planning to stop me?'

'Nope. Don't think I could if I wanted, which I don't, and anyway, the Royal Consort left word that you were free to go.'

'Thanks.'

He started following me down the corridor. 'So, what do you plan to do now?' he asked.

'Don't know,' I replied. 'Probably go for a walk and start swimming when I hit water. Actually, I'm a fairly rubbish swimmer, so I might need a boat.'

'Ah, well, this might help with that.'

I turned to see what he was holding, but his fingers were closed over his palm. 'I want you to know that I got this fair and square. Perfectly legitimate bribe.'

'So noted.'

'It's just that . . . my daughter, she recognised what it was and wouldn't stop shouting at me until I promised to give it to you, then my missus got in on the act and pretty soon I was outnumbered.'

'What are you holding, Dezerick?'

He opened his hand and held it out to me. There on his callused palm sat a single gold coin with the seal of the Greatcoats impressed on its surface. 'Someone bribed you with a *juror's coin*?'

He nodded. 'Reckon so. My little girl certainly thinks that's what it is.'

I took the coin. It was old, the symbols worn. Beneath the rubbed crown were the distinctive markings of the particular Greatcoat who'd given out the coin. They were my marks.

'Who gave this to you?' I asked.

He jerked a thumb up towards one of the windows near the ceiling. 'One of them conscripts, well, a volunteer, actually.' He chuckled. 'Who in all the hells is crazy enough to volunteer for military service? And now of all times, eh?'

I rolled the coin over in my hand. Each minting had been slightly different; this one had to be at least fifteen years old. A coin like this could feed a family for a year. To keep one unspent for so long? 'Dezerick, can you take me to the person who gave you this?'

The guard shook his head. 'Din't see 'em. It was dark and I was paying more attention to the coin than the person offering it to me.'

'What did they ask for?'

'Same as the others. "Show him kindness," he said, "or mercy if you can manage it".'

I let the weight of the coin settle into my hand, then found my fingers closing tightly around it as my feet walked me down the hall and up the stairs, through the corridors of the keep and out past the guards, through the front gate where the morning sun was just beginning to reflect off the dew on what little grass had struggled up through the rubble left in the wake of a God's destructive power.

I walked up and down the rows of tents for a while before I realised there was no point; there were far more soldiers now than when I'd first returned to the castle weeks ago and it would take me days to check all the faces slowly joining the queue for the meagre rations that passed for breakfast in this ragtag army.

How could anyone ask these people to die in a hopeless battle?

They were smiths and crafters and farmers, not soldiers. The Greatcoats and the other Orders of the "*Dal Verteri*" might have been formed to protect the country, but these men and women *were* the country. They were the ones who stoked the smithy fires or shaped wood in workshops, who turned dirt and sweat into the crops that fed a nation. If the God of War himself descended from his chariot and demanded they march in his name, I'd duel the bastard on the spot.

I started back for the castle, but the coin was still heavy in my hand, so I turned and held it aloft. 'Who brought this?' I asked, my voice loud, the words echoing across the field.

People stared at me, no doubt wondering why I was shouting at them, but I went on shouting anyway. 'Whose is this? Who here served on a jury and kept the payment unspent?'

A man in tanners' leathers took a step forward. 'I served on a jury,' he said. 'For Antrim Thomas – the King's Memory himself.' He reached into a pocket and pulled something out, holding it up high. It was a golden Greatcoat's coin and it shone in the sunlight.

'I served,' a woman just a few feet from him said, and she too held up a coin. 'Kest Murrowson, the Queen's Shield, gave me this.'

'I got mine from Talia, the King's Spear,' a young man declared proudly, holding up his own.

'Mine from Brasti!' another said. 'Along with more beer than any one man should ever drink!'

Laughter, then boasting, and more men and women held up coins, each declaring the name of the Greatcoat who'd given it to them, along with their home town or village.

'Whose coin is this, damn you?' I shouted.

A boy, no more than fourteen and far too young to die serving in an army that had no hope of winning, came forward and mumbled, 'It was my mother's, sir. She was the town blacksmith in Uttarr.'

'I remember her . . . she served on my jury on one of my first missions. Where is she now?'

'Dead, sir – last year.' He looked at the coin. 'She gave me that before she passed, said it was my job now to ensure the verdict against Lord Myrdhin remained in force.'

'But why didn't she spend it?'

The boy gave me a queer look. 'Spend it? She'd never do that, sir, not even in the hard times. Said it meant something: something that couldn't be bought for mere gold.'

'And yet you sold it for better food for a prisoner?'

'I didn't know what else to do, sir. First Cantor's in jail, I just thought . . .' He looked unsure of himself and muttered, 'Didn't know what else to do.'

I tossed him back the coin. 'Don't sell it so cheaply next time.'

'Don't you dare have a go at that boy,' Feltock said, hopping up to me, supporting himself on his crutch. 'You can't blame him if people get all sentimental around you Trattari.'

'Sentimental isn't the word I'd use for the way most people view us in this country, Feltock.'

The old man looked at me wide-eyed for a moment, then he chuckled. 'You really don't know?'

'Don't know what?'

He turned to face the worn-down, filthy, malnourished volunteers and shouted in the voice that had no doubt served him well when he'd commanded his own troops, 'Oi, you lot: how many of you served on a Greatcoat's jury?'

By way of answer, men and women all over the camp ducked into their tents for a moment, or reached into pockets or pouches or bent over to remove something from socks or shoes . . .

Saints . . . Half the army is made up of jurors!

'Falcio, there you are,' Brasti said. Kest came up on my other side. 'Nehra's up my nose about you not making a de—' He looked around and I watched as his expression took on the same mixture of confusion and hopefulness that was pasted across my own face. 'By the infinite abundance of Saint Laina's left tit . . .'

One by one those who had come to Aramor willing to sacrifice themselves in a hopeless war held their hands up high, gold coins pressed between thumbs and forefingers, catching the sunlight like a thousand stars shining in the dawn. *This*, I thought, overcome by the sight of them all. *This was Paelis' dream!* Not some paltry hundred and forty-four magistrates with our swords and our coats, but the jurors: ordinary men and woman armed with nothing.

For a while the three of us just stood there and stared at them all. I dearly wanted to cling to that moment for ever, but now I had rather a lot of work to do.

'Gentlemen,' I said to Kest and Brasti, 'I'm of a mind to attempt something rather daring and heroic.'

Brasti grinned. 'I assume this preposterous venture of yours is doomed to fail?'

'Assuredly. But we're going to do it anyway. You know why?'

Kest had a broad smile, one I'd rarely seen before. 'Because preposterous heroics are the only things we've ever been good at.'

'Tell Nehra to summon the Orders,' I told Brasti. 'Tell her the First Cantor of the Greatcoats has ruled that we're going to fight for this Gods-forsaken country of ours.'

CHAPTER SIXTY-THREE

THE TRAITOR

In a better world, the sight of all those jurors holding up their coins would have sustained me through the insanity to follow. Unfortunately, as I'd never declared war before, I found myself completely unprepared for what came next and barely had time to give those stalwart jurors another thought.

'I really think there's something inherently wrong with any country that lets *Falcio* decide if it goes to war,' Brasti said as the three of us walked up the stairs towards the King's private chambers.

'That's not *technically* what happened,' Kest observed. 'Falcio merely ruled that the Orders would support the King.'

'Yes, which just *happened* to set off a war.' Brasti slapped me on the back. 'Can't wait to see what all those Bardatti songs will say about you if this goes badly.'

'Thanks.'

I waited for the two guards in Aramor's purple livery standing outside the King's chambers to open the double-doors to let us inside.

Neither moved.

'Captain needs to speak with you first,' the more senior of the two men said at last.

'Oh, Saint Vigga-whose-shit-plugs-privies,' Brasti swore. 'Not *this* again!'

'Yes, *this* again,' Antrim said, striding down the hall towards us.

I was surprised to see he still wore the gold circles on his collar denoting his rank as leader of the Aramor Guards.

'Of course,' Brasti said, frowning. 'Falcio tries to kill a King and gets asked to lead his army, and Antrim lets *enemy* soldiers into the castle and somehow keeps his job as Captain of the Guards. I wish someone would have told me that all I needed to do to advance my career was screw up incredibly badly.'

Antrim ignored him, focusing his ire on me. 'The King, in what I think we'll have to refer to as "his infinite mercy", decided *I* wasn't to blame. *Don't* make me look like a fool again, Falcio.'

'Relax, Antrim,' Brasti said. 'Kest and I will keep an eye on him.'

'You two arseholes are staying outside.' He signalled to the two guards, who finally opened the door, but before I could walk past, Antrim said, very quietly, 'The fate of my homeland rests on your shoulders, Falcio. No more mistakes. No more losing your temper. Next time you endanger the King, it'll be me you'll face in the duelling circle.'

I was fairly certain that was the first time Antrim Thomas had ever threatened anyone in his life.

I found Filian standing over a map unfurled on a large oval table littered with coloured wooden shapes apparently representing different military divisions. Trin was standing on one side and, more surprisingly, Valiana was on the other. That she was able to look so remarkably calm and demure in the presence of the woman who had tried to kill her even more times than she'd tried to kill me was a testament to Valiana's remarkable self-control.

'Ah, Falcio, good,' the King said as I entered the room. He waved a piece of parchment in his hand. 'I'm afraid that the Duchess has been putting forward a number of entirely convincing arguments as to why I should issue a warrant for your arrest on charges of treason. I thought perhaps you might help me dissuade her.'

I hadn't been expecting a parade, exactly, but I had hoped that perhaps agreeing to throw away my life – not to mention the lives of a couple of thousand people I liked quite a bit better than our new King and his charming Consort – would keep me out of gaol for a little longer.

'Perhaps Duchess Tarindelle could be a little more specific,' I said, watching Trin. 'I've committed rather a lot of treason lately.'

She offered up her usual knowing smile, along with a slight shake of her head.

'Wrong Duchess,' Filian explained.

I turned to Valiana. '*You?* You want the King to name me traitor?'

'It's not what you think, Falcio,' she said quickly. 'The idea is to—'

'It's insurance,' Filian said, looking none too pleased by the idea himself. 'Valiana believes I shouldn't be present at the battle.'

'You see what happens?' Trin asked whimsically. 'Give a woman the Duchy of Rijou and all of a sudden she becomes as corrupt as our father.'

The urge to reach for my rapier was cut off by the sudden rage on Valiana's face. Apparently I wasn't the only one in danger of being goaded to rash acts of violence. A second later, Valiana mastered herself. 'Falcio, if you'll just let me explain—'

'You want to give the King a second chance at peace with Avares,' I said, already working through Valiana's reasoning. 'If our bid to impress the Avareans with our *rokhan* fails, they'll massacre half the country in retaliation. But if the attack comes not from the ruler of the country but from a treasonous rebel . . .'

Valiana smiled. 'Exactly. The King could claim you led the rebellion against his wishes. It's a long shot, but if there's even a remote possibility that this will open the door for a better treaty with the Avareans . . .'

She was right: the odds were slim, but slim odds were better than none. And what was even better, the Magdan would love it:

Morn gets control of the country *without* having to fulfil any Avarean obligation to destroy those who dare to resist without showing true *rokhan*, while *I* die a traitor to my own homeland. It was a depressingly brilliant ploy.

'You should sign it, your Majesty,' I said at last.

He hesitated for a moment, but then, looking older than his fifteen years, took the pen Valiana was proffering, dipped it in the inkwell and signed the decree. 'So begins my reign, with an act of ignominy and cowardice, one that my father would never even have considered.'

'Oh, he would have,' I said, thinking of the day King Paelis had ordered me to stand the Greatcoats down and sign the infamous concord that declared our order disbanded. 'He'd do whatever it took to keep people safe.'

Filian rolled up the parchment and sealed it with wax. 'It's done. Congratulations, Falcio, you're now the unlawful leader of a rebel army – none of whom realise that you've all been declared traitors to Tristia and its people.' He sounded very young as he asked, 'Can you save us?'

There was no point in hiding the truth from him, or from myself. 'Not a chance. The Avareans were dangerous even when they fought with badly made bronze swords and spears. Now they have cannon and weapons of Shan steel. Even if every single one of the Dukes rallied to us, we'd still have no hope against the Avarean horde.'

Filian took in a slow breath, visibly trying to summon his courage. 'I suppose I can hardly blame the Dukes for seceding then, can I?' he said at last. 'Not if they buy their own people a few more years of freedom.'

'Do not give up hope quite yet, your Majesty,' Valiana said gently.

He turned to her. 'Hope, my Lady?' He gestured to the coloured blocks of wood arrayed on the map on the table. 'What cause do you see here for hope?'

Valiana met my eyes, and in her smile I saw the warmth that had been absent for far too long. 'Where our people have always found it, your Majesty, in tales told by the fireside of a sharp blade wielded by a quick hand and guided by a brave and foolish heart, of friends fighting together no matter the odds.'

'Stories?' Trin said, turning the word into something small and petty. 'You really should have paid more attention to Mother's lectures on the art of warfare.'

'She wasn't my mother,' Valiana replied, refusing to take the bait.

Filian flicked one of the wooden pieces on the map, tipping it over. 'So we wager the future of the country on the hope that by, in effect, sacrificing themselves to the horde, Falcio and the others will tell such a tale of valour that our enemy's admiration will get us better terms in defeat. Yes? That's it?' He looked up at me. 'Do you really believe in all this Avarean nonsense about honour and *rokhan*, Falcio?'

I only knew one real Avarean, and he was on our side, so I didn't really have an answer for that – but fortunately, Valiana did. 'It makes little difference, your Majesty,' she said. 'Victorious nations set terms of surrender based on how dangerous they deem the conquered.'

Trin gave a smirk. 'Ah. So you *were* listening to Mother's lectures after all.'

A flash of annoyance passed across Filian's features, but he let it go and turned back to me. 'What price will you ask of me, Falcio?'

'Price?' Trin asked before I could ask the same question.

The King nodded. 'Well, I assume Falcio expects his sacrifice – and that of what will likely be a great many others – to come at some cost to me. No doubt it'll be some curtailing of royal prerogative . . . So, go on then: what would you have me do?'

Being new to the business of war, it hadn't occurred to me to ask for anything, especially as I was almost certainly going to be dead within a couple of weeks anyway. But I did like the idea of limiting Filian's – and by extension, Trin's – power over the country.

'A charter,' I said quickly.

'A *what*?' Filian asked.

I considered my next words carefully. The problem with Morn's plans for a better country was that he wanted to replace one tyranny with another, making us a judiciary rather than a monarchy. What Tristia needed was something else entirely.

'Your Majesty, if there's any kind of country left once this is done, if the Avareans leave you with anything to govern, then you'll sign a charter giving the citizenry of Tristia a voice in your rule.'

'How exactly would I do that?' Filian asked. He sounded oddly unsurprised by my demand.

No fucking idea, I thought, but as usual, Valiana understood what I was trying to say better than I did myself. 'A council,' she said suddenly, then explained, 'The monarchy has always relied on a Ducal Council for advice – your Majesty could establish a Citizens' Council, with members drawn from every walk of life, to ensure you hear the needs of those you rule.' She gestured to Trin and added, 'Your Majesty would no doubt also want a representative of the nobility on this new Citizens' Council.'

Trin looked aghast: she had just gone from being Filian's sole advisor to having to sit around a table with farmers and stonemasons. 'You *cannot* do this,' she said firmly to Filian. 'You would be overturning a thousand years of—'

'I accept your terms,' Filian said.

For a moment I was surprised at his acquiescence, then I wondered, was this exactly what he'd wanted when he'd asked what payment I expected in return for running his war? Had he known even before I did that the one thing I'd ask for would be a limit on the influence of the nobility?

What game are you playing, your Majesty?

'I believe we're done for now,' the King said.

Trin, recovering her composure, turned her gaze to Valiana and me. 'You may take your leave of us now. The King and I—'

'I would speak to the First Cantor a moment,' Filian interrupted. 'Alone.'

Valiana looked surprised, Trin incensed – and I was enjoying myself for the first time in ages. 'You know,' I said to Filian once we were alone, 'it's entirely possible that Trin wants to kill you more than me right now.'

'Tarindelle would never hurt me,' he said. 'Although I know it's hard for you to believe, I do know something of love.' He turned and pulled down a black wooden case from one of the bookshelves and set it on the table in front of me. The box was about eighteen inches long and four inches high. 'This is for you, Falcio.'

'A gift, your Majesty? I—'

'It's not from me.' He placed his hands on the box for a moment, gingerly, as if it were hot to the touch. 'I found it among my sister's things. I believe she meant to give it to you on the day of her coronation.'

I took the box from him and flipped up the twin brass clasps. The lid opened smoothly to reveal a beautifully made leather bracer filled with throwing knives, although this one had seven where my old one had only six. On top was a note written in Aline's light and elegant hand:

So you'll never be without – and because a Queen is far too busy and important to be handing you knives every time you get yourself into yet another silly old fight.

I held the bracer in my hands for a long while, letting my fingers travel over the carefully stitched leather; all the while, my eyes never left the note.

'I'm sorry,' Filian said.

I was about to ask him why he was apologising when I felt the tears dripping down my cheeks.

'I wish I'd known her better,' he said. 'Perhaps tonight you and I could talk a while, Falcio. I would like to know more about my sister.'

I carefully replaced the bracer of knives and laid the note on top, then I closed the box and tucked it under my arm.

'It's kind of you to offer, your Majesty, but if Aline were here right now, she would tell me it was past time I got on with saving your damned country now.'

I recovered my composure as best I could as I exited the room – Brasti turns it into a public event any time he catches me crying. Fortunately, he was too busy peppering me with questions to notice my appearance. 'How did it go?' he asked. 'Valiana here won't tell us *anything* and I *must* know why Trin stormed out looking as if she'd just eaten her own poisoned fruit.'

'Oh, you know,' I began, 'the usual things. So, first of all, I've agreed to be declared a traitor.'

He shrugged as if that was nothing new. 'Well, you've always been prone to a little light treason now and again.' He grinned. 'Hey, does this mean I'm no longer the Greatcoat with the worst criminal past?'

Kest was watching me. 'If I surmise correctly, we're to be named as accomplices.'

I nodded.

'Figures,' Brasti said. 'Well, doesn't matter much if we're all going to be dead in a couple of weeks – you can't hang a corpse for treason. Oh no, wait, I forgot – people *are* doing that now, aren't they?'

'It's not all bad news,' I said. 'Valiana might have just convinced the King to make Tristia into a constitutional monarchy.'

'Clever girl,' Brasti said, winking at her approvingly. 'Now, can someone explain to me what a constitutional monarchy is?'

'We'll figure it out if there's still a country in the next two weeks,'

I replied. 'For now, we'd best get the Generals in a room and tell them how this is going to work.'

'Ah, about the Generals . . .' Valiana said, suddenly looking uncomfortable.

'*What* about the Generals?'

Brasti grinned. Evidently he already knew. 'Remember when Antrim told you to keep your cool?' he asked.

'Ye-esss . . .' I replied warily.

'You'll be needing to hang onto that thought during your next meeting.'

CHAPTER SIXTY-FOUR

THE GENERAL

It is regrettably true that in Tristia, for every brave, selfless soul willing to sacrifice themselves for others, there'll be at least one complete arsehole determined to look out only for themselves. What no one had ever told me was that the arseholes most skilled at this were Tristia's military leaders.

'You can't be serious,' I said, standing nose to nose with General Herredal. Behind him was an impressive entourage of lieutenants whose primary military function appeared to be laughing on cue at their fearless leader's jokes and scowling on his behalf at any who *dared* to question his ineffable wisdom. They were doing a lot of the latter right now.

'I fail to see what confounds you, Trattari,' General Herredal repeated. He gestured at the two other Generals in the room. 'It is quite clear: we have given our terms to the King himself and none of us have any intention of altering our demands.'

Here's something else I never knew about war: in Tristia, when the King wants to send the army into battle, his Generals have the right to renegotiate the terms of their service. This strikes me as a spectacularly bad tradition, especially on those occasions when a vastly superior army has just declared war and half the Duchies have seceded, taking their troops with them. Not only were Generals Herredal, Abruni and Orzeno demanding simply *preposterous* sums of money, they also wanted lands, noble titles and – and this was the best part – *ships,* for their personal and no doubt immediate use.

It was the ships that really got to me.

'You son of a bitch,' I said, grabbing him by the collar, ignoring the lieutenants reaching for their ceremonial daggers; Kest and Brasti were kind enough to show them the error of their ways. It's amazing how educational a punch to the nose can be. 'You're already preparing to run!'.

'How *dare* you accuse the General of—'

The other lieutenant's words were cut off by another smart punch to the nose, this one delivered by Gwyn, who'd agreed to provide what intelligence he could on Avarean military practices.

'My apologies,' the young Rangieri said. 'They told me we were going to fight the enemy and I got confused.'

General Herredal was probably in his late fifties, but he was strong enough to shake off my grip and he looked ready to more than pay back the abuse we'd given his men in kind, but Valiana stopped him.

'Enough!' she cried, looking exasperated. 'All of you! The matter of payment is separate from the more pressing issue of *where* this fight will take place.'

'And I have told you—' Herredal appeared to be struggling to find a suitably insulting way to address Valiana.

'—"your Grace",' I suggested.

He sneered at that. 'Not likely. I imagine by the time she makes it to the front gates of Rijou her title will have already been taken by another.'

'Again,' Valiana said, 'a matter secondary to the more important question we must deal with today.'

'The army will remain *here*,' Herredal declared. 'It will be less costly to hold out in Aramor and wait for the enemy to come to us.'

'So you would let them march through Pertine as if the Duchy were already theirs?'

He gave her a patronising smile. 'The Duke – I'm sorry, the *Prince* of Pertine – has already signed an armistice; I'm quite sure the piss-drinking barbarians will be exceedingly polite to their new friends.'

'*Pertine*,' Valiana said, 'is still part of Tristia, General.'

She was halfway to accusing him of sedition at this point, but Herredal clearly didn't care. 'It's easier to fight here than in enemy territory, which *Pertine* will be if we try to send our troops through it.' Valiana was opening her mouth to respond, but he cut her off. 'I will not discuss military strategy with fools who have no concept of the art of war.'

'You are the fool,' Gwyn said. 'Once the Avarean horde enters Tristia it will never leave. They would lose every last man and woman among them before they ceded one inch of territory.' He turned to me. 'If you are to fight them, it must be at the border between the two lands. Only there can you have any hope of showing them this country will cost too high a price.'

'Once in Pertine, there will be no way to retreat,' Herredal added.

'And no doubt that would make it harder for you and your personal staff to reach your new ships,' I couldn't stop myself saying out loud.

Herredal locked eyes with me and smiled, practically *daring* me to hit him. 'I'm not the one who started this war, Trattari, so don't blame me that it cannot be won. And don't doubt for a moment that this new King of yours has his own ship ready and his own plans to escape the country when it falls.'

'The people who have to live in this country, General,' Valiana said, 'do not *have* ships, nor do they have the ability to flee. Their only hope now lies in us showing the Avareans that we are as great a nation of warriors as they are, in showing this . . . this *rokhan* that means so much to them. Only through courage can we—'

Herredal held up a hand. 'I will not be lectured to by you, *girl*. I have actually *fought* Avareans. No, if there is to be a fight, it will be here in Aramor.' He glanced around his entourage, who were busy nodding and murmuring assent. 'Furthermore, while I have already compromised my beliefs and agreed that women may fight – though the Gods know what punishment they'll rain down on us for that foolishness! – I will have none of this Bardatti nonsense.' With that he picked up and slowly crumpled the piece of paper upon which Nehra had set down the placement of her own warband: her drummers, musicians and singers.

'The Bardatti are part of this fight, General,' Valiana said. 'Their ways may seem strange to you, bu—'

'*Strange?*' Herredal bellowed. He turned to Nehra, sitting by the window scribbling furiously. 'You, minstrel,' he called out to her. 'What is it *exactly* you're doing right now?'

Nehra looked up and raised an eyebrow, as if the General had missed the blindingly obvious. 'I'm composing the warsong, of course.'

Okay, so even I knew that didn't sound like a particularly vital component of military strategy.

General Herredal sighed, apparently having had enough of us all. Ignoring Valiana completely, he turned to me. 'Allow me to make this very simple for you and your little King: none of you know how to fight a war; moreover, you have no idea how to even manage troop allocations, movements, supply lines – or anything else. Without me, you *have* no army. So you can either accept *my* command at *my* price, or you can find yourselves with no army whatsoever.' He patted me on the shoulder. 'Unless you fancy yourself a General now, Trattari?'

'Me? No, sir,' I said politely, 'you're quite correct: troop movements, supply lines . . . It's all rather beyond me.'

'Good, in that case . . .' He held out the document listing his demands.

I stared at him, wanting quite desperately to punch him extremely hard on his bulbous nose. The only reason I stayed my hand wasn't that it would create more problems than the momentary pleasure was worth – after all, it's not as if I'm known for my tremendous sense of restraint – but because it would be insufficiently painful and humiliating for him.

So it looked like I had two choices: I could either let the Generals command our troops as they pleased – well, at least for the few hours, until the Generals decided to run off to enjoy a life on the ocean wave – or we could find ourselves with no experienced military leadership whatsoever.

'It can't be that complicated, right?' I asked Kest.

'It's remarkably complex,' he replied.

'Your answer, Trattari?' Herredal asked.

I *hate* the way military men say the word '*Trattari*'. I swear, every single soldier I've ever met manages to make it sound even dirtier than the nobles do. Even—

Oh, I thought. *I like this idea a lot.*

'Trattari?' Herredal repeated.

'Abide a moment, if you would, General Herredal.' I took Valiana's arm and led her towards the door.

'What?' Valiana asked.

I turned back briefly. 'Brasti, do me a favour and find the General something to drink, will you? And some biscuits, if there happen to be any around.' I continued leading Valiana out through the door and into the hallway towards the main entrance to the castle. 'Time to reunite you with an old friend.'

He was even more furious than I'd expected. '*Damn you*, Falcio,' he growled, 'I begged you not to—'

'Feltock?' Valiana said, her voice as small as a child's. It had taken her a moment to recognise his face through the thick growth of beard. No doubt the missing leg and eye didn't help either.

'Aye,' he said at last, but before he'd finished turning to her,

Valiana had thrown herself on him, wrapping him in her arms and crushing him in a bear-hug, almost weeping with joy.

'I thought you were *dead*! Feltock, I cried a thousand tears over you—'

He patted her back awkwardly and muttered, 'Well, I . . . I didn't want you to see me like this.' To me he said, 'You made me a promise, Trattari.'

'I broke it and I don't care. She had a right to know. Besides, I needed her here for this.'

'For what?' Valiana asked, finally letting go of him.

'Well, I need a rather large favour and I don't think Feltock's all that positively inclined towards me right now.'

'Damned right,' Feltock said.

'What favour?' Valiana asked.

'Well, you see, before he was *Captain* Feltock, he had a different job title.'

Feltock's eyes went wide. 'Oh, hells! You can't possibly think I'd—'

'General Feltock,' I said, 'we'd all appreciate it very much if you'd be so kind as to command the Tristian army in the most hopeless battle the country has ever faced.'

CHAPTER SIXTY-FIVE

THE FIELD

I have never understood the way of soldiers. I'm troubled by all that unthinking obedience.

From the first moment I met King Paelis – well, the *second* moment, I suppose, since I'd spent the first actively trying to murder him – our relationship was built on *argument*. Every subject was open to debate, every mission questioned. If, on the odd occasion, the King finally told me to shut up and get on with it, that didn't change the fact that, while I served the Crown, I never felt like a servant.

Soldiers *are* servants. They march where you tell them to, eat when you tell them to and die for reasons they rarely understand, usually as a result of a mistake or a momentary fit of pique, rather than for any great cause.

I could never live – or die – that way, so I found myself humbled watching these men and women in ill-fitting leather armour trudging along day after day, walking the long road from Aramor to Pertine, never complaining, never questioning. No one gave them the privilege of arguing with their commanders or demanding the purpose of an order; they just did as they were told because they had faith in their commanders.

Faith has always been a bit of a problem for me.

'We march, we march, we march for one more day,' a group of

soldiers sang, their voices tired but enthusiastic, as they followed those of us on horseback. 'Our enemies run far away, but we must fight and so we say' – a short, theatrical pause, then – 'let's march, let's march, for one more day—'

Here's something else I hadn't known about armies: soldiers die without ever taking the field. They get sick on the road or break an ankle, but they keep walking until it becomes something worse. They eat rotten meat and suddenly can't breathe, or wander off for a piss in the middle of the night and fall off a cliff.

You'd think that brigands would be afraid of armies, but they aren't; armies are full of opportunities for the more enterprising sort of thug: they'll happily pick off one or two laggards, slit their throats and loot whatever paltry coins the poor sods had, then disappear into the night.

And if you're thinking the commander will gladly halt the march so that some well-meaning but ignorant Greatcoat can start an investigation and bring the killers to justice . . .

. . . well, apparently war doesn't work that way. Justice turns out to be a luxury of peacetime.

'You're fretting again,' Ethalia said, riding up beside me. The greatcoat with its subtle hues of red and copper that Aline had given her made her look far too much like a soldier.

'I'm not fretting.'

She pointed behind us. 'Every mile you look back to see if anyone's missing. There are nearly two thousand soldiers here, Falcio. You can't watch over every one of them.'

That much was certainly true. 'I wish you'd go back,' I said.

She gave me a dirty look, which I ignored.

A little way ahead of us, Nehra was still strumming a few bars on her guitar: the same fucking chords, over and over, and if there was any variation, my unmusical ears couldn't detect it. And all the while she was humming a melody, occasionally tossing in a 'dah dum, dah dum' here or there. I was fairly certain she was trying to drive me insane.

'Could you pick a different song?' I asked. 'Maybe one that, you know, ends at some point?'

'I'm rather busy, Falcio' – her fingers effortlessly plucked that maddening sequence of notes – 'so could you find someone else on whom to focus your ill-temper for a while?'

'Busy doing what?'

She raised an eyebrow. 'Still composing the warsong, of course. You can't rush these things.'

Ah. Right. Something *else* I didn't know. *Can't have a war without your own special song.* 'Maybe you should find yourself a sword instead,' I suggested. Nehra had managed to assemble nearly a hundred Bardatti, all with drums, guitars, horns, flutes . . . They'd come remarkably well prepared – if the plan were to give a very large concert.

'You know *nothing* of war, Falcio.' And Nehra turned back to her composing.

As if I hadn't figured that out already.

'How far to the border?' Ethalia interrupted, probably to keep me from getting into another argument with Nehra.

Feltock, who looked remarkably comfortable in the saddle, even with only one leg, opened his eye and glanced around. 'Eight days.'

Eight days. We'd lost forty-three soldiers in the two weeks since leaving Aramor, so assuming nothing changed, another twenty-odd unwitting men and women would die before even *seeing* the enemy.

'I'm curious, General,' Ethalia said. 'You've got the troops marching in a different formation today – and every time we stop, you order them to check their weapons . . .'

'Aye. A sword doesn't do much good if it's stuck in its scabbard, my Lady.'

'But if we're eight days from the fight . . . ?'

'Eight days from the border with Avares, my Lady.' The General shot me a glance; not that he needed to remind me that my so-called *plan* held any number of risks. 'Nobody said anything about eight days from the fight.'

'You think the Avareans could already be in Pertine?'

Feltock shook his head. 'Nah, they'll want to come through Lesteris Pass, down the Degueren Steppes. The snow's still heavy on the ground but it's beginning to melt, so they won't want to risk getting caught in an avalanche – that means they'll likely wait another two weeks. That's why Valiana was pushing for us to meet the enemy in Pertine rather than wait in Aramor: this way we get to the battlefield first and have time to prepare.'

'I just thought she was, you know, standing on principle or something,' I said.

Feltock laughed. 'Ah, she's full of principle, she is.' He tapped a finger to his forehead. 'But clever, too. She read the lie of the land just right, my girl did.'

My girl. Jillard was her true father and Feltock the man who'd protected her most of her young life. I felt like I'd lost something very precious, but I shook the thought away. *Get over yourself, idiot.*

'Forgive me, General,' Ethalia said, 'but if the Avareans won't yet be in Pertine, then who do you anticipate having to fight?'

The old man's jaw tightened. 'Our friends, my Lady. *Our friends.*'

'Your Grace,' I said calmly. It's remarkably hard to be calm when you're standing between two armies in front of a man who looks suspiciously like he's about to order you killed.

'Falcio, you damned fool,' Meillard, Duke – no, *Prince* of Pertine – started. 'Did you *really* think I'd let you march an army through my Principality?'

'I'm sorry, your Grace. I must have been confused. I'd heard you were quite happy to let armies march across your lands.'

'Falcio . . .' Valiana warned.

Meillard gazed at her with a mixture of disgust and sympathy. 'I thought better of you, Realm's Protector. Despite your inexperience and sentimentality, you've often proved to be—'

She held up a hand. 'Kindly spare me, your Grace. If you think you're the first man to patronise me this way, you must have been sleeping during all the Ducal Council's meetings.'

The old Duke's solicitude vanished instantly. 'Very well then, you want to be treated as an equal? Here's the simple truth: your army is too small and your soldiers are largely untrained, hungry and already exhausted.'

He turned to Feltock, ignoring Valiana and me as well now. 'Seventeen hells, Feltock! I knew you as a wise and steady General – did they cut out your brain when they took that eye of yours?'

Feltock showed not the slightest sign of ire or concern. 'I've wondered that same thing myself, your Grace. You see, I've discovered that even with an arrow through the eye socket, clearly damaging the brain, the mind can still—'

'Not the time,' I said.

'Ah, right.' To Meillard he said, 'I look forward to sitting down for a drink, your Grace. We can talk over the good old days.'

'I'm afraid your days are numbered, Feltock.'

'Quite likely. This Trattari bastard is apparently determined to bring me to an early grave.'

Meillard gave me one of those looks I often get from Dukes: ten gallons of condescending disappointment mixed with just under an ounce of grudging respect. 'I've never understood why powerful men and women pay such heed to a failed farmer with nothing but a half-decent sword arm and a faulty sense of self-preservation. You know nothing of politics and even less of war.' He glanced at Feltock. 'Damn it, General, you've clearly got the Trattari's ear. Speak honestly to him – *advise* him. Help him see reason.'

Feltock turned to me. 'Falcio, this plan of yours is reckless and foolhardy. You should abandon it at once.'

'So noted,' I said.

Feltock turned back to Meillard and shrugged. 'You see what I have to deal with, your Grace?'

The Duke growled, 'I should have the two of you bastards hung for traitors.'

'That part comes later,' Brasti called out from behind us. 'Also, *we're* not the ones who committed succession.'

'He means "secession",' Kest clarified.

Normally the two of them annoy me when they get like this, but the look of barely contained fury on Duke Meillard's face brought a smile to mine. 'You're going to tell your commanders to cede the road to us, your Grace, then you're going to allow five hundred of them to join our army and fight for their country, if they wish.'

'Five hundred?' Brasti walked over and looked past Meillard. 'There's a good thousand men there, Falcio.'

'True, but I figure we'll never get more than half of them to agree to join us, so we might as well make those ones feel special.'

Meillard grunted. 'You think even *one* of *my* men would join your hopeless cause?'

'Well, I admit the pay's not great, your Grace, but the food's about to get better.'

'And how do you reckon that?' Meillard asked. 'You think I didn't send scouts into Aramor? We know your supply lines are stretched – you've not enough food to last even a week.'

'True – but that's all about to change,' I explained, 'because you, Duke Meillard, are going to start supplying us with food and medicines and wood for arrows and bolts, as well as whatever billeting your people can provide without causing themselves undue suffering.'

He laughed. 'And why would I do this, exactly?'

I let the smile fall from my face and made sure he could see I was deadly serious when I said, 'Because right now I don't give a shit about the Avarean invasion force. I don't need an army bigger than theirs, your Grace. I only need one bigger than yours.'

Meillard's eyes widened, then he swore, 'You son of a bitch! You *knew* I'd block your way – you *wanted* me to do it – so you could take us on without fearing an attack to your flank.'

I gave him my best impression of a confused bystander. 'Is *that* what I did, your Grace? I do apologise. It was an accident on my part, stemming from my complete lack of knowledge of politics and warfare.'

Meillard turned on Valiana and snarled, 'You were supposed to be the Realm's Protector! Would you truly wage war on your own people? You're no better than that bitch Trin!'

As menacing as I'd tried to appear, Valiana was positively terrifying in her calm. 'You made it quite plain, *Prince* Meillard, that you considered Pertine its own country – and a country that has sided with our enemy at that. Should you try to block our way, we will destroy your army, give your people six days to flee into Aramor, and then leave Pertine such a ruin that when the Avareans come, they will see there is nothing in Tristia worth invading.'

'Still think it's a good idea to secede from Tristia?' I wondered aloud.

Meillard stared back at us, trying to work out if we really were ready to start a war between Aramor and Pertine that would end only in blood. I felt bad for him: Meillard wasn't an especially bad man; he was just a little too used to getting his way.

Well, we all learn that lesson eventually, your Grace.

'Very well,' Meillard said at last. He motioned for one of his aides to come forward and issued a quick series of orders.

When he was done, the newly restored Duke of Pertine let out a sigh. 'I've been on a knife's edge about this whole secession nonsense since the beginning,' he admitted, 'but my Generals convinced me it was the only way we could survive.'

'Those of us who fought the last wars are old men now,' Feltock said. 'Those battles were long ago, and our way of fighting as tired as we are. We're facing something new now.'

'And I suppose you've got some strategy to win, General Feltock?'

'Me?' Feltock chuckled. 'Haven't got a clue, to be honest. I can organise the troops, get 'em from one place to another with most of 'em alive, position cavalry and infantry – but *winning*? Against what's coming?' He shook his head and jerked a thumb at me. 'I'm hoping the Trattari's going to come up with something.'

Orders went down the line of both armies, and once it was done and we were amicably parting company, Meillard called out to me, 'Do you really believe you can do it, Falcio?'

'Do what, your Grace?'

'Win a war the entire country knows cannot be won.'

Hopeless causes tend to end in blood and tears, but they do give opportunities for a good line here or there.

I grinned. 'Just watch me.'

CHAPTER SIXTY-SIX

THE ABSENT CANNON

The truth is, Meillard was right: I really *don't* understand war. I've spent most of my adult life fighting duels, so steel and bloodshed are old, if regrettable, companions. But war? Battles, sieges, troop movements, supply lines? None of that makes any sense to me. And worst of all is the waiting. A duellist deals in thrusts and parries, feints and counter-attacks. Our strength is in speed: decisions made in a fraction of a second, in lightning-fast movements. Go to any duelling court and count the seconds between the two opponents entering the circle, beginning to trade blows and one or both lying dead or injured. You'll be lucky to get to sixty.

Wars take weeks, months, sometimes even years. The Shan have been at war with their Eastern neighbours for almost a century: children there are born, raised and die without ever having known peace. Do the people there spend their entire lives counting the minutes and praying the next will bring a trumpeting announcement of the end of the hostilities? Do they lie on their deathbeds, still at war, cursing the name of whichever ruler set them on this path in the first place?

On the snow-covered field of battle, our soldiers were frantically digging shallow holes and refilling them; we lacked the time and resources to build ballistae, trebuchet or other war machines that might have made a difference, so we had to put our hopes in less conventional methods.

I looked at the men and women, already exhausted, and wondered how many years would pass before the people of Tristia stopped cursing my name.

The field of battle. Through the exchange of emissaries we'd somehow agreed to this specific patch of land, this field that ends at a sheer cliff-face, the eastern edge of which separates Tristia from Avares, as the place to set about the business of killing each other.

'They're here,' Brasti said, jogging towards me, Gwyn close behind him.

'How far?' Valiana asked. She, Feltock and Nehra had been working out troop deployment by arranging Filian's coloured wooden blocks on a hastily sketched map. Who says war isn't a game?

'About two miles. It won't be long now.' He pointed towards the softly descending forest to the left of the cliff-face. 'They'll come down from there and then set up with the cliff at their backs.'

'I told you we should have set traps in the forest,' Feltock said.

'How big is the horde?' I asked Brasti.

For once, he was speechless. '*Massive*. Falcio, we couldn't go far enough to see the end of their lines. It's like . . . it's like staring at the ocean and trying to count the drops of water.'

'Would we kill them all with little traps in the hills?' I asked Feltock.

'Of course not, but—'

'Then I'd rather not piss them off. The whole point of this suicide mission is to make the Avareans see us as honourable foes, after all.' I looked back at our own soldiers. That was a lot of people to sacrifice just to make a positive impression on an implacable enemy.

'I've got some of the local volunteers from Pertine organised,' Ethalia said, coming up to stand beside me. 'We've got a dozen tents set up over there as our infirmary.'

Ethalia had always been loath to shed blood, and now she was Saint of Mercy none of us knew what price she'd pay for doing so, but she had insisted on coming. It felt good to have her standing beside me; warmer, somehow. 'I wish you weren't here,' I said.

She took my hand and drew me away from the others. 'You need to stop saying that.'

'Sorry,' I said, not very convincingly.

Abruptly, she wrapped her arms around me, so tightly I could barely breathe. 'You think I don't know, Falcio? You expect to meet your end here. You hide it well, but I see it in your face every time you think no one's watching.'

I hugged her back, suddenly afraid of the very thought she had given voice to. 'I'm not suicidal. I don't *want* to die, but I've been lucky for a very long time, Ethalia, and I think this time . . .' I could feel her cheek brushing against mine.

'You think Death himself will finally catch up to you.'

It sounded silly when she said it, but it was true, and I had nothing to offer that might comfort her.

'Do you know why I came, Falcio?' She didn't wait for a reply. 'I'm here because when . . . when it happens, when Death comes for you, I will stand in his way and refuse to let him have you.'

'I don't think it works that way, sweetheart.'

She buried her face in my shoulder. 'It *ought* to.'

We watched them come, these men and women for whom war was religion and mercy a concept so foreign that Gwyn said the closest word to it in their language actually meant 'to forget'. They jogged down the narrow, rugged path in groups of ten or twelve, huge packs on their backs, moving as easily as if this were nothing more than a pleasant hike on a fine day, rather than the beginning of the end of one of our two nations.

'This is a rather odd sensation,' Kest said.

'What's that?' I asked.

'Watching the enemy come on so slowly, seeing their ranks swell on the field and knowing there isn't a single thing we can do about it.'

I walked a little farther away from the others to watch in silence as the Avarean numbers began to surpass our own. I was filled with a growing sense of unease. Brasti had been right about that cliff-top: Morn's cannons could reach us from there, no matter how far we retreated. I'd spent an hour arguing the point with Feltock, but he and Valiana assured me that for every advantage another location further back might have, there would be just as many disadvantages. In the end, it came down to holding the line at the border between our two countries: *that* mattered, somehow.

'When do you think the fighting will begin?' I asked Feltock.

'Tomorrow sometime,' he replied. 'There will be certain formalities first, of course.'

'Such as?'

'Well, each of us offers the other the chance to surrender. Then we make some rather elaborate threats about what happens if the other refuses . . . it goes on like that for a while.'

'And then?'

The old man shrugged. 'Then the dying begins.'

That night I awoke to find Kest shaking my shoulder. 'Falcio,' he said, keeping his voice quiet. 'There's something you need to see.'

My back was sore and my muscles stiff. I've always been rubbish in the cold. 'What is it?'

'The Avarean forces have arrived.'

I rubbed the sleep from my eyes. 'Well, according to Brasti, there are more of them than anyone could ever count, so I can't imagine that's what you're waking me up to tell me.'

He shook his head. 'It's not that; it's . . . Well, you'd best come and see for yourself.'

We walked out to the edge. Our command tents were positioned on a small hill overlooking the field where our own soldiers slept uneasily, awaiting the morning. Gwyn was standing outside, waiting for us. He motioned to the other side of the field, where, at the bottom of the cliff, the Avarean forces had made their own encampment. There were thousands of them – they must have outnumbered us five to one . . . which, oddly, was not nearly as bad as I'd feared.

'I thought there would be more.' I turned to Gwyn. 'Didn't you say there were nearly fifty thousand warriors in Avares, spread out across more than two hundred warbands?'

He nodded.

'Then why am I staring at . . . What? Ten thousand soldiers?'

'A little more than seven thousand,' Kest corrected.

Seven thousand. So they only outnumber us three to one. 'Where in hells are the rest of them? You and Brasti both said you saw—'

Gwyn pointed his spear up high, towards the top of the cliff. 'There.'

I strained to see, only barely able to make out the fires, and then after a moment, the tents behind them. 'How many?' I asked Gwyn.

'All of them. More than forty thousand.'

Feltock came up behind us, Valiana with him. 'What in hells?' he asked. 'Are they *all* planning to rain arrows down on us?'

Gwyn shook his head. 'No, that is not the Avarean way. Even archers must take their place upon the field and face the enemy if they wish to earn *rokhan*. I think . . . I think they are not here to fight.'

'Then what *are* they here to do?' Brasti asked. 'Because this is a long way to travel just to enjoy the show.'

Valiana took his offhand comment poorly. 'Do not call it that,' she said, pointing at our camp. 'In a few hours, many of those men and women will rise to greet their last sunrise. Their deaths will be *real*, not some cheap performance.'

I didn't hear what Brasti said in reply, because Valiana's last words were gnawing at me powerfully – I stared at the cliff-top, at the horde, thousands upon thousands of Avareans, waiting there like an audience anticipating the opening of the curtain. Somehow, weirdly, they reminded me of the guests sitting at their elegant tables at Margrave Evidalle's wedding.

'Son of a *bitch!*' I swore.

All at once, and far too late, a dozen separate pieces locked into place: tiny questions I'd barely even considered because everything else had been so spectacularly falling apart all around me. *How* had an outsider like Morn managed to unite all the warbands in Avares? If he had such an unstoppable army, why had he bothered to sign non-aggression pacts with the Dukes? And, of course, the question I *should* have asked myself when Morn had first revealed himself to us in Avares: why had he been so quick to show me his strength when he *knew* I'd never switch to his side?

'What is it?' Valiana asked.

A sharp intake of breath from Kest told me he'd worked it out, too.

We stared at each other, silently cursing ourselves for missing the obvious – and, worst of all, for our own part in this folly.

'Morn never united the warbands of Avares, did he?' Kest asked.

I shook my head. 'How could he? Two hundred bands? That would take *decades.*'

'So he took over a few of them, as many as he could win through cunning and skill.'

Valiana pointed at the cliff-top. 'But what about them? Why are they here?'

'They're the audience,' I replied. 'They've come to see how well the Magdan leads his troops, how much *rokhan* he gains for them.'

Brasti was still staring at the horde off in the distance. 'You're saying this is some kind of *test?*'

'This is how Morn proves himself worthy of being the Warlord of all Avares,' Kest said.

The more I thought about it, the more apparent Morn's strategy became. After he'd won over his first warband, he'd doubtless challenged other Warlords, and used the skills we'd learned as Greatcoats to kill them in duels so he could take their warriors into his ever-growing army. But how far could you go with that? Eventually people would become wise to him and start uniting against him. So the second part of Morn's plan must have been to strike a deal: if he could win Tristia for Avares, they would let him carve out a piece of it for his new country that would be led by magistrates – not to mention make him the first man to command all the warbands of Avares in a thousand years. Not a bad legacy.

'I don't understand,' Brasti said. 'He's trying to invade the country with only seven thousand men? We could have brought – what—?' He turned to Feltock.

'Fifteen thousand, at least, if we had all the Dukes with us.'

'Which is too big a risk of losing,' Kest said.

'He needed to take most of our forces off the board, so he put on that little show for us in Avares,' I said, feeling sick at just how easily I'd been played. 'He made us think he had us so overpowered we could never hope to fight back. And *we* brought that message back to Tristia.'

'The Dukes,' Valiana said, understanding. 'They believed we were outnumbered, so they accepted the Magdan's offer of armistice in exchange for their seceding from Tristia.'

'Not the Magdan,' I said. That had been an illusion too, a feint. There was no Magdan. 'His name is Morn.'

'What about the cannon?' Brasti asked. 'We saw dozens of them – and racks of Shan steel weapons!'

'What we *saw*,' Kest said, and his tone told me he was kicking himself, 'were a few genuine weapons, no doubt secured at *ruinous* cost. The rest were likely fakes.' He turned to me. 'That cannon we used to escape? The one that wasn't covered up? That may well have been the only functioning one they had.'

A shadow passed across Valiana's features. 'All we had to do was stay united. Had we simply kept the country together . . . Tristia could have survived . . .'

That son of a bitch had outmanoeuvred us at every step. *You would have made an excellent First Cantor, Morn, if only you hadn't turned out to be such an arrogant prick.*

I sat down in the snow and looked at the enemy forces. Somewhere out there, Morn was sitting in his tent, polishing his sword and laughing his head off. The others were staring at me, wondering if I'd lost my mind.

'Will I have a chance to speak to Morn?' I asked Feltock. 'You said there would be an exchange of threats or whatever. Will he be there?'

'The Generals always meet. You can come if you want – but what will you say to him?'

'I'm going to challenge him to a duel.'

Brasti groaned. 'Please tell me that's not your big plan – didn't he kick your arse last time?'

'That was in the mountains. I wasn't ready for him.'

Kest looked troubled. 'Would he even accept such a duel?'

'Of course not,' I said. 'He's too smart. Even though I think he believes he can take me, he'd never risk it. He's got this all planned out far too well.'

'Then what's the point?'

I kept staring at the enemy. Ever since this had begun, I'd been letting others tell me that the world was shaped by politics, by economics, by military strategy – all things I didn't understand. I'd believed them, and let myself be pulled into an arena in which I could never hope to compete. But I'd allowed myself to be deceived. This wasn't a war between nations, nor a duel between rivals.

'It's a performance,' I said, rising to my feet.

'What?' Brasti asked.

'It's a play. This whole mess? It's a piece of theatre.' I gestured around. 'There's the stage, and there are the players, even if they don't know it.' I raised my arm towards the cliff-top. 'There's the audience. That's what this has been, right from the start.'

'A performance,' Brasti repeated. 'Only instead of a round of applause and some coins, Morn wants the audience to give him two countries.'

'Exactly.'

'Well then, we're good and buggered,' Feltock said. He looked at me. 'What's wrong with his face?'

'Oh, that's what Falcio looks like when he smiling,' Brasti explained.

'I'd dearly like to know what there is to smile about,' Feltock said.

'You asked why I was going to challenge him to a duel he'll never accept? Because while I might be rubbish at politics, I might not understand economics or military strategy – hells, I don't even know much about the theatre. But *stories*? I've spent my entire life trying to live up to the tales our people tell. I know how stories work and I'm going to use that to take Morn apart, one piece at a time.'

'They still have four times as many soldiers,' General Feltock pointed out. 'How exactly do you plan to defeat this "Morn"?'

'Simple. I'm going to tell a better story than he can.'

CHAPTER SIXTY-SEVEN

THE RITUAL

It was not yet dawn when I got up. I knew what I had to do now; I just had no idea *how* I was going to do it. Morn and his force were waiting for the next movement in this strange dance; they were sitting there patiently: row upon row of warriors in heavy chainmail and thick furs. These men knew how it all worked. They'd been bred for it.

I might not understand war but that hadn't stopped me from starting one. Now I had to end it.

'They make an impressive sight, don't they?' Nehra asked, taking up position beside me.

I had quizzed her on all the Avarean rituals of war, but right now a different question was bothering me. 'What stops them from attacking us right now?' I asked.

'Nobody sends their troops to fight in the dark.'

I knew that was true; I'd read it somewhere. 'But why is that?' I asked. 'I mean, how is it worse for one side than the other to attack at night?'

'War isn't a street-brawl, Falcio. Generals don't like uncertainty. Each engagement is carefully planned: the timing of your attacks, how best to use the terrain, how to deploy your units, when to advance, when to retreat.'

I stared at the bearded warriors across the gap. 'You make it all sound so civilised.'

'It's far more than that for the Avareans. War is a spiritual practice to them. It has commandments, rituals . . .'

I didn't understand – religion has never made much sense to me – but I did need to start making sense of their faith. 'Tell me again about the Scorn.'

'It's not complicated, Falcio. The Scorn is the ritual challenge that precedes the first engagement. So each side chooses a warrior who will ride up to the enemy line, and walk their horse along the ranks. The enemy forces will be shouting and screaming at them, seeking to unnerve them. If they so much as flinch, the enemy will fall upon them, cutting them to pieces.'

'I imagine *not* flinching takes a good deal of training.'

'Avarean children practise the Scorn even before they learn how to hold a sword.' She put a hand on my arm. 'Falcio, if you don't think you can do it . . .'

'It can't be me,' I said, which surprised her. 'Nothing I do will impress the Avareans. Even though Morn defeated me in battle, he'll have talked me up – he needs to convince them that I'm *special* somehow. So even if I do survive the Scorn, it won't make them think any better of Tristians as a people.'

'Kest has the most self-control,' Nehra suggested. 'He might even—'

'Not Kest, either. He's been the Saint of Swords. Morn will have spread that around, too.'

'Then who?'

I turned and left her standing there, not because I meant to be mysterious, but because even saying the name out loud made me sick to my stomach. It wasn't fair – but then, that was the difference between a duel and a war. In a duel, it's only your own life you throw away, not someone else's. But I had declared war and now I was going to have to get used to the idea of trading other people's lives for some small chance at Tristia's survival. That's how I'd made my choice of who to send.

I might not understand war, but I know duelling better than any man alive.

'First Cantor?' she asked, sitting cross-legged on the ground, sharpening that idiotic rusted cutlass of hers with a whetstone and cloth, oblivious to the fact that her blade had no chance of ever piercing Avarean chainmail.

'How old are you, Chalmers?' I asked.

'Eighteen.'

Eighteen years old. I wondered if she'd ever even kissed someone. Chalmers was young, guileless, and lousy with a blade. She wouldn't last five seconds in the Scorn.

'How did you become a Greatcoat, Chalmers?'

'I told you before: the King appointed me. He named me the—'

'Yes, but *why*? You couldn't have been more than thirteen years old. I doubt you'd had much training in the law and it's obvious it wasn't for any skill with a blade. So why would King Paelis make you a Greatcoat?'

She put down the whetstone and laid the sword across her lap. 'I used to spend all my time with my grandmother.'

'The quartermaster.'

She nodded. 'I liked the way she had to keep track of so many different things, find out why we had too few or too many of one item or another, who took them, and why.' Chalmers smiled. 'I really annoyed my grandmother, all my constant questions, so she started sending me out on these little missions: "Girl, there's a half-wheel of cheese that's gone missing from the food stores. Go find me the culprit!" or "Girl, there should be six hammers here but I count only five. Bring me the head of the man who has the sixth!"'

'And did you?'

Chalmers lifted her chin just a hair. 'Every time. Including the time when someone stole a small casket of elspeth leaves from the apothecary's supply room. I followed every trace of that casket, every scrap of blue-green leaves through every tower and passage in the entire castle. It took me nearly eight weeks, but eventually I found the thief.'

'Who was it?' I asked, then the answer suddenly occurred to me. 'Paelis? You caught the King stealing elspeth leaves?'

She nodded. 'They're mostly used to heal cuts, but apparently you can use them to create a paste that produces an intoxicating smoke.'

I laughed. The King had been absolutely shameless in his quest to find new and interesting ways to get himself drunk or addled. 'And so he made you a Greatcoat?'

'Not right then, no, but he asked how I'd found him out and when I explained it to him, he said to come see him when I came of age and he'd name me to the Greatcoats.'

'But if you were only thirteen when he died—'

'The night before the Dukes came for him, after he'd seen you and all the others, I went to see him. He wasn't pleased to see me, but I said that if he was so damned determined to get himself killed then I would see him fulfil his promise to me first.'

'And so he named you.'

She nodded. 'I became the King's Question that day.' She rose and put her sword in its scabbard. 'And before you make some snide comment, I'm as much a Greatcoat as you or Kest or Brasti or any of those others.'

'Maybe more so,' I said.

'How dare you—! Wait, what—?'

She was so young . . . so damned *young*. And yet, what had Aline said to me? In an unjust country we are all nothing but victims, and the best we can hope for is one chance to prove ourselves, to turn our death into a sacrifice for what we believe in rather than a fate that was set upon us.

'Greatcoat, report,' I said.

She straightened herself before me. 'My name is Chalmers, the King's Question,' she said.

'And mine is Falcio val Mond, First Cantor of the Greatcoats, once called the King's Heart. Chalmers, I have a mission for you.'

CHAPTER SIXTY-EIGHT

THE SCORN

The chill air bit through both the leather and the inner lining of my coat. The breath leaving my mouth took the form of pale clouds. It wasn't yet full winter and I'd been in colder places and times, so it was strange to me that I felt so uncomfortable. I wondered if perhaps the Avareans had some kind of magic at their disposal that froze the blood of their enemies, or if it was simply that moments such as these resist any sense of warmth.

I hate magic, but I think I hate war much more.

The crunch of footsteps in the snow drifted towards me, two sets of them. One strode, angrily, the other was quieter, more precise. Apparently Brasti and Kest had heard about the Scorn.

'Are you out of your fucking mind?' Brasti demanded.

'Probably,' I conceded.

He and Kest came alongside me. 'You're sending an eighteen-year-old girl who doesn't even have a proper greatcoat to be torn to pieces by a bunch of fucking barbarians whose only method of population control probably comes from eating their own young!'

'There's no other way.'

'You could go yourself – or send Kest, or hells, if you have to, send *me*. I'll die for your stupid cause if that's what it takes.'

'It won't work if it's one of the three of us.'

His eyes narrowed. 'What won't work?'

I didn't answer. I found the language of war too bitter on my tongue.

Kest understood, of course. 'You want to show the Avareans who we are,' he said softly.

'Except they value *strength*!' Brasti shouted, far too close to my ear. 'You're sending the weakest among us – even Valiana had more training with a sword when she took up the coat!'

'That's why he's doing it,' Kest said. He could sense my discomfort and so he spoke for me, to shield me from even that well-deserved pain. 'Nothing about us will impress them except our willingness to fight.'

Brasti stood in front of me. 'So you're sending her to die in the hope that a bunch of piss-drinking warriors *admire* us for it?'

'I don't care what the Avareans think.'

'Please, Falcio, tell me you haven't fooled yourself into believing you can make the Magdan put a stop to this by showing him just how courageous *Chalmers* is?'

'I don't care what he thinks either.'

'Then . . . *oh, you bloody fool.*'

'It's the only play,' I said.

Brasti shook his head. '*Damn you*, Falcio. Damn you and damn the King for this idiotic dream of yours. They won't change sides. They won't take down the Magdan for us.'

'I don't expect them to.'

'Then what—?'

I couldn't stand it any more, the pecking, scolding tone in his voice that was so close to the one in my head. I grabbed him by the collar of his coat and growled, 'It's all I have left, Brasti – these small, petty gambits. You seriously think I have any faith in my fellow Greatcoats any more? *They walked away from the King's dream!* They abandoned the missions he gave them, and the oaths they swore!'

Brasti pushed me off of him. 'Then what good will sacrificing Chalmers do?'

For all my anger, I couldn't answer, so Kest did it for me. 'It will slow them down.'

Brasti turned to face him. 'Slow them down?'

'Even if they've turned against us, watching Chalmers – someone near the age when most of us took up our coats – will give them pause. When the fight comes, it will make them question themselves and, if we are very lucky, it will make them hesitate, just a little.'

'So you agree?' I asked.

Kest shook his head. 'No. I understand, but that's not the same thing. Falcio, you're still thinking like a duellist. This is *war*. When the battle begins, they won't be thinking of anything except the chaos and bloodshed all around them. They will fight on instinct.'

'Maybe,' I conceded. 'But maybe you're wrong.'

'These are poor odds on which to bet a young woman's life.'

A bitter laugh came out from somewhere deep inside me. 'Is that what you think? A poor bet? Kest, once the fight starts, she'll be there, in the midst of it. She's rubbish with a blade and she has no experience with war. She'll die before the first day is out. I'm just trying to give her one chance to die for something that *matters*.'

Kest and Brasti just stood there, looking at me. I knew they were trying to gauge whether I'd lost my mind or not.

Finally Kest said, 'It is a cold logic that's guiding you, Falcio.'

'Look around,' I said, turning to set down the path from the hill to where Chalmers would ride to her death. 'It's a cold fucking country.'

The Avareans sent their warrior first. He was a broad-chested, broad-shouldered young man riding a heavy warhorse covered by ring mail, though he himself was shirtless, and sporting half a dozen red cuts on his skin. We had watched from a distance as a dozen Avareans had apparently fought each other for the privilege of riding the Scorn. They are a strange people.

'You sure about this?' Feltock asked, watching along with me.

I nodded.

The Avarean rode straight for our front line as if he intended to crash right through them. To their credit, none of them fled, though they all looked like they wished they could. Though we had more than enough experienced soldiers ready and eager to stand in that line, I had insisted we put only the smallest, least-threatening people we could find – farmers and crafters, and the worse-fitting the armour, the better. There would be no great glory for the Avareans in this ride.

'Come see the people you've come to butcher, you arrogant bastard,' I whispered.

At the last instant before he met the line, the Avarean turned his horse at a right angle and slowed to barely more than a walk as he stared down our soldiers one by one. He made faces at them, grinning or frowning, pretending to cry and then suddenly laughing and jeering at them. Following my orders, our own troops did nothing in reply, which served to aggravate the young warrior, who increased his efforts to tempt and taunt them. As he passed the halfway mark of our line, he grew frustrated, making more and more menacing gestures at our soldiers, although never touching his weapon.

Just a few more seconds, I thought, *and then this bastard can go riding back to his own troops and tell them how he couldn't get a rise out of us.*

He was almost at the end when something went very wrong. One of ours, I couldn't see whether it was a man or woman, suddenly reacted, bringing a sword up to shield themselves. The young Avarean grinned in response, and, as was his right, instantly drew his own blade and thrust it through his opponent's neck. As the body fell, the next soldier very nearly made the same mistake, only barely restraining himself in time. The Avarean laughed and said something in his own language – probably thanking us. He reached the end of the line and turned to ride back to the whoops and cheers of his own troops.

We'd lost this round: we'd proven our soldiers couldn't keep their nerve in the face of one lone warrior.

Now one of ours was going to have to ride their line.

'Any advice?' Chalmers asked, climbing up into the saddle. Every part of her was shaking. Her voice wavered, her hands barely clutched the reins. Even her feet shifted about in the stirrups, which confused the poor beast no end. I'm not sure why Chalmers chose Arsehole out of all the mounts available – maybe some small shred of spite peeking out beneath the stoic determination to do her duty. I doubted it, though. She might want to hurt me but I doubted she was the sort to take out her fears and frustrations on a horse.

'Steady, Arsehole,' I told him, patting his neck. He gave no sign that he'd understood, probably because he was a horse and not even a very bright one at that.

'Well?' Chalmers asked.

I looked out at the Avarean warriors all lined up waiting for her. It was, Nehra had explained to me, a kind of privilege to be in that line, to see the face of the enemy up close. Perhaps they would glean some secret about us, some insight into our strengths and weaknesses. Or perhaps it was no different than drunks at a bar staring each other down.

'Show them who you are,' I said to Chalmers.

'What I am is terrified.'

I looked up at her. She wasn't lying. This wasn't anticipation or anxiety. This wasn't the kind of reckless determination I'd seen in Valiana when she'd first taken up the coat, or the grim acceptance of death I'd seen in so many other Greatcoats. Most of us were fighters before we'd been magistrates; Chalmers was the opposite. She'd been drawn in by her fascination with the law, with investigation. She had no reference points for what was coming next. Eighteen and unlikely to see twenty. When I faced death, I saw the events of my life behind me. What she saw now were all the things she would never experience. There was an acrid smell in the air. She had pissed herself.

'Dismount,' I said.

Her eyes widened and a look of confusion gave way to one of delirious relief. 'First Cantor?'

'It means, "get off the horse".'

She began to lift a leg over, but she hesitated. 'Why?'

'I was wrong. My idea won't do any good. It's better if one of us goes.'

'One of us,' she repeated my words.

'I don't mean it that way. Of course you're one of us. I mean, it's better if I go, or Kest.'

Her eyes drifted away from me, up and to the right as if the answer were somewhere in the clouds. 'Yes, but why won't your idea work?'

'Just get off the—'

'I need to know,' she said, 'why won't your idea work? You said yesterday that the Avareans already expect you to go, so it won't impress them when you do.'

'Chalmers, don't start—'

'You think I'll start crying, or begging for mercy once I'm near them? You think I'll try to run away before I get to the end of their line. You expect me to fail.'

'I absolutely expect you to fail,' I admitted. 'I'm afraid you'll do so too soon and they'll laugh at us.'

The words hit her like a slap in the face, but after a few seconds she nodded. 'You're probably right.' She looked down at her shaking hands. 'I'm not even sure at this point that I'll be able to stay on the horse long enough to ride out to them.'

'It's perfectly normal. Dismount. None of our men know that you were going to ride the Scorn, and none of them ever will.'

'What would you do in my place?' she asked.

A hundred decent lies came to my lips; it wasn't hard to think of reasons to not do this foolish, futile act. But something about Chalmers, her strange devotion to knowing the truth, forced me to say, 'I would ride out to those men with their swords and their chainmail. I would show them my fear – all of it. I would let them see every ounce of terror inside me. But when the urge to turn and run came upon me? I'd think back to a girl I once met on a wedding barge, wearing her poorly made leather coat – not even a proper greatcoat, mind you – and wielding nothing but a broken cutlass as a dozen guardsmen surrounded her. I'd remember the way she held her ground as they closed in on her and asked them, "I don't suppose any of you gutless rat-faced canker-blossoms would like to surrender?"'

Chalmers laughed – a brittle, fragile thing, as much a defiance of her own fear as a reaction to what I'd said, but then she asked, 'Do you think I should try that line out on the Avareans?'

Without waiting for a reply, she kicked Arsehole's flanks and took off for the enemy line.

CHAPTER SIXTY-NINE

THE KING'S QUESTION

Imagine for a moment riding towards a line of enemy soldiers, the distance between you shrinking faster than you would have thought possible. You want to look back, to see your own people behind you, but you can't, because if you do, you'll turn the horse and flee for safety.

The line gets closer.

The terrain beneath your mount's hooves feels uneven, and you're certain that at any moment he'll fall and break a leg, leaving you tumbling down to the ground. Even when he doesn't, the cold wind assails you, making the tips of your fingers so numb that you don't think you'll be able to hold on. For all your shivering, sweat begins to trickle down your face and inside your clothes. The line of fierce, wild men grows closer, their faces wild. Feral. *Hungry.*

The line gets closer.

The shouts and hooting begin, filling your ears, creeping inside you all the way down your spine. These men are not just going to *kill* you: they're going to tear you limb from limb, laughing as they do it.

The line keeps getting closer.

It would be easy to believe you could just keep riding, that somehow you will find hard steel at your core that won't bend. Perhaps you imagine just closing your eyes and throwing your life away as if you were jumping off a cliff, uttering your own gorge prayer. Maybe you could find something – *anything* – that would keep you riding all the way to the enemy line.

And if you did? *That would be the easy part.*

'She's there,' Nehra said. I hadn't even heard her coming up. I hadn't seen her because my own eyes had been closed.

I couldn't see what the Avareans were doing, but somehow I could *feel* it, as if the air itself was vibrating as they leered at Chalmers, taunting her. No doubt Morn had made sure at least a few of them knew enough of our language to shout threats at her, promises to seek her out during the battle, to bring special torments to her when they got their hands on her.

'Why isn't she taunting them back?' Brasti asked. 'I though the whole point was to scorn the enemy and make *them* react.'

'I told her not to.'

The Avarean soldiers were jeering at her, howling like animals, and every time I heard screams I kept thinking they must be Chalmers, already torn from her horse. But this, too, was merely one of the ways they sought to make her flee.

'Why did you tell her not to give her own insults?' Nehra asked. 'It would make it easier on her.'

'Because it's not who she is.'

Tristia has never been a nation of warriors. We aren't born to the shield. Our army is weak, our people disunited. We are a country only by virtue of geography; in all other ways, we are individuals. Chalmers was an individual: a quirky woman who liked mysteries and wanted to spend her last day on this earth wearing a greatcoat even though she knew as well as any of us that it didn't mean anything any more. Let them see that. Let them see *Chalmers.*

The noise of the enemy grew louder, filling the plain. I heard the steel of the blades of those in the rear lines clanging against their shields, trying to get Chalmers to react.

'Remarkable,' Kest said.

'What is it?' I had to squint to see much more than a blur of steel and fur.

'She's reached the end of the line,' Brasti said. 'She's alive!' He turned to Nehra. 'That's it then, right? She's done the line and now she can ride back.'

'No,' I said.

'What do you mean, "no"?' Brasti asked.

I didn't answer. They would understand soon enough. I had told Chalmers that if she somehow managed to survive the first pass of the line that she should turn her horse right back around and ride it again.

'We've got to get her!' Brasti shouted, heading towards the horses.

I grabbed him by the arm and dragged him back. 'Don't. Let her do this.'

'She'll be fucking killed!' He threw off my grip. 'You made her do the scorn ride. She survived it – that's enough!'

'Brasti's right,' Kest said, his eyes narrowed as he peered out towards the enemy line. 'The Avareans are getting more and more riled up. They won't let her survive a second pass. We should—'

'If you try to rush after her, you'll make matters worse,' Nehra said. She didn't look pleased with me at all. 'The Avareans will consider it a breach of the ritual. They'll swarm over you and any goodwill we might have generated will be gone.'

Brasti glared at me. 'So we just watch her die?'

'Maybe,' I replied. 'She was ready for that possibility.'

'Possibility? It's a fucking *certainty*!'

'She's going down,' Kest said, pointing.

Out on the field, several Avarean warriors had lost any pretence at composure. Apparently they didn't like the idea that Chalmers had not only got lucky and somehow managed not to run away, but that she would ride past them a second time? That was too much and several of them grabbed at Arsehole as he went by. My copper-flanked Tivanieze surprised them all by leaping away from their grasp, even as he kept following the line, allowing Chalmers to guide him rather than fleeing like a mad beast. Damn, but he was a good horse. But the Avareans grew smart: further down the line, several of them leaped out before she reached them, ready to grab her. Chalmers tried to hold her seat, but they were too big for her and dragged her down to the ground.

'Saints,' Brasti swore, 'look at what they're—'

'Shut up,' I said.

My distance vision may be shit, but even I could tell what was happening: four Avareans, big bastards, had each taken one of Chalmers' limbs and they'd begun pulling in different directions. It's not easy to sever a human arm or leg by sheer force. This was their show of strength, their way of mocking her act of courage.

'Damn you, Falcio,' Brasti said. 'Let me—'

'It's too late,' I said. 'You'll never reach her.'

'This is on your head.'

As if I didn't know that.

'You believe this will strengthen the resolve of our side?' Kest asked me. I marvelled at the way he could keep calm at a moment like this. If I were him, I'd be beating the shit out of me.

'I don't care about resolve,' I replied.

'Then what—?'

'*There!*' Nehra said, pointing to the right, where some dozen figures on horseback were breaking ranks from the Avarean force. There were roars of outrage as they raced along the front line, heading straight for the men holding Chalmers, weapons drawn high – swords, maces, a staff here, a spear there. Most military regiments wield the same weapon for efficiency, but of course, these weren't regular soldiers. You could tell that by the long leather coats they wore.

'*Son of a bitch!*' Brasti swore.

Several Avareans, realising what was happening, tried to block their path, but the riders were moving too swiftly; they were, after all, well trained in evasion. They took out those who got in their way, and when they reached the men trying to tear Chalmers apart, they struck with speed and certainty. Three of the men let go at once, reaching instead to draw their own weapons. One man didn't. His arm landed a few feet away in the snow, spraying blood.

A moment later Chalmers was draped across a saddle and the dozen men and women were pounding towards us, with Arsehole, my brave, lunatic horse, a few yards behind, doing his best to keep up despite the arrow sticking out of his rump. In the distance behind them, I could see the Avarean commanders executing the men who'd broken the line when they'd tried to tear Chalmers apart.

'I can't believe it,' Brasti said, as the rebel Greatcoats rode past our own cheering lines towards the hill where we stood. 'How could you know they would—?'

'He didn't know,' Kest said, his eyes on me. He looked neither impressed nor forgiving. 'He bet that girl's life on this gambit.'

'Songs will be sung for a century about her ride,' Nehra said, the faraway stare in her eyes telling me she was already composing the words.

If Chalmers died, I doubted that would make me feel better.

Moments later, thirteen Greatcoats rode up to where we stood. They'd broken ranks to save Chalmers, which I might have appreciated more had we not been in this mess because of them. The one bright spot was the rider who was bearing Chalmers: Quillata, the King's Sail, Seventh Cantor of the Greatcoats.

'Falcio,' she said, nodding to me as she rode up. 'Does this belong to you?'

I lifted Chalmers from the saddle. Her eyes were closed, her face so pale I thought she might be dead from the fright. Brasti spread a saddle-blanket on the snow and I placed her upon it as gently as I could.

'She's alive,' Quil said to me. There was a quaver in her voice I didn't recognise.

'What is it?' I asked.

She shook her head, and now I could see she was trying not to weep. You have to understand, Quillata is made from raw iron, bent and shaped according to her own will and nothing else. She is as hard a woman as this world has ever made, but when she looked down at Chalmers, her voice broke. 'She kept saying she needed to go back.'

'What? Why?' Brasti asked.

Quil turned and looked at Arsehole. 'She said she needed to make sure her horse was okay.'

One of the other Greatcoats laughed at that, but I didn't. I bent down and as I lifted Chalmers up so that I could take her to her tent, Quil and I kept staring at each other. For all the disputes over the direction of the country or who should or shouldn't rule, at least we agreed on one thing. We all knew what a Greatcoat was.

CHAPTER SEVENTY

THE RETURN

'You can open your eyes now, Chalmers,' I said, laying the girl down on the cot in one of Ethalia's medical tents. 'Come on now, you're safe. Open your eyes.'

Her entire body was shaking, as if she were still lying across Quillata's horse, thundering across the field.

'Leave her be,' Brasti said, putting his hand on my shoulder and trying to pull me away. 'She's been through enough.'

I shrugged him off. I love Brasti dearly but he's never understood people like me – people like Chalmers. He does what he does because it's in his nature. Chalmers wasn't brave by nature; she had to *fight* for it, to claw at her own fears until she could *force* them to back down. If she let herself retreat, even for an instant, all that would be gone.

'Greatcoat, report,' I ordered.

Brasti grabbed at me again. 'Falcio, I swear if you don't back off I'm going to kick the shit out of you, and it'll be for the good of all humankind.'

'Greatcoat, report!' I bellowed.

The girl's eyes flickered open. I doubt she could have seen me through the flood of tears, and the shaking hadn't abated at all, but her voice was clear as a bell when she replied, 'Chalmers, granddaughter of Zagdunsky, called the King's Question.' She swallowed, then added, 'What the fuck do you want now, First Cantor?'

I took one of her trembling hands in mine. 'A hundred more like you.'

She smiled weakly and stared at the remains of the sleeve of her fake greatcoat, ripped off when an Avarean had grabbed her as he tried to tear *her* apart. It wasn't just that sleeve; the entire thing was in tatters now. 'You owe me a new coat.' she said.

'I do at that.'

Uncertainty returned to her gaze. 'Arsehole . . . is he—?'

'Unkillable?' Brasti asked. 'Gwyn barely had the arrow out of his rump before the dumb beast was already jouncing around the camp looking for someone to play with.'

Chalmer's smile became a grin as she looked at me. 'Take care of my horse, would you?'

'You want a new coat and *my* horse?'

She nodded. 'That, and one more thing.'

'Anything,' I said.

She let go of my hand. 'I think I'd like to sleep now, First Cantor.'

Because I knew she'd understand, I said, 'But just for a little while, right?'

Her eyes closed.

I found Quillata and the rest of the double-double-crossing Greatcoats huddled outside. 'How is she?' Old Tobb asked, the collar of his greatcoat turned up against the cold. I couldn't help but notice that he and the others had shed the fur cloaks they'd been wearing in Avares, as if doing so proved their renewed loyalty. I stared at him, becoming more and more convinced that his disposition, intellect, and integrity could only be improved by him being slapped silly for an hour or so. The only reason I stayed my hand was that I realised I'd been wanting to do that a lot lately.

'Chalmers is a Greatcoat,' I said. 'She doesn't break just because a few piss-drinking barbarians shake their clubs at her.'

The others glared at me, a flash of anger at what they – quite rightly – suspected was a slight at their own constancy. The King used to say the true strength of the Greatcoats was in our judgement – that our ability to render the *right* verdict was what made us worthy of the coats. I'd asked him once what our greatest weakness was and he'd not even paused to think before replying, 'Your damned pride. You're all so brave, so daring, so skilled at fighting, it's a miracle you don't all beat each other senseless on a daily basis just to prove who's tougher.'

'We thought we were saving the country,' Jakin, the King's Stone, said, strands of dark hair falling across his face as he bowed his head mournfully. He was the same age as Kest, Brasti and me but he'd always struck me as much younger, somehow – idealistic in a way that comes and goes so easily when you're a teenager.

'Then you thought wrong,' Kest said tersely. He'd recruited Jakin to the Greatcoats in the first place; that explained the unusual edge to his voice – and Jakin's stricken look.

Quil stepped forward, shielding the others from my ire. 'We're not going to drop down to our knees and beg forgiveness, if that's what you're waiting for, Falcio. The country was rotting from the inside – everyone but you three could see that! It was so *obvious* the King's plan – whatever it was – had failed.'

Murielle de Vierre, the King's Thorn, came a little closer; with her long red curls and high cheekbones she looked far too exotic for such drab surroundings. We all assumed the King had named her his 'thorn' ironically, because her remarkable and delicate beauty made 'the Rose' far more appropriate. 'Morn *promised* us, First Cantor,' she said dramatically. 'He gave *oaths* to us—'

'What did he promise?' I hadn't stopped wondering what he could possibly have said to turn more than forty Greatcoats away from everything they once believed in.

'That if we stood by him there would be no war,' she explained.

'That once the Dukes seceded, the country wouldn't be able to field an army, so no one would have to die.'

'So instead we could all live as slaves?' Brasti asked.

Murielle shook her head, wanting us to *understand*. 'No, he really did have a plan! Morn would show the horde that he was able to win the country with just a few warbands and once they'd made him the Magdan of all Avares, he'd be able to convince them to allow Tristia to remain unconquered – a kind of . . . well, a client state.'

'And how exactly did he manage to convince *you* of that rubbish?'

She looked ashamed, and I felt a little bad for it. On the night King Paelis had named Murielle to the Greatcoats she'd surprised me by asking me to come into town to celebrate with her. I'd refused, giving the excuse that I had to leave on a judicial circuit early the following morning. If not for that moment of cowardice, it might have been the start of something between us. Now I looked at her, at all these men and women who had once been more than a family to me. I'd tried so hard to prove myself worthy of the rank of First Cantor – worthy of *them*. 'How could you all have betrayed the King this way?' Of course, what I really meant was something far more petty, *How could you all have betrayed* me?

'Morn's plan made sense,' Quil answered defensively. 'Far more than the King's dream ever did, that's for certain.' She kicked at the snow. 'Damn it, Falcio, you knew Paelis best. How were all those stupid little missions he gave us supposed to save Tristia from itself?'

I'd asked myself that same question countless times and I had yet to come up with an answer that made sense. One hundred and forty-four Greatcoats, each sent off with one final enigmatic order. Would Paelis still have given those commands if he'd known the price they would extract from us?

Parrick Morran, the King's Calm, forced to save the life of Duke Jillard – a man the King himself despised.

Nile Padgeman, the King's Arm, sacrificed himself in a hopeless effort to protect Duke Roset in Luth. Harden Vitale, the King's Whisper, died trying to protect Saint Gan-who-laughs-with-dice.

'I don't know,' I admitted.

Kest caught my eye, his expression warning me against showing uncertainty in front of the others. *Kest Murrowson, the King's Blade, forced to promise that he'd kill his best friend before allowing him to become a tyrant.*

'Perhaps the King believed there was no other way,' Kest said. 'Perhaps before we could restore the rule of law, we needed to first prove to people that the laws *meant* something – that the Greatcoats would do whatever it took to uphold them, even at the cost of losing everything we'd ever fought for.'

Falcio val Mond, ordered to find and protect the one girl who could have fulfilled the King's vision for the country – only to watch her die on the cold stone floor of a broken castle.

The others were watching me. 'I don't know,' I repeated dully. Who was I to blame Quil and Tobb and all the rest for being seduced by Morn's promises of easing Tristia's suffering? What magistrate wouldn't wonder what a nation might be like if it were ruled by a judiciary instead of feckless nobles? If I hadn't had Kest and Brasti with me these past years, if Valiana hadn't come into my life, had Aline not shown herself to be so remarkable, might not I have lost hope as well?

Murielle took my hand. 'We were wrong, Falcio. Morn made his scheme sound so logical, so brilliant both in conception and execution.' Her gaze went to the field down below. 'It wasn't until we got here that we realised how far he was willing to go, how . . . *personal* this is for him.'

'He hates me *that* much?'

'Not you—' She was shaking her head. 'I mean, yes, Morn despises you – but mostly because you always stood up for the King.' She let go of my hand. 'It's *Paelis* Morn resents – for lying to us, for tricking us into believing we could somehow protect the country after his death, when in reality the King had no idea how to save Tristia.'

'So now Morn wants to destroy the country just to prove a point?' Brasti asked, sounding as incredulous as I felt.

'No, it's the opposite,' Quillata interrupted. 'He wants to prove he can do what Paelis couldn't: that he can build a better nation than the King could have even imagined.' Every line in her face echoed the regret in her voice. 'It's become an obsession for him, Falcio. It's made him cold and mean, but it's also made him . . . He's *brilliant*, Falcio, he really is – far more so than any of us ever realised.'

The noon sun was starting to rise, lending a shimmer to the snow and ice on the cliff-top where the horde waited for the next act of Morn's tantalising performance. Why was it that in Tristia, madness so often went in hand with genius? What was it about my people, that their worst desires were inextricably linked with the means to bring those desires to life?

'I've dealt with clever men before,' I said, and turned to make my way down the hill and onto the field where Morn and I would meet for the final parlay before the battle.

'Not like him,' Quillata called out. 'Morn manipulated the populations of two countries into this war and tore Tristia apart without even firing a shot. He tricked every one of us – even you – into playing a part in his plans.'

I paused for a moment. 'What's your point?'

'I'm sorry, Falcio, I truly am, but he's better at this than you are.'

CHAPTER SEVENTY-ONE

THE WAR SPEECH

'Hello, First Cantor.' Morn's tone was surprisingly amiable considering we were standing nine feet apart at the centre of a field between two armies. Apparently the distance was one of the precise requirements for this next little piece of theatre called *The Peace Parlay*, in which our two nations would have one final opportunity to avert war. This particular tradition must have come from some long-ago era when Avareans had been more civilised, for the seven thousand barbarians on the other side of the field jeering and grunting at me clearly couldn't wait to get started on the 'bloodshed' bit of the tradition.

'Did you want to surrender, Morn?' I asked pleasantly.

He shook his head, but he kept his eyes fixed on me, which told me he wasn't entirely sure I'd hold to the oath not to attack during the parley. 'It has to be war, Falcio. I couldn't stop it even if I wanted to. Tristian blood is going to drench the snow beneath our feet, and every man and woman you dragged here is going to die.'

'You sound broken-up over it, Morn. There is one option that would save everyone a lot of trouble, if you're up for it.'

'A duel? I don't think so.'

'Why not? You beat me once.'

'Because war doesn't work that way.' He gestured at my hand, which kept drifting towards the hilt of my rapier. 'By the way, the

Avareans have very strict rules when it comes to *rokhan*. If you kill me right now, I promise you our countrymen would pay the price for a thousand years and a thousand more.'

Nehra had already reminded me of the consequences of losing my temper before I'd come onto the field. Twice. So had Feltock, Kest, and Valiana. Even Brasti added his own two bits' worth. So I ignored him and asked instead, 'Remind me, how long exactly do we have to stand out here staring at each other like moon-crossed lovers?'

'Not long. Another minute or so should satisfy both sides that we made the attempt.'

'What shall we do to pass the time then? Know any good songs?'

He sighed. 'Another joke. You know what disappoints me most about you, Falcio? It's that you could have been a great man. You can outfight most soldiers and out-think most Generals. And yet all you do is throw yourself at the waves of history, hoping to beat back the ocean. And every time you nearly drown and Kest has to pull you out of the water, you point to your soggy clothes and shout, "See here? This is the blood of my enemy! If I just keep going back, eventually he'll run out!"'

'I asked for a song, not a poem.'

Morn chuckled. 'Always so clever. I wonder . . .' He paused for a moment before asking, 'Are you prepared to put that eloquent wit of yours to the test?'

'You won't duel me but you want to have a *talking* contest?'

He spread his hands. 'It's only words. What have you got to lose?'

A great deal, in fact: Nehra had already warned me that the Avareans had another little ritual up their sleeves called 'the Oration for the Dead'. The leader of each side is afforded the opportunity to speak directly to the opposing soldiers in an attempt to break their spirit. Basically, you're expected to describe in detail what will happen if they dare to fight in hopes that some significant number will turn tail and run. Nehra had made it clear that there was nothing I could say to the Avareans that would scare them, whereas there were any number of dark images Morn could describe to our soldiers that might convince them to abandon the battle. Of course, the Avareans didn't really expect us to agree to this particular tradition, which was good, because only an idiot would do so.

'Sure,' I said. 'Let's all hear what you've got to say.'

'You know me,' Morn began as he walked along the snowy ground at the front of our lines. His voice was calm, almost reassuring, and it carried surprisingly well. He would have made a passable opera singer. 'I was born in the city of Chevor, in Baern. I bet some of you were as well.'

A few heads nodded in response.

He took out a small knife from his coat, causing several of our soldiers to grab their spears tighter. Thank the Saints dead and living, no one did more than that. Feltock had spent the better part of an hour explaining *exactly* what would happen if we attacked an emissary during the Oration. Since the whole point of us coming here was to convince the Avareans to think well enough of our courage and discipline that they'd choose *not* to massacre every townsperson and villager in the country, we were going to have to stand here for a bit, listening patiently to Morn's garbage. I wondered if any army had ever had to suffer so much just to win the favour of its enemy.

'I'm one of you,' Morn said, running the knife blade across his palm. 'My blood is as Tristian as any of yours.' He put the knife back in the pocket of his coat. 'So why must it be only your blood that will be spilled on this field?' He renewed his slow walk along our line. 'I have family in Tristia, just like you do. So why must it only be your families who will weep over your death?'

'Maybe your family just doesn't like you,' Brasti shouted, setting off a smattering of laughter.

Morn smiled as if we'd just played right into his hand. 'A joke?'

he asked, once the laughter had died down. 'Is that what they offer you in return for the senseless waste of your lives? A *fucking joke*? But no. I think it's something else.' He turned and started walking back in my direction, pointing at me. 'I think this man has made you a false promise. I think Falcio, along with Filian, the boy King, Duchess Trin's *puppet*, who cost you the life of the Queen you loved, has convinced you that if you die bravely here, your families at home will be treated with respect by the Avareans once we invade.'

'It's true, isn't it?' one of our men shouted. Feltock shot him a look, but by now the soldier wasn't about to be cowed – at least, not by Feltock. 'We were told that if we fought here, life might not be so bad for our folks back home.'

Morn stopped walking and stood there for a moment, staring at the man who'd spoken. His expression was sympathetic at first, but then he began to laugh. 'I take it back,' he said, in between chuckles. 'Falcio *did* offer you a joke in return for your service.' Then his face hardened suddenly. 'Look at me, you damned fools! *I* am the Magdan of Avares. *I* am the leader of that army – seven-thousand strong – who will rip you limb from limb upon that field in the morning.' He resumed his march along the lines, and the men and women he passed flinched more than they had during the Scorn.

'*Respect?*' he demanded, then threw an arm back to point to the army on the other side. 'You think those warriors, born and bred for battle, will *respect* you? They won't even *see* you! The Avareans admire courage, that's true, but only when it's paired with skill in battle. Most of you have never even killed a man before. You'll stumble. You'll hesitate. The Avareans will run right through you, their blades slicing through the flesh and bone of your bodies like freshly sharpened scythes through dry summer grass! They'll keep running, too, all the way to your homes, to your cities and towns and villages, where they will rape and kill everyone you've ever loved. *That* is what you are doing to your wives, to your husbands, to your children. *You* are bringing the horde to their door!'

'We have to stop this,' Kest whispered to me.

'We can't,' Nehra warned. 'Once the Oration has begun, we're bound to let him finish.'

'Look at our soldiers. Morn may not even need to finish his speech before they all drop their weapons and beg for mercy. Falcio . . .'

'We play it out,' I said.

Morn must have noticed us talking because he turned to us. 'Look at them. See how they scheme against you, even now? Do you want to know the truth about Falcio val Mond and the Greatcoats? Would you like to know the *real* reason why he brought you here to die?' He paused for a moment, just to make sure I was watching him, and that I would pay attention to what he said next. 'Tell them, Falcio. Tell these brave men and women about *your wife*. Tell them why the King named his daughter after her. Tell them the finest joke ever inflicted upon a nation.'

'You should shut up now,' Kest said, just loud enough for Morn and those nearest in our front line to hear.

Morn shook his head sadly. 'It is an awful tale, to be sure: a woman raped and killed by the Duke of her own Duchy in some tavern while her husband still knelt in the shit and grime of his own land, unable to make himself stand up again because he'd failed to draw a blade when they'd taken her away.' Morn locked eyes with me. 'The others knew about your past, Falcio, but they never understood it, did they? None of them ever understood the *real* reason for the formation of the Greatcoats.'

'Why don't you tell them,' I said, though I'm not sure the words came out as anything more than breath leaving my lungs.

'It was all for *her*!' he shouted. '*All of it!*' He turned to face the troops, every one of whom looked captivated. 'King Paelis needed a fool – a *jester*; a madman who would go around the country parroting his ideas for all to hear.' Morn gestured to the other Greatcoats standing together behind the lines. 'Someone who could find other fools to do the same: not an easy job, I assure you – but who should turn up in the King's bedroom one night but Falcio val Mond.' His arm swung back to point at me. 'Do you think the justice he wants is for *you*? If so, the joke is on you, because there's only one injustice that Falcio has *ever* fought for: revenge for his wife's death!'

In the periphery of my vision, I saw dozens of pairs of eyes looking at me, waiting for me to deny it. They'd be waiting a long time.

'Have you ever wondered why the King gave his daughter a commoner's name?' Morn waited for a moment then let out a barking laugh. 'So this fool would *protect* her! That's right: had he named her Elissa or Myrin, Tessa or Jadrine, the girl would never have survived Ganath Kalila in Rijou!'

I could see the muscles in Morn's face clenched so tight his jaw looked as if it might crack from the strain. The raw outrage was so palpable that our own soldiers felt it – worse, I thought they were starting to share it. 'But do you want to know the best part?' Morn asked. 'The part which will make every one of you drop your weapons right now and begin the long march home to your families?'

My own soldiers waited, staring at me, looking very much like they might soon turn from being an army to a lynch mob.

Morn dropped to his knees.

'This,' he said at last. '*This* is the greatest joke of all, because *this* is the one thing the Greatcoats are told *never* to do, the one thing your dead Queen said *you* should never do: kneel. Oh, everyone knows that the Greatcoats *never* kneel. But do you know why?' Morn rose to his feet and bridged the distance between us until he was standing just inches away from me. 'Because Falcio val Mond was *on his knees* when his wife was being raped and killed. Because that's the *one thing* he can never allow himself to be again. Because of his cowardice on that day years ago, he will watch every one of you die without an ounce of remorse, knowing your loved ones are sure to follow. Just. So. Long. As. He. Never. Has. To. Kneel.'

Morn swung his hand back and for an instant I thought he was going to hit me, but then he squeezed his fist tighter and tighter until droplets of blood from the cut he'd made with his knife began to fall, staining the snow red. 'I am one of you,' he told the army. 'And I regret that this is all the blood I can shed for you.'

He took three steps back and gestured for me to take my turn, without uttering another word.

None were needed.

CHAPTER SEVENTY-TWO

THE FUNERAL ORATION

'Aline,' I said. 'Her name was Aline.'

'Falcio, don't,' Kest said, trying to pull me away. 'Feltock can address the troops. You don't have t—'

I shrugged off his hand. Kest sees the world in parries and thrusts, in calculation and miscalculation – and he'd just witnessed a catastrophic *mis*calculation on my part. I had underestimated Morn's rhetorical skills.

The men and women of our army glared at me, their faces flushed with outrage and resentment, but most of all, with fear. Like any gifted demagogue, Morn had stoked the terror already in their hearts until it had become a blazing bonfire, and then offered them the means to rid themselves of it by giving them a target for their wrath: me.

'Everything he said was true,' I began. 'Duke Yered came to our farm and he took my wife from me. His men killed her in a roadside tavern and all the while, I knelt in the dirt of our field, cowering, *praying* that she would come back to me.'

I looked at Kest, who was gazing at me with a mix of sympathy and confused impotence. There was no thrust to make here, no parry that could block the blow that had struck home long ago. 'It's odd . . . people talk about Aline's murder as if it had happened to *me*, as if the worst thing that had taken place that day was that *my* wife was taken from *me*.' I shook my head. 'There stands poor Falcio val Mond. His wife was killed and now he's lost.' I looked back up at the rows upon rows of faces staring back. '*Nothing* happened to *me*. *She* was killed. *Her* life was taken.'

Unbidden, my legs carried me to stand before Morn. 'This man came here to mock the death of my wife, and yet he never even said her name!'

Morn stared back at me impassively. Unconcerned. *Unimpressed.*

'Say her name,' I told him. 'Say her *fucking* name.'

'Aline,' he said idly, a parent humouring a hysterical child in the midst of a temper tantrum.

I spun around and strode back to our line, stopping in front of a young man who held his spear in both hands as if he feared I were about to attack him. 'Say her name,' I said.

'A . . . Aline,' he stuttered.

I turned to the woman standing next to him. 'Say her name.'

'Aline.'

Unable to contain the pain Morn had so skilfully ignited any longer, I leaned back and gave voice to it, shouting at the cloudless sky above. '*Her name was Aline!*'

There was a deathly silence once the echoes had faded away. 'There are no portraits of her,' I said more quietly, 'and most days I can barely remember what she looked like. Her voice . . . I'm not even sure if it was high-pitched or low any more. The feel of her skin, the scent of her hair . . . It's all gone now. *Everything* about her is gone.' I looked back at Morn. '*Except* her name.'

They stared at me, confused; their anger had faded into an obvious concern that I might well be losing my mind from grief. They weren't far wrong. 'King Paelis named his daughter after my wife. Was it to trick me into protecting her? Perhaps. Or maybe it was because of the countless hours I'd made him sit with me in his library, watching me get drunk on his wine while I told him about

Aline, repeating the same stories over and over again, as if the only way I could keep her memory alive was to carve it into another's heart.' A small, humourless chuckle escaped my lips. 'You know, the King never once met Aline, but he loved my wife almost as much as I did. I made sure of that.'

I gestured to Morn. 'He's right, you know: the Avareans *are* different from us. Tristians are farmers and labourers, crafters and merchants, liars and thieves. We are these things first, and only sometimes do we take up sword and spear to wage war. The Avareans are born to the blade. They are warriors first and everything else second.'

A shadow of a smile crossed Morn's features. I was doing his work for him.

I turned back to the army. 'Are you scared?'

Soldiers rarely admit to fear, even in the worst of circumstances, and yet a goodly number nodded.

'Why did you bring us here?' one of the men in the rear lines called out. 'You said it yourself: we aren't warriors. What is there for us to do here but die?'

Murmurs of agreement spread through the lines, a sea of pale faces trembling with fear. I glanced back at Morn, who was openly smiling now, although no doubt he was wondering what had come over me. He'd brought my troops to the very edge of breaking, taking away all the false confidence that comes from marching off to battle, singing brave songs and boasting to each other about their untried martial prowess. Now he watched, fascinated, as I took my own soldiers over the edge he'd so carefully led them to.

That was your first mistake, you bastard.

Ask any torturer – and I've known a few in my time – and they'll tell you the secret to fear and pain is to measure it out in careful doses. Increase the victim's sense of terror too much at once and you risk inuring them to your torments. My troops were so utterly consumed with fear and hopelessness now that had the Avarean commanders suddenly blown their horns and begun the charge to cut us down it would have been a huge relief.

Watch now, Morn. Watch and see the difference between you and me, between you and these people you thought you could rule.

'We are the dead,' I told them. 'Soon, we will be forgotten. But do you want to know what's worse than dying, worse than being forgotten?' I pushed past the soldiers in the front lines until I reached the man who'd spoken earlier. 'The person you love most in all the world? After tomorrow, they're going to die. They'll be forgotten, too.'

He looked back at me, his face pale, his eyes wide as that terrible thought burrowed into him.

'Do you have someone you love back home?' I asked.

He nodded.

'Give me their name.'

It took him a long time to answer, 'Ludren.'

'Speak up. I can't hear you.'

'Ludren,' the soldier shouted.

'What's so special about this "Ludren"?'

'He . . . he saved my life. Many times, actually. Even when we were boys, he . . .'

'Would you see Ludren forgotten?'

His brow furrowed. 'No.'

'But who will remember Ludren after you're dead? After everyone you know is dead?'

'I . . .'

I turned and walked back to the front of the line. 'When Tristia is gone, who will remember the names of those we loved, of those who made our lives worth living? Who will remember Ludren? Who will remember my wife? Who will remember the King's daughter: the girl who could have saved this country from itself?'

I heard a sob, and then another, and more, coming from the

rows and rows of soldiers. 'What was her name?' I asked. 'I have forgotten it already.'

'Aline,' someone called out, then another, and another: 'Aline. *Aline.*'

'That's right,' I shouted, '*Aline of Tristia*. Some of you were at Castle Aramor when the God of Fear came to call, were you not? You'd come as pilgrims, begging for relief from despair when the Saints began to die. Some of you watched as that fourteen-year-old girl – what was her name again—?'

'—Aline. Aline. *Aline—!*'

'—she stood before him – the God of Fear himself – and she *faced him down*.'

'It's truth he speaks,' a woman called out. 'I was there. I saw what she did.'

'Damned right she did!' another soldier shouted, and soon people were cheering her name – 'Aline! *Queen Aline!*' – as if they'd forgotten she was dead.

I waited until the shouts died down before I spoke again. 'Would you have her name be lost? Her tale unwritten?'

'No!' they yelled, now furious at the very suggestion. '*NO!*'

'We are the dead,' I shouted back, striding up the line. 'We are the forgotten. But Aline's name – the name of the girl who was everything that was best about this country – her name will *not* be forgotten!'

'Aline! *Aline!*'

'Do you know why?'

'Aline! Aline! *Aline!*'

I turned and faced Morn, but I stared right past him to the thousands of soldiers on the other side of that field and with all the breath in my lungs shouted, 'Because. I. Will. Not. Allow. Them. To. Forget. It!'

A rumbling was rising up in our troops, growing in strength until it practically vibrated the ground beneath our feet.

'I may be a dead man, soon to be forgotten, but I will carry Aline's name on my lips into battle tomorrow.'

'Aline,' they repeated, not shouting it now, but speaking it firmly, with unbreakable determination: no longer a name, *an oath.*

'I will carry my wife's name, too, just as each of you will carry the names of those you love best, those who *must not* be forgotten. Let those names be our battle-cries.' I gestured to the Avareans. 'Look at those warriors opposite. See how fierce and strong they are? They do not fear us. And yet from tomorrow until the day they die, those warriors will remember the names we spoke as their blades pierced our bodies. They will know the names of those for whom each of us fought and died. They will know the name of the Queen of Tristia.'

'Aline! Aline! *Aline!*'

I looked up at the horde waiting there on that cliff-top a hundred feet above us. 'And a hundred years from now, when the great-great-grandchildren of these so-called warriors see the name of an obscure little country that once knew songs and dance and love and loss, they will know what the word Tristia really means: it means *a nation of heroes.*'

The roaring cheers went on for a long, long time, and all the while Morn and I stood watching each other, listening to the sound of the soon-dead rise above fear, above even sorrow.

Only after I was done did Morn finally make the effort to smirk and say, 'Not bad, Falcio. You must have just a bit of the Bardatti in you.' As he turned to walk back to his lines, he motioned for me to follow him. 'I suppose you'll want to speak to my troops now.'

I remained where I was.

'No need,' I said. 'I already did.'

CHAPTER SEVENTY-THREE

THE DAL VERTERI

I slept unexpectedly well that night. Somehow Morn's speech had brought me a strange kind of peace. He'd been right about so many things, not least that much of what I'd tried to accomplish had been done in a vain effort to make up for my cowardice the day Aline was taken. But while I'd long ago acknowledged that to myself, I realised that Morn had also been right about the reason for my obsession with the rule that a Greatcoat never kneels; I hadn't known that.

But Morn had been an even bigger fool than I was, to believe I'd be *shamed* by those truths. I needed to make no apologies for trying to become the man Aline would have wanted me to be. We used to spend hours sitting in the dark at night, huddled under our covers like children, me telling Aline all the stories the Bardatti Bal Armidor had told me about the Greatcoats. 'Well then, my darling,' she'd say when she'd finally had enough of my rambling, 'if it's all so marvellous, then I suppose we'll need to find a decent sword and a better coat.'

'Then who would stay at the farm to protect you?' I'd asked.

I couldn't see in the dark, of course, but I knew she'd be smiling in that lopsided way of hers. 'Me? What makes you think I'm letting *you* go off to be a Greatcoat when I'm clearly better suited to the role?' She'd pat me on the cheek. 'Do look after the goats while I'm away, dear.'

The sound of chuckling woke me, and it took me a moment to realise I was the one laughing.

'Falcio?' Ethalia asked, from where she sat a few feet away in the shadows. 'Nehra's called for us.'

As I wiped the blurriness from my eyes, she looked as if she'd been sitting there for a while. 'You didn't wake me.'

'You were smiling in your sleep. I didn't want to take that away from you.'

'Come here,' I said.

She got up and walked over, and she let me take her hand in mine, but then gave me a warning glance. 'Falcio val Mond, if you so much as *think* of telling me to leave before the battle, I will set my Awe upon you with such force that even you won't be able to resist it.'

'How could I?' I asked. 'I am *perpetually* in awe of you.'

She gave me a small smile. 'Sometimes you're worse than Brasti.'

I rose and pulled her to me, revelling in the sensations of being close to her, and more, being unashamed of it. I had loved Aline: she had been my wife, and my guide, in life and in death, and I had tried my best to follow her example ever since. I would do so now, too. 'You seem to be rather a silly woman,' I told Ethalia. 'I think a sensible husband might be in order.'

She made one of her eyebrows arch. I wished I could do that. 'You will let me know when you find one for me, I hope? In the meantime, we've kept Nehra waiting long enough.'

She pulled me towards the entrance of the tent, but I held firm for a moment. When she turned and looked at me questioningly, I said, 'I won't ask you to leave, Ethalia. If you decide to fight . . . if this is where you choose to meet your end . . . then I'll be next to you when Death comes, and he'll have to answer to both of us.'

Ethalia placed her free hand behind my neck. 'Falcio val Mond!

Is the world coming to an end, or are you growing wiser with age?' Before I could answer she pulled me close and pressed her lips to mine, a kiss so filled with hope that it left no room in me for despair.

'Well, it's about time,' Rhyleis said.

Ethalia and I reluctantly separated. 'Rhyleis,' Ethalia sighed. 'Do you follow us around for no better purpose than to—'

'I do, in fact,' she replied with a grin. 'I *will* have my great love song from the two of you, even if I have to tie you both to the bed myself.'

'That sounds much less romantic than you think it does,' Ethalia said.

The young Bardatti tilted her head. 'Really? I suppose I'll have to keep practising. In the meantime, Nehra sent me to get you.'

'She sent *you*?' Ethalia asked.

'Well, it *is* possible she actually sent someone else and specifically ordered me to stay away from Falcio, but she knows me well enough by now to realise *that's* not going to happen.'

She led us outside and down the eastern slope of the hill. The moon was hanging low on the horizon, its dim light casting pale shadows in the snow of the nearly two hundred men and women waiting there. 'Hello, Ethalia, First Cantor,' Nehra said. 'Falcio, it's time you met the Dal Verteri.'

My eyes went first to my fellow Greatcoats: Kest, Brasti, Valiana, Mateo and most of the others from Castle Aramor were standing alongside those that Chalmers' Scorn ride had brought back to us: twenty-one in all, as I'd ordered Antrim and Allister to keep half a dozen of ours in Aramor to protect King Filian. I'd read enough in between fencing and swordsmanship manuals to know that war was an excellent time for assassination attempts against monarchs.

Nehra's Bardatti, next to them, held cloth-covered instruments of one kind or another: war drums, pipes and battle horns, even guitars like the one Nehra herself carried. I didn't bother making any scathing remarks about the effectiveness of singing someone to death – it was clear from the way they were all glaring at Brasti he'd already got to it.

To the left of the Bardatti were thirty Knights on horseback. They wore no livery, but their steel breastplates were inscribed with symbols; after a moment I realised they were the old pictograms used to represent Tristia's different towns and villages. I recognised Sir Elizar, even with his helm down.

'Honori,' I said, greeting him formally, 'are you the leader of this somewhat small cavalry unit?'

He shook his head. 'We have only just begun to reform the Order of Honori. We must wait for a leader who can show us the path we must take, so in the meantime, we will fight alongside you and take our orders from General Feltock.'

Thirty Knights: barely enough to qualify as a squad. We had other mounted soldiers, of course, but they lacked the steel armour and war swords, let alone the training needed to cut a swathe through the Avareans.

I was surprised to see Quentis, still in his grey coat, surrounded by a dozen other Cogneri, none of whom I recognised, thankfully. 'Planning on interrogating the enemy to death?' I asked.

The other Cogneri didn't look especially pleased with my joke, but Quentis smiled. 'Couldn't let the secular Orders have all the fun, could we? Besides, by our reckoning, these Avareans are *all* heathens. We thought we'd better do our part; it's clear they might need a fair bit of smiting.'

Then Gwyn came forward – and to my enormous surprise, he was accompanied by two others, also in long coats, though none looked alike. 'Silviene,' the woman introduced herself. Her coat was lighter than the other two, the colour of sand, and she wore a thin silk scarf masking her mouth and chin. 'I walk the desert paths and keep a watch on those who might seek to invade from the East.'

I didn't know what the appropriate response was, so I offered, 'I'm Falcio val Mond. I deal with annoying conspiracies and put the pointy end of things into arseholes.'

To my eternal embarrassment, she nodded solemnly, as if she now understood this was how Greatcoats introduced themselves. The man next to her was wearing a coat more like ours, although the cuffs reminded me of a ship captain's uniform. 'Patrus Neville,' he said, grinning broadly as he held out a hand. 'I sail the southern coasts and keep an eye on potential enemy ships.' Then he added, 'Sometimes I steal them, just to be safe.'

'A pirate?' Brasti yelled incredulously. 'Damn it, Falcio! I *told* you we should've—'

'Ignore him,' I said to Patrus Neville, because by then my eyes had caught sight of a dozen hooded figures standing a little to one side. 'Who are they?' I wondered aloud.

Ethalia went to them and said, 'It is time, brothers and sisters.'

They removed their hoods and even in the near-dark they shimmered in a dozen different hues.

'Sancti,' one of the Cogneri said, his voice filled with awe, and sank to his knees.

'Rise,' a young man glowing a delicate pale blue, with rather lustrous blond hair and fine-boned features, told him. 'Your gestures of submission are unnecessary. Also, unwanted.'

'Forgive us, Sancti,' Quentis said, grabbing his colleague by the collar and hauling him to his feet. 'Old habits die hard.'

The young Saint walked over to me and extended a hand. 'Arcanciel-who-watches-all-pass. You will know me as the new Saint of Memory.'

I was about to shake his hand but Brasti got there first. 'Brasti-who-never-misses,' he said, 'soon to be Saint of Archery.'

Arcanciel stared back at him. 'You do realise Merhan-who-rides-the-arrow is still alive, don't you? The Blacksmith's men never got to him.'

'Damn it!' Brasti swore. 'There really is no fucking justice in the world.'

'Actually,' Arcanciel said, gesturing at a woman in her middle years with close-cropped grey hair, 'Kersa-whose-scales-balance-all is the new Saint of Justice.'

She gave a slight incline of her head to me. 'Greetings, First Cantor.' Then she brought me down to earth. 'It would be unjust of us to allow you to be deceived by our presence. We cannot fight alongside you.'

'Why in all the hells not?' Brasti asked indignantly.

Saint Arcanciel answered, 'Our purpose is to inspire those whose spirits align with our natures, and to protect our people from the overreach of Gods, not to be used as weapons against foreign armies.'

'There will be precious few left to inspire if Avares conquers Tristia,' Kest said.

The other Saints looked at him oddly, as if his presence was inexplicable to them. I suppose they'd never met someone who'd given back Sainthood before. 'You may be right,' Arcanciel conceded, 'but if we use our Awe against the Avareans, we risk awakening *their* Gods, and the waves of destruction such an act would unleash upon Tristia would be endless.' He turned to Ethalia. 'But you are still determined to fight, Ethalia-who-shares-all-sorrows?'

'I am.'

'Then you must do so as a woman and not a Saint. Whatever happens, you must not use your Awe against the enemy soldiers.'

She surprised me by giving him a wicked grin. 'Boy, I've been holding men in awe of me since long before I became a Saint.'

Arcanciel returned a stilted smile, as if he wasn't quite sure what to make of her words. It must be difficult for Saints to hold onto their humanity – and I thought again how remarkable Ethalia was for fighting so hard to retain hers.

'Forgive me,' I asked the assembled Saints, 'but if you haven't come to fight, then why *are* you here?'

Saint Kersa came and took my hand, the gesture oddly gentle and reassuring. 'To be with you,' she replied. 'We are here so those who have come to sacrifice themselves know that we, at least, will remember them, and will do so for as long as we exist.'

Standing there with the Sancti under the fading stars felt like a solemn moment, a sacred one – right up until Brasti rolled his eyes and asked, 'Is there some kind of law that requires Saints to be perpetually dour? I swear, not one of you has a sense of humour.'

Saint Arcanciel gave him a pointed look. 'You know there's nothing that prevents us from setting our Awe upon *you*, don't you?'

'Did he just make a joke?' Brasti asked me.

'Enough,' Nehra said, her voice bringing all of us to attention. 'If it's laughter you want, Brasti Goodbow, then let us make preparations, for I've a mind to play a number of tricks on our enemy come first light.'

With that enigmatic pronouncement, she led what was left of the Dal Verteri, Tristia's ancient Orders of judges, spies, troubadours and other daring fools, around the hill to where we would take our places among the smallest army my country has ever fielded.

The battle for Tristia was about to begin.

CHAPTER SEVENTY-FOUR

THE WARSONG

Even after the commanders had received their orders, even as we stood on our little hill with our soldiers below waiting for the order to attack, Feltock, Valiana, Nehra and Kest continued to debate the plan. I *really* hoped Morn couldn't see us bickering from his vantage point on the other side of the field.

The four of them were staring down at the little coloured blocks of wood set out on the map of the field. The lie of the land had been carefully noted; every rise and dip, every bush and outcropping of rock that might serve as temporary cover was illustrated. They had argued every movement, every tactic, even the parts that made no sense to half of them. Nehra knew little about cavalry charges and out-flanking manoeuvres, while Feltock couldn't begin to evaluate any of what the Bardatti proposed. Of course Valiana was apparently able to hold it all in her head at once, periodically turning to Kest to ask his estimation of what would happen if this number of soldiers happened to arrive at that precise location on the field just before those Avareans *there* could get to them, then she would explain it so it made sense to the others. The four of them were like clockmakers, carefully placing invisible gears and levers inside an imaginary machine and tuning it to perfection.

Me? I was just waiting for someone to point me in the direction of whoever I needed to kill before one got to me.

'Morn has trained his soldiers to work in formation,' Kest warned. 'You can't assume th—'

'Look, boy,' Feltock said, 'I've actually *fought* against the Avareans, and I'm telling you: these bastards spend their entire lives making themselves fierce and fearless. This "Magdan" might have taught them to march on command, but when the blood gets up, you're going to witness what absolute and uncontrollable violence really looks like.'

'That doesn't sound good for us,' I said.

'Well, that all depends,' Feltock said.

Valiana said, 'Patriana used to say that the very thing that made the Avareans so dangerous was also their weakness.'

'They're ferocious, but they lack discipline,' Feltock explained. 'It's all about the smell of blood, of battle, of *rokhan* for them.'

'So if we get them to break formation, we'll have a better chance?'

The old man looked dour. 'If we were fighting with a proper army, with experienced soldiers? Yes. If our troops could hold to their own formations we'd have a chance, at least for a little while.'

'But not many of our own people have ever been in a battle,' Kest said.

'Aye.' Feltock stared down at the map, extended a hand to reach for one of the wooden pieces, then stopped himself. 'Hells. No point in playing with the damn thing any longer.' He turned to me. 'We have two problems: if the Avareans don't break formation, they'll overrun us. If they *do* break formation, but our soldiers fail to hold their own lines, then . . . Well, then you'll see what a real massacre looks like up close.'

Even the Greatcoats, who'd faced death over and over in the course of their duties, would be hard-pressed not to break in the face of *that* – so how could we expect farmers and stonemasons and carpenters to withstand the sight of seven thousand madmen coming for them?

Brasti had been uncharacteristically silent until now. 'How in the name of Saint—?' He turned to Kest. 'Who was the prissy one? The one with the unnaturally pretty hair?'

'Arcanciel-who-watches-all-pass?'

'Right. How in the name of Arca-what's-his-name are we supposed to make the Avareans go berserk *and* keep our own troops from panicking long enough to put up a fight?'

Feltock jerked a thumb at Nehra. 'Ask her.'

We turned to look at the Bardatti, but her eyes were now closed.

'Nehra?' I asked.

'Shhh . . . I'm finding the tuning. It changes a little as the temperature rises in the morning.'

'You do realise that no one but you knows what that means, right?'

Nehra opened her eyes, but instead of answering me, she walked over to one of her musicians and spoke to her. The musician started tweaking the tuning of her guitar, then relayed the message to the drummer next to her, who fiddled with the straps around the barrel of his drum before whispering to the piper next to him, and so it went on down the line.

After a few minutes, Nehra said, 'We're ready. It's time.'

Something huge, unswallowable, pressed against the inside of my throat. I'd been in fights before – hells, I'd probably been in more duels than anyone else alive. But this was *different*. This was *war*. When I fought a duel, I won or I lost. I lived, or died. There was no *winning* here: people would die, no matter which side prevailed. I looked down at our troops, standing there so bravely, awaiting their moment to fight. My gaze went to the enemy across the field, and to my surprise, I felt a kind of sympathy for them, too. No matter how ferocious, some of them would be dying right alongside us.

'How does it begin?' I asked.

Nehra turned and motioned for a young man – barely more than a boy, really – to come over. He handed a bright silver horn to her and she gave it to me. 'The Avareans sent word last night: in honour of Chalmers' Scorn ride, the privilege of sounding the first charge goes to us.'

I held the horn in my hand, its smooth surface cold against the skin of my palm. This shining instrument was about to unleash hells upon my homeland. I stared at Kest and Brasti, Valiana and Feltock, and they each nodded to me. Still not satisfied, my gaze went to the Bardatti, rows upon rows of them, looking like musicians awaiting only the rise and fall of the conductor's hand – until you saw the determination in their faces. The drummers' sticks were shaking – but then I realised they weren't trembling but *vibrating*: they were already locked into a rhythm and pattern. The Bardatti were ready, but still I couldn't bring myself to sound that damned horn.

'Falcio?' I hadn't even noticed Valiana coming up alongside me. 'It's time.'

I looked down at the army below. I had no way of knowing if they were truly ready for what was about to happen.

Kest and Brasti came to stand with me. 'Do you suppose we should have warned them?' Brasti asked.

'Who?' I asked.

'The Avareans.'

'Warned them about what?'

Kest put a hand on my shoulder. 'That some of us believe in the virtue of daring heroics. That for all its flaws, Tristia just might be a nation of heroes.'

I felt something quiet the shaking inside me: not a calm, exactly, more like a stillness. *Valour, if you're out there somewhere*, I thought, as I tilted my head back and brought the horn to my lips, *I'd really appreciate it if you could make sure I can blow this thing properly.*

CHAPTER SEVENTY-FIVE

THE BARDATTI WAR

They came for *us*. Even though we'd sounded the attack, the instant I blew the horn, the first boom of the Avarean war drums suddenly filled the air between us, a roaring rumble that made it seem as if the Avarean warriors were giants, and the earth was crumbling beneath their mighty footsteps. In perfect lines they came for us, following the drumbeat, chanting their damned warsongs. *Coordinated. Controlled.*

'General Feltock?' Valiana said. There was a trembling in her voice that made me wonder if the enemy really were shaking the ground beneath our feet.

'My Lady?'

'The weather looks fair.'

Feltock gazed out across the field. 'A clear day, my Lady. Does it please you?'

'It does not.'

The General grinned, then signalled to a Bardatti horn player standing next to him. 'Let's do something about that, shall we?'

The Bardatti sounded three short, piercing bursts, and from our right flank two dozen horses leaped onto the field, their riders carrying flaming torches in their hands. They were fast and furious – but they scattered long before they reached the enemy, as if their nerve had already broken. If the Avareans were watching closely, they'd have seen each rider dropping their torch on a small mound; we'd dug them when we'd first arrived, then covered them with snow.

If the Avareans were surprised by this odd manoeuvre, they showed no sign, only continued their march towards us. The torches hissed in the snow, but their amberlight flames didn't go out. Instead they slowly melted the snow into water which soaked into the powder piled underneath until thick, billowing grey clouds started to rise from the ground. Nightmist filled the air, blanketing the field.

'I'm starting to develop a real fondness for that stuff,' Brasti remarked.

Feltock gave another signal, and suddenly our divisions, which had been slowly but steadily moving forward, changed direction, everyone running swiftly towards locations now hidden by the nightmist. Avarean archers fired on command, but their arrows were wasted; they could only guess where our troops might be. The advancing Avareans were beginning to look less certain: they were still marching in formation, but clearly not sure why.

'They look confused,' Brasti said. 'I hope they don't get upset.'

The drumbeat changed as the Avarean commanders issued new orders and the warriors, looking happy again – *everything was under control* – moved smoothly in their new directions, still singing their songs.

I turned to Nehra. 'What now?'

'Like us, they use drum-signals for troop movements. They use their songs to keep their warriors in line and focused.' The smile on her face was fiercer than I'd ever seen on her before.

She walked over to her first war-drummer. The young man's powerful arms and shoulders were bare despite the cold, except for the leather harness he wore over his neck and back, supporting his huge drum. 'Merrick, let's show them how the Bardatti wage war.'

The muscles on the young man's arms tensed as he began. Unlike the Avareans, his strokes were precise, measured, each beat made up of the initial percussive strike and then a kind of echoing flutter. After a few moments, the other drummers picked up the rhythm. A moment later, the horns joined in, then the pipes, and then guitarists began playing, their sound muted in comparison to the melody of the horns and yet somehow just as potent, like a prickling feeling on the skin. The more I listened, the stronger the sensation was. The drumbeat felt raw, powerful. Looking down at those of our troops advancing on the enemy, I could see they looked more coordinated than before, and far more unified than the Avareans. But there was something strange going on: some weird chordal arrangement that the guitars played underneath the horns: it wasn't unpleasant, but somehow . . . *dangerous*.

I knew something important was taking place, I just didn't know what it was.

'What song are your people playing?' I asked Nehra. 'I don't recognise it.'

'Listen,' she said.

'I am – I don't—'

'Not just to our players.' She gestured towards the Avareans on the other side of the field. 'Listen to the whole orchestra.'

I turned my attention outwards, to the Avarean drummers, whose rhythms now seemed confused, rambling. Their warriors were still singing, but they sounded . . . *off*, somehow . . . discordant. 'What's happening to them? Why have they changed their song?'

'They haven't,' Nehra said, standing before her musicians. As she waved her hands in careful patterns in the air, I could suddenly see how she was *changing* the music. 'The Avareans play the same rhythms, sing the same notes as before.'

'Then what—?'

'Did you think warsongs were nothing more than jolly tunes to amuse the troops as they go into battle? I composed us a *war*song, Falcio. Our drumbeats are syncopating against theirs, breaking down the rhythms their troops use to stay coordinated. The notes we're playing combine with the melodies they're singing to create chords that are unnatural to the Avarean ear. *This* was why I had you bring back their songs to me.'

The Avarean front lines had not just lost their even pace; they had lost that sense of unity I'd seen before. Now they looked confused, anxious.

Nehra left her musicians to play on as she turned to see the effects of her work herself. 'You came to take our country?' she called out to them, her voice an instrument in itself, challenging them, taunting them. 'You sought to destroy our culture, *our music*? Let's see you come for us when your own hearts begin to beat too fast, too anxiously. Come for us as the rhythms of your own drums are brought crashing down upon you! Let's see your vaunted skill in battle as we play the melodies that shatter your concentration, that make your ears beg for an ending, that take your own songs and drive you mad with them. *This* is our weapon. *This* is how the Bardatti wage war!'

As if this were his cue, Feltock gave the signal and the horn player next to him seamlessly added a series of blasts into the music, and suddenly, from inside thick pockets of the nightmist, arrows flew out into the Avarean troops. We'd not only sent spearmen into those patches of fog, but archers too.

I could barely make out Morn, let alone see his face, but I fancied he wasn't pleased at all.

'Cannon,' Kest warned.

In the distance we could see eight of them being rolled forward, their barrels aiming at our rear lines. Eight cannon might not be a lot, but they're enough to create no small amount of havoc.

'We've got to take those out,' I told Feltock. 'Let me and the rest of the Greatcoats—'

'You'll never get through their lines,' he interrupted.

'We have to try!'

'Oh, I wouldn't waste your time,' Darriana said, and I turned to see her and Gwyn coming up behind me. They looked pale and were shivering as they brushed snow off their coats.

'Where have you two been?' I asked.

Darri smiled. 'Visiting our neighbours.'

I turned back to see the Avarean cannon-master raise his fist, then bring it swiftly down, and a moment later torches were held to the wicks. For a moment nothing happened.

'You wet down their powder? How did the two of you even—?'

'We're the fucking Dashini and Rangieri,' Darri answered, grinning. 'Sneaking in and out of places is what we do. Now shush. I've always enjoyed fireworks.'

'I thought you—'

Suddenly the sound of thunder rolled over the drumming, overpowering the warsongs, the noise of battle. Fire and sparks exploded dramatically from one of the cannon, followed by another great crack of thunder, then another cannon exploded. Avareans were fleeing the flames, trying to dodge the bits of metal flying at them as the barrels broken apart in fast-moving lethally sharp shards – the noise became so loud I could hear nothing at all save a great ringing in my ears. I might not be able to listen to what was happening, but my eyes were fixed on the chaos raging among our enemies as we all struggled to comprehend what had just happened.

The Magdan's mighty warbands had finally met Tristia's paltry army on the battlefield.

They were not enjoying the experience.

CHAPTER SEVENTY-SIX

THE HUNDRED NAMES

It was a good first day, or so they told me. We lost nearly four hundred soldiers in those opening exchanges across the snow-covered field. The enemy had lost many more. I had no idea how Feltock could look across the carnage spread out before us and make such calculations, but he estimated that a thousand Avareans had met their ancestors at the hands of a people they'd believed wouldn't last an hour.

That night music rang throughout our camp. The Bardatti went among our troops, leading them in tunes and tales, some of which I recognised, others which I strongly suspected they were making up on the spot. I couldn't bring myself to go along to share in the momentary joy of death denied for one more night, instead choosing to visit a less jovial part of our camp. Oddly, Brasti joined me.

'Is there nothing more we can do?' he asked, as we walked along the rows of the wounded and dying. Most were shivering despite the fires set to warm them.

Ethalia was directing physicians and assistants, comforting those who broke down as patient after patient died from injuries too severe to treat, then, sometimes forcefully, sending them back to work. Every spare moment found her sitting with the wounded, using her Saintly presence to give them comfort, the Gods of any country that might disapprove be damned.

Sometimes a soldier would call me, ask me to hold their hands for a moment, as if that might do some good, and as I hadn't the heart to tell them otherwise, I smiled and told the lies you tell the dying, because sometimes that's all that's left.

'What's your name?' I asked a young man whose leg was being bound tightly in preparation for amputation.

'Idoren, sir,' he replied, then suddenly broke into tears. At first I assumed it was at the prospect of losing his leg, but then he said, 'I failed, sir. I failed him.'

'Failed who?'

'My son. I failed my son.'

I squeezed Idoren's hand harder. 'You failed no one, soldier. There's no—'

'You don't understand, sir! I . . . I didn't even fight!' He raised his other hand to his eyes. 'I went out with my squad into a patch of nightmist where I was supposed to shoot arrows at the enemy. My hands were shaking so bad I dropped my quiver. I reached down to get it but tripped on a rock and fell. Two of my own arrows pierced my leg.'

I looked down at the bandaged wounds. How could that lead to amputation?

Idoren saw me staring. 'I couldn't move – I spent hours there lying on the ground in the snow and the nightmist. I couldn't move and the cold – well, it got into the wound and now they say I have to lose the leg or it'll spread.'

'I'm sorry,' I said uselessly, remembering Trin's self-mutilated fingers.

He gripped my hand harder. 'I never even met the enemy, sir. I never got to say my boy's name.' A great racking sob broke from him. 'He's a good lad, sir. His name ought to be remembered.'

'Tell me his name.'

'Myken, sir. It's Myken.'

I nodded. 'Tomorrow, Idoren, I'm going to go out on that field and I'll carry Myken's name with me. I'll speak his name when next we meet the enemy.'

The soldier brought my hand to his lips and kissed it. 'Thank you, sir. Thank you.'

A physician carrying a bone saw discreetly hidden under a cloth signalled it was time for me to leave him to his work. I let go of Idoren's hand and moved on, only to have another soldier stop me – a thickset woman with a soaked bandage across her head covering a wound that wouldn't stop bleeding. 'My name's Marsi, my man's name is Felsan,' she said, 'like the Saint. He has a wasting disease in his legs so he can't walk – I came to fight for him, and for our two daughters, Lida and Iphissa. Will you carry their names for me, First Cantor?'

'And my boy's,' another of the wounded called out. 'His name is Terrick.'

A sick feeling crept inside me. I had been the one to convince these soldiers that somehow carrying the name of someone they loved would make some difference to the world. One by one those who had tried to fight but been taken down before they could even face the enemy begged me to carry the names of their loved ones, to make sure the enemy heard them, and knew whose lives they were destroying. 'I . . . I can't,' I said helplessly. 'I'm sorry, there's just too m—'

'Tell me,' Brasti said, and he crouched on the floor and started taking the arrows out of his quiver. He laid them on the ground, then reached inside his coat for a small, sharp knife. 'Tell me their names,' he said, and as they did, he set about carving those names into his arrows.

We stayed there for another two hours, pausing only to call for more arrows, and when he was done, forty-six shafts bore the names of some village boy or girl or spouse or parent. It was impossible to hope each one would find a target, but Brasti just stood up and said, 'Rest easy tonight, for tomorrow every one of these arrows will fly across that field, and if each one of the Avareans they strike learns only one word of our language, it will be the name *you* sent them.'

A lot of the wounded died that night. It would be too much to hope that this strange ritual Brasti had devised would take the pain from their passing, but for some at least, it did give solace. Brasti may never become a Saint, but for those few hours, he was theirs.

I got back to my tent exhausted beyond measure and desperate for whatever sleep remained to me, but I'd only just removed my coat and unslung my rapiers when Kest appeared.

'Can it wait until morning?' I asked.

'I'm afraid not. We got word a couple of hours ago: a contingent of soldiers is coming from the south. They'll be here soon.'

'Any idea who's leading them?'

'Rhetan,' Kest said, then added, 'Duke of Baern, apparently. It seems Ossia has abdicated.'

'A death sentence will do that to you.' I sighed, put my coat and sword belt back on, then checked to ensure the cold hadn't frozen the blades in their scabbards. 'I don't suppose the new Duke has given any indication as to whether he intends to die alongside us or hasten our deaths in exchange for some heretofore unknown favour from Avares?'

'It's Rhetan,' Kest reminded me, holding the tent flap open for me. 'I imagine that's up for negotiation.'

'You're rather late, your Grace,' I said, walking up to Rhetan who stood warming his hands by the fire. Several sturdy looking men I assumed to be his lieutenants stood close by.

The new Duke of Baern surveyed the darkened field ahead of us. 'Oh, I expect we're here in plenty of time for our share of the bloodshed. Besides, I didn't want to overtire my soldiers by forcing too fast a march. It's as I've told you before: patience in all things.'

When he caught my gaze, he must have seen my suspicion there. 'We'll fight with you, Falcio, to whatever end awaits us all.'

'I must confess, I was wondering if Baern might perhaps—'

'Secede? Like Domaris and Pulnam?' He reached up to scratch at the sparse beard he must have started growing on the way here. 'I'll admit I did give it some consideration. However, it appears that I have little choice in the matter.'

He gestured behind us, to a woman only now dismounting from her horse. I almost didn't recognise the Lady Mareina at first; she was no longer the beaten-up, emaciated woman I'd first encountered some months ago. Now she looked . . . well, she looked very like her sister Cestina, but what I saw in her eyes was something different entirely. Rhetan shook his head at the sight of her. 'This Damina you foisted upon me? She had the gall to threaten that should Baern secede from Tristia, then the newly minted Condate of Revancia would secede from Baern. Worse, she somehow managed to convince two Viscounts and a Margrave to go along with her. It appears that conspiracy and sedition runs thick in her family's blood.'

Mareina gave me the barest nod in acknowledgment before walking right past me. I turned to see her destination and found her embracing Chalmers. 'Three hundred soldiers,' Rhetan said a little bitterly as he clapped me on the shoulder. 'That's what your little Greatcoat's reckless determination to rescue a stranger has bought you.'

I watched as Chalmers and the Lady Mareina talked for a few minutes, then suddenly burst into laughter, and I wondered what they were discussing, and what bond had formed between them in those moments aboard Margrave Evidalle's wedding barge.

'Eh?' Rhetan asked. 'What was that you just said?'

I hadn't realised I'd spoken aloud, so it took me a moment to remember. 'Forgive me, your Grace. I believe I said, "Fuck anyone who ever doubts the purpose of daring acts of heroism".'

*

Rhetan wasn't the only nobleman to arrive that night. He'd met up with Pastien, Ducal Protector of Luth, on the road, bringing nearly a hundred and fifty of his own soldiers with him. We now had roughly four hundred more soldiers than we'd started with.

On the other hand, we also had Pastien.

The boy was kneeling in front of Valiana when I found him, ignoring Feltock entirely. 'What little I have . . .' Pastien – I suppose he was simply 'Lord Pastien' at that point, since the title of Ducal Protector had been stripped from him; all he had left was some pathetically small Condate with half a dozen villages and a town barely big enough to earn the name. 'What strength the Condate of Guillard has to offer is yours, Realm's Protector.'

Kick him in the face. Please, if some small part of you still considers yourself my daughter, just kick him in the face, just once, for your old Da.

She reached a hand down and bid him to rise. 'If Tristia is to survive, it will not be on the might of our numbers but on the strength of our hearts. Thank you, Lord Pastien. You and your soldiers are most welcome indeed.'

The boy's face brightened, then went a little red. He spoke more quietly when he said, 'Valiana, I . . . I also hope that this action on my part might persuade you to once again allow me to come to you, for you to teach me how to make you mine once ag—'

Rolling her eyes, she cut him off. 'Oh, for the sake of Gods alive and dead, Pastien, are you entirely incapable of doing *anything* because it's what you *believe* in, rather than some coin to exchange for that which you could not earn yourself?' Before he could reply, she leaned in close, and spoke so quietly I doubt anyone but Pastien and I could hear her. 'And if you ever, *ever* try to "make me yours" again, the only thing I will "teach" you is the first rule of the sword.'

Now *that's* my girl.

CHAPTER SEVENTY-SEVEN

THE INEVITABLE

If our first day of battle had brought us good fortune, the second looked – for a while, at least – like a miracle. The addition of Rhetan and Pastien's troops had ignited fresh enthusiasm in our existing forces and had enabled Feltock to adjust his positions to good effect. For every one of ours who fell that morning, the enemy lost nearly three.

But war is a game of numbers, and ours were far too small.

'They've altered their tactics,' Kest shouted as we rode away from the enemy flank with the rest of the Greatcoats and Sir Elizar's Knights. For the third time they'd repelled our charge. 'The Avarean commanders have found a way to communicate their orders without interference from the Bardatti warsong.'

A scream from behind me caused me to glance back and I saw Old Tobb – not only a Greatcoat but a former Domaris cavalry officer – fall from his horse with three spears sticking out of his back. He wasn't the first Greatcoat to die that day, nor was he the last.

Fear and exhaustion began to wear on me. A duellist puts every ounce of energy he has into a few brief minutes in the circle. A soldier must fight on and on, hour after hour, until either a halt is called or he dies on the field.

Worse than the physical effects was the fog obscuring my thoughts, thick as nightmist. The constant rise and fall of frantic, violent action followed by desperate retreat were wearing on me, turning the battle into a roiling assault on my senses – flashes of steel, splatters of blood, the rapturous roaring of the enemy as they attacked, the panicked screams of our own soldiers as they fell to the ground, the mad, grinning faces of the Avarean warriors hacking them to pieces the last thing they saw.

By the time the sun set and that strange, unspoken agreement to cease fighting for the day had come once again, I could swear I felt Death himself breathing at my neck, chasing after me as I stumbled up the small hill to collapse beside Kest.

'They fought with all their hearts,' Feltock said quietly, standing at the hill's edge as he looked down at our men as they nursed their wounds and took what rest they could. 'May what Gods there are damn any man who says otherwise.'

'How many?' I asked. I couldn't summon enough strength for any more words.

'We lost eight hundred,' he replied, then turned and grinned. 'The Avareans lost two thousand.'

'Two thousand?' We'd fared better than I'd thought, but the look in Feltock's eyes told me it wasn't good enough.

'It's the numbers. They still have four thousand to our less than sixteen hundred.'

'So what happens now?' I asked.

He glanced at Valiana and Nehra, as if waiting for one of them to explain what should be blindingly obvious, and when neither spoke, asked, 'Now?' He gestured down at the weary soldiers huddled together on the field. 'Those people did what you asked of them, Falcio: they proved our worth to the enemy. They have displayed as much damned *rokhan* as any of us could hope for. If the Avareans have an ounce of honour or decency or whatever it is that makes a man show mercy to his enemy, then there's a chance our people back home will survive.'

'But our troops,' I said. 'What happens tomorrow?'

'Tomorrow Morn's warriors will overrun us, Falcio.' He looked down at the soldiers preparing for sleep. 'Tomorrow we die. Every last one of us.'

It's hard, deciding what to do with your last hours of life. I spent a little time with Valiana, mostly trying to convince her to leave the field. *That* didn't go down well. Despite my promise to Ethalia, I tried to do the same with her, but she did me the kindness of clamping a hand over my mouth before I could speak.

'It hardly seems a suitable end for the song Rhyleis has worked so hard on, that it should end with you sitting alone in a tent with a bloody nose, Falcio.'

I gently removed her hand. 'You know, people are starting to wonder just how merciful the Saint of Mercy really is.'

'I've told you many times, Falcio val Mond, it's in my nature to be mysterious. I am a Sister of the Order of Mysterious Light, after all.'

'I thought it was supposed to be *Merciful* Light.'

She kissed me then, and held the kiss for a long time before she said, 'And here I thought you and I agreed that we could be more than just one thing.'

I expected that kiss to become something more, but then she took my hand and led me outside. 'Where are we going?' I asked.

'To where you would want to be, no matter how persuasive my charms.'

We walked hand in hand in the darkness, guided as much by the soft sound of Nehra's guitar as the fire around which Kest, Brasti and Valiana were sitting. I thought she meant us all to share the remaining hours together, but instead, Nehra and Valiana got up, and they, along with Ethalia, left the fire to Kest, Brasti and me.

'Well, Falcio,' Brasti said, 'I think you're taking far too long to concoct a daring plan that saves us all from total annihilation.'

'I suspect the odds are rather unfavourable for any of Falcio's plans to work,' Kest said.

I felt a sudden urge to shout at them both, to tell Brasti to stop making everything into a joke and Kest to stop finding new ways to tell me we were screwed. Ethalia had given us this time together and for once I just wanted to sit with my best friends and speak plainly, *honestly*, to stop playing the fools and instead admit that we loved each other without pretext or artifice. But that's not who we were; it wasn't how we had lived and it likely wouldn't be how we died. The three of us had survived a thousand dangers and a million heartaches not just with our wits and weapons, but with the little jokes, the jibes, the small – perhaps even petty – defiances against a world that was determined to kill us.

'It's that damned cliff that bugs me,' Brasti went on, 'even more than the horde. It feels like the Avareans could send all that snow crashing down on us at any damn time they want.'

'It's too far away,' Kest said. 'The snow wouldn't reach us here.'

Brasti shook his head. 'You really are thick sometimes, you know that? I was being metaphysical.'

'You mean *metaphorical*.'

'Oh, really? My mistake.'

Kest suddenly looked at him. I mean *really* looked at him. 'But you already knew that, didn't you? How long have you been pretending—?'

Brasti grinned. 'Sometimes I like letting you feel superior.'

For a long while Kest just sat there, eyes narrowed as he tried to work out how many times Brasti's incompetence with words had been genuine, and how many times he'd been poking fun at him. Finally he leaned back and laughed, loudly, uproariously. It was infectious, and soon Brasti and I were roaring with laughter too.

Who says being fools is such a bad thing?

When tiredness and the reality of our situation finally settled over us again, I stared out across the field and tried to guess which tent belonged to Morn. Was he feeling triumphant at the certainty of his eventual success, I wondered? Or enraged over the luck we'd had and whatever respect or *rokhan* that might have cost him among the Avareans?

I'd give just about anything to meet you out on the field, Morn.

'He won't,' Kest said.

I looked up. I hadn't realised I'd spoken aloud.

'Maybe if you asked him *very* nicely,' Brasti said, and set about changing the string on his bow, whistling all the while.

Kest looked annoyed. 'Is there a reason why you *insist* on whistling *that* particular song over and over?'

'It's cheerful,' Brasti replied. 'I'm entitled to a bit of cheer on the night before my death, aren't I?'

'You do realise your cheery melody is an *Avarean* song?'

'No, it's not – I distinctly remember hearing it in a tavern ten years ago.'

'You heard it ten *weeks* ago. *In Avares.*'

I stood up, leaving them to their debate, and peered up at the cliff where the horde was encamped so that they could look down on us like Gods. *No,* I reminded myself, *not Gods. An audience.* It felt important to remember that somehow. However many thousands of warriors there were they weren't some grand pantheon of deities sitting in judgement of us, but an audience of spectators, sitting in the cheap seats and waiting for the final act to begin.

How many miles had they travelled just to be here? How much had it cost, how much time and labour wasted, for no better purpose than to watch Morn's little stage play?

'Are you really so captivated by all this?' I shouted at them in futile frustration. 'Or are you simply captives of your own stupid tales?'

'Falcio?' Brasti asked. He and Kest were staring at me. 'Who are you yelling at?'

I shook my head. I was no better, was I? How much of my life had been shaped by the stories of Greatcoats from ages past? Were the Avareans any worse, that they lived and died by songs like the one Brasti had been whistling incessantly?

'*There*,' he said suddenly.

'What is it?' I asked.

He stood and came closer, staring at me. 'You've got something.'

'No, I don't.'

He pointed at my face. 'Yes, you do. I can see it in that stupid expression of yours.'

'It's not what you think,' I said, realising he'd confused my bitter laughter for something else. 'I'm just—'

'No, I'd recognise that look anywhere.'

'Leave him be,' Kest said, coming to stand with us.

'I will not. I *know* that face. Falcio's got something.'

'Look,' I said, 'I think I'd know if I had a plan.'

'Maybe not. You're brilliant, but not always very bright.'

'That's literally—' Kest began.

'I know, damn it, but I'm telling you, Falcio's got something.'

'What's happening?' Valiana asked, running towards us with Ethalia and Nehra close behind. 'We heard shouting.'

'Falcio's got a plan,' Brasti said.

I started to deny it again, but there *was* something tickling at the back of my mind, and I turned back to look up at the cliff-top again, then down at Morn's troops encamped below. There was *something* there: something I could use. *What was I missing?*

Brasti started whistling again, even as he kept watching me.

'What are you doing?' I asked.

'I was whistling when you thought of your ingenious plan,' he replied, then went back to his tune.

'You'll let me know when you want me to hit him?' Kest asked.

Now would be an excellent time, I was about to say, only at that moment the pieces finally fell into place and I reached out and grabbed Brasti by the shoulders. 'You know, for a very dim man you're really rather bright.'

'See?' he said to Kest.

'Those two things are literally the opposite of one another.'

I ignored them and turned to Nehra. 'Your Bardatti – how quickly can you teach them a different song?'

Nehra snorted, making it clear what she thought of *my* intellect. 'I won't have to. They wouldn't *be* Bardatti if they didn't already know all the important Tristian songs.'

I smiled. 'Who said anything about a *Tristian* song?'

CHAPTER SEVENTY-EIGHT

THE FINAL GAMBIT

Considering just how terrible my plan was, I encountered surprisingly little resistance, perhaps because in the end the worst that could happen would be that seven people would end up dying looking rather stupid. The real argument was over who would be going.

'Enough!' I said when the sun peeked out over the horizon and I'd had my limit of listening to the others argue. 'I've made my decision.'

Darriana looked up at me quizzically. 'Where did you get the idea that any of us were letting *you* decide?'

'It's . . . well, technically it's my plan,' I said defensively.

She reached up and patted me on the head. 'That's nice. It's a nice plan.'

In the end, it was agreed that Kest, Brasti and I were the most skilled and experienced at fighting together. Valiana would go because – as she so succinctly put it – whether she was Realm's Protector or Duchess of Rijou, she outranked the rest of us. Darriana said we could choose whomever we wanted, but that she would kill one of us at random to take our spot rather than let Valiana go without her. When Ethalia arrived bearing a pair of two-foot lengths of wood, Darriana barked out a laugh and asked what good she hoped to do with those. Less than three seconds later, Darri was staring up at her from the ground, a look of total and incredulous confusion on her face.

'I spent my life among an Order whose vocation was to bring joy and pleasure to the worst and most violent of men in the hope of changing their paths. Did you think we never trained to deal with those who instead sought to inflict *their* violence upon *us*?' She reached down a hand and helped Darriana up. 'Still keen to meet me in the circle one day?'

Darri grinned. 'More than ever, Sister.'

'Well, that's six,' Brasti said, 'assuming these two don't kill each other before we even start.'

'Seven,' Chalmers said, walking unsteadily towards us. Despite the injuries she'd sustained during the Scorn, she'd insisted on trying to fight on the second day of the battle. Ignoring my orders, she'd planned to ride out, but Arsehole clearly sensed something was wrong and promptly dumped her on her arse every time she'd tried to mount him.

'Chalmers . . .' I was determined to refuse her, but I found I couldn't. Her courage had taken away any right I had to deny her the chance to fight for her country.

'I'm going,' she said, her voice strident – then her eyes fluttered closed and she dropped to the ground. Behind her was Quillata. She quickly stoppered the tiny vial in her hand before taking in a breath.

'Grey Slumber?' Kest asked, covering his own nose in case any of the fumes could still reach him.

Quil nodded. 'I've had it since the old days – wasn't sure it would still work.' She looked down at Chalmers. 'You've already shown yourself a hero, little one. Time to give the rest of us a chance.'

I turned to Nehra. 'Your people are ready?'

For once she skipped over the part where she tells me I'm an idiot for asking. 'It will be a performance not soon forgotten, First Cantor.'

I looked at Kest and Brasti, Darri and Valiana, at Ethalia, part of me wishing she'd stay behind, but the larger part of me grateful she'd be with me at the end, and finally at Quillata.

She stared back at me with a wry smile. 'I knew you'd end up dragging me into your heroic nonsense one of these days.'

I set off down the hill, the others following, as murmurs spread throughout the army, soldiers wondering aloud what we were doing now. We'd told only our General; Feltock needed to know so that he could keep them from chasing after us. We couldn't take a chance that word of what we planned might reach the other side. For this to work, it had to come out of the blue, leaving no chance for Morn to devise any counter-move.

The first inkling either side had that something had changed, that today wouldn't simply begin with two armies charging at each other once again, was when Nehra brought forward one of her Bardatti singers. The girl looked barely thirteen, but she wore her troubadour's colours proudly. She stood up on the hill and opened her mouth to sing the first notes of a song no Tristian had ever sung. Well, except for Brasti, sort of. It was called 'Seven for a Thousand', and as first our soldiers and then the Avareans across the field looked up in wonder, the people I loved best in the world joined me in a final act of reckless daring to fulfil not the heroic tales of our own people, but those of our enemy..

'Any final commands, First Cantor?' Brasti asked, his bow in hand and an arrow at the ready.

'Just one,' I replied, as the seven of us set off at a run straight for the four thousand warriors across the field. 'Don't die.'

CHAPTER SEVENTY-NINE

THE WAR OF SEVEN

It took the Avareans a few seconds to understand what was happening, but when they did, it was as if the very ground beneath our feet was coming apart, cracked open by the strange, almost obscene mix of rage and joy we'd aroused in them. As the Bardatti musicians took up the song, the pipes and horns on the melody, the drummers pounding the fierce beat and the guitarists strumming so loud I could hear them echoing across the field, the horde watching from the cliff-top above cheered so loudly I thought the entire mountain would fall beneath them.

Soon the rest of Nehra's war singers had joined in, stacking harmony upon harmony, their voices rising above the instruments, intermingling and stirring all of us as if we too were strings to be plucked by their nimble hands. However many centuries the song had been sung in Avares, surely it had *never* been performed like this.

Soon even Morn's warriors were shaking their fists and raising their weapons, their faces taking on fierce, proud grins even as a thousand of them came for us.

We had shown them the kind of respect that they had never anticipated from us, but one they understood, and they were going to return it in kind.

Now we just needed to survive – not for long, just long enough.

The first problem, of course, was the difference in terrain. 'Seven for a Thousand' told the tale of the small, half-starved band of Avareans who'd held a mountain pass near the Western Sea against the thousand soldiers who'd come from across the water intending to raid their lands. The pass in question was narrow – barely six feet across – with seventy-foot cliffs on either side, which meant no more than twenty of the enemy could attack them at one time. Since the field upon which we fought was rather barren, save for the few outcroppings of rock we'd already marked, Kest, Brasti, Valiana, Ethalia, Darriana, Quil and I had to *pretend* there were cliff walls on either side of us, and hope the Avareans would do the same.

Come on, you bastards, I thought, as the seven of us stood there while the enemy charged at us. *Show me how much you hold to your songs and legends. Show the horde above your* rokhan.

'I can't believe it,' Quil said in awe. 'I think they're—'

Her words were cut off when an Avarean axe came spinning in the air towards her, but Kest's shield went up and the axe blade bit into it and got no further. But she was right.

Suddenly the Avareans were upon us, and there was no more time for words, no more time for anything except this one last fight, this final act of defiance the seven of us performed in the name of a King long dead, of his daughter taken too soon, and of the dream that had been the Greatcoats.

'Nuria,' Brasti said, firing an arrow in the name of the daughter of a woman who'd died in the infirmary last night. 'Lida. Iphissa.' I couldn't tell how he knew which names were carved into each arrow he nocked and fired at the enemy, but perhaps he'd simply memorised them all and called each out in turn, regardless of which arrow was in his hand at that moment.

Quillata fought in a heavy-handed style, swinging her longsword to help keep as many of the Avareans at bay at one time as she could while Darriana and I used our lighter weapons to deliver thrusts and lunges that sent warriors falling to the ground until they were stacked like cordwood and their fellow Avareans were forced to push them aside to get to us. Ethalia fought beside me, using her sticks with surprising grace and speed. Her blows never killed – that wasn't her way – but they broke noses and sent blood into men's eyes, blinding them and making them as much a danger to their own fellows as to us.

'Falcio . . .' Kest warned, 'it needs to happen soon.'

'It will,' I promised. After all, it wasn't as if he'd be able to say *I told you so* if I turned out to be wrong.

We were relying heavily on Kest's speed and skill with his shield, blocking the arrows and spears that came hurtling our way. The Avareans were going half-mad with joy and bloodthirst, and those with bows were shooting more of their arrows into their own men than at us. Some got through, though; Quil was the first to take an arrow, when the bone plates in her coat failed to block the narrow point; it stuck in her left shoulder, rendering that arm useless. Of course she continued to fight with the longsword in her right hand.

It wouldn't be long now, but we needed more time. 'Valiana,' I said, 'it has to be now.'

Even as she batted away a spear coming for her, she glanced at me uncertainly. 'Falcio, I don't know if—'

'Do it,' Kest said. He was the only one who had some sense of what we were asking of her. 'I will watch over you. Let the red flow.'

Kest had been dealing with the Saint's Fever and not the *Adoracia fidelis* which was still coursing through Valiana's veins, but the effect was not dissimilar. The instant she let the adoracia take over, you could *see* the red rage inside her eyes. Suddenly the heavy blade she'd brought with her looked almost too light in her hands and within seconds she was cutting into our enemies with so much speed and force that the first man barely had time to see that he'd lost his left arm at the shoulder before Valiana took his head. Again and again she swung without regard for the Avareans' armour or weapons, oblivious to everything around her. It was enough to shake the confidence even of the war-mad Avareans, but before long they began focusing their attacks on her.

'Kest!' I shouted as an archer from their rear took aim.

'I see it.' He leaped up high, just to Valiana's right and raised his shield over her head, but even as he deflected the arrow, Kest had to spin away – in Valiana's uncontrolled rage she'd nearly sliced him with her blade.

'Damn, Falcio,' Quil said, thrusting her longsword into the belly of the man I was fighting. 'Where are you getting these new Greatcoats from?'

I didn't answer; I was too busy working through how long we had left, because however much the Avareans loved their song, 'Seven for a Thousand' was almost certainly bullshit. Seven fighters, no matter how skilled, cannot long withstand a thousand enemies. Fortunately, we only needed to survive long enough to make one thing happen – and it finally did. Morn, seeing his own warriors and the horde above beginning to look upon him with doubt, was forced to join the fight.

Come and get me, you bastard.

He came at me with that great long glaive of his, the sixteen-inch curved blade at the end of the seven-foot-long spear slicing the air on an angle as it came for my neck. I pushed off on my back leg into a diagonal lunge, ducking under his blade and thrusting my rapier for his belly, but I came up short. That damned glaive gave him too much reach.

'You stupid shit,' he spat, smoothly bringing his weapon back up only to bring it crashing down on me as if it were a hammer and I a nail. 'You think this changes *anything*?'

'Actually,' I replied, jumping to my right and letting the blade of his weapon slam into the ground next to me, 'I think it might just change everything.'

I tried to step on the shaft – a reflex from fighting too many men with spears – but Morn spun it in his grip, turning the sharp-bladed end up and pulling hard towards himself. I lifted my foot but still felt the edge cut into the sole of my boot. The sting hurt like seven hells – its only virtue was that it meant the cut had been too shallow to reach the tendons. The only problem was now I was limping.

'Falcio!' I heard Darriana call out.

'Stick to the plan,' I shouted back.

'The plan?' Morn asked. '*The plan*? Is that what you call this suicide?'

He started to press me back and the others made way for him even as they continued to hold off the rest of our attackers. Morn was deadly fast with his glaive, using the long weapon to slice through the air, forcing me to back away, only to suddenly drive straight for me, leaving me no choice but to push off my injured foot and dive to the right. Soon he'd left the narrow confines of the imaginary cliff walls we'd all so politely pretended existed, but I refused to do the same, staying on my own small patch. I could see some of his own men were gaping at him, horrified that the song they so glorified was being dishonoured in this way.

'We could have worked *together*, Falcio!' he bellowed at me. 'We could have ushered in a new era.'

'I hardly think Tyanny is new, Morn,' I said, stumbling back to stay out of the way of his weapon, 'but I hardly think tyranny is all that new.'

He screamed something incoherent at me, swinging his glaive in ever-wilder arcs. A glaive is a versatile weapon, and it can even be graceful, wielded by a master like Morn, but it isn't *light*, and for all his outrage, Morn was beginning to slow. Though the pain in my foot and a dozen other small wounds I'd not even noticed before were wearing me down, I'd been conserving my strength. I needed only one opening; one small gap in Morn's defences and I would ignore the creeping agony in my foot and execute one long lunge too fast for him to evade. I thought I had it, too. For just a second, as he brought his glaive up for a downward strike, I truly believed I'd found that opening – then I saw Morn's smile and remembered: *he's a better actor than I am.*

Somehow, as he'd been forcing me away from the others and I'd been moving in ever-so-slight increments to angle him where I wanted him, we had both achieved our aims. The problem was, Morn had *cheated*: suddenly two of his men were on either side of me, breaking the unspoken rules their fellow warriors had followed. They grabbed my arms and twisted hard, forcing me to drop both my rapiers.

'How in the name of every Saint have you stayed alive this long?' Morn asked.

'Well, it's a little complicated,' I replied, 'but if you want, I'd be happy to explain it to you.'

'What I want,' Morn began, signalling to his men, who grabbed onto me tighter and began to slowly force me to the ground, 'is for you to finally do what the world has been waiting for all these years, Falcio. I want you to *kneel*.'

It's actually not as easy as you might think to force a man down to his knees, but Morn's warriors were brutally strong and I knew I wasn't going to be able to hold out for long. 'Why, Morn,' I said, 'didn't you know? If you wanted me to kneel, all you had to do was *ask*.'

And with that, I dropped down to my knees and my two captors, unprepared for the sudden lack of resistance, came with me. Morn blinked furiously as the sun behind me went straight into his eyes, preventing him from seeing Darriana – who for once had followed my orders – had waited until that exact moment to run straight for us, leaping first onto my back and using me to propel herself high up into the air. Morn tried to get his weapon up to block her, but with the sun in his eyes and her having the advantage of being far above him, he couldn't reach her in time. Darriana's arm extended, joining the narrow blade of her sword to form a perfect line, and for just an instant it was like staring at a painter's masterpiece, an image so perfect it could only exist in the mind of an artist. Darriana was, in that moment, what swordsmiths dreamed of when they forged their weapons: the flawless union of body and blade.

She winked at me.

The tip of her sword drove into Morn's chest, but not into his heart – this, too, had been part of my orders, although I hadn't been at all sure if she would follow that one. Instead of dying instantly, Morn took the blade just a fraction below his left lung.

A better man would have been grateful.

He shouted something in Avarean, and I didn't need a translator to tell me he was commanding his men to kill us. I shook off the two men who'd been holding me – they were now blessedly distracted by the blade in Morn's chest – and threw myself into a roll, coming up to retrieve my rapiers so I could fight for what little time was left.

I saw Valiana stumble as the strength and ferocity the *Adoracia fidelis* had lent her finally gave out. Quentis was down, and Quilatta – who'd only met him days before – fought with all her ruthless determination to protect him from an enemy's spear. Darriana abandoned her blade to run for Brasti, whose bow had splintered under the blow of an Avarean sword. I felt Ethalia's hand brush mine one last time as she raised her sticks to guard my flank. Kest caught my eye, and nodded once as if to say goodbye before racing to try to shield the others for as long as he could.

I'm not sure if the other Avareans would have followed through with Morn's command, or whether tradition bound them to the spirit of their song, but it didn't matter, because somewhere high above us, a horn blew.

The Avarean warriors, their faces still full of battle-lust and fury, froze, and every single one of them dropped to one knee, leaving only the seven of us standing. We looked at each other, our eyes searching each other for signs of mortal wounds, each praying they would find none. All of us were injured, some worse than others. Quil looked pale, and I could see she'd taken a stab wound to the thigh that she was having to hold closed with her one good hand. Ethalia had a cut on her forehead that was bleeding into her eyes and blinding her; even so, she was hanging on to Valiana, whispering soothing words to her as she fought to bring the adoracia in Valiana's veins back under control. We needed medical care, all of us, but we looked oddly more alive than we had any right to be.

'You *fools!*' Morn roared, Darriana's blade still sticking out of his chest. For once, though, he wasn't yelling at us; he was yelling at the horde on the cliff-top above. 'I could have given you this damned country. They wouldn't have lasted even one more day – but you let yourselves be taken in by a stupid fucking *song*?'

The horde looked down from the cliff-top, silent save for a single word that kept being repeated, over and over. *Kujandis, Kujandis, Kujandis.* It was the Avarean word for coward.

'You know what that is?' Brasti asked, holding his bleeding arm and stumbling over to stand in front of Morn. 'That's the audience telling you they didn't enjoy the performance.'

Kest and I stared at him.

Brasti narrowed his eyes. 'What?'

'Seriously?' I asked. '"That's the audience telling you they didn't enjoy the performance"?'

'You didn't like it? I thought it was clever.'

'It was a bit on the nose,' Ethalia said, unsteady on her feet as she came towards us, Darriana uncharacteristically rushing to help support her.

'Your opinion doesn't count,' Brasti said. 'You always side with Falcio; you're in love with him.'

She smiled at me. 'Well, maybe just a little.'

I took her from Darriana, deciding that I'd be the one to help her walk back to our camp and somehow forgetting that I could barely stand on my left foot and would likely need someone to support *me* before long.

'What now?' Brasti asked, staring at the Avareans, who still looked like they'd quite like to kill us. A lot. None of them moved to attack, though. They didn't even rise to their feet. Apparently they were waiting for some kind of signal. I hoped it wasn't supposed to come from me, because if it was, they'd be waiting a long time.

'Let's go home,' I said. 'I've never much liked Pertine this time of year.'

CHAPTER EIGHTY

THE LAST TYRANT

Tristian legends abound with tales of brave heroes gone to war, facing insurmountable odds and yet somehow emerging victorious. In none of those stories do those same heroes then have to suffer through negotiating an armistice treaty. Note that I didn't say '*peace* treaty', because it turns out the Avareans have no word for peace.

'Truce,' repeated the Avarean negotiator, a man named Kugriek, whose command of Tristian was only slightly better than that of my old friend Reyek. 'We give you good truce.'

We sat on opposite sides of a hastily constructed table set in the middle of the very same field upon which we'd shed each other's blood only days before. The injured had been taken away and the dead burned or buried as each nation's customs called for, but there were more than enough remnants of the carnage to make me glad of the cold, for once.

The *good truce* of which Kugriek spoke promised a cessation of hostilities between our two nations in exchange for what the Avarean negotiator called 'the rightful return of *bludlandeg*', which, Gwyn explained, meant 'blood lands' – or in this context, the entire Duchies of Orison and Hervor.

When I realised what was being demanded of us, I suggested they could have Orison and Hervor but only if they agreed to take Pulnam and Domaris as well. No one but me thought that was funny.

'They will not relent in this, First Cantor,' Gwyn said. 'The Avareans believe it is their duty to take back the *bludlandeg* – not simply because those lands were part of their territory in the past, but because they would consider it cowardice on their part to abandon the families who live there to the uncaring rule of Tristia.'

When a horde of bloodthirsty barbarians tells you that you haven't been taking good enough care of your people, it's hard not to cringe a little.

In the end, it came down to this: we either gave up those two Duchies or we named the date and place where our armies would meet once again to wage war. The best I could do was to negotiate a provision that gave every citizen of Orison and Hervor a year to decide whether to stay as part of Avares or depart for the south, unhindered, with their families and belongings. The Avarean Warlords who stood around Kugriek laughed when this was explained to them, apparently finding the thought of *anyone* choosing to remain Tristian when they could instead live under Avarean protection as hilarious as it was preposterous. I suspected they might be right.

In exchange for our concessions, we were offered a truce, to be upheld for three generations. I'd never heard of the duration of treaties being described in such terms, but Gwyn explained that blood-feuds were common in Avares, and holding to such a truce ensured the children and grandchildren of those who'd died in the war would not seek vengeance.

'Very well,' I told Kugriek, and the agreement was carefully inscribed in both languages on the rounded surfaces of two steel-fronted shields taken from the battlefield: another charming Avarean tradition. 'I will take this to my King and—'

Kugriek cut me off with a wave of his hand and proceeded to translate for the other Avarean Warlords. A great deal of bellowing followed. Finally, Kugriek pointed a thick finger at me and said, 'We make truce only with ruler.'

I sighed and turned to Gwyn. 'Could you please explain to them – *again* – that I am *not* the King of Tristia. If they give us two weeks we can get Filian here to—'

'Speak to me!' Kugriek demanded, slamming his meaty fist down on the flimsy negotiating table. 'I speak you language good!'

'A moment, if you please,' Valiana told the negotiator before turning to me. The Avareans never seemed to interrupt *her*. Having seen her fight under the influence of the *Adoracia fidelis*, they'd promptly named her *Bludyirdan*, which meant 'Champion of Blood' or some such thing. Whenever 'Bludyirdan' spoke, they were all remarkably polite. 'They won't let us wait for the King, Falcio. I don't think they'd recognise Filian's authority even if he were here: he didn't lead the battle and so he has no standing in their eyes.'

'Fine, then make Feltock sign the damned thing.'

'Leave me out of it,' the General said. 'I'd as soon not be hanged for a traitor the moment we get home.'

Excellent.

'You sign,' Kugriek said to me. 'We make truce with Magdan of Tristia.'

The Magdan of Tristia. I was fairly sure that was going to come back to haunt me one day.

Also on the subject of Magdans, the Avarean Warlords had demanded – on pain of abandoning the truce altogether – that they be given the right to execute Morn and punish those who'd followed him, in accordance with Avarean law.

Since I really didn't give a shit about Morn, other than ensuring he could never threaten my homeland again, I'd agreed – but I'd demanded one concession of my own: the return of the rebel Greatcoats. The Avareans considered this a fair trade; one of the Warlords was even kind enough to offer me his favourite beheading axe – a magnanimous gesture, I thought.

The Greatcoats who'd sided with Morn were traitors, according to Tristian law, which carried the death penalty. Instead, I tried them as deserters, a lesser crime which afforded the leniency of exile. They could take a ship and depart this troubled continent for ever. You'd've thought they would have been a little more grateful.

'Fuck them,' Brasti told me as we made preparations for our return to Aramor. 'None of them were deserving of the coat in the first place.'

'I suspect they might have shown Falcio a bit more gratitude had he allowed them to keep theirs, actually,' Kest observed.

That had been one of *my* non-negotiable terms. I'd given them their lives and their freedom. The coats came back with me.

'Don't think this counts as you giving me a *proper* greatcoat,' Chalmers complained. I'd found one of the twenty-seven coats we'd retrieved was a perfect fit for her, and actually in much better condition than mine, but she still considered it a poor offering.

'Stop bellyaching,' I told her. 'It's a thing – an object. It's nothing but leather with bone plates sewn inside the lining and a bunch of pockets with a few tools and tricks.'

Kest and Brasti stared at me disapprovingly and Chalmers looked hurt. 'You make it sound meaningless,' she said.

I sighed. I was going to have to stop being an arse at some point, so it might as well be now. 'Put it on,' I told her.

She slid her arms through the sleeves and then set about adjusting the straps and doing up the buttons.

Kest, Bresti and I watched with a kind of reverance as she went through those simple motions. There's a sacredness in bearing witness when a man or woman – not a God or Saint, but just a regular person – readies themselves to give up everything in service to this strange creation of humanity that we call the Law.

When Chalmers was done I reached out and adjusted her collar. 'There,' I said. '*Now* it's a greatcoat.'

*

My final lesson in the art of warfare turned out to be the discovery that disbanding an army is actually more work than recruiting it in the first place. In all the chaos caused by two heirs to the throne, the secession of half the country and the sudden threat of invasion, there had never been time for proper records to keep track of who had joined, where and when and under what terms. No pensions had been established for the sixteen hundred who'd survived and for the families of more than a thousand who hadn't, so yet again it fell to me to set terms and sign declarations promising payment for the veterans and families of Tristia's three-day war.

As if that weren't enough, Pertine was suddenly intent on rejoining the country, but required assurances: no reprisals, no punitive taxes. I tried suggesting this was for the King to deal with, but Duke Meillard had cannily worked out that we were in dire need of provisions and support to get our soldiers home.

So by the time I finally returned to Aramor and presented myself in the new throne room (which looked suspiciously like my old courtroom, swiftly renovated for its new purpose), I did so with several decrees in hand, all of which entailed costly promises on behalf of a young and inexperienced King whose own coffers were nearly empty. Fortunately – well, depending on where you stood and how many weapons were pointed at you – Trin had a solution for all of this.

'Worthless scraps of paper,' she declared, and slapped the arm of the man holding the agreements I'd brought with me, scattering them on the floor. I'd have tried to pick them up, but there were a great many guards surrounding me at the time.

'*This* is the only decree that matters,' Trin said, and held out a rolled-up piece of parchment which I recognised as the one declaring me a traitor and all those who had fought with me insurrectionists. Apparently even winning a Gods-damned war doesn't buy you out of trouble in this country.

'I don't suppose we could get the King's opinion on the matter?' I asked, noting the empty throne. 'Where is our new monarch, by the way?'

'Attending to matters far more important than this.' Trin glanced down at the large shield with the Avarean armistice treaty inscribed upon it that was being held out for her by one of the clerks. After a minute or so her face lost all colour and her expression became even more terrifying than usual. I guessed she'd got to the part where I'd given up Orison and her own Duchy in exchange for the truce.

'You will *hang* for this,' she said. 'You will all . . .' She turned to one of the guards, only now noticing something that no doubt would have occurred earlier to her had she not been quite so irritated by my return on horseback rather than in a coffin. 'Where are the others?' she demanded. 'Where are Kest and Brasti and the rest of your tatter—'

'I imagine they're waiting to break him out of prison again,' Filian said, walking through one of the side doors. 'That *is* why you came here alone, isn't it, Falcio?'

The King of Tristia wore what I assumed to be the latest fashion in royal couture. To my eyes it looked like a particularly elaborate bathrobe. His hair was elegantly groomed and a new – and properly fitted – gold circlet sat on his head. Beyond the rich clothes, though, he looked tired and his skin had a grey-green pallor to it. I wondered if perhaps Trin had already begun to poison him.

'Your Majesty,' I said, as he approached the throne. 'You look like shit.'

'I've been a trifle ill.'

The clerk holding the shield stared at me, aghast. 'Who are you that you would dare speak to the King so?'

Filian glanced down at the Avarean shield for a moment. 'According to this he's the Magdan of Tristia.' He looked up at me. 'A rather ostentatious title for a magistrate, don't you think?'

The question sounded flippant, but he was trying to decide what I intended to do with my newfound influence. No doubt having had to hide here in his castle while someone else led his army to war also stung. 'It's really more of a honorary sort of thing, your Majesty,' I said.

He nodded at that, as though we'd come to some sort of agreement, which I suppose we had. 'I imagine you're hoping that I'll go ahead with that charter you proposed? You don't *really* expect me to create some preposterous "Council of Citizens", do you?'

I locked eyes with him. It's not as if I hadn't considered the possibility that Filian would turn out to be faithless. I'd just hoped for better. 'I suppose it all depends on what type of King you want to be, your Majesty.'

Trin had evidently assessed the situation and now she looked upon me with something vaguely like sympathy. 'A King's power cannot be circumscribed by those he rules, Falcio.' She motioned to two of the guards standing behind me. 'Just as he cannot allow the continued existence of those who might threaten his authority.'

'I never looked to garner power or influence,' I said, oddly heart-broken by this utterly predictable duplicity. 'I never wanted songs or stories written about me. All I wanted was to bring back the rule of law. I just wanted life to be a little more fair.'

Trin nodded as if she understood – and maybe she did, in her own way, but it didn't matter. She waved forward another clerk who carried with him an inch-thick sheaf of papers, along with a small golden tray containing a pen and inkwell. Trin took them and placed them on the wide arm of the throne. 'This is the first of King Filian's Laws,' she said. 'It revokes the rights and privileges of the Greatcoats immediately and for all time, names those who do not cease their activities as traitors to the country and orders their swift arrest and execution.'

I looked at Filian, who had taken a seat on his throne. He sat there placidly, watching the last traces of his father's dream being wiped from existence. *This* was what Filian's life had all been about: raised to believe he was destined to become King of a country that was diseased and needed swift and decisive action to cut out the infection, taught the ways of power by the incomparably manipulative Duchess Patriana and worst of all, deeply in love with Trin.

She handed him the pen and he dipped it in the inkwell. He looked up at her and I saw such adoration in his eyes. Was it magic of some kind? Spells or powders or potions administered over years to make him devoted to her? I wished I could pretend it was, but this was simply the very real love of a boy for a girl he found both beautiful and brilliant: a love that allowed him to believe she did terrible things only because this was a terrible world and a price must be paid to establish order.

She leaned over and kissed him on the lips.

'No,' he said.

Trin's eyes went wide in disbelief.

Without prompting, Filian repeated the word. 'No.'

What I saw play out on her face took any joy from the moment. All the layers of deception and guile slid away, leaving only the terrible sadness and hurt that comes from complete betrayal.

'I thought you loved me.'

'I do,' he said. 'And I know you love me, but that isn't enough, Tarindelle. You scheme and plot, you manipulate everyone around you, even me. When I first came to Castle Aramor, you sowed the seeds of discord and fear: you made it clear to everyone that either Aline or I had to die, and in so doing you weakened this country.'

'She was weak: a foolish girl, a child—'

'She was my sister,' Filian said. 'Those few days we had together . . . I came to see how much wisdom and courage was in her. She could have helped me rule this country. She could have helped save it – and yet when she died, you laughed.'

'I . . . Filian, you don't *understand*. You don't know what these people – these damnable, *heartless* people – have taken from me.'

'I do know,' he said, then he placed the pen down on the tray and rose from the throne. He put his arms around her. 'I love you now as I have always loved you – as I always will love you. But I was trained to govern as a King and you would have me rule as a Tyrant.'

'I gave you a throne,' she said numbly.

'And in return, I give you your life.' He let her go and turned to all of us. 'The Lady Trin will be leaving now. Let no one try to interfere with her departure.'

He turned back to her, his face weary and sorrowful. 'If she ever attempts to return to Tristia, she is to be killed on sight.'

CHAPTER EIGHTY-ONE

THE LAST CANTOR

There wasn't nearly as much chaos as one might have expected. Trin left with remarkable grace, probably because she didn't much care for the alternative. Filian signed documents declaring that the agreements I had negotiated were done so on his behalf and carried the full weight of his authority. He even gave me the decree naming me a traitor as a gift.

He offered me rooms at the castle, but I'd already told the others to meet me back at the Busted Scales, the abandoned old Greatcoats tavern. Ethalia was waiting for me in one of the rooms upstairs with fresh bandages and salves to re-dress each other's injuries. I wasn't used to the idea of her being injured in battle, and I found the experience of treating her wounds, no matter how slight, to be profoundly unsettling. I quickly learned not to comment on it.

For my part, it turned out I'd been hurt quite badly during the three-day war, though I hadn't noticed it at the time. My lack of awareness struck me as odd considering how meticulous I usually was about such things after a duel. Feltock had said this was normal, that soldiers often go into a kind of shock after a battle: just one of the *many* ways in which war is different from duelling.

Ethalia and I didn't speak much while she was changing my dressings. Maybe I *was* still in shock. It's rather hard to tell sometimes.

When she was done, I heard myself ask, 'Do you love me?'

She took my hand and kissed it and then led me to the bed. 'Rest,' she said, and lay down beside me.

Rest. Such a strange word. I had slept plenty on the way back from Pertine, but I couldn't remember the last time I felt at rest.

Suddenly it was much later, and I awoke with her head on my chest. I could tell from her breathing that she was already awake, so I took hold of her chin and turned her head up so I could see her eyes. 'Ethalia, will you—?'

'Don't,' she said.

'I was going to—'

'Don't ask me to marry you, Falcio.'

I felt as if I'd just been struck with the flat of a blade. I let go of her chin and started to pull away but she caught me by the wrist and pulled me back.

'Why?' I asked.

'I told you before, there are complications between us. You need time to heal, to let the weight of the world slip from your shoulders. Maybe then you'll know what it is you truly want.'

'I don't understand,' I said.

Ethalia gave me a weary smile. 'Of course you don't.' She pushed herself up on one elbow. 'You're injured, beaten and heartsick. You're full of grief and barely contained rage. I know you care for me, Falcio, but when you look at me . . . sometimes it's as if you've forgotten I'm a woman; you think instead I'm the Goddess Love herself.'

'Some people would take that as a compliment.'

'*I* don't.' She looked through the window at the night sky for a moment. I thought the moonlight was reflecting on her face, then I realised it was the glow of her Sainthood. 'It's more difficult than you know to be . . . *myself*, sometimes.'

'And me being in love with you makes that harder?'

'Sometimes.'

It is fair to say that I have absolutely no understanding of women at all.

Ethalia sensed my confusion and tried to explain. 'You look at me as if I'm your salvation, Falcio, when I *want* to be – what I *am* – is a woman of Tristia. Nothing more, nothing less. Is that so hard to understand?'

I couldn't think of anything clever to say, and a banging on the door interrupted whatever else she might have said. 'Falcio, you've got a visitor,' Brasti shouted.

'Tell them to bugger off.'

'Sure thing. Bugger off, your Majesty,' Brasti declared loudly.

I rose and quickly put on my trousers and a shirt. At least I had the sense to wait until Ethalia dressed before opening the door.

'Forgive my intrusion,' Filian said.

'Nice outfit, your Majesty,' I said, noting the rich red and gold brocade robes he was wearing, despite us being in a rather shabby area of town. 'Very discreet.'

He looked at me for a moment with a confused expression. 'Ah, you're being funny. Did my father find it endearing?'

'I don't know, but he had the good grace to pretend, anyway.'

Filian sighed. 'Something else I'll have to learn, I suppose. May I come in?'

I turned to Ethalia. She nodded.

'It's your country,' I said. 'Who am I to—?'

'Stop testing me, Falcio,' the King said, entering the room. He handed me a document, which I guessed from the flowery writing was another decree. 'I thought you might like to see this.'

I looked down and glanced through the handful of paragraphs above a line where his signature should be. 'You're reinstating the Greatcoats permanently?'

'I am.'

'I can't help but notice you haven't signed the document.'

'There's something I want in return.'

I shook my head. 'If you've come to me with some list of promises and demands, your Majesty, then you're wasting your time. The Greatcoats don't work that way. Besides, you convicted me of treason, remember? I have a nice scroll that explains it in detail. I'm not the First Cantor any more.'

'I have only one demand,' he said.

'What?'

'That you return as First Cantor.'

'I . . . find that surprising, your Majesty, given I—'

'Nearly stabbed me with a sword?'

'I was going to say, preached open sedition and treason against the Crown, but I do recall something about a sword in there.'

'I suppose I should be flattered,' the King said, leaning back against the small desk and folding his arms. 'After all, didn't you begin your relationship with my father by trying to kill him?'

'There were . . . *circumstances*, your Majesty.'

'No doubt. Well, I won't be so presumptuous as to ask that you try to refrain from doing that in future since I suspect you can't stop yourself from the occasional act of attempted regicide.'

'I . . . are you making a joke, your Majesty?'

'I don't know. Is it funny?'

I shrugged. 'It's not bad. Your father would have inserted something sexual in there.'

Filian looked confused. 'How?'

'I don't know. It was a gift he had.'

'Well, I'll keep practising. In the meantime, will you accede to my request?'

'Will you really refuse to reinstate the Greatcoats if I don't?'

He sighed and reached into the folds of his robes to pull out a small case. He opened it and removed an elaborately carved wooden pen and a small bottle of ink, both of which he set on the desk.

He pulled the stopper, dipped the pen and signed his name to the decree. 'No more ultimatums. No more drama. I would as soon be known as the most boring King in the history of our country.' He turned back to me. 'Now, will you retake your position?'

I looked at Ethalia, who said, 'This is your decision, Falcio. Don't ask me to make it for you.'

The King stared at her with a mystified expression. 'Who are you, exactly, my Lady, that the man who has shaken the foundations of this country, who once duelled a God and found a way to win an unwinnable war, should seek your permission?'

'Just some woman,' I said.

I thought it sounded funny at the time.

Filian's eyes were still on Ethalia. 'No, my Lady,' he said. 'Whatever Falcio says, I do not believe you are just "some woman".' He bowed then, which made me like him a little more, but didn't change anything.

'I'm sorry, your Majesty,' I said. 'I can't be First Cantor of the Greatcoats any more.'

He looked a little annoyed, a little sad and a little scared. 'I . . . Falcio, I need—'

'I'm broken,' I said.

'I don't understand.' Fillion's confused expression betrayed his youthfulness; he hadn't yet seen enough of the world to understand it.

'I know you don't, your Majesty. But unfortunately, I don't know of any better way to say it. I'm broken. I've given everything I had to this country and now I need to stop, at least for a while.'

He looked as though he were about to protest but then held back, which I thought showed remarkable wisdom. 'What will you do?' he asked finally.

I looked at Ethalia again, wondering briefly whether if I asked her to marry me right then and there in front of the King she'd feel obliged to say yes, to spare me the humiliation of a refusal. Then

I came to my senses and said instead, 'I'm not sure, your Majesty. There's a little island off the coast of Baern which I'm told is a nice place to recuperate for a while.'

'Very well,' he said. 'When will you leave?'

'Soon, but first I need to . . .'

It started as a sigh that took too much breath from me. I simply couldn't finish that sentence, couldn't speak at all. Right there in front of the woman who'd just told me she didn't want me to ask her to marry me, in front of my new King who was all of fifteen years old, I started crying.

'Ah,' Filian said gently, after a while. 'Of course. You have one final duty to perform.'

CHAPTER EIGHTY-TWO

THE COTTAGE

I found her where I'd first met her, in a little cottage on a road a mile or so outside of Aramor whose only distinction was that if you kept walking it long enough it just happened to lead all the way back to a small farm in Pertine where a foolish boy had once been born, had spent his childhood dreaming of Greatcoats, had met a girl and had, for a very short while, been happy.

'I wondered when you'd come,' Magrit Denezia said, though to me she would always be the Tailor. She led me inside and then sat heavily in the room's only chair, content, apparently, for me to stand.

'You might have been waiting a long time. I'd never imagined I'd live this long.'

She gave me that sour grin of hers. 'Ah, that's the thing about people like you and me, Falcio: our curse is to keep living, when those we love best die.'

'Well, that cheered me right up,' I said. I glanced around the small cottage and was surprised to see all of her books and furnishings arrayed around the room in a remarkably familiar configuration. 'You realise you've recreated your cell in Aramor, don't you?'

She waved a hand. 'It suited me fine while I was there. Why go to the trouble of rethinking it all?' She set down her sewing and rose from her chair. She walked, a little stiffly, I thought, to a set of coats hanging from a rack on the far side of her cell. 'The black,

I think,' she said, taking one down. 'It's best for a journey such as this.'

I was going to ask how she knew why I'd come, but then she would have said, 'I'm a Tailor, Falcio. I know where every thread starts and where it ends.' And frankly, I wasn't in the mood.

'Come on,' I said. 'We'll need to walk back to the castle, but there will be a cart waiting for us there.'

She followed me out of the cottage and leaned a hand against my arm. 'It's kind of you to let me come.'

'Paelis would have wanted me to bring you.'

'No, he wouldn't,' the Tailor said. 'But thank you for pretending.'

Outside the gates of Aramor was a simple horse-cart with a seat at the front wide enough for two and a longer space in the back. The stable boys weren't there and neither were the promised horses, but I wasn't angry as the explanation for their absence stood in front of me, her wide muzzle nuzzling at the black silk that shrouded the body.

'You decided to show up,' I said.

Monster opened her mouth, revealing sharp teeth and a belly-full of rage. She neighed in that way of hers that always sounds more like the growl of a mountain cat than it does anything that should come from a horse.

'Don't pick fights,' the Tailor said. 'We have a long journey and it'll be easier if you have both hands.'

It was a fair point, but more importantly, there was nothing I could say to Monster that didn't apply equally well to myself. So I walked round to the long wooden bearing poles. 'Come on then,' I said to the Greathorse.

It's hard to imagine a creature simultaneously so noble and belligerent. Monster was nearly twice the size of a normal horse and I had no doubt she could pull us all the way to Phan without breaking a sweat. What surprised me was her willingness. Monster was not an animal meant for service. Nonetheless she walked slowly towards the front of the cart and let me attach the breeching straps around her front, then to the poles. I didn't bother with the bridle or the reins. She didn't need them and wouldn't have tolerated them.

'Falcio,' the Tailor said quietly, and when I turned to see what she wanted, she was pointing to the western edge of the castle grounds. There, peeking out from the trees, were a pair of large horses, their coats black as night itself. It took me a moment to realise that they weren't *grown* horses at all, but foals who had no business being anywhere near that size. The sight of them took my breath away.

Greathorses.

I patted Monster on the neck. 'Nicely done, old girl.'

She growled at me in response.

'Give us a hand then,' the Tailor said, lifting one foot onto the step of the cart.

I went up the other side and reached down to give her my arm for support until she was seated on the bench. 'I don't recall you ever needing help before.'

'Misery wears on the body as it does the soul,' she replied as Monster began pulling the cart down the long road that led out of Aramor. 'I shouldn't need to remind you of that.'

CHAPTER EIGHTY-THREE

THE COMPANION

Our journey took us north and east, up the winding trade route called the Bow. After almost a month on the road, I would have expected the body to be rotting, but whenever I removed the black cloth from Aline's corpse she still lay there, perfectly white and perfectly still, like a porcelain doll.

'That deathhouse keeper at Aramor did a good job with the preserving oils,' the Tailor said.

I grunted something, my reply probably not an actual word.

At first we'd ridden in silence, neither of us being especially fond of the other these days and there being nothing to say. But sometimes grief demands sharing, and what started as the occasional snide remark about our mutual failure to protect the King's daughter had, over the days and miles, become reminiscences and, eventually, stories. The early ones were those we both knew, mostly about King Paelis and his odd ways. After a while we each sought to find tales that the other hadn't known – to elicit an unexpected laugh or tear.

Sometimes we grew so weary that one of us would repeat a story for the second, third, or even fourth time. The other always knew, but by unspoken mutual agreement we each pretended not to have heard it before. I talked a lot about the King – about the early days, when he and I roved around the country on horseback looking for new Greatcoats to recruit. The Tailor would remind me that the King was a terrible rider and that I was lying atrociously about his skills.

For her part, the Tailor would recount the events of Aline's girlhood, tales of her fierce intellect and bold ways when confronting every petty injustice done to a servant or anyone less fortunate than herself. We would both pretend that this was the Aline we had brought to Aramor with us, rather than the broken, sometimes child-like creature we'd tried to put on the throne, the girl who had overcome those tragedies only to sacrifice herself for the kingdom.

'Filian is your grandson,' I said, one evening as we rode past the northern border of Domaris into the Duchy of Pulnam.

'Thanks for clearing that up,' the Tailor replied, biting on a piece of the mercilessly tough and ridiculously expensive dried beef we'd splurged on the day before.

'I mean . . . don't you want to . . . I don't know. Support him? Get to know him?'

She handed me the last of the beef. 'And what will I find in him?' She wiped her mouth on the sleeve of her coat. 'If he's like Patriana I'll want to kill him and if he's like Paelis I'll want to kill myself.'

'Rage or sorrow,' I said. 'Is that all that's left to us?'

'It'll be all right, Falcio. The sun will keep shining.' She patted a patronising hand against my arm but then, curiously, left it there. Perhaps even more curiously, I was glad she did.

I suppose there was no choice left but to admit that I loved the old woman.

I'm not sure what I expected to find at the end of the uneven little road that ended like a sigh in the middle of the Duchy of Pulnam. Whatever it was I hoped or feared to see, it wasn't the Gods of Love, Death and Valour waiting for me.

'Perfect,' the Tailor muttered when she noticed them standing in the shadows of the small hill where we intended to lay Aline to rest.

I hopped down from the seat atop the horse-cart. 'I'll deal with them.'

'Keep a civil tongue and try not to challenge them to a duel.'

I loosened my rapier in its scabbard. 'No promises.'

Monster growled, which I took as endorsement of any violence I might choose to instigate.

Valour still looked like Tommer to me: a young boy with unruly black hair and eyes that were quick and bright. Death wore a simple cowl, his face hidden in its shadows. I felt rather certain I wouldn't want to see it up close. And the Goddess of Love? It turned out that despite Ethalia's protestations, the Goddess of Love looked exactly like her to my eyes. I would have felt smug were I not so irritated by the presence here of these divine figures.

'Welcome, Falcio,' Valour said. He bowed a little, as did Love. Death just stood there looking awkward.

'This is a private ceremony,' I said. 'I'm afraid I'm going to have to ask you to fuck off.'

The Tailor ambled over to stand beside me. 'This is your idea of a civil tongue?'

'It's an uncivil world,' I replied.

If the three Gods were offended, they gave no sign. 'We will respect your wishes in this matter, Falcio,' Valour said. 'However we – the three of us – have a gift we wish to give.'

'Is it money?' the Tailor asked. 'Because we ran out a few days ago.'

'No gifts,' I said. 'There is nothing the Gods have that I want.'

'The gift is not for you,' Valour said.

That surprised me. 'Then who—?'

The sound of shuffling movement caught my ears above the mild desert breeze and I spun, my weapon already drawn.

'Falcio?'

My rapier fell soundlessly to the sandy ground. Aline was stepping down from the horse-cart. She rubbed her eyes, then took a few steps towards me.

'Don't,' the Tailor said, the fingers of her hand hard as steel as they gripped my shoulder. 'You mustn't touch her.'

'She's right,' Valour said. 'You may not hold her, Falcio. My brother is moved to gentleness this night but Death kneels for no man.'

'You're playing with forces you shouldn't,' the Tailor said. 'And in poor taste.'

The boy – or God – looked completely unashamed. 'The veil is weaker here, and my brother only recently returned. He has . . . a little leeway . . . in restoring the balance.'

'Just like a God,' she said, 'to think you get to make such decisions.'

They argued a little longer but I barely heard any of it; all I wanted to do was to tear away from the Tailor and reach out to hold Aline.

Just once. Just one last time let me hold her and tell her I'm sorry.

'I've been very tired, Falcio,' Aline said. 'Have we been on an especially long journey?' She looked around. 'Monster?'

'Don't,' I said, before she could run to the Greathorse. 'Come over here, sweetling.'

Aline frowned at me. 'How many times have I asked you not to call me that?' She started walking towards me. 'Are we back in Phan? What are we doing here?'

'I . . .' I turned back to the three Gods. 'Stop this, damn you! What kind of gift is it, to let me see her when—?'

'I said the gift wasn't for you,' Valour interrupted me gently.

'Then for whom?'

He nodded towards Aline. 'It is for her.'

Aline took a few steps closer. 'Hello,' she said, as though she had only just then noticed the three figures standing behind us. 'I don't believe we've met. May I ask your names? Are you friends of Falcio's? Because he doesn't look very pleased to see you.'

Valour stepped in front of me then bowed at the waist. 'My name isn't very important, my Lady, but I am something of a friend to your father.'

She curtsied in response to his bow and then looked up at the stars and sighed. 'It seems everyone knew my father except for me.'

'That's terrible,' Valour said gently. 'Would you like to meet him?'

Aline smiled uncertainly, as if this might be some sort of joke. 'Is . . . is that possible?'

Valour turned and pointed up the little hill. There, standing near the top, waving, was a tall man, though a little rounded at the shoulders and with rather bad posture.

'This can't be . . .' I said, although I'm not sure the words made it out of my mouth.

'Come along, dear,' the Goddess Love said to Aline. 'I'll take you to him.'

Aline looked up at me. 'Is it all right if I go see him, Falcio? Because if you're going to get into a fight with these people then you might need me to hold onto your bracer for you.'

'Why in the world would I need to fight? These are . . . *friends*.'

Her eyes narrowed. 'Why do you always assume I'm an idiot?'

'Go on,' I said. 'I'll be waiting here when you're done.'

She grinned. 'Try not to start the duel before I get back.'

Love reached out a hand and placed it gently on Aline's shoulders and walked with her up the path to the hilltop.

'Thank you,' I said at last to Valour and Death.

Death didn't speak, but I saw perhaps the slightest tilt of his head.

The Tailor sat down unceremoniously on the ground and crossed her legs. 'What a load of nonsense,' she said, but even I heard the catch in her voice.

'I don't understand,' I said to Valour. 'Is she . . . is she going to be with her father? If so, why did you have to do all this?'

He looked as if he were about to reply then stopped himself.

Valour and Death shared a glance and finally Valour said, 'It's a little complicated, Falcio.'

The Tailor snorted. 'By which he means that the Gods themselves don't know.' She waved a hand at Death. 'Even you, eh? A God of Death who knows next to nothing about his domain? What are you, some sort of celestial absentee landlord?'

I felt as if my mind was slowly wrapping itself around something which might be important. 'They had to meet in this world, didn't they? That's ... *necessary*, somehow, isn't it?'

Valour nodded. 'That's as good a way of looking at it as any other.'

A thousand questions came to mind but I guessed they would never be answered, so I just stood there rather uncomfortably with the Gods Valour and Death and a rather nasty old woman who passed the time by trying to come up with ever more elaborate insults for them. *Now who's forgotten a civil tongue?*

Love came back down the path towards us, and I was surprised to see Aline close behind her.

'How ... how was it?' I asked the dead girl who'd just been to see her long-dead father.

She smiled. 'Strange. Wonderful. Confusing. He's a bit like you.' She turned to look down at the Tailor who was still seated on the ground. 'A little like you, as well, though that only makes sense, I suppose. He's rather silly for a King, isn't he?'

I chuckled, although if I'm honest, it was more of a sob. 'Far too silly for a *proper* King.'

Aline reached out a hand towards me then stopped herself. 'Go to him, Falcio. He's asking for you.'

CHAPTER EIGHTY-FOUR

THE DEAD

I walked like a man asleep, keeping my eyes on King Paelis as I stumbled up the winding little path, fearful that he would disappear if I blinked.

'Come on then,' he said. 'Are you really going to keep your King waiting?'

His voice was a bit less reedy than I remembered it. All the way up the hill I'd convinced myself this would be just some illusion of him, another hallucination conjured from memory and grief. It wasn't. I knew, I *knew* this was the real Paelis. My King. My friend.

He looked a little different than he had in my imaginings. His hair was scragglier, he wasn't quite as tall, but he wasn't quite so skinny, either. His smile was exactly the same. 'Death seems to agree with you,' I said.

'Death agrees with no man, Falcio. Don't let the clerics tell you otherwise.'

'I've learned to take everything the clerics say with a grain of salt, your Majesty.'

'Good fellow.' He sat down on a large flat rock and pointed to a similar – though slightly less grand one – for me. 'Don't stand there with your mouth hanging open like a boy brought to his first brothel. Your King commands you to sit down.'

I complied, though I wasn't entirely sure he had the right to command anything.

'You have questions,' he said.

'I . . . yes, it's safe to say I have a few, your Majesty.'

He nodded thoughtfully. 'Very well, but you may ask only one before I am called away.'

'Really?' I asked. 'It actually works that way?'

He grinned. 'Nah. Well, actually I don't know. Death doesn't make you smarter, that much I'll tell you for free. Just ask what you want.'

It might be hard to imagine but I swear that at that precise moment I couldn't think of a single question. Perhaps that's because I wanted to grab him by the collar and shake him so badly. 'You left us with *nothing*,' I said at last. 'No plan. No resources. No—'

He leaned his head back and started laughing and went on for far too long before he paused enough to get out, 'Only you, Falcio, would choose to use our brief time together to launch into a speech about the unfairness of the world.'

'I don't suppose death is any fairer?' I asked.

'Not really. Worse in some ways.' He looked at me and the smile went away. 'Come on, Falcio, say what you really want to say.'

It took a moment to get the words out. 'I failed you,' I said simply.

'Is that so?'

'In every way imaginable.'

He ran a hand through his rather feeble attempt at a short beard. 'Well then, I suppose you should dedicate yourself to a life of agonising penitence.' He stood up and raised one hand in the air. 'Despise yourself, Falcio van Mond! Blame yourself for every bad thing in this world! Shun every solace! Push away those who love you! Suffer in glorious, unmatched self-flagellation . . .' He paused for a moment, then looked down at me. 'Oh, wait. You've already been doing that, haven't you?'

'You know, you still have a shitty sense of humour, your Majesty.'

He shrugged. 'It's still a shitty world, Falcio. And if you're waiting for the afterlife to be better, well' – he waved a hand at the Gods at the bottom of the hill – 'you've got a taste of the kinds of morons who govern that domain.'

'You mean the kinds of morons who give people enigmatic quests that make no sense?' A thought occurred to me then, and I finally understood which question I most wanted to ask. 'Was Aline really the Charoite, or was it Filian all along?'

'I'm sorry?'

I rose to my feet to stand before him. 'The *Charoite*, damn you! Your final command to me, the thing you told me I had to seek out: the reason I found Aline in the first place and fought every damned assassin, tyrant and God who tried to take over your damned country in the meantime! Once and for all, your Majesty, who was the true Charoite?'

Paelis looked at me then, and said nothing. After a few seconds his head tilted a little, and just as he faded away into nothingness, he asked, 'What's a "charoite"?'

I wound my way back down the little hill expecting to see only the Tailor there, but nothing had changed. Love, Death, and Valour stood next to Aline. The Tailor still sat on the ground.

'Well?' the Tailor asked. 'How was he?'

I thought about my answer for a moment. 'If he weren't already dead, I'm fairly sure I'd kill him myself.'

She chuckled. 'That's my boy.'

'Falcio?'

I looked down to see Aline staring up at me. 'I . . . I think I have to go now, Falcio.' She looked back at the Gods standing behind her. 'I want to say goodbye properly but they say I can't touch you.'

The infinite grey sadness that had been filling me drop by drop turned all at once to a deep, burning red. I was so sick of the arbitrariness of death, the unfairness of life. I knelt down and opened my arms. 'Come here, sweetheart.'

She looked uncertain for a moment then rushed to me.

The Tailor shouted, 'Aline, no!'

It was too late. Aline wrapped her arms around me and I did the same to her. Her skin wasn't cold as I'd expected it, but warm and alive. Her hair tickled at my nose and her cheek pressed into mine. I held onto her like that, waiting for the end to come.

When it didn't, I opened my eyes and looked past her shoulder. There, down on one knee, was Death, his arms spread as if in supplication.

When Valour spoke, his voice was full of awe. 'Death kneels for you . . .'

'You're damned right he does,' I said.

Aline let go of me and stood back, looking at me. I suppose I must have been looking at her, too, because she asked, 'What are you staring at?'

'A dishevelled young woman with messy hair and a nose entirely too pointy to be a *proper* Queen. What are you staring at?'

Her eyes narrowed. 'A smelly man who hasn't bathed in a month with a scratchy beard who is entirely too insolent for such grand company.'

'We make a fine pair then, don't we?'

'The finest.' She yawned then, and brought a hand to her mouth. 'I'm very tired now, Falcio. Is it all right if I go back to sleep on the cart?'

'Of course, sweetheart,' I said, managing to keep the heartache out of my voice. 'I'll wake you when it's time to go.'

She smiled. 'Okay, then.' She turned and went back to the cart. When I turned to follow, she was under the black shroud, every fold in the fabric exactly as it had been before.

'Thank you,' I said to Valour.

The young God shrugged. 'For what? I told you the gift wasn't for you.'

'Thank you anyway.'

'Don't waste your thanks on them,' the Tailor said. 'The Gods never do anything out of generosity.'

I was inclined to agree when Death, who had not spoken until then, finally said, 'You really are a truly foul old creature, aren't you?'

For the first time since I'd known her, the Tailor was speechless.

Maybe the Gods aren't really so bad after all.

'We have to go,' Valour said. He and the others turned towards the east. 'Your friends come, and the one with the bow is prone to . . . unwise threats.'

For just an instant, I thought of calling on him to wait, to ask whether Death would let me see my wife Aline one last time, but I stopped myself. She above all deserved peace now, from the cares of this world, and from a foolish and reckless man who once and for all needed to find a way to stop living in the past.

I turned and saw horses coming in the distance. 'I've made a decision,' I said suddenly.

They paused in their steps. 'What decision is that?' Valour asked.

'I've decided your name is Tommer.'

'You would impose your will upon the Gods?' he asked, with the half-smile of a boy who's just been caught at mischief.

'Someone has to,' I replied.

Valour turned, and for a brief moment I saw something behind those clear, bright eyes. Something familiar. 'Tommer, God of Valour?' He grinned. 'It's as good a name as any, I suppose.'

CHAPTER EIGHTY-FIVE

THE DEPARTURE

You would think that the Gods would leave the earth in a flash of light or a puff of smoke, but these didn't; they just began walking east, towards the empty desert. I wondered what they would do if we simply decided to follow them.

'Gods,' the Tailor spat. 'Of all man's useless inventions, they are surely the most pointless.'

Five horses arrived. Kest, Brasti, Valiana, Ethalia and Chalmers dismounted. When first Ethalia came towards me I thought it might be some trick – that the God Love had once again taken her form – because she was glowing a little, though not in the way her Sainthood usually caused her to. On the other hand, it had been a month since I'd last seen her, so I might have just been imagining it.

Brasti, who's always had the best vision of all of us, ran to where the Tailor and I stood and looked out towards the desert. 'Are those the fucking Gods again?'

'Three of them, anyway,' I replied.

Ethalia came into my arms and I squeezed her. 'Not so hard,' she said. 'It's been a long ride.'

'Sorry,' I said, a little hurt.

Brasti took a couple of steps towards the desert. 'Don't even think of coming back,' he shouted, 'or you'll have Brasti God-Slayer, Vanquisher of the Avarean Horde, to answer to!'

'Vanquisher of the *what?*'

'He's been saying that all the way here,' Valiana said, rolling her eyes. 'Every tavern and inn we stopped at he'd rush in looking to see if he could find a Bardatti or even a travelling minstrel to hear the tale of how *he* came up with the brilliant plan to defeat the Avareans simply by whistling their own song. When the troubadours showed no interest, he just started rattling it off to every drunk he could find.'

Brasti turned back to us. 'Look, I understand how those among you who haven't defeated an undefeatable army or killed a God might feel a trifle' – here he looked at Kest – '*reduced* by your lack of accomplishment. But please don't hold it against those of us posessed of more . . . substantial virtues.'

Kest and I shared a brief glance and the two of us had to struggle to keep from breaking out into a fit of laughter. Oh how this unprepared world would suffer on the day that Brasti Goodbow finally learned that one of his dirty jokes helped defeat the Saint of Swords. 'Why were the Gods here?' Kest asked, once the risk of inexplicable giggling on his part had passed.

I was going to say something clever about how visits from the Gods had become such a frequent occurrence that I really don't pay attention any more, but then I realised that the others might take some solace in what had happened with Aline.

'That's . . . surprisingly decent of them,' Kest said, once the tale had been told.

'It'll come back to haunt us,' the Tailor countered, 'just wait and see. Nothing good comes from consorting with Gods or the dead.'

'So,' Brasti said. 'After all of that, what did the King have to say?'

'He said the whole world could have been saved if only you'd learned how to use a sword properly.'

Brasti pointed to himself. 'Hello? Man who repeatedly saves the world here? Can I get a modicum of respect?'

'You're very impressive, dear,' I said.

'Finally. Thank you.' He leaned towards me and whispered in a voice that could likely have been heard miles away, 'I'll have you know I didn't let Ethalia anywhere near my bed, no matter how much she pleaded with me.'

'"*Pleaded* with you"?'

'Well, not so much openly. I mean, she didn't actually beg out loud. It was more in the eyes.'

Ethalia looked down at the ground. 'It's . . . not entirely untrue. I did have . . . thoughts . . . of coming to your room at night.'

'Really?' Brasti asked.

She grinned wickedly. 'Yes, but only to ask if you could stop snoring. The walls of the inn were shaking.'

He threw up his hands. 'Lies. I'm surrounded by liars.'

'Did the King reveal anything to you?' Valiana asked.

'Only that he was a bigger arsehole than I remembered.'

'Well, some of us knew that already,' Kest said, surprising me with his grin.

'Oh, for Saints' sake,' the Tailor growled. 'Will one of you help me bury my granddaughter next to my son so I can get back to my cottage and die of old age in peace?'

We buried Aline in a little plot at the top of the hill next to where the Tailor had laid her son years before. It would have been a silent ceremony, but for Brasti's periodic attempts at humour, Kest's glances, which shut him up, Valiana's tears and Ethalia's song. I hadn't even known that she could sing. The woman insisted on continually surprising me. Sister of Mystery indeed.

The Tailor said nothing nor made any sound, but when she and I looked at each other I knew the depths of her sorrow. It was mirrored in my own heart.

It was too late to begin the journey back, so we made camp near the horse-cart. The Tailor stayed by Aline's grave.

I unbuckled the breaching straps and expected Monster to race back towards Aramor and her new herd, out of our lives for ever, but instead, she walked a few yards away and looked up at the hilltop.

Brasti organised a meal, but I couldn't tell you what it was. My taste for food had largely vanished, along with my taste for most other things in life.

'Our new monarch is turning out to be a bit of a mess, in case you're wondering,' Brasti said, finally, as we sat around the fire.

'King Filian's not as bad as all that,' Valiana countered.

'Well,' Brasti smiled evilly, 'the Greatcoats have gone straight for the hells since he picked his new First Cantor.'

I'd hoped the King would choose Valiana, though her new status as Duchess of Rijou made that politically complicated. Quilatta was the next most likely given she'd been a Cantor before. 'Who did he choose?' I asked.

He turned and nodded to Chalmers, who was studiously looking down at her plate.

I was about to say something stupid when Ethalia squeezed my hand so hard I felt my knuckles crack together.

Chalmers stared at me with an uncharacteristically pleading look in her eyes. 'You have to take the job back, Falcio. The other Greatcoats *hate* me! Most of them won't talk to me and the ones who do only tell me how unqualified I am – which is true, by the way. And it's not just them, either: I've had three Dukes already make veiled threats to me and the King just tells me it's up to me to deal with them.'

I couldn't help but smile at that.

'It's not funny!' she said.

'Chalmers, having everyone hate you and threaten your life at every turn is precisely how you can tell you're the right person to be the First Cantor of the Greatcoats.'

She set her plate down on the ground. 'Great. Any advice? Or should I just slit my own throat now and save my enemies the trouble?'

Without meaning to, my gaze went to Kest and Brasti. 'Find two friends,' I told her. 'Make sure they're belligerent and annoying and that they get you into trouble at every turn.'

'And get you out of it,' Kest said.

'That, too. Most of all, though, pick two people for whom you'd gladly die.'

Brasti looked back at me, for once without a trace of smugness or irony. 'And who'd just as gladly die for you.'

Chalmers rolled her eyes at us, but then asked, 'Are you really leaving the Greatcoats?'

'For now,' I said.

'It isn't fair. All of you are abandoning me.'

'All of us?' I looked at the others. 'What are you—?'

'I'm the Duchess of Rijou now,' Valiana said, 'although I suspect that foetid worm Shiballe already has a hundred spies and assassins waiting for me.'

I reached out a hand to take hers for a moment. 'Try not to kill them all. You'll need *someone* to rule over.' I turned to Brasti. 'And you? Is Darriana really crazy enough to marry you?'

'She is – but not for a while yet. Darri's got it into her head to reform the Dashini. She thinks there might be records in the old Dashini monastery that describe how their Order functioned in the past when they were spies for the country rather than just assassins.'

'Please tell me *you're* not going to become a Dashini, Brasti.'

I'd only been joking, but he looked oddly uncomfortable. 'Actually, I'm . . . well, I'm joining the Rangieri.' He held up a hand. 'For a while, at least.' He looked west to the far mountains. 'There are only three of them left, at least that we know of, and with everything happening out there, someone needs to start keeping an eye on the long view.'

The notion of Brasti being the one who thinks to the future terrified me no end. 'And you?' I said to Kest.

He opened his mouth to speak, but didn't get the chance, because Brasti had got to his feet, chortling gleefully.

'You're not going to believe this,' he announced, 'but Kest Murrowson here is – wait for it! – becoming a fucking *Knight!*'

Valiana and Ethalia both sighed and I got the sense this had been discussed at length on their journey here. Still . . .

'A Knight?' I asked.

'It's not as simple as Brasti makes it sound. Sir Elizar approached me after the battle.' He paused as though trying to remember a prepared speech. 'How many times have we found the country weakened from within because the Knights were manipulated or tricked into following the wrong path? How many lives could we have saved if they were – well, protectors rather than thugs?'

'It's a nice thought, Kest, but—'

'Hear me out. These are all fighting men, usually second or third sons with weapons and armour and skill but no sense of what that should mean. They do the things they do because—'

'Because they're arseholes,' Brasti said.

'No, because they're seeking something they don't know how to find.' Kest looked at me. 'Falcio, I know something of what it's like to always be seeking purpose by following someone else.'

'Well . . .' I really couldn't wrap my head around it. 'Which Duchy do you plan to join?'

'None of them,' he replied. 'I'm going on a journey, with Sir Elizar and the others, to reform the Honori. We're going to start a new Order of Knights, Falcio, who will serve the smaller towns and villages across the country.'

'*Hamlet Knights*,' Brasti said, as if it were the funniest thing in the world.

'It's not the worst idea I've ever heard.' I stood up to stretch my legs. Ethalia joined me. 'And you?' I asked. 'How does the Saint of Mercy plan to spend the next few years? Healing the sick? Ending all wars?'

She smiled. 'I have no illusions of saving the world. My ambitions are slightly narrower. There's a particular swordsman who is in dire need of saving.'

'If by "saving", you mean . . .' The words faded before they even left my mouth. Standing there, under that sky, not a hundred yards from where Aline lay buried next to her father, the weight of it all suddenly came down upon me. I wasn't angry or even sad. I was simply *exhausted*. The very act of taking air into my lungs felt so full of effort and so lacking in any significance that I wondered if I could just stop breathing. But Ethalia was looking at me so I summoned the energy to say, 'I don't suppose you have a way to start my heart beating again, the way you once did for Kest, do you?'

She reached out and took my hand between both of hers and placed it against her chest. I could feel the strong, steady beat of her heart. It served only to make my own feel feeble. 'I don't think it's—'

She pulled my hand down lower, to her belly.

'What are you—?'

And then, suddenly, without warning . . . *there*.

A small, sudden pressure against my fingertips.

I looked at Ethalia and she was smiling. My eyes went down to her belly and only then did I notice the slight roundness which had been hidden by her coat.

'I believe I warned you some time ago that there were . . . *complications* we needed to discuss.'

What I had felt hadn't been a beat, but a *kick*.

And again.

Thunder.

Life.

'A daughter, I think,' Ethalia said.

Brasti, Kest and Valiana stood and joined us. Brasti removed his bow from over his shoulder and placed it in on the ground next to us. 'My bow is hers,' he said, without a trace of sarcasm for once, and knelt down.

'Greatcoats don't kneel,' I reminded him but he just smiled back at me. His gesture was a gift: not an act of weakness or shame, but of love.

'My blade is hers,' Valiana said, and she too knelt.

Kest laid his shield down next. 'My life is hers.'

'I—'

A sound from behind me drew my attention: Monster was walking towards us. She jostled me aside and then sniffed at Ethalia's face, then at her belly.

Then the Greathorse knelt down in front of us.

'Your daughter will *never* want for protectors,' Chalmers said.

I looked at these daring fools I loved more than anyhing in the world. 'That's not what matters.' I wanted to tell them what *did* matter was that my daughter would have the truest of friends; that she would love and be loved, but I didn't give any grand speech. Sometimes the words just don't need to be said.

My name is Falcio val Mond.

I might just be the luckiest man who ever lived.

THE END

POSTSCRIPT

Dear Fellow Traveller,

We meet here at the end. The Greatcoats Quartet and its recounting of the victories and tragedies of a particularly idealistic and romantic (as well as reckless and occasionally self-deceiving) duellist has reached its conclusion. Falcio has – in spite of all the improbabilities laid upon the world by the ill-intentioned actions of Gods and Saints alike – saved his country from conspiracy, civil war, divine retribution and, ultimately, the Greatcoats themselves. Of course, he did this with the indefatigable loyalty of Kest, the dauntlessness of Valiana, the inspiration and courage of two very different women named Aline, the love and wisdom of Ethalia and . . . I'm sure there was some other guy, but I forget now.

My ambition with the Greatcoats was to write a series of swashbuckling adventure novels that could sit on the shelf alongside Dumas' Three Musketeers and C.S. Forester's Horatio Hornblower; that would speak to people whose hearts soared when they watched Errol Flynn in *The Adventures of Robin Hood* or *Captain Blood*, and to those who discovered swashbuckling through *The Princess Bride*'s unparallelled homage to that remarkable heritage. Most of all, though, I wanted to write stories a reader would choose to go back to every once in a while, wanting to spend a little more time with Falcio, Kest and Brasti in their moments of friendly banter, daring heroism – and yes, heartbreaking loss.

So whether you bought this book from a store (be nice to bookshops – there wouldn't be authors without them), borrowed it from a library (be even nicer to librarians – you might marry one some day and begin the adventure of a lifetime) or surreptitiously lifted it from a friend's bookshelf (they'll understand – really), you have my sincere gratitude and my promise that while the Greatcoats Quartet has come to an end, those troublesome travelling magistrates will one day return.

All my best,

Sebastien de Castell
twitter: @decastell
web: www.decastell.com
Vancouver, Canada
March 2017

ACKNOWLEDGEMENTS

Court documents will one day conclusively prove that Jo Fletcher, my redoubtable editor and acclaimed publisher, assured me without equivocation that the final book in a series is by far the easiest to write. 'A piece of cake', I believe she called it. 'Practically writes itself!'

In all fairness, I could be lying on this point and she may – I say may – not only have warned me well in advance of the challenge I was undertaking with *Tyrant's Throne*, but also devoted herself to countless hours reading, editing, re-reading and re-editing innumerable chapters of the book – all of which I sent to her in somewhat random order. Jo informs me that this particular authorial practice falls under the provisions of justifiable homicide.

I'd like to thank the following rather remarkable people for their invaluable support (as well as sneak in a few secrets about the Greatcoats you won't find anywhere else):

The Saints:

(Also called *The Sancti*, also called extremely often by me at all hours of the day and night by me begging for help.)

Christina de Castell, who I promise I will not make read seven unfinished drafts of my books again.

Jo Fletcher, who I promise I will make read seven unfinished drafts of my books again.

Heather Adams, the world's most wonderful literary agent, who may have created a monster.

Eric Torin, who taught me aspects of writing that I couldn't have learned anywhere else.

Kim Tough, whose boundless passion for story and character you will one day adore in her books.

The Inquisitors:

(Possibly more accurately referred to as the Order of Noble Torturers)

Wil Arndt (@warndt)

Brad Dehnert (@BradDehnert)

Jim Hull (www.narrativefirst.com)

Shuran, leader of the Black Tabards, was once a member of the Dashini. Patriana paid him to assassinate King Paelis after he was deposed for fear that her fellow Dukes might balk at shedding royal blood when the time came.

The Inlaudati:

(Secretive, often unseen figures performing their strange magic in the shadows.)

Nathaniel Marunas, my favourite person to talk books with. 'Gotta poo, Todd. Gotta poo.'

Olivia Mead, to whom I plan to be much less irritating this year.

Sam Bradbury, who, like Olivia, is destined to be a shining star in the industry.

Patrick Carpenter; the books never would have looked so amazing without you.

Melanie Thompson; the books never would have actually been made without you.

By the time Shuran and his *azu* (Dashini partner) arrived at Aramor, Falcio had already helped Paelis die on his own terms. Rather than commit suicide for his failure, Shuran killed his *azu* and burned the Dashini markings from his own face, thus dishonouring his order long before his fellow assassins failed to kill Falcio.

Ian Binnie, who brings the artistry of typesetting to the UK editions.

Sharona Selby, whose proofreading saved us all from my roughly one thousand errors.

Dave Murphy and Ron Beard, for heroically kidnapping bookstore buyers until they agreed to stock the series.

Frances Doyle and Katie Day, for making sure the ebooks got *everywhere*.

The Bardatti:

It takes a lot of luck for a fantasy series to do well, and what I mean by luck is specifically the great good fortune to have people choose to actively champion your series. The Greatcoats could have ended up struggling to find a readership, had it not been for the enthusiasm and evangelism of bloggers, booksellers, librarians, fellow authors and fellow readers from all around the world. I am profoundly grateful to all of you, and I apologise that I can mention only a few people here:

- Agnes Meszaros, whom I finally got to meet at Fantasy in the Court last year, who is just as delightful in person as she is online.
- Amanda Craig, renowned author and journalist, for her kind words about the Greatcoats.
- Peter Darbyshire of the Vancouver Province and a hell of an author in his own right. Stop getting me in trouble with George R.R. Martin fans.

- Which is why Shuran is always referred to as a foreigner in *Knight's Shadow* but no one knows where exactly he's from.
- Walter & Jill of White Dwarf Books, Vancouver's amazing fantasy & sci-fi bookstore.
- Alex, Danie and everyone at Forbidden Planet, London's amazing fantasy & sci-fi bookstore.
- Penny Bullock from Waterstones Lancaster – also amazing, though they sell other things, too.
- David, Harry, Pavla and the rest of the fine crew at Goldsboro Books whose early support really helped the series take off.
- Trin was the one person who knew Shuran's secret, and her admiration for his deviousness and daring is one of the reasons she deemed him worthy to be her co-conspirator.
- The wonderful French book blog, *L'ours Inculte* (ours-inculte.fr), who are kind enough to review even the English editions of the books!
- The character of Darriana was named by Laura, a.k.a. Stars_Cascade, and was partially based on a nineteenth century actress from Zanesville, Ohio, named Ella Hattan.
- Tracy Erickson, who was kind enough to hang out with me at WorldCon.
- Joel Pearson, who has no excuse for not having come to World-Con.
- Andrew Mather from The Quill To Live (thequilltolive.com), who called me underrated, thus proving we've never met in person.
- Charlie Hopkins of A Reading Machine (areadingmachine.com) for sending me an actual hand-written card.
- Che from Che Adventure (youtube.com/CheAdventureBooks) for her lovely book vlog.
- Samantha from Sam's Nonsense (facebook.com/novelsandnon-sense) for my favourite video posts about the series.
- Ella Hattan, sometimes called 'La Jaguarina', was quite possibly

the finest sword fighter of her era, and made her living challenging any male fencers who would face her to public duels. She was posthumously inducted into the US Fencing Hall of Fame.

- Petros of Booknest (Booknest.eu) for his tireless work on the Fabulous Fantasy Fundraiser
- Linda Akerman, the Book Girl of Mur-y-Castell (books-forlife.blogspot.com)
- Stephenie Sheung at The Bibliosanctum (bibliosanctum.com)
- Jasper de Joode of The Book Plank (thebookplank.blogspot.com), who I think did my very first interview.
- Sachin Dev / Smorgasbord Fantasia (fantasy-smorgasbord.blogspot.ca)
- Marc Aplin, and all the wonderful folks at Fantasy Faction (fantasy-faction.com) for – well, there're too many things to list at this point!
- Valiana's mother, the woman who called herself Viscountess Belletrice and had a love affair with Jillard, is in fact still alive.
- Sarah Avery at Black Gate Magazine (blackgate.com)
- Lisa at Over The Effing Rainbow (overtheeffingrainbow.co.uk)
- Liz Barnsley of Liz Loves Books (lizlovesbooks.com)
- Cindy from Draumr Kopa (draumrkopablog.wordpress.com)
- Rob Matheny & Phil Overby of the Grimdark podcast (thegrimtidingspodcast.com) Thanks for immortalising my horrible Irish whistle playing.
- Bob Milne of Beauty In Ruins (beauty-in-ruins.blogspot.com) whose review of *Saint's Blood* made me terrified of what would happen if *Tyrant's Throne* wasn't as good.
- Nazia Khatun, who is still my favourite.
- To all of you who take the time to write me with your thoughts and questions about the Greatcoats, know that your emails are the highlights of my day.

Falcio, Kest and Brasti will return . . .

One day . . .